# The Parisians -Complete

*by*

Edward Bulwer-Lytton

Double9 BOOKS

# The Parisians -Complete
## by Edward Bulwer-Lytton



ISBN: 978-93-58591-77-4

**Published by**

**DOUBLE 9 BOOKS**
2/13-B, Ansari Road
Daryaganj, New Delhi – 110002
info@double9books.com
www.double9books.com
Tel. 011-40042856

# ABOUT THE AUTHOR

Edward George Bulwer Lytton was a prolific English author, poet, novelist and politician, he served at the prestigious post of Secretary of the State for the Colonies of the United Kingdom. He was born in London on 23 May 1803. His father was General William Bulwer of Heydon Hall, mother was Elizabeth Barbara Lytton. He was a delicate child but a rapid learner. He started writing verses at ten years of age. He went to Trinity College of Cambridge. For English verse Sculpture he won the Chancellor Gold Medal. His first novel, the glorious Byronic romance Falkland, was not liked by people. But his second novel, Pelham or The Adventure of a Gentleman, was a hit and he began his successful fluent career in literary writing. He joined politics as a member of the Whigs, liberal political party. He died on 18 January 1873. His notable works - Pelham, The Last Days of Pompeii, The Coming Race, The Haunted and Haunters, Zanoni: A Rosicrucian Tale, Harold : The Last of Saxon Kings, Alice or the Mysteries, Athens : It's Rise and Fall etc. Lytton used some considerable phrases - 'It was dark and Stormy night', 'Almighty dollar, the pen is mightier than the sword' etc.

# CONTENTS

# INTRODUCTORY CHAPTER.

They who chance to have read the "Coming Race" may perhaps remember that I, the adventurous discoverer of the land without a sun, concluded the sketch of my adventures by a brief reference to the malady which, though giving no perceptible notice of its encroachments, might, in the opinion of my medical attendant, prove suddenly fatal.

I had brought my little book to this somewhat melancholy close a few years before the date of its publication, and in the meanwhile I was induced to transfer my residence to Paris, in order to place myself under the care of an English physician, renowned for his successful treatment of complaints analogous to my own.

I was the more readily persuaded to undertake this journey,—partly because I enjoyed a familiar acquaintance with the eminent physician referred to, who had commenced his career and founded his reputation in the United States; partly because I had become a solitary man, the ties of home broken, and dear friends of mine were domiciled in Paris, with whom I should be sure of tender sympathy and cheerful companionship. I had reason to be thankful for this change of residence: the skill of Dr. C______ soon restored me to health. Brought much into contact with various circles of Parisian society, I became acquainted with the persons and a witness of the events that form the substance of the tale I am about to submit to the public, which has treated my former book with so generous an indulgence. Sensitively tenacious of that character for strict and unalloyed veracity which, I flatter myself, my account of the abodes and manners of the Vril-ya has established, I could have wished to preserve the following narrative no less jealously guarded than its predecessor from the vagaries of fancy. But Truth undisguised, never welcome in any civilized community above ground, is exposed at this time to especial dangers in Paris; and my life would not be worth an hour's purchase if I exhibited her 'in puris naturalibus' to the eyes of a people wholly unfamiliarized to a spectacle so indecorous. That care for one's personal safety which is the first duty of thoughtful man compels me therefore to reconcile the appearance of 'la Verite' to the 'bienseances' of the polished society in which 'la Liberte' admits no opinion not dressed after the last fashion.

Attired as fiction, Truth may be peacefully received; and, despite the necessity thus imposed by prudence, I indulge the modest hope that I do not in these pages unfaithfully represent certain prominent types of the brilliant population which has invented so many varieties of Koom-Posh;

*[Koom-Posh, Glek-Nas. For the derivation of these terms and their metaphorical signification, I must refer the reader to the "Coming Race," chapter xii., on the language of the Vril-ya. To those who have not read or have forgotten that historical composition, it may be convenient to state briefly that Koom-Posh with the Vril-ya is the name for the government of the many, or the ascendency of the most ignorant or hollow, and may be loosely rendered Hollow-Bosh. When Koom-Posh degenerates from popular ignorance into the popular ferocity which precedes its decease, the name for that state of things is Glek-Nas; namely, the universal strife-rot.]*

and even when it appears hopelessly lost in the slough of a Glek-Nas, re-emerges fresh and lively as if from an invigorating plunge into the Fountain of Youth. O Paris, 'foyer des idees, et oeil du monde!'—animated contrast to the serene tranquillity of the Vril-ya, which, nevertheless, thy noisiest philosophers ever pretend to make the goal of their desires: of all communities on which shines the sun and descend the rains of heaven, fertilizing alike wisdom and folly, virtue and vice; in every city men have yet built on this earth,—mayest thou, O Paris, be the last to brave the wands of the Coming Race and be reduced into cinders for the sake of the common good!

*TISH.*

PARIS, August 28, 1872.

# BOOK I.

## CHAPTER I.

It was a bright day in the early spring of 1869. All Paris seemed to have turned out to enjoy itself. The Tuileries, the Champs Elysees, the Bois de Boulogne, swarmed with idlers. A stranger might have wondered where Toil was at work, and in what nook Poverty lurked concealed. A millionaire from the London Exchange, as he looked round on the magasins, the equipages, the dresses of the women; as he inquired the prices in the shops and the rent of apartments,—might have asked himself, in envious wonder, How on earth do those gay Parisians live? What is their fortune? Where does it come from?

As the day declined, many of the scattered loungers crowded into the Boulevards; the cafes and restaurants began to light up.

About this time a young man, who might be some five or six and twenty, was walking along the Boulevard des Italiens, heeding little the throng through which he glided his solitary way: there was that in his aspect and bearing which caught attention. He looked a somebody; but though unmistakably a Frenchman, not a Parisian. His dress was not in the prevailing mode: to a practised eye it betrayed the taste and the cut of a provincial tailor. His gait was not that of the Parisian,—less lounging, more stately; and, unlike the Parisian, he seemed indifferent to the gaze of others.

Nevertheless there was about him that air of dignity or distinction which those who are reared from their cradle in the pride of birth acquire so unconsciously that it seems hereditary and inborn. It must also be confessed that the young man himself was endowed with a considerable share of that nobility which Nature capriciously distributes among her favourites with little respect for their pedigree and blazon, the nobility of form and face. He was tall and well shaped, with graceful length of limb and fall of shoulders; his face was handsome, of the purest type of French masculine beauty,—the nose inclined to be aquiline, and delicately thin, with finely-cut open nostrils; the complexion clear,—the eyes large, of a light hazel, with dark lashes,—the hair of a chestnut brown, with no tint of auburn,—

the beard and mustache a shade darker, clipped short, not disguising the outline of lips, which were now compressed, as if smiles had of late been unfamiliar to them; yet such compression did not seem in harmony with the physiognomical character of their formation, which was that assigned by Lavater to temperaments easily moved to gayety and pleasure.

Another man, about his own age, coming quickly out of one of the streets of the Chausee d'Antin, brushed close by the stately pedestrian above described, caught sight of his countenance, stopped short, and exclaimed, "Alain!" The person thus abruptly accosted turned his eye tranquilly on the eager face, of which all the lower part was enveloped in black beard; and slightly lifting his hat, with a gesture of the head that implied, "Sir, you are mistaken; I have not the honour to know you," continued his slow indifferent way. The would-be acquaintance was not so easily rebuffed. "Peste," he said, between his teeth, "I am certainly right. He is not much altered: of course I AM; ten years of Paris would improve an orang-outang." Quickening his step, and regaining the side of the man he had called "Alain," he said, with a well-bred mixture of boldness and courtesy in his tone and countenance,

"Ten thousand pardons if I am wrong. Put surely I accost Alain de Kerouec, son of the Marquis de Rochebriant."

"True, sir; but—"

"But you do not remember me, your old college friend, Frederic Lemercier?"

"Is it possibly?" cried Alain, cordially, and with an animation which charged the whole character of his countenance. "My dear Frederic, my dear friend, this is indeed good fortune! So you, too, are at Paris?"

"Of course; and you? Just come, I perceive," he added, somewhat satirically, as, linking his arm in his new-found friend's, he glanced at the cut of that friend's coat-collar.

"I have been here a fortnight," replied Alain.

"Hem! I suppose you lodge in the old Hotel de Rochebriant. I passed it yesterday, admiring its vast facade, little thinking you were its inmate."

"Neither am I; the hotel does not belong to me; it was sold some years ago by my father."

"Indeed! I hope your father got a good price for it; those grand hotels have trebled their value within the last five years. And how is your father? Still the same polished grand seigneur? I never saw him but once, you know;

and I shall never forget his smile, style grand monarque, when he patted me on the head and tipped me ten napoleons."

"My father is no more," said Alain, gravely; "he has been dead nearly three years."

"Ciel! forgive me; I am greatly shocked. Hem! so you are now the Marquis de Rochebriant, a great historical name, worth a large sum in the market. Few such names left. Superb place your old chateau, is it not?"

"A superb place, no—a venerable ruin, yes!"

"Ah, a ruin! so much the better. All the bankers are mad after ruins: so charming an amusement to restore them. You will restore yours, without doubt. I will introduce you to such an architect! has the 'moyen age' at his fingers' ends. Dear,—but a genius."

The young Marquis smiled,—for since he had found a college friend, his face showed that it could smile,—smiled, but not cheerfully, and answered,

"I have no intention to restore Rochebriant. The walls are solid: they have weathered the storms of six centuries, they will last my time, and with me the race perishes."

"Bah! the race perish, indeed! you will marry. 'Parlez moi de ca': you could not come to a better man. I have a list of all the heiresses at Paris, bound in russia leather. You may take your choice out of twenty. Ah, if I were but a Rochebriant! It is an infernal thing to come into the world a Lemercier. I am a democrat, of course. A Lemercier would be in a false position if he were not. But if any one would leave me twenty acres of land, with some antique right to the De and a title, faith, would not I be an aristocrat, and stand up for my order? But now we have met, pray let us dine together. Ah! no doubt you are engaged every day for a month. A Rochebriant just new to Paris must be 'fete' by all the Faubourg."

"No," answered Alain, simply, "I am not engaged; my range of acquaintance is more circumscribed than you suppose."

"So much the better for me. I am luckily disengaged today, which is not often the case, for I am in some request in my own set, though it is not that of the Faubourg. Where shall we dine?—at the Trois Freres?"

"Wherever you please. I know no restaurant at Paris, except a very ignoble one, close by my lodging."

"'Apropos', where do you lodge?"

"Rue de l'Universite, Numero —."

"A fine street, but 'triste'. If you have no longer your family hotel, you have no excuse to linger in that museum of mummies, the Faubourg St. Germain; you must go into one of the new quarters by the Champs Elysees. Leave it to me; I'll find you a charming apartment. I know one to be had a bargain,—a bagatelle,—five hundred naps a-year. Cost you about two or three thousand more to furnish tolerably, not showily. Leave all to me. In three days you shall be settled. Apropos! horses! You must have English ones. How many?—three for the saddle, two for your 'coupe'? I'll find them for you. I will write to London to-morrow: Reese [Rice] is your man."

"Spare yourself that trouble, my dear Frederic. I keep no horses and no coupe. I shall not change my apartment." As he said this, Rochebriant drew himself up somewhat haughtily.

"Faith," thought Lemercier, "is it possible that the Marquis is poor? No. I have always heard that the Rochebriants were among the greatest proprietors in Bretagne. Most likely, with all his innocence of the Faubourg St. Germain, he knows enough of it to be aware that I, Frederic Lemercier, am not the man to patronize one of its greatest nobles. 'Sacre bleu!' if I thought that; if he meant to give himself airs to me, his old college friend,—I would—I would call him out."

Just as M. Lemercier had come to that bellicose resolution, the Marquis said, with a smile which, though frank, was not without a certain grave melancholy in its expression, "My dear Frederic, pardon me if I seem to receive your friendly offers ungraciously. But I believe that I have reasons you will approve for leading at Paris a life which you certainly will not envy;" then, evidently desirous to change the subject, he said in a livelier tone, "But what a marvellous city this Paris of ours is! Remember I had never seen it before: it burst on me like a city in the Arabian Nights two weeks ago. And that which strikes me most—I say it with regret and a pang of conscience—is certainly not the Paris of former times, but that Paris which M. Buonaparte—I beg pardon, which the Emperor—has called up around him, and identified forever with his reign. It is what is new in Paris that strikes and enthrals me. Here I see the life of France, and I belong to her tombs!"

"I don't quite understand you," said Lemercier. "If you think that because your father and grandfather were Legitimists, you have not the fair field of living ambition open to you under the Empire, you never were more mistaken. 'Moyen age,' and even rococo, are all the rage. You have no idea how valuable your name would be either at the Imperial Court or in a Commercial Company. But with your fortune you are independent of all but fashion and the Jockey Club.

"And 'apropos' of that, pardon me,—what villain made your coat?—let me know; I will denounce him to the police." Half amused, half amazed, Alain Marquis de Rochebriant looked at Frederic Lemercier much as a good-tempered lion may look upon a lively poodle who takes a liberty with his mane, and after a pause he replied curtly, "The clothes I wear at Paris were made in Bretagne; and if the name of Rochebriant be of any value at all in Paris, which I doubt, let me trust that it will make me acknowledged as 'gentilhomme,' whatever my taste in a coat or whatever the doctrines of a club composed—of jockeys."

"Ha, ha!" cried Lemercier, freeing himself from the arm of his friend, and laughing the more irresistibly as he encountered the grave look of the Marquis. "Pardon me,—I can't help it,—the Jockey Club,—composed of jockeys!—it is too much!—the best joke. My dear, Alain, there is some of the best blood of Europe in the Jockey Club; they would exclude a plain bourgeois like me. But it is all the same: in one respect you are quite right. Walk in a blouse if you please: you are still Rochebriant; you would only be called eccentric. Alas! I am obliged to send to London for my pantaloons: that comes of being a Lemercier. But here we are in the Palais Royal."

# CHAPTER II.

The salons of the Trois Freres were crowded; our friends found a table with some little difficulty. Lemercier proposed a private cabinet, which, for some reason known to himself, the Marquis declined.

Lemercier spontaneously and unrequested ordered the dinner and the wines.

While waiting for their oysters, with which, when in season, French 'bon-vivants' usually commence their dinner, Lemercier looked round the salon with that air of inimitable, scrutinizing, superb impertinence which distinguishes the Parisian dandy. Some of the ladies returned his glance coquettishly, for Lemercier was 'beau garcon;' others turned aside indignantly, and muttered something to the gentlemen dining with them. The said gentlemen, when old, shook their heads, and continued to eat unmoved; when young, turned briskly round, and looked at first fiercely at M. Lemercier, but, encountering his eye through the glass which he had screwed into his socket, noticing the hardihood of his countenance and the squareness of his shoulders, even they turned back to the tables, shook their heads, and continued to eat unmoved, just like the old ones.

"Ah!" cried Lemercier, suddenly, "here comes a man you should know, 'mon cher.' He will tell you how to place your money,—a rising man, a coming man, a future minister. Ah! 'bon jour,' Duplessis, 'bon jour,'" kissing his hand to a gentleman who had just entered and was looking about him for a seat. He was evidently well and favourably known at the Trois Freres. The waiters had flocked round him, and were pointing to a table by the window, which a saturnine Englishman, who had dined off a beefsteak and potatoes, was about to vacate.

M. Duplessis, having first assured himself, like a prudent man, that his table was secure, having ordered his oysters, his chablis, and his 'potage a la bisque,' now paced calmly and slowly across the salon, and halted before Lemercier.

Here let me pause for a moment, and give the reader a rapid sketch of the two Parisians.

Frederic Lemercier is dressed, somewhat too showily, in the extreme of the prevalent fashion. He wears a superb pin in his cravat,—a pin worth two thousand francs; he wears rings on his fingers, 'breloques' to his watch-chain. He has a warm though dark complexion, thick black eyebrows, full lips, a nose somewhat turned up, but not small, very fine large dark eyes, a bold, open, somewhat impertinent expression of countenance; withal decidedly handsome, thanks to colouring, youth, and vivacity of regard.

Lucien Duplessis, bending over the table, glancing first with curiosity at the Marquis de Rochebriant, who leans his cheek on his hand and seems not to notice him, then concentrating his attention on Frederic Lemercier, who sits square with his hands clasped,—Lucien Duplessis is somewhere between forty and fifty, rather below the middle height, slender, but not slight,—what in English phrase is called "wiry." He is dressed with extreme simplicity: black frockcoat buttoned up; black cravat worn higher than men who follow the fashions wear their neckcloths nowadays; a hawk's eye and a hawk's beak; hair of a dull brown, very short, and wholly without curl; his cheeks thin and smoothly shaven, but he wears a mustache and imperial, plagiarized from those of his sovereign, and, like all plagiarisms, carrying the borrowed beauty to extremes, so that the points of mustache and imperial, stiffened and sharpened by cosmetics which must have been composed of iron, looked like three long stings guarding lip and jaw from invasion; a pale olive-brown complexion, eyes small, deep-sunk, calm, piercing; his expression of face at first glance not striking, except for quiet immovability. Observed more heedfully, the expression was keenly intellectual,—determined about the lips, calculating about the brows: altogether the face of no ordinary man, and one not, perhaps, without fine and high qualities, concealed from the general gaze by habitual reserve, but justifying the confidence of those whom he admitted into his intimacy.

"Ah, mon cher," said Lemercier, "you promised to call on me yesterday at two o'clock. I waited in for you half an hour; you never came."

"No; I went first to the Bourse. The shares in that Company we spoke of have fallen; they will fall much lower: foolish to buy in yet; so the object of my calling on you was over. I took it for granted you would not wait if I failed my appointment. Do you go to the opera to-night?"

"I think not; nothing worth going for: besides, I have found an old friend, to whom I consecrate this evening. Let me introduce you to the Marquis de Rochebriant. Alain, M. Duplessis."

The two gentlemen bowed.

"I had the honour to be known to Monsieur your father," said Duplessis.

"Indeed," returned Rochebriant. "He had not visited Paris for many years before he died."

"It was in London I met him, at the house of the Russian Princess C____."

The Marquis coloured high, inclined his head gravely, and made no reply. Here the waiter brought the oysters and the chablis, and Duplessis retired to his own table.

"That is the most extraordinary man," said Frederic, as he squeezed the lemon over his oysters, "and very much to be admired."

"How so? I see nothing at least to admire in his face," said the Marquis, with the bluntness of a provincial.

"His face. Ah! you are a Legitimist,—party prejudice. He dresses his face after the Emperor; in itself a very clever face, surely."

"Perhaps, but not an amiable one. He looks like a bird of prey."

"All clever men are birds of prey. The eagles are the heroes, and the owls the sages. Duplessis is not an eagle nor an owl. I should rather call him a falcon, except that I would not attempt to hoodwink him."

"Call him what you will," said the Marquis, indifferently; "M. Duplessis can be nothing to me."

"I am not so sure of that," answered Frederic, somewhat nettled by the phlegm with which the Provincial regarded the pretensions of the Parisian. "Duplessis, I repeat it, is an extraordinary man. Though untitled, he descends from your old aristocracy; in fact, I believe, as his name shows, from the same stem as the Richelieus. His father was a great scholar, and I believe he has read much himself. Might have distinguished himself in literature or at the bar, but his parents died fearfully poor; and some distant relations in commerce took charge of him, and devoted his talents to the 'Bourse.' Seven years ago he lived in a single chamber, 'au quatrieme,' near the Luxembourg. He has now a hotel, not large but charming, in the Champs Elysees, worth at least six hundred thousand francs. Nor has he made his own fortune alone, but that of many others; some of birth as high as your own. He has the genius of riches, and knocks off a million as a poet does an ode, by the force of inspiration. He is hand-in-glove with the Ministers, and has been invited to Compiegne by the Emperor. You will find him very useful."

Alain made a slight movement of incredulous dissent, and changed the conversation to reminiscences of old school-boy days.

The dinner at length came to a close. Frederic rang for the bill,—glanced over it. "Fifty-nine francs," said he, carelessly flinging down his napoleon and a half. The Marquis silently drew forth his purse and extracted the same sum. When they were out of the restaurant, Frederic proposed adjourning to his own rooms. "I can promise you an excellent cigar, one of a box given to me by an invaluable young Spaniard attached to the Embassy here. Such cigars are not to be had at Paris for money, nor even for love; seeing that women, however devoted and generous, never offer you anything better than a cigarette. Such cigars are only to be had for friendship. Friendship is a jewel."

"I never smoke," answered the Marquis, "but I shall be charmed to come to your rooms; only don't let me encroach on your good-nature. Doubtless you have engagements for the evening."

"None till eleven o'clock, when I have promised to go to a soiree to which I do not offer to take you; for it is one of those Bohemian entertainments at which it would do you harm in the Faubourg to assist,—at least until you have made good your position. Let me see, is not the Duchesse de Tarascon a relation of yours?"

"Yes; my poor mother's first cousin."

"I congratulate you. 'Tres grande dame.' She will launch you in 'puro cielo,' as Juno might have launched one of her young peacocks."

"There has been no acquaintance between our houses," returned the Marquis, dryly, "since the mesalliance of her second nuptials."

"Mesalliance! second nuptials! Her second husband was the Duc de Tarascon."

"A duke of the First Empire, the grandson of a butcher."

"Diable! you are a severe genealogist, Monsieur le Marquis. How can you consent to walk arm-in-arm with me, whose great-grandfather supplied bread to the same army to which the Due de Tarascon's grandfather furnished the meat?"

"My dear Frederic, we two have an equal pedigree, for our friendship dates from the same hour. I do not blame the Duchesse de Tarascon for marrying the grandson of a butcher, but for marrying the son of a man made duke by a usurper. She abandoned the faith of her house and the cause of her sovereign. Therefore her marriage is a blot on our scutcheon."

Frederic raised his eyebrows, but had the tact to pursue the subject no further. He who interferes in the quarrels of relations must pass through life without a friend.

The young men now arrived at Lemercier's apartment, an entresol looking on the Boulevard des Italiens, consisting of more rooms than a bachelor generally requires; low-pitched, indeed, but of good dimensions, and decorated and furnished with a luxury which really astonished the provincial, though, with the high-bred pride of an oriental, he suppressed every sign of surprise.

Florentine cabinets, freshly retouched by the exquisite skill of Mombro; costly specimens of old Sevres and Limoges; pictures and bronzes and marble statuettes,—all well chosen and of great price, reflected from mirrors in Venetian frames,—made a 'coup d'oeil' very favourable to that respect which the human mind pays to the evidences of money. Nor was comfort less studied than splendour. Thick carpets covered the floors, doubled and quilted portieres excluded all draughts from chinks in the doors. Having allowed his friend a few minutes to contemplate and admire the 'salle a manger' and 'salon' which constituted his more state apartments, Frederic then conducted him into a small cabinet, fitted up with scarlet cloth and gold fringes, whereon were artistically arranged trophies of Eastern weapons and Turkish pipes with amber mouthpieces.

There, placing the Marquis at ease on a divan and flinging himself on another, the Parisian exquisite ordered a valet, well dressed as himself, to bring coffee and liqueurs; and after vainly pressing one of his matchless cigars on his friend, indulged in his own Regalia.

"They are ten years old," said Frederic, with a tone of compassion at Alain's self-inflicted loss,—"ten years old. Born therefore about the year in which we two parted—"

"When you were so hastily summoned from college," said the Marquis, "by the news of your father's illness. We expected you back in vain. Have you been at Paris ever since?"

"Ever since; my poor father died of that illness. His fortune proved much larger than was suspected: my share amounted to an income from investments in stocks, houses, etc., to upwards of sixty thousand francs a-year; and as I wanted six years to my majority of course the capital on attaining my majority would be increased by accumulation. My mother desired to keep me near her; my uncle, who was joint guardian with her, looked with disdain on our poor little provincial cottage; so promising an heir should acquire his finishing education under masters at Paris. Long before I was of age, I was initiated into politer mysteries of our capital than those celebrated by Eugene Sue. When I took possession of my fortune five years ago, I was considered a Croesus; and really for that patriarchal time I was wealthy. Now, alas! my accumulations have vanished in my outfit;

and sixty thousand francs a-year is the least a Parisian can live upon. It is not only that all prices have fabulously increased, but that the dearer things become, the better people live. When I first came out, the world speculated upon me; now, in order to keep my standing, I am forced to speculate on the world. Hitherto I have not lost; Duplessis let me into a few good things this year, worth one hundred thousand francs or so. Croesus consulted the Delphic Oracle. Duplessis was not alive in the time of Croesus, or Croesus would have consulted Duplessis."

Here there was a ring at the outer door of the apartment, and in another minute the valet ushered in a gentleman somewhere about the age of thirty, of prepossessing countenance, and with the indefinable air of good-breeding and 'usage du monde.' Frederic started up to greet cordially the new-comer, and introduced him to the Marquis under the name of "Sare Grarm Varn."

"Decidedly," said the visitor, as he took off his paletot and seated himself beside the Marquis,—"decidedly, my dear Lemercier," said he, in very correct French, and with the true Parisian accent and intonation, "you Frenchmen merit that praise for polished ignorance of the language of barbarians which a distinguished historian bestows on the ancient Romans. Permit me, Marquis, to submit to you the consideration whether Grarm Varn is a fair rendering of my name as truthfully printed on this card."

The inscription on the card, thus drawn from its case and placed in Alain's hand, was—

*MR. GRAHAM VANE,*

*No. __ Rue d'Anjou.*

The Marquis gazed at it as he might on a hieroglyphic, and passed it on to Lemercier in discreet silence.

That gentleman made another attempt at the barbarian appellation.

"'Grar—ham Varne.' 'C'est ca!' I triumph! all difficulties yield to French energy."

Here the coffee and liqueurs were served; and after a short pause the Englishman, who had very quietly been observing the silent Marquis, turned to him and said, "Monsieur le Marquis, I presume it was your father whom I remember as an acquaintance of my own father at Ems. It is many years ago; I was but a child. The Count de Chambord was then at that enervating little spa for the benefit of the Countess's health. If our friend Lemercier does not mangle your name as he does mine, I understand him to say that you are the Marquis de Rochebriant."

"That is my name: it pleases me to hear that my father was among those who flocked to Ems to do homage to the royal personage who deigns to assume the title of Count de Chambord."

"My own ancestors clung to the descendants of James II. till their claims were buried in the grave of the last Stuart, and I honour the gallant men who, like your father, revere in an exile the heir to their ancient kings."

The Englishman said this with grace and feeling; the Marquis's heart warmed to him at once.

"The first loyal 'gentilhome' I have met at Paris," thought the Legitimist; "and, oh, shame! not a Frenchman!" Graham Vane, now stretching himself and accepting the cigar which Lemercier offered him, said to that gentleman "You who know your Paris by heart—everybody and everything therein worth the knowing, with many bodies and many things that are not worth it—can you inform me who and what is a certain lady who every fine day may be seen walking in a quiet spot at the outskirts of the Bois de Boulogne, not far from the Baron de Rothschild's villa? The said lady arrives at this selected spot in a dark-blue coupe without armorial bearings, punctually at the hour of three. She wears always the same dress,—a kind of gray pearl-coloured silk, with a 'cachemire' shawl. In age she may be somewhat about twenty—a year or so more or less—and has a face as haunting as a Medusa's; not, however, a face to turn a man into a stone, but rather of the two turn a stone into a man. A clear paleness, with a bloom like an alabaster lamp with the light flashing through. I borrow that illustration from Sare Scott, who applied it to Milor Bee-ren."

"I have not seen the lady you describe," answered Lemercier, feeling humiliated by the avowal; "in fact, I have not been in that sequestered part of the Bois for months; but I will go to-morrow: three o'clock you say,—leave it to me; to-morrow evening, if she is a Parisienne, you shall know all about her. But, mon cher, you are not of a jealous temperament to confide your discovery to another."

"Yes, I am of a very jealous temperament," replied the Englishman; "but jealousy comes after love, and not before it. I am not in love; I am only haunted. To-morrow evening, then, shall we dine at Philippe's, seven o'clock?"

"With all my heart," said Lemercier; "and you too, Alain?"

"Thank you, no," said the Marquis, briefly; and he rose, drew on his gloves, and took up his hat.

At these signals of departure, the Englishman, who did not want tact nor delicacy, thought that he had made himself 'de trop' in the 'tete-a-tete' of two friends of the same age and nation; and, catching up his paletot, said hastily, "No, Marquis, do not go yet, and leave our host in solitude; for I have an engagement which presses, and only looked in at Lemercier's for a moment, seeing the light at his windows. Permit me to hope that our acquaintance will not drop, and inform me where I may have the honour to call on you."

"Nay," said the Marquis; "I claim the right of a native to pay my respects first to the foreigner who visits our capital, and," he added in a lower tone, "who speaks so nobly of those who revere its exiles."

The Englishman saluted, and walked slowly towards the door; but on reaching the threshold turned back and made a sign to Lemercier, unperceived by Alain.

Frederic understood the sign, and followed Graham Vane into the adjoining room, closing the door as he passed.

"My dear Lemercier, of course I should not have intruded on you at this hour on a mere visit of ceremony. I called to say that the Mademoiselle Duval whose address you sent me is not the right one,—not the lady whom, knowing your wide range of acquaintance, I asked you to aid me in finding out."

"Not the right Duval? Diable! she answered your description, exactly."

"Not at all."

"You said she was very pretty and young,—under twenty."

"You forgot that I said she deserved that description twenty-one years ago."

"Ah, so you did; but some ladies are always young. 'Age,' says a wit in the 'Figaro,' 'tis a river which the women compel to reascend to its source when it has flowed onward more than twenty years.' Never mind: 'soyez tranquille;' I will find your Duval yet if she is to be found. But why could not the friend who commissioned you to inquire choose a name less common? Duval! every street in Paris has a shop-door over which is inscribed the name of Duval."

"Quite true, there is the difficulty; however, my dear Lemercier, pray continue to look out for a Louise Duval who was young and pretty twenty-one years ago: this search ought to interest me more than that which I entrusted to you tonight, respecting the pearly-robed lady; for in the last I but gratify my own whim, in the first I discharge a promise to a friend. You, so perfect a Frenchman, know the difference; honour is engaged to the first. Be sure you let me know if you find any other Madame or Mademoiselle

Duval; and of course you remember your promise not to mention to any one the commission of inquiry you so kindly undertake. I congratulate you on your friendship for M. de Rochebriant. What a noble countenance and manner!"

Lemercier returned to the Marquis. "Such a pity you can't dine with us to-morrow. I fear you made but a poor dinner to-day. But it is always better to arrange the menu beforehand. I will send to Philippe's tomorrow. Do not be afraid."

The Marquis paused a moment, and on his young face a proud struggle was visible. At last he said, bluntly and manfully,

"My dear Frederic, your world and mine are not and cannot be the same. Why should I be ashamed to own to my old schoolfellow that I am poor,—very poor; that the dinner I have shared with you to-day is to me a criminal extravagance? I lodge in a single chamber on the fourth-story; I dine off a single plat at a small restaurateur's; the utmost income I can allow to myself does not exceed five thousand francs a year: my fortunes I cannot hope much to improve. In his own country Alain de Rochebriant has no career." Lemercier was so astonished by this confession that he remained for some moments silent, eyes and mouth both wide open; at length he sprang up, embraced his friend well-nigh sobbing, and exclaimed, "'Tant mieux pour moi!' You must take your lodging with me. I have a charming bedroom to spare. Don't say no. It will raise my own position to say 'I and Rochebriant keep house together.' It must be so. Come here to-morrow. As for not having a career,—bah! I and Duplessis will settle that. You shall be a millionaire in two years. Meanwhile we will join capitals: I my paltry notes, you your grand name. Settled!"

"My dear, dear Frederic," said the young noble, deeply affected, "on reflection you will see what you propose is impossible. Poor I may be without dishonour; live at another man's cost I cannot do without baseness. It does not require to be 'gentilhomme' to feel that: it is enough to be a Frenchman. Come and see me when you can spare the time. There is my address. You are the only man in Paris to whom I shall be at home. Au revoir." And breaking away from Lemercier's clasp, the Marquis hurried off.

# CHAPTER III.

Alain reached the house in which he lodged. Externally a fine house, it had been the hotel of a great family in the old regime. On the first floor were still superb apartments, with ceilings painted by Le Brun, with walls on which the thick silks still seemed fresh. These rooms were occupied by a rich 'agent de change;' but, like all such ancient palaces, the upper stories were wretchedly defective even in the comforts which poor men demand nowadays: a back staircase, narrow, dirty, never lighted, dark as Erebus, led to the room occupied by the Marquis, which might be naturally occupied by a needy student or a virtuous 'grisette.' But there was to him a charm in that old hotel, and the richest 'locataire' therein was not treated with a respect so ceremonious as that which at tended the lodger on the fourth story. The porter and his wife were Bretons; they came from the village of Rochebriant; they had known Alain's parents in their young days; it was their kinsman who had recommended him to the hotel which they served: so, when he paused at the lodge for his key, which he had left there, the porter's wife was in waiting for his return, and insisted on lighting him upstairs and seeing to his fire, for after a warm day the night had turned to that sharp biting cold which is more trying in Paris than even in London.

The old woman, running up the stairs before him, opened the door of his room, and busied herself at the fire. "Gently, my good Marthe," said he, "that log suffices. I have been extravagant to-day, and must pinch for it."

"M. le Marquis jests," said the old woman, laughing.

"No, Marthe; I am serious. I have sinned, but I shall reform. 'Entre nous,' my dear friend, Paris is very dear when one sets one's foot out of doors: I must soon go back to Rochebriant."

"When M. le Marquis goes back to Rochebriant he must take with him a Madame la Marquise,—some pretty angel with a suitable dot."

"A dot suitable to the ruins of Rochebriant would not suffice to repair them, Marthe: give me my dressing-gown, and good-night."

"'Bon repos, M. le Marquis! beaux reves, et bel avenir.'"

"'Bel avenir!'" murmured the young man, bitterly, leaning his cheek on his hand; "what fortune fairer than the present can be mine? yet inaction in youth is more keenly felt than in age. How lightly I should endure poverty if it brought poverty's ennobling companion, Labour,—denied to me! Well, well; I must go back to the old rock: on this ocean there is no sail, not even an oar, for me."

Alain de Rochebriant had not been reared to the expectation of poverty. The only son of a father whose estates were large beyond those of most nobles in modern France, his destined heritage seemed not unsuitable to his illustrious birth. Educated at a provincial academy, he had been removed at the age of sixteen to Rochebriant, and lived there simply and lonelily enough, but still in a sort of feudal state, with an aunt, an elder and unmarried sister to his father.

His father he never saw but twice after leaving college. That brilliant seigneur visited France but rarely, for very brief intervals, residing wholly abroad. To him went all the revenues of Rochebriant save what sufficed for the manage of his son and his sister. It was the cherished belief of these two loyal natures that the Marquis secretly devoted his fortune to the cause of the Bourbons; how, they knew not, though they often amused themselves by conjecturing: and, the young man, as he grew up, nursed the hope that he should soon hear that the descendant of Henri Quatre had crossed the frontier on a white charger and hoisted the old gonfalon with its 'fleur-de-lis.' Then, indeed, his own career would be opened, and the sword of the Kerouecs drawn from its sheath. Day after day he expected to hear of revolts, of which his noble father was doubtless the soul. But the Marquis, though a sincere Legitimist, was by no means an enthusiastic fanatic. He was simply a very proud, a very polished, a very luxurious, and, though not without the kindliness and generosity which were common attributes of the old French noblesse, a very selfish grand seigneur.

Losing his wife (who died the first year of marriage in giving birth to Alain) while he was yet very young, he had lived a frank libertine life until he fell submissive under the despotic yoke of a Russian Princess, who, for some mysterious reason, never visited her own country and obstinately refused to reside in France. She was fond of travel, and moved yearly from London to Naples, Naples to Vienna, Berlin, Madrid, Seville, Carlsbad, Baden-Baden,—anywhere for caprice or change, except Paris. This fair wanderer succeeded in chaining to herself the heart and the steps of the Marquis de Rochebriant.

She was very rich; she lived semi-royally. Hers was just the house in which it suited the Marquis to be the 'enfant qate.' I suspect that, cat-like, his attachment was rather to the house than to the person of his mistress. Not that he was domiciled with the Princess; that would have been somewhat too much against the proprieties, greatly too much against the Marquis's notions of his own dignity. He had his own carriage, his own apartments, his own suite, as became so grand a seigneur and the lover of so grand a dame. His estates, mortgaged before he came to them, yielded no income sufficient for his wants; he mortgaged deeper and deeper, year after year, till he could mortgage them no more. He sold his hotel at Paris; he accepted without scruple his sister's fortune; he borrowed with equal 'sang froid' the two hundred thousand francs which his son on coming of age inherited from his mother. Alain yielded that fortune to him without a murmur,—nay, with pride; he thought it destined to go towards raising a regiment for the fleur-de-lis.

To do the Marquis justice, he was fully persuaded that he should shortly restore to his sister and son what he so recklessly took from them. He was engaged to be married to his Princess so soon as her own husband died. She had been separated from the Prince for many years, and every year it was said he could not last a year longer. But he completed the measure of his conjugal iniquities by continuing to live; and one day, by mistake, Death robbed the lady of the Marquis instead of the Prince.

This was an accident which the Marquis had never counted upon. He was still young enough to consider himself young; in fact, one principal reason for keeping Alain secluded in Bretagne was his reluctance to introduce into the world a son "as old as myself" he would say pathetically. The news of his death, which happened at Baden after a short attack of bronchitis caught in a supper 'al fresco' at the old castle, was duly transmitted to Rochebriant by the Princess; and the shock to Alain and his aunt was the greater because they had seen so little of the departed that they regarded him as a heroic myth, an impersonation of ancient chivalry, condemning himself to voluntary exile rather than do homage to usurpers. But from their grief they were soon roused by the terrible doubt whether Rochebriant could still be retained in the family. Besides the mortgagees, creditors from half the capitals in Europe sent in their claims; and all the movable effects transmitted to Alain by his father's confidential Italian valet, except sundry carriages and horses which were sold at Baden for what they would fetch, were a magnificent dressing-case, in the secret drawer of which were some bank-notes amounting to thirty thousand francs, and three large boxes containing the Marquis's correspondence, a few miniature female portraits, and a great many locks of hair.

Wholly unprepared for the ruin that stared him in the face, the young Marquis evinced the natural strength of his character by the calmness with which he met the danger, and the intelligence with which he calculated and reduced it.

By the help of the family notary in the neighbouring town, he made himself master of his liabilities and his means; and he found that, after paying all debts and providing for the interest of the mortgages, a property which ought to have realized a rental of L10,000 a year yielded not more than L400. Nor was even this margin safe, nor the property out of peril; for the principal mortgagee, who was a capitalist in Paris named Louvier, having had during the life of the late Marquis more than once to wait for his half-yearly interest longer than suited his patience,—and his patience was not enduring,—plainly declared that if the same delay recurred he should put his right of seizure in force; and in France still more than in England, bad seasons seriously affect the security of rents. To pay away L9,600 a year regularly out of L10,000, with the penalty of forfeiting the whole if not paid,—whether crops may fail, farmers procrastinate, and timber fall in price,—is to live with the sword of Damocles over one's head.

For two years and more, however, Alain met his difficulties with prudence and vigour; he retrenched the establishment hitherto kept at the chateau, resigned such rural pleasures as he had been accustomed to indulge, and lived like one of his petty farmers. But the risks of the future remained undiminished.

"There is but one way, Monsieur le Marquis," said the family notary, M. Hebert, "by which you can put your estate in comparative safety. Your father raised his mortgages from time to time, as he wanted money, and often at interest above the average market interest. You may add considerably to your income by consolidating all these mortgages into one at a lower percentage, and in so doing pay off this formidable mortgagee, M. Louvier, who, I shrewdly suspect, is bent upon becoming the proprietor of Rochebriant. Unfortunately those few portions of your land which were but lightly charged, and, lying contiguous to small proprietors, were coveted by them, and could be advantageously sold, are already gone to pay the debts of Monsieur the late Marquis. There are, however, two small farms which, bordering close on the town of S______, I think I could dispose of for building purposes at high rates; but these lands are covered by M. Louvier's general mortgage, and he has refused to release them, unless the whole debt be paid. Were that debt therefore transferred to another mortgagee, we might stipulate for their exception, and in so doing secure a sum of more than 100,000 francs, which you could keep in reserve for a pressing or unforeseen occasion, and make the nucleus of a capital devoted to the gradual liquidation of the charges on the estate. For with a little capital, Monsieur le Marquis, your rent-roll might be very greatly increased, the forests and orchards improved, those meadows round S_____ drained and irrigated. Agriculture is beginning to be understood in Bretagne, and your estate would soon double its value in the hands of a spirited capitalist. My advice to you, therefore, is to go to Paris, employ a good 'avoue,' practised in such branch of his profession, to negotiate the consolidation of your mortgages upon terms that will enable you to sell outlying portions, and so pay off the charge by instalments agreed upon; to see if some safe company or rich individual can be found to undertake for a term of years the management of your forests, the draining of the S_____ meadows, the superintendence of your fisheries, etc. They, it is true, will monopolize the profits for many years,—perhaps twenty; but you are a young man: at the end of that time you will reenter on your estate with a rental so improved that the mortgages, now so awful, will seem to you comparatively trivial."

In pursuance of this advice, the young Marquis had come to Paris fortified with a letter from M. Hebert to an 'avoue' of eminence, and with many letters from his aunt to the nobles of the Faubourg connected with his house. Now one reason why M. Hebert had urged his client to undertake this important business in person, rather than volunteer his own services in Paris, was somewhat extra-professional. He had a sincere and profound affection for Alain; he felt compassion for that young life so barrenly wasted in seclusion and severe privations; he respected, but was too practical a man of business to share, those chivalrous sentiments of loyalty to an exiled dynasty which disqualified the man for the age he lived in, and, if not greatly modified, would cut him off from the hopes and aspirations of his eager generation. He thought plausibly enough that the air of the grand metropolis was necessary to the mental health, enfeebled and withering amidst the feudal mists of Bretagne; that once in Paris, Alain would imbibe the ideas of Paris, adapt himself to some career leading to honour and to fortune, for which he took facilities from his high birth, an historical name too national for any dynasty not to welcome among its adherents, and an intellect not yet sharpened by contact and competition with others, but in itself vigorous, habituated to thought, and vivified by the noble aspirations which belong to imaginative natures.

At the least, Alain would be at Paris in the social position which would afford him the opportunities of a marriage, in which his birth and rank would be readily accepted as an equivalent to some ample fortune that would serve to redeem the endangered seigneuries. He therefore warned Alain that the affair for which he went to Paris might be tedious, that lawyers were always slow, and advised him to calculate on remaining several months, perhaps a year; delicately suggesting that his rearing hitherto had been too secluded for his age and rank, and that a year at Paris, even if he failed in the object which took him there, would not be thrown away in the knowledge of men and things that would fit him better to grapple with his difficulties on his return.

Alain divided his spare income between his aunt and himself, and had come to Paris resolutely determined to live within the L200 a year which remained to his share. He felt the revolution in his whole being that commenced when out of sight of the petty principality in which he was the object of that feudal reverence, still surviving in the more unfrequented parts of Bretagne, for the representatives of illustrious names connected with the immemorial legends of the province.

The very bustle of a railway, with its crowd and quickness and unceremonious democracy of travel, served to pain and confound and humiliate that sense of individual dignity in which he had been nurtured. He felt that, once away from Rochebriant, he was but a cipher in the sum of human beings. Arrived at Paris, and reaching the gloomy hotel to which he had been recommended, he greeted even the desolation of that solitude which is usually so oppressive to a stranger in the metropolis of his native land. Loneliness was better than the loss of self in the reek and pressure of an unfamiliar throng. For the first few days he had wandered over Paris without calling even on the 'avoue' to whom M. Hebert had directed him. He felt with the instinctive acuteness of a mind which, under sounder training, would have achieved no mean distinction, that it was a safe precaution to imbue himself with the atmosphere of the place, and seize on those general ideas which in great capitals are so contagious that they are often more accurately caught by the first impressions than by subsequent habit, before he brought his mind into collision with those of the individuals he had practically to deal with.

At last he repaired to the 'avoue,' M. Gandrin, Rue St. Florentin. He had mechanically formed his idea of the abode and person of an 'avoue' from his association with M. Hebert. He expected to find a dull house in a dull street near the centre of business, remote from the haunts of idlers, and a grave man of unpretending exterior and matured years.

He arrived at a hotel newly fronted, richly decorated, in the fashionable quartier close by the Tuileries. He entered a wide 'porte cochere,' and was directed by the concierge to mount 'au premier.' There, first detained in an office faultlessly neat, with spruce young men at smart desks, he was at length admitted into a noble salon, and into the presence of a gentleman lounging in an easy-chair before a magnificent bureau of 'marqueterie, genre Louis Seize,' engaged in patting a white curly lapdog, with a pointed nose and a shrill bark.

The gentleman rose politely on his entrance, and released the dog, who, after sniffing the Marquis, condescended not to bite.

"Monsieur le Marquis," said M. Gandrin, glancing at the card and the introductory note from M. Hebert, which Alain had sent in, and which lay on the 'secretaire' beside heaps of letters nicely arranged and labelled, "charmed to make the honour of your acquaintance; just arrived at Paris? So M. Hebert—a very worthy person whom I have never seen, but with whom I have had correspondence—tells me you wish for my advice; in fact, he wrote to me some days ago, mentioning the business in question,—consolidation of mortgages. A very large sum wanted, Monsieur le Marquis, and not to be had easily."

"Nevertheless," said Alain, quietly, "I should imagine that there must be many capitalists in Paris willing to invest in good securities at fair interest."

"You are mistaken, Marquis; very few such capitalists. Men worth money nowadays like quick returns and large profits, thanks to the magnificent system of 'Credit Mobilier,' in which, as you are aware, a man may place his money in any trade or speculation without liabilities beyond his share. Capitalists are nearly all traders or speculators."

"Then," said the Marquis, half rising, "I am to presume, sir, that you are not likely to assist me."

"No, I don't say that, Marquis. I will look with care into the matter. Doubtless you have with you an abstract of the necessary documents, the conditions of the present mortgages, the rental of the estate, its probable prospects, and so forth."

"Sir, I have such an abstract with me at Paris; and having gone into it myself with M. Hebert, I can pledge you my word that it is strictly faithful to the facts."

The Marquis said this with naive simplicity, as if his word were quite sufficient to set that part of the question at rest. M. Gandrin smiled politely and said, "'Eh bien,' M. le Marquis: favour me with the abstract; in a week's time you shall have my opinion. You enjoy Paris? Greatly improved under the Emperor. 'Apropos,' Madame Gandrin receives tomorrow evening; allow me that opportunity to present you to her." Unprepared for the proffered hospitality, the Marquis had no option but to murmur his gratification and assent.

In a minute more he was in the streets. The next evening he went to Madame Gandrin's,—a brilliant reception,—a whole moving flower-bed of "decorations" there. Having gone through the ceremony of presentation to Madame Gandrin,—a handsome woman dressed to perfection, and conversing with the secretary to an embassy,—the young noble ensconced himself in an obscure and quiet corner, observing all and imagining that he escaped observation. And as the young men of his own years glided by him, or as their talk reached his ears, he became aware that from top to toe, within and without, he was old-fashioned, obsolete, not of his race, not of his day. His rank itself seemed to him a waste-paper title-deed to a heritage long lapsed. Not thus the princely seigneurs of Rochebriant made their 'debut' at the capital of their nation. They had had the 'entree' to the cabinets of their kings; they had glittered in the halls of Versailles; they had held high posts of distinction in court and camp; the great Order of St. Louis had seemed their hereditary appanage. His father, though a voluntary exile in manhood, had been in childhood a king's page, and throughout life remained the associate of princes; and here, in an 'avoue's soiree,' unknown, unregarded, an expectant on an 'avoue's' patronage, stood the last lord of Rochebriant.

It is easy to conceive that Alain did not stay long. But he stayed long enough to convince him that on L200 a year the polite society of Paris, even as seen at M. Gandrin's, was not for him. Nevertheless, a day or two after, he resolved to call upon the nearest of his kinsmen to whom his aunt had given him letters. With the Count de Vandemar, one of his fellow-nobles of the sacred Faubourg, he should be no less Rochebriant, whether in a garret or a palace. The Vandemars, in fact, though for many generations before the First Revolution a puissant and brilliant family, had always recognized the Rochebriants as the head of their house,—the trunk from which they had been slipped in the fifteenth century, when a younger son of the Rochebriants married a wealthy heiress and took the title with the lands of Vandemar.

Since then the two families had often intermarried. The present count had a reputation for ability, was himself a large proprietor, and might furnish advice to guide Alain in his negotiations with M. Gandrin. The Hotel do Vandemar stood facing the old Hotel de Rochebriant; it was less spacious, but not less venerable, gloomy, and prison-like.

As he turned his eyes from the armorial scutcheon which still rested, though chipped and mouldering, over the portals of his lost ancestral house, and was about to cross the street, two young men, who seemed two or three years older than himself, emerged on horseback from the Hotel de Vandemar.

Handsome young men, with the lofty look of the old race, dressed with the punctilious care of person which is not foppery in men of birth, but seems part of the self-respect that appertains to the old chivalric point of honour. The horse of one of these cavaliers made a caracole which brought it nearly upon Alain as he was about to cross. The rider, checking his steed, lifted his hat to Alain and uttered a word of apology in the courtesy of ancient high-breeding, but still with condescension as to an inferior. This little incident, and the slighting kind of notice received from coevals of his own birth, and doubtless his own blood,—for he divined truly that they were the sons of the Count de Vandemar,—disconcerted Alain to a degree which perhaps a Frenchman alone can comprehend. He had even half a mind to give up his visit and turn back. However, his native manhood prevailed over that morbid sensitiveness which, born out of the union of pride and poverty, has all the effects of vanity, and yet is not vanity itself.

The Count was at home, a thin spare man with a narrow but high forehead, and an expression of countenance keen, severe, and 'un peu moqueuse.'

He received the Marquis, however, at first with great cordiality, kissed him on both sides of his cheek, called him "cousin," expressed immeasurable regret that the Countess was gone out on one of the missions of charity in which the great ladies of the Faubourg religiously interest themselves, and that his sons had just ridden forth to the Bois.

As Alain, however, proceeded, simply and without false shame, to communicate the object of his visit at Paris, the extent of his liabilities, and the penury of his means, the smile vanished from the Count's face. He somewhat drew back his fauteuil in the movement common to men who wish to estrange themselves from some other man's difficulties; and when Alain came to a close, the Count remained some moments seized with a slight cough; and, gazing intently on the carpet, at length he said, "My dear young friend, your father behaved extremely ill to you,—dishonourably, fraudulently."

"Hold!" said the Marquis, colouring high. "Those are words no man can apply to my father in my presence."

The Count stared, shrugged his shoulders, and replied with 'sang froid,' "Marquis, if you are contented with your father's conduct, of course it is no business of mine: he never injured me. I presume, however, that, considering my years and my character, you come to me for advice: is it so?"

Alain bowed his head in assent.

"There are four courses for one in your position to take," said the Count, placing the index of the right hand successively on the thumb and three fingers of the left,—"four courses, and no more.

"First. To do as your notary recommended: consolidate your mortgages, patch up your income as you best can, return to Rochebriant, and devote the rest of your existence to the preservation of your property. By that course your life will be one of permanent privation, severe struggle; and the probability is that you will not succeed: there will come one or two bad seasons, the farmers will fail to pay, the mortgagee will foreclose, and you may find yourself, after twenty years of anxiety and torment, prematurely old and without a sou.

"Course the second. Rochebriant, though so heavily encumbered as to yield you some such income as your father gave to his chef de cuisine, is still one of those superb 'terres' which bankers and Jews and stock-jobbers court and hunt after, for which they will give enormous sums. If you place it in good hands, I do not doubt that you could dispose of the property within three months, on terms that would leave you a considerable surplus, which, invested with judgment, would afford you whereon you could live at Paris in a way suitable to your rank and age. Need we go further?—does this course smile to you?"

"Pass on, Count; I will defend to the last what I take from my ancestors, and cannot voluntarily sell their roof-tree and their tombs."

"Your name would still remain, and you would be just as well received in Paris, and your 'noblesse' just as implicitly conceded, if all Judaea encamped upon Rochebriant. Consider how few of us 'gentilshommes' of the old regime have any domains left to us. Our names alone survive: no revolution can efface them."

"It may be so, but pardon me; there are subjects on which we cannot reason,—we can but feel. Rochebriant may be torn from me, but I cannot yield it."

"I proceed to the third course. Keep the chateau and give up its traditions; remain 'de facto' Marquis of Rochebriant, but accept the new order of things. Make yourself known to the people in power. They will be charmed to welcome you a convert from the old noblesse is a guarantee of stability to the new system. You will be placed in diplomacy; effloresce into an ambassador, a minister,—and ministers nowadays have opportunities to become enormously rich."

"That course is not less impossible than the last. Till Henry V. formally resign his right to the throne of Saint Louis, I can be servant to no other man seated on that throne."

"Such, too, is my creed," said the Count, "and I cling to it; but my estate is not mortgaged, and I have neither the tastes nor the age for public employments. The last course is perhaps better than the rest; at all events it is the easiest. A wealthy marriage; even if it must be a 'mesalliance.' I think at your age, with your appearance, that your name is worth at least two million francs in the eyes of a rich 'roturier' with an ambitious daughter."

"Alas!" said the young man, rising, "I see I shall have to go back to Rochebriant. I cannot sell my castle, I cannot sell my creed, and I cannot sell my name and myself."

"The last all of us did in the old 'regime,' Marquis. Though I still retain the title of Vandemar, my property comes from the Farmer-General's daughter, whom my great-grandfather, happily for us, married in the days of Louis Quinze. Marriages with people of sense and rank have always been 'marriages de convenance' in France. It is only in 'le petit monde' that men having nothing marry girls having nothing, and I don't believe they are a bit the happier for it. On the contrary, the 'quarrels de menage' leading to frightful crimes appear by the 'Gazette des Tribunaux' to be chiefly found among those who do not sell themselves at the altar."

The old Count said this with a grim 'persiflage.' He was a Voltairian.

Voltairianism, deserted by the modern Liberals of France, has its chief cultivation nowadays among the wits of the old 'regime.' They pick up its light weapons on the battle-field on which their fathers perished, and re-feather against the 'canaille' the shafts which had been pointed against the 'noblesse.'

"Adieu, Count," said Alain, rising; "I do not thank you less for your advice because I have not the wit to profit by it."

"'Au revoir,' my cousin; you will think better of it when you have been a month or two at Paris. By the way, my wife receives every Wednesday; consider our house yours."

"Count, can I enter into the world which Madame la Comtesse receives, in the way that becomes my birth, on the income I take from my fortune?"

The Count hesitated. "No," said he at last, frankly; "not because you will be less welcome or less respected, but because I see that you have all the pride and sensitiveness of a 'seigneur de province.' Society would therefore give you pain, not pleasure. More than this, I know, by the remembrance of my own youth and the sad experience of my own sons, that you would be irresistibly led into debt, and debt in your circumstances would be the loss of Rochebriant. No; I invite you to visit us. I offer you the most select but not the most brilliant circles of Paris, because my wife is religious, and frightens away the birds of gay plumage with the scarecrows of priests and bishops. But if you accept my invitation and my offer, I am bound, as an old man of the world to a young kinsman, to say that the chances are that you will be ruined."

"I thank you, Count, for your candour; and I now acknowledge that I have found a relation and a guide," answered the Marquis, with nobility of mien that was not without a pathos which touched the hard heart of the old man.

"Come at least whenever you want a sincere if a rude friend;" and though he did not kiss his cousin's cheek this time, he gave him, with more sincerity, a parting shake of the hand.

And these made the principal events in Alain's Paris life till he met Frederic Lemercier. Hitherto he had received no definite answer from M. Gandrin, who had postponed an interview, not having had leisure to make himself master of all the details in the abstract sent to him.

# CHAPTER IV.

The next day, towards the afternoon, Frederic Lemercier, somewhat breathless from the rapidity at which he had ascended to so high an eminence, burst into Alain's chamber.

"'Br-r! mon cher;' what superb exercise for the health—how it must strengthen the muscles and expand the chest! After this who should shrink from scaling Mont Blanc? Well, well. I have been meditating on your business ever since we parted. But I would fain know more of its details. You shall confide them to me as we drive through the Bois. My coupe is below, and the day is beautiful; come."

To the young Marquis, the gayety, the heartiness of his college friend were a cordial. How different from the dry counsels of the Count de Vandemar! Hope, though vaguely, entered into his heart. Willingly he accepted Frederic's invitation, and the young men were soon rapidly borne along the Champs Elysees. As briefly as he could Alain described the state of his affairs, the nature of his mortgages, and the result of his interview with M. Gandrin.

Frederic listened attentively. "Then Gandrin has given you as yet no answer?"

"None; but I have a note from him this morning asking me to call to-morrow."

"After you have seen him, decide on nothing,—if he makes you any offer. Get back your abstract, or a copy of it, and confide it to me. Gandrin ought to help you; he transacts affairs in a large way. 'Belle clientele' among the millionnaires. But his clients expect fabulous profits, and so does he. As for your principal mortgagee, Louvier, you know, of course, who he is."

"No, except that M. Hebert told me that he was very rich."

"'Rich' I should think so; one of the Kings of Finance, Ah! observe those young men on horseback."

Alain looked forth and recognized the two cavaliers whom he had conjectured to be the sons of the Count de Vandemar.

"Those 'beaux garcons' are fair specimens of your Faubourg," said Frederic; "they would decline my acquaintance because my grandfather kept a shop, and they keep a shop between them."

"A shop! I am mistaken, then. Who are they?"

"Raoul and Enguerrand, sons of that mocker of man, the Count de Vandemar."

"And they keep a shop! You are jesting."

"A shop at which you may buy gloves and perfumes, Rue de la Chaussee d'Antin. Of course they don't serve at the counter; they only invest their pocket-money in the speculation; and, in so doing, treble at least their pocket-money, buy their horses, and keep their grooms."

"Is it possible! nobles of such birth! How shocked the Count would be if he knew it!"

"Yes, very much shocked if he was supposed to know it. But he is too wise a father not to give his sons limited allowances and unlimited liberty, especially the liberty to add to the allowances as they please. Look again at them; no better riders and more affectionate brothers since the date of Castor and Pollux. Their tastes indeed differ—Raoul is religious and moral, melancholy and dignified; Enguerrand is a lion of the first water,—elegant to the tips of his nails. These demigods nevertheless are very mild to mortals. Though Enguerrand is the best pistol-shot in Paris, and Raoul the best fencer, the first is so good-tempered that you would be a brute to quarrel with him, the last so true a Catholic, that if you quarrelled with him you need not fear his sword. He would not die in the committal of what the Church holds a mortal sin."

"Are you speaking ironically? Do you mean to imply that men of the name of Vandemar are not brave?"

"On the contrary, I believe that, though masters of their weapons, they are too brave to abuse their skill; and I must add that, though they are sleeping partners in a shop, they would not cheat you of a farthing. Benign stars on earth, as Castor and Pollux were in heaven."

"But partners in a shop!"

"Bah! when a minister himself, like the late M. de M______, kept a shop, and added the profits of 'bons bons' to his revenue, you may form some idea of the spirit of the age. If young nobles are not generally sleeping partners in shops, still they are more or less adventurers in commerce. The Bourse is the profession of those who have no other profession. You have visited the Bourse?"

"No."

"No! this is just the hour. We have time yet for the Bois. Coachman, drive to the Bourse."

"The fact is," resumed Frederic, "that gambling is one of the wants of civilized men. The 'rouge-et-noir' and 'roulette' tables are forbidden; the hells closed: but the passion for making money without working for it must have its vent, and that vent is the Bourse. As instead of a hundred wax-lights you now have one jet of gas, so instead of a hundred hells you have now one Bourse, and—it is exceedingly convenient; always at hand; no discredit being seen there as it was to be seen at Frascati's; on the contrary, at once respectable, and yet the mode."

The coupe stops at the Bourse, our friends mount the steps, glide through the pillars, deposit their canes at a place destined to guard them, and the Marquis follows Frederic up a flight of stairs till he gains the open gallery round a vast hall below. Such a din! such a clamour! disputations, wrangling, wrathful.

Here Lemercier distinguished some friends, whom he joined for a few minutes.

Alain left alone, looked down into the hall. He thought himself in some stormy scene of the First Revolution. An English contested election in the market-place of a borough when the candidates are running close on each other—the result doubtful, passions excited, the whole borough in civil war—is peaceful compared to the scene at the Bourse.

Bulls and bears screaming, bawling, gesticulating, as if one were about to strangle the other; the whole, to an uninitiated eye, a confusion, a Babel, which it seems absolutely impossible to reconcile to the notion of quiet mercantile transactions, the purchase and sale of shares and stocks. As Alain gazed bewildered, he felt himself gently touched, and, looking round, saw the Englishman.

"A lively scene!" whispered Mr. Vane. "This is the heart of Paris: it beats very loudly."

"Is your Bourse in London like this?"

"I cannot tell you: at our Exchange the general public are not admitted: the privileged priests of that temple sacrifice their victims in closed penetralia, beyond which the sounds made in the operation do not travel to ears profane. But had we an Exchange like this open to all the world, and placed, not in a region of our metropolis unknown to fashion, but in some elegant square in St. James's or at Hyde Park Corner, I suspect that our national character would soon undergo a great change, and that all our idlers and sporting-men would make their books there every day, instead of waiting long months in 'ennui' for the Doncaster and the Derby. At present we have but few men on the turf; we should then have few men not on

Exchange, especially if we adopt your law, and can contrive to be traders without risk of becoming bankrupts. Napoleon I. called us a shopkeeping nation. Napoleon III. has taught France to excel us in everything, and certainly he has made Paris a shopkeeping city."

Alain thought of Raoul and Enguerrand, and blushed to find that what he considered a blot on his countrymen was so familiarly perceptible to a foreigner's eye.

"And the Emperor has done wisely, at least for the time," continued the Englishman, with a more thoughtful accent. "He has found vent thus for that very dangerous class in Paris society to which the subdivision of property gave birth; namely the crowd of well-born, daring young men without fortune and without profession. He has opened the 'Bourse' and said, 'There, I give you employment, resource, an 'avenir.'' He has cleared the byways into commerce and trade, and opened new avenues of wealth to the noblesse, whom the great Revolution so unwisely beggared. What other way to rebuild a 'noblesse' in France, and give it a chance of power be side an access to fortune? But to how many sides of your national character has the Bourse of Paris magnetic attraction! You Frenchmen are so brave that you could not be happy without facing danger, so covetous of distinction that you would pine yourselves away without a dash, coute quo coute, at celebrity and a red ribbon. Danger! look below at that arena: there it is; danger daily, hourly. But there also is celebrity; win at the Bourse, as of old in a tournament, and paladins smile on you, and ladies give you their scarves, or, what is much the same, they allow you to buy their cachemires. Win at the Bourse,—what follows? the Chamber, the Senate, the Cross, the Minister's 'portefeuille.' I might rejoice in all this for the sake of Europe,—could it last, and did it not bring the consequences that follow the demoralization which attends it. The Bourse and the Credit Mobilier keep Paris quiet, at least as quiet as it can be. These are the secrets of this reign of splendour; these the two lions couchants on which rests the throne of the Imperial reconstructor."

Alain listened surprised and struck. He had not given the Englishman credit for the cast of mind which such reflections evinced.

Here Lemercier rejoined them, and shook hands with Graham Vane, who, taking him aside, said, "But you promised to go to the Bois, and indulge my insane curiosity about the lady in the pearl-coloured robe?"

"I have not forgotten; it is not half-past two yet; you said three. 'Soyez tranquille;' I drive thither from the Bourse with Rochebriant."

"Is it necessary to take with you that very good-looking Marquis?"

"I thought you said you were not jealous, because not yet in love. However, if Rochebriant occasions you the pang which your humble servant failed to inflict, I will take care that he do not see the lady."

"No," said the Englishman; "on consideration, I should be very much obliged to any one with whom she would fall in love. That would disenchant me. Take the Marquis by all means."

Meanwhile Alain, again looking down, saw just under him, close by one of the pillars, Lucien Duplessis. He was standing apart from the throng, a small space cleared round himself, and two men who had the air of gentlemen of the 'beau monde,' with whom he was conferring. Duplessis, thus seen, was not like the Duplessis at the restaurant. It would be difficult to explain what the change was, but it forcibly struck Alain: the air was more dignified, the expression keener; there was a look of conscious power and command about the man even at that distance; the intense, concentrated intelligence of his eye, his firm lip, his marked features, his projecting, massive brow, would have impressed a very ordinary observer. In fact, the man was here in his native element; in the field in which his intellect gloried, commanded, and had signalized itself by successive triumphs. Just thus may be the change in the great orator whom you deemed insignificant in a drawing-room, when you see his crest rise above a reverential audience; or the great soldier, who was not distinguishable from the subaltern in a peaceful club, could you see him issuing the order to his aids-de-camp amidst the smoke and roar of the battle-field.

"Ah, Marquis!" said Graham Vane, "are you gazing at Duplessis? He is the modern genius of Paris. He is at once the Cousin, the Guizot, and the Victor Hugo of speculation. Philosophy, Eloquence, audacious Romance,—all Literature now is swallowed up in the sublime epic of 'Agiotage,' and Duplessis is the poet of the Empire."

"Well said, M. Grarm Varn," cried Frederic, forgetting his recent lesson in English names. "Alain underrates that great man. How could an Englishman appreciate him so well?"

"'Ma foi!'" returned Graham, quietly. "I am studying to think at Paris, in order some day or other to know how to act in London. Time for the Bois. Lemercier, we meet at seven,—Philippe's."

# CHAPTER V.

"What do you think of the Bourse?" asked Lemercier, as their carriage took the way to the Bois.

"I cannot think of it yet; I am stunned. It seems to me as if I had been at a 'Sabbat,' of which the wizards were 'agents de change,' but not less bent upon raising Satan."

"Pooh! the best way to exorcise Satan is to get rich enough not to be tempted by him. The fiend always loved to haunt empty places; and of all places nowadays he prefers empty purses and empty stomachs."

"But do all people get rich at the Bourse? or is not one man's wealth many men's ruin?"

"That is a question not very easy to answer; but under our present system Paris gets rich, though at the expense of individual Parisians. I will try and explain. The average luxury is enormously increased even in my experience; what were once considered refinements and fopperies are now called necessary comforts. Prices are risen enormously, house-rent doubled within the last five or six years; all articles of luxury are very much dearer; the very gloves I wear cost twenty per cent more than I used to pay for gloves of the same quality. How the people we meet live, and live so well, is an enigma that would defy AEdipus if AEdipus were not a Parisian. But the main explanation is this: speculation and commerce, with the facilities given to all investments, have really opened more numerous and more rapid ways to fortune than were known a few years ago.

"Crowds are thus attracted to Paris, resolved to venture a small capital in the hope of a large one; they live on that capital, not on their income, as gamesters do. There is an idea among us that it is necessary to seem rich in order to become rich. Thus there is a general extravagance and profusion. English milords marvel at our splendour. Those who, while spending their capital as their income, fail in their schemes of fortune, after one, two, three, or four years, vanish. What becomes of them, I know no more than I do what becomes of the old moons. Their place is immediately supplied by new candidates. Paris is thus kept perennially sumptuous and splendid by the gold it engulfs. But then some men succeed,—succeed prodigiously, preternaturally; they make colossal fortunes, which are magnificently expended. They set an example of show and pomp, which is of course the more contagious because so many men say, 'The other day those millionnaires were as poor as we are; they never economized; why should we?' Paris is thus doubly enriched,—by the fortunes it swallows up, and by the fortunes it casts up; the last being always reproductive, and the first never lost except to the individuals."

"I understand: but what struck me forcibly at the scene we have left was the number of young men there; young men whom I should judge by their appearance to be gentlemen, evidently not mere spectators,—eager, anxious, with tablets in their hands. That old or middle-aged men should find a zest in the pursuit of gain I can understand, but youth and avarice seem to me a new combination, which Moliere never divined in his 'Avare.'"

"Young men, especially if young gentlemen, love pleasure; and pleasure in this city is very dear. This explains why so many young men frequent the Bourse. In the old gaining now suppressed, young men were the majority; in the days of your chivalrous forefathers it was the young nobles, not the old, who would stake their very mantles and swords on a cast of the die. And, naturally enough, mon cher; for is not youth the season of hope, and is not hope the goddess of gaming, whether at rouge-et-noir or the Bourse?"

Alain felt himself more and more behind his generation. The acute reasoning of Lemercier humbled his amour propre. At college Lemercier was never considered Alain's equal in ability or book-learning. What a stride beyond his school-fellow had Lemercier now made! How dull and stupid the young provincial felt himself to be as compared with the easy cleverness and half-sportive philosophy of the Parisian's fluent talk!

He sighed with a melancholy and yet with a generous envy. He had too fine a natural perception not to acknowledge that there is a rank of mind as well as of birth, and in the first he felt that Lemercier might well walk before a Rochebriant; but his very humility was a proof that he underrated himself.

Lemercier did not excel him in mind, but in experience. And just as the drilled soldier seems a much finer fellow than the raw recruit, because he knows how to carry himself, but after a year's discipline the raw recruit may excel in martial air the upright hero whom he now despairingly admires, and never dreams he can rival; so set a mind from a village into the drill of a capital, and see it a year after; it may tower a head higher than its recruiting-sergeant.

# CHAPTER VI.

"I believe," said Lemercier, as the coupe rolled through the lively alleys of the Bois de Boulogne, "that Paris is built on a loadstone, and that every Frenchman with some iron globules in his blood is irresistibly attracted towards it. The English never seem to feel for London the passionate devotion that we feel for Paris. On the contrary, the London middle class, the commercialists, the shopkeepers, the clerks, even the superior artisans compelled to do their business in the capital, seem always scheming and pining to have their home out of it, though but in a suburb."

"You have been in London, Frederic?"

"Of course; it is the mode to visit that dull and hideous metropolis."

"If it be dull and hideous, no wonder the people who are compelled to do business in it seek the pleasures of home out of it."

"It is very droll that though the middle class entirely govern the melancholy Albion, it is the only country in Europe in which the middle class seem to have no amusements; nay, they legislate against amusement. They have no leisure-day but Sunday; and on that day they close all their theatres, even their museums and picture-galleries. What amusements there may be in England are for the higher classes and the lowest."

"What are the amusements of the lowest class?"

"Getting drunk."

"Nothing else?"

"Yes. I was taken at night under protection of a policeman to some cabarets, where I found crowds of that class which is the stratum below the working class; lads who sweep crossings and hold horses, mendicants, and, I was told, thieves, girls whom a servant-maid would not speak to, very merry, dancing quadrilles and waltzes, and regaling themselves on sausages,—the happiest-looking folks I found in all London; and, I must say, conducting themselves very decently."

"Ah!" Here Lemercier pulled the check-string. "Will you object to a walk in this quiet alley? I see some one whom I have promised the Englishman to—But heed me, Alain, don't fall in love with her."

# CHAPTER VII.

The lady in the pearl-coloured dress! Certainly it was a face that might well arrest the eye and linger long on the remembrance.

There are certain "beauty-women" as there are certain "beauty-men," in whose features one detects no fault, who are the show figures of any assembly in which they appear, but who, somehow or other, inspire no sentiment and excite no interest; they lack some expression, whether of mind, or of soul, or of heart, without which the most beautiful face is but a beautiful picture. This lady was not one of those "beauty-women." Her features taken singly were by no means perfect, nor were they set off by any brilliancy of colouring. But the countenance aroused and impressed the imagination with a belief that there was some history attached to it, which you longed to learn. The hair, simply parted over a forehead unusually spacious and high for a woman, was of lustrous darkness; the eyes, of a deep violet blue, were shaded with long lashes.

Their expression was soft and mournful, but unobservant. She did not notice Alain and Lemercier as the two men slowly passed her. She seemed abstracted, gazing into space as one absorbed in thought or revery. Her complexion was clear and pale, and apparently betokened delicate health.

Lemercier seated himself on a bench beside the path, and invited Alain to do the same. "She will return this way soon," said the Parisian, "and we can observe her more attentively and more respectfully thus seated than if we were on foot; meanwhile, what do you think of her? Is she French? is she Italian? can she be English?"

"I should have guessed Italian, judging by the darkness of the hair and the outline of the features; but do Italians have so delicate a fairness of complexion?"

"Very rarely; and I should guess her to be French, judging by the intelligence of her expression, the simple neatness of her dress, and by that nameless refinement of air in which a Parisienne excels all the descendants of Eve,—if it were not for her eyes. I never saw a Frenchwoman with eyes of that peculiar shade of blue; and if a Frenchwoman had such eyes, I flatter myself she would have scarcely allowed us to pass without making some use of them."

"Do you think she is married?" asked Alain.

"I hope so; for a girl of her age, if comme il faut, can scarcely walk alone in the Bois, and would not have acquired that look so intelligent,—more than intelligent,—so poetic."

"But regard that air of unmistakable distinction; regard that expression of face,-so pure, so virginal: comme il faut she must be."

As Alain said these last words, the lady, who had turned back, was approaching them, and in full view of their gaze. She seemed unconscious of their existence as before, and Lemercier noticed that her lips moved as if she were murmuring inaudibly to herself.

She did not return again, but continued her walk straight on till at the end of the alley she entered a carriage in waiting for her, and was driven off.

"Quick, quick!" cried Lemercier, running towards his own coupe; "we must give chase."

Alain followed somewhat less hurriedly, and, agreeably to instructions Lemercier had already given to his coachman, the Parisian's coupe set off at full speed in the track of the strange lady's, which was still in sight.

In less than twenty minutes the carriage in chase stopped at the grille of one of those charming little villas to be found in the pleasant suburb of A——; a porter emerged from the lodge, opened the gate; the carriage drove in, again stopped at the door of the house, and the two gentlemen could not catch even a glimpse of the lady's robe as she descended from the carriage and disappeared within the house.

"I see a cafe yonder," said Lemercier; "let us learn all we can as to the fair unknown, over a sorbet or a petit verre." Alain silently, but not reluctantly, consented. He felt in the fair stranger an interest new to his existence.

They entered the little cafe, and in a few minutes Lemercier, with the easy savoir vivre of a Parisian, had extracted from the garcon as much as probably any one in the neighbourhood knew of the inhabitants of the villa.

It had been hired and furnished about two months previously in the name of Signora Venosta; but, according to the report of the servants, that lady appeared to be the gouvernante or guardian of a lady much younger, out of whose income the villa was rented and the household maintained.

It was for her the coupe was hired from Paris. The elder lady very rarely stirred out during the day, but always accompanied the younger in any evening visits to the theatre or the houses of friends.

It was only within the last few weeks that such visits had been made.

The younger lady was in delicate health, and under the care of an English physician famous for skill in the treatment of pulmonary complaints. It was by his advice that she took daily walking exercise in the Bois. The establishment consisted of three servants, all Italians, and speaking but imperfect French. The garcon did not know whether either of the ladies was married, but their mode of life was free from all scandal or suspicion; they probably belonged to the literary or musical world, as the garcon had observed as their visitors the eminent author M. Savarin and his wife; and, still more frequently, an old man not less eminent as a musical composer.

"It is clear to me now," said Lemercier, as the two friends reseated themselves in the carriage, "that our pearly ange is some Italian singer of repute enough in her own country to have gained already a competence; and that, perhaps on account of her own health or her friend's, she is living quietly here in the expectation of some professional engagement, or the absence of some foreign lover."

"Lover! do you think that?" exclaimed Alain, in a tone of voice that betrayed pain.

"It is possible enough; and in that case the Englishman may profit little by the information I have promised to give him."

"You have promised the Englishman?"

"Do you not remember last night that he described the lady, and said that her face haunted him: and I—"

"Ah! I remember now. What do you know of this Englishman? He is rich, I suppose."

"Yes, I hear he is very rich now; that an uncle lately left him an enormous sum of money. He was attached to the English Embassy many years ago, which accounts for his good French and his knowledge of Parisian life. He comes to Paris very often, and I have known him some time. Indeed he has intrusted to me a difficult and delicate commission. The English tell me that his father was one of the most eminent members of their Parliament, of ancient birth, very highly connected, but ran out his fortune and died poor; that our friend had for some years to maintain himself, I fancy, by his pen; that he is considered very able; and, now that his uncle has enriched him, likely to enter public life and run a career as distinguished as his father's."

"Happy man! happy are the English," said the Marquis, with a sigh; and as the carriage now entered Paris, he pleaded the excuse of an engagement, bade his friend goodby, and went his way musing through the crowded streets.

# CHAPTER VIII.

## LETTER FROM ISAURA CICOGNA TO MADAME DE GRANTMESNIL.

*VILLA D'— —-, A— — —.*

I can never express to you, my beloved Eulalie, the strange charm which a letter from you throws over my poor little lonely world for days after it is received. There is always in it something that comforts, something that sustains, but also a something that troubles and disquiets me. I suppose Goethe is right, "that it is the property of true genius to disturb all settled ideas," in order, no doubt, to lift them into a higher level when they settle down again.

Your sketch of the new work you are meditating amid the orange groves of Provence interests me intensely; yet, do you forgive me when I add that the interest is not without terror? I do not find myself able to comprehend how, amid those lovely scenes of Nature, your mind voluntarily surrounds itself with images of pain and discord. I stand in awe of the calm with which you subject to your analysis the infirmities of reason and the tumults of passion. And all those laws of the social state which seem to me so fixed and immovable you treat with so quiet a scorn, as if they were but the gossamer threads which a touch of your slight woman's hand could brush away. But I cannot venture to discuss such subjects with you. It is only the skilled enchanter who can stand safely in the magic circle, and compel the spirits that he summons, even if they are evil, to minister to ends in which he foresees a good.

We continue to live here very quietly, and I do not as yet feel the worse for the colder climate. Indeed, my wonderful doctor, who was recommended to me as American, but is in reality English, assures me that a single winter spent here under his care will suffice for my complete re-establishment. Yet that career, to the training for which so many years have been devoted, does not seem to me so alluring as it once did.

I have much to say on this subject, which I defer till I can better collect my own thoughts on it; at present they are confused and struggling. The great Maestro has been most gracious.

In what a radiant atmosphere his genius lives and breathes! Even in his cynical moods, his very cynicism has in it the ring of a jocund music,—the laugh of Figaro, not of Mephistopheles.

We went to dine with him last week. He invited to meet us Madame S———, who has this year conquered all opposition, and reigns alone, the great S———; Mr. T————, a pianist of admirable promise; your friend M. Savarin, wit, critic, and poet, with his pleasant, sensible wife; and a few others, who, the Maestro confided to me in a whisper, were authorities in the press. After dinner S——- sang to us, magnificently, of course. Then she herself graciously turned to me, said how much she had heard from the Maestro in my praise, and so and so. I was persuaded to sing after her. I need not say to what disadvantage. But I forgot my nervousness; I forgot my audience; I forgot myself, as I always do when once my soul, as it were, finds wing in music, and buoys itself in the air, relieved from the sense of earth. I knew not that I had succeeded till I came to a close, and then my eyes resting on the face of the grand prima donna, I was seized with an indescribable sadness, with a keen pang of remorse. Perfect artiste though she be, and with powers in her own realm of art which admit of no living equal, I saw at once that I had pained her: she had grown almost livid; her lips were quivering, and it was only with a great effort that she muttered out some faint words intended for applause. I comprehended by an instinct how gradually there can grow upon the mind of an artist the most generous that jealousy which makes the fear of a rival annihilate the delight in art. If ever I should achieve S——-'s fame as a singer, should I feel the same jealousy?—I think not now, but I have not been tested. She went away abruptly. I spare you the recital of the compliments paid to me by my other auditors, compliments that gave me no pleasure; for on all lips, except those of the Maestro, they implied, as the height of eulogy, that I had inflicted torture upon S——-. "If so," said he, "she would be as foolish as a rose that was jealous of the whiteness of a lily. You would do yourself great wrong, my child, if you tried to vie with the rose in its own colour."

He patted my bended head as he spoke, with that kind of fatherly king-like fondness with which he honours me; and I took his hand in mine, and kissed it gratefully. "Nevertheless," said Savarin, "when the lily comes out there will be a furious attack on it, made by the clique that devotes itself to the rose: a lily clique will be formed en revanche, and I foresee a fierce paper war. Do not be frightened at its first outburst: every fame worth having must be fought for."

Is it so? have you had to fight for your fame, Eulalie? and do you hate all contests as much as I do?

Our only other gayety since I last wrote was a soiree at M. Louvier's. That republican millionaire was not slow in attending to the kind letter you addressed to him recommending us to his civilities. He called at once, placed his good offices at our disposal, took charge of my modest fortune, which he has invested, no doubt, as safely as it is advantageously in point of interest, hired our carriage for us, and in short has been most amiably useful.

At his house we met many to me most pleasant, for they spoke with such genuine appreciation of your works and yourself. But there were others whom I should never have expected to meet under the roof of a Croesus who has so great a stake in the order of things established. One young man—a noble whom he specially presented to me, as a politician who would be at the head of affairs when the Red Republic was established—asked me whether I did not agree with him that all private property was public spoliation, and that the great enemy to civilization was religion, no matter in what form.

He addressed to me these tremendous questions with an effeminate lisp, and harangued on them with small feeble gesticulations of pale dirty fingers covered with rings.

I asked him if there were many who in France shared his ideas.

"Quite enough to carry them some day," he answered with a lofty smile. "And the day may be nearer than the world thinks, when my confreres will be so numerous that they will have to shoot down each other for the sake of cheese to their bread."

That day nearer than the world thinks! Certainly, so far as one may judge the outward signs of the world at Paris, it does not think of such things at all. With what an air of self-content the beautiful city parades her riches! Who can gaze on her splendid palaces, her gorgeous shops, and believe that she will give ear to doctrines that would annihilate private rights of property; or who can enter her crowded churches, and dream that she can ever again install a republic too civilized for religion?

*Adieu. Excuse me for this dull letter. If I have written on much that has little interest even for me, it is that I wish to distract my mind from brooding over the question that interests me most, and on which I most need your counsel. I will try to approach it in my next.*

*ISAURA.*

*FROM THE SAME TO THE SAME.*

Eulalie, Eulalie!—What mocking spirit has been permitted in this modern age of ours to place in the heart of woman the ambition which is the prerogative of men? You indeed, so richly endowed with a man's genius, have a right to man's aspirations. But what can justify such ambition in me? Nothing but this one unintellectual perishable gift of a voice that does but please in uttering the thoughts of others. Doubtless I could make a name familiar for its brief time to the talk of Europe,—a name, what name? a singer's name. Once I thought that name a glory. Shall I ever forget the day when you first shone upon me; when, emerging from childhood as from a dim and solitary bypath, I stood forlorn on the great thoroughfare of life, and all the prospects before me stretched sad in mists and in rain? You beamed on me then as the sun coming out from the cloud and changing the face of earth; you opened to my sight the fairy-land of poetry and art; you took me by the hand and said, "Courage! there is at each step some green gap in the hedgerows, some, soft escape from the stony thoroughfare. Beside the real life expands the ideal life to those who seek it. Droop not, seek it: the ideal life has its sorrows, but it never admits despair; as on the ear of him who follows the winding course of a stream, the stream ever varies the note of its music,—now loud with the rush of the falls; now low and calm as it glides by the level marge of smooth banks; now sighing through the stir of the reeds; now babbling with a fretful joy as some sudden curve on the shore stays its flight among gleaming pebbles,—so to the soul of the artist is the voice of the art ever fleeting beside and before him. Nature gave thee the bird's gift of song: raise the gift into art, and make the art thy companion.

"Art and Hope were twin-born, and they die together." See how faithfully I remember, methinks, your very words. But the magic of the words, which I then but dimly understood, was in your smile and in your eye, and the queen-like wave of your hand as if beckoning to a world which lay before you, visible and familiar as your native land. And how devotedly, with what earnestness of passion, I gave myself up to the task of raising my gift into an art! I thought of nothing else, dreamed of nothing else; and oh, now sweet to me then were words of praise! "Another year yet," at length said the masters, "and you ascend your throne among the queens of song." Then—then—I would have changed for no other throne on earth my hope of that to be achieved in the realms of my art. And then came that long fever: my strength broke down, and the Maestro said, "Rest, or your voice is gone, and your throne is lost forever." How hateful that rest seemed to me! You again came to my aid. You said, "The time you think lost should be but time improved. Penetrate your mind with other songs than the trash of Libretti. The more you habituate yourself to the forms, the more you imbue yourself with the spirit, in which passions have been expressed and character delineated by great writers, the more completely you will accomplish yourself in your own special art of singer and actress." So, then, you allured me to a new study. Ah! in so doing did you dream that you diverted me from the old ambition? My knowledge of French and Italian, and my rearing in childhood, which had made English familiar to me, gave me the keys to the treasure-houses of three languages. Naturally I began with that in which your masterpieces are composed. Till then I had not even read your works. They were the first I chose. How they impressed, how they startled me! what depths in the mind of man, in the heart of woman, they revealed to me! But I owned to you then, and I repeat it now, neither they nor any of the works in romance and poetry which form the boast of recent French literature satisfied yearnings for that calm sense of beauty, that divine joy in a world beyond this world, which you had led me to believe it was the prerogative of ideal art to bestow. And when I told you this with the rude frankness you had bid me exercise in talk with you, a thoughtful, melancholy shade fell over your face, and you said quietly, "You are right, child; we, the French of our time, are the offspring of revolutions that settled nothing, unsettled all: we resemble those troubled States which rush into war abroad in order to re-establish peace at home. Our books suggest problems to men for reconstructing some social system in which the calm that belongs to art may be found at last: but such books should not be in your hands; they are not for the innocence and youth of women as yet unchanged by the systems which exist." And the next day you brought me 'l'asso's great poem, the "Gerusalemme Liberata," and said, smiling, "Art in its calm is here."

You remember that I was then at Sorrento by the order of my physician. Never shall I forget the soft autumn day when I sat amongst the lonely rocklets to the left of the town,—the sea before me, with scarce a ripple; my very heart steeped in the melodies of that poem, so marvellous for a strength disguised in sweetness, and for a symmetry in which each proportion blends into the other with the perfectness of a Grecian statue. The whole place seemed to me filled with the presence of the poet to whom it had given birth. Certainly the reading of that poem formed an era in my existence: to this day I cannot acknowledge the faults or weaknesses which your criticisms pointed out; I believe because they are in unison with my own nature, which yearns for harmony, and, finding that, rests contented. I shrink from violent contrasts, and can discover nothing tame and insipid in a continuance of sweetness and serenity. But it was not till after I had read "La Gerusalemme" again and again, and then sat and brooded over it, that I recognized the main charm of the poem in the religion which clings to it as the perfume clings to a flower,—a religion sometimes melancholy, but never to me sad. Hope always pervades it. Surely if, as you said, "Hope is twin-born with art," it is because art at its highest blends itself unconsciously with religion, and proclaims its affinity with hope by its faith in some future good more perfect than it has realized in the past.

Be this as it may, it was in this poem so pre-eminently Christian that I found the something which I missed and craved for in modern French masterpieces; even yours,—a something spiritual, speaking to my own soul, calling it forth; distinguishing it as an essence apart from mere human reason; soothing, even when it excited; making earth nearer to heaven. And when I ran on in this strain to you after my own wild fashion, you took my head between your hands and kissed me, and said, "Happy are those who believe! long may that happiness be thine!" Why did I not feel in Dante the Christian charm that I felt in Tasso? Dante in your eyes, as in those of most judges, is infinitely the greater genius; but reflected on the dark stream of that genius the stars are so troubled, the heaven so threatening.

Just as my year of holiday was expiring, I turned to English literature; and Shakspeare, of course, was the first English poet put into my hands. It proves how childlike my mind still was, that my earliest sensation in reading him was that of disappointment. It was not only that, despite my familiarity with English (thanks chiefly to the care of him whom I call my second father), there is much in the metaphorical diction of Shakspeare which I failed to comprehend; but he seemed to me so far like the modern French writers who affect to have found inspiration in his muse, that he obtrudes images of pain and suffering without cause or motive sufficiently clear to ordinary understandings, as I had taught myself to think it ought to be in the drama.

He makes Fate so cruel that we lose sight of the mild deity behind her. Compare, in this, Corneille's "Polyeucte," with the "Hamlet." In the first an equal calamity befalls the good, but in their calamity they are blessed. The death of the martyr is the triumph of his creed. But when we have put down the English tragedy,—when Hamlet and Ophelia are confounded in death with Polonius and the fratricidal king, we see not what good end for humanity is achieved. The passages that fasten on our memory do not make us happier and holier: they suggest but terrible problems, to which they give us no solution.

In the "Horaces" of Corneille there are fierce contests, rude passions, tears drawn from some of the bitterest sources of human pity; but then through all stands out, large and visible to the eyes of all spectators, the great ideal of devoted patriotism. How much of all that has been grandest in the life of France, redeeming even its worst crimes of revolution in the love of country, has had its origin in the "Horaces" of Corneille. But I doubt if the fates of Coriolanus and Caesar and Brutus and Antony, in the giant tragedies of Shakspeare, have made Englishmen more willing to die for England. In fine, it was long before—I will not say I understood or rightly appreciated Shakspeare, for no Englishman would admit that I or even you could ever do so, but before I could recognize the justice of the place his country claims for him as the genius without an equal in the literature of Europe. Meanwhile the ardour I had put into study, and the wear and tear of the emotions which the study called forth, made themselves felt in a return of my former illness, with symptoms still more alarming; and when the year was out I was ordained to rest for perhaps another year before I could sing in public, still less appear on the stage. How I rejoiced when I heard that fiat! for I emerged from that year of study with a heart utterly estranged from the profession in which I had centred my hopes before—Yes, Eulalie, you had bid me accomplish myself for the arts of utterance; by the study of arts in which thoughts originate the words they employ; and in doing so I had changed myself into another being. I was forbidden all fatigue of mind: my books were banished, but not the new self which the books had formed. Recovering slowly through the summer, I came hither two months since, ostensibly for the advice of Dr. C————, but really in the desire to commune with my own heart and be still.

And now I have poured forth that heart to you, would you persuade me still to be a singer? If you do, remember at least how jealous and absorbing the art of the singer and the actress is,—how completely I must surrender myself to it, and live among books or among dreams no more. Can I be anything else but singer? and if not, should I be contented merely to read and to dream?

I must confide to you one ambition which during the lazy Italian summer took possession of me; I must tell you the ambition, and add that I have renounced it as a vain one. I had hoped that I could compose, I mean in music. I was pleased with some things I did: they expressed in music what I could not express in words; and one secret object in coming here was to submit them to the great Maestro. He listened to them patiently: he complimented me on my accuracy in the mechanical laws of composition; he even said that my favourite airs were "touchants et gracieux."

And so he would have left me, but I stopped him timidly, and said, "Tell me frankly, do you think that with time and study I could compose music such as singers equal to myself would sing to?"

"You mean as a professional composer?"

"Well, yes."

"And to the abandonment of your vocation as a singer?"

"Yes."

"My dear child, I should be your worst enemy if I encouraged such a notion: cling to the career in which you call be greatest; gain but health, and I wager my reputation on your glorious success on the stage. What can you be as a composer? You will set pretty music to pretty words, and will be sung in drawing-rooms with the fame a little more or less that generally attends the compositions of female amateurs. Aim at something higher, as I know you would do, and you will not succeed. Is there any instance in modern times, perhaps in any times, of a female composer who attains even to the eminence of a third-rate opera-writer? Composition in letters may be of no sex. In that Madame Dudevant and your friend Madame de Grantmesnil can beat most men; but the genius of musical composition is homme, and accept it as a compliment when I say that you are essentially femme."

He left me, of course, mortified and humbled; but I feel he is right as regards myself, though whether in his depreciation of our whole sex I cannot say. But as this hope has left me, I have become more disquieted, still more restless. Counsel me, Eulalie; counsel, and, if possible, comfort me. ISAURA. FROM THE SAME TO THE SAME.

No letter from you yet, and I have left you in peace for ten days. How do you think I have spent them? The Maestro called on us with M. Savarin, to insist on our accompanying them on a round of the theatres. I had not been to one since my arrival. I divined that the kind-hearted composer had a motive in this invitation. He thought that in witnessing the applauses bestowed on actors, and sharing in the fascination in which theatrical illusion holds an audience, my old passion for the stage, and with it the longing for an artiste's fame, would revive.

In my heart I wished that his expectations might be realized. Well for me if I could once more concentrate all my aspirations on a prize within my reach!

We went first to see a comedy greatly in vogue, and the author thoroughly understands the French stage of our day. The acting was excellent in its way. The next night we went to the Odeon, a romantic melodrama in six acts, and I know not how many tableaux. I found no fault with the acting there. I do not give you the rest of our programme. We visited all the principal theatres, reserving the opera and Madame S——— for the last. Before I speak of the opera, let me say a word or two on the plays.

There is no country in which the theatre has so great a hold on the public as in France; no country in which the successful dramatist has so high a fame; no country perhaps in which the state of the stage so faithfully represents the moral and intellectual condition of the people. I say this not, of course, from my experience of countries which I have not visited, but from all I hear of the stage in Germany and in England.

The impression left on my mind by the performances I witnessed is, that the French people are becoming dwarfed. The comedies that please them are but pleasant caricatures of petty sections in a corrupt society. They contain no large types of human nature; their witticisms convey no luminous flashes of truth; their sentiment is not pure and noble,—it is a sickly and false perversion of the impure and ignoble into travesties of the pure and noble.

Their melodramas cannot be classed as literature: all that really remains of the old French genius is its vaudeville. Great dramatists create great parts. One great part, such as a Rachel would gladly have accepted, I have not seen in the dramas of the young generation.

High art has taken refuge in the opera; but that is not French opera. I do not complain so much that French taste is less refined. I complain that French intellect is lowered. The descent from "Polyeucte" to "Ruy Blas" is great, not so much in the poetry of form as in the elevation of thought; but the descent from "Ruy Blas" to the best drama now produced is out of poetry altogether, and into those flats of prose which give not even the glimpse of a mountain-top.

But now to the opera. S——— in Norma! The house was crowded, and its enthusiasm as loud as it was genuine. You tell me that S——— never rivalled Pasta, but certainly her Norma is a great performance. Her voice has lost less of its freshness than I had been told, and what is lost of it her practised management conceals or carries off.

The Maestro was quite right: I could never vie with her in her own line; but conceited and vain as I may seem even to you in saying so, I feel in my own line that I could command as large an applause,—of course taking into account my brief-lived advantage of youth. Her acting, apart from her voice, does not please me. It seems to me to want intelligence of the subtler feelings, the under-current of emotion which constitutes the chief beauty of the situation and the character. Am I jealous when I say this? Read on and judge.

On our return that night, when I had seen the Venosta to bed, I went into my own room, opened the window, and looked out. A lovely night, mild as in spring at Florence,—the moon at her full, and the stars looking so calm and so high beyond our reach of their tranquillity. The evergreens in the gardens of the villas around me silvered over, and the summer boughs, not yet clothed with leaves, were scarcely visible amid the changeless smile of the laurels. At the distance lay Paris, only to be known by its innumerable lights. And then I said to myself,

"No, I cannot be an actress; I cannot resign my real self for that vamped-up hypocrite before the lamps. Out on those stage-robes and painted cheeks! Out on that simulated utterance of sentiments learned by rote and practised before the looking-glass till every gesture has its drill!"

Then I gazed on those stars which provoke our questionings, and return no answer, till my heart grew full,—so full,—and I bowed my head and wept like a child.

FROM THE SAME TO THE SAME.

And still no letter from you! I see in the journals that you have left Nice. Is it that you are too absorbed in your work to have leisure to write to me? I know you are not ill, for if you were, all Paris would know of it. All Europe has an interest in your health. Positively I will write to you no more till a word from yourself bids me do so.

I fear I must give up my solitary walks in the Bois de Boulogne: they were very dear to me, partly because the quiet path to which I confined myself was that to which you directed me as the one you habitually selected when at Paris, and in which you had brooded over and revolved the loveliest of your romances; and partly because it was there that, catching, alas! not inspiration but enthusiasm from the genius that had hallowed the place, and dreaming I might originate music, I nursed my own aspirations and murmured my own airs. And though so close to that world of Paris to which all artists must appeal for judgment or audience, the spot was so undisturbed, so sequestered. But of late that path has lost its solitude, and therefore its charm.

Six days ago the first person I encountered in my walk was a man whom I did not then heed. He seemed in thought, or rather in revery, like myself; we passed each other twice or thrice, and I did not notice whether he was young or old, tall or short; but he came the next day, and a third day, and then I saw that he was young, and, in so regarding him, his eyes became fixed on mine. The fourth day he did not come, but two other men came, and the look of one was inquisitive and offensive. They sat themselves down on a bench in the walk, and though I did not seem to notice them, I hastened home; and the next day, in talking with our kind Madame Savarin, and alluding to these quiet walks of mine, she hinted, with the delicacy which is her characteristic, that the customs of Paris did not allow demoiselles comme il faut to walk alone even in the most sequestered paths of the Bois.

I begin now to comprehend your disdain of customs which impose chains so idly galling on the liberty of our sex.

We dined with the Savarins last evening: what a joyous nature he has! Not reading Latin, I only know Horace by translations, which I am told are bad; but Savarin seems to me a sort of half Horace,—Horace on his town-bred side, so playfully well-bred, so good-humoured in his philosophy, so affectionate to friends, and so biting to foes. But certainly Savarin could not have lived in a country farm upon endives and mallows. He is town-bred and Parisian, jusqu'au bout des ongles. How he admires you, and how I love him for it! Only in one thing he disappoints me there. It is your style that he chiefly praises: certainly that style is matchless; but style is only the clothing of thought, and to praise your style seems to me almost as invidious as the compliment to some perfect beauty, not on her form and face, but on her taste and dress.

We met at dinner an American and his wife,—a Colonel and Mrs. Morley: she is delicately handsome, as the American women I have seen generally are, and with that frank vivacity of manner which distinguishes them from English women. She seemed to take a fancy to me, and we soon grew very good friends.

She is the first advocate I have met, except yourself, of that doctrine upon the rights of Women, of which one reads more in the journals than one hears discussed in salons. Naturally enough I felt great interest in that subject, more especially since my rambles in the Bois were forbidden; and as long as she declaimed on the hard fate of the women who, feeling within them powers that struggle for air and light beyond the close precinct of household duties, find themselves restricted from fair rivalry with men in such fields of knowledge and toil and glory as men since the world began have appropriated to themselves, I need not say that I went with her cordially: you can guess that by my former letters. But when she entered into the detailed catalogue of our exact wrongs and our exact rights, I felt all the pusillanimity of my sex and shrank back in terror.

Her husband, joining us when she was in full tide of eloquence, smiled at me with a kind of saturnine mirth. "Mademoiselle, don't believe a word she says: it is only tall talk! In America the women are absolute tyrants, and it is I who, in concert with my oppressed countrymen, am going in for a platform agitation to restore the Rights of Men."

Upon this there was a lively battle of words between the spouses, in which, I must own, I thought the lady was decidedly worsted.

No, Eulalie, I see nothing in these schemes for altering our relations towards the other sex which would improve our condition. The inequalities we suffer are not imposed by law,—not even by convention: they are imposed by nature.

Eulalie, you have had an experience unknown to me: you have loved. In that day did you,—you, round whom poets and sages and statesmen gather, listening to your words as to an oracle,—did you feel that your pride of genius had gone out from you, that your ambition lived in whom you loved, that his smile was more to you than the applause of a world?

I feel as if love in a woman must destroy her rights of equality, that it gives to her a sovereign even in one who would be inferior to herself if her love did not glorify and crown him. Ah! if I could but merge this terrible egotism which oppresses me, into the being of some one who is what I would wish to be were I man! I would not ask him to achieve fame. Enough if I felt that he was worthy of it, and happier methinks to console him when he failed than to triumph with him when he won. Tell me, have you felt this? When you loved did you stoop as to a slave, or did you bow down as to a master?

FROM MADAME DE GRANTMESNIL TO ISAURA CICOGNA.

Chere enfant,—All your four letters have reached me the same day. In one of my sudden whims I set off with a few friends on a rapid tour along the Riviera to Genoa, thence to Turin on to Milan. Not knowing where we should rest even for a day, my letters were not forwarded.

I came back to Nice yesterday, consoled for all fatigues in having insured that accuracy in description of localities which my work necessitates.

You are, my poor child, in that revolutionary crisis through which genius passes in youth before it knows its own self, and longs vaguely to do or to be a something other than it has done or has been before. For, not to be unjust to your own powers, genius you have,—that inborn undefinable essence, including talent, and yet distinct from it. Genius you have, but genius unconcentrated, undisciplined. I see, though you are too diffident to say so openly, that you shrink from the fame of singer, because, fevered by your reading, you would fain aspire to the thorny crown of author. I echo the hard saying of the Maestro: I should be your worst enemy did I encourage you to forsake a career in which a dazzling success is so assured, for one in which, if it were your true vocation, you would not ask whether you were fit for it; you would be impelled to it by the terrible star which presides over the birth of poets.

Have you, who are so naturally observant, and of late have become so reflective, never remarked that authors, however absorbed in their own craft, do not wish their children to adopt it? The most successful author is perhaps the last person to whom neophytes should come for encouragement. This I think is not the case with the cultivators of the sister arts.

The painter, the sculptor, the musician, seem disposed to invite disciples and welcome acolytes. As for those engaged in the practical affairs of life, fathers mostly wish their sons to be as they have been.

The politician, the lawyer, the merchant, each says to his children, "Follow my steps." All parents in practical life would at least agree in this,—they would not wish their sons to be poets. There must be some sound cause in the world's philosophy for this general concurrence of digression from a road of which the travellers themselves say to those whom they love best, "Beware!"

Romance in youth is, if rightly understood, the happiest nutriment of wisdom in after-years; but I would never invite any one to look upon the romance of youth as a thing

*"To case in periods and embalm in ink."*

Enfant, have you need of a publisher to create romance? Is it not in yourself? Do not imagine that genius requires for its enjoyment the scratch of the pen and the types of the printer. Do not suppose that the poet, the romancier, is most poetic, most romantic, when he is striving, struggling, labouring, to check the rush of his ideas, and materialize the images which visit him as souls into such tangible likenesses of flesh and blood that the highest compliment a reader can bestow on them is to say that they are lifelike: No: the poet's real delight is not in the mechanism of composing; the best part of that delight is in the sympathies he has established with innumerable modifications of life and form, and art and Nature, sympathies which are often found equally keen in those who have not the same gift of language. The poet is but the interpreter. What of?—Truths in the hearts of others. He utters what they feel. Is the joy in the utterance? Nay, it is in the feeling itself. So, my dear, dark-bright child of song, when I bade thee open, out of the beaten thoroughfare, paths into the meads and river-banks at either side of the formal hedgerows, rightly dost thou add that I enjoined thee to make thine art thy companion. In the culture of that art for which you are so eminently gifted, you will find the ideal life ever beside the real. Are you not ashamed to tell me that in that art you do but utter the thoughts of others? You utter them in music; through the music you not only give to the thoughts a new character, but you make them reproductive of fresh thoughts in your audience.

You said very truly that you found in composing you could put into music thoughts which you could not put into words. That is the peculiar distinction of music. No genuine musician can explain in words exactly what he means to convey in his music.

How little a libretto interprets an opera; how little we care even to read it! It is the music that speaks to us; and how?—Through the human voice. We do not notice how poor are the words which the voice warbles. It is the voice itself interpreting the soul of the musician which enchants and enthralls us. And you who have that voice pretend to despise the gift. What! despise the power of communicating delight!—the power that we authors envy; and rarely, if ever, can we give delight with so little alloy as the singer.

And when an audience disperses, can you guess what griefs the singer may have comforted? what hard hearts he may have softened? what high thoughts he may have awakened?

You say, "Out on the vamped-up hypocrite! Out on the stage-robes and painted cheeks!"

I say, "Out on the morbid spirit which so cynically regards the mere details by which a whole effect on the minds and hearts and souls of races and nations can be produced!"

There, have I scolded you sufficiently? I should scold you more, if I did not see in the affluence of your youth and your intellect the cause of your restlessness. Riches are always restless. It is only to poverty that the gods give content.

You question me about love; you ask if I have ever bowed to a master, ever merged my life in another's: expect no answer on this from me. Circe herself could give no answer to the simplest maid, who, never having loved, asks, "What is love?"

In the history of the passions each human heart is a world in itself; its experience profits no others. In no two lives does love play the same part or bequeath the same record.

I know not whether I am glad or sorry that the word "love" now falls on my ear with a sound as slight and as faint as the dropping of a leaf in autumn may fall on thine.

I volunteer but this lesson, the wisest I can give, if thou canst understand it: as I bade thee take art into thy life, so learn to look on life itself as an art. Thou couldst discover the charm in Tasso; thou couldst perceive that the requisite of all art, that which pleases, is in the harmony of proportion. We lose sight of beauty if we exaggerate the feature most beautiful.

Love proportioned adorns the homeliest existence; love disproportioned deforms the fairest.

Alas! wilt thou remember this warning when the time comes in which it may be needed?

E— —- G— — —.

# BOOK II.

## CHAPTER I.

It is several weeks after the date of the last chapter; the lime-trees in the Tuileries are clothed in green.

In a somewhat spacious apartment on the ground-floor in the quiet locality of the Rue d'Anjou, a man was seated, very still and evidently absorbed in deep thought, before a writing-table placed close to the window.

Seen thus, there was an expression of great power both of intellect and of character in a face which, in ordinary social commune, might rather be noticeable for an aspect of hardy frankness, suiting well with the clear-cut, handsome profile, and the rich dark auburn hair, waving carelessly over one of those broad open foreheads, which, according to an old writer, seem the "frontispiece of a temple dedicated to Honour."

The forehead, indeed, was the man's most remarkable feature. It could not but prepossess the beholder. When, in private theatricals, he had need to alter the character of his countenance, he did it effectually, merely by forcing down his hair till it reached his eyebrows. He no longer then looked like the same man.

The person I describe has been already introduced to the reader as Graham Vane. But perhaps this is the fit occasion to enter into some such details as to his parentage and position as may make the introduction more satisfactory and complete.

His father, the representative of a very ancient family, came into possession, after a long minority, of what may be called a fair squire's estate, and about half a million in moneyed investments, inherited on the female side. Both land and money were absolutely at his disposal, unencumbered by entail or settlement. He was a man of a brilliant, irregular genius, of princely generosity, of splendid taste, of a gorgeous kind of pride closely allied to a masculine kind of vanity. As soon as he was of age he began to build, converting his squire's hall into a ducal palace. He then stood for the county; and in days before the first Reform Bill, when a county election was to the estate of a candidate what a long war is to the debt of a nation. He won the election; he obtained early successes in Parliament. It was said by good authorities in political circles that, if he chose, he might aspire to lead his party, and ultimately to hold the first rank in the government of his country.

That may or may not be true; but certainly he did not choose to take the trouble necessary for such an ambition. He was too fond of pleasure, of luxury, of pomp. He kept a famous stud of racers and hunters. He was a munificent patron of art. His establishments, his entertainments, were on a par with those of the great noble who represented the loftiest (Mr. Vane would not own it to be the eldest) branch of his genealogical tree.

He became indifferent to political contests, indolent in his attendance at the House, speaking seldom, not at great length nor with much preparation, but with power and fire, originality and genius; so that he was not only effective as an orator, but combining with eloquence advantages of birth, person, station, the reputation of patriotic independence, and genial attributes of character, he was an authority of weight in the scales of party.

This gentleman, at the age of forty, married the dowerless daughter of a poor but distinguished naval officer, of noble family, first cousin to the Duke of Alton.

He settled on her a suitable jointure, but declined to tie up any portion of his property for the benefit of children by the marriage. He declared that so much of his fortune was invested either in mines, the produce of which was extremely fluctuating, or in various funds, over rapid transfers in which it was his amusement and his interest to have control, unchecked by reference to trustees, that entails and settlements on children were an inconvenience he declined to incur.

Besides, he held notions of his own as to the wisdom of keeping children dependent on their father. "What numbers of young men," said he, "are ruined in character and in fortune by knowing that when their father dies they are certain of the same provision, no matter how they displease him; and in the meanwhile forestalling that provision by recourse to usurers." These arguments might not have prevailed over the bride's father a year or two later, when, by the death of intervening kinsmen, he became Duke of Alton; but in his then circumstances the marriage itself was so much beyond the expectations which the portionless daughter of a sea-captain has the right to form that Mr. Vane had it all his own way, and he remained absolute master of his whole fortune, save of that part of his landed estate on which his wife's jointure was settled; and even from this incumbrance he was very soon freed. His wife died in the second year of marriage, leaving an only son,—Graham. He grieved for her loss with all the passion of an impressionable, ardent, and powerful nature. Then for a while he sought distraction to his sorrow by throwing himself into public life with a devoted energy he had not previously displayed.

His speeches served to bring his party into power, and he yielded, though reluctantly, to the unanimous demand of that party that he should accept one of the highest offices in the new Cabinet. He acquitted himself well as an administrator, but declared, no doubt honestly, that he felt like Sinbad released from the old man on his back, when, a year or two afterwards, he went out of office with his party. No persuasions could induce him to come in again; nor did he ever again take a very active part in debate. "No," said he, "I was born to the freedom of a private gentleman: intolerable to me is the thraldom of a public servant. But I will bring up my son so that he may acquit the debt which I decline to pay to my country." There he kept his word. Graham had been carefully educated for public life, the ambition for it dinned into his ear from childhood. In his school vacations his father made him learn and declaim chosen specimens of masculine oratory; engaged an eminent actor to give him lessons in elocution; bade him frequent theatres, and study there the effect which words derive from looks and gesture; encouraged him to take part himself in private theatricals. To all this the boy lent his mind with delight. He had the orator's inborn temperament; quick, yet imaginative, and loving the sport of rivalry and contest. Being also, in his boyish years, good-humoured and joyous, he was not more a favourite with the masters in the schoolroom than with the boys in the play-ground. Leaving Eton at seventeen, he then entered at Cambridge, and became, in his first term, the most popular speaker at the Union.

But his father cut short his academical career, and decided, for reasons of his own, to place him at once in diplomacy. He was attached to the Embassy at Paris, and partook of the pleasures and dissipations of that metropolis too keenly to retain much of the sterner ambition to which he had before devoted himself. Becoming one of the spoiled darlings of fashion, there was great danger that his character would relax into the easy grace of the Epicurean, when all such loiterings in the Rose Garden were brought to abrupt close by a rude and terrible change in his fortunes.

His father was killed by a fall from his horse in hunting; and when his affairs were investigated, they were found to be hopelessly involved: apparently the assets would not suffice for the debts. The elder Vane himself was probably not aware of the extent of his liabilities. He had never wanted ready money to the last. He could always obtain that from a money-lender, or from the sale of his funded investments. But it became obvious, on examining his papers, that he knew at least how impaired would be the heritage he should bequeath to a son whom he idolized. For that reason he had given Graham a profession in diplomacy, and for that reason he had privately applied to the Ministry for the Viceroyalty of India, in the event of its speedy vacancy. He was eminent enough not to anticipate refusal, and with economy in that lucrative post much of his pecuniary difficulties might have been redeemed, and at least an independent provision secured for his son.

Graham, like Alain de Rochebriant, allowed no reproach on his father's memory; indeed, with more reason than Alain, for the elder Vane's fortune had at least gone on no mean and frivolous dissipation.

It had lavished itself on encouragement to art, on great objects of public beneficence, on public-spirited aid of political objects; and even in more selfish enjoyments there was a certain grandeur in his princely hospitalities, in his munificent generosity, in a warm-hearted carelessness for money. No indulgence in petty follies or degrading vices aggravated the offence of the magnificent squanderer.

"Let me look on my loss of fortune as a gain to myself," said Graham, manfully. "Had I been a rich man, my experience of Paris tells me that I should most likely have been a very idle one. Now that I have no gold, I must dig in myself for iron."

The man to whom he said this was an uncle-in-law,—if I may use that phrase,—the Right Hon. Richard King, popularly styled "the blameless King."

This gentleman had married the sister of Graham's mother, whose loss in his infancy and boyhood she had tenderly and anxiously sought to supply. It is impossible to conceive a woman more fitted to invite love and reverence than was Lady Janet King, her manners were so sweet and gentle, her whole nature so elevated and pure.

Her father had succeeded to the dukedom when she married Mr. King, and the alliance was not deemed quite suitable. Still it was not one to which the Duke would have been fairly justified in refusing his assent.

Mr. King could not indeed boast of noble ancestry, nor was even a landed proprietor; but he was a not-undistinguished member of Parliament, of irreproachable character, and ample fortune inherited from a distant kinsman, who had enriched himself as a merchant. It was on both sides a marriage of love.

It is popularly said that a man uplifts a wife to his own rank: it as often happens that a woman uplifts her husband to the dignity of her own character. Richard King rose greatly in public estimation after his marriage with Lady Janet.

She united to a sincere piety a very active and a very enlightened benevolence. She guided his ambition aside from mere party politics into subjects of social and religious interest, and in devoting himself to these he achieved a position more popular and more respected than he could ever have won in the strife of party.

When the Government of which the elder Vane became a leading Minister was formed, it was considered a great object to secure a name as high in the religious world, so beloved by the working classes, as that of Richard King; and he accepted one of those places which, though not in the cabinet, confers the rank of Privy Councillor.

When that brief-lived Administration ceased, he felt the same sensation of relief that Vane had felt, and came to the same resolution never again to accept office, but from different reasons, all of which need not now be detailed. Amongst them, however, certainly this: he was exceedingly sensitive to opinion, thin-skinned as to abuse, and very tenacious of the respect due to his peculiar character of sanctity and philanthropy. He writhed under every newspaper article that had made "the blameless King" responsible for the iniquities of the Government to which he belonged. In the loss of office he seemed to recover his former throne.

Mr. King heard Graham's resolution with a grave approving smile, and his interest in the young man became greatly increased. He devoted himself strenuously to the object of saving to Graham some wrecks of his paternal fortunes, and having a clear head and great experience in the transaction of business, he succeeded beyond the most sanguine expectations formed by the family solicitor. A rich manufacturer was found to purchase at a fancy price the bulk of the estate with the palatial mansion, which the estate alone could never have sufficed to maintain with suitable establishments.

So that when all debts were paid, Graham found himself in possession of a clear income of about L500 a year, invested in a mortgage secured on a part of the hereditary lands, on which was seated an old hunting-lodge bought by a brewer.

With this portion of the property Graham parted very reluctantly. It was situated amid the most picturesque scenery on the estate, and the lodge itself was a remnant of the original residence of his ancestors before it had been abandoned for that which, built in the reign of Elizabeth, had been expanded into a Trenthain-like palace by the last owner.

But Mr. King's argument reconciled him to the sacrifice. "I can manage," said the prudent adviser, "if you insist on it, to retain that remnant of the hereditary estate which you are so loath to part with. But how? by mortgaging it to an extent that will scarcely leave you L50. a year net from the rents. This is not all. Your mind will then be distracted from the large object of a career to the small object of retaining a few family acres; you will be constantly hampered by private anxieties and fears; you could do nothing for the benefit of those around you,—could not repair a farmhouse for a better class of tenant, could not rebuild a labourer's dilapidated cottage. Give up an idea that might be very well for a man whose sole ambition was to remain a squire, however beggarly. Launch yourself into the larger world of metropolitan life with energies wholly unshackled, a mind wholly undisturbed, and secure of an income which, however modest, is equal to that of most young men who enter that world as your equals."

Graham was convinced, and yielded, though with a bitter pang. It is hard for a man whose fathers have lived on the soil to give up all trace of their whereabouts. But none saw in him any morbid consciousness of change of fortune, when, a year after his father's death, he reassumed his place in society. If before courted for his expectations, he was still courted for himself; by many of the great who had loved his father, perhaps even courted more.

He resigned the diplomatic career, not merely because the rise in that profession is slow, and in the intermediate steps the chances of distinction are slight and few, but more because he desired to cast his lot in the home country, and regarded the courts of other lands as exile.

It was not true, however, as Lemercier had stated on report, that he lived on his pen. Curbing all his old extravagant tastes, L500 a year amply supplied his wants. But he had by his pen gained distinction, and created great belief in his abilities for a public career. He had written critical articles, read with much praise, in periodicals of authority, and had published one or two essays on political questions which had created yet more sensation. It was only the graver literature, connected more or less with his ultimate object of a public career, in which he had thus evinced his talents of composition. Such writings were not of a nature to bring him much money, but they gave him a definite and solid station. In the old time, before the first Reform Bill, his reputation would have secured him at once a seat in Parliament; but the ancient nurseries of statesmen are gone, and their place is not supplied.

He had been invited, however, to stand for more than one large and populous borough, with very fair prospects of success; and, whatever the expense, Mr. King had offered to defray it. But Graham would not have incurred the latter obligation; and when he learned the pledges which his supporters would have exacted, he would not have stood if success had been certain and the cost nothing. "I cannot," he said to his friends, "go into the consideration of what is best for the country with my thoughts manacled; and I cannot be both representative and slave of the greatest ignorance of the greatest number. I bide my time, and meanwhile I prefer to write as I please, rather than vote as I don't please."

Three years went by, passed chiefly in England, partly in travel; and at the age of thirty, Graham Vane was still one of those of whom admirers say, "He will be a great man some day;" and detractors reply, "Some day seems a long way off."

The same fastidiousness which had operated against that entrance into Parliament, to which his ambition not the less steadily adapted itself, had kept him free from the perils of wedlock. In his heart he yearned for love and domestic life, but he had hitherto met with no one who realized the ideal he had formed. With his person, his accomplishments, his connections, and his repute, he might have made many an advantageous marriage. But somehow or other the charm vanished from a fair face, if the shadow of a money-bag fell on it; on the other hand, his ambition occupied so large a share in his thoughts that he would have fled in time from the temptation of a marriage that would have overweighted him beyond the chance of rising. Added to all, he desired in a wife an intellect that, if not equal to his own, could become so by sympathy,—a union of high culture and noble aspiration, and yet of loving womanly sweetness which a man seldom finds out of books; and when he does find it, perhaps it does not wear the sort of face that he fancies. Be that as it may, Graham was still unmarried and heart-whole.

And now a new change in his life befell him. Lady Janet died of a fever contracted in her habitual rounds of charity among the houses of the poor. She had been to him as the most tender mother, and a lovelier soul than hers never alighted on the earth. His grief was intense; but what was her husband's?—one of those griefs that kill.

To the side of Richard King his Janet had been as the guardian angel. His love for her was almost worship: with her, every object in a life hitherto so active and useful seemed gone. He evinced no noisy passion of sorrow. He shut himself up, and refused to see even Graham. But after some weeks had passed, he admitted the clergyman in whom on spiritual matters he habitually confided, and seemed consoled by the visits; then he sent for his lawyer and made his will; after which he allowed Graham to call on him daily, on the condition that there should be no reference to his loss. He spoke to the young man on other subjects, rather drawing him out about himself, sounding his opinion on various grave matters, watching his face while he questioned, as if seeking to dive into his heart, and sometimes pathetically sinking into silence, broken but by sighs. So it went on for a few more weeks; then he took the advice of his physician to seek change of air and scene. He went away alone, without even a servant, not leaving word where he had gone. After a little while he returned, more ailing, more broken than before. One morning he was found insensible,—stricken by paralysis. He regained consciousness, and even for some days rallied strength. He might have recovered, but he seemed as if he tacitly refused to live. He expired at last, peacefully, in Graham's arms.

At the opening of his will it was found that he had left Graham his sole heir and executor. Deducting government duties, legacies to servants, and donations to public charities, the sum thus bequeathed to his lost wife's nephew was two hundred and twenty thousand pounds.

With such a fortune, opening indeed was made for an ambition so long obstructed. But Graham affected no change in his mode of life; he still retained his modest bachelor's apartments, engaged no servants, bought no horses, in no way exceeded the income he had possessed before. He seemed, indeed, depressed rather than elated by the succession to a wealth which he had never anticipated.

Two children had been born from the marriage of Richard King: they had died young, it is true, but Lady Janet at the time of her own decease was not too advanced in years for the reasonable expectation of other offspring; and even after Richard King became a widower, he had given to Graham no hint of his testamentary dispositions. The young man was no blood-relation to him, and naturally supposed that such relations would become the heirs. But in truth the deceased seemed to have no blood-relations: none had ever been known to visit him; none raised a voice to question the justice of his will.

Lady Janet had been buried at Kensal Green; her husband's remains were placed in the same vault.

For days and days Graham went his way lonelily to the cemetery. He might be seen standing motionless by that tomb, with tears rolling down his cheeks; yet his was not a weak nature,—not one of those that love indulgence of irremediable grief. On the contrary, people who did not know him well said "that he had more head than heart," and the character of his pursuits, as of his writings, was certainly not that of a sentimentalist. He had not thus visited the tomb till Richard King had been placed within it. Yet his love for his aunt was unspeakably greater than that which he could have felt for her husband. Was it, then, the husband that he so much more acutely mourned; or was there something that, since the husband's death, had deepened his reverence for the memory of her whom he had not only loved as a mother, but honoured as a saint?

These visits to the cemetery did not cease till Graham was confined to his bed by a very grave illness,—the only one he had ever known. His physician said it was nervous fever, and occasioned by moral shock or excitement; it was attended with delirium. His recovery was slow, and when it was sufficiently completed he quitted England; and we find him now, with his mind composed, his strength restored, and his spirits braced, in that gay city of Paris; hiding, perhaps, some earnest purpose amid his participation in its holiday enjoyments. He is now, as I have said, seated before his writing-table in deep thought. He takes up a letter which he had already glanced over hastily, and reperuses it with more care.

The letter is from his cousin, the Duke of Alton, who had succeeded a few years since to the family honours,—an able man, with no small degree of information, an ardent politician, but of very rational and temperate opinions; too much occupied by the cares of a princely estate to covet office for himself; too sincere a patriot not to desire office for those to whose hands he thought the country might be most safely entrusted; an intimate friend of Graham's. The contents of the letter are these:—

*MY DEAR GRAHAM,—I trust that you will welcome the brilliant opening*
*into public life which these lines are intended to announce to you. Vavasour has just been with me to say that he intends to resign his seat for the county when Parliament meets, and agreeing with me that there is no one so fit to succeed him as yourself, he suggests the keeping his intention secret until you have arranged your committee and are prepared to take the field. You cannot hope to escape a contest; but I have examined the Register, and the party has gained rather than lost since the last election, when Vavasour was so triumphantly returned. The expenses for this county, where there are so many outvoters to bring up, and so many agents to retain, are always large in comparison with some other counties; but that consideration is all in your favour, for it deters Squire Hunston, the only man who could beat you, from starting; and to your resources a thousand pounds more or less are a trifle not worth discussing. You know how difficult it is nowadays to find a seat for a man of moderate opinions like yours and mine. Our county would exactly suit you. The constituency is so evenly divided*

*between the urban and rural populations, that its representative must fairly consult the interests of both. He can be neither an ultra-Tory nor a violent Radical. He is left to the enviable freedom, to which you say you aspire, of considering what is best for the country as a whole.*

*Do not lose so rare an opportunity. There is but one drawback to your triumphant candidature. It will be said that you have no longer an acre in the county in which the Vanes have been settled so long. That drawback can be removed. It is true that you can never hope to buy back the estates which you were compelled to sell at your father's death: the old manufacturer gripes them too firmly to loosen his hold; and after all, even were your income double what it is, you would be overhoused in the vast pile in which your father buried so large a share of his fortune. But that beautiful old hunting-lodge, the Stamm Schloss of your family, with the adjacent farms, can be now repurchased very reasonably. The brewer who bought them is afflicted with an extravagant son, whom he placed in the—Hussars, and will gladly sell the property for L5,000 more than he gave: well worth the difference, as he has improved the farm-buildings and raised the rental. I think, in addition to the sum you have on mortgage, L3,000 will be accepted, and as a mere investment pay you nearly three per cent. But to you it is worth more than double the money; it once more identifies your ancient name with the county. You would be a greater personage with that moderate holding in the district in which your race took root, and on which your father's genius threw such a lustre, than you would be if you invested all your wealth in a county in which every squire and farmer would call you "the new man." Pray think over this most seriously, and instruct your solicitor to open negotiations with the brewer at once. But rather put yourself into the train, and come back to England straight to me. I will ask Vavasour to meet you. What news from Paris? Is the Emperor as ill as the papers insinuate? And is the revolutionary party gaining ground?*

*Your affectionate cousin,*

*ALTON.*

As he put down this letter, Graham heaved a short impatient sigh.

"The old Stamm Schloss," he muttered,—"a foot on the old soil once more! and an entrance into the great arena with hands unfettered. Is it possible!—is it?—is it?"

At this moment the door-bell of the apartment rang, and a servant whom Graham had hired at Paris as a laquais de place announced "Ce Monsieur."

Graham hurried the letter into his portfolio, and said, "You mean the person to whom I am always at home?"

"The same, Monsieur."

"Admit him, of course."

There entered a wonderfully thin man, middle-aged, clothed in black, his face cleanly shaven, his hair cut very short, with one of those faces which, to use a French expression, say "nothing." It was absolutely without expression: it had not even, despite its thinness, one salient feature. If you had found yourself anywhere seated next to that man, your eye would have passed him over as too insignificant to notice; if at a cafe, you would have gone on talking to your friend without lowering your voice. What mattered it whether a bete like that overheard or not? Had you been asked to guess his calling and station, you might have said, minutely observing the freshness of his clothes and the undeniable respectability of his tout ensemble, "He must be well off, and with no care for customers on his mind,—a ci-devant chandler who has retired on a legacy."

Graham rose at the entrance of his visitor, motioned him courteously to a seat beside him, and waiting till the laquais had vanished, then asked, "What news?"

"None, I fear, that will satisfy Monsieur. I have certainly hunted out, since I had last the honour to see you, no less than four ladies of the name of Duval, but only one of them took that name from her parents, and was also christened Louise."

"Ah—Louise!"

"Yes, the daughter of a perfumer, aged twenty-eight. She, therefore, is not the Louise you seek. Permit me to refer to your instructions." Here M. Renard took out a note-book, turned over the leaves, and resumed, "Wanted, Louise Duval, daughter of Auguste Duval, a French drawing-master, who lived for many years at Tours, removed to Paris in 1845, lived at No. 12, Rue de S—— at Paris for some years, but afterwards moved to a different guartier of the town, and died 1848, in Rue I——, No. 39. Shortly after his death, his daughter Louise left that lodging, and could not be traced. In 1849 official documents reporting her death were forwarded from Munich to a person (a friend of yours, Monsieur). Death, of course, taken for granted; but nearly five years afterwards, this very person encountered the said Louise Duval at Aix-la-Chapelle, and never heard nor saw more of her. Demande submitted, to find out said Louise Duval or any children of hers born in 1848-9; supposed in 1852-3 to have one child, a girl, between four and five years old. Is that right, Monsieur?"

"Quite right."

"And this is the whole information given to me. Monsieur on giving it asked me if I thought it desirable that he should commence inquiries at Aix-la-Chapelle, where Louise Duval was last seen by the person interested to discover her. I reply, No; pains thrown away. Aix-la-Chapelle is not a place where any Frenchwoman not settled there by marriage would remain. Nor does it seem probable that the said Duval would venture to select for her residence Munich, a city in which she had contrived to obtain certificates of her death. A Frenchwoman who has once known Paris always wants to get back to it; especially, Monsieur, if she has the beauty which you assign to this lady. I therefore suggested that our inquiries should commence in this capital. Monsieur agreed with me, and I did not grudge the time necessary for investigation."

"You were most obliging. Still I am beginning to be impatient if time is to be thrown away."

"Naturally. Permit me to return to my notes. Monsieur informs me that twenty-one years ago, in 1848, the Parisian police were instructed to find out this lady and failed, but gave hopes of discovering her through her relations. He asks me to refer to our archives; I tell him that is no use. However, in order to oblige him, I do so. No trace of such inquiry: it must have been, as Monsieur led me to suppose, a strictly private one, unconnected with crime or with politics; and as I have the honour to tell Monsieur, no record of such investigations is preserved in our office. Great scandal would there be, and injury to the peace of families, if we preserved the results of private inquiries intrusted to us—by absurdly jealous husbands, for instance. Honour,—Monsieur, honour forbids it. Next I suggest to Monsieur that his simplest plan would be an advertisement in the French journals, stating, if I understand him right, that it is for the pecuniary interest of Madame or Mademoiselle Duval, daughter of Auguste Duval, artiste en dessin, to come forward. Monsieur objects to that."

"I object to it extremely; as I have told you, this is a strictly confidential inquiry; and an advertisement which in all likelihood would be practically useless (it proved to be so in a former inquiry) would not be resorted to unless all else failed, and even then with reluctance."

"Quite so. Accordingly, Monsieur delegates to me, who have been recommended to him as the best person he can employ in that department of our police which is not connected with crime or political surveillance, a task the most difficult. I have, through strictly private investigations, to discover the address and prove the identity of a lady bearing a name among the most common in France, and of whom nothing has been heard for fifteen years, and then at so migratory an endroit as Aix-la-Chapelle. You will not or cannot inform me if since that time the lady has changed her name by marriage."

"I have no reason to think that she has; and there are reasons against the supposition that she married after 1849."

"Permit me to observe that the more details of information Monsieur can give me, the easier my task of research will be."

"I have given you all the details I can, and, aware of the difficulty of tracing a person with a name so much the reverse of singular, I adopted your advice in our first interview, of asking some Parisian friend of mine, with a large acquaintance in the miscellaneous societies of your capital, to inform me of any ladies of that name whom he might chance to encounter; and he, like you, has lighted upon one or two, who alas! resemble the right one in name and nothing more."

"You will do wisely to keep him on the watch as well as myself. If it were but a murderess or a political incendiary, then you might trust exclusively to the enlightenment of our corps, but this seems an affair of sentiment, Monsieur. Sentiment is not in our way. Seek the trace of that in the haunts of pleasure."

M. Renard, having thus poetically delivered himself of that philosophical dogma, rose to depart.

Graham slipped into his hand a bank-note of sufficient value to justify the profound bow he received in return.

When M. Renard had gone, Graham heaved another impatient sigh, and said to himself, "No, it is not possible,—at least not yet."

Then, compressing his lips as a man who forces himself to something he dislikes, he dipped his pen into the inkstand, and wrote rapidly thus to his kinsman:

> *MY DEAR COUSIN,—I lose not a post in replying to your kind and considerate letter. It is not in my power at present to return to England. I need not say how fondly I cherish the hope of representing the dear old county some day. If Vavasour could be induced to defer his resignation of the seat for another session, or*

*at least for six or seven months, why then I might be free to avail myself of the opening; at present I am not. Meanwhile I am sorely tempted to buy back the old Lodge; probably the brewer would allow me to leave on mortgage the sum I myself have on the property, and a few additional thousands. I have reasons for not wishing to transfer at present much of the money now invested in the Funds. I will consider this point, which probably does not press.*

*I reserve all Paris news till my next; and begging you to forgive so curt and unsatisfactory a reply to a letter so important that it excites me more than I like to own, believe me your affectionate friend and cousin,*
*GRAHAM.*

# CHAPTER II.

AT about the same hour on the same day in which the Englishman held the conference with the Parisian detective just related, the Marquis de Rochebriant found himself by appointment in the cabinet d'affaires of his avoue M. Gandrin that gentleman had hitherto not found time to give him a definite opinion as to the case submitted to his judgment. The avoue received Alain with a kind of forced civility, in which the natural intelligence of the Marquis, despite his inexperience of life, discovered embarrassment.

"Monsieur le Marquis," said Gandrin, fidgeting among the papers on his bureau, "this is a very complicated business. I have given not only my best attention to it, but to your general interests. To be plain, your estate, though a fine one, is fearfully encumbered—fearfully— frightfully."

"Sir," said the Marquis, haughtily, "that is a fact which was never disguised from you."

"I do not say that it was, Marquis; but I scarcely realized the amount of the liabilities nor the nature of the property. It will be difficult—nay, I fear, impossible—to find any capitalist to advance a sum that will cover the mortgages at an interest less than you now pay. As for a Company to take the whole trouble off your hands, clear off the mortgages, manage the forests, develop the fisheries, guarantee you an adequate income, and at the end of twenty-one years or so render up to you or your heirs the free enjoyment of an estate thus improved, we must dismiss that prospect as a wild dream of my good friend M. Hebert. People in the provinces do dream; in Paris everybody is wide awake."

"Monsieur," said the Marquis, with that inborn imperturbable loftiness of sang froid which has always in adverse circumstances characterized the French noblesse, "be kind enough to restore my papers. I see that you are not the man for me. Allow me only to thank you, and inquire the amount of my debt for the trouble I have given."

"Perhaps you are quite justified in thinking I am not the man for you, Monsieur le Marquis; and your papers shall, if you decide on dismissing me, be returned to you this evening. But as to my accepting remuneration where I have rendered no service, I request M. le Marquis to put that out of the question. Considering myself, then, no longer your avoue, do not think I take too great a liberty in volunteering my counsel as a friend,—or a friend at least to M. Hebert, if you do not vouchsafe my right so to address yourself."

M. Gandrin spoke with a certain dignity of voice and manner which touched and softened his listener.

"You make me your debtor far more than I pretend to repay," replied Alain. "Heaven knows I want a friend, and I will heed with gratitude and respect all your counsels in that character."

"Plainly and briefly, my advice is this: M. Louvier is the principal mortgagee. He is among the six richest capitalists of Paris. He does not, therefore, want money, but, like most self-made men, he is very accessible to social vanities. He would be proud to think he had rendered a service to a Rochebriant. Approach him, either through me, or, far better, at once introduce yourself, and propose to consolidate all your other liabilities in one mortgage to him, at a rate of interest lower than that which is now paid to some of the small mortgagees. This would add considerably to your income and would carry out M. Hebert's advice."

"But does it not strike you, dear M. Gandrin, that such going cap-in-hand to one who has power over my fate, while I have none over his, would scarcely be consistent with my self-respect, not as Rochebriant only, but as Frenchman?"

"It does not strike me so in the least; at all events, I could make the proposal on your behalf, without compromising yourself, though I should be far more sanguine of success if you addressed M. Louvier in person."

"I should nevertheless prefer leaving it in your hands; but even for that I must take a few days to consider. Of all the mortgagees M. Louvier has been hitherto the severest and most menacing, the one whom Hebert dreads the most; and should he become sole mortgagee, my whole estate would pass to him if, through any succession of bad seasons and failing tenants, the interest was not punctually paid."

"It could so pass to him now."

"No; for there have been years in which the other mortgagees, who are Bretons and would be loath to ruin a Rochebriant, have been lenient and patient."

"If Louvier has not been equally so, it is only because he knew nothing of you, and your father no doubt had often sorely tasked his endurance.

Come, suppose we manage to break the ice easily. Do me the honour to dine here to meet him; you will find that he is not an unpleasant man."

The Marquis hesitated, but the thought of the sharp and seemingly hopeless struggle for the retention of his ancestral home to which he would be doomed if he returned from Paris unsuccessful in his errand overmastered his pride. He felt as if that self-conquest was a duty he owed to the very tombs of his fathers. "I ought not to shrink from the face of a creditor," said he, smiling somewhat sadly, "and I accept the proposal you so graciously make."

"You do well, Marquis, and I will write at once to Louvier to ask him to give me his first disengaged day."

The Marquis had no sooner quitted the house than M. Gandrin opened a door at the side of his office, and a large portly man strode into the room,—stride it was rather than step,—firm, self-assured, arrogant, masterful.

"Well, mon ami," said this man, taking his stand at the hearth, as a king might take his stand in the hall of his vassal, "and what says our petit muscadin?"

"He is neither petit nor muscadin, Monsieur Louvier," replied Gandrin, peevishly; "and he will task your powers to get him thoroughly into your net. But I have persuaded him to meet you here. What day can you dine with me? I had better ask no one else."

"To-morrow I dine with my friend O——-, to meet the chiefs of the Opposition," said M. Louvier, with a sort of careless rollicking pomposity. "Thursday with Pereire; Saturday I entertain at home. Say Friday. Your hour?"

"Seven."

"Good! Show me those Rochebriant papers again; there is something I had forgotten to note. Never mind me. Go on with your work as if I were not here."

Louvier took up the papers, seated himself in an armchair by the fireplace, stretched out his legs, and read at his ease, but with a very rapid eye, as a practised lawyer skims through the technical forms of a case to fasten upon the marrow of it.

"Ah! as I thought. The farms could not pay even the interest on my present mortgage; the forests come in for that. If a contractor for the yearly sale of the woods was bankrupt and did not pay, how could I get my interest? Answer me that, Gandrin."

"Certainly you must run the risk of that chance."

"Of course the chance occurs, and then I foreclose, seize,—Rochebriant and its seigneuries are mine."

As he spoke he laughed, not sardonically,—a jovial laugh,—and opened wide, to reshut as in a vice, the strong iron hand which had doubtless closed over many a man's all.

"Thanks. On Friday, seven o'clock." He tossed the papers back on the bureau, nodded a royal nod, and strode forth imperiously as he had strode in.

# CHAPTER III.

MEANWHILE the young Marquis pursued his way thoughtfully through the streets, and entered the Champs Elysees. Since we first, nay, since we last saw him, he is strikingly improved in outward appearances. He has unconsciously acquired more of the easy grace of the Parisian in gait and bearing. You would no longer detect the Provincial—perhaps, however, because he is now dressed, though very simply, in habiliments that belong to the style of the day. Rarely among the loungers in the Champs Elysees could be seen a finer form, a comelier face, an air of more unmistakable distinction.

The eyes of many a passing fair one gazed on him, admiringly or coquettishly. But he was still so little the true Parisian that they got no smile, no look in return. He was wrapped in his own thoughts; was he thinking of M. Louvier?

He had nearly gained the entrance of the Bois de Boulogne, when he was accosted by a voice behind, and turning round saw his friend Lemercier arm-in-arm with Graham Vane.

"Bonjour, Alain," said Lemercier, hooking his disengaged arm into Rochebriant's. "I suspect we are going the same way."

Alain felt himself change countenance at this conjecture, and replied coldly, "I think not; I have got to the end of my walk, and shall turn back to Paris;" addressing himself to the Englishman, he said with formal politeness, "I regret not to have found you at home when I called some weeks ago, and no less so to have been out when you had the complaisance to return my visit."

"At all events," replied the Englishman, "let me not lose the opportunity of improving our acquaintance which now offers. It is true that our friend Lemercier, catching sight of me in the Rue de Rivoli, stopped his coupe and carried me off for a promenade in the Bois. The fineness of the day tempted us to get out of his carriage as the Bois came in sight. But if you are going back to Paris I relinquish the Bois and offer myself as your companion."

Frederic (the name is so familiarly English that the reader might think me pedantic did I accentuate it as French) looked from one to the other of his two friends, half amused and half angry.

"And am I to be left alone to achieve a conquest, in which, if I succeed, I shall change into hate and envy the affection of my two best friends? Be it so.

*"' Un veritable amant ne connait point d'amis.'"*

"I do not comprehend your meaning," said the Marquis, with a compressed lip and a slight frown.

"Bah!" cried Frederic; "come, franc jeu; cards on the table. M. Gram Varn was going into the Bois at my suggestion on the chance of having another look at the pearl-coloured angel; and you, Rochebriant, can't deny that you were going into the Bois for the same object."

"One may pardon an enfant terrible," said the Englishman, laughing, "but an ami terrible should be sent to the galleys. Come, Marquis, let us walk back and submit to our fate. Even were the lady once more visible, we have no chance of being observed by the side of a Lovelace so accomplished and so audacious!"

"Adieu, then, recreants: I go alone. Victory or death." The Parisian beckoned his coachman, entered his carriage, and with a mocking grimace kissed his hand to the companions thus deserting or deserted.

Rochebriant touched the Englishman's arm, and said, "Do you think that Lemercier could be impertinent enough to accost that lady?"

"In the first place," returned the Englishman, "Lemercier himself tells me that the lady has for several weeks relinquished her walks in the Bois, and the probability is, therefore, that he will not have the opportunity to accost her. In the next place, it appears that when she did take her solitary walk, she did not stray far from her carriage, and was in reach of the protection of her laquais and coachman. But to speak honestly, do you, who know Lemercier better than I, take him to be a man who would commit an impertinence to a woman unless there were viveurs of his own sex to see him do it?"

Alain smiled. "No. Frederic's real nature is an admirable one, and if he ever do anything that he ought to be ashamed of, 'twill be from the pride of showing how finely he can do it. Such was his character at college, and such it still seems at Paris. But it is true that the lady has forsaken her former walk; at least I—I have not seen her since the day I first beheld her in company with Frederic. Yet—yet, pardon me, you were going to the Bois on the chance of seeing her. Perhaps she has changed the direction of her walk, and—and—"

The Marquis stopped short, stammering and confused.

The Englishman scanned his countenance with the rapid glance of a practised observer of men and things, and after a short pause said: "If the lady has selected some other spot for her promenade, I am ignorant of it; nor have I ever volunteered the chance of meeting with her, since I learned—first from Lemercier, and afterwards from others—that her destination is the stage. Let us talk frankly, Marquis. I am accustomed to take much exercise on foot, and the Bois is my favourite resort: one day I there found myself in the allee which the lady we speak of used to select for her promenade, and there saw her. Something in her face impressed me; how shall I describe the impression? Did you ever open a poem, a romance, in some style wholly new to you, and before you were quite certain whether or not its merits justified the interest which the novelty inspired, you were summoned away, or the book was taken out of your hands? If so, did you not feel an intellectual longing to have another glimpse of the book? That illustration describes my impression, and I own that I twice again went to the same allee. The last time I only caught sight of the young lady as she was getting into her carriage. As she was then borne away, I perceived one of the custodians of the Bois; and learned, on questioning him, that the lady was in the habit of walking always alone in the same allee at the same hour on most fine days, but that he did not know her name or address. A motive of curiosity—perhaps an idle one—then made me ask Lemercier, who boasts of knowing his Paris so intimately, if he could inform me who the lady was. He undertook to ascertain."

"But," interposed the Marquis, "he did not ascertain who she was; he only ascertained where she lived, and that she and an elder companion were Italians;—whom he suspected, without sufficient ground, to be professional singers."

"True; but since then I ascertained more detailed particulars from two acquaintances of mine who happen to know her,—M. Savarin, the distinguished writer, and Mrs. Morley, an accomplished and beautiful American lady, who is more than an acquaintance. I may boast the honour of ranking among her friends. As Savarin's villa is at A———, I asked him incidentally if he knew the fair neighbour whose face had so attracted me; and Mrs. Morley being present, and overhearing me, I learned from both what I now repeat to you.

"The young lady is a Signorina Cicogna,—at Paris, exchanging (except among particular friends), as is not unusual, the outlandish designation of Signorina for the more conventional one of Mademoiselle. Her father was a member of the noble Milanese family of the same name, therefore the young lady is well born. Her father has been long dead; his widow married again an English gentleman settled in Italy, a scholar and antiquarian; his name was Selby. This gentleman, also dead, bequeathed the Signorina a small but sufficient competence. She is now an orphan, and residing with a companion, a Signora Venosta, who was once a singer of some repute at the Neapolitan Theatre, in the orchestra of which her husband was principal performer; but she relinquished the stage several years ago on becoming a widow, and gave lessons as a teacher. She has the character of being a scientific musician, and of unblemished private respectability. Subsequently she was induced to give up general teaching, and undertake the musical education and the social charge of the young lady with her. This girl is said to have early given promise of extraordinary excellence as a singer, and excited great interest among a coterie of literary critics and musical cognoscenti. She was to have come out at the Theatre of Milan a year or two ago, but her career has been suspended in consequence of ill-health, for which she is now at Paris under the care of an English physician, who has made remarkable cures in all complaints of the respiratory organs. ———, the great composer, who knows her, says that in expression and feeling she has no living superior, perhaps no equal since Malibran."

"You seem, dear Monsieur, to have taken much pains to acquire this information."

"No great pains were necessary; but had they been I might have taken them, for, as I have owned to you, Mademoiselle Cicogna, while she was yet a mystery to me, strangely interested my thoughts or my fancies. That interest has now ceased. The world of actresses and singers lies apart from mine."

"Yet," said Alain, in a tone of voice that implied doubt, "if I understand Lemercier aright, you were going with him to the Bois on the chance of seeing again the lady in whom your interest has ceased."

"Lemercier's account was not strictly accurate. He stopped his carriage to speak to me on quite another subject, on which I have consulted him, and then proposed to take me on to the Bois. I assented; and it was not till we were in the carriage that he suggested the idea of seeing whether the pearly-robed lady had resumed her walk in the allee. You may judge how indifferent I was to that chance when I preferred turning back with you to going on with him. Between you and me, Marquis, to men of our age, who have the business of life before them, and feel that if there be aught in which noblesse oblige it is a severe devotion to noble objects, there is nothing more fatal to such devotion than allowing the heart to be blown hither and thither at every breeze of mere fancy, and dreaming ourselves into love with some fair creature whom we never could marry consistently with the career we have set before our ambition. I could not marry an actress,—

neither, I presume, could the Marquis de Rochebriant; and the thought of a courtship which excluded the idea of marriage to a young orphan of name unblemished, of virtue unsuspected, would certainly not be compatible with 'devotion to noble objects.'"

Alain involuntarily bowed his head in assent to the proposition, and, it may be, in submission to an implied rebuke.

The two men walked in silence for some minutes, and Graham first spoke, changing altogether the subject of conversation. "Lemercier tells me you decline going much into this world of Paris, the capital of capitals, which appears so irresistibly attractive to us foreigners."

"Possibly; but, to borrow your words, I have the business of life before me."

"Business is a good safeguard against the temptations to excess in pleasure, in which Paris abounds. But there is no business which does not admit of some holiday, and all business necessitates commerce with mankind. A propos, I was the other evening at the Duchese de Tarascon's,—a brilliant assembly, filled with ministers, senators, and courtiers. I heard your name mentioned."

"Mine?"

"Yes; Duplessis, the rising financier—who rather to my surprise was not only present among these official and decorated celebrities, but apparently quite at home among them—asked the Duchess if she had not seen you since your arrival at Paris. She replied, 'No; that though you were among her nearest connections, you had not called on her;' and bade Duplessis tell you that you were a monstre for not doing so. Whether or not Duplessis will take that liberty I know not; but you must pardon me if I do. She is a very charming woman, full of talent; and that stream of the world which reflects the stars, with all their mythical influences on fortune, flows through her salons."

"I am not born under those stars. I am a Legitimist."

"I did not forget your political creed; but in England the leaders of opposition attend the salons of the Prime Minister. A man is not supposed to compromise his opinions because he exchanges social courtesies with those to whom his opinions are hostile. Pray excuse me if I am indiscreet, I speak as a traveller who asks for information: but do the Legitimists really believe that they best serve their cause by declining any mode of competing with its opponents? Would there not be a fairer chance of the ultimate victory of their principles if they made their talents and energies individually prominent; if they were known as skilful generals, practical statesmen, eminent diplomatists, brilliant writers? Could they combine,—not to sulk and exclude themselves from the great battle-field of the world, but in their several ways to render themselves of such use to their country that some day or other, in one of those revolutionary crises to which France, alas! must long be subjected, they would find themselves able to turn the scale of undecided councils and conflicting jealousies."

"Monsieur, we hope for the day when the Divine Disposer of events will strike into the hearts of our fickle and erring countrymen the conviction that there will be no settled repose for France save under the sceptre of her rightful kings. But meanwhile we are,—I see it more clearly since I have quitted Bretagne,—we are a hopeless minority."

"Does not history tell us that the great changes of the world have been wrought by minorities,—but on the one condition that the minorities shall not be hopeless? It is almost the other day that the Bonapartists were in a minority that their adversaries called hopeless, and the majority for the Emperor is now so preponderant that I tremble for his safety. When a majority becomes so vast that intellect disappears in the crowd, the date of its destruction commences; for by the law of reaction the minority is installed against it. It is the nature of things that minorities are always more intellectual than multitudes, and intellect is ever at work in sapping numerical force. What your party want is hope; because without hope there is no energy. I remember hearing my father say that when he met the Count de Chambord at Ems, that illustrious personage delivered himself of a belle phrase much admired by his partisans. The Emperor was then President of the Republic, in a very doubtful and dangerous position. France seemed on the verge of another convulsion. A certain distinguished politician recommended the Count de Chambord to hold himself ready to enter at once as a candidate for the throne. And the Count, with a benignant smile on his handsome face, answered, 'All wrecks come to the shore: the shore does not go to the wrecks.'"

"Beautifully said!" exclaimed the Marquis.

"Not if 'Le beau est toujours le vrai.' My father, no inexperienced nor unwise politician, in repeating the royal words, remarked: 'The fallacy of the Count's argument is in its metaphor. A man is not a shore. Do you not think that the seamen on board the wrecks would be more grateful to him who did not complacently compare himself to a shore, but considered himself a human being like themselves, and risked his own life in a boat, even though it were a cockleshell, in the chance of saving theirs?"

Alain de Rochebriant was a brave man, with that intense sentiment of patriotism which characterizes Frenchmen of every rank and persuasion, unless they belong to the Internationalists; and, without pausing to consider, he cried, "Your father was right."

The Englishman resumed: "Need I say, my dear Marquis, that I am not a Legitimist? I am not an Imperialist, neither am I an Orleanist nor a Republican. Between all those political divisions it is for Frenchmen to make their choice, and for Englishmen to accept for France that government which France has established. I view things here as a simple observer. But it strikes me that if I were a Frenchman in your position, I should think myself unworthy my ancestors if I consented to be an insignificant looker-on."

"You are not in my position," said the Marquis, half mournfully, half haughtily, "and you can scarcely judge of it even in imagination."

"I need not much task my imagination; I judge of it by analogy. I was very much in your position when I entered upon what I venture to call my career; and it is the curious similarity between us in circumstances, that made me wish for your friendship when that similarity was made known to me by Lemercier, who is not less garrulous than the true Parisian usually is. Permit me to say that, like you, I was reared in some pride of no inglorious ancestry. I was reared also in the expectation of great wealth. Those expectations were not realized: my father had the fault of noble natures,—generosity pushed to imprudence: he died poor and in debt. You retain the home of your ancestors; I had to resign mine."

The Marquis had felt deeply interested in this narrative, and as Graham now paused, took his hand and pressed it. "One of our most eminent personages said to me about that time, 'Whatever a clever man of your age determines to do or to be, the odds are twenty to one that he has only to live on in order to do or to be it.' Don't you think he spoke truly? I think so."

"I scarcely know what to think," said Rochebriant; "I feel as if you had given me so rough a shake when I was in the midst of a dull dream, that I am not yet quite sure whether I am asleep or awake."

Just as he said this, and towards the Paris end of the Champs Elysees, there was a halt, a sensation among the loungers round them; many of them uncovered in salute.

A man on the younger side of middle age, somewhat inclined to corpulence, with a very striking countenance, was riding slowly by. He returned the salutations he received with the careless dignity of a Personage accustomed to respect, and then reined in his horse by the side of a barouche, and exchanged some words with a portly gentleman who was its sole occupant. The loungers, still halting, seemed to contemplate this parley—between him on horseback and him in the carriage—with very eager interest. Some put their hands behind their ears and pressed forward, as if trying to overhear what was said.

"I wonder," quoth Graham, "whether, with all his cleverness, the Prince has in any way decided what he means to do or to be."

"The Prince!" said Rochebriant, rousing himself from revery; "what Prince?"

"Do you not recognize him by his wonderful likeness to the first Napoleon,—him on horseback talking to Louvier, the great financier."

"Is that stout bourgeois in the carriage Louvier,—my mortgagee, Louvier?"

"Your mortgagee, my dear Marquis? Well, he is rich enough to be a very lenient one upon pay-day."

"Hein!—I doubt his leniency," said Alain. "I have promised my avoue to meet him at dinner. Do you think I did wrong?"

"Wrong! of course not; he is likely to overwhelm you with civilities. Pray don't refuse if he gives you an invitation to his soiree next Saturday; I am going to it. One meets there the notabilities most interesting to study,—artists, authors, politicians, especially those who call themselves Republicans. He and the Prince agree in one thing; namely, the cordial reception they give to the men who would destroy the state of things upon which Prince and financier both thrive. Hillo! here comes Lemercier on return from the Bois."

Lemercier's coupe stopped beside the footpath. "What tidings of the Belle Inconnue?" asked the Englishman. "None; she was not there. But I am rewarded: such an adventure! a dame of the haute volee; I believe she is a duchess. She was walking with a lap-dog, a pure Pomeranian. A strange poodle flew at the Pomeranian, I drove off the poodle, rescued the Pomeranian, received the most gracious thanks, the sweetest smile: femme superbe, middle aged. I prefer women of forty. Au revoir, I am due at the club."

Alain felt a sensation of relief that Lemercier had not seen the lady in the pearl-coloured dress, and quitted the Englishman with a lightened heart.

# CHAPTER IV.

"Piccola, piccola! com e cortese! another invitation from M. Louvier for next Saturday,—conversazione." This was said in Italian by an elderly lady bursting noisily into the room,—elderly, yet with a youthful expression of face, owing perhaps to a pair of very vivacious black eyes. She was dressed, after a somewhat slatternly fashion, in a wrapper of crimson merino much the worse for wear, a blue handkerchief twisted turban-like round her head, and her feet encased in list slippers. The person to whom she addressed herself was a young lady with dark hair, which, despite its evident repugnance, was restrained into smooth glossy braids over the forehead, and at the crown of the small graceful head into the simple knot which Horace has described as "Spartan." Her dress contrasted the speaker's by an exquisite neatness.

We have seen her before as the lady in the pearl-coloured robe; but seen now at home she looks much younger. She was one of those whom, encountered in the streets or in society, one might guess to be married,—probably a young bride; for thus seen there was about her an air of dignity and of self-possession which suits well with the ideal of chaste youthful matronage; and in the expression of the face there was a pensive thoughtfulness beyond her years. But as she now sat by the open window arranging flowers in a glass bowl, a book lying open on her lap, you would never have said, "What a handsome woman!" you would have said, "What a charming girl!" All about her was maidenly, innocent, and fresh. The dignity of her bearing was lost in household ease, the pensiveness of her expression in an untroubled serene sweetness.

Perhaps many of my readers may have known friends engaged in some absorbing cause of thought, and who are in the habit when they go out, especially if on solitary walks, to take that cause of thought with them. The friend may be an orator meditating his speech, a poet his verses, a lawyer a difficult case, a physician an intricate malady. If you have such a friend, and you observe him thus away from his home, his face will seem to you older and graver. He is absorbed in the care that weighs on him. When you see him in a holiday moment at his own fireside, the care is thrown aside; perhaps he mastered while abroad the difficulty that had troubled him; he is cheerful, pleasant, sunny. This appears to be very much the case with persons of genius. When in their own houses we usually find them very playful and childlike. Most persons of real genius, whatever they may seem out of doors, are very sweet-tempered at home, and sweet temper is sympathizing and genial in the intercourse of private life. Certainly, observing this girl as she now bends over the flowers, it would be difficult to believe her to be the Isaura Cicogna whose letters to Madame de Grantinesnil exhibit the doubts and struggles of an unquiet, discontented, aspiring mind. Only in one or two passages in those letters would you have guessed at the writer in the girl as we now see her. It is in those passages where she expresses her love of harmony, and her repugnance to contest: those were characteristics you might have read in her face.

Certainly the girl is very lovely: what long dark eyelashes! what soft, tender, dark-blue eyes! now that she looks up and smiles, what a bewitching smile it is! by what sudden play of rippling dimples the smile is enlivened and redoubled! Do you notice one feature? In very showy beauties it is seldom noticed; but I, being in my way a physiognomist, consider that it is always worth heeding as an index of character. It is the ear. Remark how delicately it is formed in her: none of that heaviness of lobe which is a sure sign of sluggish intellect and coarse perception. Hers is the artist's ear. Note next those hands: how beautifully shaped! small, but not doll-like hands,—ready and nimble, firm and nervous hands, that could work for a helpmate. By no means very white, still less red, but somewhat embrowned as by the sun, such as you may see in girls reared in southern climes, and in her perhaps betokening an impulsive character which had not accustomed itself, when at sport in the open air, to the thraldom of gloves,—very impulsive people even in cold climates seldom do.

In conveying to us by a few bold strokes an idea of the sensitive, quick-moved, warm-blooded Henry II., the most impulsive of the Plantagenets, his contemporary chronicler tells us that rather than imprison those active hands of his, even in hawking-gloves, he would suffer his falcon to fix its sharp claws into his wrist. No doubt there is a difference as to what is befitting between a burly bellicose creature like Henry II. and a delicate young lady like Isaura Cicogna; and one would not wish to see those dainty wrists of hers seamed and scarred by a falcon's claws. But a girl may not be less exquisitely feminine for slight heed of artificial prettiness. Isaura had no need of pale bloodless hands to seem one of Nature's highest grade of gentlewomen even to the most fastidious eyes. About her there was a charm apart from her mere beauty, and often disturbed instead of heightened by her mere intellect: it consisted in a combination of exquisite artistic refinement, and of a generosity of character by which refinement was animated into vigour and warmth.

The room, which was devoted exclusively to Isaura, had in it much that spoke of the occupant. That room, when first taken furnished, had a good deal of the comfortless showiness which belongs to ordinary furnished apartments in France, especially in the Parisian suburbs, chiefly let for the summer: thin limp muslin curtains that decline to draw; stiff mahogany chairs covered with yellow Utrecht velvet; a tall secretaire in a dark corner; an oval buhl-table set in tawdry ormolu, islanded in the centre of a poor but gaudy Scotch carpet; and but one other table of dull walnut-wood, standing clothless before a sofa to match the chairs; the eternal ormolu clock flanked by the two eternal ormolu candelabra on the dreary mantelpiece. Some of this garniture had been removed, others softened into cheeriness and comfort. The room somehow or other—thanks partly to a very moderate expenditure in pretty twills with pretty borders, gracefully simple table-covers, with one or two additional small tables and easy-chairs, two simple vases filled with flowers; thanks still more to a nameless skill in re-arrangement, and the disposal of the slight knick-knacks and well-bound volumes, which, even in travelling, women who have cultivated the pleasures of taste carry about them—had been coaxed into that quiet harmony, that tone of consistent subdued colour, which corresponded with the characteristics of the inmate. Most people might have been puzzled where to place the piano, a semi-grand, so as not to take up too much space in the little room; but where it was placed it seemed so at home that you might have supposed the room had been built for it.

There are two kinds of neatness,—one is too evident, and makes everything about it seem trite and cold and stiff; and another kind of neatness disappears from our sight in a satisfied sense of completeness,—like some exquisite, simple, finished style of writing, an Addison's or a St. Pierre's.

This last sort of neatness belonged to Isaura, and brought to mind the well-known line of Catullus when on recrossing his threshold he invokes its welcome,—a line thus not inelegantly translated by Leigh Hunt,

*"Smile every dimple on the cheek of Home."*

I entreat the reader's pardon for this long descriptive digression; but Isaura is one of those characters which are called many-sided, and therefore not very easy to comprehend. She gives us one side of her character in her correspondence with Madame de Grantmesnil, and another side of it in her own home with her Italian companion,—half nurse, half chaperon.

"Monsieur Louvier is indeed very courteous," said Isaura, looking up from the flowers with the dimpled smile we have noticed. "But I think, Madre, that we should do well to stay at home on Saturday,—not peacefully, for I owe you your revenge at Euchre."

"You can't mean it, Piecola!" exclaimed the Signora, in evident consternation. "Stay at home!—why stay at home? Euchre is very well when there is nothing else to do: but change is pleasant; le bon Dieu likes it,

*"'Ne caldo ne gelo*
*Resta mai in cielo.'*

"And such beautiful ices one gets at M. Louvier's! Did you taste the pistachio ice? What fine rooms, and so well lit up! I adore light. And the ladies so beautifully dressed: one sees the fashions. Stay at home! play at Euchre indeed! Piccola, you cannot be so cruel to yourself: you are young."

"But, dear Madre, just consider; we are invited because we are considered professional singers: your reputation as such is of course established,—mine is not; but still I shall be asked to sing, as I was asked before; and you know Dr. C. forbids me to do so except to a very small audience; and it is so ungracious always to say 'No;' and besides, did you not yourself say, when we came away last time from M. Louvier's, that it was very dull, that you knew nobody, and that the ladies had such superb toilets that you felt mortified—and—"

"Zitto! zitto! you talk idly, Piccola,—very idly. I was mortified then in my old black Lyons silk; but have I not bought since then my beautiful Greek jacket,—scarlet and gold lace? and why should I buy it if I am not to show it?"

"But, dear Madre, the jacket is certainly very handsome, and will make an effect in a little dinner at the Savarins or Mrs. Morley's; but in a great formal reception like M. Louvier's will it not look—"

"Splendid!" interrupted the Signora.

"But singolare."

"So much the better; did not that great English Lady wear such a jacket, and did not every one admire her, piu tosto invidia the compassione?"

Isaura sighed. Now the jacket of the Signora was a subject of disquietude to her friend. It so happened that a young English lady of the highest rank and the rarest beauty had appeared at M. Louvier's, and indeed generally in the beau monde of Paris, in a Greek jacket that became her very much. The jacket had fascinated, at M. Louvier's, the eyes of the Signora. But of this Isaura was unaware. The Signora, on returning home from M. Louvier's, had certainly lamented much over the mesquin appearance of her old-fashioned Italian habiliments compared with the brilliant toilette of the gay Parisiennes; and Isaura—quite woman enough to sympathize with woman in such womanly vanities—proposed the next day to go with the Signora to one of the principal couturieres of Paris, and adapt the Signora's costume to the fashions of the place. But the Signora having predetermined on a Greek jacket, and knowing by instinct that Isaura would be disposed to thwart that splendid predilection, had artfully suggested that it would be better to go to the couturiere with Madame Savarin, as being a more experienced adviser,—and the coupe only held two.

As Madame Savarin was about the same age as the Signora, and dressed as became her years and in excellent taste, Isaura thought this an admirable suggestion; and pressing into her chaperon's hand a billet de banque sufficient to re-equip her cap-a pie, dismissed the subject from her mind. But the Signora was much too cunning to submit her passion for the Greek jacket to the discouraging comments of Madame Savarin. Monopolizing the coupe, she became absolute mistress of the situation. She went to no fashionable couturiere's. She went to a magasin that she had seen advertised in the Petites Afiches as supplying superb costumes for fancy-balls and amateur performers in private theatricals. She returned home triumphant, with a jacket still more dazzling to the eye than that of the English lady.

When Isaura first beheld it, she drew back in a sort of superstitious terror, as of a comet or other blazing portent.

"Cosa stupenda!" (stupendous thing!) She might well be dismayed when the Signora proposed to appear thus attired in M. Louvier's salon. What might be admired as coquetry of dress in a young beauty of rank so great that even a vulgarity in her would be called distinguee, was certainly an audacious challenge of ridicule in the elderly ci-devant music-teacher.

But how could Isaura, how can any one of common humanity, say to a woman resolved upon wearing a certain dress, "You are not young and handsome enough for that?" Isaura could only murmur, "For many reasons I would rather stay at home, dear Madre."

"Ah! I see you are ashamed of me," said the Signora, in softened tones: "very natural. When the nightingale sings no more, she is only an ugly brown bird;" and therewith the Signora Venosta seated herself submissively, and began to cry.

On this Isaura sprang up, wound her arms round the Signora's neck, soothed her with coaxing, kissed and petted her, and ended by saying, "Of course we will go;" and, "but let me choose you another dress,—a dark-green velvet trimmed with blonde: blonde becomes you so well."

"No, no: I hate green velvet; anybody can wear that. Piccola, I am not clever like thee; I cannot amuse myself like thee with books. I am in a foreign land. I have a poor head, but I have a big heart" (another burst of tears); "and that big heart is set on my beautiful Greek jacket."

"Dearest Madre," said Isaura, half weeping too, "forgive me, you are right. The Greek jacket is splendid; I shall be so pleased to see you wear it: poor Madre! so pleased to think that in the foreign land you are not without something that pleases you!"

# CHAPTER V.

CONFORMABLY with his engagement to meet M. Louvier, Alain found himself on the day and at the hour named in M. Gandrin's salon. On this occasion Madame Gandrin did not appear. Her husband was accustomed to give diners d'hommes. The great man had not yet arrived. "I think, Marquis," said M. Gandrin, "that you will not regret having followed my advice: my representations have disposed Louvier to regard you with much favour, and he is certainly flattered by being permitted to make your personal acquaintance."

The avoue had scarcely finished this little speech, when M. Louvier was announced. He entered with a beaming smile, which did not detract from his imposing presence. His flatterers had told him that he had a look of Louis Philippe; therefore he had sought to imitate the dress and the bonhomie of that monarch of the middle class. He wore a wig, elaborately piled up, and shaped his whiskers in royal harmony with the royal wig. Above all, he studied that social frankness of manner with which the able sovereign dispelled awe of his presence or dread of his astuteness. Decidedly he was a man very pleasant to converse and to deal with—so long as there seemed to him something to gain and nothing to lose by being pleasant. He returned Alain's bow by a cordial offer of both expansive hands, into the grasp of which the hands of the aristocrat utterly disappeared. "Charmed to make your acquaintance, Marquis; still more charmed if you will let me be useful during your sejour at Paris. Ma foi, excuse my bluntness, but you are a fort beau garcon. Monsieur your father was a handsome man, but you beat him hollow. Gandrin, my friend, would not you and I give half our fortunes for one year of this fine fellow's youth spent at Paris? Peste! what love-letters we should have, with no need to buy them by billets de banque!" Thus he ran on, much to Alain's confusion, till dinner was announced. Then there was something grandiose in the frank bourgeois style wherewith he expanded his napkin and twisted one end into his waistcoat; it was so manly a renunciation of the fashions which a man so repandu in all circles might be supposed to follow,—as if he were both too great and too much in earnest for such frivolities. He was evidently a sincere bon vivant, and M. Gandrin had no less evidently taken all requisite pains to gratify his taste. The Montrachet served with the oysters was of precious vintage; that vin de madere which accompanied the potage a la bisque would have contented an American. And how radiant became Louvier's face when amongst the entrees he came upon laitances de carpes! "The best thing in the world," he cried, "and one gets it so seldom since the old Rocher de Cancale has lost its renown. At private houses, what does one get now? blanc de poulet, flavourless trash. After all, Gandrin, when we lose the love-letters, it is some consolation that laitances de carpes and sautes de foie gras are still left to fill up the void in our hearts. Marquis, heed my counsel; cultivate betimes the taste for the table,—that and whist are the sole resources of declining years. You never met my old friend Talleyrand—ah, no! he was long before your time. He cultivated both, but he made two mistakes. No man's intellect is perfect on all sides. He confined himself to one meal a day, and he never learned to play well at whist. Avoid his errors, my young friend,—avoid them. Gandrin, I guess this pineapple is English,—it is superb."

"You are right,—a present from the Marquis of H———-."

"Ah! instead of a fee, I wager. The Marquis gives nothing for nothing, dear man! Droll people the English. You have never visited England, I presume, cher Rochebriant?" The affable financier had already made vast progress in familiarity with his silent fellow-guest.

When the dinner was over and the three men had reentered the salon for coffee and liqueurs, Gandrin left Louvier and Alain alone, saying he was going to his cabinet for cigars which he could recommend. Then Louvier, lightly patting the Marquis on the shoulder, said with what the French call effusion, "My dear Rochebriant, your father and I did not quite understand each other. He took a tone of grand seigneur that sometimes wounded me; and I in turn was perhaps too rude in asserting my rights—as creditor, shall I say?—no, as fellow-citizen; and Frenchmen are so vain, so over-susceptible; fire up at a word; take offence when none is meant. We two, my dear boy, should be superior to such national foibles. Bref—I have a mortgage on your lands. Why should that thought mar our friendship? At my age, though I am not yet old, one is flattered if the young like us, pleased if we can oblige them, and remove from their career any little obstacle in its way. Gandrin tells me you wish to consolidate all the charges on your estate into one on a lower rate of interest. Is it so?"

"I am so advised," said the Marquis.

"And very rightly advised; come and talk with me about it some day next week. I hope to have a large sum of money set free in a few days. Of course, mortgages on land don't pay like speculations at the Bourse; but I am rich enough to please myself. We will see, we will see."

Here Gandrin returned with the cigars; but Alain at that time never smoked, and Louvier excused himself, with a laugh and a sly wink, on the plea that he was going to pay his respects—as doubtless that joli garcon was going to do likewise—to a belle dame who did not reckon the smell of tobacco among the perfumes of Houbigant or Arabia.

"Meanwhile," added Louvier, turning to Gandrin, "I have something to say to you on business about the contract for that new street of mine. No hurry,—after our young friend has gone to his 'assignation.'"

Alain could not misinterpret the hint; and in a few moments took leave of his host, more surprised than disappointed that the financier had not invited him, as Graham had assumed he would, to his soiree the following evening.

When Alain was gone, Louvier's jovial manner disappeared also, and became bluffly rude rather than bluntly cordial. "Gandrin, what did you mean by saying that that young man was no muscadin! Muscadin, aristocrate, offensive from top to toe."

"You amaze me; you seemed to take to him so cordially."

"And pray, were you too blind to remark with what cold reserve he responded to my condescensions; how he winced when I called him Rochebriant; how he coloured when I called him 'dear boy'? These aristocrats think we ought to thank them on our knees when they take our money, and" here Louvier's face darkened—"seduce our women." "Monsieur Louvier, in all France I do not know a greater aristocrat than yourself."

I don't know whether M. Gandrin meant that speech as a compliment, but M. Louvier took it as such,—laughed complacently and rubbed his hands. "Ay, ay, millionnaires are the real aristocrats, for they have power, as my beau Marquis will soon find. I must bid you good night. Of course I shall see Madame Gandrin and yourself to-morrow. Prepare for a motley gathering,—lots of democrats and foreigners, with artists and authors, and such creatures."

"Is that the reason why you did not invite the Marquis?"

"To be sure; I would not shock so pure a Legitimist by contact with the sons of the people, and make him still colder to myself. No; when he comes to my house he shall meet lions and viveurs of the haut ton, who will play into my hands by teaching him how to ruin himself in the quickest manner and in the genre Regence. Bon soir, mon vieux."

# CHAPTER VI.

The next night Graham in vain looked round for Alain in M. Louvier's salons, and missed his high-bred mien and melancholy countenance. M. Louvier had been for some four years a childless widower, but his receptions were not the less numerously attended, nor his establishment less magnificently monde for the absence of a presiding lady: very much the contrary; it was noticeable how much he had increased his status and prestige as a social personage since the death of his unlamented spouse.

To say truth, she had been rather a heavy drag on his triumphal car. She had been the heiress of a man who had amassed a great deal of money,—not in the higher walks of commerce, but in a retail trade.

Louvier himself was the son of a rich money-lender; he had entered life with an ample fortune and an intense desire to be admitted into those more brilliant circles in which fortune can be dissipated with eclat. He might not have attained this object but for the friendly countenance of a young noble who was then—

*"The glass of fashion and the mould of form;"*

but this young noble, of whom later we shall hear more, came suddenly to grief, and when the money-lender's son lost that potent protector, the dandies, previously so civil, showed him a very cold shoulder.

Louvier then became an ardent democrat, and recruited the fortune he had impaired by the aforesaid marriage, launched into colossal speculations, and became enormously rich. His aspirations for social rank now revived, but his wife sadly interfered with them. She was thrifty by nature; sympathized little with her husband's genius for accumulation; always said he would end in a hospital; hated Republicans; despised authors and artists, and by the ladies of the beau monde was pronounced common and vulgar.

So long as she lived, it was impossible for Louvier to realize his ambition of having one of the salons which at Paris establish celebrity and position. He could not then command those advantages of wealth which he especially coveted. He was eminently successful in doing this now. As soon as she was safe in Pere la Chaise, he enlarged his hotel by the purchase and annexation of an adjoining house; redecorated and refurnished it, and in this task displayed, it must be said to his credit, or to that of the administrators he selected for the purpose, a nobleness of taste rarely exhibited nowadays. His collection of pictures was not large, and consisted exclusively of the French school, ancient and modern, for in all things Louvier affected the patriot. But each of those pictures was a gem; such Watteaus, such Greuzes, such landscapes by Patel, and, above all, such masterpieces by Ingres, Horace Vernet, and Delaroche were worth all the doubtful originals of Flemish and Italian art which make the ordinary boast of private collectors.

These pictures occupied two rooms of moderate size, built for their reception, and lighted from above. The great salon to which they led contained treasures scarcely less precious; the walls were covered with the richest silks which the looms of Lyons could produce. Every piece of furniture here was a work of art in its way: console-tables of Florentine mosaic, inlaid with pearl and lapis-lazuli; cabinets in which the exquisite designs of the Renaissance were carved in ebony; colossal vases of Russian malachite, but wrought by French artists. The very knick-knacks scattered carelessly about the room might have been admired in the cabinets of the Palazzo Pitti. Beyond this room lay the salle de danse, its ceiling painted by ———, supported by white marble columns, the glazed balcony and the angles of the room filled with tiers of exotics. In the dining-room, on the same floor, on the other side of the landing-place, were stored in glazed buffets not only vessels and salvers of plate, silver and gold, but, more costly still, matchless specimens of Sevres and Limoges, and mediaeval varieties of Venetian glass. On the ground-floor, which opened on the lawn of a large garden, Louvier had his suite of private apartments, furnished, as he said, "simply, according to English notions of comfort;"—Englishmen would have said, "according to French notions of luxury." Enough of these details, which a writer cannot give without feeling himself somewhat vulgarized in doing so, but without a loose general idea of which a reader would not have an accurate conception of something not vulgar,—of something grave, historical, possibly tragical,—the existence of a Parisian millionaire at the date of this narrative.

The evidence of wealth was everywhere manifest at M. Louvier's, but it was everywhere refined by an equal evidence of taste. The apartments devoted to hospitality ministered to the delighted study of artists, to whom free access was given, and of whom two or three might be seen daily in the "show-rooms," copying pictures or taking sketches of rare articles of furniture or effects for palatian interiors.

Among the things which rich English visitors of Paris most coveted to see was M. Louvier's hotel, and few among the richest left it without a sigh of envy and despair. Only in such London houses as belong to a Sutherland or a Holford could our metropolis exhibit a splendour as opulent and a taste as refined.

M. Louvier had his set evenings for popular assemblies. At these were entertained the Liberals of every shade, from tricolor to rouge, with the artists and writers most in vogue, pele-mele with decorated diplomatists, ex-ministers, Orleanists, and Republicans, distinguished foreigners, plutocrats of the Bourse, and lions male and female from the arid nurse of that race, the Chaussee d'Antin. Of his more select reunions something will be said later.

"And how does this poor Paris metamorphosed please Monsieur Vane?" asked a Frenchman with a handsome, intelligent countenance, very carefully dressed though in a somewhat bygone fashion, and carrying off his tenth lustrum with an air too sprightly to evince any sense of the weight. This gentleman, the Vicomte de Breze, was of good birth, and had a legitimate right to his title of Vicomte,—which is more than can be said of many vicomtes one meets at Paris. He had no other property, however, than a principal share in an influential journal, to which he was a lively and sparkling contributor. In his youth, under the reign of Louis Philippe, he had been a chief among literary exquisites; and Balzac was said to have taken him more than once as his model for those brilliant young vauriens who figure in the great novelist's comedy of Human Life. The Vicomte's fashion expired with the Orleanist dynasty.

"Is it possible, my dear Vicomte," answered Graham, "not to be pleased with a capital so marvellously embellished?"

"Embellished it may be to foreign eyes," said the Vicomte, sighing, "but not improved to the taste of a Parisian like me. I miss the dear Paris of old,—the streets associated with my beaux jours are no more. Is there not something drearily monotonous in those interminable perspectives? How frightfully the way lengthens before one's eyes! In the twists and curves of the old Paris one was relieved from the pain of seeing how far one had to go from one spot to another,—each tortuous street had a separate idiosyncrasy; what picturesque diversities, what interesting recollections,—all swept away! Mon Dieu! and what for,—miles of florid facades staring and glaring at one with goggle-eyed pitiless windows; house-rents trebled, and the consciousness that if you venture to grumble underground railways, like concealed volcanoes, can burst forth on you at any moment with an eruption of bayonets and muskets. This maudit empire seeks to keep its hold on France much as a grand seigneur seeks to enchain a nymph of the ballet,—tricks her out in finery and baubles, and insures her infidelity the moment he fails to satisfy her whims."

"Vicomte," answered Graham, "I have had the honour to know you since I was a small boy at a preparatory school home for the holidays, and you were a guest at my father's country-house. You were then fete as one of the most promising writers among the young men of the day, especially favoured by the princes of the reigning family. I shall never forget the impression made on me by your brilliant appearance and your no less brilliant talk."

"Ah! ces beaux jours! ce bon Louis Philippe, ce cher petit Joinville," sighed the Vicomte.

"But at that day you compared le bon Louis Philippe to Robert Macaire. You described all his sons, including, no doubt, ce cher petit Joinville, in terms of resentful contempt, as so many plausible gamins whom Robert Macaire was training to cheat the public in the interest of the family firm. I remember my father saying to you in answer, 'No royal house in Europe has more sought to develop the literature of an epoch and to signalize its representatives by social respect and official honours than that of the Orleans dynasty. You, Monsieur de Breze, do but imitate your elders in seeking to destroy the dynasty under which you flourish; should you succeed, you hommes de plume will be the first sufferers and the loudest complainers.'"

"Cher Monsieur Vane," said the Vicomte, smiling complacently, "your father did me great honour in classing me with Victor Hugo, Alexandre Dumas, Emile de Girardin, and the other stars of the Orleanist galaxy, including our friend here, M. Savarin. A very superior man was your father."

"And," said Savarin, who, being an Orleanist, had listened to Graham's speech with an approving smile,—"and if I remember right, my dear De Breze, no one was more brilliantly severe than yourself on poor De Lamartine and the Republic that succeeded Louis Philippe; no one more emphatically expressed the yearning desire for another Napoleon to restore order at home and renown abroad. Now you have got another Napoleon."

"And I want change for my Napoleon," said De Breze, laughing.

"My dear Vicomte," said Graham, "one thing we may all grant,—that in culture and intellect you are far superior to the mass of your fellow Parisians; that you are therefore a favourable type of their political character."

"Ah, mon cher, vous etes trop aimable."

"And therefore I venture to say this,—if the archangel Gabriel were permitted to descend to Paris and form the best government for France that the wisdom of seraph could devise, it would not be two years—I doubt if it would be six months—before out of this Paris, which you call the Foyer des Idees, would emerge a powerful party, adorned by yourself and other hommes de plume, in favour of a revolution for the benefit of ce bon Satan and ce cher petit Beelzebub."

"What a pretty vein of satire you have, mon cher!" said the Vicomte, good-humouredly; "there is a sting of truth in your witticism. Indeed, I must send you some articles of mine in which I have said much the same thing,—les beaux, esprits se rencontrent. The fault of us French is impatience, desire of change; but then it is that desire which keeps the world going and retains our place at the head of it. However, at this time we are all living too fast for our money to keep up with it, and too slow for our intellect not to flag. We vie with each other on the road to ruin, for in literature all the old paths to fame are shut up."

Here a tall gentleman, with whom the Vicomte had been conversing before he accosted Vane, and who had remained beside De Breze listening in silent attention to this colloquy, interposed, speaking in the slow voice of one accustomed to measure his words, and with a slight but unmistakable German accent. "There is that, Monsieur de Breze, which makes one think gravely of what you say so lightly. Viewing things with the unprejudiced eyes of a foreigner, I recognize much for which France should be grateful to the Emperor. Under his sway her material resources have been marvellously augmented; her commerce has been placed by the treaty with England on sounder foundations, and is daily exhibiting richer life; her agriculture had made a prodigious advance wherever it has allowed room for capitalists, and escaped from the curse of petty allotments and peasant-proprietors, a curse which would have ruined any country less blessed by Nature; turbulent factions have been quelled; internal order maintained; the external prestige of France, up at least to the date of the Mexican war, increased to an extent that might satisfy even a Frenchman's amour propre; and her advance in civilization has been manifested by the rapid creation of a naval power which should put even England on her mettle. But, on the other hand—"

"Ay, on the other hand," said the Vicomte.

"On the other hand there are in the imperial system two causes of decay and of rot silently at work. They may not be the faults of the Emperor, but they are such misfortunes as may cause the fall of the Empire. The first is an absolute divorce between the political system and the intellectual culture of the nation. The throne and the system rest on universal suffrage,—on a suffrage which gives to classes the most ignorant a power that preponderates over all the healthful elements of knowledge. It is the tendency of all ignorant multitudes to personify themselves, as it were, in one individual. They cannot comprehend you when you argue for a principle; they do comprehend you when you talk of a name. The Emperor Napoleon is to them a name, and the prefects and officials who influence their votes are paid for incorporating all principles in the shibboleth of that single name. You have thus sought the well-spring of a political system in the deepest stratum of popular ignorance. To rid popular ignorance of its normal revolutionary bias, the rural peasants are indoctrinated with the conservatism that comes from the fear which appertains to property. They have their roots of land or their shares in a national loan. Thus you estrange the crassitude of an ignorant democracy still more from the intelligence of the educated classes by combining it with the most selfish and abject of all the apprehensions that are ascribed to aristocracy and wealth. What is thus embedded in the depths of your society makes itself shown on the surface. Napoleon III. has been compared to Augustus; and there are many startling similitudes between them in character and in fate. Each succeeds to the heritage of a great name that had contrived to unite autocracy with the popular cause; each subdued all rival competitors, and inaugurated despotic rule in the name of freedom; each mingled enough of sternness with ambitious will to stain with bloodshed the commencement of his power,—but it would be an absurd injustice to fix the same degree of condemnation on the coup d'etat as humanity fixes on the earlier cruelties of Augustus; each, once firm in his seat, became mild and clement,—Augustus perhaps from policy, Napoleon III. from a native kindliness of disposition which no fair critic of character can fail to acknowledge. Enough of similitudes; now for one salient difference. Observe how earnestly Augustus strove, and how completely he succeeded in the task, to rally round him all the leading intellects in every grade and of every party,—the followers of Antony, the friends of Brutus; every great captain, every great statesman, every great writer, every mail who could lend a ray of mind to his own Julian constellation, and make the age of Augustus an era in the annals of human intellect and genius. But this has not been the good fortune of your Emperor. The result of his system has been the suppression of intellect in every department. He has rallied round him not one great statesman; his praises are hymned by not one great poet. The celebrates of a former day stand aloof; or, preferring exile to constrained allegiance, assail him with unremitting missiles from their asylum in foreign shores. His reign is sterile of new celebrites. The few that arise enlist themselves against him. Whenever he shall venture to give full freedom to the press and to the legislature, the intellect thus suppressed or thus hostile will burst forth in collected volume. His partisans have not been trained and disciplined to meet such assailants. They will be as weak as no doubt they will be violent. And the worst is, that the intellect thus rising in mass against him will be warped and distorted, like captives who, being kept in chains, exercise their limbs on escaping in vehement jumps without definite object. The directors of emancipated opinion may thus be terrible enemies to the Imperial Government, but they will be very unsafe councillors to France. Concurrently with this divorce between the Imperial system and the national intellect,—a divorce so complete that even your salons have lost their wit, and even your caricatures their point,—a corruption of manners which the Empire, I own, did not originate, but inherit, has become so common that every one owns and nobody blames it. The gorgeous ostentation of the Court has perverted the habits of the people. The intelligence abstracted from other vents betakes itself to speculating for a fortune; and the greed of gain and the passion for show are sapping the noblest elements of the old French manhood. Public opinion stamps with no opprobrium a minister or favourite who profits by a job; and I fear you will find that jobbing pervades all your administrative departments."

"All very true," said De Breze, with a shrug of the shoulders and in a tone of levity that seemed to ridicule the assertion he volunteered; "Virtue and Honour banished from courts and salons and the cabinet of authors ascend to fairer heights in the attics of ouvriers."

"The ouvriers, ouvriers of Paris!" cried this terrible German.

"Ay, Monsieur le Comte, what can you say against our ouvriers? A German count cannot condescend to learn anything about ces petites gens."

"Monsieur," replied the German, "in the eyes of a statesman there are no petites gens, and in those of a philosopher no petites choses. We in Germany have too many difficult problems affecting our working classes to solve, not to have induced me to glean all the information I can as to the ouvriers of Paris. They have among them men of aspirations as noble as can animate the souls of philosophers and poets, perhaps not the less noble because common-sense and experience cannot follow their flight; but as a body the ouvriers of Paris have not been elevated in political morality by the benevolent aim of the Emperor to find them ample work and good wages independent of the natural laws that regulate the markets of labour. Accustomed thus to consider the State bound to maintain them, the moment the State fails in that impossible task, they will accommodate their honesty to a rush upon property under the name of social reform.

"Have you not noticed how largely increased within the last few years is the number of those who cry out, 'La Propriete, cest le vol'? Have you considered the rapid growth of the International Association? I do not say that for all these evils—the Empire is exclusively responsible. To a certain degree they are found in all rich communities, especially where democracy is more or less in the ascendant. To a certain extent they exist in the large towns of Germany; they are conspicuously increasing in England; they are acknowledged to be dangerous in the United States of America; they are,

I am told on good authority, making themselves visible with the spread of civilization in Russia. But under the French Empire they have become glaringly rampant, and I venture to predict that the day is not far off when the rot at work throughout all layers and strata of French society will insure a fall of the fabric at the sound of which the world will ring.

"There is many a fair and stately tree which continues to throw out its leaves and rear its crest till suddenly the wind smites it, and then, and not till then, the trunk which seems so solid is found to be but the rind to a mass of crumbled powder."

"Monsieur le Comte," said the Vicomte, "you are a severe critic and a lugubrious prophet; but a German is so safe from revolution that he takes alarm at the stir of movement which is the normal state of the French esprit."

"French esprit may soon evaporate into Parisian betise. As to Germany being safe from revolution, allow me to repeat a saying of Goethe's-but has Monsieur le Vicomte ever heard of Goethe?"

"Goethe, of course,—tres joli ecrivain."

"Goethe said to some one who was making much the same remark as yourself, 'We Germans are in a state of revolution now, but we do things so slowly that it will be a hundred years before we Germans shall find it out; but when completed, it will be the greatest revolution society has yet seen, and will last like the other revolutions that, beginning, scarce noticed, in Germany, have transformed the world.'"

"Diable, Monsieur le Comte! Germans transformed the world! What revolutions do you speak of?"

"The invention of gunpowder, the invention of printing, and the expansion of a monk's quarrel with his Pope into the Lutheran revolution."

Here the German paused, and asked the Vicomte to introduce him to Vane, which De Breze did by the title of Count von Rudesheim. On hearing Vane's name, the Count inquired if he were related to the orator and statesman, George Graham Vane, whose opinions, uttered in Parliament, were still authoritative among German thinkers. This compliment to his deceased father immensely gratified but at the same time considerably surprised the Englishman. His father, no doubt, had been a man of much influence in the British House of Commons,—a very weighty speaker, and, while in office, a first-rate administrator; but Englishmen know what a House of Commons reputation is,—how fugitive, how little cosmopolitan; and that a German count should ever have heard of his father delighted but amazed him. In stating himself to be the son of George Graham Vane, he intimated not only the delight but the amaze, with the frank savoir vivre which was one of his salient characteristics.

"Sir," replied the German, speaking in very correct English, but still with his national accent, "every German reared to political service studies England as the school for practical thought distinct from impracticable theories. Long may you allow us to do so! Only excuse me one remark,—never let the selfish element of the practical supersede the generous element. Your father never did so in his speeches, and therefore we admired him. At the present day we don't so much care to study English speeches; they may be insular,—they are not European. I honour England; Heaven grant that you may not be making sad mistakes in the belief that you can long remain England if you cease to be European." Herewith the German bowed, not uncivilly,—on the contrary, somewhat ceremoniously,—and disappeared with a Prussian Secretary of Embassy, whose arm he linked in his own, into a room less frequented.

"Vicomte, who and what is your German count?" asked Vane.

"A solemn pedant," answered the lively Vicomte,—"a German count, que voulez-vous de plus?"

## CHAPTER VII.

A LITTLE later Graham found himself alone amongst the crowd. Attracted by the sound of music, he had strayed into one of the rooms whence it came, and in which, though his range of acquaintance at Paris was for an Englishman large and somewhat miscellaneous, he recognized no familiar countenance. A lady was playing the pianoforte—playing remarkably well—with accurate science, with that equal lightness and strength of finger which produces brilliancy of execution; but to appreciate her music one should be musical one's self. It wanted the charm that fascinates the uninitiated. The guests in the room were musical connoisseurs,—a class with whom Graham Vane had nothing in common. Even if he had been more capable of enjoying the excellence of the player's performance, the glance he directed towards her would have sufficed to chill him into indifference. She was not young, and with prominent features and puckered skin, was twisting her face into strange sentimental grimaces, as if terribly overcome by the beauty and pathos of her own melodies. To add to Vane's displeasure, she was dressed in a costume wholly antagonistic to his views of the becoming,—in a Greek jacket of gold and scarlet, contrasted by a Turkish turban.

Muttering "What she-mountebank have we here?" he sank into a chair behind the door, and fell into an absorbed revery. From this he was aroused by the cessation of the music and the hum of subdued approbation by which it was followed. Above the hum swelled the imposing voice of M. Louvier as he rose from a seat on the other side of the piano, by which his bulky form had been partially concealed.

"Bravo! perfectly played! excellent! Can we not persuade your charming young countrywoman to gratify us even by a single song?" Then turning aside and addressing some one else invisible to Graham he said, "Does that tyrannical doctor still compel you to silence, Mademoiselle?"

A voice so sweetly modulated that if there were any sarcasm in the words it was lost in the softness of pathos, answered, "Nay, Monsieur Louvier, he rather overtasks the words at my command in thankfulness to those who like yourself, so kindly regard me as something else than a singer."

It was not the she-mountebank who thus spoke. Graham rose and looked round with instinctive curiosity. He met the face that he said had haunted him. She too had risen, standing near the piano, with one hand tenderly resting on the she-mountebank's scarlet and gilded shoulder,—the face that haunted him, and yet with a difference. There was a faint blush on the clear pale cheek, a soft yet playful light in the grave dark-blue eyes, which had not been visible in the countenance of the young lady in the pearl-coloured robe. Graham did not hear Louvier's reply, though no doubt it was loud enough for him to hear. He sank again into revery. Other guests now came into the room, among them Frank Morley, styled Colonel,—eminent military titles in the United States do not always denote eminent military services,—a wealthy American, and his sprightly and beautiful wife. The Colonel was a clever man, rather stiff in his deportment, and grave in speech, but by no means without a vein of dry humour. By the French he was esteemed a high-bred specimen of the kind of grand seigneur which democratic republics engender. He spoke French like a Parisian, had an imposing presence, and spent a great deal of money with the elegance of a man of taste and the generosity of a man of heart. His high breeding was not quite so well understood by the English, because the English are apt to judge breeding by little conventional rules not observed by the American Colonel. He had a slight nasal twang, and introduced "sir" with redundant ceremony in addressing Englishmen, however intimate he might be with them, and had the habit (perhaps with a sly intention to startle or puzzle them) of adorning his style of conversation with quaint Americanisms.

Nevertheless, the genial amiability and the inherent dignity of his character made him acknowledged as a thorough gentleman by every Englishman, however conventional in tastes, who became admitted into his intimate acquaintance.

Mrs. Morley, ten or twelve years younger than her husband, had no nasal twang, and employed no Americanisms in her talk, which was frank, lively, and at times eloquent. She had a great ambition to be esteemed of a masculine understanding; Nature unkindly frustrated that ambition in rendering her a model of feminine grace. Graham was intimately acquainted with Colonel Morley; and with Mrs. Morley had contracted one of those cordial friendships, which, perfectly free alike from polite flirtation and Platonic attachment, do sometimes spring up between persons of opposite sexes without the slightest danger of changing their honest character into morbid sentimentality or unlawful passion. The Morleys stopped to accost Graham, but the lady had scarcely said three words to him, before, catching sight of the haunting face, she darted towards it. Her husband, less emotional, bowed at the distance, and said, "To my taste, sir, the Signorina Cicogna is the loveliest girl in the present bee,* and full of mind, sir."

*[*Bee, a common expression in "the West" for a meeting or gathering ]of people.*

"Singing mind," said Graham, sarcastically, and in the ill-natured impulse of a man striving to check his inclination to admire.

"I have not heard her sing," replied the American, dryly; "and the words 'singing mind' are doubtless accurately English, since you employ them; but at Boston the collocation would be deemed barbarous. You fly off the handle. The epithet, sir, is not in concord with the substantive."

"Boston would be in the right, my dear Colonel. I stand rebuked; mind has little to do with singing."

"I take leave to deny that, sir. You fire into the wrong flock, and would not hazard the remark if you had conversed as I have with Signorina Cicogna."

Before Graham could answer, Signorina Cicogna stood before him, leaning lightly on Mrs. Morley's arm.

"Frank, you must take us into the refreshment-room," said Mrs. Morley to her husband; and then, turning to Graham, added, "Will you help to make way for us?"

Graham bowed, and offered his arm to the fair speaker. "No," said she, taking her husband's. "Of course you know the Signorina, or, as we usually call her, Mademoiselle Cicogna. No? Allow me to present you. Mr. Graham Vane, Mademoiselle Cicogna. Mademoiselle speaks English like a native."

And thus abruptly Graham was introduced to the owner of the haunting face. He had lived too much in the great world all his life to retain the innate shyness of an Englishman; but he certainly was confused and embarrassed when his eyes met Isaura's, and he felt her hand on his arm. Before quitting the room she paused and looked back. Graham's look followed her own, and saw behind them the lady with the scarlet jacket escorted by some portly and decorated connoisseur. Isaura's face brightened to another kind of brightness,—a pleased and tender light.

"Poor dear Madre," she murmured to herself in Italian. "Madre!" echoed Graham, also in Italian. "I have been misinformed, then; that lady is your mother."

Isaura laughed a pretty, low, silvery laugh, and replied in English, "She is not my mother; but I call her Madre, for I know no name more loving."

Graham was touched, and said gently, "Your own mother was evidently very dear to you."

Isaura's lip quivered, and she made a slight movement as if she would have withdrawn her hand from his arm. He saw that he had offended or wounded her, and with the straightforward frankness natural to him, resumed quickly, "My remark was impertinent in a stranger; forgive it."

"There is nothing to forgive, Monsieur."

The two now threaded their way through the crowd, both silent. At last Isaura, thinking she ought to speak first in order to show that Graham had not offended her, said,

"How lovely Mrs. Morley is!"

"Yes; and I like the spirit and ease of her American manner. Have you known her long, Mademoiselle?"

"No; we met her for the first time some weeks ago at M. Savarin's."

"Was she very eloquent on the rights of women?"

"What! you have heard her on that subject?"

"I have rarely heard her on any other, though she is the best and perhaps the cleverest friend I have at Paris; but that may be my fault, for I like to start it. It is a relief to the languid small-talk of society to listen to any one thoroughly in earnest upon turning the world topsy-turvy."

"Do you suppose poor Mrs. Morley would seek to do that if she had her rights?" asked Isaura, with her musical laugh.

"Not a doubt of it; but perhaps you share her opinions."

"I scarcely know what her opinions are, but—"

"Yes?—but—"

"There is a—what shall I call it?—a persuasion, a sentiment, out of which the opinions probably spring, that I do share."

"Indeed? a persuasion, a sentiment, for instance, that a woman should have votes in the choice of legislators, and, I presume, in the task of legislation?"

"No, that is not what I mean. Still, that is an opinion, right or wrong, which grows out of the sentiment I speak of."

"Pray explain the sentiment."

"It is always so difficult to define a sentiment; but does it not strike you that in proportion as the tendency of modern civilization has been to raise women more and more to an intellectual equality with men, in proportion as they read and study and think, an uneasy sentiment, perhaps querulous, perhaps unreasonable, grows up within their minds that the conventions of the world are against the complete development of the faculties thus aroused and the ambition thus animated; that they cannot but rebel, though it may be silently, against the notions of the former age, when women were not thus educated, notions that the aim of the sex should be to steal through life unremarked; that it is a reproach to be talked of; that women are plants to be kept in a hothouse and forbidden the frank liberty of growth in the natural air and sunshine of heaven? This, at least, is a sentiment which has sprung up within myself; and I imagine that it is the sentiment which has given birth to many of the opinions or doctrines that seem absurd, and very likely are so, to the general public. I don't pretend even to have considered those doctrines; I don't pretend to say what may be the remedies for the restlessness and uneasiness I feel. I doubt if on this earth there be any remedies; all I know is, that I feel restless and uneasy."

Graham gazed on her countenance as she spoke with an astonishment not unmingled with tenderness and compassion, astonishment at the contrast between a vein of reflection so hardy, expressed in a style of language that seemed to him so masculine, and the soft velvet dreamy eyes, the gentle tones, and delicate purity of hues rendered younger still by the blush that deepened their bloom.

At this moment they had entered the refreshment-room; but a dense group being round the table, and both perhaps forgetting the object for which Mrs. Morley had introduced them to each other, they had mechancially seated themselves on an ottoman in a recess while Isaura was yet speaking. It must seem as strange to the reader as it did to Graham that such a speech should have been spoken by so young a girl to an acquaintance so new; but in truth Isaura was very little conscious of Graham's presence. She had got on a subject that perplexed and tormented her solitary thoughts; she was but thinking aloud.

"I believe," said Graham, after a pause, "that I comprehend your sentiment much better than I do Mrs. Morley's opinions; but permit me one observation. You say truly that the course of modern civilization has more or less affected the relative position of woman cultivated beyond that level on which she was formerly contented to stand,—the nearer perhaps to the heart of man because not lifting her head to his height,—and hence a sense of restlessness, uneasiness; but do you suppose that, in this whirl and dance of the atoms which compose the rolling ball of the civilized world, it is only women that are made restless and uneasy? Do you not see amid the masses congregated in the wealthiest cities of the world, writhings and struggles against the received order of things? In this sentiment of discontent there is a certain truthfulness, because it is an element of human nature, and how best to deal with it is a problem yet unsolved; but in the opinions and doctrines to which, among the masses, the sentiment gives birth, the wisdom of the wisest detects only the certainty of a common ruin, offering for reconstruction the same building-materials as the former edifice,—materials not likely to be improved because they may be defaced. Ascend from the working classes to all others in which civilized culture prevails, and you will find that same restless feeling,—the fluttering of untried wings against the bars between wider space and their longings. Could you poll all the educated ambitious young men in England,—perhaps in Europe,—at least half of them, divided between a reverence for the past and a curiosity as to the future, would sigh, 'I am born a century too late or a century too soon!'"

Isaura listened to this answer with a profound and absorbing interest. It was the first time that a clever young man talked thus sympathetically to her, a clever young girl.

Then, rising, he said, "I see your Madre and our American friends are darting angry looks at me. They have made room for us at the table, and are wondering why I should keep you thus from the good things of this little life. One word more ere we join them,—consult your own mind, and consider whether your uneasiness and unrest are caused solely by conventional shackles on your sex. Are they not equally common to the youth of ours,—common to all who seek in art, in letters, nay, in the stormier field of active life, to clasp as a reality some image yet seen but as a dream?"

# CHAPTER VIII.

No further conversation in the way of sustained dialogue took place that evening between Graham and Isaura.

The Americans and the Savarins clustered round Isaura when they quitted the refreshment-room. The party was breaking up. Vane would have offered his arm again to Isaura, but M. Savarin had forestalled him. The American was despatched by his wife to see for the carriage; and Mrs. Morley said, with her wonted sprightly tone of command,

"Now, Mr. Vane, you have no option but to take care of me to the shawl-room."

Madame Savarin and Signora Venosta had each found their cavaliers, the Italian still retaining hold of the portly connoisseur, and the Frenchwoman accepting the safeguard of the Vicomte de Breze. As they descended the stairs, Mrs. Morley asked Graham what he thought of the young lady to whom she had presented him.

"I think she is charming," answered Graham.

"Of course; that is the stereotyped answer to all such questions, especially by you Englishmen. In public or in private, England is the mouthpiece of platitudes."

"It is natural for an American to think so. Every child that has just learned to speak uses bolder expressions than its grandmamma; but I am rather at a loss to know by what novelty of phrase an American would have answered your question."

"An American would have discovered that Isaura Cicogna had a soul, and his answer would have confessed it."

"It strikes me that he would then have uttered a platitude more stolid than mine. Every Christian knows that the dullest human being has a soul. But, to speak frankly, I grant that my answer did not do justice to the Signorina, nor to the impression she makes on me; and putting aside the charm of the face, there is a charm in a mind that seems to have gathered stores of reflection which I should scarcely have expected to find in a young lady brought up to be a professional singer."

"You add prejudice to platitude, and are horribly prosaic to-night; but here we are in the shawl-room. I must take another opportunity of attacking you. Pray dine with us tomorrow; you will meet our Minister and a few other pleasant friends."

"I suppose I must not say, 'I shall be charmed,'" answered Vane; "but I shall be."

"Bon Dieu! that horrid fat man has deserted Signora Venosta,—looking for his own cloak, I dare say; selfish monster! Go and hand her to her carriage; quick, it is announced!"

Graham, thus ordered, hastened to offer his arm to the she-mountebank. Somehow she had acquired dignity in his eyes, and he did not feel the least ashamed of being in contact with the scarlet jacket.

The Signora grappled to him with a confiding familiarity. "I am afraid," she said in Italian, as they passed along the spacious hall to the porte cochere,—"I am afraid that I did not make a good effect to-night. I was nervous; did not you perceive it?"

"No, indeed; you enchanted us all;" replied the dissimulator.

"How amiable you are to say so! You must think that I sought for a compliment. So I did; you gave me more than I deserved. Wine is the milk of old men, and praise of old women; but an old man may be killed by too much wine, and an old woman lives all the longer for too much praise. Buona notte."

Here she sprang, lithesomely enough, into the carriage, and Isaura followed, escorted by M. Savarin. As the two men returned towards the shawl-room, the Frenchman said, "Madame Savarin and I complain that you have not let us see so much of you as we ought. No doubt you are greatly sought after; but are you free to take your soup with us the day after to-morrow? You will meet the Count von Rudesheim, and a few others more lively if less wise."

"The day after to-morrow I will mark with a white stone. To dine with M. Savarin is an event to a man who covets distinction."

"Such compliments reconcile an author to his trade. You deserve the best return I can make you. You will meet la belle Isaura. I have just engaged her and her chaperon. She is a girl of true genius; and genius is like those objects of virtu which belong to a former age, and become every day more scarce and more precious."

Here they encountered Colonel Morley and his wife hurrying to their carriage. The American stopped Vane, and whispered, "I am glad, sir, to hear from my wife that you dine with us to-morrow. Sir, you will meet Mademoiselle Cicogna, and I am not without a kinkle [notion] that you will be enthused."

"This seems like a fatality," soliloquized Vane as he walked through the deserted streets towards his lodging. "I strove to banish that haunting face from my mind. I had half forgotten it, and now—" Here his murmur sank into silence. He was deliberating in very conflicted thought whether or not he should write to refuse the two invitations he had accepted.

"Pooh!" he said at last, as he reached the door of his lodging, "is my reason so weak that it should be influenced by a mere superstition? Surely I know myself too well, and have tried myself too long, to fear that I should be untrue to the duty and ends of my life, even if I found my heart in danger of suffering."

Certainly the Fates do seem to mock our resolves to keep our feet from their ambush, and our hearts from their snare! How our lives may be coloured by that which seems to us the most trivial accident, the merest chance! Suppose that Alain de Rochebriant had been invited to that reunion at M. Louvier's, and Graham Vane had accepted some other invitation and passed his evening elsewhere, Alain would probably have been presented to Isaura—what then might have happened? The impression Isaura had already made upon the young Frenchman was not so deep as that made upon Graham; but then, Alain's resolution to efface it was but commenced that day, and by no means yet confirmed. And if he had been the first clever young man to talk earnestly to that clever young girl, who can guess what impression he might have made upon her? His conversation might have had less philosophy and strong sense than Graham's, but more of poetic sentiment and fascinating romance.

However, the history of events that do not come to pass is not in the chronicle of the Fates.

# BOOK III.

## CHAPTER I.

The next day the guests at the Morleys' had assembled when Vane entered. His apology for unpunctuality was cut short by the lively hostess. "Your pardon is granted without the humiliation of asking for it; we know that the characteristic of the English is always to be a little behindhand."

She then proceeded to introduce him to the American Minister, to a distinguished American poet, with a countenance striking for mingled sweetness and power, and one or two other of her countrymen sojourning at Paris; and this ceremony over, dinner was announced, and she bade Graham offer his arm to Mademoiselle Cicogna.

"Have you ever visited the United States, Mademoiselle?" asked Vane, as they seated themselves at the table.

"No."

"It is a voyage you are sure to make soon."

"Why so?"

"Because report says you will create a great sensation at the very commencement of your career; and the New World is ever eager to welcome each celebrity that is achieved in the Old,—more especially that which belongs to your enchanting art."

"True, sir," said an American senator, solemnly striking into the conversation; "we are an appreciative people; and if that lady be as fine a singer as I am told, she might command any amount of dollars."

Isaura coloured, and turning to Graham, asked him in a low voice if he were fond of music.

"I ought of course to say 'yes,'" answered Graham, in the same tone; "but I doubt if that 'yes' would be an honest one. In some moods, music—if a kind of music I like—affects me very deeply; in other moods, not at all. And I cannot bear much at a time. A concert wearies me shamefully; even an opera always seems to me a great deal too long. But I ought to add that I am no judge of music; that music was never admitted into my education; and, between ourselves, I doubt if there be one Englishman in five hundred who would care for opera or concert if it were not the fashion to say he did. Does my frankness revolt you?"

"On the contrary, I sometimes doubt, especially of late, if I am fond of music myself."

"Signorina,—pardon me,—it is impossible that you should not be. Genius can never be untrue to itself, and must love that in which it excels, that by which it communicates joy, and," he added, with a half-suppressed sigh, "attains to glory."

"Genius is a divine word, and not to be applied to a singer," said Isaura, with a humility in which there was an earnest sadness.

Graham was touched and startled; but before he could answer, the American Minister appealed to him across the table, asking if he had quoted accurately a passage in a speech by Graham's distinguished father, in regard to the share which England ought to take in the political affairs of Europe.

The conversation now became general, very political and very serious. Graham was drawn into it, and grew animated and eloquent.

Isaura listened to him with admiration. She was struck by what seemed to her a nobleness of sentiment which elevated his theme above the level of commonplace polemics. She was pleased to notice, in the attentive silence of his intelligent listeners, that they shared the effect produced on herself. In fact, Graham Vane was a born orator, and his studies had been those of a political thinker. In common talk he was but the accomplished man of the world, easy and frank and genial, with a touch of good-natured sarcasm; but when the subject started drew him upward to those heights in which politics become the science of humanity, he seemed a changed being. His cheek glowed, his eye brightened, his voice mellowed into richer tones, his language be came unconsciously adorned. In such moments there might scarcely be an audience, even differing from him in opinion, which would not have acknowledged his spell.

When the party adjourned to the salon, Isaura said softly to Graham, "I understand why you did not cultivate music; and I think, too, that I can now understand what effects the human voice can produce on human minds without recurring to the art of song."

"Ah," said Graham, with a pleased smile, "do not make me ashamed of my former rudeness by the revenge of compliment; and, above all, do not disparage your own art by supposing that any prose effect of voice in its utterance of mind can interpret that which music alone can express, even to listeners so uncultured as myself. Am I not told truly by musical composers, when I ask them to explain in words what they say in their music, that such explanation is impossible, that music has a language of its own untranslatable by words?"

"Yes," said Isaura, with thoughtful brow but brightening eyes, "you are told truly. It was only the other day that I was pondering over that truth."

"But what recesses of mind, of heart, of soul, this untranslatable language penetrates and brightens up! How incomplete the grand nature of man—though man the grandest—would be, if you struck out of his reason the comprehension of poetry, music, and religion! In each are reached and are sounded deeps in his reason otherwise concealed from himself. History, knowledge, science, stop at the point in which mystery begins. There they meet with the world of shadow. Not an inch of that world can they penetrate without the aid of poetry and religion, two necessities of intellectual man much more nearly allied than the votaries of the practical and the positive suppose. To the aid and elevation of both those necessities comes in music, and there has never existed a religion in the world which has not demanded music as its ally. If, as I said frankly, it is only in certain moods of my mind that I enjoy music, it is only because in certain moods of my mind I am capable of quitting the guidance of prosaic reason for the world of shadow; that I am so susceptible as at every hour, were my nature perfect, I should be to the mysterious influences of poetry and religion. Do you understand what I wish to express?"

"Yes, I do, and clearly."

"Then, Signorina, you are forbidden to undervalue the gift of song. You must feel its power over the heart, when you enter the opera-house; over the soul, when you kneel in a cathedral."

"Oh," cried Isaura, with enthusiasm, a rich glow mantling over her lovely face, "how I thank you! Is it you who say you do not love music? How much better you understand it than I did till this moment!"

Here Mrs. Morley, joined by the American poet, came to the corner in which the Englishman and the singer had niched themselves. The poet began to talk, the other guests gathered round, and every one listened reverentially till the party broke up. Colonel Morley handed Isaura to her carriage; the she-mountebank again fell to the lot of Graham.

"Signor," said she, as he respectfully placed her shawl round her scarlet-and-gilt jacket, "are we so far from Paris that you cannot spare the time to call? My child does not sing in public, but at home you can hear her. It is not every woman's voice that is sweetest at home."

Graham bowed, and said he would call on the morrow. Isaura mused in silent delight over the words which had so extolled the art of the singer. Alas, poor child! she could not guess that in those words, reconciling her to the profession of the stage, the speaker was pleading against his own heart.

There was in Graham's nature, as I think it commonly is in that of most true orators, a wonderful degree of intellectual conscience which impelled him to acknowledge the benignant influences of song, and to set before the young singer the noblest incentives to the profession to which he deemed her assuredly destined; but in so doing he must have felt that he was widening the gulf between her life and his own. Perhaps he wished to widen it in proportion as he dreaded to listen to any voice in his heart which asked if the gulf might not be overleapt.

# CHAPTER II.

ON the morrow Graham called at the villa at A———. The two ladies received him in Isaura's chosen sitting-room.

Somehow or other, conversation at first languished. Graham was reserved and distant, Isaura shy and embarrassed. The Venosta had the frais of making talk to herself. Probably at another time Graham would have been amused and interested in the observation of a character new to him, and thoroughly southern,—lovable not more from its naive simplicity of kindliness than from various little foibles and vanities, all of which were harmless, and some of them endearing as those of a child whom it is easy to make happy, and whom it seems so cruel to pain; and with all the Venosta's deviations from the polished and tranquil good taste of the beau monde, she had that indescribable grace which rarely deserts a Florentine, so that you might call her odd but not vulgar; while, though uneducated, except in the way of her old profession, and never having troubled herself to read anything but a libretto and the pious books commended to her by her confessor, the artless babble of her talk every now and then flashed out with a quaint humour, lighting up terse fragments of the old Italian wisdom which had mysteriously embedded themselves in the groundwork of her mind.

But Graham was not at this time disposed to judge the poor Venosta kindly or fairly. Isaura had taken high rank in his thoughts. He felt an impatient resentment mingled with anxiety and compassionate tenderness at a companionship which seemed to him derogatory to the position he would have assigned to a creature so gifted, and unsafe as a guide amidst the perils and trials to which the youth, the beauty, and the destined profession of Isaura were exposed. Like most Englishmen—especially Englishmen wise in the knowledge of life—he held in fastidious regard the proprieties and conventions by which the dignity of woman is fenced round; and of those proprieties and conventions the Venosta naturally appeared to him a very unsatisfactory guardian and representative.

Happily unconscious of these hostile prepossessions, the elder Signora chatted on very gayly to the visitor. She was in excellent spirits; people had been very civil to her both at Colonel Morley's and M. Louvier's. The

American Minister had praised the scarlet jacket. She was convinced she had made a sensation two nights running. When the amour propre is pleased, the tongue is freed.

The Venosta ran on in praise of Paris and the Parisians; of Louvier and his soiree and the pistachio ice; of the Americans, and a certain creme de maraschino which she hoped the Signor Inglese had not failed to taste,—the creme de maraschino led her thoughts back to Italy. Then she grew mournful. How she missed the native beau ciel! Paris was pleasant, but how absurd to call it "le Paradis des Femmes,"—as if les Femmes could find Paradise in a brouillard!

"But," she exclaimed, with vivacity of voice and gesticulation, "the Signor does not come to hear the parrot talk; he is engaged to come that he may hear the nightingale sing. A drop of honey attracts the fly more than a bottle of vinegar."

Graham could not help smiling at this adage. "I submit," said he, "to your comparison as regards myself; but certainly anything less like a bottle of vinegar than your amiable conversation I cannot well conceive. However, the metaphor apart, I scarcely know how I dare ask Mademoiselle to sing after the confession I made to her last night."

"What confession?" asked the Venosta.

"That I know nothing of music and doubt if I can honestly say that I am fond of it."

"Not fond of music! Impossible! You slander yourself. He who loves not music would have a dull time of it in heaven. But you are English, and perhaps have only heard the music of your own country. Bad, very bad—a heretic's music! Now listen."

Seating herself at the piano, she began an air from the "Lucia," crying out to Isaura to come and sing to her accompaniment.

"Do you really wish it?" asked Isaura of Graham, fixing on him questioning, timid eyes.

"I cannot say how much I wish to hear you."

Isaura moved to the instrument, and Graham stood behind her. Perhaps he felt that he should judge more impartially of her voice if not subjected to the charm of her face.

But the first note of the voice held him spell-bound. In itself the organ was of the rarest order, mellow and rich, but so soft that its power was lost in its sweetness, and so exquisitely fresh in every note.

But the singer's charm was less in voice than in feeling; she conveyed to the listener so much more than was said by the words, or even implied by the music. Her song in this caught the art of the painter who impresses the mind with the consciousness of a something which the eye cannot detect on the canvas.

She seemed to breathe out from the depths of her heart the intense pathos of the original romance, so far exceeding that of the opera,-the human tenderness, the mystic terror of a tragic love-tale more solemn in its sweetness than that of Verona.

When her voice died away no applause came,—not even a murmur. Isaura bashfully turned round to steal a glance at her silent listener, and beheld moistened eyes and quivering lips. At that moment she was reconciled to her art. Graham rose abruptly and walked to the window.

"Do you doubt now if you are fond of music?" cried the Venosta.

"This is more than music," answered Graham, still with averted face. Then, after a short pause, he approached Isaura, and said, with a melancholy half-smile,—

"I do not think, Mademoiselle, that I could dare to hear you often; it would take me too far from the hard real world: and he who would not be left behindhand on the road that he must journey cannot indulge frequent excursions into fairyland."

"Yet," said Isaura, in a tone yet sadder, "I was told in my childhood, by one whose genius gives authority to her words, that beside the real world lies the ideal. The real world then seemed rough to me. 'Escape,' said my counsellor, 'is granted from that stony thoroughfare into the fields beyond its formal hedgerows. The ideal world has its sorrows, but it never admits despair.' That counsel then, methought, decided my choice of life. I know not now if it has done so."

"Fate," answered Graham, slowly and thoughtfully, "Fate, which is not the ruler but the servant of Providence, decides our choice of life, and rarely from outward circumstances. Usually the motive power is within. We apply the word 'genius' to the minds of the gifted few; but in all of us there is a genius that is inborn, a pervading something which distinguishes our very identity, and dictates to the conscience that which we are best fitted to do and to be. In so dictating it compels our choice of life; or if we resist the dictate, we find at the close that we have gone astray. My choice of life thus compelled is on the stony thoroughfares, yours in the green fields."

As he thus said, his face became clouded and mournful. The Venosta, quickly tired of a conversation in which she had no part, and having various little household matters to attend to, had during this dialogue slipped unobserved from the room; yet neither Isaura nor Graham felt the sudden consciousness that they were alone which belongs to lovers. "Why," asked Isaura, with that magic smile reflected in countless dimples which, even when her words were those of a man's reasoning, made them seem gentle with a woman's sentiment,—"why must your road through the world be so exclusively the stony one? It is not from necessity, it can not be from taste; and whatever definition you give to genius, surely it is not your own inborn genius that dictates to you a constant exclusive adherence to the commonplace of life."

"Ah, Mademoiselle, do not misrepresent me. I did not say that I could not sometimes quit the real world for fairyland,—I said that I could not do so often. My vocation is not that of a poet or artist."

"It is that of an orator, I know," said Isaura, kindling; "so they tell me, and I believe them. But is not the orator somewhat akin to the poet? Is not oratory an art?"

"Let us dismiss the word orator; as applied to English public life, it is a very deceptive expression. The Englishman who wishes to influence his countrymen by force of words spoken must mix with them in their beaten thoroughfares; must make himself master of their practical views and interests; must be conversant with their prosaic occupations and business; must understand how to adjust their loftiest aspirations to their material welfare; must avoid as the fault most dangerous to himself and to others that kind of eloquence which is called oratory in France, and which has helped to make the French the worst politicians in Europe. Alas! Mademoiselle, I fear that an English statesman would appear to you a very dull orator."

"I see that I spoke foolishly,—yes, you show me that the world of the statesman lies apart from that of the artist. Yet—"

"Yet what?"

"May not the ambition of both be the same?"

"How so?"

"To refine the rude, to exalt the mean; to identify their own fame with some new beauty, some new glory, added to the treasure-house of all."

Graham bowed his head reverently, and then raised it with the flush of enthusiasm on his cheek and brow.

"Oh, Mademoiselle," he exclaimed, "what a sure guide and what a noble inspirer to a true Englishman's ambition nature has fitted you to be, were it not—" He paused abruptly.

This outburst took Isaura utterly by surprise. She had been accustomed to the language of compliment till it had begun to pall, but a compliment of this kind was the first that had ever reached her ear. She had no words in answer to it; involuntarily she placed her hand on her heart as if to still its beatings. But the unfinished exclamation, "Were it not," troubled her more than the preceding words had flattered, and mechanically she murmured, "Were it not—what?"

"Oh," answered Graham, affecting a tone of gayety, "I felt too ashamed of my selfishness as man to finish my sentence."

"Do so, or I shall fancy you refrained lest you might wound me as woman."

"Not so; on the contrary, had I gone on it would have been to say that a woman of your genius, and more especially of such mastery in the most popular and fascinating of all arts, could not be contented if she inspired nobler thoughts in a single breast,—she must belong to the public, or rather the public must belong to her; it is but a corner of her heart that an individual can occupy, and even that individual must merge his existence in hers, must be contented to reflect a ray of the light she sheds on admiring thousands. Who could dare to say to you, 'Renounce your career; confine your genius, your art, to the petty circle of home'? To an actress, a singer, with whose fame the world rings, home would be a prison. Pardon me, pardon—"

Isaura had turned away her face to hide tears that would force their way; but she held out her hand to him with a childlike frankness, and said softly, "I am not offended." Graham did not trust himself to continue the same strain of conversation. Breaking into a new subject, he said, after a constrained pause, "Will you think it very impertinent in so new an acquaintance, if I ask how it is that you, an Italian, know our language as a native; and is it by Italian teachers that you have been trained to think and to feel?"

"Mr. Selby, my second father, was an Englishman, and did not speak any other language with comfort to himself. He was very fond of me; and had he been really my father I could not have loved him more. We were constant companions till—till I lost him."

"And no mother left to console you!"

Isaura shook her head mournfully, and the Venosta here re-entered. Graham felt conscious that he had already stayed too long, and took leave.

They knew that they were to meet that evening at the Savarins'.

To Graham that thought was not one of unmixed pleasure; the more he knew of Isaura, the more he felt self-reproach that he had allowed himself to know her at all.

But after he had left, Isaura sang low to herself the song which had so affected her listener; then she fell into abstracted revery, but she felt a strange and new sort of happiness. In dressing for M. Savarin's dinner, and twining the classic ivy wreath in her dark locks, her Italian servant exclaimed, "How beautiful the Signorina looks to-night!"

# CHAPTER III.

M. Savarin was one of the most brilliant of that galaxy of literary men which shed lustre on the reign of Louis Philippe.

His was an intellect peculiarly French in its lightness and grace. Neither England nor Germany nor America has produced any resemblance to it. Ireland has, in Thomas Moore; but then in Irish genius there is so much that is French.

M. Savarin was free from the ostentatious extravagance which had come into vogue with the Empire. His house and establishment were modestly maintained within the limit of an income chiefly, perhaps entirely, derived from literary profits.

Though he gave frequent dinners, it was but to few at a time, and without show or pretence. Yet the dinners, though simple, were perfect of their kind; and the host so contrived to infuse his own playful gayety into the temper of his guests, that the feasts at his house were considered the pleasantest at Paris. On this occasion the party extended to ten, the largest number his table admitted.

All the French guests belonged to the Liberal party, though in changing tints of the tricolor. Place aux dames! first to be named were the Countess de Craon and Madame Vertot, both without husbands. The Countess had buried the Count, Madame Vertot had separated from Monsieur. The Countess was very handsome, but she was sixty; Madame Vertot was twenty years younger, but she was very plain. She had quarrelled with the distinguished author for whose sake she had separated from Monsieur, and no man had since presumed to think that he could console a lady so plain for the loss of an author so distinguished.

Both these ladies were very clever. The Countess had written lyrical poems entitled "Cries of Liberty," and a drama of which Danton was the hero, and the moral too revolutionary for admission to the stage; but at heart the Countess was not at all a revolutionist,—the last person in the world to do or desire anything that could bring a washerwoman an inch nearer to a countess. She was one of those persons who play with fire in order to appear enlightened.

Madame Vertot was of severer mould. She had knelt at the feet of M. Thiers, and went into the historico-political line. She had written a remarkable book upon the modern Carthage (meaning England), and more recently a work that had excited much attention upon the Balance of Power, in which she proved it to be the interest of civilization and the necessity of Europe that Belgium should be added to France, and Prussia circumscribed to the bounds of its original margraviate. She showed how easily these two objects could have been effected by a constitutional monarch instead of an egotistical Emperor. Madame Vertot was a decided Orleanist.

Both these ladies condescended to put aside authorship in general society. Next amongst our guests let me place the Count de Passy and Madame son espouse. The Count was seventy-one, and, it is needless to add, a type of Frenchman rapidly vanishing, and not likely to find itself renewed. How shall I describe him so as to make my English reader understand? Let me try by analogy. Suppose a man of great birth and fortune, who in his youth had been an enthusiastic friend of Lord Byron and a jocund companion of George IV.; who had in him an immense degree of lofty romantic sentiment with an equal degree of well-bred worldly cynicism, but who, on account of that admixture, which is so rare, kept a high rank in either of the two societies into which, speaking broadly, civilized life divides itself,—the romantic and the cynical. The Count de Passy had been the most ardent among the young disciples of Chateaubriand, the most brilliant among the young courtiers of Charles X. Need I add that he had been a terrible lady-killer?

But in spite of his admiration of Chateaubriand and his allegiance to Charles X., the Count had been always true to those caprices of the French noblesse from which he descended,—caprices which destroyed them in the old Revolution; caprices belonging to the splendid ignorance of their nation in general and their order in particular. Speaking without regard to partial exceptions, the French gentilhomme is essentially a Parisian; a Parisian is essentially impressionable to the impulse or fashion of the moment. Is it a la mode for the moment to be Liberal or anti-Liberal? Parisians embrace and kiss each other, and swear through life and death to adhere forever to the mode of the moment. The Three Days were the mode of the moment,—the Count de Passy became an enthusiastic Orleanist. Louis Philippe was very gracious to him. He was decorated; he was named prefet of his department; he was created senator; he was about to be sent Minister to a German Court when Louis Philippe fell. The Republic was proclaimed. The Count caught the popular contagion, and after exchanging tears and kisses with patriots whom a week before he had called canaille, he swore eternal fidelity to the

Republic. The fashion of the moment suddenly became Napoleonic, and with the coup d'etat the Republic was metamorphosed into an Empire. The Count wept on the bosoms of all the Vieilles Moustaches he could find, and rejoiced that the sun of Austerlitz had re-arisen. But after the affair of Mexico the sun of Austerlitz waxed very sickly. Imperialism was fast going out of fashion. The Count transferred his affection to Jules Favre, and joined the ranks of the advanced Liberals. During all these political changes, the Count had remained very much the same man in private life; agreeable, good-natured, witty, and, above all, a devotee of the fair sex. When he had reached the age of sixty-eight he was still fort bel homme, unmarried, with a grand presence and charming manner. At that age he said, "Je me range," and married a young lady of eighteen. She adored her husband, and was wildly jealous of him; while the Count did not seem at all jealous of her, and submitted to her adoration with a gentle shrug of the shoulders.

The three other guests who, with Graham and the two Italian ladies, made up the complement of ten, were the German Count von Rudesheim, a celebrated French physician named Bacourt, and a young author whom Savarin had admitted into his clique and declared to be of rare promise. This author, whose real name was Gustave Rameau, but who, to prove, I suppose, the sincerity of that scorn for ancestry which he professed, published his verses under the patrician designation of Alphonse de Valcour, was about twenty-four, and might have passed at the first glance for younger; but, looking at him closely, the signs of old age were already stamped on his visage.

He was undersized, and of a feeble slender frame. In the eyes of women and artists the defects of his frame were redeemed by the extraordinary beauty of the face. His black hair, carefully parted in the centre, and worn long and flowing, contrasted the whiteness of a high though narrow forehead, and the delicate pallor of his cheeks. His feature, were very regular, his eyes singularly bright; but the expression of the face spoke of fatigue and exhaustion; the silky locks were already thin, and interspersed with threads of silver; the bright eyes shone out from sunken orbits; the lines round the mouth were marked as they are in the middle age of one who has lived too fast.

It was a countenance that might have excited a compassionate and tender interest but for something arrogant and supercilious in the expression,-something that demanded not tender pity but enthusiastic admiration. Yet that expression was displeasing rather to men than to women; and one could well conceive that, among the latter, the enthusiastic admiration it challenged would be largely conceded.

The conversation at dinner was in complete contrast to that at the Americans' the day before. There the talk, though animated, had been chiefly earnest and serious; here it was all touch and go, sally and repartee. The subjects were the light on lots and lively anecdotes of the day, not free from literature and politics, but both treated as matters of persiflage, hovered round with a jest and quitted with an epigram. The two French lady authors, the Count de Passy, the physician, and the host far outspoke all the other guests. Now and then, however, the German Count struck in with an ironical remark condensing a great deal of grave wisdom, and the young author with ruder and more biting sarcasm. If the sarcasm told, he showed his triumph by a low-pitched laugh; if it failed, he evinced his displeasure by a contemptuous sneer or a grim scowl.

Isaura and Graham were not seated near each other, and were for the most part contented to be listeners.

On adjourning to the salon after dinner, Graham, however, was approaching the chair in which Isaura had placed herself, when the young author, forestalling him, dropped into the seat next to her, and began a conversation in a voice so low that it might have passed for a whisper. The Englishman drew back and observed them. He soon perceived, with a pang of jealousy not unmingled with scorn, that the author's talk appeared to interest Isaura. She listened with evident attention; and when she spoke in return, though Graham did not hear her words, he could observe on her expressive countenance an increased gentleness of aspect.

"I hope," said the physician, joining Graham, as most of the other guests gathered round Savarin, who was in his liveliest vein of anecdote and wit,— "I hope that the fair Italian will not allow that ink-bottle imp to persuade her that she has fallen in love with him."

"Do young ladies generally find him so seductive?" asked Graham, with a forced smile.

"Probably enough. He has the reputation of being very clever and very wicked, and that is a sort of character which has the serpent's fascination for the daughters of Eve."

"Is the reputation merited?"

"As to the cleverness, I am not a fair judge. I dislike that sort of writing which is neither manlike nor womanlike, and in which young Rameau excels. He has the knack of finding very exaggerated phrases by which to express commonplace thoughts. He writes verses about love in words so stormy that you might fancy that Jove was descending upon Semele; but when you examine his words, as a sober pathologist like myself is disposed to do, your fear for the peace of households vanishes,—they are Fox et proeterea nihil; no man really in love would use them. He writes prose about the wrongs of humanity. You feel for humanity; you say, 'Grant the wrongs, now for the remedy,'—and you find nothing but balderdash. Still I am bound to say that both in verse and prose Gustave Rameau is in unison with a corrupt taste of the day, and therefore he is coming into vogue. So much as to his writings; as to his wickedness, you have only to look at him to feel sure that he is not a hundredth part so wicked as he wishes to seem. In a word, then, M. Gustave Rameau is a type of that somewhat numerous class among the youth of Paris, which I call 'the lost Tribe of Absinthe.' There is a set of men who begin to live full gallop while they are still boys. As a general rule, they are originally of the sickly frames which can scarcely even trot, much less gallop without the spur of stimulants, and no stimulant so fascinates their peculiar nervous system as absinthe. The number of patients in this set who at the age of thirty are more worn out than septuagenarians increases so rapidly as to make one dread to think what will be the next race of Frenchmen. To the predilection for absinthe young Rameau and the writers of his set add the imitation of Heine, after, indeed, the manner of caricaturists, who effect a likeness striking in proportion as it is ugly. It is not easy to imitate the pathos and the wit of Heine; but it is easy to imitate his defiance of the Deity, his mockery of right and wrong, his relentless war on that heroic standard of thought and action which the writers who exalt their nation intuitively preserve. Rameau cannot be a Heine, but he can be to Heine what a misshapen snarling dwarf is to a mangled blaspheming Titan. Yet he interests the women in general, and he evidently interests the fair Signorina in especial."

Just as Bacourt finished that last sentence, Isaura lifted the head which had hitherto bent in an earnest listening attitude that seemed to justify the Doctor's remarks, and looked round. Her eyes met Graham's with the fearless candour which made half the charm of their bright yet soft intelligence; but she dropped them suddenly with a half-start and a change of colour, for the expression of Graham's face was unlike that which she had hitherto seen on it,—it was hard, stern, and somewhat disdainful. A minute or so afterwards she rose, and in passing across the room towards the group round the host, paused at a table covered with books and prints near to which Graham was standing alone. The Doctor had departed in company with the German Count.

Isaura took up one of the prints.

"Ah!" she exclaimed, "Sorrento, my Sorrento. Have you ever visited Sorrento, Mr. Vane?"

Her question and her movement were evidently in conciliation. Was the conciliation prompted by coquetry, or by a sentiment more innocent and artless?

Graham doubted, and replied coldly, as he bent over the print,—

"I once stayed there a few days, but my recollection of it is not sufficiently lively to enable me to recognize its features in this design."

"That is the house, at least so they say, of Tasso's father; of course you visited that?"

"Yes, it was a hotel in my time; I lodged there."

"And I too. There I first read 'The Gerusalemine.'" The last words were said in Italian, with a low measured tone, inwardly and dreamily.

A somewhat sharp and incisive voice speaking in French here struck in and prevented Graham's rejoinder: "Quel joli dessin! What is it, Mademoiselle?"

Graham recoiled; the speaker was Gustave Rameau, who had, unobserved, first watched Isaura, then rejoined her side.

"A view of Sorrento, Monsieur, but it does not do justice to the place. I was pointing out the house which belonged to Tasso's father."

"Tasso! Hein! and which is the fair Eleonora's?"

"Monsieur," answered Isaura, rather startled at that question, from a professed homme de lettres, "Eleonora did not live at Sorrento."

"Tant pis pour Sorrente," said the homme de lettres, carelessly. "No one would care for Tasso if it were not for Eleonora."

"I should rather have thought," said Graham, "that no one would have cared for Eleonora if it were not for Tasso."

Rameau glanced at the Englishman superciliously. "Pardon, Monsieur, in every age a love-story keeps its interest; but who cares nowadays for le clinquant du Tasse?"

"Le clinquant du Tasse!" exclaimed Isaura, indignantly.

"The expression is Boileau's, Mademoiselle, in ridicule of the 'Sot de qualite,' who prefers—

*"'Le clinquant du Tasse a tout l'or de Virgile.'*

"But for my part I have as little faith in the last as the first."

"I do not know Latin, and have therefore not read Virgil," said Isaura.

"Possibly," remarked Graham, "Monsieur does not know Italian, and has therefore not read Tasso."

"If that be meant in sarcasm," retorted Rameau, "I construe it as a compliment. A Frenchman who is contented to study the masterpieces of modern literature need learn no language and read no authors but his own."

Isaura laughed her pleasant silvery laugh. "I should admire the frankness of that boast, Monsieur, if in our talk just now you had not spoken as contemptuously of what we are accustomed to consider French masterpieces as you have done of Virgil and Tasso."

"Ah, Mademoiselle! it is not my fault if you have had teachers of taste so rococo as to bid you find masterpieces in the tiresome stilted tragedies of Corneille and Racine. Poetry of a court, not of a people, one simple novel, one simple stanza that probes the hidden recesses of the human heart, reveals the sores of this wretched social state, denounces the evils of superstition, kingcraft, and priestcraft, is worth a library of the rubbish which pedagogues call 'the classics.' We agree, at least, in one thing, Mademoiselle; we both do homage to the genius of your friend Madame de Grantmesnil."

"Your friend, Signorina!" cried Graham, incredulously; "is Madame de Grantmesnil your friend?"

"The dearest I have in the world."

Graham's face darkened; he turned away in silence, and in another minute vanished from the room, persuading himself that he felt not one pang of jealousy in leaving Gustave Rameau by the side of Isaura. "Her dearest friend Madame de Grantmesnil!" he muttered.

A word now on Isaura's chief correspondent. Madame de Grantmesnil was a woman of noble birth and ample fortune. She had separated from her husband in the second year after marriage. She was a singularly eloquent writer, surpassed among contemporaries of her sex in popularity and renown only by Georges Sand.

At least as fearless as that great novelist in the frank exposition of her views, she had commenced her career in letters by a work of astonishing power and pathos, directed against the institution of marriage as regulated in Roman Catholic communities. I do not know that it said more on this delicate subject than the English Milton has said; but then Milton did not write for a Roman Catholic community, nor adopt a style likely to captivate the working classes. Madame de Grantmesnil's first book was deemed an attack on the religion of the country, and captivated those among the working classes who had already abjured that religion. This work was followed up by others more or less in defiance of "received opinions,"—some with political, some with social revolutionary aim and tendency, but always with a singular purity of style. Search all her books, and however you might revolt from her doctrine, you could not find a hazardous expression. The novels of English young ladies are naughty in comparison. Of late years, whatever might be hard or audacious in her political or social doctrines softened itself into charm amid the golden haze of romance. Her writings had grown more and more purely artistic,—poetizing what is good and beautiful in the realities of life rather than creating a false ideal out of what is vicious and deformed. Such a woman, separated young from her husband, could not enunciate such opinions and lead a life so independent and uncontrolled as Madame de Grantmesnil had done, without scandal, without calumny. Nothing, however, in her actual life had ever been so proved against her as to lower the high position she occupied in right of birth, fortune, renown. Wherever she went she was fetee, as in England foreign princes, and in America foreign authors, are fetes. Those who knew her well concurred in praise of her lofty, generous, lovable qualities. Madame de Grantmesnil had known Mr. Selby; and when, at his death, Isaura, in the innocent age between childhood and youth, had been left the most sorrowful and most lonely creature on the face of the earth, this famous woman, worshipped by the rich for her intellect, adored by the poor for her beneficence, came to the orphan's friendless side, breathing love once more into her pining heart, and waking for the first time the desires of genius, the aspirations of art, in the dim self-consciousness of a soul between sleep and waking.

But, my dear Englishman, put yourself in Graham's place, and suppose that you were beginning to fall in love with a girl whom for many good reasons you ought not to marry; suppose that in the same hour in which you were angrily conscious of jealousy on account of a man whom it wounds your self-esteem to consider a rival, the girl tells you that her dearest friend is a woman who is famed for her hostility to the institution of marriage!

# CHAPTER IV.

On the same day in which Graham dined with the Savarins, M. Louvier assembled round his table the elite of the young Parisians who constituted the oligarchy of fashion, to meet whom he had invited his new friend the Marquis de Rochebriant. Most of them belonged to the Legitimist party, the noblesse of the faubourg; those who did not, belonged to no political party at all,—indifferent to the cares of mortal States as the gods of Epicurus. Foremost among this Jeunesse doree were Alain's kinsmen, Raoul and Enguerrand de Vandemar. To these Louvier introduced him with a burly parental bonhomie, as if he were the head of the family. "I need not bid you, young folks, to make friends with each other. A Vandemar and a Rochebriant are not made friends,—they are born friends." So saying he turned to his other guests.

Almost in an instant Alain felt his constraint melt away in the cordial warmth with which his cousins greeted him. These young men had a striking family likeness to each other, and yet in feature, colouring, and expression, in all save that strange family likeness, they were contrasts. Raoul was tall, and, though inclined to be slender, with sufficient breadth of shoulder to indicate no inconsiderable strength of frame. His hair worn short and his silky beard worn long were dark; so were his eyes, shaded by curved drooping lashes; his complexion was pale, but clear and healthful. In repose the expression of his face was that of a somewhat melancholy indolence, but in speaking it became singularly sweet, with a smile of the exquisite urbanity which no artificial politeness can bestow; it must emanate from that native high breeding which has its source in goodness of heart.

Enguerrand was fair, with curly locks of a golden chestnut. He wore no beard, only a small mustache rather darker than his hair. His complexion might in itself be called effeminate, its bloom was so fresh and delicate; but there was so much of boldness and energy in the play of his countenance, the hardy outline of the lips, and the open breadth of the forehead, that "effeminate" was an epithet no one ever assigned to his aspect. He was somewhat under the middle height, but beautifully proportioned, carried himself well, and somehow or other did not look short even by the side of tall men. Altogether he seemed formed to be a mother's darling, and spoiled by women, yet to hold his own among men with a strength of will more evident in his look and his bearing than it was in those of his graver and statelier brother.

Both were considered by their young co-equals models in dress, but in Raoul there was no sign that care or thought upon dress had been bestowed; the simplicity of his costume was absolute and severe. On his plain shirt-front there gleamed not a stud, on his fingers there sparkled not a ring. Enguerrand, on the contrary, was not without pretension in his attire; the broderie in his shirt-front seemed woven by the Queen of the Fairies. His rings of turquoise and opal, his studs and wrist-buttons of pearl and brilliants, must have cost double the rental of Rochebriant, but probably they cost him nothing. He was one of those happy Lotharios to whom Calistas make constant presents. All about him was so bright that the atmosphere around seemed gayer for his presence.

In one respect at least the brothers closely resembled each other,—in that exquisite graciousness of manner for which the genuine French noble is traditionally renowned; a graciousness that did not desert them even when they came reluctantly into contact with roturiers or republicans; but the graciousness became egalite, fraternite, towards one of their caste and kindred.

"We must do our best to make Paris pleasant to you," said Raoul, still retaining in his grasp the hand he had taken.

"Vilain cousin," said the livelier Enguerrand, "to have been in Paris twenty-four hours, and without letting us know."

"Has not your father told you that I called upon him?"

"Our father," answered Raoul, "was not so savage as to conceal that fact; but he said you were only here on business for a day or two, had declined his invitation, and would not give your address. Pauvre pere! we scolded him well for letting you escape from us thus. My mother has not forgiven him yet; we must present you to her to-morrow. I answer for your liking her almost as much as she will like you."

Before Alain could answer dinner was announced. Alain's place at dinner was between his cousins. How pleasant they made themselves! It was the first time in which Alain had been brought into such familiar conversation with countrymen of his own rank as well as his own age. His heart warmed to them. The general talk of the other guests was strange to his ear; it ran much upon horses and races, upon the opera and the ballet; it was enlivened with satirical anecdotes of persons whose names were unknown to the Provincial; not a word was said that showed the smallest interest in politics or the slightest acquaintance with literature. The world of these well-born guests seemed one from which all that concerned the great mass of mankind was excluded, yet the talk was that which could only be found in a very polished society. In it there was not much wit, but there was a prevalent vein of gayety, and the gayety was never violent, the laughter was never loud; the scandals circulated might imply cynicism the most absolute, but in language the most refined. The Jockey Club of Paris has its perfume.

Raoul did not mix in the general conversation; he devoted himself pointedly to the amusement of his cousin, explaining to him the point of the anecdotes circulated, or hitting off in terse sentences the characters of the talkers.

Enguerrand was evidently of temper more vivacious than his brother, and contributed freely to the current play of light gossip and mirthful sally.

Louvier, seated between a duke and a Russian prince, said little except to recommend a wine or an entree, but kept his eye constantly on the Vandemars and Alain.

Immediately after coffee the guests departed. Before they did so, however, Raoul introduced his cousin to those of the party most distinguished by hereditary rank or social position. With these the name of Rochebriant was too historically famous not to insure respect of its owner; they welcomed him among them as if he were their brother.

The French duke claimed him as a connection by an alliance in the fourteenth century; the Russian prince had known the late Marquis, and trusted that the son would allow him to improve into friendship the acquaintance he had formed with the father.

Those ceremonials over, Raoul linked his arm in Alain's and said: "I am not going to release you so soon after we have caught you. You must come with me to a house in which I at least spend an hour or two every evening. I am at home there. Bah! I take no refusal. Do not suppose I carry you off to Bohemia,—a country which, I am sorry to say, Enguerrand now and then visits, but which is to me as unknown as the mountains of the moon. The house I speak of is comme il faut to the utmost. It is that of the Contessa di Rimini,—a charming Italian by marriage, but by birth and in character on ne peut plus Francaise. My mother adores her."

That dinner at M. Louvier's had already effected a great change in the mood and temper of Alain de Rochebriant; he felt, as if by magic, the sense of youth, of rank, of station, which had been so suddenly checked and stifled, warmed to life within his veins. He should have deemed himself a boor had he refused the invitation so frankly tendered.

But on reaching the coupe which the brothers kept in common, and seeing it only held two, he drew back.

"Nay, enter, mon cher," said Raoul, divining the cause of his hesitation; "Enguerrand has gone on to his club."

# CHAPTER V.

"Tell me," said Raoul, when they were in the carriage, "how you came to know M. Louvier."

"He is my chief mortgagee."

"H'm! that explains it. But you might be in worse hands; the man has a character for liberality."

"Did your father mention to you my circumstances, and the reason that brings me to Paris?"

"Since you put the question point-blank, my dear cousin, he did."

"He told you how poor I am, and how keen must be my lifelong struggle to keep Rochebriant as the home of my race?"

"He told us all that could make us still more respect the Marquis de Rochebriant, and still more eagerly long to know our cousin and the head of our house," answered Raoul, with a certain nobleness of tone and manner.

Alain pressed his kinsman's hand with grateful emotion. "Yet," he said falteringly, "your father agreed with me that my circumstances would not allow me to—"

"Bah!" interrupted Raoul, with a gentle laugh; "my father is a very clever man, doubtless, but he knows only the world of his own day, nothing of the world of ours. I and Enguerrand will call on you to-morrow, to take you to my mother, and before doing so, to consult as to affairs in general. On this last matter Enguerrand is an oracle. Here we are at the Contessa's."

# CHAPTER VI.

The Contessa di Rimini received her visitors in a boudoir furnished with much apparent simplicity, but a simplicity by no means inexpensive. The draperies were but of chintz, and the walls covered with the same material,—a lively pattern, in which the prevalents were rose-colour and white; but the ornaments on the mantelpiece, the china stored in the cabinets or arranged on the shelves, the small knickknacks scattered on the tables, were costly rarities of art.

The Contessa herself was a woman who had somewhat passed her thirtieth year,—not strikingly handsome, but exquisitely pretty. "There is," said a great French writer, "only one way in which a woman can be handsome, but a hundred thousand ways in which she can be pretty;" and it would be impossible to reckon up the number of ways in which Adeline di Rimini carried off the prize in prettiness.

Yet it would be unjust to the personal attractions of the Contessa to class them all under the word "prettiness." When regarded more attentively, there was an expression in her countenance that might almost be called divine, it spoke so unmistakably of a sweet nature and an untroubled soul. An English poet once described her by repeating the old lines,

*"Her face is like the milky way I' the sky,*
*—A meeting of gentle lights without a name."*

She was not alone; an elderly lady sat on an armchair by the fire, engaged in knitting; and a man, also elderly, and whose dress proclaimed him an ecclesiastic, sat at the opposite corner, with a large Angora cat on his lap.

"I present to you, Madame," said Raoul, "my new-found cousin, the seventeenth Marquis de Rochebriant, whom I am proud to consider on the male side the head of our house, representing its eldest branch. Welcome him for my sake,—in future he will be welcome for his own."

The Contessa replied very graciously to this introduction, and made room for Alain on the divan from which she had risen.

The old lady looked up from her knitting; the ecclesiastic removed the cat from his lap. Said the old lady, "I announce myself to M. le Marquis. I knew his mother well enough to be invited to his christening; otherwise I have no pretension to the acquaintance of a cavalier si beau, being old, rather deaf, very stupid, exceedingly poor—"

"And," interrupted Raoul, "the woman in all Paris the most adored for bonte, and consulted for savoir vivre by the young cavaliers whom she deigns to receive. Alain, I present you to Madame de Maury, the widow of a distinguished author and academician, and the daughter of the brave Henri de Gerval, who fought for the good cause in La Vendee. I present you also to the Abbe Vertpre, who has passed his life in the vain endeavour to make other men as good as himself."

"Base flatterer!" said the Abbe, pinching Raoul's ear with one hand, while he extended the other to Alain. "Do not let your cousin frighten you from knowing me, Monsieur le Marquis; when he was my pupil, he so convinced me of the incorrigibility of perverse human nature, that I now chiefly address myself to the moral improvement of the brute creation. Ask the Contessa if I have not achieved a beau succes with her Angora cat. Three months ago that creature had the two worst propensities of man,—he was at once savage and mean; he bit, he stole. Does he ever bite now? No. Does he ever steal? No. Why? I have awakened in that cat the dormant conscience, and that done, the conscience regulates his actions; once made aware of the difference between wrong and right, the cat maintains it unswervingly, as if it were a law of nature. But if, with prodigious labour, one does awaken conscience in a human sinner, it has no steady effect on his conduct,—he continues to sin all the same. Mankind at Paris, Monsieur le Marquis, is divided between two classes,-one bites and the other steals. Shun both; devote yourself to cats."

The Abbe delivered this oration with a gravity of mien and tone which made it difficult to guess whether he spoke in sport or in earnest, in simple playfulness or with latent sarcasm.

But on the brow and in the eye of the priest there was a general expression of quiet benevolence, which made Alain incline to the belief that he was only speaking as a pleasant humourist; and the Marquis replied gayly,—

"Monsieur L'Abbe, admitting the superior virtue of cats when taught by so intelligent a preceptor, still the business of human life is not transacted by cats; and since men must deal with men, permit me, as a preliminary caution, to inquire in which class I must rank yourself. Do you bite or do you steal?"

This sally, which showed that the Marquis was already shaking off his provincial reserve, met with great success. Raoul and the Contessa laughed merrily; Madame de Maury clapped her hands, and cried "Bien!"

The Abbe replied, with unmoved gravity, "Both. I am a priest; it is my duty to bite the bad and steal from the good, as you will see, Monsieur le Marquis, if you will glance at this paper."

Here he handed to Alain a memorial on behalf of an afflicted family who had been burnt out of their home, and reduced from comparative ease to absolute want. There was a list appended of some twenty subscribers, the last being the Contessa, fifty francs, and Madame de Maury, five.

"Allow me, Marquis," said the Abbe, "to steal from you. Bless you two-fold, mon fils!" (taking the napoleon Alain extended to him) "first for your charity; secondly, for the effect of its example upon the heart of your cousin. Raoul de Vandemar, stand and deliver. Bah! what! only ten francs."

Raoul made a sign to the Abbe, unperceived by the rest, as he answered, "Abbe, I should excel your expectations of my career if I always continue worth half as much as my cousin."

Alain felt to the bottom of his heart the delicate tact of his richer kinsman in giving less than himself, and the Abbe replied, "Niggard, you are pardoned. Humility is a more difficult virtue to produce than charity, and in your case an instance of it is so rare that it merits encouragement."

The "tea equipage" was now served in what at Paris is called the English fashion; the Contessa presided over it, the guests gathered round the table, and the evening passed away in the innocent gayety of a domestic circle. The talk, if not especially intellectual, was at least not fashionable. Books were not discussed, neither were scandals; yet somehow or other it was cheery and animated, like that of a happy family in a country-house. Alain thought still the better of Raoul that, Parisian though he was, he could appreciate the charm of an evening so innocently spent.

On taking leave, the Contessa gave Alain a general invitation to drop in whenever he was not better engaged.

"I except only the opera nights," said she. "My husband has gone to Milan on his affairs, and during his absence I do not go to parties; the opera I cannot resist."

Raoul set Alain down at his lodgings. "Au revoir; tomorrow at one o'clock expect Enguerrand and myself."

# CHAPTER VII.

Raul and Enguerrand called on Alain at the hour fixed. "In the first place," said Raoul, "I must beg you to accept my mother's regrets that she cannot receive you to-day. She and the Contessa belong to a society of ladies formed for visiting the poor, and this is their day; but to-morrow you must dine with us en famille. Now to business. Allow me to light my cigar while you confide the whole state of affairs to Enguerrand. Whatever he counsels, I am sure to approve."

Alain, as briefly as he could, stated his circumstances, his mortgages, and the hopes which his avow had encouraged him to place in the friendly disposition of M. Louvier. When he had concluded, Enguerrand mused for a few moments before replying. At last he said, "Will you trust me to call on Louvier on your behalf? I shall but inquire if he is inclined to take on himself the other mortgages; and if so, on what terms. Our relationship gives me the excuse for my interference; and to say truth, I have had much familiar intercourse with the man. I too am a speculator, and have often profited by Louvier's advice. You may ask what can be his object in serving me; he can gain nothing by it. To this I answer, the key to his good offices is in his character. Audacious though he be as a speculator, he is wonderfully prudent as a politician. This belle France of ours is like a stage tumbler; one can never be sure whether it will stand on its head or its feet. Louvier very wisely wishes to feel himself safe whatever party comes uppermost. He has no faith in the duration of the Empire; and as, at all events, the Empire will not confiscate his millions, he takes no trouble in conciliating Imperialists. But on the principle which induces certain savages to worship the devil and neglect the bon Dieu, because the devil is spiteful and the bon Dieu is too beneficent to injure them, Louvier, at heart detesting as well as dreading a republic, lays himself out to secure friends with the Republicans of all classes, and pretends to espouse their cause; next to them, he is very conciliatory to the Orleanists; lastly, though he thinks the Legitimists have no chance, he desires to keep well with the nobles of that party, because they exercise a considerable influence over that sphere of opinion which belongs to fashion,—for fashion is never powerless in Paris. Raoul and myself are no mean authorities in salons and clubs, and a good word from us is worth having.

"Besides, Louvier himself in his youth set up for a dandy; and that deposed ruler of dandies, our unfortunate kinsman, Victor de Mauleon, shed some of his own radiance on the money-lender's son. But when Victor's star was eclipsed, Louvier ceased to gleam. The dandies cut him. In his heart he exults that the dandies now throng to his soirees.

"Bref, the millionaire is especially civil to me,—the more so as I know intimately two or three eminent journalists; and Louvier takes pains to plant garrisons in the press. I trust I have explained the grounds on which I may be a better diplomatist to employ than your avoue; and with your leave I will go to Louvier at once."

"Let him go," said Raoul. "Enguerrand never fails in anything he undertakes; especially," he added, with a smile half sad, half tender, "when one wishes to replenish one's purse."

"I too gratefully grant such an ambassador all powers to treat," said Alain. "I am only ashamed to consign to him a post so much beneath his genius," and "his birth" he was about to add, but wisely checked himself. Enguerrand said, shrugging his shoulders, "You can't do me a greater kindness than by setting my wits at work. I fall a martyr to ennui when I am not in action;" he said, and was gone.

"It makes me very melancholy at times," said Raoul, flinging away the end of his cigar, "to think that a man so clever and so energetic as Enguerrand should be as much excluded from the service of his country as if he were an Iroquois Indian. He would have made a great diplomatist."

"Alas!" replied Alain, with a sigh, "I begin to doubt whether we Legitimists are justified in maintaining a useless loyalty to a sovereign who renders us morally exiles in the land of our birth."

"I have no doubt on the subject," said Raoul. "We are not justified on the score of policy, but we have no option at present on the score of honour. We should gain so much for ourselves if we adopted the State livery and took the State wages that no man would esteem us as patriots; we should only be despised as apostates. So long as Henry V. lives, and does not resign his claim, we cannot be active citizens; we must be mournful lookers-on. But what matters it? We nobles of the old race are becoming rapidly extinct. Under any form of government likely to be established in France we are equally doomed. The French people, aiming at an impossible equality, will never again tolerate a race of gentilshommes. They cannot prevent, without destroying commerce and capital altogether, a quick succession of men of the day, who form nominal aristocracies much more opposed to equality than any hereditary class of nobles; but they refuse these fleeting substitutes of born patricians all permanent stake in the country, since whatever estate they buy must be subdivided at their death my poor Alain, you are making it the one ambition of your life to preserve to your posterity the home and lands of your forefathers. How is that possible, even supposing you could redeem the mortgages? You marry some day; you have children, and Rochebriant must then be sold to pay for their separate portions. How this condition of things, while rendering us so ineffective to perform the normal functions of a noblesse in public life, affects us in private life, may be easily conceived.

"Condemned to a career of pleasure and frivolity, we can scarcely escape from the contagion of extravagant luxury which forms the vice of the time. With grand names to keep up, and small fortunes whereon to keep them, we readily incur embarrassment and debt. Then neediness conquers pride. We cannot be great merchants, but we can be small gamblers on the Bourse, or, thanks to the Credit Mobilier, imitate a cabinet minister, and keep a shop under another name. Perhaps you have heard that Enguerrand and I keep a shop. Pray, buy your gloves there. Strange fate for men whose ancestors fought in the first Crusade—mais que voulez-vous?"

"I was told of the shop," said Alain; "but the moment I knew you I disbelieved the story."

"Quite true. Shall I confide to you why we resorted to that means of finding ourselves in pocket-money? My father gives us rooms in his hotel; the use of his table, which we do not much profit by; and an allowance, on which we could not live as young men of our class live at Paris. Enguerrand had his means of spending pocket-money, I mine; but it came to the same thing,—the pockets were emptied. We incurred debts. Two years ago my father straitened himself to pay them, saying, 'The next time you come to me with debts, however small, you must pay them yourselves, or you must marry, and leave it to me to find you wives.' This threat appalled us both. A month afterwards, Enguerrand made a lucky hit at the Bourse, and proposed to invest the proceeds in a shop. I resisted as long as I could; but Enguerrand triumphed over me, as he always does. He found an excellent deputy in a bonne who had nursed us in childhood, and married a journeyman perfumer who understands the business. It answers well; we are not in debt, and we have preserved our freedom."

After these confessions Raoul went away, and Alain fell into a mournful revery, from which he was roused by a loud ring at his bell. He opened the door, and beheld M. Louvier. The burly financier was much out of breath after making so steep an ascent. It was in gasps that he muttered, "Bon jour; excuse me if I derange you." Then entering and seating himself on a chair, he took some minutes to recover speech, rolling his eyes staringly round the meagre, unluxurious room, and then concentrating their gaze upon its occupier.

"Peste, my dear Marquis!" he said at last, "I hope the next time I visit you the ascent may be less arduous. One would think you were in training to ascend the Himalaya."

The haughty noble writhed under this jest, and the spirit inborn in his order spoke in his answer.

"I am accustomed to dwell on heights, Monsieur Louvier; the castle of Rochebriant is not on a level with the town." An angry gleam shot out from the eyes of the millionaire, but there was no other sign of displeasure in his answer. "Bien dit, mon cher; how you remind me of your father! Now, give me leave to speak on affairs. I have seen your cousin Enguerrand de Vandemar. Homme de moyens, though joli garcon. He proposed that you should call on me. I said 'no' to the cher petit Enguerrand,—a visit from me was due to you. To cut matters short, M. Gandrin has allowed me to look into your papers. I was disposed to serve you from the first; I am still more disposed to serve you now. I undertake to pay off all your other mortgages, and become sole mortgagee, and on terms that I have jotted down on this paper, and which I hope will content you."

He placed a paper in Alain's hand, and took out a box, from which he extracted a jujube, placed it in his mouth, folded his hands, and reclined back in his chair, with his eyes half closed, as if exhausted alike by his ascent and his generosity.

In effect, the terms were unexpectedly liberal. The reduced interest on the mortgages would leave the Marquis an income of L1,000 a year instead of L400. Louvier proposed to take on himself the legal cost of transfer, and to pay to the Marquis 25,000 francs, on the completion of the deed, as a bonus. The mortgage did not exempt the building-land, as Hebert desired. In all else it was singularly advantageous, and Alain could but feel a thrill of grateful delight at an offer by which his stinted income was raised to comparative affluence. "Well, Marquis," said Louvier, "what does the castle say to the town?"

"Monsieur Louvier," answered Alain, extending his hand with cordial eagerness, "accept my sincere apologies for the indiscretion of my metaphor. Poverty is proverbially sensitive to jests on it. I owe it to you if I cannot hereafter make that excuse for any words of mine that may displease you. The terms you propose are most liberal, and I close with them at once."

"Bon," said Louvier, shaking vehemently the hand offered to him; "I will take the paper to Gandrin, and instruct him accordingly. And now, may

I attach a condition to the agreement which is not put down on paper? It may have surprised you perhaps that I should propose a gratuity of 25,000 francs on completion of the contract. It is a droll thing to do, and not in the ordinary way of business, therefore I must explain. Marquis, pardon the liberty I take, but you have inspired me with an interest in your future. With your birth, connections, and figure you should push your way in the world far and fast. But you can't do so in a province. You must find your opening at Paris. I wish you to spend a year in the capital, and live, not extravagantly, like a nouveau riche, but in a way not unsuited to your rank, and permitting you all the social advantages that belong to it. These 25,000 francs, in addition to your improved income, will enable you to gratify my wish in this respect. Spend the money in Paris; you will want every sou of it in the course of the year. It will be money well spent. Take my advice, cher Marquis. Au plaisir."

The financier bowed himself out. The young Marquis forgot all the mournful reflections with which Raoul's conversation had inspired him. He gave a new touch to his toilette, and sallied forth with the air of a man on whose morning of life a sun heretofore clouded has burst forth and bathed the landscape in its light.

# CHAPTER VIII.

Since the evening spent at the Savarins', Graham had seen no more of Isaura. He had avoided all chance of seeing her; in fact, the jealousy with which he had viewed her manner towards Rameau, and the angry amaze with which he had heard her proclaim her friendship for Madame de Grantmesnil, served to strengthen the grave and secret reasons which made him desire to keep his heart yet free and his hand yet unpledged. But alas! the heart was enslaved already. It was under the most fatal of all spells,—first love conceived at first sight. He was wretched; and in his wretchedness his resolves became involuntarily weakened. He found himself making excuses for the beloved. What cause had he, after all, for that jealousy of the young poet which had so offended him; and if in her youth and inexperience Isaura had made her dearest friend of a great writer by whose genius she might be dazzled, and of whose opinions she might scarcely be aware, was it a crime that necessitated her eternal banishment from the reverence which belongs to all manly love? Certainly he found no satisfactory answers to such self-questionings. And then those grave reasons known only to himself, and never to be confided to another—why he should yet reserve his hand unpledged—were not so imperative as to admit of no compromise. They might entail a sacrifice, and not a small one to a man of Graham's views and ambition. But what is love if it can think any sacrifice, short of duty and honour, too great to offer up unknown uncomprehended, to the one beloved? Still, while thus softened in his feelings towards Isaura, he became, perhaps in consequence of such softening, more and more restlessly impatient to fulfil the object for which he had come to Paris, the great step towards which was the discovery of the undiscoverable Louise Duval.

He had written more than once to M. Renard since the interview with that functionary already recorded, demanding whether Renard had not made some progress in the research on which he was employed, and had received short unsatisfactory replies preaching patience and implying hope.

The plain truth, however, was that M. Renard had taken no further pains in the matter. He considered it utter waste of time and thought to attempt a discovery to which the traces were so faint and so obsolete. If the discovery were effected, it must be by one of those chances which occur without labour or forethought of our own. He trusted only to such a chance in continuing the charge he had undertaken. But during the last day or two Graham had become yet more impatient than before, and peremptorily requested another visit from this dilatory confidant.

In that visit, finding himself pressed hard, and though naturally willing, if possible, to retain a client unusually generous, yet being on the whole an honest member of his profession, and feeling it to be somewhat unfair to accept large remuneration for doing nothing, M. Renard said frankly, "Monsieur, this affair is beyond me; the keenest agent of our police could make nothing of it. Unless you can tell me more than you have done, I am utterly without a clew. I resign, therefore, the task with which you honoured me, willing to resume it again if you can give me information that could render me of use."

"What sort of information?"

"At least the names of some of the lady's relations who may yet be living."

"But it strikes me that, if I could get at that piece of knowledge, I should not require the services of the police. The relations would tell me what had become of Louise Duval quite as readily as they would tell a police agent."

"Quite true, Monsieur. It would really be picking your pockets if I did not at once retire from your service. Nay, Monsieur, pardon me, no further payments; I have already accepted too much. Your most obedient servant."

Graham, left alone, fell into a very gloomy revery. He could not but be sensible of the difficulties in the way of the object which had brought him to Paris, with somewhat sanguine expectations of success founded on a belief in the omniscience of the Parisian police, which is only to be justified when they have to deal with a murderess or a political incendiary. But the name of Louise Duval is about as common in France as that of Mary Smith in England; and the English reader may judge what would be the likely result of inquiring through the ablest of our detectives after some Mary Smith of whom you could give little more information than that she was the daughter of a drawing-master who had died twenty years ago, that it was about fifteen years since anything had been heard of her, that you could not say if through marriage or for other causes she had changed her name or not, and you had reasons for declining resort to public advertisements. In the course of inquiry so instituted, the probability would be that you might hear of a great many Mary Smiths, in the pursuit of whom your employee would lose all sight and scent of the one Mary Smith for whom the chase was instituted.

In the midst of Graham's despairing reflections his laquais announced M. Frederic Lemercier.

"Cher Grarm-Varn. A thousand pardons if I disturb you at this late hour of the evening; but you remember the request you made me when you first arrived in Paris this season?"

"Of course I do,—in case you should ever chance in your wide round of acquaintance to fall in with a Madame or Mademoiselle Duval of about the age of forty, or a year or so less, to let me know; and you did fall in with two ladies of that name, but they were not the right one, not the person whom my friend begged me to discover; both much too young."

"Eh bien, mon cher. If you will come with me to the bal champetre in the Champs Elysees to-night, I can show you a third Madame Duval,—her Christian name is Louise, too, of the age you mention,—though she does her best to look younger, and is still very handsome. You said your Duval was handsome. It was only last evening that I met this lady at a soiree given by Mademoiselle Julie Caumartin, coryphee distinguee, in love with young Rameau."

"In love with young Rameau? I am very glad to hear it. He returns the love?"

"I suppose so. He seems very proud of it. But apropos of Madame Duval, she has been long absent from Paris, just returned, and looking out for conquests. She says she has a great penchant for the English; promises me to be at this ball. Come."

"Hearty thanks, my dear Lemercier. I am at your service."

# CHAPTER IX.

The bal champetre was gay and brilliant, as such festal scenes are at Paris. A lovely night in the midst of May, lamps below and stars above; the society mixed, of course. Evidently, when Graham has singled out Frederic Lemercier from all his acquaintances at Paris to conjoin with the official aid of M. Renard in search of the mysterious lady, he had conjectured the probability that she might be found in the Bohemian world so familiar to Frederic; if not as an inhabitant, at least as an explorer. Bohemia was largely represented at the bal champetre, but not without a fair sprinkling of what we call the "respectable classes," especially English and Americans, who brought their wives there to take care of them. Frenchmen, not needing such care, prudently left their wives at home. Among the Frenchmen of station were the Comte de Passy and the Vicomte de Breze.

On first entering the gardens, Graham's eye was attracted and dazzled by a brilliant form. It was standing under a festoon of flowers extended from tree to tree, and a gas jet opposite shone full upon the face,—the face of a girl in all the freshness of youth. If the freshness owed anything to art, the art was so well disguised that it seemed nature. The beauty of the countenance was Hebe-like, joyous, and radiant; and yet one could not look at the girl without a sentiment of deep mournfulness. She was surrounded by a group of young men, and the ring of her laugh jarred upon Graham's ear. He pressed Frederic's arm, and directing his attention to the girl, asked who she was.

"Who? Don't you know? That is Julie Caumartin. A little while ago her equipage was the most admired in the Bois, and great ladies condescended to copy her dress or her coiffure; but she has lost her splendour, and dismissed the rich admirer who supplied the fuel for its blaze, since she fell in love with Gustave Rameau. Doubtless she is expecting him to-night. You ought to know her; shall I present you?"

"No," answered Graham, with a compassionate expression in his manly face. "So young; seemingly so gay. How I pity her!"

"What! for throwing herself away on Rameau? True. There is a great deal of good in that girl's nature, if she had been properly trained. Rameau wrote a pretty poem on her which turned her head and won her heart, in which she is styled the 'Ondine of Paris,'—a nymph-like type of Paris itself."

"Vanishing type, like her namesake; born of the spray, and vanishing soon into the deep," said Graham. "Pray go and look for the Duval; you will find me seated yonder."

Graham passed into a retired alley, and threw himself on a solitary bench, while Lemercier went in search of Madame Duval. In a few minutes the Frenchman reappeared. By his side was a lady well dressed, and as she passed under the lamps Graham perceived that, though of a certain age, she was undeniably handsome. His heart beat more quickly. Surely this was the Louise Duval he sought.

He rose from his seat, and was presented in due form to the lady, with whom Frederic then discreetly left him. "M. Lemercier tells me that you think that we were once acquainted with each other."

"Nay, Madame; I should not fail to recognize you were that the case. A friend of mine had the honour of knowing a lady of your name; and should I be fortunate enough to meet that lady, I am charged with a commission that may not be unwelcome to her. M. Lemercier tells me your nom de bapteme is Louise."

"Louise Corinne, Monsieur."

"And I presume that Duval is the name you take from your parents?"

"No; my father's name was Bernard. I married, when I was a mere child, M. Duval, in the wine trade at Bordeaux."

"Ah, indeed!" said Graham, much disappointed, but looking at her with a keen, searching eye, which she met with a decided frankness. Evidently, in his judgment, she was speaking the truth.

"You know English, I think, Madame," he resumed, addressing her in that language.

"A leetle; speak un peu."

"Only a little?"

Madame Duval looked puzzled, and replied in French, with a laugh, "Is it that you were told that I spoke English by your countryman, Milord Sare Boulby? Petit scelerat, I hope he is well. He sends you a commission for me,—so he ought; he behaved to me like a monster."

"Alas! I know nothing of Milord Sir Boulby. Were you never in England yourself?"

"Never," with a coquettish side-glance; "I should like so much to go. I have a foible for the English in spite of that vilain petit Boulby. Who is it gave you the commission for me? Ha! I guess, le Capitaine Nelton."

"No. What year, Madame, if not impertinent, were you at Aix-la-Chapelle?"

"You mean Baden? I was there seven years ago, when I met le Capitaine Nelton, bel homme aux cheveux rouges."

"But you have been at Aix?"

"Never."

"I have, then, been mistaken, Madame, and have only to offer my most humble apologies."

"But perhaps you will favour me with a visit, and we may on further conversation find that you are not mistaken. I can't stay now, for I am engaged to dance with the Belgian of whom, no doubt, M. Lemercier has told you."

"No, Madame, he has not."

"Well, then, he will tell you. The Belgian is very jealous; but I am always at home between three and four; this is my card."

Graham eagerly took the card, and exclaimed, "Is this you're your own handwriting, Madame?"

"Yes, indeed."

"Tres belle ecriture," said Graham, and receded with a ceremonious bow. "Anything so unlike her handwriting! Another disappointment," muttered the Englishman as the lady went back to the ball.

A few minutes later Graham joined Lemercier, who was talking with De Passy and De Breze.

"Well," said Lemercier, when his eye rested on Graham, "I hit the right nail on the head this time, eh?"

Graham shook his head.

"What! is she not the right Louise Duval?"

"Certainly not."

The Count de Passy overheard the name, and turned. "Louise Duval," he said; "does Monsieur Vane know a Louise Duval?"

"No; but a friend asked me to inquire after a lady of that name whom he had met many years ago at Paris." The Count mused a moment, and said, "Is it possible that your friend knew the family De Mauleon?"

"I really can't say. What then?"

"The old Vicomte de Mauleon was one of my most intimate associates. In fact, our houses are connected. And he was extremely grieved, poor man, when his daughter Louise married her drawing-master, Auguste Duval."

"Her drawing-master, Auguste Duval? Pray say on. I think the Louise Duval my friend knew must have been her daughter. She was the only child of a drawing-master or artist named Auguste Duval, and probably enough her Christian name would have been derived from her mother. A Mademoiselle de Mauleon, then, married M. Auguste Duval?"

"Yes; the old Vicomte had espoused en premieres noces Mademoiselle Camille de Chavigny, a lady of birth equal to his own; had by her one daughter, Louise. I recollect her well,—a plain girl, with a high nose and a sour expression. She was just of age when the first Vicomtesse died, and by the marriage settlement she succeeded at once to her mother's fortune, which was not large. The Vicomte was, however, so poor that the loss of that income was no trifle to him. Though much past fifty, he was still very handsome. Men of that generation did not age soon, Monsieur," said the Count, expanding his fine chest and laughing exultingly.

"He married, en secondes noces, a lady of still higher birth than the first, and with a much larger dot. Louise was indignant at this, hated her stepmother; and when a son was born by the second marriage she left the paternal roof, went to reside with an old female relative near the Luxembourg, and there married this drawing-master. Her father and the family did all they could to prevent it; but in these democratic days a woman who has attained her majority can, if she persist in her determination, marry to please herself and disgrace her ancestors. After that mesalliance her father never would see her again. I tried in vain to soften him. All his parental affections settled on his handsome Victor.

"Ah! you are too young to have known Victor de Mauleon during his short reign at Paris, as roi des viveurs."

"Yes, he was before my time; but I have heard of him as a young man of great fashion; said to be very clever, a duellist, and a sort of Don Juan."

"Exactly."

"And then I remember vaguely to have heard that he committed, or was said to have committed, some villanous action connected with a great lady's jewels, and to have left Paris in consequence."

"Ah, yes; a sad scrape. At that time there was a political crisis; we were under a Republic; anything against a noble was believed. But I am sure

Victor de Mauleon was not the man to commit a larceny. However, it is quite true that he left Paris, and I don't know what has become of him since." Here he touched De Breze, who, though still near, had not been listening to this conversation, but interchanging jest and laughter with Lemercier on the motley scene of the dance.

"De Breze, have you ever heard what became of poor dear Victor de Mauleon?—you knew him."

"Knew him? I should think so. Who could be in the great world and not know le beau Victor? No; after he vanished I never heard more of him; doubtless long since dead. A good-hearted fellow in spite of all his sins."

"My dear Monsieur de Breze, did you know his half-sister?" asked Graham,—"a Madame Duval?"

"No. I never heard he had a half-sister. Halt there; I recollect that I met Victor once, in the garden at Versailles, walking arm-in-arm with the most beautiful girl I ever saw; and when I complimented him afterwards at the Jockey Club on his new conquest, he replied very gravely that the young lady was his niece. 'Niece!' said I; 'why, there can't be more than five or six years between you.' 'About that, I suppose,' said he; 'my half-sister, her mother, was more than twenty years older than I at the time of my birth.' I doubted the truth of his story at the time; but since you say he really had a sister, my doubt wronged him."

"Have you never seen that same young lady since?"

"Never."

"How many years ago was this?"

"Let me see, about twenty or twenty-one years ago. How time flies!"

Graham still continued to question, but could learn no further particulars. He turned to quit the gardens just as the band was striking up for a fresh dance, a wild German waltz air; and mingled with that German music his ear caught the sprightly sounds of the French laugh, one laugh distinguished from the rest by a more genuine ring of light-hearted joy, the laugh that he had heard on entering the gardens, and the sound of which had then saddened him. Looking towards the quarter from which it came, he again saw the "Ondine of Paris." She was not now the centre of a group. She had just found Gustave Rameau, and was clinging to his arm with a look of happiness in her face, frank and innocent as a child's; and so they passed amid the dancers down a solitary lamplit alley, till lost to the Englishman's lingering gaze.

# CHAPTER X.

The next morning Graham sent again for M. Renard. "Well," he cried, when that dignitary appeared and took a seat beside him, "chance has favoured me."

"I always counted on chance, Monsieur. Chance has more wit in its little finger than the Paris police in its whole body."

"I have ascertained the relations, on the mother's side, of Louise Duval, and the only question is how to get at them." Here Graham related what he had heard, and ended by saying, "This Victor de Mauleon is therefore my Louise Duval's uncle. He was, no doubt, taking charge of her in the year that the persons interested in her discovery lost sight of her in Paris; and surely he must know what became of her afterwards."

"Very probably; and chance may befriend us yet in the discovery of Victor de Mauleon. You seem not to know the particulars of that story about the jewels which brought him into some connection with the police, and resulted in his disappearance from Paris."

"No; tell me the particulars."

"Victor de Mauleon was heir to some 60,000 or 70,000 francs a year, chiefly on the mother's side; for his father, though the representative of one of the most ancient houses in Normandy, was very poor, having little of his own except the emoluments of an appointment in the Court of Louis Philippe.

"But before, by the death of his parents, Victor came into that inheritance, he very largely forestalled it. His tastes were magnificent. He took to 'sport,' kept a famous stud, was a great favourite with the English, and spoke their language fluently. Indeed he was considered very accomplished, and of considerable intellectual powers. It was generally said that some day or other, when he had sown his wild oats, he would, if he took to politics, be an eminent man. Altogether he was a very strong creature. That was a very strong age under Louis Philippe. The viveurs of Paris were fine types for the heroes of Dumas and Sue,—full of animal life and spirits. Victor de Mauleon was a romance of Dumas, incarnated."

"Monsieur Renard, forgive me that I did not before do justice to your taste in polite literature."

"Monsieur, a man in my profession does not attain even to my humble eminence if he be not something else than a professional. He must study mankind wherever they are described, even in les romans. To return to Victor de Mauleon. Though he was a 'sportman,' a gambler, a Don Juan, a duel list, nothing was ever said against his honour. On the contrary, on matters of honour he was a received oracle; and even though he had fought several duels (that was the age of duels), and was reported without a superior, almost without an equal, in either weapon, the sword or the pistol, he is said never to have wantonly provoked an encounter, and to have so used his skill that he contrived never to slay, nor even gravely to wound, an antagonist.

"I remember one instance of his generosity in this respect; for it was much talked of at the time. One of your countrymen, who had never handled a fencing-foil nor fired a pistol, took offence at something M. de Mauleon had said in disparagement of the Duke of Wellington, and called him out. Victor de Mauleon accepted the challenge, discharged his pistol, not in the air—that might have been an affront—but so as to be wide of the mark, walked up to the lines to be shot at, and when missed, said, 'Excuse the susceptibility of a Frenchman loath to believe that his countryman can be beaten save by accident, and accept every apology one gentleman can make to another for having forgotten the respect due to one of the most renowned of your national heroes.' The Englishman's name was Vane. Could it have been your father?"

"Very probably; just like my father to call out any man who insulted the honour of his country, as represented by its men. I hope the two combatants became friends?"

"That I never heard; the duel was over; there my story ends."

"Pray go on."

"One day—it was in the midst of political events which would have silenced most subjects of private gossip—the beau monde was startled by the news that the Vicomte (he was then, by his father's death, Vicomte) de Mauleon had been given into the custody of the police on the charge of stealing the jewels of the Duchesse de (the wife of a distinguished foreigner). It seems that some days before this event, the Duc, wishing to make Madame his spouse an agreeable surprise, had resolved to have a diamond necklace belonging to her, and which was of setting so old-fashioned that she had not lately worn it, reset for her birthday. He therefore secretly possessed himself of the key to an iron safe in a cabinet adjoining her dressing-room (in which safe her more valuable jewels were kept), and took from it the necklace. Imagine his dismay when the jeweller in the Rue Vivienne to whom he carried it recognized the pretended diamonds as imitation paste which he himself had some days previously inserted into an empty setting brought to him by a Monsieur with whose name he was unacquainted. The Duchesse was at that time in delicate health; and as the Duc's suspicions naturally fell on the servants, especially on the femme de chambre, who was in great favour with his wife, he did not like to alarm Madame, nor through her to put the servants on their guard. He resolved, therefore, to place the matter in the hands of the famous ————, who was then the pride and ornament of the Parisian police. And the very night afterwards the Vicomte de Mauleon was caught and apprehended in the cabinet where the jewels were kept, and to which he had got access by a false key, or at least a duplicate key, found in his possession. I should observe that M. de Mauleon occupied the entresol in the same hotel in which the upper rooms were devoted to the Duc and Duchesse and their suite. As soon as this charge against the Vicomte was made known (and it was known the next morning), the extent of his debts and the utterness of his ruin (before scarcely conjectured or wholly unheeded) became public through the medium of the journals, and furnished an obvious motive for the crime of which he was accused. We Parisians, Monsieur, are subject to the most startling reactions of feeling. The men we adore one day we execrate the next. The Vicomte passed at once from the popular admiration one bestows on a hero to the popular contempt with which one regards a petty larcener. Society wondered how it had ever condescended to receive into its bosom the gambler, the duellist, the Don Juan. However, one compensation in the way of amusement he might still afford to society for the grave injuries he had done it. Society would attend his trial, witness his demeanour at the bar, and watch the expression of his face when he was sentenced to the galleys. But, Monsieur, this wretch completed the measure of his iniquities. He was not tried at all. The Duc and Duchesse quitted Paris for Spain, and the Duc instructed his lawyer to withdraw his charge, stating his conviction of the Vicomte's complete innocence of any other offence than that which he himself had confessed."

"What did the Vicomte confess? You omitted to state that."

"The Vicomte, when apprehended, confessed that, smitten by an insane passion for the Duchesse, which she had, on his presuming to declare it, met with indignant scorn, he had taken advantage of his lodgment in the same house to admit himself into the cabinet adjoining her dressing-room by means of a key which he had procured, made from an impression of the key-hole taken in wax.

"No evidence in support of any other charge against the Vicomte was forthcoming,—nothing, in short, beyond the infraction du domicile caused by the madness of youthful love, and for which there was no prosecution. The law, therefore, could have little to say against him. But society was more rigid; and exceedingly angry to find that a man who had been so conspicuous for luxury should prove to be a pauper, insisted on believing that M. de Mauleon was guilty of the meaner, though not perhaps, in the eyes of husbands and fathers, the more heinous, of the two offences. I presume that the Vicomte felt that he had got into a dilemma from which no pistol-shot or sword-thrust could free him, for he left Paris abruptly, and has not since reappeared. The sale of his stud and effects sufficed, I believe, to pay his debts, for I will do him the justice to say that they were paid."

"But though the Vicomte de Mauleon has disappeared, he must have left relations at Paris, who would perhaps know what has become of him and of his niece."

"I doubt it. He had no very near relations. The nearest was an old celibataire of the same name, from whom he had some expectations, but who died shortly after this esclandre, and did not name the Vicomte in his will. M. Victor had numerous connections among the highest families, the Rochebriants, Chavignys, Vandemars, Passys, Beauvilliers; but they are not likely to have retained any connection with a ruined vaurien, and still less with a niece of his who was the child of a drawing-master. But now you have given me a clew, I will try to follow it up. We must find the Vicomte, and I am not without hope of doing so. Pardon me if I decline to say more at present. I would not raise false expectations; but in a week or two I will have the honour to call again upon Monsieur."

"Wait one instant. You have really a hope of discovering M. de Mauleon?"

"Yes. I cannot say more at present."

M. Renard departed. Still that hope, however faint it might prove, served to reanimate Graham; and with that hope his heart, as if a load had been lifted from its mainspring, returned instinctively to the thought of Isaura. Whatever seemed to promise an early discharge of the commission connected with the discovery of Louise Duval seemed to bring Isaura nearer to him, or at least to excuse his yearning desire to see more of her, to understand her better. Faded into thin air was the vague jealousy of Gustave Rameau which he had so unreasonably conceived; he felt as if it were impossible that the man whom the "Ondine of Paris" claimed as her lover could dare to woo or hope to win an Isaura. He even forgot the friendship with the eloquent denouncer of the marriage-bond, which a little while ago had seemed to him an unpardonable offence. He remembered only the lovely face, so innocent, yet so intelligent; only the sweet voice, which had for the first time breathed music into his own soul; only the gentle hand, whose touch had for the first time sent through his veins the thrill which distinguishes from all her sex the woman whom we love. He went forth elated and joyous, and took his way to Isaura's villa. As he went, the leaves on the trees under which he passed seemed stirred by the soft May breeze in sympathy with his own delight. Perhaps it was rather the reverse: his own silent delight sympathized with all delight in awakening Nature. The lover seeking reconciliation with the loved one from whom some trifle has unreasonably estranged him, in a cloudless day of May,—if he be not happy enough to feel a brotherhood in all things happy,—a leaf in bloom, a bird in song,—then indeed he may call himself lover, but he does not know what is love.

# BOOK IV.

## CHAPTER I.

### FROM ISAURA CICOGNA TO MADAME DE GRANTMESNIL.

It is many days since I wrote to you, and but for your delightful note just received, reproaching me for silence, I should still be under the spell of that awe which certain words of M. Savarin were well fitted to produce. Chancing to ask him if he had written to you lately, he said, with that laugh of his, good-humouredly ironical, "No, Mademoiselle, I am not one of the Facheux whom Moliere has immortalized. If the meeting of lovers should be sacred from the intrusion of a third person, however amiable, more sacred still should be the parting between an author and his work. Madame de Grantmesnil is in that moment so solemn to a genius earnest as hers,—she is bidding farewell to a companion with whom, once dismissed into the world, she can never converse familiarly again; it ceases to be her companion when it becomes ours. Do not let us disturb the last hours they will pass together."

These words struck me much. I suppose there is truth in them. I can comprehend that a work which has long been all in all to its author, concentrating his thoughts, gathering round it the hopes and fears of his inmost heart, dies, as it were, to him when he has completed its life for others, and launched it into a world estranged from the solitude in which it was born and formed. I can almost conceive that, to a writer like you, the very fame which attends the work thus sent forth chills your own love for it. The characters you created in a fairyland, known but to yourself, must lose something of their mysterious charm when you hear them discussed and cavilled at, blamed or praised, as if they were really the creatures of streets and salons.

I wonder if hostile criticism pains or enrages you as it seems to do such other authors as I have known. M. Savarin, for instance, sets down in his tablets as an enemy to whom vengeance is due the smallest scribbler who wounds his self-love, and says frankly, "To me praise is food, dispraise is poison. Him who feeds me I pay; him who poisons me I break on the wheel." M. Savarin is, indeed, a skilful and energetic administrator to his own reputation. He deals with it as if it were a kingdom,—establishes fortifications for its defence, enlists soldiers to fight for it. He is the soul and centre of a confederation in which each is bound to defend the territory of the others, and all those territories united constitute the imperial realm of M. Savarin. Don't think me an ungracious satirist in what I am thus saying of our brilliant friend. It is not I who here speak; it is himself. He avows his policy with the naivete which makes the charm of his style as writer. "It is the greatest mistake," he said to me yesterday, "to talk of the Republic of Letters. Every author who wins a name is a sovereign in his own domain, be it large or small. Woe to any republican who wants to dethrone me!" Somehow or other, when M. Savarin thus talks I feel as if he were betraying the cause of, genius. I cannot bring myself to regard literature as a craft,—to me it is a sacred mission; and in hearing this "sovereign" boast of the tricks by which he maintains his state, I seem to listen to a priest who treats as imposture the religion he professes to teach. M. Savarin's favourite eleve now is a young contributor to his journal, named Gustave Rameau. M. Savarin said the other day in my hearing, "I and my set were Young France; Gustave Rameau and his set are New Paris."

"And what is the distinction between the one and the other?" asked my American friend, Mrs. Morley.

"The set of 'Young France,'" answered M. Savarin, "had in it the hearty consciousness of youth; it was bold and vehement, with abundant vitality and animal spirits; whatever may be said against it in other respects, the power of thews and sinews must be conceded to its chief representatives. But the set of 'New Paris' has very bad health, and very indifferent spirits. Still, in its way, it is very clever; it can sting and bite as keenly as if it were big and strong. Rameau is the most promising member of the set. He will be popular in his time, because he represents a good deal of the mind of his time,—namely, the mind and the time of 'New Paris.'"

Do you know anything of this young Rameau's writings? You do not know himself, for he told me so, expressing a desire, that was evidently very sincere, to find some occasion on which to render you his homage. He said this the first time I met him at M. Savarin's, and before he knew how dear to me are yourself and your fame. He came and sat by me after dinner, and won my interest at once by asking me if I had heard that you were busied on a new work; and then, without waiting for my answer, he launched forth into praises of you, which made a notable contrast to the scorn with which he spoke of all your contemporaries,—except indeed M. Savarin, who, however, might not have been pleased to hear his favourite pupil style him "a great writer in small things." I spare you his epigrams on Dumas and

Victor Hugo and my beloved Lamartine. Though his talk was showy, and dazzled me at first, I soon got rather tired of it, even the first time we met. Since then I have seen him very often, not only at M. Savarin's, but he calls here at least every other day, and we have become quite good friends. He gains on acquaintance so far that one cannot help feeling how much he is to be pitied. He is so envious! and the envious must be so unhappy. And then he is at once so near and so far from all the things that he envies. He longs for riches and luxury, and can only as yet earn a bare competence by his labours. Therefore he hates the rich and luxurious. His literary successes, instead of pleasing him, render him miserable by their contrast with the fame of the authors whom he envies and assails. He has a beautiful head, of which he is conscious, but it is joined to a body without strength or grace. He is conscious of this too,—but it is cruel to go on with this sketch. You can see at once the kind of person who, whether he inspire affection or dislike, cannot fail to create an interest, painful but compassionate.

You will be pleased to hear that Dr. C. considers my health so improved that I may next year enter fairly on the profession for which I was intended and trained. Yet I still feel hesitating and doubtful. To give myself wholly up to the art in which I am told I could excel must alienate me entirely from the ambition that yearns for fields in which, alas! it may perhaps never appropriate to itself a rood for culture,—only wander, lost in a vague fairyland, to which it has not the fairy's birthright. O thou great Enchantress, to whom are equally subject the streets of Paris and the realm of Faerie, thou who hast sounded to the deeps that circumfluent ocean called "practical human life," and hast taught the acutest of its navigators to consider how far its courses are guided by orbs in heaven,—canst thou solve this riddle which, if it perplexes me, must perplex so many? What is the real distinction between the rare genius and the commonalty of human souls that feel to the quick all the grandest and divinest things which the rare genius places before them, sighing within themselves, "This rare genius does but express that which was previously familiar to us, so far as thought and sentiment extend"? Nay, the genius itself, however eloquent, never does, never can, express the whole of the thought or the sentiment it interprets; on the contrary, the greater the genius is, the more it leaves a something of incomplete satisfaction on our minds,—it promises so much more than it performs; it implies so much more than it announces. I am impressed with the truth of what I thus say in proportion as I re-peruse and re-study the greatest writers that have come within my narrow range of reading; and by the greatest writers I mean those who are not exclusively reasoners (of such I cannot judge), nor mere poets (of whom, so far as concerns the union of words with music, I ought to be able to judge), but the few who unite reason and poetry, and appeal at once to the common-sense of the multitude and the imagination of the few. The highest type of this union to me is Shakspeare; and I can comprehend the justice of no criticism on him which does not allow this sense of incomplete satisfaction augmenting in proportion as the poet soars to his highest. I ask again, In what consists this distinction between the rare genius and the commonalty of minds that exclaim, "He expresses what we feel, but never the whole of what we feel"? Is it the mere power over language, a larger knowledge of dictionaries, a finer ear for period and cadence, a more artistic craft in casing our thoughts and sentiments in well-selected words? Is it true what Buffon says, "that the style is the man"? Is it true what I am told Goethe said, "Poetry is form"? I cannot believe this; and if you tell me it is true, then I no longer pine to be a writer. But if it be not true, explain to me how it is that the greatest genius is popular in proportion as it makes itself akin to us by uttering in better words than we employ that which was already within us, brings to light what in our souls was latent, and does but correct, beautify, and publish the correspondence which an ordinary reader carries on privately every day between himself and his mind or his heart. If this superiority in the genius be but style and form, I abandon my dream of being something else than a singer of words by another to the music of another. But then, what then? My knowledge of books and art is wonderfully small. What little I do know I gather from very few books and from what I hear said by the few worth listening to whom I happen to meet; and out of these, in solitude and revery, not by conscious effort, I arrive at some results which appear to my inexperience original. Perhaps, indeed, they have the same kind of originality as the musical compositions of amateurs who effect a cantata or a quartette made up of borrowed details from great masters, and constituting a whole so original that no real master would deign to own it. Oh, if I could get you to understand how unsettled, how struggling my whole nature at this moment is! I wonder what is the sensation of the chrysalis which has been a silkworm, when it first feels the new wings stirring within its shell,—wings, alas! they are but those of the humblest and shortest-lived sort of moth, scarcely born into daylight before it dies. Could it reason, it might regret its earlier life, and say, "Better be the silkworm than the moth."

FROM THE SAME TO THE SAME.

Have you known well any English people in the course of your life? I say well, for you must have had acquaintance with many. But it seems to me so difficult to know an Englishman well. Even I, who so loved and revered Mr. Selby,—I, whose childhood was admitted into his companionship by that love which places ignorance and knowledge, infancy and age, upon ground so equal that heart touches heart, cannot say that I understand the

English character to anything like the extent to which I fancy I understand the Italian and the French. Between us of the Continent and them of the island the British Channel always flows. There is an Englishman here to whom I have been introduced, whom I have met, though but seldom, in that society which bounds the Paris world to me. Pray, pray tell me, did you ever know, ever meet him? His name is Graham Vane. He is the only son, I am told, of a man who was a celebrite in England as an orator and statesman, and on both sides he belongs to the haute aristocratic. He himself has that indescribable air and mien to which we apply the epithet 'distinguished.' In the most crowded salon the eye would fix on him, and involuntarily follow his movements. Yet his manners are frank and simple, wholly without the stiffness or reserve which are said to characterize the English. There is an inborn dignity in his bearing which consists in the absence of all dignity assumed. But what strikes me most in this Englishman is an expression of countenance which the English depict by the word 'open,'—that expression which inspires you with a belief in the existence of sincerity. Mrs. Morley said of him, in that poetic extravagance of phrase by which the Americans startle the English, "That man's forehead would light up the Mammoth Cave." Do you not know, Eulalie, what it is to us cultivators of art—art being the expression of truth through fiction—to come into the atmosphere of one of those souls in which Truth stands out bold and beautiful in itself, and needs no idealization through fiction? Oh, how near we should be to heaven could we live daily, hourly, in the presence of one the honesty of whose word we could never doubt, the authority of whose word we could never disobey! Mr. Vane professes not to understand music, not even to care for it, except rarely, and yet he spoke of its influence over others with an enthusiasm that half charmed me once more back to my destined calling; nay, might have charmed me wholly, but that he seemed to think that I—that any public singer—must be a creature apart from the world,—the world in which such men live. Perhaps that is true.

# CHAPTER II.

It was one of those lovely noons towards the end of May in which a rural suburb has the mellow charm of summer to him who escapes awhile from the streets of a crowded capital. The Londoner knows its charm when he feels his tread on the softening swards of the Vale of Health, or, pausing at Richmond under the budding willow, gazes on the river glittering in the warmer sunlight, and hears from the villa-gardens behind him the brief trill of the blackbird. But the suburbs round Paris are, I think, a yet more pleasing relief from the metropolis; they are more easily reached, and I know not why, but they seem more rural,—perhaps because the contrast of their repose with the stir left behind, of their redundance of leaf and blossom compared with the prim efflorescence of trees in the Boulevards and Tuileries, is more striking. However that may be, when Graham reached the pretty suburb in which Isaura dwelt, it seemed to him as if all the wheels of the loud busy life were suddenly smitten still. The hour was yet early; he felt sure that he should find Isaura at home. The garden-gate stood unfastened and ajar; he pushed it aside and entered. I think I have before said that the garden of the villa was shut out from the road and the gaze of neighbours by a wall and thick belts of evergreens; it stretched behind the house somewhat far for the garden of a suburban villa. He paused when he had passed the gateway, for he heard in the distance the voice of one singing,—singing low, singing plaintively. He knew it was the voice of Isaura-he passed on, leaving the house behind him, and tracking the voice till he reached the singer.

Isaura was seated within an arbour towards the farther end of the garden,—an arbour which, a little later in the year, must indeed be delicate and dainty with lush exuberance of jessamine and woodbine; now into its iron trelliswork leaflets and flowers were insinuating their gentle way. Just at the entrance one white rose—a winter rose that had mysteriously survived its relations—opened its pale hues frankly to the noonday sun. Graham approached slowly, noiselessly, and the last note of the song had ceased when he stood at the entrance of the arbour. Isaura did not perceive him at first, for her face was bent downward musingly, as was often her wont after singing, especially when alone; but she felt that the place was darkened, that something stood between her and the sunshine. She raised her face, and a quick flush mantled over it as she uttered his name, not loudly, not as in surprise, but inwardly and whisperingly, as in a sort of fear.

"Pardon me, Mademoiselle," said Graham, entering; "but I heard your voice as I came into the garden, and it drew me onward involuntarily. What a lovely air! and what simple sweetness in such of the words as reached me! I am so ignorant of music that you must not laugh at me if I ask whose is the music and whose are the words? Probably both are so well known as to convict me of a barbarous ignorance."

"Oh, no," said Isaura, with a still heightened colour, and in accents embarrassed and hesitating. "Both the words and music are by an unknown and very humble composer, yet not, indeed, quite original,—they have not even that merit; at least they were suggested by a popular song in the Neapolitan dialect which is said to be very old."

"I don't know if I caught the true meaning of the words, for they seemed to me to convey a more subtle and refined sentiment than is common in the popular songs of southern Italy."

"The sentiment in the original is changed in the paraphrase, and not, I fear, improved by the change."

"Will you explain to me the sentiment in both, and let me judge which I prefer?"

"In the Neapolitan song a young fisherman, who has moored his boat under a rock on the shore, sees a beautiful face below the surface of the waters; he imagines it to be that of a Nereid, and casts in his net to catch this supposed nymph of the ocean. He only disturbs the water, loses the image, and brings up a few common fishes. He returns home disappointed, and very much enamoured of the supposed Nereid. The next day he goes again to the same place, and discovers that the face which had so charmed him was that of a mortal girl reflected on the waters from the rock behind him, on which she had been seated, and on which she had her home. The original air is arch and lively; just listen to it." And Isaura warbled one of those artless and somewhat meagre tunes to which light-stringed instruments are the fitting accompaniment.

"That," said Graham, "is a different music indeed from the other, which is deep and plaintive, and goes to the heart."

"But do you not see how the words have been altered? In the song you first heard me singing, the fisherman goes again to the spot, again and again sees the face in the water, again and again seeks to capture the Nereid, and never knows to the last that the face was that of the mortal on the rock close behind him, and which he passed by without notice every day. Deluded by an ideal image, the real one escapes from his eye."

"Is the verse that is recast meant to symbolize a moral in love?"

"In love? nay, I know not; but in life, yes,—at least the life of the artist."

"The paraphrase of the original is yours, Signorina, words and music both. Am I not right? Your silence answers 'Yes.' Will you pardon me if I say that, though there can be no doubt of the new beauty you have given to the old song, I think that the moral of the old was the sounder one, the truer to human life. We do not go on to the last duped by an allusion. If enamoured by the shadow on the waters, still we do look around us and discover the image it reflects."

Isaura shook her head gently, but made no answer. On the table before her there were a few myrtle-sprigs and one or two buds from the last winter rose, which she had been arranging into a simple nosegay; she took up these, and abstractedly began to pluck and scatter the rose-leaves.

"Despise the coming May flowers if you will, they will soon be so plentiful," said Graham; "but do not cast away the few blossoms which winter has so kindly spared, and which even summer will not give again;" and placing his hand on the winter buds, it touched hers,—lightly, indeed, but she felt the touch, shrank from it, coloured, and rose from her seat.

"The sun has left this side of the garden, the east wind is rising, and you must find it chilly here," she said, in an altered tone; "will you not come into the house?"

"It is not the air that I feel chilly," said Graham, with a half-smile; "I almost fear that my prosaic admonitions have displeased you."

"They were not prosaic; and they were kind and very wise," she added, with her exquisite laugh,—laugh so wonderfully sweet and musical. She now had gained the entrance of the arbour; Graham joined her, and they walked towards the house. He asked her if she had seen much of the Savarins since they had met.

"Once or twice we have been there of an evening."

"And encountered, no doubt, the illustrious young minstrel who despises Tasso and Corneille?"

"M. Rameau? Oh, yes; he is constantly at the Savarins. Do not be severe on him. He is unhappy, he is struggling, he is soured. An artist has thorns in his path which lookers-on do not heed."

"All people have thorns in their path, and I have no great respect for those who want lookers-on to heed them whenever they are scratched. But

M. Rameau seems to me one of those writers very common nowadays, in France and even in England; writers who have never read anything worth studying, and are, of course, presumptuous in proportion to their ignorance. I should not have thought an artist like yourself could have recognized an artist in a M. Rameau who despises Tasso without knowing Italian."

Graham spoke bitterly; he was once more jealous.

"Are you not an artist yourself? Are you not a writer? M. Savarin told me you were a distinguished man of letters."

"M. Savarin flatters me too much. I am not an artist, and I have a great dislike to that word as it is now hackneyed and vulgarized in England and in France. A cook calls himself an artist; a tailor does the same; a man writes a gaudy melodrame, a spasmodic song, a sensational novel, and straightway he calls Himself an artist, and indulges in a pedantic jargon about 'essence' and 'form,' assuring us that a poet we can understand wants essence, and a poet we can scan wants form. Thank heaven, I am not vain enough to call myself artist. I have written some very dry lucubrations in periodicals, chiefly political, or critical upon other subjects than art. But why, a propos of M. Rameau, did you ask me that question respecting myself?"

"Because much in your conversation," answered Isaura, in rather a mournful tone, "made me suppose you had more sympathies with art and its cultivators than you cared to avow; and if you had such sympathies, you would comprehend what a relief it is to a poor aspirant to art like myself to come into communication with those who devote themselves to any art distinct from the common pursuits of the world, what a relief it is to escape from the ordinary talk of society. There is a sort of instinctive freemasonry among us, including masters and disciples; and one art has a fellowship with other arts. Mine is but song and music, yet I feel attracted towards a sculptor, a painter, a romance-writer, a poet, as much as towards a singer, a musician. Do you understand why I cannot contemn M. Rameau as you do? I differ from his tastes in literature; I do not much admire such of his writings as I have read; I grant that he overestimates his own genius, whatever that be,—yet I like to converse with him. He is a struggler upwards, though with weak wings, or with erring footsteps, like myself."

"Mademoiselle," said Graham, earnestly, "I cannot say how I thank you for this candour. Do not condemn me for abusing it, if—" he paused.

"If what?"

"If I, so much older than yourself,—I do not say only in years, but in the experience of life, I whose lot is cast among those busy and 'positive' pursuits, which necessarily quicken that unromantic faculty called common-sense,—if, I say, the deep interest with which you must inspire all whom you admit into an acquaintance even as unfamiliar as that now between us makes me utter one caution, such as might be uttered by a friend or brother. Beware of those artistic sympathies which you so touchingly confess; beware how, in the great events of life, you allow fancy to misguide your reason. In choosing friends on whom to rely, separate the artist from the human being. Judge of the human being for what it is in itself. Do not worship the face on the waters, blind to the image on the rock. In one word, never see in an artist like a M. Rameau the human being to whom you could intrust the destinies of your life. Pardon me, pardon me; we may meet little hereafter, but you are a creature so utterly new to me, so wholly unlike any woman I have ever before encountered and admired, and to me seem endowed with such wealth of mind and soul, exposed to such hazard, that—that—" again he paused, and his voice trembled as he concluded—"that it would be a deep sorrow to me if, perhaps years hence, I should have to say, 'Alas'! by what mistake has that wealth been wasted!'"

While they had thus conversed, mechanically they had turned away from the house, and were again standing before the arbour.

Graham, absorbed in the passion of his adjuration, had not till now looked into the face of the companion by his side. Now, when he had concluded, and heard no reply, he bent down and saw that Isaura was weeping silently.

His heart smote him.

"Forgive me," he exclaimed, drawing her hand into his; "I have had no right to talk thus; but it was not from want of respect; it was—it was—"

The hand which was yielded to his pressed it gently, timidly, chastely.

"Forgive!" murmured Isaura; "do you think that I, an orphan, have never longed for a friend who would speak to me thus?" And so saying, she lifted her eyes, streaming still, to his bended countenance,—eyes, despite their tears, so clear in their innocent limpid beauty, so ingenuous, so frank, so virgin-like, so unlike the eyes of 'any other woman he had encountered and admired.'

"Alas!" he said, in quick and hurried accents, "you may remember, when we have before conversed, how I, though so uncultured in your art, still recognized its beautiful influence upon human breasts; how I sought to combat your own depreciation of its rank among the elevating agencies of humanity; how, too, I said that no man could venture to ask you to renounce the boards, the lamps,—resign the fame of actress, of singer. Well, now that you accord to me the title of friend, now that you so touchingly remind me that you are an orphan, thinking of all the perils the young and the beautiful of your sex must encounter when they abandon private life for public, I think that a true friend might put the question, 'Can you resign the fame of actress, of singer?'"

"I will answer you frankly. The profession which once seemed to me so alluring began to lose its charms in my eyes some months ago. It was your words, very eloquently expressed, on the ennobling effects of music and song upon a popular audience, that counteracted the growing distaste to rendering up my whole life to the vocation of the stage; but now I think I should feel grateful to the friend whose advice interpreted the voice of my own heart, and bade me relinquish the career of actress."

Graham's face grew radiant. But whatever might have been his reply was arrested; voices and footsteps were heard behind. He turned round and saw the Venosta, the Savarins, and Gustave Rameau.

Isaura heard and saw also, started in a sort of alarmed confusion, and then instinctively retreated towards the arbour. Graham hurried on to meet the Signora and the visitors, giving time to Isaura to compose herself by arresting them in the pathway with conventional salutations.

A few minutes later Isaura joined them, and there was talk to which Graham scarcely listened, though he shared in it by abstracted monosyllables. He declined going into the house, and took leave at the gate. In parting, his eyes fixed themselves on Isaura. Gustave Rameau was by her side. That nosegay which had been left in the arbour was in her hand; and though she was bending over it, she did not now pluck and scatter the rose-leaves. Graham at that moment felt no jealousy of the fair-faced young poet beside her.

As he walked slowly back, he muttered to himself, "But am I yet in the position to hold myself wholly free? Am I, am I? Were the sole choice before me that between her and ambition and wealth, how soon it would be made! Ambition has no prize equal to the heart of such a woman; wealth no sources of joy equal to the treasures of her love."

# CHAPTER III.

## FROM ISAURA CICOGNA TO MADAME DE GRANTMESNIL.

The day after I posted my last, Mr. Vane called on us. I was in our little garden at the time. Our conversation was brief, and soon interrupted by visitors,—the Savarins and M. Rameau. I long for your answer. I wonder how he impressed you, if you have met him; how he would impress, if you met him now. To me he is so different from all others; and I scarcely know why his words ring in my ears, and his image rests in my thoughts. It is strange altogether; for though he is young, he speaks to me as if he were so much older than I,—so kindly, so tenderly, yet as if I were a child, and much as the dear Maestro might do, if he thought I needed caution or counsel. Do not fancy, Eulalie, that there is any danger of my deceiving myself as to the nature of such interest as he may take in me. Oh, no! There is a gulf between us there which he does not lose sight of, and which we could not pass. How, indeed, I could interest him at all, I cannot guess. A rich, high-born Englishman, intent on political life; practical, prosaic—no, not prosaic; but still with the kind of sense which does not admit into its range of vision that world of dreams which is familiar as their daily home to Romance and to Art. It has always seemed to me that for love, love such as I conceive it, there must be a deep and constant sympathy between two persons,—not, indeed, in the usual and ordinary trifles of taste and sentiment, but in those essentials which form the root of character, and branch out in all the leaves and blooms that expand to the sunshine and shrink from the cold,—that the worldling should wed the worldling, the artist the artist. Can the realist and the idealist blend together, and hold together till death and beyond death? If not, can there be true love between them?

By true love, I mean the love which interpenetrates the soul, and once given can never die. Oh, Eulalie, answer me, answer!

P. S.—I have now fully made up my mind to renounce all thought of the stage.

FROM MADAME DE GRANTMESNIL TOISAURA CICOGNA.

MY DEAR CHILD,—how your mind has grown since you left me, the sanguine and aspiring votary of an art which, of all arts, brings the most immediate reward to a successful cultivator, and is in itself so divine in its immediate effects upon human souls! Who shall say what may be the after-results of those effects which the waiters on posterity presume to despise because they are immediate? A dull man, to whose mind a ray of that vague starlight undetected in the atmosphere of workday life has never yet travelled; to whom the philosopher, the preacher, the poet appeal in vain,—nay, to whom the conceptions of the grandest master of instrumental music are incomprehensible; to whom Beethoven unlocks no portal in heaven; to whom Rossini has no mysteries on earth unsolved by the critics of the pit,—suddenly hears the human voice of the human singer, and at the sound of that voice the walls which enclosed him fall. The something far from and beyond the routine of his commonplace existence becomes known to him. He of himself, poor man, can make nothing of it. He cannot put it down on paper, and say the next morning, "I am an inch nearer to heaven than I was last night;" but the feeling that he is an inch nearer to heaven abides with him. Unconsciously he is gentler, he is less earthly, and, in being nearer to heaven, he is stronger for earth. You singers do not seem to me to understand that you have—to use your own word, so much in vogue that it has become abused and trite—a mission! When you talk of missions, from whom comes the mission? Not from men. If there be a mission from man to men, it must be appointed from on high.

Think of all this; and in being faithful to your art, be true to yourself. If you feel divided between that art and the art of the writer, and acknowledge the first to be too exacting to admit a rival, keep to that in which you are sure to excel. Alas, my fair child! do not imagine that we writers feel a happiness in our pursuits and aims more complete than that which you can command. If we care for fame (and, to be frank, we all do), that fame does not come up before us face to face, a real, visible, palpable form, as it does to the singer, to the actress. I grant that it may be more enduring, but an endurance on the length of which we dare not reckon. A writer cannot be sure of immortality till his language itself be dead; and then he has but a share in an uncertain lottery. Nothing but fragments remains of the Phrynichus who rivalled AEschylus; of the Agathon who perhaps excelled Euripides; of the Alcaeus, in whom Horace acknowledged a master and a model; their renown is not in their works, it is but in their names. And, after all, the names of singers and actors last perhaps as long. Greece retains the name of Polus, Rome of Roscius, England of Garrick, France of Talma, Italy of Pasta, more lastingly than posterity is likely to retain mine. You address to me a question, which

I have often put to myself,—"What is the distinction between the writer and the reader, when the reader says, 'These are my thoughts, these are my feelings; the writer has stolen them, and clothed them in his own words'?" And the more the reader says this, the more wide is the audience, the more genuine the renown, and, paradox though it seems, the more consummate the originality, of the writer. But no, it is not the mere gift of expression, it is not the mere craft of the pen, it is not the mere taste in arrangement of word and cadence, which thus enables the one to interpret the mind, the heart, the soul of the many. It is a power breathed into him as he lay in his cradle, and a power that gathered around itself, as he grew up, all the influences he acquired, whether from observation of external nature, or from study of men and books, or from that experience of daily life which varies with every human being. No education could make two intellects exactly alike, as no culture can make two leaves exactly alike. How truly you describe the sense of dissatisfaction which every writer of superior genius communicates to his admirers! how truly do you feel that the greater is the dissatisfaction in proportion to the writer's genius, and the admirer's conception of it! But that is the mystery which makes—let me borrow a German phrase—the cloud-land between the finite and the infinite. The greatest philosopher, intent on the secrets of Nature, feels that dissatisfaction in Nature herself. The finite cannot reduce into logic and criticism the infinite.

Let us dismiss these matters, which perplex the reason, and approach that which touches the heart, which in your case, my child, touches the heart of woman. You speak of love, and deem that the love which lasts—the household, the conjugal love—should be based upon such sympathies of pursuit that the artist should wed the artist.

This is one of the questions you do well to address to me; for whether from my own experience, or from that which I have gained from observation extended over a wide range of life, and quickened and intensified by the class of writing that I cultivate, and which necessitates a calm study of the passions, I am an authority on such subjects, better than most women can be. And alas, my child, I come to this result: there is no prescribing to men or to women whom to select, whom to refuse. I cannot refute the axiom of the ancient poet, "In love there is no wherefore." But there is a time—it is often but a moment of time—in which love is not yet a master, in which we can say, "I will love, I will not love."

Now, if I could find you in such a moment, I would say to you, "Artist, do not love, do not marry, an artist." Two artistic natures rarely combine. The artistic nature is wonderfully exacting. I fear it is supremely egotistical,—so jealously sensitive that it writhes at the touch of a rival. Racine was the happiest of husbands; his wife adored his genius, but could not understand his plays. Would Racine have been happy if he had married a Corneille in petticoats? I who speak have loved an artist, certainly equal to myself. I am sure that he loved me. That sympathy in pursuits of which you speak drew us together, and became very soon the cause of antipathy. To both of us the endeavour to coalesce was misery.

I don't know your M. Rameau. Savarin has sent me some of his writings; from these I judge that his only chance of happiness would be to marry a commonplace woman, with separation de biens. He is, believe me, but one of the many with whom New Paris abounds, who because they have the infirmities of genius imagine they have its strength.

I come next to the Englishman. I see how serious is your questioning about him. You not only regard him as a being distinct from the crowd of a salon; he stands equally apart in the chamber of your thoughts,—you do not mention him in the same letter as that which treats of Rameau and Savarin. He has become already an image not to be lightly mixed up with others. You would rather not have mentioned him at all to me, but you could not resist it. The interest you feel in him so perplexed you, that in a kind of feverish impatience you cry out to me, "Can you solve the riddle? Did you ever know well Englishmen? Can an Englishman be understood out of his island?" etc. Yes, I have known well many Englishmen; in affairs of the heart they are much like all other men. No; I do not know this Englishman in particular, nor any one of his name.

Well, my child, let us frankly grant that this foreigner has gained some hold on your thoughts, on your fancy, perhaps also on your heart. Do not fear that he will love you less enduringly, or that you will become alienated from him, because he is not an artist. If he be a strong nature, and with some great purpose in life, your ambition will fuse itself in his; and knowing you as I do, I believe you would make an excellent wife to an Englishman whom you honoured as well as loved; and sorry though I should be that you relinquished the singer's fame, I should be consoled in thinking you safe in the woman's best sphere,—a contented home, safe from calumny, safe from gossip. I never had that home; and there has been no part in my author's life in which I would not have given all the celebrity it won for the obscure commonplace of such woman-lot. Could I move human beings as pawns on a chessboard, I should indeed say that the most suitable and congenial mate for you, for a woman of sentiment and genius, would be a well-born and well-educated German; for such a German unites, with domestic habits and a strong sense of family ties, a romance of sentiment, a love of art, a predisposition towards the poetic side of life, which is very rare among Englishmen of the same class. But as the German is not forthcoming, I give my vote for the Englishman, provided only you love him. Ah, child, be sure of that. Do not mistake fancy for love. All women do not require love in marriage, but without it that which is best and highest in you would wither and die. Write to me often and tell me all. M. Savarin is right. My book is no longer my companion. It is gone from me, and I am once more alone in the world.

Yours affectionately.

P. S.—Is not your postscript a woman's? Does it not require a woman's postscript in reply? You say in yours that you have fully made up your mind to renounce all thoughts of the stage. I ask in mine, "What has the Englishman to do with that determination?"

# CHAPTER IV.

Some weeks have passed since Graham's talk with Isaura in the garden; he has not visited the villa since. His cousins the D'Altons have passed through Paris on their way to Italy, meaning to stay a few days; they stayed nearly a month, and monopolized much of Graham's companionship. Both these were reasons why, in the habitual society of the Duke, Graham's persuasion that he was not yet free to court the hand of Isaura became strengthened, and with that persuasion necessarily came a question equally addressed to his conscience. "If not yet free to court her hand, am I free to expose myself to the temptation of seeking to win her affection?" But when his cousin was gone, his heart began to assert its own rights, to argue its own case, and suggest modes of reconciling its dictates to the obligations which seemed to oppose them. In this hesitating state of mind he received the following note:—

*VILLA ———, LAC D'ENGHIEN.*

MY DEAR MR. VANE,—We have retreated from Paris to the banks of this beautiful little lake. Come and help to save Frank and myself from quarrelling with each other, which, until the Rights of Women are firmly established, married folks always will do when left to themselves, especially if they are still lovers, as Frank and I are. Love is a terribly quarrelsome thing. Make us a present of a few days out of your wealth of time. We will visit Montmorency and the haunts of Rousseau, sail on the lake at moonlight, dine at gypsy restaurants under trees not yet embrowned by summer heats, discuss literature and politics, "Shakspeare and the musical glasses,"—and be as sociable and pleasant as Boccaccio's tale-tellers, at Fiesole. We shall be but a small party, only the Savarins, that unconscious sage and humourist Signora Venosta, and that dimple-cheeked Isaura, who embodies the song of nightingales and the smile of summer. Refuse, and Frank shall not have an easy moment till he sends in his claims for thirty millions against the Alabama.

*Yours, as you behave,*
*LIZZIE MORLEY.*

Graham did not refuse. He went to Enghien for four days and a quarter. He was under the same roof as Isaura. Oh, those happy days! so happy that they defy description. But though to Graham the happiest days he had ever known, they were happier still to Isaura. There were drawbacks to his happiness, none to hers,—drawbacks partly from reasons the weight of which the reader will estimate later; partly from reasons the reader may at once comprehend and assess. In the sunshine of her joy, all the vivid colourings of Isaura's artistic temperament came forth, so that what I may call the homely, domestic woman-side of her nature faded into shadow. If, my dear reader, whether you be man or woman, you have come into familiar contact with some creature of a genius to which, even assuming that you yourself have a genius in its own way, you have no special affinities, have you not felt shy with that creature? Have you not, perhaps, felt how intensely you could love that creature, and doubted if that creature could possibly love you? Now I think that shyness and that disbelief are common with either man or woman, if, however conscious of superiority in the prose of life, he or she recognizes inferiority in the poetry of it. And yet this self-abasement is exceedingly mistaken. The poetical kind of genius is so grandly indulgent, so inherently deferential, bows with such unaffected modesty to the superiority in which it fears it may fail (yet seldom does fail),—the superiority of common-sense. And when we come to women, what marvellous truth is conveyed by the woman who has had no superior in intellectual gifts among her own sex! Corinne, crowned at the Capitol, selects out of the whole world as the hero of her love no rival poet and enthusiast, but a cold-blooded, sensible Englishman.

Graham Vane, in his strong masculine form of intellect—Graham Vane, from whom I hope much, if he live to fulfil his rightful career—had, not unreasonably, the desire to dominate the life of the woman whom he selected as the partner of his own; but the life of Isaura seemed to escape him. If at moments, listening to her, he would say to himself, "What a companion! life could never be dull with her," at other moments he would say, "True, never dull, but would it be always safe?" And then comes in that mysterious power of love which crushes all beneath its feet, and makes us end self-commune by that abject submission of reason, which only murmurs, "Better be unhappy with the one you love than happy with one whom you do not." All such self-communes were unknown to Isaura. She lived in the bliss of the hour. If Graham could have read her heart, he would have dismissed all doubt whether he could dominate her life. Could a Fate or an Angel have said to her, "Choose,—on one side I promise you the glories of a Catalani, a Pasta, a Sappho, a De Stael, a Georges Sand, all combined into one immortal name; or, on the other side, the whole heart of the man who would estrange himself from you if you had such combination of glories,"—her answer would have brought Graham Vane to her feet. All scruples, all doubts, would have vanished; he would have exclaimed, with the generosity inherent in the higher order of man, "Be glorious, if your nature wills it so. Glory enough to me that you would have resigned glory itself to become mine." But how is it that men worth a woman's loving become so diffident when they love intensely? Even in ordinary cases of love there is so ineffable a delicacy in virgin woman, that a man, be he how refined soever, feels himself rough and rude and coarse in comparison; and while that sort of delicacy was pre-eminent in this Italian orphan, there came, to increase the humility of the man so proud and so confident in himself when he had only men to deal with, the consciousness that his intellectual nature was hard and positive beside the angel-like purity and the fairy-like play of hers.

There was a strong wish on the part of Mrs. Morley to bring about the union of these two. She had a great regard and a great admiration for both. To her mind, unconscious of all Graham's doubts and prejudices, they were exactly suited to each other. A man of intellect so cultivated as Graham's, if married to a commonplace English "Miss," would surely feel as if life had no sunshine and no flowers. The love of an Isaura would steep it in sunshine, pave it with flowers. Mrs. Morley admitted—all American Republicans of gentle birth do admit—the instincts which lead "like" to match with "like," an equality of blood and race. With all her assertion of the Rights of Woman, I do not think that Mrs. Morley would ever have conceived the possibility of consenting that the richest and prettiest and cleverest girl in the States could become the wife of a son of hers if the girl had the taint of negro blood, even though shown nowhere save the slight distinguishing hue of her finger-nails. So had Isaura's merits been threefold what they were and she had been the wealthy heiress of a retail grocer, this fair Republican would have opposed (more strongly than many an English duchess, or at least a Scotch duke, would do, the wish of a son), the thought of an alliance between Graham Vane and the grocer's daughter! But Isaura was a Cicogna, an offspring of a very ancient and very noble house. Disparities of fortune, or mere worldly position, Mrs. Morley supremely despised. Here were the great parities of alliance,—parities in years and good looks and mental culture. So, in short, she in the invitation given to them had planned for the union between Isaura and Graham. To this plan she had an antagonist, whom she did not even guess, in Madame Savarin. That lady, as much attached to Isaura as was Mrs. Morley herself, and still more desirous of seeing a girl, brilliant and parentless, transferred from the companionship of Signora Venosta to the protection of a husband, entertained no belief in the serious attentions of Graham Vane. Perhaps she exaggerated his worldly advantages, perhaps she undervalued the warmth of his affections; but it was not within the range of her experience, confined much to Parisian life, nor in harmony with her notions of the frigidity and morgue of the English national character, that a rich and high-born young man, to whom a great career in practical public life was predicted, should form a matrimonial alliance with a foreign orphan girl, who, if of gentle birth, had no useful connections, would bring no correspondent dot, and had been reared and intended for the profession of the stage. She much more feared that the result of any attentions on the part of such a man would be rather calculated to compromise the orphan's name, or at least to mislead her expectations, than to secure her the shelter of a wedded home. Moreover, she had cherished plans of her own for Isaura's future. Madame Savarin had conceived for Gustave Rameau a friendly regard, stronger than that which Mrs. Morley entertained for Graham Vane, for it was more motherly. Gustave had been familiarized to her sight and her thoughts since he had first been launched into the literary world under her husband's auspices; he had confided to her his mortification in his failures, his joy in his successes. His beautiful countenance, his delicate health, his very infirmities and defects, had endeared him to her womanly heart. Isaura was the wife of all others who, in Madame Savarin's opinion, was made for Rameau. Her fortune, so trivial beside the wealth of the Englishman, would be a competence to Rameau; then that competence might swell into vast riches if Isaura succeeded on the stage. She found with extreme displeasure that Isaura's mind had become estranged from the profession to which she had been destined, and divined that a deference to the Englishman's prejudices had something to do with that estrangement. It was not to be expected that a Frenchwoman, wife to a sprightly man of letters, who had intimate friends and allies in every department of the artistic world, should cherish any prejudice whatever against the exercise of an art in which success achieved riches and renown; but she was prejudiced, as most Frenchwomen are, against allowing to unmarried girls the same freedom and independence of action that are the rights of women—French women—when married; and she would have disapproved the entrance of Isaura on her professional career until she could enter it as a wife, the wife of an artist, the wife of Gustave Rameau.

Unaware of the rivalry between these friendly diplomatists and schemers, Graham and Isaura glided hourly more and more down the current, which as yet ran smooth. No words by which love is spoken were exchanged between them; in fact, though constantly together, they were very rarely, and then but for moments, alone with each other. Mrs. Morley artfully schemed more than once to give them such opportunities for that mutual explanation of heart which, she saw, had not yet taken place; with art more practised and more watchful, Madame Savarin contrived to baffle her hostess's intention. But, indeed, neither Graham nor Isaura sought to make opportunities for themselves. He, as we know, did not deem himself wholly justified in uttering the words of love by which a man of honour binds himself for life; and she!—what girl pure-hearted and loving truly does not shrink from seeking the opportunities which it is for the man to court? Yet Isaura needed no words to tell her that she was loved,—no, nor even a pressure of the hand, a glance of the eye; she felt it instinctively, mysteriously, by the glow of her own being in the presence of her lover. She knew that she herself could not so love unless she were beloved.

Here woman's wit is keener and truthfuller than man's. Graham, as I have said, did not feel confident that he had reached the heart of Isaura. He was conscious that he had engaged her interest, that he had attracted her fancy; but often, when charmed by the joyous play of her imagination, he would sigh to himself, "To natures so gifted what single mortal can be the all in all."

They spent the summer mornings in excursions round the beautiful neighbourhood, dined early, and sailed on the calm lake at moonlight. Their talk was such as might be expected from lovers of books in summer holidays. Savarin was a critic by profession; Graham Vane, if not that, at least owed such literary reputation as he had yet gained to essays in which the rare critical faculty was conspicuously developed.

It was pleasant to hear the clash of these two minds encountering each other; they differed perhaps less in opinions than in the mode by which opinions are discussed. The Englishman's range of reading was wider than the Frenchman's, and his scholarship more accurate; but the Frenchman had a compact neatness of expression, a light and nimble grace, whether in the advancing or the retreat of his argument, which covered deficiencies, and often made them appear like merits. Graham was compelled, indeed, to relinquish many of the forces of superior knowledge or graver eloquence, which with less lively antagonists he could have brought into the field, for the witty sarcasm of Savarin would have turned them aside as pedantry or declamation. But though Graham was neither dry nor diffuse, and the happiness at his heart brought out the gayety of humour which had been his early characteristic, and yet rendered his familiar intercourse genial and playful, still there was this distinction between his humour and Savarin's wit,—that in the first there was always something earnest, in the last always something mocking. And in criticism Graham seemed ever anxious to bring out a latent beauty, even in writers comparatively neglected; Savarin was acutest when dragging forth a blemish never before discovered in writers universally read.

Graham did not perhaps notice the profound attention with which Isaura listened to him in these intellectual skirmishes with the more glittering Parisian. There was this distinction she made between him and Savarin,—when the last spoke she often chimed in with some happy sentiment of her own; but she never interrupted Graham, never intimated a dissent from his theories of art, or the deductions he drew from them; and she would remain silent and thoughtful for some minutes when his voice ceased. There was passing from his mind into hers an ambition which she imagined, poor girl, that he would be pleased to think he had inspired, and which might become a new bond of sympathy between them. But as yet the ambition was vague and timid,—an idea or a dream to be fulfilled in some indefinite future.

The last night of this short-lived holiday-time, the party, after staying out on the lake to a later hour than usual, stood lingering still on the lawn of the villa; and their host, who was rather addicted to superficial studies of the positive sciences, including, of course, the most popular of all, astronomy, kept his guests politely listening to speculative conjectures on the probable size of the inhabitants of Sirius, that very distant and very gigantic inhabitant of heaven who has led philosophers into mortifying reflections upon the utter insignificance of our own poor little planet, capable of producing nothing greater than Shakspeares and Newtons, Aristotles and Caesars,—mannikins, no doubt, beside intellects proportioned to the size of the world in which they flourish.

As it chanced, Isaura and Graham were then standing close to each other and a little apart from the rest. "It is very strange," said Graham, laughing low, "how little I care about Sirius. He is the sun of some other system, and is perhaps not habitable at all, except by Salamanders. He cannot be one of the stars with which I have established familiar acquaintance, associated with fancies and dreams and hopes, as most of us do, for instance, with Hesperus, the moon's harbinger and comrade. But amid all those stars there is one—not Hesperus—which has always had from my childhood a mysterious fascination for me. Knowing as little of astrology as I do of astronomy, when I gaze upon that star I become credulously superstitious, and fancy it has an influence on my life. Have you, too, any favourite star?"

"Yes," said Isaura; "and I distinguish it now, but I do not even know its name, and never would ask it."

"So like me. I would not vulgarize my unknown source of beautiful illusions by giving it the name it takes in technical catalogues. For fear of learning that name I never have pointed it out to any one before. I too at this moment distinguish it apart from all its brotherhood. Tell me which is yours."

Isaura pointed and explained. The Englishman was startled. By what strange coincidence could they both have singled out from all the host of heaven the same favourite star? "Cher Vane," cried Savarin, "Colonel Morley declares that what America is to the terrestrial system Sirius is to the heavenly. America is to extinguish Europe, and then Sirius is to extinguish the world."

"Not for some millions of years; time to look about us," said the Colonel, gravely. "But I certainly differ from those who maintain that Sirius recedes from us. I say that he approaches. The principles of a body so enlightened must be those of progress." Then addressing Graham in English, he added, "there will be a mulling in this fogified planet some day, I predicate. Sirius is a keener!"

"I have not imagination lively enough to interest myself in the destinies of Sirius in connection with our planet at a date so remote," said Graham, smiling. Then he added in a whisper to Isaura, "My imagination does not carry me further than to wonder whether this day twelvemonth—the 8th of July-we two shall both be singling out that same star, and gazing on it as now, side by side."

This was the sole utterance of that sentiment in which the romance of love is so rich that the Englishman addressed to Isaura during those memorable summer days at Enghien.

# CHAPTER V.

The next morning the party broke up. Letters had been delivered both to Savarin and to Graham, which, even had the day for departure not been fixed, would have summoned them away. On reading his letter, Savarin's brow became clouded. He made a sign to his wife after breakfast, and wandered away with her down an alley in the little garden. His trouble was of that nature which a wife either soothes or aggravates, according sometimes to her habitual frame of mind, sometimes to the mood of temper in which she may chance to be,—a household trouble, a pecuniary trouble.

Savarin was by no means an extravagant man. His mode of living, though elegant and hospitable, was modest compared to that of many French authors inferior to himself in the fame which at Paris brings a very good return in francs; but his station itself as the head of a powerful literary clique necessitated many expenses which were too congenial to his extreme good-nature to be regulated by strict prudence. His hand was always open to distressed writers and struggling artists, and his sole income was derived from his pen and a journal in which he was chief editor and formerly sole proprietor. But that journal had of late not prospered. He had sold or pledged a considerable share in the proprietorship. He had been compelled also to borrow a sum large for him, and the debt obtained from a retired bourgeois who lent out his moneys "by way," he said, "of maintaining an excitement and interest in life," would in a few days become due. The letter was not from that creditor; but it was from his publisher, containing a very disagreeable statement of accounts, pressing for settlement, and declining an offer of Savarin for a new book (not yet begun) except upon terms that the author valued himself too highly to accept. Altogether, the situation was unpleasant. There were many times in which Madame Savarin presumed to scold her distinguished husband for his want of prudence and thrift. But those were never the times when scolding could be of no use. It could clearly be of no use now. Now was the moment to cheer and encourage him; to reassure him as to his own undiminished powers and popularity, for he talked dejectedly of himself as obsolete and passing out of fashion; to convince him also of the impossibility that the ungrateful publisher whom Savarin's more brilliant successes had enriched could encounter the odium of hostile proceedings; and to remind him of all the authors, all the artists, whom he in their earlier difficulties had so liberally assisted, and from whom a sum sufficing to pay the bourgeois creditor when the day arrived could now be honourably asked and would be readily contributed. In this last suggestion the homely prudent good-sense of Madame Savarin failed her. She did not comprehend that delicate pride of honour which, with all his Parisian frivolities and cynicism, dignified the Parisian man of genius. Savarin could not, to save his neck from a rope, have sent round the begging-hat to friends whom he had obliged. Madame Savarin was one of those women with large-lobed ears, who can be wonderfully affectionate, wonderfully sensible, admirable wives and mothers, and yet are deficient in artistic sympathies with artistic natures. Still, a really good honest wife is such an incalculable blessing to her lord, that, at the end of the talk in the solitary alley, this man of exquisite finesse, of the undefinably high-bred temperament, and, alas! the painful morbid susceptibility, which belongs to the genuine artistic character, emerged into the open sunlit lawn with his crest uplifted, his lip curved upward in its joyous mockery, and perfectly persuaded that somehow or other he should put down the offensive publisher, and pay off the unoffending creditor when the day for payment came. Still he had judgment enough to know that to do this he must get back to Paris, and could not dawdle away precious hours in discussing the principles of poetry with Graham Vane.

There was only one thing, apart from "the begging-hat," in which Savarin dissented from his wife.—She suggested his starting a new journal in conjunction with Gustave Rameau, upon whose genius and the expectations to be formed from it (here she was tacitly thinking of Isaura wedded to Rameau, and more than a Malibran on the stage) she insisted vehemently. Savarin did not thus estimate Gustave Rameau, thought him a clever, promising young writer in a very bad school of writing, who might do well some day or other. But that a Rameau could help a Savarin to make a fortune! No; at that idea he opened his eyes, patted his wife's shoulder, and called her "enfant."

Graham's letter was from M. Renard, and ran thus:—

*MONSIEUR,—I had the honour to call at your apartment this morning,*
*and I write this line to the address given to me by your concierge*
*to say that I have been fortunate enough to ascertain that the*
*relation of the missing lady is now at Paris. I shall hold myself*
*in readiness to attend your summons. Deign to accept, Monsieur, the*
*assurance of my profound consideration.*
*J. RENARD.*

This communication sufficed to put Graham into very high spirits. Anything that promised success to his research seemed to deliver his thoughts from a burden and his will from a fetter. Perhaps in a few days he might frankly and honourably say to Isaura words which would justify his retaining longer, and pressing more ardently, the delicate hand which trembled in his as they took leave.

On arriving at Paris, Graham despatched a note to M. Renard requesting to see him, and received a brief line in reply that M. Renard feared he should be detained on other and important business till the evening, but hoped to call at eight o'clock. A few minutes before that hour he entered Graham's apartment.

"You have discovered the uncle of Louise Duval!" exclaimed Graham; "of course you mean M. de Mauleon, and he is at Paris?"

"True so far, Monsieur; but do not be too sanguine as to the results of the information I can give you. Permit me, as briefly as possible, to state the circumstances. When you acquainted me with the fact that M. de Mauleon was the uncle of Louise Duval, I told you that I was not without hopes of finding him out, though so long absent from Paris. I will now explain why. Some months ago, one of my colleagues engaged in the political department (which I am not) was sent to Lyons, in consequence of some suspicions conceived by the loyal authorities there of a plot against the emperor's life. The suspicions were groundless, the plot a mare's nest. But my colleague's attention was especially drawn towards a man not mixed up with the circumstances from which a plot had been inferred, but deemed in some way or other a dangerous enemy to the Government. Ostensibly, he exercised a modest and small calling as a sort of courtier or agent de change; but it was noticed that certain persons familiarly frequenting his apartment, or to whose houses he used to go at night, were disaffected to the Government,—not by any means of the lowest rank,—some of them rich malcontents who had been devoted Orleanists; others, disappointed aspirants to office or the 'cross;' one or two well-born and opulent fanatics dreaming of another Republic. Certain very able articles in the journals of the excitable Midi, though bearing another signature, were composed or dictated by this man,—articles evading the censure and penalties of the law, but very mischievous in their tone. All who had come into familiar communication with this person were impressed with a sense of his powers; and also with a vague belief that he belonged to a higher class in breeding and education than that of a petty agent de change. My colleague set himself to watch the man, and took occasions of business at his little office to enter into talk with him. Not by personal appearance, but by voice, he came to a conclusion that the man was not wholly a stranger to him,—a peculiar voice with a slight Norman breadth of pronunciation, though a Parisian accent; a voice very low, yet very distinct; very masculine, yet very gentle. My colleague was puzzled till late one evening he observed the man coming out of the house of one of these rich malcontents, the rich malcontent himself accompanying him. My colleague, availing himself of the dimness of light, as the two passed into a lane which led to the agent's apartment, contrived to keep close behind and listen to their conversation; but of this he heard nothing,—only, when at the end of the lane, the rich man turned abruptly, shook his companion warmly by the hand, and parted from him, saying, 'Never fear; all shall go right with you, my dear Victor.' At the sound of that name 'Victor,' my colleague's memories, before so confused, became instantaneously clear. Previous to entering our service, he had been in the horse business, a votary of the turf; as such he had often seen the brilliant 'sportman,' Victor de Mauleon; sometimes talked to him. Yes, that was the voice,—the slight Norman intonation (Victor de Mauleon's father had it strongly, and Victor had passed some of his early childhood in Normandy), the subdued modulation of speech which had made so polite the offence to men, or so winning the courtship to women,—that was Victor de Mauleon. But why there in that disguise? What was his real business and object? My confrere had no time allowed to him to prosecute such inquiries. Whether Victor or the rich malcontent had observed him at their heels, and feared he might have overheard their words, I know not; but the next day appeared in one of the popular journals circulating among the ouvriers a paragraph stating that a Paris spy had been seen at Lyons, warning all honest men against his machinations, and containing a tolerably accurate description of his person. And that very day, on venturing forth, my estimable colleague suddenly found himself hustled by a ferocious throng, from whose hands he was with great difficulty rescued by the municipal guard. He left Lyons that night; and for recompense of his services received a sharp reprimand from his chief. He had committed the worst offence in our profession, trop de zele. Having only heard the outlines of this story from another, I repaired to my confrere after my last interview with Monsieur, and learned what I now tell you from his own lips. As he was not in my branch of the service, I could not order him to return to Lyons; and I doubt whether his chief would have allowed it. But I went to Lyons myself, and there ascertained that our supposed Vicomte had left that town for Paris some months ago, not long after the adventure of my colleague. The man bore a very good character generally,—was said to be very honest and inoffensive; and the notice taken of him by persons of higher rank was attributed generally to a respect for his talents, and not on account of any sympathy in political opinions. I found that the confrere mentioned, and who alone could identify M. de Mauleon in the disguise which the Vicomte had assumed, was absent on one of those missions abroad in which he is chiefly employed. I had to wait for his return, and it was only the day before yesterday that I obtained the following particulars. M. de Mauleon bears the same name as he did at Lyons,—that name is Jean Lebeau; he exercises the ostensible profession of a 'letter-writer,' and a sort of adviser on business among the workmen and petty bourgeoisie, and he nightly frequents the cafe Jean Jacques, Rue Faubourg Montmartre. It is not yet quite half-past eight, and, no doubt, you could see him at the cafe this very night, if you thought proper to go."

"Excellent! I will go! Describe him!"

"Alas! that is exactly what I cannot do at present; for after hearing what I now tell you, I put the same request you do to my colleague, when, before he could answer me, he was summoned to the bureau of his chief, promising to return and give me the requisite description. He did not return; and I find that he was compelled, on quitting his chief, to seize the first train starting for Lille upon an important political investigation which brooked no delay. He will be back in a few days, and then Monsieur shall have the description."

"Nay; I think I will seize time by the forelock, and try my chance tonight. If the man be really a conspirator, and it looks likely enough, who knows but what he may see quick reason to take alarm and vanish from Paris at any hour?—Cafe Jean Jacques, Rue ———; I will go. Stay; you have seen Victor de Mauleon in his youth: what was he like then?"

"Tall, slender, but broad-shouldered, very erect, carrying his head high, a profusion of dark curls, a small black mustache, fair clear complexion, light-coloured eyes with dark lashes, fort bel homme. But he will not look like that now."

"His present age?"

"Forty-seven or forty-eight. But before you go, I must beg you to consider well what you are about. It is evident that M. de Mauleon has some strong reason, whatever it be, for merging his identity in that of Jean Lebeau. I presume, therefore, that you could scarcely go up to M. Lebeau, when you have discovered him, and say, 'Pray, Monsieur le Vicomte, can you give me some tidings of your niece, Louise Duval?' If you thus accosted him, you might possibly bring some danger on yourself, but you would certainly gain no information from him."

"True."

"On the other hand, if you make his acquaintance as M. Lebeau, how can you assume him to know anything about Louise Duval?"

"Parbleu! Monsieur Renard, you try to toss me aside on both horns of the dilemma; but it seems to me that, if I once make his acquaintance as M.

Lebeau, I might gradually and cautiously feel my way as to the best mode of putting the question to which I seek reply. I suppose, too, that the man must be in very poor circumstances to adopt so humble a calling, and that a small sum of money may smooth all difficulties."

"I am not so sure of that," said M. Renard, thoughtfully; "but grant that money may do so, and grant also that the Vicomte, being a needy man, has become a very unscrupulous one,—is there anything in your motives for discovering Louise Duval which might occasion you trouble and annoyance, if it were divined by a needy and unscrupulous man; anything which might give him a power of threat or exaction? Mind, I am not asking you to tell me any secret you have reasons for concealing, but I suggest that it might be prudent if you did not let M. Lebeau know your real name and rank; if, in short, you could follow his example, and adopt a disguise. But no; when I think of it, you would doubtless be so unpractised in the art of disguise that he would detect you at once to be other than you seem; and if suspecting you of spying into his secrets, and if those secrets be really of a political nature, your very life might not be safe."

"Thank you for your hint; the disguise is an excellent idea, and combines amusement with precaution. That this Victor de Mauleon must be a very unprincipled and dangerous man is, I think, abundantly clear. Granting that he was innocent of all design of robbery in the affair of the jewels, still, the offence which he did own—that of admitting himself at night by a false key into the rooms of a wife, whom he sought to surprise or terrify into dishonour—was a villanous action; and his present course of life is sufficiently mysterious to warrant the most unfavourable supposition. Besides, there is another motive for concealing my name from him: you say that he once had a duel with a Vane, who was very probably my father, and I have no wish to expose myself to the chance of his turning up in London some day, and seeking to renew there the acquaintance that I had courted at Paris. As for my skill in playing any part I may assume, do not fear; I am no novice in that. In my younger days I was thought clever in private theatricals, especially in the transformations of appearance which belong to light comedy and farce. Wait a few minutes, and you shall see."

Graham then retreated into his bedroom, and in a few minutes reappeared so changed, that Renard at first glance took him for a stranger. He had doffed his dress—which habitually, when in Capitals, was characterized by the quiet, indefinable elegance that to a man of the great world, high-bred and young, seems "to the manner born"—for one of those coarse suits which Englishmen are wont to wear in their travels, and by which they are represented in French or German caricatures,—loose jacket of tweed with redundant pockets, waistcoat to match, short dust-coloured trousers. He had combed his hair straight over his forehead, which, as I have said somewhere before, appeared in itself to alter the character of his countenance, and, without any resort to paints or cosmetics, had somehow or other given to the expression of his face an impudent, low-bred expression, with a glass screwed on to his right eye,—such a look as a cockney journeyman, wishing to pass for a "swell" about town, may cast on a servant-maid in the pit of a suburban theatre.

"Will it do, old fellow?" he exclaimed, in a rollicking, swaggering tone of voice, speaking French with a villanous British accent.

"Perfectly," said Renard, laughing. "I offer my compliments, and if ever you are ruined, Monsieur, I will promise you a place in our police. Only one caution,—take care not to overdo your part."

"Right. A quarter to nine; I'm off."

# CHAPTER VI.

There is generally a brisk exhilaration of spirits in the return to any special amusement or light accomplishment associated with the pleasant memories of earlier youth; and remarkably so, I believe, when the amusement or accomplishment has been that of the amateur stage-player. Certainly I have known persons of very grave pursuits, of very dignified character and position, who seem to regain the vivacity of boyhood when disguising look and voice for a part in some drawing-room comedy or charade. I might name statesmen of solemn repute rejoicing to raise and to join in a laugh at their expense in such travesty of their habitual selves.

The reader must not therefore be surprised, nor, I trust, deem it inconsistent with the more serious attributes of Graham's character, if the Englishman felt the sort of joyful excitement I describe, as, in his way to the cafe Jean Jacques, he meditated the role he had undertaken; and the joyousness was heightened beyond the mere holiday sense of humouristic pleasantry by the sanguine hope that much to effect his lasting happiness might result from the success of the object for which his disguise was assumed.

It was just twenty minutes past nine when he arrived at the cafe Jean Jacques. He dismissed the fiacre and entered.

The apartment devoted to customers comprised two large rooms. The first was the cafe properly speaking; the second, opening on it, was the billiard-room. Conjecturing that he should probably find the person of whom he was in quest employed at the billiard-table, Graham passed thither at once. A tall man, who might be seven-and-forty, with a long black beard, slightly grizzled, was at play with a young man of perhaps twenty-eight, who gave him odds,—as better players of twenty-eight ought to give odds to a player, though originally of equal force, whose eye is not so quick, whose hand is not so steady, as they were twenty years ago. Said Graham to himself, "The bearded man is my Vicomte." He called for a cup of coffee, and seated himself on a bench at the end of the room.

The bearded man was far behind in the game. It was his turn to play; the balls were placed in the most awkward position for him. Graham himself was a fair billiard-player, both in the English and the French game. He said to himself, "No man who can make a cannon there should accept odds." The bearded man made a cannon; the bearded man continued to make cannons; the bearded man did not stop till he had won the game. The gallery of spectators was enthusiastic. Taking care to speak in very bad, very English-French, Graham expressed to one of the enthusiasts seated beside him his admiration of the bearded man's playing, and ventured to ask if the bearded man were a professional or an amateur player.

"Monsieur," replied the enthusiast, taking a short cutty-pipe from his mouth, "it is an amateur, who has been a great player in his day, and is so proud that he always takes less odds than he ought of a younger man. It is not once in a month that he comes out as he has done to-night; but to-night he has steadied his hand. He has had six petits verres."

"Ah, indeed! Do you know his name?"

"I should think so: he buried my father, my two aunts, and my wife."

"Buried?" said Graham, more and more British in his accent; "I don't understand."

"Monsieur, you are English."

"I confess it."

"And a stranger to the Faubourg Montmartre."

"True."

"Or you would have heard of M. Giraud, the liveliest member of the State Company for conducting funerals. They are going to play La Poule."

Much disconcerted, Graham retreated into the cafe, and seated himself haphazard at one of the small tables. Glancing round the room, he saw no one in whom he could conjecture the once brilliant Vicomte.

The company appeared to him sufficiently decent, and especially what may be called local. There were some blouses drinking wine, no doubt of the cheapest and thinnest; some in rough, coarse dresses, drinking beer. These were evidently English, Belgian, or German artisans. At one table, four young men, who looked like small journeymen, were playing cards. At three other tables, men older, better dressed, probably shop-keepers, were playing dominos. Graham scrutinized these last, but among them all could detect no one corresponding to his ideal of the Vicomte de Mauleon. "Probably," thought he, "I am too late, or perhaps he will not be here this evening. At all events, I will wait a quarter of an hour." Then, the garcon approaching his table, he deemed it necessary to call for something, and, still in strong English accent, asked for lemonade and an evening journal. The garcon nodded and went his way. A monsieur at the round table next his own politely handed to him the "Galignani," saying in very good English, though unmistakably the good English of a Frenchman, "The English journal, at your service."

Graham bowed his head, accepted the "Galignani," and inspected his courteous neighbour. A more respectable-looking man no Englishman could see in an English country town. He wore an unpretending flaxen wig, with limp whiskers that met at the chin, and might originally have been the same colour as the wig, but were now of a pale gray,—no beard, no mustache. He was dressed with the scrupulous cleanliness of a sober citizen,—a high white neckcloth, with a large old-fashioned pin, containing a little knot of hair covered with glass or crystal, and bordered with a black framework, in which were inscribed letters,—evidently a mourning pin, hallowed to the memory of lost spouse or child,—a man who, in England, might be the mayor of a cathedral town, at least the town-clerk. He seemed suffering from some infirmity of vision, for he wore green spectacles. The expression of his face was very mild and gentle; apparently he was about sixty years old,—somewhat more.

Graham took kindly to his neighbour, insomuch that, in return for the "Galignani," he offered him a cigar, lighting one himself.

His neighbour refused politely.

"Merci! I never smoke, never; mon medecin forbids it. If I could be tempted, it would be by, an English cigar. Ah, how you English beat us in all things,—your ships, your iron, your tabac,—which you do not grow!"

This speech rendered literally as we now render it may give the idea of a somewhat vulgar speaker. But there was something in the man's manner, in his smile, in his courtesy, which did not strike Graham as vulgar; on the contrary, he thought within himself, "How instinctive to all Frenchmen good breeding is!"

Before, however, Graham had time to explain to his amiable neighbour the politico-economical principle according to which England, growing no tobacco, had tobacco much better than France, which did grow it, a rosy middle-aged monsieur made his appearance, saying hurriedly to Graham's neighbour, "I'm afraid I'm late, but there is still a good half-hour before us if you will give me my revenge."

"Willingly, Monsieur Georges. Garcon, the dominos."

"Have you been playing at billiards?" asked M. Georges.

"Yes, two games."

"With success?"

"I won the first, and lost the second through the defect of my eyesight; the game depended on a stroke which would have been easy to an infant,—I missed it."

Here the dominos arrived, and M. Georges began shuffling them; the other turned to Graham and asked politely if he understood the game.

"A little, but not enough to comprehend why it is said to require so much skill."

"It is chiefly an affair of memory with me; but M. Georges, my opponent, has the talent of combination, which I have not."

"Nevertheless," replied M. Georges, gruffly, "you are not easily beaten; it is for you to play first, Monsieur Lebeau." Graham almost started. Was it possible! This mild, limp-whiskered, flaxen-wigged man Victor de Mauleon, the Don Juan of his time; the last person in the room he should have guessed. Yet, now examining his neighbour with more attentive eye, he wondered at his stupidity in not having recognized at once the ci-devant gentilhomme and beau garcon. It happens frequently that our imagination plays us this trick; we form to ourselves an idea of some one eminent for good or for evil,—a poet, a statesman, a general, a murderer, a swindler, a thief. The man is before us, and our ideas have gone into so different a groove that he does not excite a suspicion; we are told who he is, and immediately detect a thousand things that ought to have proved his identity.

Looking thus again with rectified vision at the false Lebeau, Graham observed an elegance and delicacy of feature which might, in youth, have made the countenance very handsome, and rendered it still good-looking, nay, prepossessing. He now noticed, too, the slight Norman accent, its native harshness of breadth subdued into the modulated tones which bespoke the habits of polished society. Above all, as M. Lebeau moved his dominos with one hand, not shielding his pieces with the other (as M. Georges warily did), but allowing it to rest carelessly on the table, he detected the hands of the French aristocrat,—hands that had never done work; never (like those of the English noble of equal birth) been embrowned or freckled, or roughened or enlarged by early practice in athletic sports; but hands seldom seen save in the higher circles of Parisian life,—partly perhaps of hereditary formation, partly owing their texture to great care begun in early youth, and continued mechanically in after life,—with long taper fingers and polished nails; white and delicate as those of a woman, but not slight, not feeble; nervous and sinewy as those of a practised swordsman.

Graham watched the play, and Lebeau good-naturedly explained to him its complications as it proceeded; though the explanation, diligently attended to by M. Georges, lost Lebeau the game.

The dominos were again shuffled, and during that operation M. Georges said, "By the way, Monsieur Lebeau, you promised to find me a locataire for my second floor; have you succeeded?"

"Not yet. Perhaps you had better advertise in 'Les Petites Affiches.' You ask too much for the habitues of this neighbourhood,—one hundred francs a month."

"But the lodging is furnished, and well too, and has four rooms. One hundred francs are not much."

A thought flashed upon Graham. "Pardon, Monsieur," he said, "have you an appartement de garcon to let furnished?"

"Yes, Monsieur, a charming one. Are you in search of an apartment?"

"I have some idea of taking one, but only by the month. I am but just arrived at Paris, and I have business which may keep me here a few weeks. I do but require a bedroom and a small cabinet, and the rent must be modest. I am not a milord."

"I am sure we could arrange, Monsieur," said M. Georges, "though I could not well divide my logement. But one hundred francs a month is not much!"

"I fear it is more than I can afford; however, if you will give me your address, I will call and see the rooms,—say the day after to-morrow. Between this and then, I expect letters which may more clearly decide my movements."

"If the apartments suit you," said M. Lebeau, "you will at least be in the house of a very honest man, which is more than can be said of every one who lets furnished apartments. The house, too, has a concierge, with a handy wife who will arrange your rooms and provide you with coffee—or tea, which you English prefer—if you breakfast at home." Here M. Georges handed a card to Graham, and asked what hour he would call.

"About twelve, if that hour is convenient," said Graham, rising. "I presume there is a restaurant in the neighbourhood where I could dine reasonably."

"Je crois bien, half-a-dozen. I can recommend to you one where you can dine en prince for thirty sous. And if you are at Paris on business, and want any letters written in private, I can also recommend to you my friend here, M. Lebeau. Ay, and on affairs his advice is as good as a lawyer's, and his fee a bagatelle."

"Don't believe all that Monsieur Georges so flatteringly says of me," put in M. Lebeau, with a modest half-smile, and in English. "I should tell you that I, like yourself, am recently arrived at Paris, having bought the business and goodwill of my predecessor in the apartment I occupy; and it is only to the respect due to his antecedents, and on the score of a few letters of recommendation which I bring from Lyons, that I can attribute the confidence shown to me, a stranger in this neighbourhood. Still I have some knowledge of the world, and I am always glad if I can be of service to the English. I love the English"—he said this with a sort of melancholy earnestness which seemed sincere; and then added in a more careless tone,—"I have met with much kindness from them in the course of a chequered life."

"You seem a very good fellow,—in fact, a regular trump, Monsieur Lebeau," replied Graham, in the same language. "Give me your address. To say truth, I am a very poor French scholar, as you must have seen, and am awfully bother-headed how to manage some correspondence on matters with which I am entrusted by my employer, so that it is a lucky chance which has brought me acquainted with you."

M. Lebeau inclined his head gracefully, and drew from a very neat morocco case a card, which Graham took and pocketed. Then he paid for his coffee and lemonade, and returned home well satisfied with the evening's adventure.

# CHAPTER VII.

The next morning Graham sent for M. Renard, and consulted with that experienced functionary as to the details of the plan of action which he had revolved during the hours of a sleepless night.

"In conformity with your advice," said he, "not to expose myself to the chance of future annoyance, by confiding to a man so dangerous as the false Lebeau my name and address, I propose to take the lodging offered to me, as Mr. Lamb, an attorney's clerk, commissioned to get in certain debts, and transact other matters of business, on behalf of his employer's clients. I suppose there will be no difficulty with the police in this change of name, now that passports for the English are not necessary?"

"Certainly not. You will have no trouble in that respect."

"I shall thus be enabled very naturally to improve acquaintance with the professional letter-writer, and find an easy opportunity to introduce the name of Louise Duval. My chief difficulty, I fear, not being a practical actor, will be to keep up consistently the queer sort of language I have adopted, both in French and in English. I have too sharp a critic in a man so consummate himself in stage trick and disguise as M. Lebeau not to feel the necessity of getting through my role as quickly as I can. Meanwhile, can you recommend me to some magasin where I can obtain a suitable change of costume? I can't always wear a travelling suit, and I must buy linen of coarser texture than mine, and with the initials of my new name inscribed on it."

"Quite right to study such details; I will introduce you to a magasin near the Temple, where you will find all you want."

"Next, have you any friends or relations in the provinces unknown to M. Lebeau, to whom I might be supposed to write about debts or business matters, and from whom I might have replies?"

"I will think over it, and manage that for you very easily. Your letters shall find their way to me, and I will dictate the answers."

After some further conversation on that business, M. Renard made an appointment to meet Graham at a cafe near the Temple later in the afternoon, and took his departure.

Graham then informed his laquais de place that, though he kept on his lodgings, he was going into the country for a few days, and should not want the man's services till he returned. He therefore dismissed and paid him off at once, so that the laquais might not observe, when he quitted his rooms the next day, that he took with him no change of clothes, etc.

# CHAPTER VIII.

Graham Vane has been for some days in the apartment rented of M. Georges. He takes it in the name of Mr. Lamb,—a name wisely chosen, less common than Thompson and Smith, less likely to be supposed an assumed name, yet common enough not to be able easily to trace it to any special family. He appears, as he had proposed, in the character of an agent employed by a solicitor in London to execute sundry commissions and to collect certain outstanding debts. There is no need to mention the name of the solicitor; if there were, he could give the name of his own solicitor, to whose discretion he could trust implicitly. He dresses and acts up to his assumed character with the skill of a man who, like the illustrious Charles Fox, has, though in private representations, practised the stage-play in which Demosthenes said the triple art of oratory consisted; who has seen a great deal of the world, and has that adaptability of intellect which knowledge of the world lends to one who is so thoroughly in earnest as to his end that he agrees to be sportive as to his means.

The kind of language he employs when speaking English to Lebeau is that suited to the role of a dapper young underling of vulgar mind habituated to vulgar companionships. I feel it due, if not to Graham himself, at least to the memory of the dignified orator whose name he inherits, so to modify and soften the hardy style of that peculiar diction in which he disguises his birth and disgraces his culture, that it is only here and there that I can venture to indicate the general tone of it; but in order to supply my deficiencies therein, the reader has only to call to mind the forms of phraseology which polite novelists in vogue, especially young-lady novelists, ascribe to well-born gentlemen, and more emphatically to those in the higher ranks of the Peerage. No doubt Graham, in his capacity of critic, had been compelled to read, in order to review, those contributions to refined literature, and had familiarized himself to a vein of conversation abounding with "swell" and "stunner" and "awfully jolly," in its libel on manners and outrage on taste.

He has attended nightly the cafe Jean Jacques; he has improved acquaintance with M. Georges and M. Lebeau; he has played at billiards, he has played at dominos, with the latter. He has been much surprised at the unimpeachable honesty which M. Lebeau has exhibited in both these games. In billiards, indeed, a man cannot cheat except by disguising his strength; it is much the same in dominos,—it is skill combined with luck, as in whist; but in whist there are modes of cheating which dominos do not allow,—you can't mark a domino as you can a card. It was perfectly clear to Graham that M. Lebeau did not gain a livelihood by billiards or dominos at the cafe Jean Jacques. In the former he was not only a fair but a generous player. He played exceedingly well, despite his spectacles; but he gave, with something of a Frenchman's lofty fanfaronnade, larger odds to his adversary than his play justified. In dominos, where such odds could not well be given, he insisted on playing such small stakes as two or three francs might cover. In short, M. Lebeau puzzled Graham. All about M. Lebeau, his manner, his talk, was irreproachable, and baffled suspicion; except in this,—Graham gradually discovered that the cafe had a quasi-political character. Listening to talkers round him, he overheard much that might well have shocked the notions of a moderate Liberal; much that held in disdain the objects to which, in 1869, an English Radical directed his aspirations. Vote by ballot, universal suffrage, etc.,—such objects the French had already attained. By the talkers at the cafe Jean Jacques they were deemed to be the tricky contrivances of tyranny. In fact, the talk was more scornful of what Englishmen understand by radicalism or democracy than Graham ever heard from the lips of an ultra-Tory. It assumed a strain of philosophy far above the vulgar squabbles of ordinary party politicians,—a philosophy which took for its fundamental principles the destruction of religion and of private property. These two objects seemed dependent the one on the other. The philosophers of the Jean Jacques held with that expounder of Internationalism, Eugene Dupont, "Nous ne voulons plus de religion, car les religions etouffent l'intelligence."

*[Discours par Eugene Dupont a la Cloture du Congres de Bruxelles, Sept. 3, 1868]*

Now and then, indeed, a dissentient voice was raised as to the existence of a Supreme Being, but, with one exception, it soon sank into silence. No voice was raised in defence of private property. These sages appeared for the most part to belong to the class of ouvriers or artisans. Some of them were foreigners,—Belgian, German, English; all seemed well off for their calling. Indeed they must have had comparatively high wages, to judge by their dress and the money they spent on regaling themselves. The language of several was well chosen, at times eloquent. Some brought with them women who seemed respectable, and who often joined in the conversation, especially when it turned upon the law of marriage as a main obstacle to all personal liberty and social improvement. If this was a subject on which the women did not all agree, still they discussed it, without prejudice and with admirable sang froid. Yet many of them looked like wives and mothers. Now and then a young journeyman brought with him a young lady of more doubtful aspect, but such a couple kept aloof from the others. Now and then, too, a man evidently of higher station than that of ouvrier, and who was received by the philosophers with courtesy and respect, joined one of the tables and ordered a bowl of punch for general participation. In such occasional visitors, Graham, still listening, detected a writer of the press; now and then, a small artist or actor or medical student. Among the habitues there was one man, an ouvrier, in whom Graham could not help feeling an interest. He was called Monnier, sometimes more familiarly Armand, his baptismal appellation. This man had a bold and honest expression of countenance. He talked like one who, if he had not read much, had thought much on the subjects he loved to discuss. He argued against the capital of employers quite as ably as Mr. Mill has argued against the rights of property in land. He was still more eloquent against the laws of marriage and Heritage. But his was the one voice not to be silenced in favour of a Supreme Being. He had at least the courage of his opinions, and was always thoroughly in earnest. M. Lebeau seemed to know this man, and honoured him with a nod and a smile, when passing by him to the table he generally occupied. This familiarity with a man of that class, and of opinions so extreme, excited Graham's curiosity. One evening he said to Lebeau, "A queer fellow that you have just nodded to.

"How so?"

"Well, he has queer notions."

"Notions shared, I believe, by many of your countrymen?"

"I should think not many. Those poor simpletons yonder may have caught 'em from their French fellow-workmen, but I don't think that even the gobemouches in our National Reform Society open their mouths to swallow such wasps."

"Yet I believe the association to which most of those ouvriers belong had its origin in England."

"Indeed! what association?"

"The International."

"Ah, I have heard of that."

Lebeau turned his green spectacles full on Graham's face as he said slowly, "And what do you think of it?"

Graham prudently checked the disparaging reply that first occurred to him, and said, "I know so little about it that I would rather ask you."

"I think it might become formidable if it found able leaders who knew how to use it. Pardon me, how came you to know of this cafe? Were you recommended to it?"

"No; I happened to be in this neighbourhood on business, and walked in, as I might into any other cafe."

"You don't interest yourself in the great social questions which are agitated below the surface of this best of all possible worlds?"

"I can't say that I trouble my head much about them."

"A game at dominos before M. Georges arrives?"

"Willingly. Is M. Georges one of those agitators below the surface?"

"No, indeed. It is for you to play."

Here M. Georges arrived, and no further conversation on political or social questions ensued.

Graham had already called more than once at M. Lebeau's office, and asked him to put into good French various letters on matters of business, the subjects of which had been furnished by M. Renard. The office was rather imposing and stately, considering the modest nature of M. Lebeau's ostensible profession. It occupied the entire ground-floor of a corner house, with a front-door at one angle and a back-door at the other. The anteroom to his cabinet, and in which Graham had generally to wait some minutes before he was introduced, was generally well filled, and not only by persons who, by their dress and outward appearance, might be fairly supposed sufficiently illiterate to require his aid as polite letter-writers,—not only by servant-maids and grisettes, by sailors, zouaves, and journeymen workmen,—but not unfrequently by clients evidently belonging to a higher, or at least a richer, class of society,—men with clothes made by a fashionable tailor; men, again, who, less fashionably attired; looked like opulent tradesmen and fathers of well-to-do families,—the first generally young, the last generally middle-aged. All these denizens of a higher world were introduced by a saturnine clerk into M. Lebeau's reception-room, very quickly and in precedence of the ouvriers and grisettes.

"What can this mean?" thought Graham; "is it really that this humble business avowed is the cloak to some political conspiracy concealed,—the International Association?" And so pondering, the clerk one day singled him from the crowd and admitted him into M. Lebeau's cabinet. Graham thought the time had now arrived when he might safely approach the subject that had brought him to the Faubourg Montmartre.

"You are very good," said Graham, speaking in the English of a young earl in our elegant novels,—"you are very good to let me in while you have so many swells and nobs waiting for you in the other room. But, I say, old fellow, you have not the cheek to tell me that they want you to correct their cocker or spoon for them by proxy?"

"Pardon me," answered M. Lebeau in French, "if I prefer my own language in replying to you. I speak the English I learned many years ago, and your language in the beau monde, to which you evidently belong, is strange to me. You are quite right, however, in your surmise that I have other clients than those who, like yourself, think I could correct their verbs or their spelling. I have seen a great deal of the world,—I know something of it, and something of the law; so that many persons come to me for advice and for legal information on terms more moderate than those of an avoue. But my ante-chamber is full, I am pressed for time; excuse me if I ask you to say at once in what I can be agreeable to you to-day."

"Ah!" said Graham, assuming a very earnest look, "you do know the world, that is clear; and you do know the law of France, eh?"

"Yes, a little."

"What I wanted to say at present may have something to do with French law, and I meant to ask you either to recommend to me a sharp lawyer, or to tell me how I can best get at your famous police here."

"Police?"

"I think I may require the service of one of those officers whom we in England call detectives; but if you are busy now, I can call to-morrow."

"I spare you two minutes. Say at once, dear Monsieur, what you want with law or police."

"I am instructed to find out the address of a certain Louise Duval, daughter of a drawing-master named Adolphe Duval, living in the Rue ——in the year 1848."

Graham, while he thus said, naturally looked Lebeau in the face,—not pryingly, not significantly, but as a man generally does look in the face the other man whom he accosts seriously. The change in the face he regarded was slight, but it was unmistakable. It was the sudden meeting of the eyebrows, accompanied with the sudden jerk of the shoulder and bend of the neck, which betoken a man taken by surprise, and who pauses to reflect before he replies. His pause was but momentary,

"For what object is this address required?"

"That I don't know; but evidently for some advantage to Madame or Mademoiselle Duval, if still alive, because my employer authorizes me to spend no less than L100 in ascertaining where she is, if alive, or where she was buried, if dead; and if other means fail, I am instructed to advertise to the effect that if Louise Duval, or, in case of her death, any children of hers living in the year 1849, will communicate with some person whom I may appoint at Paris, such intelligence, authenticated, may prove to the advantage of the party advertised for. I am, however, told not to resort to this means without consulting either with a legal adviser or the police."

"Hem! have you inquired at the house where this lady was, you say, living in 1848?"

"Of course I have done that; but very clumsily, I dare say, through a friend, and learned nothing. But I must not keep you now. I think I shall apply at once to the police. What should I say when I get to the bureau?"

"Stop, Monsieur, stop. I do not advise you to apply to the police. It would be waste of time and money. Allow me to think over the matter. I shall see you this evening at the cafe Jean Jacques at eight o'clock. Till then do nothing."

"All right; I obey you. The whole thing is out of my way of business awfully. Bonjour."

# CHAPTER IX.

Punctually at eight o'clock Graham Vane had taken his seat at a corner table at the remote end of the cafe Jean Jacques, called for his cup of coffee and his evening journal, and awaited the arrival of M. Lebeau. His patience was not tasked long. In a few minutes the Frenchman entered, paused at the comptoir, as was his habit, to address a polite salutation to the well-dressed lady who there presided, nodded as usual to Armand Monnier, then glanced round, recognized Graham with a smile, and approached his table with the quiet grace of movement by which he was distinguished.

Seating himself opposite to Graham, and speaking in a voice too low to be heard by others, and in French, he then said,

"In thinking over your communication this morning, it strikes me as probable, perhaps as certain, that this Louise Duval or her children, if she have any, must be entitled to some moneys bequeathed to her by a relation or friend in England. What say you to that assumption, Monsieur Lamb?"

"You are a sharp fellow," answered Graham. "Just what I say to myself. Why else should I be instructed to go to such expense in finding her out? Most likely, if one can't trace her, or her children born before the date named, any such moneys will go to some one else; and that some one else, whoever he be, has commissioned my employer to find out. But I don't imagine any sum due to her or her heirs can be much, or that the matter is very important; for, if so, the thing would not be carelessly left in the hands of one of the small fry like myself, and clapped in along with a lot of other business as an off-hand job."

"Will you tell me who employed you?"

"No, I don't feel authorized to do that at present; and I don't see the necessity of it. It seems to me, on consideration, a matter for the police to ferret out; only, as I asked before, how should I get at the police?"

"That is not difficult. It is just possible that I might help you better than any lawyer or any detective."

"Why, did you ever know this Louise Duval?"

"Excuse me, Monsieur Lamb; you refuse me your full confidence; allow me to imitate your reserve."

"Oho!" said Graham; "shut up as close as you like; it is nothing to me. Only observe, there is this difference between us, that I am employed by another. He does not authorize me to name him, and if I did commit that indiscretion, I might lose my bread and cheese. Whereas you have nobody's secret to guard but your own, in saying whether or not you ever knew a Madame or Mademoiselle Duval; and if you have some reason for not getting me the information I am instructed to obtain, that is also a reason for not troubling you further. And after all, old boy" (with a familiar slap on Lebeau's stately shoulder), "after all, it is I who would employ you; you don't employ me. And if you find out the lady, it is you who would get the L100., not I."

M. Lebeau mechanically brushed, with a light movement of hand, the shoulder which the Englishman had so pleasantly touched, drew himself and chair some inches back, and said slowly,—

"Monsieur Lamb, let us talk as gentleman to gentleman. Put aside the question of money altogether; I must first know why your employer wants to hunt out this poor Louise Duval. It may be to her injury, and I would do her none if you offered thousands where you offer pounds. I forestall the condition of mutual confidence; I own that I have known her,—it is many years ago; and, Monsieur Lamb, though a Frenchman very often injures a woman from love, he is in a worse plight for bread and cheese than I am if he injures her for money."

"Is he thinking of the duchess's jewels?" thought Graham. "Bravo, mon vieux," he said aloud; "but as I don't know what my employer's motive in his commission is, perhaps you can enlighten me. How could his inquiry injure Louise Duval?"

"I cannot say; but you English have the power to divorce your wives. Louise Duval may have married an Englishman, separated from him, and he wants to know where he can find, in order to criminate and divorce her, or it may be to insist on her return to him."

"Bosh! that is not likely."

"Perhaps, then, some English friend she may have known has left her a bequest, which would of course lapse to some one else if she be not living."

"By gad!" cried Graham, "I think you hit the right nail on the head: c'est cela. But what then?"

"Well, if I thought any substantial benefit to Louise Duval might result from the success of your inquiry, I would really see if it were in my power to help you. But I must have time to consider."

"How long?"

"I can't exactly say; perhaps three or four days."

"Bon! I will wait. Here comes M. Georges. I leave you to dominos and him. Good-night."

Late that night M. Lebeau was seated alone in a chamber connected with the cabinet in which he received visitors. A ledger was open before him, which he scanned with careful eyes, no longer screened by spectacles. The survey seemed to satisfy him. He murmured, "It suffices, the time has come," closed the book, returned it to his bureau, which he locked up, and then wrote in cipher the letter here reduced into English:—

> *"DEAR AND NOBLE FRIEND,—Events march; the Empire is everywhere undermined. Our treasury has thriven in my hands; the sums subscribed and received by me through you have become more than quadrupled by advantageous speculations, in which M. Georges has been a most trustworthy agent. A portion of them I have continued to employ in the mode suggested,—namely, in bringing together men discreetly chosen as being in their various ways representatives and ringleaders of the motley varieties that, when united at the right moment, form a Parisian mob. But from that right moment we are as yet distant. Before we can call passion into action, we must prepare opinion for change. I propose now to devote no inconsiderable portion of our fund towards the inauguration of a journal which shall gradually give voice to our designs. Trust me to insure its success, and obtain the aid of writers who will have no notion of the uses to which they ultimately contribute. Now that the time has come to establish for ourselves an organ in the press, addressing higher orders of intelligence than those which are needed to destroy and incapable of reconstructing, the time has also arrived for the reappearance in his proper name and rank of the man in whom you take so gracious an interest. In vain you have pressed him to do so before; till now he had not amassed together, by the slow process of petty gains and constant savings, with such additions as prudent speculations on his own account might contribute, the modest means necessary to his resumed position; and*

*as he always contended against your generous offers, no consideration should ever tempt him either to appropriate to his personal use a single sou intrusted to him for a public purpose, or to accept from friendship the pecuniary aid which would abase him into the hireling of a cause. No! Victor de Mauleon despises too much the tools that he employs to allow any man hereafter to say, 'Thou also wert a tool, and hast been paid for thy uses.'*

*"But to restore the victim of calumny to his rightful place in this gaudy world, stripped of youth and reduced in fortune, is a task that may well seem impossible. To-morrow he takes the first step towards the achievement of the impossible. Experience is no bad substitute for youth, and ambition is made stronger by the goad of poverty.*

*"Thou shalt hear of his news soon."*

# BOOK V.

## CHAPTER I.

The next day at noon M. Louvier was closeted in his study with M. Gandrin.

"Yes," cried Louvier, "I have behaved very handsomely to the beau Marquis. No one can say to the contrary."

"True," answered Gandrin. "Besides the easy terms for the transfer of the mortgages, that free bonus of one thousand louis is a generous and noble act of munificence."

"Is it not! and my youngster has already begun to do with it as I meant and expected. He has taken a fine apartment; he has bought a coupe and horses; he has placed himself in the hands of the Chevalier de Finisterre; he is entered at the Jockey Club. Parbleu, the one thousand louis will be soon gone."

"And then?"

"And then! why, he will have tasted the sweets of Parisian life; he will think with disgust of the vieux manoir. He can borrow no more. I must remain sole mortgagee, and I shall behave as handsomely in buying his estates as I have behaved in increasing his income."

Here a clerk entered and said that a monsieur wished to see M. Louvier for a few minutes in private, on urgent business.

"Tell him to send in his card."

"He has declined to do so, but states that he has already the honour of your acquaintance."

"A writer in the press, perhaps; or is he an artist?"

"I have not seen him before, Monsieur, but he has the air tres comme il faut."

"Well, you may admit him. I will not detain you longer, my dear Gandrin. My homages to Madame. Bonjour."

Louvier bowed out M. Gandrin, and then rubbed his hands complacently. He was in high spirits. "Aha, my dear Marquis, thou art in my trap now. Would it were thy father instead," he muttered chucklingly, and then took his stand on the hearth, with his back to the fireless grate. There entered a gentleman exceedingly well dressed,—dressed according to the fashion, but still as became one of ripe middle age, not desiring to pass for younger than he was.

He was tall, with a kind of lofty ease in his air and his movements; not slight of frame, but spare enough to disguise the strength and endurance which belong to sinews and thews of steel, freed from all superfluous flesh, broad across the shoulders, thin in the flanks. His dark hair had in youth been luxuriant in thickness and curl; it was now clipped short, and had become bare at the temples, but it still retained the lustre of its colour and the crispness of its ringlets. He wore neither beard nor mustache, and the darkness of his hair was contrasted by a clear fairness of complexion, healthful, though somewhat pale, and eyes of that rare gray tint which has in it no shade of blue,—peculiar eyes, which give a very distinct character to the face. The man must have been singularly handsome in youth; he was handsome still, though probably in his forty-seventh or forty-eighth year, doubtless a very different kind of comeliness. The form of the features and the contour of the face were those that suit the rounded beauty of the Greek outline, and such beauty would naturally have been the attribute of the countenance in earlier days; but the cheeks were now thin, and with lines of care and sorrow between nostril and lip, so that the shape of the face seemed lengthened, and the features had become more salient.

Louvier gazed at his visitor with a vague idea that he had seen him before, and could not remember where or when; but at all events he recognized at the first glance a man of rank and of the great world.

"Pray be seated, Monsieur," he said, resuming his own easy-chair.

The visitor obeyed the invitation with a very graceful bend of his head, drew his chair near to the financier's, stretched his limbs with the ease of a man making himself at home, and fixing his calm bright eyes quietly on Louvier, said, with a bland smile,—

"My dear old friend, do you not remember me? You are less altered than I am."

Louvier stared hard and long; his lip fell, his cheek paled, and at last he faltered out, "Ciel! is it possible! Victor, the Vicomte de Mauleon?"

"At your service, my dear Louvier."

There was a pause; the financier was evidently confused and embarrassed, and not less evidently the visit of the "dear old friend" was unwelcome.

"Vicomte," he said at last, "this is indeed a surprise; I thought you had long since quitted Paris for good."

"'L'homme propose,' etc. I have returned, and mean to enjoy the rest of my days in the metropolis of the Graces and the Pleasures. What though we are not so young as we were, Louvier,—we have more vigour in us than the new generation; and though it may no longer befit us to renew the gay carousals of old, life has still excitements as vivid for the social temperament and ambitious mind. Yes, the roi des viveurs returns to Paris for a more solid throne than he filled before."

"Are you serious?"

"As serious as the French gayety will permit one to be."

"Alas, Monsieur le Vicomte! can you flatter yourself that you will regain the society you have quitted, and the name you have—"

Louvier stopped short; something in the Vicomte's eye daunted him.

"The name I have laid aside for convenience of travel. Princes travel incognito, and so may a simple gentilhomme. 'Regain my place in society,' say you? Yes; it is not that which troubles me."

"What does?"

"The consideration whether on a very modest income I can be sufficiently esteemed for myself to render that society more pleasant than ever. Ah, mon cher! why recoil? why so frightened? Do you think I am going to ask you for money? Have I ever done so since we parted; and did I ever do so before without repaying you? Bah! you roturiers are worse than the Bourbons. You never learn or unlearn. 'Fors non mutat genus.'"

The magnificent millionaire, accustomed to the homage of grandees from the Faubourg and lions from the Chaussee d'Antin, rose to his feet in superb wrath, less at the taunting words than at the haughtiness of mien with which they were uttered.

"Monsieur, I cannot permit you to address me in that tone. Do you mean to insult me?"

"Certainly not. Tranquillize your nerves, reseat yourself, and listen,—reseat yourself, I say."

Louvier dropped into his chair.

"No," resumed the Vicomte, politely, "I do not come here to insult you, neither do I come to ask money; I assume that I am in my rights when I ask Monsieur Louvier what has become of Louise Duval?"

"Louise Duval! I know nothing about her."

"Possibly not now; but you did know her well enough, when we two parted, to be a candidate for her hand. You did know her enough to solicit my good offices in promotion of your suit; and you did, at my advice, quit Paris to seek her at Aix-la-Chapelle."

"What! have you, Monsieur de Mauleon, not heard news of her since that day?"

"I decline to accept your question as an answer to mine. You went to Aix-la-Chapelle; you saw Louise Duval, at my urgent request she condescended to accept your hand."

"No, Monsieur de Mauleon, she did not accept my hand. I did not even see her. The day before I arrived at Aix-la-Chapelle she had left it,—not alone,—left it with her lover."

"Her lover! You do not mean the miserable Englishman who—"

"No Englishman," interrupted Louvier, fiercely. "Enough that the step she took placed an eternal barrier between her and myself. I have never even sought to hear of her since that day. Vicomte, that woman was the one love of my life. I loved her, as you must have known, to folly, to madness. And how was my love requited? Ah! you open a very deep wound, Monsieur le Vicomte."

"Pardon me, Louvier; I did not give you credit for feelings so keen and so genuine, nor did I think myself thus easily affected by matters belonging to a past life so remote from the present. For whom did Louise forsake you?"

"It matters not; he is dead."

"I regret to hear that; I might have avenged you."

"I need no one to avenge my wrong. Let this pass."

"Not yet. Louise, you say, fled with a seducer? So proud as she was, I can scarcely believe it."

"Oh, it was not with a roturier she fled; her pride would not have allowed that."

"He must have deceived her somehow. Did she continue to live with him?"

"That question, at least, I can answer; for though I lost all trace of her life, his life was pretty well known to me till its end; and a very few months after she fled he was enchained to another. Let us talk of her no more."

"Ay, ay," muttered De Mauleon, "some disgraces are not to be redeemed, and therefore not to be discussed. To me, though a relation, Louise Duval was but little known, and after what you tell me, I cannot dispute your right to say, 'Talk of her no more.' You loved her, and she wronged you. My poor Louvier, pardon me if I made an old wound bleed afresh."

These words were said with a certain pathetic tenderness; they softened Louvier towards the speaker.

After a short pause the Vicomte swept his hand over his brow, as if to dismiss from his mind a painful and obtrusive thought; then with a changed expression of countenance,—an expression frank and winning,—with voice and with manner in which no vestige remained of the irony or the haughtiness with which he had resented the frigidity of his reception, he drew his chair still nearer to Louvier's, and resumed: "Our situations, Paul Louvier, are much changed since we two became friends. I then could say, 'Open sesame' to whatever recesses, forbidden to vulgar footsteps, the adventurer whom I took by the hand might wish to explore. In those days my heart was warm; I liked you, Louvier,—honestly liked you. I think our personal acquaintance commenced in some gay gathering of young viveurs, whose behaviour to you offended my sense of good breeding?"

Louvier coloured and muttered inaudibly. De Mauleon continued: "I felt it due to you to rebuke their incivilities, the more so as you evinced on that occasion your own superiority in sense and temper, permit me to add, with no lack of becoming spirit."

Louvier bowed his head, evidently gratified.

"From that day we became familiar. If any obligation to me were incurred, you would not have been slow to return it. On more than one occasion when I was rapidly wasting money—and money was plentiful with you—you generously offered me your purse. On more than one occasion I accepted the offer; and you would never have asked repayment if I had not insisted on repaying. I was no less grateful for your aid." Louvier made a movement as if to extend his hand, but he checked the impulse.

"There was another attraction which drew me towards you. I recognized in your character a certain power in sympathy with that power which I imagined lay dormant in myself, and not to be found among the freluquets and lions who were my more habitual associates. Do you not remember some hours of serious talk we have had together when we lounged in the

Tuileries, or sipped our coffee in the garden of the Palais Royal?—hours when we forgot that those were the haunts of idlers, and thought of the stormy actions affecting the history of the world of which they had been the scene; hours when I confided to you, as I confided to no other man, the ambitious hopes for the future which my follies in the present, alas! were hourly tending to frustrate."

"Ay, I remember the starlit night; it was not in the gardens of the Tuileries nor in the Palais Royal,—it was on the Pont de la Concorde, on which we had paused, noting the starlight on the waters, that you said, pointing towards the walls of the Corps Legislatif, 'Paul, when I once get into the Chamber, how long will it take me to become First Minister of France?'"

"Did I say so?—possibly; but I was too young then for admission to the Chamber, and I fancied I had so many years yet to spare in idle loiterings at the Fountain of Youth. Pass over these circumstances. You became in love with Louise. I told you her troubled history; it did not diminish your love; and then I frankly favoured your suit. You set out for Aix-la-Chapelle a day or two afterwards; then fell the thunderbolt which shattered my existence, and we have never met again till this hour. You did not receive me kindly, Paul Louvier."

"But," said Louvier, falteringly, "but since you refer to that thunderbolt, you cannot but be aware that—that—"

"I was subjected to a calumny which I expect those who have known me as well as you did to assist me now to refute."

"If it be really a calumny."

"Heavens, man! could you ever doubt that?" cried De Mauleon, with heat; "ever doubt that I would rather have blown out my brains than allowed them even to conceive the idea of a crime so base?"

"Pardon me," answered Louvier, meekly, "but I did not return to Paris for months after you had disappeared. My mind was unsettled by the news that awaited me at Aix; I sought to distract it by travel,—visited Holland and England; and when I did return to Paris, all that I heard of your story was the darker side of it. I willingly listen to your own account. You never took, or at least never accepted, the Duchesse de — — —'s jewels; and your friend M. de — —- never sold them to one jeweller and obtained their substitutes in paste from another?"

The Vicomte made a perceptible effort to repress an impulse of rage; then reseating himself in his chair, and with that slight shrug of the shoulder by which a Frenchman implies to himself that rage would be out of place, replied calmly, "M. de N. did as you say, but of course not employed by me, nor with my knowledge. Listen; the truth is this,—the time has come to tell it. Before you left Paris for Aix I found myself on the brink of ruin. I had glided towards it with my characteristic recklessness, with that scorn of money for itself, that sanguine confidence in the favour of fortune, which are vices common to every roi des viveurs. Poor mock Alexanders that we spendthrifts are in youth! we divide all we have among others, and when asked by some prudent friend, 'What have you left for your own share?' answer, 'Hope.' I knew, of course, that my patrimony was rapidly vanishing; but then my horses were matchless. I had enough to last me for years on their chance of winning—of course they would win. But you may recollect when we parted that I was troubled,—creditors' bills before me—usurers' bills too,—and you, my dear Louvier, pressed on me your purse, were angry when I refused it. How could I accept? All my chance of repayment was in the speed of a horse. I believed in that chance for myself; but for a trustful friend, no. Ask your own heart now,—nay, I will not say heart,—ask your own common-sense, whether a man who then put aside your purse—spendthrift, vaurien, though he might be—was likely to steal or accept a woman's jewels. Va, mon pauvre Louvier, again I say, 'Fors non mutat genus.'"

Despite the repetition of the displeasing patrician motto, such reminiscences of his visitor's motley character—irregular, turbulent, the reverse of severe, but, in its own loose way, grandly generous and grandly brave—struck both on the common-sense and the heart of the listener; and the Frenchman recognized the Frenchman. Louvier doubted De Mauleon's word no more, bowed his head, and said, "Victor de Mauleon, I have wronged you; go on."

"On the day after you left for Aix came that horse-race on which my all depended: it was lost. The loss absorbed the whole of my remaining fortune; it absorbed about twenty thousand francs in excess, a debt of honour to De N., whom you called my friend. Friend he was not; imitator, follower, flatterer, yes. Still I deemed him enough my friend to say to him, 'Give me a little time to pay the money; I must sell my stud, or write to my only living relation from whom I have expectations.' You remember that relation,—Jacques de Mauleon, old and unmarried. By De N.'s advice I did write to my kinsman. No answer came; but what did come were fresh bills from creditors. I then calmly calculated my assets. The sale of my stud and effects might suffice to pay every sou that I owed, including my debt to De N.; but that was not quite certain. At all events, when the debts were paid I should be beggared. Well, you know, Louvier, what we Frenchmen are: how Nature has denied to us the quality of patience; how involuntarily suicide presents itself to us when hope is lost; and suicide seemed to me here due to honour, namely, to the certain discharge of my liabilities,—for the stud and effects of Victor de Mauleon, roi des viveurs, would command much higher prices if he died like Cato than if he ran away from his fate like Pompey. Doubtless De N. guessed my intention from my words or my manner; but on the very day in which I had made all preparations for quitting the world from which sunshine had vanished, I received in a blank envelope bank-notes amounting to seventy thousand francs, and the post-mark on the envelope was that of the town of Fontainebleau, near to which lived my rich kinsman Jacques. I took it for granted that the sum came from him. Displeased as he might have been with my wild career, still I was his natural heir. The sum sufficed to pay my debt to De N., to all creditors, and leave a surplus. My sanguine spirits returned. I would sell my stud; I would retrench, reform, go to my kinsman as the penitent son. The fatted calf would be killed, and I should wear purple yet. You understand that, Louvier?"

"Yes, yes; so like you. Go on."

"Now, then, came the thunderbolt! Ah! in those sunny days you used to envy me for being so spoilt by women. The Duchesse de — — — had conceived for me one of those romantic fancies which women without children and with ample leisure for the waste of affection do sometimes conceive for very ordinary men younger than themselves, but in whom they imagine they discover sinners to reform or heroes to exalt. I had been honoured by some notes from the Duchesse in which this sort of romance was owned. I had not replied to them encouragingly. In truth, my heart was then devoted to another,—the English girl whom I had wooed as my wife; who, despite her parents' retraction of their consent to our union when they learned how dilapidated were my fortunes, pledged herself to remain faithful to me, and wait for better days." Again De Mauleon paused in suppressed emotion, and then went on hurriedly: "No, the Duchesse did not inspire me with guilty passion, but she did inspire me with an affectionate respect. I felt that she was by nature meant to be a great and noble creature, and was, nevertheless, at that moment wholly misled from her right place amongst women by an illusion of mere imagination about a man who happened then to be very much talked about, and perhaps resembled some Lothario in the novels which she was always reading. We lodged, as you may remember, in the same house."

"Yes, I remember. I remember how you once took me to a great ball given by the Duchesse; how handsome I thought her, though no longer young; and you say right—how I did envy you, that night!"

"From that night, however, the Duc, not unnaturally, became jealous. He reproved the Duchesse for her too amiable manner towards a mauvais sujet like myself, and forbade her in future to receive my visits. It was then that these notes became frequent and clandestine, brought to me by her maid, who took back my somewhat chilling replies.

"But to proceed. In the flush of my high spirits, and in the insolence of magnificent ease with which I paid De N——— the trifle I owed him, something he said made my heart stand still."

"I told him that the money received had come from Jacques de Mauleon, and that I was going down to his house that day to thank him. He replied, 'Don't go; it did not come from him.' 'It must; see the post-mark of the envelope,—Fontainebleau.' 'I posted it at Fontainebleau.' 'You sent me the money, you!' 'Nay, that is beyond my means. Where it came from,' said this miserable, 'much more may yet come;' and then be narrated, with that cynicism so in vogue at Paris, how he had told the Duchesse (who knew him as my intimate associate) of my stress of circumstance, of his fear that I meditated something desperate; how she gave him the jewels to sell and to substitute; how, in order to baffle my suspicion and frustrate my scruples, he had gone to Fontainebleau and there posted the envelope containing the bank-notes, out of which he secured for himself the payment he deemed otherwise imperilled. De N. having made this confession, hurried down the stairs swiftly enough to save himself a descent by the window. Do you believe me still?"

"Yes; you were always so hot-blooded, and De N. so considerate of self, I believe you implicitly."

"Of course I did what any man would do; I wrote a hasty letter to the Duchesse, stating all my gratitude for an act of pure friendship so noble; urging also the reasons that rendered it impossible for a man of honour to profit by such an act. Unhappily, what had been sent was paid away ere I knew the facts; but I could not bear the thought of life till my debt to her was acquitted; in short, Louvier, conceive for yourself the sort of letter which I—which any honest man—would write, under circumstances so cruel."

"H'm!" grunted Louvier.

"Something, however, in my letter, conjoined with what De N. had told her as to my state of mind, alarmed this poor woman, who had deigned to take in me an interest so little deserved. Her reply, very agitated and incoherent, was brought to me by her maid, who had taken my letter, and by whom, as I before said, our correspondence had been of late carried on. In her reply she implored me to decide, to reflect on nothing till I had seen her; stated how the rest of her day was pre-engaged; and since to visit her openly had been made impossible by the Due's interdict, enclosed the key to the private entrance to her rooms, by which I could gain an interview with her at ten o'clock that night, an hour at which the Duc had informed her he should be out till late at his club. Now, however great the indiscretion which the Duchesse here committed, it is due to her memory to say that I am convinced that her dominant idea was that I meditated self-destruction; that no time was to be lost to save me from it; and for the rest she trusted to the influence which a woman's tears and adjurations and reasonings have over even the strongest and hardest men. It is only one of those coxcombs in whom the world of fashion abounds who could have admitted a thought that would have done wrong to the impulsive, generous, imprudent eagerness of a woman to be in time to save from death by his own hand a fellow-being for whom she had conceived an interest. I so construed her note. At the hour she named I admitted myself into the rooms by the key she sent. You know the rest: I was discovered by the Duc and by the agents of police in the cabinet in which the Duchesse's jewels were kept. The key that admitted me into the cabinet was found in my possession."

De Mauleon's voice here faltered, and he covered his face with a convulsive hand. Almost in the same breath he recovered from visible sign of emotion, and went on with a half laugh.

"Ah! you envied me, did you, for being spoiled by the women? Enviable position indeed was mine that night! The Duc obeyed the first impulse of his wrath. He imagined that I had dishonoured him; he would dishonour me in return. Easier to his pride, too, a charge against the robber of jewels than against a favoured lover of his wife. But when I, obeying the first necessary obligation of honour, invented on the spur of the moment the story by which the Duchesse's reputation was cleared from suspicion, accused myself of a frantic passion and the trickery of a fabricated key, the Due's true nature of gentilhomme came back. He retracted the charge which he could scarcely even at the first blush have felt to be well-founded; and as the sole charge left was simply that which men comme il faut do not refer to criminal courts and police investigations, I was left to make my bow unmolested and retreat to my own rooms, awaiting there such communciations as the Duc might deem it right to convey to me on the morrow.

"But on the morrow the Duc, with his wife and personal suite, quitted Paris en route for Spain; the bulk of his retinue, including the offending Abigail, was discharged; and, whether through these servants or through the police, the story before evening was in the mouth of every gossip in club or cafe,—exaggerated, distorted, to my ignominy and shame. My detection in the cabinet, the sale of the jewels, the substitution of paste by De N., who was known to be my servile imitator and reputed to be my abject tool, all my losses on the turf, my debts,—all these scattered fibres of flax were twisted together in a rope that would have hanged a dog with a much better name than mine. If some disbelieved that I could be a thief, few of those who should have known me best held me guiltless of a baseness almost equal to that of theft,—the exaction of profit from the love of a foolish woman."

"But you could have told your own tale, shown the letters you had received from the Duchesse, and cleared away every stain on your honour."

"How?—shown her letters, ruined her character, even stated that she had caused her jewels to be sold for the uses of a young roue! Ah, no, Louvier! I would rather have gone to the galleys."

"H'm!" grunted Louvier again.

"The Duc generously gave me better means of righting myself. Three days after he quitted Paris I received a letter from him, very politely written, expressing his great regret that any words implying the suspicion too monstrous and absurd to need refutation should have escaped him in the surprise of the moment; but stating that since the offence I had owned was one that he could not overlook, he was under the necessity of asking the only reparation I could make. That if it 'deranged' me to quit Paris, he would return to it for the purpose required; but that if I would give him the additional satisfaction of suiting his convenience, he should prefer to await my arrival at Bayonne, where he was detained by the indisposition of the Duchesse."

"You have still that letter?" asked Louvier, quickly. "Yes; with other more important documents constituting what I may call my pieces justificatives.

"I need not say that I replied stating the time at which I should arrive at Bayonne, and the hotel at which I should await the Duc's command. Accordingly I set out that same day, gained the hotel named, despatched to the Duc the announcement of my arrival, and was considering how I should obtain a second in some officer quartered in the town—for my soreness and resentment at the marked coldness of my former acquaintances at Paris had forbidden me to seek a second among any of that faithless number—when the Due himself entered my room. Judge of my amaze at seeing him in person; judge how much greater the amaze became when he advanced with a grave but cordial smile, offering me his hand!

"'Monsieur de Mauleon,' said he, 'since I wrote to you, facts have become known to me which would induce me rather to ask your friendship than call on you to defend your life. Madame la Duchesse has been seriously ill since we left Paris, and I refrained from all explanations likely to add to the hysterical excitement under which she was suffering. It is only this day that her mind became collected, and she herself then gave me her entire confidence. Monsieur, she insisted on my reading the letters that you addressed to her. Those letters, Monsieur, suffice to prove your innocence of any design against my peace. The Duchesse has so candidly avowed her own indiscretion, has so clearly established the distinction between indiscretion and guilt, that I have granted her my pardon with a lightened heart and a firm belief that we shall be happier together than we have been yet.'

"The Due continued his journey the next day, but he subsequently honoured me with two or three letters written as friend to friend, and in which you will find repeated the substance of what I have stated him to say by word of mouth."

"But why not then have returned to Paris? Such letters, at least, you might have shown, and in braving your calumniators you would have soon lived them down."

"You forget that I was a ruined man. When, by the sale of my horses, etc., my debts, including what was owed to the Duchesse, and which I remitted to the Duc, were discharged, the balance left to me would not have maintained me a week at Paris. Besides, I felt so sore, so indignant. Paris and the Parisians had become to me so hateful. And to crown all, that girl, that English girl whom I had so loved, on whose fidelity I had so counted—well, I received a letter from her, gently but coldly bidding me farewell forever. I do not think she believed me guilty of theft; but doubtless the offence I had confessed, in order to save the honour of the Duchesse, could but seem to her all sufficient! Broken in spirit, bleeding at heart to the very core, still self-destruction was no longer to be thought of. I would not die till I could once more lift up my head as Victor de Mauleon."

"What then became of you, my poor Victor?"

"Ah! that is a tale too long for recital. I have played so many parts that I am puzzled to recognize my own identity with the Victor de Mauleon whose name I abandoned. I have been a soldier in Algeria, and won my cross on the field of battle,—that cross and my colonel's letter are among my pieces justificatives; I have been a gold-digger in California, a speculator in New York, of late in callings obscure and humble. But in all my adventures, under whatever name, I have earned testimonials of probity, could manifestations of so vulgar a virtue be held of account by the enlightened people of Paris. I come now to a close. The Vicomte de Mauleon is about to re-appear in Paris, and the first to whom he announces that sublime avatar is Paul Louvier. When settled in some modest apartment, I shall place in your hands my pieces justificatives. I shall ask you to summon my surviving relations or connections, among which are the Counts de Vandemar, Beauvilliers, De Passy, and the Marquis de Rochebriant, with any friends of your own who sway the opinions of the Great World. You will place my justification before them, expressing your own opinion that it suffices; in a word, you will give me the sanction of your countenance. For the rest, I trust to myself to propitiate the kindly and to silence the calumnious. I have spoken; what say you?"

"You overrate my power in society. Why not appeal yourself to your high-born relations?"

"No, Louvier; I have too well considered the case to alter my decision. It is through you, and you alone, that I shall approach my relations. My vindicator must be a man of whom the vulgar cannot say, 'Oh, he is a relation,—a fellow-noble; those aristocrats whitewash each other.' It must be an authority with the public at large,—a bourgeois, a millionaire, a roi de la Bourse. I choose you, and that ends the discussion."

Louvier could not help laughing good-humouredly at the sang froid of the Vicomte. He was once more under the domination of a man who had for a time dominated all with whom he lived.

De Mauleon continued: "Your task will be easy enough. Society changes rapidly at Paris. Few persons now exist who have more than a vague recollection of the circumstances which can be so easily explained to my complete vindication when the vindication comes from a man of your solid respectability and social influence. Besides, I have political objects in view. You are a Liberal; the Vandemars and Rochebriants are Legitimists. I prefer a godfather on the Liberal side. Pardieu, mon ami, why such coquettish hesitation? Said and done. Your hand on it."

"There is my hand then. I will do all I can to help you."

"I know you will, old friend; and you do both kindly and wisely." Here De Mauleon cordially pressed the hand he held, and departed.

On gaining the street, the Vicomte glided into a neighbouring courtyard, in which he had left his fiacre, and bade the coachman drive towards the Boulevard Sebastopol. On the way, he took from a small bag that he had left in the carriage the flaxen wig and pale whiskers which distinguished M. Lebeau, and mantled his elegant habiliments in an immense cloak, which he had also left in the fiacre. Arrived at the Boulevard Sebastopol, he drew up the collar of the cloak so as to conceal much of his face, stopped the driver, paid him quickly, and, bag in hand, hurried on to another stand of fiacres at a little distance, entered one, drove to the Faubourg Montmartre, dismissed the vehicle at the mouth of a street not far from M. Lebeau's office, and gained on foot the private side-door of the house, let himself in with his latchkey, entered the private room on the inner side of his office, locked the door, and proceeded leisurely to exchange the brilliant appearance which the Vicomte de Mauleon had borne on his visit to the millionaire for the sober raiment and bourgeois air of M. Lebeau, the letter-writer.

Then after locking up his former costume in a drawer of his secretaire, he sat himself down and wrote the following lines:—

> *DEAR MONSIEUR GEORGES,—I advise you strongly, from information that*
> *has just reached me, to lose no time in pressing M. Savarin to repay the sum I recommended you to lend him, and for which you hold his bill due this day. The scandal of legal measures against a writer so distinguished should be avoided if possible. He will avoid it and get the money somehow; but he must be urgently pressed. If you neglect this warning, my responsibility is past. Agreez mes sentimens les plus sinceres.*
> *J. L.*

# CHAPTER II.

The Marquis de Rochebriant is no longer domiciled in an attic in the gloomy Faubourg. See him now in a charming appartement de garcon an premier in the Rue du Helder, close by the promenades and haunts of the mode. It had been furnished and inhabited by a brilliant young provincial from Bordeaux, who, coming into an inheritance of one hundred thousand francs, had rushed up to Paris to enjoy himself, and make his million at the Bourse. He had enjoyed himself thoroughly,—he had been a darling of the demi monde; he had been a successful and an inconstant gallant. Zelie had listened to his vows of eternal love, and his offers of unlimited cachemires; Desiree, succeeding Zelie, had assigned to him her whole heart—or all that was left of it—in gratitude for the ardour of his passion, and the diamonds and coupe which accompanied and attested the ardour; the superb Hortense, supplanting Desiree, received his visits in the charming apartment he furnished for her, and entertained him and his friends at the most delicate little suppers, for the moderate sum of four thousand francs a month. Yes, he had enjoyed himself thoroughly, but he had not made a million at the Bourse. Before the year was out, the one hundred thousand francs were gone. Compelled to return to his province, and by his hard-hearted relations ordained, on penalty of starvation, to marry the daughter of an avoue, for the sake of her dot and a share in the hated drudgery of the avoue's business,—his apartment was to be had for a tenth part of the original cost of its furniture. A certain Chevalier de Finisterre, to whom Louvier had introduced the Marquis as a useful fellow who knew Paris, and would save him from being cheated, had secured this bijou of an apartment for Alain, and concluded the bargain for the bagatelle of L500. The Chevalier took the same advantageous occasion to purchase the English well-bred hack and the neat coupe and horses which the Bordelais was also necessitated to dispose of. These purchases made, the Marquis had some five thousand francs (L200) left out of Louvier's premium of L1,000. The Marquis, however, did not seem alarmed or dejected by the sudden diminution of capital so expeditiously effected. The easy life thus commenced seemed to him too natural to be fraught with danger; and easy though it was, it was a very simple and modest sort of life compared with that of many other men of his age to whom Enguerrand had introduced him, though most of them had an income less than his, and few, indeed, of them were his equals in dignity of birth. Could a Marquis de Rochebriant, if he lived at Paris at all, give less than three thousand francs a year for his apartment, or mount a more humble establishment than that confined to a valet and a tiger, two horses for his coupe and one for the saddle? "Impossible," said the Chevalier de Finisterre, decidedly; and the Marquis bowed to so high an authority. He thought within himself, "If I find in a few months that I am exceeding my means, I can but dispose of my rooms and my horses, and return to Rochebriant a richer man by far than I left it."

To say truth, the brilliant seductions of Paris had already produced their effect, not only on the habits, but on the character and cast of thought, which the young noble had brought with him from the feudal and melancholy Bretagne.

Warmed by the kindness with which, once introduced by his popular kinsmen, he was everywhere received, the reserve or shyness which is the compromise between the haughtiness of self-esteem and the painful doubt of appreciation by others rapidly melted away. He caught insensibly the polished tone, at once so light and so cordial, of his new-made friends. With all the efforts of the democrats to establish equality and fraternity, it is among the aristocrats that equality and fraternity are most to be found. All gentilshommes in the best society are equals; and whether they embrace or fight each other, they embrace or fight as brothers of the same family. But with the tone of manners Alain de Rochebriant imbibed still more insensibly the lore of that philosophy which young idlers in pursuit of pleasure teach to each other. Probably in all civilized and luxurious capitals that philosophy is very much the same among the same class of idlers at the same age; probably it flourishes in Pekin not less than at Paris. If Paris has the credit, or discredit, of it more than any other capital, it is because in Paris more than in any other capital it charms the eye by grace and amuses the ear by wit. A philosophy which takes the things of this life very easily; which has a smile and a shrug of the shoulders for any pretender to the Heroic; which subdivides the wealth of passion into the pocket-money of caprices, is always in or out of love ankle-deep, never venturing a plunge; which, light of heart as of tongue, turns "the solemn plausibilities" of earth into subjects for epigrams and bons mots,—jests at loyalty to kings and turns up its nose at enthusiasm for commonwealths, abjures all grave studies and shuns all profound emotions. We have crowds of such philosophers in London; but there they are less noticed, because the agreeable attributes of the sect are there dimmed and obfuscated. It is not a philosophy that flowers richly in the reek of fogs and in the teeth of east winds; it wants for full development the light atmosphere of Paris. Now this philosophy began rapidly to exercise its charms upon Alain de Rochebriant. Even in the society of professed Legitimists, he felt that faith had deserted the Legitimist creed or taken refuge only as a companion of religion in the hearts of high-born women and a small minority of priests. His chivalrous loyalty still struggled to keep its ground, but its roots were very much loosened. He saw—for his natural intellect was keen—that the cause of the Bourbon was hopeless, at least for the present, because it had ceased, at least for the present, to be a cause. His political creed thus shaken, with it was shaken also that adherence to the past which had stifled his ambition of a future. That ambition began to breathe and to stir, though he owned it not to others, though, as yet, he scarce distinguished its whispers, much less directed its movements towards any definite object. Meanwhile, all that he knew of his ambition was the new-born desire for social success.

We see him, then, under the quick operation of this change in sentiments and habits, reclined on the fauteuil before his fireside, and listening to his college friend, of whom we have so long lost sight, Frederic Lemercier. Frederic had breakfasted with Alain,—a breakfast such as might have contented the author of the "Almanach des Gourmands," and provided from the cafe Anglais. Frederic has just thrown aside his regalia.

"Pardieu! my dear Alain. If Louvier has no sinister object in the generosity of his dealings with you, he will have raised himself prodigiously in my estimation. I shall forsake, in his favour, my allegiance to Duplessis, though that clever fellow has just made a wondrous coup in the Egyptians, and I gain forty thousand francs by having followed his advice. But if Duplessis has a head as long as Louvier's, he certainly has not an equal greatness of soul. Still, my dear friend, will you pardon me if I speak frankly, and in the way of a warning homily?"

"Speak; you cannot oblige me more."

"Well, then, I know that you can no more live at Paris in the way you are doing, or mean to do, without some fresh addition to your income, than a lion could live in the Jardin des Plantes upon an allowance of two mice a week."

"I don't see that. Deducting what I pay to my aunt,—and I cannot get her to take more than six thousand francs a year,—I have seven hundred napoleons left, net and clear. My rooms and stables are equipped, and I have twenty-five hundred francs in hand. On seven hundred napoleons a year, I calculate that I can very easily live as I do; and if I fail—well, I must return to Pochebriant. Seven hundred napoleons a year will be a magnificent rental there."

Frederic shook his head. "You do not know how one expense leads to another. Above all, you do not calculate the chief part of one's expenditure,—the unforeseen. You will play at the Jockey Club, and lose half your income in a night."

"I shall never touch a card."

"So you say now, innocent as a lamb of the force of example. At all events, beau seigneur, I presume you are not going to resuscitate the part of the Ermite de la Chaussee d'Antin; and the fair Parisiennes are demons of extravagance."

"Demons whom I shall not court."

"Did I say you would? They will court you. Before another month has flown you will be inundated with billets-doux."

"It is not a shower that will devastate my humble harvest. But, mon cher, we are falling upon very gloomy topics. Laissez-moi tranquille in my illusions, if illusions they be. Ah, you cannot conceive what a new life opens to the man who, like myself, has passed the dawn of his youth in privation and fear, when he suddenly acquires competence and hope. If it lasts only a year, it will be something to say 'Vixi.'"

"Alain," said Frederic; very earnestly, "believe me, I should not have assumed the ungracious and inappropriate task of Mentor, if it were only a year's experience at stake, or if you were in the position of men like myself,—free from the encumbrance of a great name and heavily mortgaged lands. Should you fail to pay regularly the interest due to Louvier, he has the power to put up at public auction, and there to buy in for himself, your chateau and domain."

"I am aware that in strict law he would have such power, though I doubt if he would use it. Louvier is certainly a much better and more generous fellow than I could have expected; and if I believe De Finisterre, he has taken a sincere liking to me on account of affection to my poor father. But why should not the interest be paid regularly? The revenues from Rochebriant are not likely to decrease, and the charge on them is lightened by the contract with Louvier. And I will confide to you a hope I entertain of a very large addition to my rental."

"How?"

"A chief part of my rental is derived from forests, and De Finisterre has heard of a capitalist who is disposed to make a contract for their sale at the fall this year, and may probably extend it to future years, at a price far exceeding that which I have hitherto obtained."

"Pray be cautious. De Finisterre is not a man I should implicitly trust in such matters."

"Why? Do you know anything against him? He is in the best society,—perfect gentilhomme,—and, as his name may tell you, a fellow-Breton. You yourself allow, and so does Enguerrand, that the purchases he made for me—in this apartment, my horses, etc.—are singularly advantageous."

"Quite true; the Chevalier is reputed sharp and clever, is said to be very amusing, and a first-rate piquet-player. I don't know him personally,—I am not in his set. I have no valid reason to disparage his character, nor do I conjecture any motive he could have to injure or mislead you. Still, I say, be cautious how far you trust to his advice or recommendation."

"Again I ask why?"

"He is unlucky to his friends. He attaches himself much to men younger than himself; and somehow or other I have observed that most of them have come to grief. Besides, a person in whose sagacity I have great confidence warned me against making the Chevalier's acquaintance, and said to me, in his blunt way, 'De Finisterre came to Paris with nothing; he has succeeded to nothing; he belongs to no ostensible profession by which anything can be made. But evidently now he has picked up a good deal; and in proportion as any young associate of his becomes poorer, De Finisterre seems mysteriously to become richer. Shun that sort of acquaintance.'"

"Who is your sagacious adviser!"

"Duplessis."

"Ah, I thought so. That bird of prey fancies every other bird looking out for pigeons. I fancy that Duplessis is, like all those money-getters, a seeker after fashion, and De Finisterre has not returned his bow."

"My dear Alain, I am to blame; nothing is so irritating as a dispute about the worth of the men we like. I began it, now let it be dropped; only make me one promise,—that if you should be in arrear, or if need presses, you will come at once to me. It was very well to be absurdly proud in an attic, but that pride will be out of place in your appartement au premier."

"You are the best fellow in the world, Frederic, and I make you the promise you ask," said Alain, cheerfully, but yet with a secret emotion of tenderness and gratitude. "And now, mon cher, what day will you dine with me to meet Raoul and Enguerrand, and some others whom you would like to know?"

"Thanks, and hearty ones, but we move now in different spheres, and I shall not trespass on yours. Je suis trop bourgeois to incur the ridicule of le bourgeois gentilhomme."

"Frederic, how dare you speak thus? My dear fellow, my friends shall honour you as I do."

"But that will be on your account, not mine. No; honestly that kind of society neither tempts nor suits me. I am a sort of king in my own walk; and I prefer my Bohemian royalty to vassalage in higher regions. Say no more of it. It will flatter my vanity enough if you will now and then descend to my coteries, and allow me to parade a Rochebriant as my familiar crony, slap him on the shoulder, and call him Alain."

"Fie! you who stopped me and the English aristocrat in the Champs Elysees, to humble us with your boast of having fascinated une grande dame,—I think you said a duchesse."

"Oh," said Lemercier, conceitedly, and passing his hand through his scented locks, "women are different; love levels all ranks. I don't blame Ruy Blas for accepting the love of a queen, but I do blame him for passing himself off as a noble,—a plagiarism, by the by, from an English play. I do not love the English enough to copy them. A propos, what has become of ce beau Grarm Varn? I have not seen him of late."

"Neither have I."

"Nor the belle Italienne?"

"Nor her," said Alain, slightly blushing.

At this moment Enguerrand lounged into the room. Alain stopped Lemercier to introduce him to his kinsman. "Enguerrand, I present to you M. Lemercier, my earliest and one of my dearest friends."

The young noble held out his hand with the bright and joyous grace which accompanied all his movements, and expressed in cordial words his delight to make M. Lemercier's acquaintance. Bold and assured as Frederic was in his own circles, he was more discomposed than set at ease by the gracious accost of a lion, whom he felt at once to be of a breed superior to his own. He muttered some confused phrases, in which ravi and flatte were alone audible, and evanished.

"I know M. Lemercier by sight very well," said Enguerrand, seating himself. "One sees him very often in the Bois; and I have met him in the Coulisses and the Bal Mabille. I think, too, that he plays at the Bourse, and is lie with M. Duplessis, who bids fair to rival Louvier one of these days. Is Duplessis also one of your dearest friends?"

"No, indeed. I once met him, and was not prepossessed in his favour."

"Nevertheless, he is a man much to be admired and respected."

"Why so?"

"Because he understands so well the art of making what we all covet,—money. I will introduce you to him."

"I have been already introduced."

"Then I will re-introduce you. He is much courted in a society which I have recently been permitted by my father to frequent,—the society, of the Imperial Court."

"You frequent that society, and the Count permits it?"

"Yes; better the Imperialists than the Republicans; and my father begins to own that truth, though he is too old or too indolent to act on it."

"And Raoul?"

"Oh, Raoul, the melancholy and philosophical Raoul, has no ambition of any kind, so long as—thanks somewhat to me—his purse is always replenished for the wants of his stately existence, among the foremost of which wants are the means to supply the wants of others. That is the true reason why he consents to our glove-shop. Raoul belongs, with some other young men of the Faubourg, to a society enrolled under the name of Saint Francois de Sales, for the relief of the poor. He visits their houses, and is at home by their sickbeds as at their stinted boards. Nor does he confine his visitations to the limits of our Faubourg; he extends his travels to Montmartre and Belleville. As to our upper world, he does not concern himself much with its changes. He says that we have destroyed too much ever to rebuild solidly; and that whatever we do build could be upset any day by a Paris mob, which he declares to be the only institution we have left. A wonderful fellow is Raoul,—full of mind, though he does little with it; full of heart, which he devotes to suffering humanity, and to a poetic, knightly reverence (not to be confounded with earthly love, and not to be degraded into that sickly sentiment called Platonic affection) for the Comtesse di Rimini, who is six years older than himself, and who is very faithfully attached to her husband, Raoul's intimate friend, whose honour he would guard as his own. It is an episode in the drama of Parisian life, and one not so uncommon as the malignant may suppose. Di Rimini knows and approves of his veneration; my mother, the best of women, sanctions it, and deems truly that it preserves Raoul safe from all the temptations to which ignobler youth is exposed. I mention this lest you should imagine there was anything in Raoul's worship of his star less pure than it is. For the rest, Raoul, to the grief and amazement of that disciple of Voltaire, my respected father, is one of the very few men I know in our circles who is sincerely religious,—an orthodox Catholic,—and the only man I know who practises the religion he professes; charitable, chaste, benevolent; and no bigot, no intolerant ascetic. His only weakness is his entire submission to the worldly common-sense of his good-for-nothing, covetous, ambitious brother Enguerrand. I cannot say how I love him for that. If he had not such a weakness, his excellence would gall me, and I believe I should hate him."

Alain bowed his head at this eulogium. Such had been the character that a few months ago he would have sought as example and model. He seemed to gaze upon a flattered portrait of himself as he had been.

"But," said Enguerrand, "I have not come here to indulge in the overflow of brotherly affection. I come to take you to your relation, the Duchesse of Tarascon. I have pledged myself to her to bring you, and she is at home on purpose to receive you."

"In that case I cannot be such a churl as to refuse. And, indeed, I no longer feel quite the same prejudices against her and the Imperialists as I brought from Bretagne. Shall I order my carriage?"

"No; mine is at the door. Yours can meet you where you will, later. Allons."

# CHAPTER III.

The Duchesse de Tarascon occupied a vast apartment in the Rue Royale, close to the Tuileries. She held a high post among the ladies who graced the brilliant court of the Empress. She had survived her second husband the duke, who left no issue, and the title died with him.

Alain and Enguerrand were ushered up the grand staircase, lined with tiers of costly exotics as if for a fete; but in that and in all kinds of female luxury, the Duchesse lived in a state of fete perpetuelle. The doors on the landing-place were screened by heavy portieres of Genoa velvet, richly embroidered in gold with the ducal crown and cipher. The two salons through which the visitors passed to the private cabinet or boudoir were decorated with Gobelin tapestries, fresh, with a mixture of roseate hues, and depicting incidents in the career of the first emperor; while the effigies of the late duke's father—the gallant founder of a short-lived race figured modestly in the background. On a table of Russian malachite within the recess of the central window lay, preserved in glass cases, the baton and the sword, the epaulettes and the decorations of the brave Marshal. On the consoles and the mantelpieces stood clocks and vases of Sevres that could scarcely be eclipsed by those in the Imperial palaces. Entering the cabinet, they found the Duchesse seated at her writing-table, with a small Skye terrier, hideous in the beauty of the purest breed, nestled at her feet. This room was an exquisite combination of costliness and comfort,—Luxury at home. The hangings were of geranium-coloured silk, with double curtains of white satin; near to the writing-table a conservatory, with a white marble fountain at play in the centre, and a trellised aviary at the back. The walls were covered with small pictures,—chiefly portraits and miniatures of the members of the imperial family, of the late Duc, of his father the Marshal and Madame la Marechale, of the present Duchesse herself, and of some of the principal ladies of the court.

The Duchesse was still in the prime of life. She had passed her fortieth year, but was so well "conserved" that you might have guessed her to be ten years younger. She was tall; not large, but with rounded figure inclined to en bon point; with dark hair and eyes, but fair complexion, injured in effect rather than improved by pearl-powder, and that atrocious barbarism of a dark stain on the eyelids which has of late years been a baneful fashion; dressed,—I am a man, and cannot describe her dress; all I know is that she had the acknowledged fame of the best-dressed subject of France. As she rose from her seat there was in her look and air the unmistakable evidence of grande dame,—a family likeness in feature to Alain himself, a stronger likeness to the picture of her first cousin (his mother) which was preserved at Rochebriant. Her descent was indeed from ancient and noble houses. But to the distinction of race she added that of fashion, crowning both with a tranquil consciousness of lofty position and unblemished reputation.

"Unnatural cousin!" she said to Alain, offering her hand to him, with a gracious smile,—"all this age in Paris, and I see you for the first time. But there is joy on earth as in heaven over sinners who truly repent. You repent truly—n'est ce pas?"

It is impossible to describe the caressing charm which the Duchesse threw into her words, voice, and look. Alain was fascinated and subdued.

"Ah, Madame la Duchesse," said he, bowing over the fait hand he lightly held, "it was not sin, unless modesty be a sin, which made a rustic hesitate long before he dared to offer his homage to the queen of the graces."

"Not badly said for a rustic," cried Enguerrand; "eh, Madame?"

"My cousin, you are pardoned," said the Duchesse. "Compliment is the perfume of gentilhommerie; and if you brought enough of that perfume from the flowers of Rochebriant to distribute among the ladies at court, you will be terribly the mode there. Seducer!"—here she gave the Marquis a playful tap on the cheek, not in a coquettish but in a mother-like familiarity, and looking at him attentively, said: "Why, you are even handsomer than your father. I shall be proud to present to their Imperial Majesties so becoming a cousin. But seat yourselves here, Messieurs, close to my arm-chair, caussons."

The Duchesse then took up the ball of the conversation. She talked without any apparent artifice, but with admirable tact; put just the questions about Rochebriant most calculated to please Alain, shunning all that might have pained him; asking him for descriptions of the surrounding scenery, the Breton legends; hoping that the old castle would never be spoiled by modernizing restorations; inquiring tenderly after his aunt, whom she had in her childhood once seen, and still remembered with her sweet, grave face; paused little for replies; then turned to Enguerrand with sprightly small-talk on the topics of the day, and every now and then bringing Alain into the pale of the talk, leading on insensibly until she got Enguerrand himself to introduce the subject of the emperor, and the political troubles which were darkening a reign heretofore so prosperous and splendid.

Her countenance then changed; it became serious, and even grave in its expression.

"It is true," she said, "that the times grow menacing, menacing not only to the throne, but to order and property and France. One by one they are removing all the breakwaters which the empire had constructed between the executive and the most fickle and impulsive population that ever shouted 'long live' one day to the man whom they would send to the guillotine the next. They are denouncing what they call personal government. Grant that it has its evils; but what would they substitute,—a constitutional monarchy like the English? That is impossible with universal suffrage and without an hereditary chamber. The nearest approach to it was the monarchy of Louis Philippe,—we know how sick they became of that. A republic?—mon Dieu! composed of Republicans terrified out of their wits at each other. The moderate men, mimics of the Girondins, with the Reds and the Socialists and the Communists, ready to tear them to pieces. And then—What then?—the commercialists, the agriculturists, the middle class combining to elect some dictator who will cannonade the mob and become a mimic Napoleon, grafted on a mimic Necker or a mimic Danton. Oh, Messieurs, I am French to the core. You inheritors of such names must be as French as I am; and yet you men insist on remaining more useless to France in the midst of her need than I am,—I, a woman who can but talk and weep."

The Duchesse spoke with a warmth of emotion which startled and profoundly affected Alain. He remained silent, leaving it to Enguerrand to answer.

"Dear Madame," said the latter, "I do not see how either myself or our kinsman can merit your reproach. We are not legislators. I doubt if there is a single department in France that would elect us, if we offered ourselves. It is not our fault if the various floods of revolution leave men of our birth and opinions stranded wrecks of a perished world. The emperor chooses his own advisers, and if they are bad ones, his Majesty certainly will not ask Alain and me to replace them."

"You do not answer—you evade me," said the Duchesse; with a mournful smile. "You are too skilled a man of the world, Monsieur Enguerrand, not to know that it is not only legislators and ministers that are necessary to the support of a throne, and the safeguard of a nation. Do you not see how great a help it is to both throne and nation when that section of public opinion which is represented by names illustrious in history, identified with records of chivalrous deeds and loyal devotion, rallies round the order established? Let that section of public opinion stand aloof, soured and discontented, excluded from active life, lending no counter-balance to the perilous oscillations of democratic passion, and tell me if it is not an enemy to itself as well as a traitor to the principles it embodies?"

"The principles it embodies, Madame," said Alain, "are those of fidelity to a race of kings unjustly set aside, less for the vices than the virtues of ancestors. Louis XV. was the worst of the Bourbons,—he was the bien aime: he escapes. Louis XVI. was in moral attributes the best of the Bourbons,—he dies the death of a felon. Louis XVIII., against whom much may be said, restored to the throne by foreign bayonets, reigning as a disciple of Voltaire might reign, secretly scoffing alike at the royalty and the religion which were crowned in his person, dies peacefully in his bed. Charles X., redeeming the errors of his youth by a reign untarnished by a vice, by a religion earnest and sincere, is sent into exile for defending established order from the very inroads which you lament. He leaves an heir against whom calumny cannot invent a tale, and that heir remains an outlaw simply because he descends from Henry IV., and has a right to reign. Madame, you appeal to us as among the representatives of the chivalrous deeds and loyal devotion which characterized the old nobility of France. Should we deserve that character if we forsook the unfortunate, and gained wealth and honour in forsaking?"

"Your words endear you to me. I am proud to call you cousin," said the Duchesse. "But do you, or does any man in his senses believe that if you upset the Empire you could get back the Bourbons; that you would not be in imminent danger of a Government infinitely more opposed to the theories on which rests the creed of Legitimists than that of Louis Napoleon? After all, what is there in the loyalty of you Bourbonites that has in it the solid worth of an argument which can appeal to the comprehension of mankind, except it be the principle of a hereditary monarchy? Nobody nowadays can maintain the right divine of a single regal family to impose itself upon a nation. That dogma has ceased to be a living principle; it is only a dead reminiscence. But the institution of monarchy is a principle strong and vital, and appealing to the practical interests of vast sections of society. Would you sacrifice the principle which concerns the welfare of millions, because you cannot embody it in the person of an individual utterly insignificant in himself? In a word, if you prefer monarchy to the hazard of republicanism for such a country as France, accept the monarchy you find, since it is quite clear you cannot rebuild the monarchy you would prefer. Does it not embrace all the great objects for which you call yourself Legitimist? Under it religion is honoured, a national Church secured, in reality if not in name; under it you have united the votes of millions to the establishment of the throne; under it all the material interests of the country, commercial, agricultural, have advanced with an unequalled rapidity of progress; under it Paris has become the wonder of the world for riches, for splendour, for grace and beauty; under it the old traditional enemies of France have been humbled and rendered impotent. The policy of Richelieu has been achieved in the abasement of Austria; the policy of Napoleon I. has been consummated in the salvation of Europe from the semi-barbarous ambition of Russia. England no longer casts her trident in the opposition scale of the balance of European power. Satisfied with the honour of our alliance, she has lost every other ally; and her forces neglected, her spirit enervated, her statesmen dreaming believers in the safety of their island, provided they withdraw from the affairs of Europe, may sometimes scold us, but will certainly not dare to fight. With France she is but an inferior satellite; without France she is—nothing. Add to all this a court more brilliant than that of Louis XIV., a sovereign not indeed without faults and errors, but singularly mild in his nature, warm-hearted to friends, forgiving to foes, whom personally no one could familiarly know and not be charmed with a bonte of character, lovable as that of Henri IV.,—and tell me what more than all this could you expect from the reign of a Bourbon?"

"With such results," said Alain, "from the monarchy you so eloquently praise, I fail to discover what the emperor's throne could possibly gain by a few powerless converts from an unpopular, and you say, no doubt truly, from a hopeless cause."

"I say monarchy gains much by the loyal adhesion of any man of courage, ability, and honour. Every new monarchy gains much by conversions from the ranks by which the older monarchies were strengthened and adorned. But I do not here invoke your aid merely to this monarchy, my cousin; I demand your devotion to the interests of France; I demand that you should not rest an outlaw from her service. Ah, you think that France is in no danger, that you may desert or oppose the Empire as you list, and that society will remain safe! You are mistaken. Ask Enguerrand."

"Madame," said Enguerrand, "you overrate my political knowledge in that appeal; but, honestly speaking, I subscribe to your reasonings. I agree with you that the empire sorely needs the support of men of honour; it has one cause of rot which now undermines it,—dishonest jobbery in its administrative departments; even in that of the army, which apparently is so heeded and cared for. I agree with you that France is in danger, and may need the swords of all her better sons, whether against the foreigner or against her worst enemies,—the mobs of her great towns. I myself received a military education, and but for my reluctance to separate myself from my father and Raoul, I should be a candidate for employments more congenial to me than those of the Bourse and my trade in the glove-shop. But Alain is happily free from all family ties, and Alain knows that my advice to him is not hostile to your exhortations."

"I am glad to think he is under so salutary an influence," said the Duchesse; and seeing that Alain remained silent and thoughtful, she wisely changed the subject, and shortly afterwards the two friends took leave.

# CHAPTER IV.

Three days elapsed before Graham again saw M. Lebeau. The letter-writer did not show himself at the cafe, and was not to be found at his office, the ordinary business of which was transacted by his clerk, saying that his master was much engaged on important matters that took him from home.

Graham naturally thought that these matters concerned the discovery of Louise Duval, and was reconciled to suspense. At the cafe, awaiting Lebeau, he had slid into some acquaintance with the ouvrier Armand Monnier, whose face and talk had before excited his interest. Indeed, the acquaintance had been commenced by the ouvrier, who seated himself at a table near to Graham's, and, after looking at him earnestly for some minutes, said, "You are waiting for your antagonist at dominos, M. Lebeau,—a very remarkable man."

"So he seems. I know, however, but little of him. You, perhaps, have known him longer?"

"Several months. Many of your countrymen frequent this cafe, but you do not seem to care to associate with the blouses."

"It is not that; but we islanders are shy, and don't make acquaintance with each other readily. By the way, since you so courteously accost me, I may take the liberty of saying that I overheard you defend the other night, against one of my countrymen, who seemed to me to talk great nonsense, the existence of le bon Dieu. You had much the best of it. I rather gathered from your argument that you went somewhat further, and were not too enlightened to admit of Christianity."

Armand Monnier looked pleased. He liked praise; and he liked to hear himself talk, and he plunged at once into a very complicated sort of Christianity,—partly Arian, partly Saint Simonian, with a little of Rousseau and a great deal of Armand Monnier. Into this we need not follow him; but, in sum, it was a sort of Christianity, the main heads of which consisted in the removal of your neighbour's landmarks, in the right of the poor to appropriate the property of the rich, in the right of love to dispense with marriage, and the duty of the State to provide for any children that might result from such union,—the parents being incapacitated to do so, as whatever they might leave was due to the treasury in common. Graham listened to these doctrines with melancholy not unmixed with contempt. "Are these opinions of yours," he asked, "derived from reading or your own reflection?"

"Well, from both, but from circumstances in life that induced me to read and reflect. I am one of the many victims of the tyrannical law of marriage. When very young I married a woman who made me miserable, and then forsook me. Morally, she has ceased to be my wife; legally, she is. I then met with another woman who suits me, who loves me. She lives with me; I cannot marry her; she has to submit to humiliations, to be called contemptuously an ouvrier's mistress. Then, though before I was only a Republican, I felt there was something wrong in society which needed a greater change than that of a merely political government; and then, too, when I was all troubled and sore, I chanced to read one of Madame de Grantmesnil's books. A glorious genius that woman's!"

"She has genius, certainly," said Graham, with a keen pang at his heart,—Madame de Grantmesnil, the dearest friend of Isaura! "But," he added, "though I believe that eloquent author has indirectly assailed certain social institutions, including that of marriage, I am perfectly persuaded that she never designed to effect such complete overthrow of the system which all civilized communities have hitherto held in reverence as your doctrines would attempt; and, after all, she but expresses her ideas through the medium of fabulous incidents and characters. And men of your sense should not look for a creed in the fictions of poets and romance-writers."

"Ah," said Monnier, "I dare say neither Madame de Grantmesnil nor even Rousseau ever even guessed the ideas they awoke in their readers; but one idea leads on to another. And genuine poetry and romance touch the heart so much more than dry treatises. In a word, Madame de Grantmesnil's book set me thinking; and then I read other books, and talked with clever men, and educated myself. And so I became the man I am." Here, with a self-satisfied air, Monnier bowed to the Englishman, and joined a group at the other end of the room.

The next evening, just before dusk, Graham Vane was seated musingly in his own apartment in the Faubourg Montmartre, when there came a slight knock at his door. He was so wrapped in thought that he did not hear the sound, though twice repeated. The door opened gently, and M. Lebeau appeared on the threshold. The room was lighted only by the gas-lamp from the street without.

Lebeau advanced through the gloom, and quietly seated himself in the corner of the fireplace opposite to Graham before he spoke. "A thousand pardons for disturbing your slumbers, Monsieur Lamb."

Startled then by the voice so near him, Graham raised his head, looked round, and beheld very indistinctly the person seated so near him.

"Monsieur Lebeau?"

"At your service. I promise to give an answer to your question; accept my apologies that it has been deferred so long. I shall not this evening go to our cafe. I took the liberty of calling—"

"Monsieur Lebeau, you are a brick."

"A what, Monsieur!—a brique?"

"I forgot; you are not up to our fashionable London idioms. A brick means a jolly fellow, and it is very kind in you to call. What is your decision?"

"Monsieur, I can give you some information, but it is so slight that I offer it gratis, and forego all thought of undertaking further inquiries. They could only be prosecuted in another country, and it would not be worth my while to leave Paris on the chance of gaining so trifling a reward as you propose. Judge for yourself. In the year 1849, and in the month of July, Louise Duval left Paris for Aix-la-Chapelle. There she remained some weeks, and then left it. I can learn no further traces of her movements."

"Aix-la-Chapelle! What could she do there?"

"It is a Spa in great request; crowded during the summer season with visitors from all countries. She might have gone there for health or for pleasure."

"Do you think that one could learn more at the Spa itself if one went there?"

"Possibly. But it is so long,—twenty years ago."

"She might have revisited the place."

"Certainly; but I know no more." "Was she there under the same name,—Duval?"

"I am sure of that."

"Do you think she left it alone or with others? You tell me she was awfully belle; she might have attracted admirers."

"If," answered Lebeau, reluctantly, "I could believe the report of my informant, Louise Duval left Aix not alone, but with some gallant; not an Englishman. They are said to have parted soon, and the man is now dead.

But, speaking frankly, I do not think Mademoiselle Duval would have thus compromised her honour and sacrificed her future. I believe she would have scorned all proposals that were not those of marriage. But all I can say for certainty is that nothing is known to me of her fate since she quitted Aix-la-Chapelle."

"In 1849? She had then a child living."

"A child? I never heard that she had any child; and I do not believe she could have had any child in 1849."

Graham mused. Somewhat less than five years after 1849 Louise Duval had been seen at Aix-la-Chapelle. Possibly she found some attraction at that place, and might yet be discovered there. "Monsieur Lebeau," said Graham, "you know this lady by sight; you would recognize her in spite of the lapse of years. Will you go to Aix and find out there what you can? Of course, expenses will be paid, and the reward will be given if you succeed."

"I cannot oblige you. My interest in this poor lady is not very strong, though I should be willing to serve her, and glad to know that she were alive. I have now business on hand which interests me much more, and which will take me from Paris, but not in the direction of Aix."

"If I wrote to my employer, and got him to raise the reward to some higher amount, that might make it worth your while?"

"I should still answer that my affairs will not permit such a journey. But if there be any chance of tracing Louise Duval at Aix,—and there may be,—you would succeed quite as well as I should. You must judge for yourself if it be worth your trouble to attempt such a task; and if you do attempt it, and do succeed, pray let me know.—A line to my office will reach me for some little time, even if I am absent from Paris. Adieu, Monsieur Lamb."

Here M. Lebeau Lose and departed.

Graham relapsed into thought; but a train of thought much more active, much more concentred than before. "No," thus ran his meditations,—"no, it would not be safe to employ that man further. The reasons that forbid me to offer any very high reward for the discovery of this woman operate still more strongly against tendering to her own relation a sum that might indeed secure his aid, but would unquestionably arouse his suspicions, and perhaps drag into light all that must be concealed. Oh, this cruel mission! I am, indeed, an impostor to myself till it be fulfilled. I will go to Aix, and take Renard with me. I am impatient till I set out, but I cannot quit Paris without once more seeing Isaura. She consents to relinquish the stage; surely I could wean her too from intimate friendship with a woman whose genius has so fatal an effect upon enthusiastic minds. And then—and then?"

He fell into a delightful revery; and contemplating Isaura as his future wife, he surrounded her sweet image with all those attributes of dignity and respect with which an Englishman is accustomed to invest the destined bearer of his name, the gentle sovereign of his household, the sacred mother of his children. In this picture the more brilliant qualities of Isaura found, perhaps, but faint presentation. Her glow of sentiment, her play of fancy, her artistic yearnings for truths remote, for the invisible fairyland of beautiful romance, receded into the background of the picture. It was all these, no doubt, that had so strengthened and enriched the love at first sight, which had shaken the equilibrium of his positive existence; and yet he now viewed all these as subordinate to the one image of mild decorous matronage into which wedlock was to transform the child of genius, longing for angel wings and unlimited space.

# CHAPTER V.

On quitting the sorry apartment of the false M. Lamb, Lebeau walked on with slow steps and bended head, like a man absorbed in thought. He threaded a labyrinth of obscure streets, no longer in the Faubourg Montmartre, and dived at last into one of the few courts which preserve the cachet of the moyen age untouched by the ruthless spirit of improvement which during the second empire has so altered the face of Paris. At the bottom of the court stood a large house, much dilapidated, but bearing the trace of former grandeur in pilasters and fretwork in the style of the Renaissance, and a defaced coat of arms, surmounted with a ducal coronet, over the doorway. The house had the aspect of desertion: many of the windows were broken; others were jealously closed with mouldering shutters. The door stood ajar; Lebeau pushed it open, and the action set in movement a bell within a porter's lodge. The house, then, was not uninhabited; it retained the dignity of a concierge. A man with a large grizzled beard cut square, and holding a journal in his hand, emerged from the lodge, and moved his cap with a certain bluff and surly reverence on recognizing Lebeau.

"What! so early, citizen?"

"Is it too early?" said Lebeau, glancing at his watch. "So it is; I was not aware of the time. But I am tired with waiting; let me into the salon. I will wait for the rest; I shall not be sorry for a little repose."

"Bon," said the porter, sententiously; "while man reposes men advance."

"A profound truth, citizen Le Roux; though if they advance on a reposing foe, they have blundering leaders unless they march through unguarded by-paths and with noiseless tread."

Following the porter up a dingy broad staircase, Lebeau was admitted into a large room, void of all other furniture than a table, two benches at its sides, and a fauteuil at its head. On the mantelpiece there was a huge clock, and some iron sconces were fixed on the panelled walls.

Lebeau flung himself, with a wearied air, into the fauteuil. The porter looked at him with a kindly expression. He had a liking to Lebeau, whom he had served in his proper profession of messenger or commissionnaire before being placed by that courteous employer in the easy post he now held. Lebeau, indeed, had the art, when he pleased, of charming inferiors; his knowledge of mankind allowed him to distinguish peculiarities in each individual, and flatter the amour propre by deference to such eccentricities. Marc le Roux, the roughest of "red caps," had a wife of whom he was very proud. He would have called the empress Citoyenne Eugenie, but he always spoke of his wife as Madame. Lebeau won his heart by always asking after Madame.

"You look tired, citizen," said the porter; "let me bring you a glass of wine."

"Thank you, mon ami, no. Perhaps later, if I have time, after we break up, to pay my respects to Madame."

The porter smiled, bowed, and retired muttering, "Nom d'un petit bonhomme; il n'y a rien de tel que les belles manieres."

Left alone, Lebeau leaned his elbow on the table, resting his chin on his hand, and gazing into the dim space,—for it was now, indeed, night, and little light came through the grimy panes of the one window left unclosed by shutters. He was musing deeply. This man was, in much, an enigma to himself. Was he seeking to unriddle it? A strange compound of contradictory elements. In his stormy youth there had been lightning-like flashes of good instincts, of irregular honour, of inconsistent generosity,—a puissant wild nature, with strong passions of love and of hate, without fear, but not without shame. In other forms of society that love of applause which had made him seek and exult in the notoriety which he mistook for fame might have settled down into some solid and useful ambition. He might have become great in the world's eye, for at the service of his desires there were no ordinary talents. Though too true a Parisian to be a severe student, still, on the whole, he had acquired much general information, partly from books, partly from varied commerce with mankind. He had the gift, both by tongue and by pen, of expressing himself with force and warmth; time and necessity had improved that gift. Coveting, during his brief career of fashion, the distinctions which necessitate lavish expenditure, he had been the most reckless of spendthrifts; but the neediness which follows waste had never destroyed his original sense of personal honour. Certainly Victor de Mauleon was not, at the date of his fall, a man to whom the thought of accepting, much less of stealing, the jewels of a woman who loved him could have occurred as a possible question of casuistry between honour and temptation. Nor could that sort of question have, throughout the sternest trials or the humblest callings to which his after-life had been subjected, forced admission into his brain. He was one of those men, perhaps the most terrible though unconscious criminals, who are the offsprings produced by intellectual power and egotistical ambition. If you had offered to Victor de Mauleon the crown of the Caesars, on condition of his doing one of those base things which "a gentleman" cannot do, pick a pocket, cheat at cards,—Victor de Mauleon would have refused the crown. He would not have refused on account of any laws of morality affecting the foundations of the social system, but from the pride of his own personality. "I, Victor de Mauleon! I pick a pocket! I cheat at cards! I!" But when something incalculably worse for the interests of society than picking a pocket or cheating at cards was concerned; when for the sake either of private ambition or political experiment hitherto untested, and therefore very doubtful, the peace and order and happiness of millions might be exposed to the release of the most savage passions, rushing on revolutionary madness or civil massacre, then this French dare-devil would have been just as unscrupulous as any English philosopher whom a metropolitan borough might elect as its representative. The system of the empire was in the way of Victor de Mauleon,—in the way of his private ambition, in the way of his political dogmas; and therefore it must be destroyed, no matter what nor whom it crushed beneath its ruins. He was one of those plotters of revolutions not uncommon in democracies, ancient and modern, who invoke popular agencies with the less scruple because they have a supreme contempt for the populace. A man with mental powers equal to De Mauleon's, and who sincerely loves the people and respects the grandeur of aspiration with which, in the great upheaving of their masses, they so often contrast the irrational credulities of their ignorance and the blind fury of their wrath, is always exceedingly loath to pass the terrible gulf that divides reform from revolution. He knows how rarely it happens that genuine liberty is not disarmed in the passage, and what sufferings must be undergone by those who live by their labour during the dismal intervals between the sudden destruction of one form of society and the gradual settlement of another. Such a man, however, has no type in a Victor de Mauleon. The circumstances of his life had placed this strong nature at war with society, and corrupted into misanthropy affections that had once been ardent. That misanthropy made his ambition more intense, because it increased his scorn for the human instruments it employed.

Victor de Mauleon knew that however innocent of the charges that had so long darkened his name, and however—thanks to his rank, his manners, his savoir vivre, the aid of Louvier's countenance and the support of his own high-born connections—he might restore himself to his rightful grade in private life, the higher prizes in public life would scarcely be within reach, to a man of his antecedents and stinted means, in the existent form and conditions of established political order. Perforce, the aristocrat must make himself democrat if he would become a political chief. Could he assist in turning upside down the actual state of things, he trusted to his individual force of character to find himself among the uppermost in the general bouleversement. And in the first stage of popular revolution the mob has no greater darling than the noble who deserts his order, though in the second stage it may guillotine him at the denunciation of his cobbler. A mind so sanguine and so audacious as that of Victor de Mauleon never thinks of the second step if it sees a way to the first.

# CHAPTER VI.

The room was in complete darkness, save where a ray from a gas-lamp at the mouth of the court came aslant through the window, when citizen Le Roux re-entered, closed the window, lighted two of the sconces, and drew forth from a drawer in the table implements of writing, which he placed thereon noiselessly, as if he feared to disturb M. Lebeau, whose head, buried in his hands, rested on the table. He seemed in a profound sleep. At last the porter gently touched the arm of the slumberer, and whispered in his ear, "It is on the stroke of ten, citizen; they will be here in a minute or so." Lebeau lifted his head drowsily.

"Eh," said he—"what?"

"You have been asleep."

"I suppose so, for I have been dreaming. Ha! I hear the door-bell. I am wide awake now."

The porter left him, and in a few minutes conducted into the salon two men wrapped in cloaks, despite the warmth of the summer night. Lebeau shook hands with them silently, and not less silently they laid aside their cloaks and seated themselves. Both these men appeared to belong to the upper section of the middle class. One, strongly built, with a keen expression of countenance, was a surgeon considered able in his profession, but with limited practice, owing to a current suspicion against his honour in connection with a forged will. The other, tall, meagre, with long grizzled hair and a wild unsettled look about the eyes, was a man of science; had written works well esteemed upon mathematics and electricity, also against the existence of any other creative power than that which he called "nebulosity," and defined to be the combination of heat and moisture. The surgeon was about the age of forty, the atheist a few years older. In another minute or so, a knock was heard against the wall. One of the men rose and touched a spring in the panel, which then flew back, and showed an opening upon a narrow stair, by which, one after the other, entered three other members of the society. Evidently there was more than one mode of ingress and exit.

The three new-comers were not Frenchmen,—one might see that at a glance; probably they had reasons for greater precaution than those who entered by the front door. One, a tall, powerfully-built man, with fair hair and beard, dressed with a certain pretension to elegance,—faded threadbare elegance,—exhibiting no appearance of linen, was a Pole. One, a slight bald man, very dark and sallow, was an Italian. The third, who seemed like an ouvrier in his holiday clothes, was a Belgian.

Lebeau greeted them all with an equal courtesy, and each with an equal silence took his seat at the table.

Lebeau glanced at the clock. "Confreres," he said, "our number as fixed for this seance still needs two to be complete, and doubtless they will arrive in a few minutes. Till they come, we can but talk upon trifles. Permit me to offer you my cigar-case." And so saying, he who professed to be no smoker handed his next neighbour, who was the Pole, a large cigar-case amply furnished; and the Pole, helping himself to two cigars, handed the case to the man next him,—two only declining the luxury, the Italian and the Belgian. But the Pole was the only man who took two cigars.

Steps were now heard on the stairs, the door opened, and citizen Le Toux ushered in, one after the other, two men, this time unmistakably French,—to an experienced eye unmistakably Parisians: the one, a young beardless man, who seemed almost boyish, with a beautiful face, and a stinted, meagre frame; the other, a stalwart man of about eight-and twenty, dressed partly as an ouvrier, not in his Sunday clothes, rather affecting the blouse,—not that he wore that antique garment, but that he was in rough costume unbrushed and stained, with thick shoes and coarse stockings, and a workman's cap. But of all who gathered round the table at which M. Lebeau presided, he had the most distinguished exterior,—a virile honest exterior, a massive open forehead, intelligent eyes, a handsome clear-cut incisive profile, and solid jaw. The expression of the face was stern, but not mean,—an expression which might have become an ancient baron as well as a modern workman; in it plenty of haughtiness and of will, and still more of self-esteem.

"Confreres," said Lebeau, rising, and every eye turned to him, "our number for the present seance is complete. To business. Since we last met, our cause has advanced with rapid and not with noiseless stride. I need not tell you that Louis Bonaparte has virtually abnegated Les idees Napoleoniennes,—a fatal mistake for him, a glorious advance for us. The liberty of the press must very shortly be achieved, and with it personal government must end. When the autocrat once is compelled to go by the advice of his ministers, look for sudden changes. His ministers will be but weathercocks, turned hither and thither according as the wind chops at Paris; and Paris is the temple of the winds. The new revolution is almost at hand. [Murmurs of applause.] It would move the laughter of the Tuileries and its ministers, of the Bourse and of its gamblers, of every dainty salon of this silken city of would-be philosophers and wits, if they were told that here within this mouldering baraque, eight men, so little blessed by fortune, so little known to fame as ourselves, met to concert the fall of an empire. The Government would not deem us important enough to notice our existence."

"I know not that," interrupted the Pole.

"Ah, pardon," resumed the orator; "I should have confined my remark to the five of us who are French. I did injustice to the illustrious antecedents of our foreign allies. I know that you, Thaddeus Loubisky, that you, Leonardo Raselli, have been too eminent for hands hostile to tyrants not to be marked with a black cross in the books of the police; I know that you, Jan Vanderstegen, if hitherto unscarred by those wounds in defence of freedom which despots and cowards would fain miscall the brands of the felon, still owe it to your special fraternity to keep your movements rigidly concealed. The tyrant would suppress the International Society, and forbids it the liberty of congress. To you three is granted the secret entrance to our council-hall. But we Frenchmen are as yet safe in our supposed insignificance. Confreres, permit me to impress on you the causes why, insignificant as we seem, we are really formidable. In the first place, we are few: the great mistake in most secret associations has been to admit many councillors; and disunion enters wherever many tongues can wrangle. In the next place, though so few in council, we are legion when the time comes for action; because we are representative men, each of his own section, and each section is capable of an indefinite expansion.

"You, valiant Pole, you, politic Italian, enjoy the confidence of thousands now latent in unwatched homes and harmless callings, but who, when you lift a finger, will, like the buried dragon's teeth, spring up into armed men. You, Jan Vanderstegen, the trusted delegate from Verviers, that swarming camp of wronged labour in its revolt from the iniquities of capital,—you, when the hour arrives, can touch the wire that flashes the telegram 'Arise' through all the lands in which workmen combine against their oppressors.

"Of us five Frenchmen, let me speak more modestly. You, sage and scholar, Felix Ruvigny, honoured alike for the profundity of your science and the probity of your manners, induced to join us by your abhorrence of priestcraft and superstition,—you made a wide connection among all the enlightened reasoners who would emancipate the mind of man from the trammels of Church-born fable, and when the hour arrives in which it is safe to say, 'Delenda est Roma,' you know where to find the pens that are more victorious than swords against a Church and a Creed. You" (turning to the surgeon)—"you, Gaspard le Noy, whom a vile calumny has robbed of the throne in your profession so justly due to your skill, you, nobly scorning the rich and great, have devoted yourself to tend and heal the humble and the penniless, so that you have won the popular title of the 'Medecin des Pauvres,' when the time comes wherein soldiers shall fly before the sansculottes, and the mob shall begin the work which they who move mobs will complete, the clients of Gaspard le Noy will be the avengers of his wrongs.

"You, Armand Monnier, simple ouvrier, but of illustrious parentage, for your grandsire was the beloved friend of the virtuous Robespierre, your father perished a hero and a martyr in the massacre of the coup d'etat; you, cultured in the eloquence of Robespierre himself, and in the persuasive philosophy of Robespierre's teacher, Rousseau; you, the idolized orator of the Red Republicans,—you will be indeed a chief of dauntless bands when the trumpet sounds for battle. Young publicist and poet, Gustave Rameau,—I care not which you are at present, I know what you will be soon, you need nothing for the development of your powers over the many but an organ for their manifestation. Of that anon. I now descend into the bathos of egotism. I am compelled lastly to speak of myself. It was at Marseilles and Lyons, as you already know, that I first conceived the plan of this representative association. For years before I had been in familiar intercourse with the friends of freedom,—that is, with the foes of the Empire. They are not all poor; some few are rich and generous. I do not say these rich and few concur in the ultimate objects of the poor and many; 'but they concur in the first object, the demolition of that which exists,—the Empire. In the course of my special calling of negotiator or agent in the towns of the Midi, I formed friendships with some of these prosperous malcontents; and out of these friendships I conceived the idea which is embodied in this council.

"According to that conception, while the council may communicate as it will with all societies, secret or open, having revolution for their object, the council refuses to merge itself in any other confederation; it stands aloof and independent; it declines to admit into its code any special articles of faith in a future beyond the bounds to which it limits its design and its force. That design unites us; to go beyond would divide. We all agree to destroy the Napoleonic dynasty; none of us might agree as to what we should place in its stead. All of us here present might say, 'A republic.' Ay, but of what kind? Vanderstegen would have it socialistic; Monnier goes further, and would have it communistic, on the principles of Fourier; Le Noy adheres to the policy of Danton, and would commence the republic by a reign of terror; our Italian ally abhors the notion of general massacre, and advocates individual assassination. Ruvigny would annihilate the worship of a Deity; Monnier holds with Voltaire and Robespierre, that, 'if there were no Deity, it would be necessary to man to create one.' Bref, we could not agree upon any plan for the new edifice, and therefore we refuse to discuss one till the ploughshare has gone over the ruins of the old. But I have another and more practical reason for keeping our council distinct from all societies with professed objects beyond that of demolition. We need a certain command of money. It is I who bring to you that, and—how? Not from my own resources,—they but suffice to support myself; not by contributions from ouvriers who, as you well know, will subscribe only for their own ends in the victory of workmen over masters. I bring money to you from the coffers of the rich malcontents. Their politics are not those of most present; their politics are what they term moderate. Some are indeed for a republic, but for a republic strong in defence of order, in support of property; others—and they are more numerous and the more rich—for a constitutional monarchy, and, if possible, for the abridgment of universal suffrage, which in their eyes tends only to anarchy in the towns and arbitrary rule under priestly influence in the rural districts. They would not subscribe a sou if they thought it went to further the designs whether of Ruvigny the atheist, or of Monnier, who would enlist the Deity of Rousseau on the side of the drapeau rouge; not a sou if they knew I had the honour to boast such confreres as I see around me. They subscribe, as we concert, for the fall of Bonaparte. The policy I adopt I borrow from the policy of the English Liberals. In England, potent millionnaires, high-born dukes, devoted Churchmen, belonging to the Liberal party, accept the services of men who look forward to measures which would ruin capital, eradicate aristocracy, and destroy the Church, provided these men combine with them in some immediate step onward against the Tories. They have a proverb which I thus adapt to French localities: if a train passes Fontainebleau on its way to Marseilles, why should I not take it to Fontainebleau because other passengers are going on to Marseilles?

"Confreres, it seems to me the moment has come when we may venture some of the fund placed at my disposal to other purposes than those to which it has been hitherto devoted. I propose, therefore, to set up a journal under the auspices of Gustave Rameau as editor-in-chief,—a journal which, if he listen to my advice, will create no small sensation. It will begin with a tone of impartiality; it will refrain from all violence of invective; it will have wit, it will have sentiment, and eloquence; it will win its way into the salons and cafes of educated men; and then, and then, when it does change from polished satire into fierce denunciation and sides with the blouses, its effect will be startling and terrific. Of this I will say more to citizen Rameau in private. To you I need not enlarge upon the fact that, at Paris, a combination of men, though immeasurably superior to us in status or influence, without a journal at command is nowhere; with such a journal, written not to alarm but to seduce fluctuating opinions, a combination of men immeasurably inferior to us may be anywhere.

"Confreres, this affair settled, I proceed to distribute amongst you sums of which each who receives will render me an account, except our valued confrere the Pole. All that we can subscribe to the cause of humanity a representative of Poland requires for himself." (A suppressed laugh among all but the Pole, who looked round with a grave, imposing air, as much as to say, "What is there to laugh at?—a simple truth.")

M. Lebeau then presented to each of his confreres a sealed envelope, containing no doubt a bank-note, and perhaps also private instructions as to its disposal. It was one of his rules to make the amount of any sum granted to an individual member of the society from the fund at his disposal a confidential secret between himself and the recipient. Thus jealousy was avoided if the sums were unequal; and unequal they generally were. In the present instance the two largest sums were given to the "Medecin des Pauvres" and to the delegate from Verviers. Both were no doubt to be distributed among "the poor," at the discretion of the trustee appointed.

Whatever rules with regard to the distribution of money M. Lebeau laid down were acquiesced in without demur, for the money was found exclusively by himself, and furnished without the pale of the Secret Council, of which he had made himself founder and dictator. Some other business was then discussed, sealed reports from each member were handed to the president, who placed them unopened in his pocket, and resumed, "Confreres, our seance is now concluded. The period for our next meeting must remain indefinite, for I myself shall leave Paris as soon as I have set on foot the journal, on the details of which I will confer with citizen Rameau. I am not satisfied with the progress made by the two travelling missionaries who complete our Council of Ten; and though I do not question their zeal, I think my experience may guide it if I take a journey to the towns of Bordeaux and Marseilles, where they now are. But should circumstances demanding concert or action arise, you may be sure that I will either summon a meeting or transmit instructions to such of our members as may be most usefully employed. For the present, confreres, you are relieved. Remain only you, dear young author."

# CHAPTER VII.

Left alone with Gustave Rameau, the President of the Secret Council remained silently musing for some moments; but his countenance was no longer moody and overcast,—his nostrils were dilated, as in triumph; there was a half-smile of pride on his lips. Rameau watched him curiously and admiringly. The young man had the impressionable, excitable temperament common to Parisian genius,—especially when it nourishes itself on absinthe. He enjoyed the romance of belonging to a secret society; he was acute enough to recognize the sagacity by which this small conclave was kept out of those crazed combinations for impracticable theories more likely to lead adventurers to the Tarpeian Rock than to the Capitol, while yet those crazed combinations might, in some critical moment, become strong instruments in the hands of practical ambition. Lebeau fascinated him, and took colossal proportions in his intoxicated vision,—vision indeed intoxicated at this moment, for before it floated the realized image of his aspirations,—a journal of which he was to be the editor-in-chief; in which his poetry, his prose, should occupy space as large as he pleased; through which his name, hitherto scarce known beyond a literary clique, would resound in salon and club and cafe, and become a familiar music on the lips of fashion. And he owed this to the man seated there,—a prodigious man.

"Cher poete," said Lebeau, breaking silence, "it gives me no mean pleasure to think I am opening a career to one whose talents fit him for those goals on which they who reach write names that posterity shall read. Struck with certain articles of yours in the journal made celebrated by the wit and gayety of Savarin, I took pains privately to inquire into your birth, your history, connections, antecedents. All confirmed my first impression,—that you were exactly the writer I wish to secure to our cause. I therefore sought you in your rooms, unintroduced and a stranger, in order to express my admiration of your compositions. Bref, we soon became friends; and after comparing minds, I admitted you, at your request, into this Secret Council. Now, in proposing to you the conduct of the journal I would establish, for which I am prepared to find all necessary funds, I am compelled to make imperative conditions. Nominally you will be editor-in-chief: that station, if the journal succeeds, will secure you position and fortune; if it fail, you fail with it. But we will not speak of failure; I must have it succeed. Our interest, then, is the same. Before that interest all puerile vanities fade away. Nominally, I say, you are editor-in-chief; but all the real work of editing will, at first, be done by others."

"Ah!" exclaimed Rameau, aghast and stunned. Lebeau resumed,

"To establish the journal I propose needs more than the genius of youth; it needs the tact and experience of mature years."

Rameau sank back on his chair with a sullen sneer on his pale lips. Decidedly Lebeau was not so great a man as he had thought.

"A certain portion of the journal," continued Lebeau, "will be exclusively appropriated to your pen."

Rameau's lip lost the sneer.

"But your pen must be therein restricted to compositions of pure fancy, disporting in a world that does not exist; or, if on graver themes connected with the beings of the world that does exist, the subjects will be dictated to you and revised. Yet even in the higher departments of a journal intended to make way at its first start, we need the aid, not indeed of men who write better than you, but of men whose fame is established,—whose writings, good or bad, the public run to read, and will find good even if they are bad. You must consign one column to the playful comments and witticisms of Savarin."

"Savarin? But he has a journal of his own. He will not, as an author, condescend to write in one just set up by me; and as a politician, he as certainly will not aid in an ultrademocratic revolution. If he care for politics at all, he is a constitutionalist, an Orleanist."

"Enfant! as an author Savarin will condescend to contribute to your journal, first, because it in no way attempts to interfere with his own; secondly,—I can tell you a secret, Savarin's journal no longer suffices for his existence. He has sold more than two-thirds of its property; he is in debt, and his creditor is urgent; and to-morrow you will offer Savarin thirty thousand francs for one column from his pen, and signed by his name, for two months from the day the journal starts. He will accept, partly because the sum will clear off the debt that hampers him, partly because he will take care that the amount becomes known; and that will help him to command higher terms for the sale of the remaining shares in the journal he now edits, for the new book which you told me he intended to write, and for the new journal which he will be sure to set up as soon as he has disposed of the old one. You say that, as a politician, Savarin, an Orleanist, will not aid in an ultra-democratic revolution. Who asks him to do so? Did I not imply at the meeting that we commence our journal with politics the mildest? Though revolutions are not made with rose-water, it is rose-water that nourishes their roots. The polite cynicism of authors, read by those who float on the surface of society, prepares the way for the social ferment in its deeps. Had there been no Voltaire, there would have been no Camille Desmoulins; had there been no Diderot, there would have been no Marat. We start as polite cynics. Of all cynics Savarin is the politest. But when I bid high for him, it is his clique that I bid for. Without his clique he is but a wit; with his clique, a power. Partly out of that clique, partly out of a circle beyond it, which Savarin can more or less influence, I select ten. Here is the list of them; study it. Entre nous, I esteem their writings as little as I do artificial flies; but they are the artificial flies at which, in this particular season of the year, the public rise. You must procure at least five of the ten; and I leave you carte blanche as to the terms. Savarin gained, the best of them will be proud of being his associates. Observe, none of these messieurs of brilliant imagination are to write political articles; those will be furnished to you anonymously, and inserted without erasure or omission. When you have secured Savarin, and five at least of the collaborateurs in the list, write to me at my office. I give you four days to do this; and the day the journal starts you enter into the income of fifteen thousand francs a year, with a rise in salary proportioned to profits. Are you contented with the terms?"

"Of course I am; but supposing I do not gain the aid of Savarin, or five at least of the list you give, which I see at a glance contains names the most a la mode in this kind of writing, more than one of them of high social rank, whom it is difficult for me even to approach,—if, I say, I fail?"

"What! with a carte blanche of terms? fie! Are you a Parisian? Well, to answer you frankly, if you fail in so easy a task, you are not the man to edit our journal, and I shall find another. Allez, courage! Take my advice; see Savarin the first thing to-morrow morning. Of course, my name and calling you will keep a profound secret from him, as from all. Say as mysteriously as you can that parties you are forbidden to name instruct you to treat with M. Savarin, and offer him the terms I have specified, the thirty thousand francs paid to him in advance the moment he signs the simple memorandum of agreement. The more mysterious you are, the more you will impose,—that is, wherever you offer money and don't ask for it."

Here Lebeau took up his hat, and, with a courteous nod of adieu, lightly descended the gloomy stairs.

# CHAPTER VIII.

At night, after this final interview with Lebeau, Graham took leave for good of his lodgings in Montmartre, and returned to his apartment in the Rue d'Anjou. He spent several hours of the next morning in answering numerous letters accumulated during his absence. Late in the afternoon he had an interview with M. Renard, who, as at that season of the year he was not over-busied with other affairs, engaged to obtain leave to place his services at Graham's command during the time requisite for inquiries at Aix, and to be in readiness to start the next day. Graham then went forth to pay one or two farewell visits; and these over, bent his way through the Champs Elysees towards Isaura's villa, when he suddenly encountered Rochebriant on horseback. The Marquis courteously dismounted, committing his horse to the care of the groom, and linking his arm in Graham's, expressed his pleasure at seeing him again; then, with some visible hesitation and embarrassment, he turned the conversation towards the political aspects of France.

"There was," he said, "much in certain words of yours, when we last walked together in this very path, that sank deeply into my mind at the time, and over which I have of late still more earnestly reflected. You spoke of the duties a Frenchman owed to France, and the 'impolicy' of remaining aloof from all public employment on the part of those attached to the Legitimist cause."

"True; it cannot be the policy of any party to forget that between the irrevocable past and the uncertain future there intervenes the action of the present time."

"Should you, as an impartial bystander, consider it dishonourable in me if I entered the military service under the ruling sovereign?"

"Certainly not, if your country needed you."

"And it may, may it not? I hear vague rumours of coming war in almost every salon I frequent. There has been gunpowder in the atmosphere we breathe ever since the battle of Sadowa. What think you of German arrogance and ambition? Will they suffer the swords of France to rust in their scabbards?"

"My dear Marquis, I should incline to put the question otherwise. Will the jealous amour propre of France permit the swords of Germany to remain sheathed? But in either case, no politician can see without grave apprehension two nations so warlike, close to each other, divided by a borderland that one covets and the other will not yield, each armed to the teeth,—the one resolved to brook no rival, the other equally determined to resist all aggression. And therefore, as you say, war is in the atmosphere; and we may also hear, in the clouds that give no sign of dispersion, the growl of the gathering thunder. War may come any day; and if France be not at once the victor—"

"France not at once the victor?" interrupted Alain, passionately; "and against a Prussian! Permit me to say no Frenchman can believe that."

"Let no man despise a foe," said Graham, smiling half sadly. "However, I must not incur the danger of wounding your national susceptibilities. To return to the point you raise. If France needed the aid of her best and bravest, a true descendant of Henri Quatre ought to blush for his ancient noblesse were a Rochebriant to say, 'But I don't like the colour of the flag.'"

"Thank you," said Alain, simply; "that is enough." There was a pause, the young men walking on slowly, arm in arm. And then there flashed across Graham's mind the recollection of talk on another subject in that very path. Here he had spoken to Alain in deprecation of any possible alliance with Isaura Cicogna, the destined actress and public; singer. His cheek flushed; his heart smote him. What! had he spoken slightingly of her—of her? What if she became his own wife? What! had he himself failed in the respect which he would demand as her right from the loftiest of his high-born kindred? What, too, would this man, of fairer youth than himself, think of that disparaging counsel, when he heard that the monitor had won the prize from which he had warned another? Would it not seem that he had but spoken in the mean cunning dictated by the fear of a worthier rival? Stung by these thoughts, he arrested his steps, and, looking the Marquis full in the face, said, "You remind me of one subject in our talk many weeks since; it is my duty to remind you of another. At that time you, and, speaking frankly, I myself, acknowledged the charm in the face of a young Italian lady. I told you then that, on learning she was intended for the stage, the charm for me had vanished. I said bluntly that it should vanish perhaps still more utterly for a noble of your illustrious name; you remember?"

"Yes," answered Alain, hesitatingly, and with a look of surprise.

"I wish now to retract all I said thereon. Mademoiselle Cicogna is not bent on the profession for which she was educated. She would willingly renounce all idea of entering it. The only counterweight which, viewed whether by my reason or my prejudices, could be placed in the opposite scale to that of the excellences which might make any man proud to win her, is withdrawn. I have become acquainted with her since the date of our conversation. Hers is a mind which harmonizes with the loveliness of her face. In one word, Marquis, I should deem myself honoured, as well as blest, by such a bride. It was due to her that I should say this; it was due also to you, in case you should retain the impression I sought in ignorance to efface. And I am bound, as a gentleman, to obey this twofold duty, even though in so doing I bring upon myself the affliction of a candidate for the hand to which I would fain myself aspire,—a candidate with pretensions in every way far superior to my own."

An older or a more cynical man than Alain de Rochebriant might well have found something suspicious in a confession thus singularly volunteered; but the Marquis was himself so loyal that he had no doubt of the loyalty of Graham.

"I reply to you," he said, "with a frankness which finds an example in your own. The first fair face which attracted my fancy since my arrival at Paris was that of the Italian demoiselle of whom you speak in terms of such respect. I do think if I had then been thrown into her society, and found her to be such as you no doubt truthfully describe, that fancy might have become a very grave emotion. I was then so poor, so friendless, so despondent! Your words of warning impressed me at the time, but less durably than you might suppose; for that very night as I sat in my solitary attic I said to myself, 'Why should I shrink, with an obsolete old-world prejudice, from what my forefathers would have termed a mesalliance? What is the value of my birthright now? None,—worse than none. It excludes me from all careers; my name is but a load that weighs me down. Why should I make that name a curse as well as a burden? Nothing is left to me but that which is permitted to all men,—wedded and holy love. Could I win to my heart the smile of a woman who brings me that dower, the home of my fathers would lose its gloom.' And therefore, if at that time I had become familiarly acquainted with her who had thus attracted my eye and engaged my thoughts, she might have become my destiny; but now!"

"But now?"

"Things have changed. I am no longer poor, friendless, solitary. I have entered the world of my equals as a Rochebriant; I have made myself responsible for the dignity of my name. I could not give that name to one, however peerless in herself, of whom the world would say, 'But for her marriage she would have been a singer on the stage!' I will own more: the fancy I conceived for the first fair face, other fair faces have dispelled. At this moment, however, I have no thought of marriage; and having known the anguish of struggle, the privations of poverty, I would ask no woman to share the hazard of my return to them. You might present me, then, safely to this beautiful Italian,—certain, indeed, that I should be her admirer; equally certain that I could not become your rival."

There was something in this speech that jarred upon Graham's sensitive pride; but on the whole, he felt relieved, both in honour and in heart. After a few more words, the two young men shook hands and parted. Alain remounted his horse. The day was now declining. Graham hailed a vacant fiacre, and directed the driver to Isaura's villa.

# CHAPTER IX.

## ISAURA.

The sun was sinking slowly as Isaura sat at her window, gazing dreamily on the rose-hued clouds that made the western borderland between earth and heaven. On the table before her lay a few sheets of manuscript hastily written, not yet reperused. That restless mind of hers had left its trace on the manuscript.

It is characteristic perhaps of the different genius of the sexes, that woman takes to written composition more impulsively, more intuitively, than man,—letter-writing, to him a task-work, is to her a recreation. Between the age of sixteen and the date of marriage, six well-educated clever girls out of ten keep a journal; not one well-educated man in ten thousand does. So, without serious and settled intention of becoming an author, how naturally a girl of ardent feeling and vivid fancy seeks in poetry or romance a confessional,—an outpouring of thought and sentiment, which are mysteries to herself till she has given them words, and which, frankly revealed on the page, she would not, perhaps could not, utter orally to a living ear.

During the last few days, the desire to create in the realm of fable beings constructed by her own breath, spiritualized by her own soul, had grown irresistibly upon this fair child of song. In fact, when Graham's words had decided the renunciation of her destined career, her instinctive yearnings for the utterance of those sentiments or thoughts which can only find expression in some form of art, denied the one vent, irresistibly impelled her to the other. And in this impulse she was confirmed by the thought that here at least there was nothing which her English friend could disapprove,—none of the perils that beset the actress. Here it seemed as if, could she but succeed, her fame would be grateful to the pride of all who loved her. Here was a career ennobled by many a woman, and side by side in rivalry with renowned men. To her it seemed that, could she in this achieve an honoured name, that name took its place at once amid the higher ranks of the social world, and in itself brought a priceless dowry and a starry crown. It was, however, not till after the visit to Enghien that this ambition took practical life and form. One evening after her return to Paris, by an effort so involuntary that it seemed to her no effort, she had commenced a tale,—without plan, without method, without knowing in one page what would fill the next. Her slight fingers hurried on as if, like the pretended spirit manifestations, impelled by an invisible agency without the pale of the world. She was intoxicated by the mere joy of inventing ideal images. In her own special art an elaborate artist, here she had no thought of art; if art was in her work, it sprang unconsciously from the harmony between herself and her subject,—as it is, perhaps, with the early soarings of the genuine lyric poets, in contrast to the dramatic. For the true lyric poet is intensely personal, intensely subjective. It is himself that he expresses, that he represents; and he almost ceases to be lyrical when he seeks to go out of his own existence into that of others with whom he has no sympathy, no rapport. This tale was vivid with genius as yet untutored,—genius in its morning freshness, full of beauties, full of faults. Isaura distinguished not the faults from the beauties. She felt only a vague persuasion that there was a something higher and brighter—a something more true to her own idiosyncrasy—than could be achieved by the art that "sings other people's words to other people's music." From the work thus commenced she had now paused; and it seemed to her fancies that between her inner self and the scene without, whether in the skies and air and sunset, or in the abodes of men stretching far and near till lost amid the roofs and domes of the great city, she had fixed and riveted the link of a sympathy hitherto fluctuating, unsubstantial, evanescent, undefined. Absorbed in her revery, she did not notice the deepening of the short twilight, till the servant entering drew the curtains between her and the world without, and placed the lamp on the table beside her. Then she turned away with a restless sigh; her eyes fell on the manuscript, but the charm of it was gone. A sentiment of distrust in its worth had crept into her thoughts, unconsciously to herself, and the page open before her at an uncompleted sentence seemed unwelcome and wearisome as a copy-book is to a child condemned to relinquish a fairy tale half told, and apply himself to a task half done. She fell again into a revery, when, starting as from a dream, she heard herself addressed by name, and turning round saw Savarin and Gustave Rameau in the room.

"We are come, Signorina," said Savarin, "to announce to you a piece of news, and to hazard a petition. The news is this: my young friend here has found a Maecenas who has the good taste so to admire his lucubrations under the nom de plume of Alphonse de Valcour as to volunteer the expenses for starting a new journal, of which Gustave Rameau is to be editor-in-chief; and I have promised to assist him as contributor for the first two months. I have given him notes of introduction to certain other feuilletonistes and critics whom he has on his list. But all put together would not serve to float the journal like a short roman from Madame de Grantmesnil. Knowing your intimacy with that eminent artist, I venture to back Rameau's supplication that you would exert your influence on his, behalf. As to the honoraires, she has but to name them."

"Carte blanche," cried Rameau, eagerly.

"You know Eulalie too well, Monsieur Savarin," answered Isaura, with a smile half reproachful, "to suppose that she is a mercenary in letters, and sells her services to the best bidder."

"Bah, belle enfant!" said Savarin, with his gay light laugh. "Business is business, and books as well as razors are made to sell. But, of course, a proper prospectus of the journal must accompany your request to write in it. Meanwhile Rameau will explain to you, as he has done to me, that the journal in question is designed for circulation among readers of haute classe it is to be pleasant and airy, full of bons mots and anecdote; witty, but not ill-natured. Politics to be Liberal, of course, but of elegant admixture,—champagne and seltzer-water. In fact, however, I suspect that the politics will be a very inconsiderable feature in this organ of fine arts and manners; some amateur scribbler in the beau monde will supply them. For the rest, if my introductory letters are successful, Madame de Grantmesnil will not be in bad company."

"You will write to Madame de Grantmesnil?" asked Rameau, pleadingly.

"Certainly I will, as soon—"

"As soon as you have the prospectus, and the names of the collaborateurs," interrupted Rameau. "I hope to send you these in a very few days."

While Rameau was thus speaking, Savarin had seated himself by the table, and his eye mechanically resting on the open manuscript lighted by chance upon a sentence—an aphorism—embodying a very delicate sentiment in very felicitous diction,—one of those choice condensations of thought, suggesting so much more than is said, which are never found in mediocre writers, and, rare even in the best, come upon us like truths seized by surprise.

"Parbleu!" exclaimed Savarin, in the impulse of genuine admiration, "but this is beautiful; what is more, it is original,"—and he read the words aloud. Blushing with shame and resentment, Isaura turned and hastily placed her hand on the manuscript.

"Pardon," said Savarin, humbly; "I confess my sin, but it was so unpremeditated that it does not merit a severe penance. Do not look at me so reproachfully. We all know that young ladies keep commonplace books in which they enter passages that strike them in the works they read; and you have but shown an exquisite taste in selecting this gem. Do tell me where you found it. Is it somewhere in Lamartine?"

"No," answered Isaura, half inaudibly, and with an effort to withdraw the paper. Savarin gently detained her hand, and looking earnestly into her tell-tale face, divined her secret.

"It is your own, Signorina! Accept the congratulations of a very practised and somewhat fastidious critic. If the rest of what you write resembles this sentence, contribute to Rameau's journal, and I answer for its success."

Rameau approached, half incredulous, half envious.

"My dear child," resumed Savarin, drawing away the manuscript from Isaura's coy, reluctant clasp, "do permit me to cast a glance over these papers. For what I yet know, there may be here more promise of fame than even you could gain as a singer."

The electric chord in Isaura's heart was touched. Who cannot conceive what the young writer feels, especially the young woman-writer, when hearing the first cheery note of praise from the lips of a writer of established fame?

"Nay, this cannot be worth your reading," said Isaura, falteringly; "I have never written anything of the kind before, and this is a riddle to me. I know not," she added, with a sweet low laugh, "why I began, nor how I should end it."

"So much the better," said Savarin; and he took the manuscript, withdrew to a recess by the farther window, and seated himself there, reading silently and quickly, but now and then with a brief pause of reflection.

Rameau placed himself beside Isaura on the divan, and began talking with her earnestly,—earnestly, for it was about himself and his aspiring hopes. Isaura, on the other hand, more woman-like than author-like, ashamed even to seem absorbed in herself and her hopes, and with her back turned, in the instinct of that shame, against the reader of her manuscript,—Isaura listened and sought to interest herself solely in the young fellow-author. Seeking to do so she succeeded genuinely, for ready sympathy was a prevalent characteristic of her nature.

"Oh," said Rameau, "I am at the turning-point of my life. Ever since boyhood I have been haunted with the words of Andre Chenier on the morning he was led to the scaffold 'And yet there was something here,' striking his forehead. Yes, I, poor, low-born, launching myself headlong in the chase of a name; I, underrated, uncomprehended, indebted even for a hearing to the patronage of an amiable trifler like Savarin, ranked by petty rivals in a grade below themselves,—I now see before me, suddenly, abruptly presented, the expanding gates into fame and fortune. Assist me, you!"

"But how?" said Isaura, already forgetting her manuscript; and certainly Rameau did not refer to that.

"How!" echoed Rameau; "how! But do you not see—or at least, do you not conjecture—this journal of which Savarin speaks contains my present and my future? Present independence, opening to fortune and renown. Ay,—and who shall say? renown beyond that of the mere writer. Behind the gaudy scaffolding of this rickety Empire, a new social edifice unperceived arises; and in that edifice the halls of State shall be given to the men who help obscurely to build it,—to men like me." Here, drawing her hand into his own, fixing on her the most imploring gaze of his dark persuasive eyes, and utterly unconscious of bathos in his adjuration, he added: "Plead for me with your whole mind and heart; use your uttermost influence with the illustrious writer whose pen can assure the fates of my journal."

Here the door suddenly opened, and following the servant, who announced unintelligibly his name, there entered Graham Vane.

# CHAPTER X.

The Englishman halted at the threshold. His eye, passing rapidly over the figure of Savarin reading in the window-niche, rested upon Rameau and Isaura seated on the same divan, he with her hand clasped in both his own, and bending his face towards hers so closely that a loose tress of her hair seemed to touch his forehead.

The Englishman halted, and no revolution which changes the habitudes and forms of States was ever so sudden as that which passed without a word in the depths of his unconjectured heart. The heart has no history which philosophers can recognize. An ordinary political observer, contemplating the condition of a nation, may very safely tell us what effects must follow the causes patent to his eyes; but the wisest and most far-seeing sage, looking at a man at one o'clock, cannot tell us what revulsions of his whole being may be made ere the clock strike two.

As Isaura rose to greet her visitor, Savarin came from the window-niche, the manuscript in his hand.

"Son of perfidious Albion," said Savarin, gayly, "we feared you had deserted the French alliance. Welcome back to Paris, and the entente cordiale."

"Would I could stay to enjoy such welcome! but I must again quit Paris."

"Soon to return, n'est ce pas? Paris is an irresistible magnet to les beaux esprits. A propos of beaux esprits, be sure to leave orders with your bookseller, if you have one, to enter your name as subscriber to a new journal."

"Certainly, if Monsieur Savarin recommends it."

"He recommends it as a matter of course; he writes in it," said Rameau.

"A sufficient guarantee for its excellence. What is the name of the journal?"

"Not yet thought of," answered Savarin. "Babes must be born before they are christened; but it will be instruction enough to your bookseller to order the new journal to be edited by Gustave Rameau."

Bowing ceremoniously to the editor in prospect, Graham said, half ironically, "May I hope that in the department of criticism you will not be too hard upon poor Tasso?"

"Never fear; the Signorina, who adores Tasso, will take him under her special protection," said Savarin, interrupting Rameau's sullen and embarrassed reply.

Graham's brow slightly contracted. "Mademoiselle," he said, "is then to be united in the conduct of this journal with M. Gustave Rameau?"

"No, indeed!" exclaimed Isaura, somewhat frightened at the idea.

"But I hope," said Savarin, "that the Signorina may become a contributor too important for an editor to offend by insulting her favourites, Tasso included. Rameau and I came hither to entreat her influence with her intimate and illustrious friend, Madame de Grantmesnil, to insure the success of our undertaking by sanctioning the announcement of her name as a contributor."

"Upon social questions,—such as the laws of marriage?" said Graham, with a sarcastic smile, which concealed the quiver of his lip and the pain in his voice.

"Nay," answered Savarin, "our journal will be too sportive, I hope, for matters so profound. We would rather have Madame de Grantmesnil's aid in some short roman, which will charm the fancy of all and offend the opinions of none. But since I came into the room, I care less for the Signorina's influence with the great authoress," and he glanced significantly at the manuscript.

"How so?" asked Graham, his eye following the glance.

"If the writer of this manuscript will conclude what she has begun, we shall be independent of Madame de Grantmesnil."

"Fie!" cried Isaura, impulsively, her face and neck bathed in blushes,—"fie! such words are a mockery."

Graham gazed at her intently, and then turned his eyes on Savarin. He guessed aright the truth. "Mademoiselle then is an author? In the style of her friend Madame de Grantmesnil?"

"Bah!" said Savarin, "I should indeed be guilty of mockery if I paid the Signorina so false a compliment as to say that in a first effort she attained to the style of one of the most finished sovereigns of language that has ever swayed the literature of France. When I say, 'Give us this tale completed, and I shall be consoled if the journal does not gain the aid of Madame de Grantmesnil,' I mean that in these pages there is that nameless charm of freshness and novelty which compensates for many faults never committed by a practised pen like Madame de Grantmesnil's. My dear young lady, go on with this story,—finish it; when finished, do not disdain any suggestions

I may offer in the way of correction,—and I will venture to predict to you so brilliant a career as author, that you will not regret should you resign for that career the bravoes you could command as actress and singer."

The Englishman pressed his hand convulsively to his heart, as if smitten by a sudden spasm. But as his eyes rested on Isaura's face, which had become radiant with the enthusiastic delight of genius when the path it would select opens before it as if by a flash from heaven, whatever of jealous irritation, whatever of selfish pain he might before have felt; was gone, merged in a sentiment of unutterable sadness and compassion. Practical man as he was, he knew so well all the dangers, all the snares, all the sorrows, all the scandals menacing name and fame, that in the world of Paris must beset the fatherless girl who, not less in authorship than on the stage, leaves the safeguard of private life forever behind her, who becomes a prey to the tongues of the public. At Paris, how slender is the line that divides the authoress from the Bohemienne! He sank into his chair silently, and passed his hand over his eyes, as if to shut out a vision of the future.

Isaura in her excitement did not notice the effect on her English visitor. She could not have divined such an effect as possible. On the contrary, even subordinate to her joy at the thought that she had not mistaken the instincts which led her to a nobler vocation than that of the singer, that the cage-bar was opened, and space bathed in sunshine was inviting the new-felt wings,—subordinate even to that joy was a joy more wholly, more simply woman's. "If," thought she, in this joy, "if this be true, my proud ambition is realized; all disparities of worth and fortune are annulled between me and him to whom I would bring no shame of mesalliance!" Poor dreamer, poor child!

"You will let me see what you have written," said Rameau, somewhat imperiously, in the sharp voice habitual to him, and which pierced Graham's ear like a splinter of glass.

"No, not now; when finished."

"You will finish it?"

"Oh, yes; how can I help it after such encouragement?" She held out her hand to Savarin, who kissed it gallantly; then her eyes intuitively sought Graham's. By that time he had recovered his self-possession. He met her look tranquilly, and with a smile; but the smile chilled her, she knew not why.

The conversation then passed upon books and authors of the day, and was chiefly supported by the satirical pleasantries of Savarin, who was in high good-spirits.

Graham, who, as we know, had come with the hope of seeing Isaura alone, and with the intention of uttering words which, however guarded, might yet in absence serve as links of union, now no longer coveted that interview, no longer meditated those words. He soon rose to depart.

"Will you dine with me to-morrow?" asked Savarin. "Perhaps I may induce the Signorina and Rameau to offer you the temptation of meeting them."

"By to-morrow I shall be leagues away."

Isaura's heart sank. This time the manuscript was fairly forgotten.

"You never said you were going so soon," cried Savarin. "When do you come back, vile deserter?"

"I cannot even guess. Monsieur Rameau, count me among your subscribers. Mademoiselle, my best regards to Signora Venosta. When I see you again, no doubt you will have become famous."

Isaura here could not control herself. She rose impulsively, and approached him, holding out her hand, and attempting a smile.

"But not famous in the way that you warned me from," she said in whispered tones. "You are friends with me still?" It was like the piteous wail of a child seeking to make it up with one who wants to quarrel, the child knows not why. Graham was moved, but what could he say? Could he have the right to warn her from this profession also; forbid all desires, all roads of fame to this brilliant aspirant? Even a declared and accepted lover might well have deemed that that would be to ask too much. He replied, "Yes, always a friend, if you could ever need one." Her hand slid from his, and she turned away wounded to the quick.

"Have you your coupe at the door?" asked Savarin.

"Simply a fiacre."

"And are going back at once to Paris?"

"Yes."

"Will you kindly drop me in the Rue de Rivoli?"

"Charmed to be of use."

# CHAPTER XI.

As the fiacre bore to Paris Savarin and Graham, the former said, "I cannot conceive what rich simpleton could entertain so high an opinion of Gustave Rameau as to select a man so young, and of reputation though promising so undecided, for an enterprise which requires such a degree of tact and judgment as the conduct of a new journal,—and a journal, too, which is to address itself to the beau monde. However, it is not for me to criticise a selection which brings a god-send to myself."

"To yourself? You jest; you have a journal of your own. It can only be through an excess of good-nature that you lend your name and pen to the service of M. Gustave Rameau."

"My good-nature does not go to that extent. It is Rameau who confers a service upon me. Peste! mon cher, we French authors have not the rents of you rich English milords. And though I am the most economical of our tribe, yet that journal of mine has failed me of late; and this morning I did not exactly see how I was to repay a sum I had been obliged to borrow of a money-lender,—for I am too proud to borrow of friends, and too sagacious to borrow of publishers,—when in walks ce cher petit Gustave with an offer, for a few trifles towards starting this new-born journal, which makes a new man of me. Now I am in the undertaking, my amour propre and my reputation are concerned in its success; and I shall take care that collaborateurs of whose company I am not ashamed are in the same boat. But that charming girl, Isaura! What an enigma the gift of the pen is! No one can ever guess who has it until tried."

"The young lady's manuscript, then, really merits the praise you bestowed on it?"

"Much more praise, though a great deal of blame, which I did not bestow,—for in a first work faults insure success as much as beauties. Anything better than tame correctness. Yes, her first work, to judge by what is written, must make a hit,—a great hit. And that will decide her career. A singer, an actress, may retire,—often does when she marries an author; but once an author always an author."

"Ah! is it so? If you had a beloved daughter, Savarin, would you encourage her to be an author?"

"Frankly, no: principally because in that case the chances are that she would marry an author; and French authors, at least in the imaginative school, make very uncomfortable husbands."

"Ah! you think the Signorina will marry one of those uncomfortable husbands,—M. Rameau, perhaps?"

"Rameau! Hein! nothing more likely. That beautiful face of his has its fascination. And to tell you the truth, my wife, who is a striking illustration of the truth that what woman wills heaven wills, is bent upon that improvement in Gustave's moral life which she thinks a union with Mademoiselle Cicogna would achieve. At all events, the fair Italian would have in Rameau a husband who would not suffer her to bury her talents under a bushel. If she succeeds as a writer (by succeeding I mean making money), he will see that her ink-bottle is never empty; and if she don't succeed as a writer, he will take care that the world shall gain an actress or a singer. For Gustave Rameau has a great taste for luxury and show; and whatever his wife can make, I will venture to say that he will manage to spend."

"I thought you had an esteem and regard for Mademoiselle Cicogna. It is Madame your wife, I suppose, who has a grudge against her?"

"On the contrary, my wife idolizes her."

"Savages sacrifice to their idols the things they deem of value; civilized Parisians sacrifice their idols themselves, and to a thing that is worthless."

"Rameau is not worthless; he has beauty and youth and talent. My wife thinks more highly of him than I do; but I must respect a man who has found admirers so sincere as to set him up in a journal, and give him carte blanche for terms to contributors. I know of no man in Paris more valuable to me. His worth to me this morning is thirty thousand francs. I own I do not think him likely to be a very safe husband; but then French female authors and artists seldom take any husbands except upon short leases. There are no vulgar connubial prejudices in the pure atmosphere of art. Women of genius, like Madame de Grantmesnil, and perhaps like our charming young friend, resemble canary-birds,—to sing their best you must separate them from their mates."

The Englishman suppressed a groan, and turned the conversation.

When he had set down his lively companion, Vane dismissed his fiacre, and walked to his lodgings musingly.

"No," he said inly; "I must wrench myself from the very memory of that haunting face,—the friend and pupil of Madame de Grantmesnil, the associate of Gustave Rameau, the rival of Julie Caumartin, the aspirant to that pure atmosphere of art in which there are no vulgar connubial prejudices! Could I—whether I be rich or poor—see in her the ideal of an English wife? As it is—as it is—with this mystery which oppresses me, which, till solved, leaves my own career insoluble,—as it is, how fortunate that I did not find her alone; did not utter the words that would fain have leaped from my heart; did not say, 'I may not be the rich man I seem, but in that case I shall be yet more ambitious, because struggle and labour are the sinews of ambition! Should I be rich, will you adorn my station? Should I be poor, will you enrich poverty with your smile? And can you, in either case, forego—really, painlessly forego, as you led me to hope—the pride in your own art?' My ambition were killed did I marry an actress, a singer. Better that than the hungerer after excitements which are never allayed, the struggler in a career which admits of no retirement,—the woman to whom marriage is no goal, who remains to the last the property of the public, and glories to dwell in a house of glass into which every bystander has a right to peer. Is this the ideal of an Englishman's wife and home? No, no!—woe is me, no!"

# BOOK VI.

## CHAPTER I.

A few weeks after the date of the preceding chapter, a gay party of men were assembled at supper in one of the private salons of the Maison Doree. The supper was given by Frederic Lemercier, and the guests were, though in various ways, more or less distinguished. Rank and fashion were not unworthily represented by Alain de Rochebriant and Enguerrand de Vandemar, by whose supremacy as "lion" Frederic still felt rather humbled, though Alain had contrived to bring them familiarly together. Art, Literature, and the Bourse had also their representatives in Henri Bernard, a rising young portrait-painter, whom the Emperor honoured with his patronage, the Vicomte de Braze, and M. Savarin. Science was not altogether forgotten, but contributed its agreeable delegate in the person of the eminent physician to whom we have been before introduced,—Dr. Bacourt. Doctors in Paris are not so serious as they mostly are in London; and Bacourt, a pleasant philosopher of the school of Aristippus, was no unfrequent nor ungenial guest at any banquet in which the Graces relaxed their zones. Martial glory was also represented at that social gathering by a warrior, bronzed and decorated, lately arrived from Algiers, on which arid soil he had achieved many laurels and the rank of Colonel. Finance contributed Duplessis. Well it might; for Duplessis had just assisted the host to a splendid coup at the Bourse.

"Ah, cher Monsieur Savarin," says Enguerrand de Vandemar, whose patrician blood is so pure from revolutionary taint that he is always instinctively polite, "what a masterpiece in its way is that little paper of yours in the 'Sens Commun,' upon the connection between the national character and the national diet! so genuinely witty!—for wit is but truth made amusing."

"You flatter me," replied Savarin, modestly; "but I own I do think there is a smattering of philosophy in that trifle. Perhaps, however, the character of a people depends more on its drinks than its food. The wines of Italy, heady, irritable, ruinous to the digestion, contribute to the character which belongs to active brains and disordered livers. The Italians conceive great plans, but they cannot digest them. The English common-people drink beer, and the beerish character is stolid, rude, but stubborn and enduring. The English middle-class imbibe port and sherry; and with these strong potations their ideas become obfuscated. Their character has no liveliness; amusement is not one of their wants; they sit at home after dinner and doze away the fumes of their beverage in the dulness of domesticity. If the English aristocracy are more vivacious and cosmopolitan, it is thanks to the wines of France, which it is the mode with them to prefer; but still, like all plagiarists, they are imitators, not inventors; they borrow our wines and copy our manners. The Germans—"

"Insolent barbarians!" growled the French Colonel, twirling his mustache; "if the Emperor were not in his dotage, their Sadowa would ere this have cost them their Rhine."

"The Germans," resumed Savarin, unheeding the interruption, "drink acrid wines, varied with beer, to which last their commonalty owes a quasi resemblance in stupidity and endurance to the English masses. Acrid wines rot the teeth Germans are afflicted with toothache from infancy. All people subject to toothache are sentimental. Goethe was a martyr to toothache. 'Werther' was written in one of those paroxysms which predispose genius to suicide. But the German character is not all toothache; beer and tobacco step in to the relief of Rhenish acridities, blend philosophy with sentiment, and give that patience in detail which distinguishes their professors and their generals. Besides, the German wines in themselves have other qualities than that of acridity. Taken with sourkrout and stewed prunes, they produce fumes of self-conceit. A German has little of French vanity; he has German self-esteem. He extends the esteem of self to those around him; his home, his village, his city, his country,—all belong to him. It is a duty he owes to himself to defend them. Give him his pipe and his sabre, and, Monsieur le Colonel, believe me, you will never take the Rhine from him."

"P-r-r," cried the Colonel; "but we have had the Rhine."

"We did not keep it. And I should not say I had a francpiece if I borrowed it from your purse and had to give it back the next day."

Here there arose a very general hubbub of voices, all raised against M. Savarin. Enguerrand, like a man of good ton, hastened to change the conversation.

"Let us leave these poor wretches to their sour wines and toothaches. We drinkers of the champagne, all our own, have only pity for the rest of the human race. This new journal 'Le Sens Commun' has a strange title, Monsieur Savarin."

"Yes; 'Le Sens Commun' is not common in Paris, where we all have too much genius for a thing so vulgar."

"Pray," said the young painter, "tell me what you mean by the title 'Le Sens Commun.' It is mysterious."

"True," said Savarin; "it may mean the Sensus communis of the Latins, or the Good Sense of the English. The Latin phrase signifies the sense of the common interest; the English phrase, the sense which persons of understanding have in common. I suppose the inventor of our title meant the latter signification."

"And who was the inventor?" asked Bacourt.

"That is a secret which I do not know myself," answered Savarin.

"I guess," said Enguerrand, "that it must be the same person who writes the political leaders. They are most remarkable; for they are so unlike the articles in other journals, whether those journals be the best or the worst. For my own part, I trouble my head very little about politics, and shrug my shoulders at essays which reduce the government of flesh and blood into mathematical problems. But these articles seem to be written by a man of the world, and as a man of the world myself, I read them."

"But," said the Vicomte de Breze, who piqued himself on the polish of his style, "they are certainly not the composition of any eminent writer. No eloquence, no sentiment; though I ought not to speak disparagingly of a fellow-contributor."

"All that may be very true;" said Savarin; "but M. Enguerrand is right. The papers are evidently the work of a man of the world, and it is for that reason that they have startled the public, and established the success of 'Le Sens Commun.' But wait a week or two longer, Messieurs, and then tell me what you think of a new roman by a new writer, which we shall announce in our impression to-morrow. I shall be disappointed, indeed, if that does not charm you. No lack of eloquence and sentiment there."

"I am rather tired of eloquence and sentiment," said Enguerrand. "Your editor, Gustave Rameau, sickens me of them with his 'Starlit Meditations in the Streets of Paris,' morbid imitations of Heine's enigmatical 'Evening Songs.' Your journal would be perfect if you could suppress the editor."

"Suppress Gustave Rameau!" cried Bernard, the painter; "I adore his poems, full of heart for poor suffering humanity."

"Suffering humanity so far as it is packed up in himself," said the physician, dryly,—"and a great deal of the suffering is bile. But a propos of your new journal, Savarin, there is a paragraph in it to-day which excites my curiosity. It says that the Vicomte de Mauleon has arrived in Paris, after many years of foreign travel; and then, referring modestly enough to the reputation for talent which he had acquired in early youth, proceeds to indulge in a prophecy of the future political career of a man who, if he have a grain of sens common, must think that the less said about him the better. I remember him well; a terrible mauvais sujet, but superbly handsome. There was a shocking story about the jewels of a foreign duchess, which obliged him to leave Paris."

"But," said Savarin, "the paragraph you refer to hints that that story is a groundless calumny, and that the true reason for De Mauleon's voluntary self-exile was a very common one among young Parisians,—he had lavished away his fortune. He returns, when, either by heritage or his own exertions, he has secured elsewhere a competence."

"Nevertheless I cannot think that society will receive him," said Bacourt. "When he left Paris, there was one joyous sigh of relief among all men who wished to avoid duels, and keep their wives out of temptation. Society may welcome back a lost sheep, but not a reinvigorated wolf."

"I beg your pardon, mon cher," said Enguerrand; "society has already opened its fold to this poor ill-treated wolf. Two days ago Louvier summoned to his house the surviving relations or connections of De Mauleon—among whom are the Marquis de Rochebriant, the Counts de Passy, De Beauvilliers, De Chavigny, my father, and of course his two sons—and submitted to us the proofs which completely clear the Vicomte de Mauleon of even a suspicion of fraud or dishonour in the affair of the jewels. The proofs include the written attestation of the Duke himself, and letters from that nobleman after De Mauleon's disappearance from Paris, expressive of great esteem, and indeed, of great admiration, for the Vicomte's sense of honour and generosity of character. The result of this family council was that we all went in a body to call on De Mauleon; and he dined with my father that same day. You know enough of the Comte de Vandemar, and, I may add, of my mother, to be sure that they are both, in their several ways, too regardful of social conventions to lend their countenance even to a relation without well weighing the pros and cons. And as for Raoul, Bayard himself could not be a greater stickler on the point of honour."

This declaration was followed by a silence that had the character of stupor.

At last Duplessis said, "But what has Louvier to do in this galere? Louvier is no relation of that well-born vaurien; why should he summon your family council?"

"Louvier excused his interference on the ground of early and intimate friendship with De Mauleon, who, he said, came to consult him on arriving at Paris, and who felt too proud or too timid to address relations with whom he had long dropped all intercourse. An intermediary was required, and Louvier volunteered to take that part on himself; nothing more natural nor more simple. By the way, Alain, you dine with Louvier to-morrow, do you not?—a dinner in honour of our rehabilitated kinsman. I and Raoul go."

"Yes, I shall be charmed to meet again a man who, whatever might be his errors in youth, on which," added Alain, slightly colouring, "it certainly does not become me to be severe, must have suffered the most poignant anguish a man of honour can undergo,—namely, honour suspected; and who now, whether by years or sorrow, is so changed that I cannot recognize a likeness to the character I have just heard given to him as mauvais sujet and vaurien."

"Bravo!" cried Enguerrand; "all honour to courage!—and at Paris it requires great courage to defend the absent."

"Nay," answered Alain, in a low voice. "The gentilhomme who will not defend another gentilhomme traduced, would, as a soldier, betray a citadel and desert a flag."

"You say M. de Mauleon is changed," said De Breze; "yes, he must be growing old. No trace left of his good looks?"

"Pardon me," said Enguerrand; "he is bien conserve, and has still a very handsome head and an imposing presence. But one cannot help doubting whether he deserved the formidable reputation he acquired in youth; his manner is so singularly mild and gentle, his conversation so winningly modest, so void of pretence, and his mode of life is as simple as that of a Spanish hidalgo."

"He does not, then, affect the role of Monte Cristo," said Duplessis, "and buy himself into notice like that hero of romance?"

"Certainly not: he says very frankly that he has but a very small income, but more than enough for his wants,—richer than in his youth, for he has learned content. We may dismiss the hint in 'Le Sens Commun' about his future political career,—at least he evinces no such ambition."

"How could he as a Legitimist?" said Alain, bitterly. "What department would elect him?"

"But is he a Legitimist?" asked De Breze.

"I take it for granted that he must be that," answered Alain, haughtily, "for he is a De Mauleon."

"His father was as good a De Mauleon as himself, I presume," rejoined De Breze, dryly; "and he enjoyed a place at the Court of Louis Philippe, which a Legitimist could scarcely accept. Victor did not, I fancy, trouble his head about politics at all, at the time I remember him; but to judge by his chief associates, and the notice he received from the Princes of the House of Orleans, I should guess that he had no predilections in favour of Henri V."

"I should regret to think so," said Alain, yet more haughtily, "since the De Mauleons acknowledge the head of their house in the representative of the Rochebriants."

"At all events," said Duplessis, "M. de Mauleon appears to be a philosopher of rare stamp. A Parisian who has known riches and is contented to be poor is a phenomenon I should like to study."

"You have that chance to-morrow evening, Monsieur Duplessis," said Enguerrand.

"What! at M. Louvier's dinner? Nay, I have no other acquaintance with M. Louvier than that of the Bourse, and the acquaintance is not cordial."

"I did not mean at M. Louvier's dinner, but at the Duchesse de Tarascon's ball. You, as one of her special favourites, will doubtless honour her reunion."

"Yes; I have promised my daughter to go to the ball. But the Duchesse is Imperialist. M. de Mauleon seems to be either a Legitimist, according to Monsieur le Marquis, or an Orleanist, according to our friend De Breze."

"What of that? Can there be a more loyal Bourbonite than De Rochebriant?—and he goes to the ball. It is given out of the season, in celebration of a family marriage. And the Duchesse de Tarascon is connected with Alain, and therefore with De Mauleon, though but distantly."

"Ah! excuse my ignorance of genealogy."

"As if the genealogy of noble names were not the history of France," muttered Alain, indignantly.

# CHAPTER II.

Yes, the "Sens Commun" was a success: it had made a sensation at starting; the sensation was on the increase. It is difficult for an Englishman to comprehend the full influence of a successful journal at Paris; the station—political, literary, social—which it confers on the contributors who effect the success. M. Lebeau had shown much more sagacity in selecting Gustave Rameau for the nominal editor than Savarin supposed or my reader might detect. In the first place, Gustave himself, with all his defects of information and solidity of intellect, was not without real genius,—and a sort of genius that when kept in restraint, and its field confined to sentiment or sarcasm, was in unison with the temper of the day; in the second place, it was only through Gustave that Lebeau could have got at Savarin, and the names which that brilliant writer had secured at the outset would have sufficed to draw attention to the earliest numbers of the "Sens Commun," despite a title which did not seem alluring. But these names alone could not have sufficed to circulate the new journal to the extent it had already reached. This was due to the curiosity excited by leading articles of a style new to the Parisian public, and of which the authorship defied conjecture. They were signed Pierre Firmin,—supposed to be a nom de plume, as, that name was utterly unknown in the world of letters. They affected the tone of an impartial observer; they neither espoused nor attacked any particular party; they laid down no abstract doctrines of government. But somehow or other, in language terse yet familiar, sometimes careless yet never vulgar, they expressed a prevailing sentiment of uneasy discontent, a foreboding of some destined change in things established, without defining the nature of such change, without saying whether it would be for good or for evil. In his criticisms upon individuals, the writer was guarded and moderate—the keenest-eyed censor of the press could not have found a pretext for interference with expression of opinions so polite. Of the Emperor these articles spoke little, but that little was not disrespectful; yet, day after day, the articles contributed to sap the Empire. All malcontents of every shade comprehended, as by a secret of freemasonry, that in this journal they had an ally. Against religion not a word was uttered, yet the enemies of religion bought that journal; still, the friends of religion bought it too, for those articles treated with irony the philosophers on paper who thought that their contradictory crotchets could fuse themselves into any single Utopia, or that any social edifice, hurriedly run up by the crazy few, could become a permanent habitation for the turbulent many, without the clamps of a creed.

The tone of these articles always corresponded with the title of the journal,—"Common-sense." It was to common-sense that it appealed,—appealed in the utterance of a man who disdained the subtle theories, the vehement declamation, the credulous beliefs, or the inflated bombast, which constitute so large a portion of the Parisian press. The articles rather resembled certain organs of the English press, which profess to be blinded by no enthusiasm for anybody or anything, which find their sale in that sympathy with ill-nature to which Huet ascribes the popularity of Tacitus, and, always quietly undermining institutions with a covert sneer, never pretend to a spirit of imagination so at variance with common-sense as a conjecture how the institutions should be rebuilt or replaced.

Well, somehow or other the journal, as I was saying, hit the taste of the Parisian public. It intimated, with the easy grace of an unpremeditated agreeable talker, that French society in all its classes was rotten; and each class was willing to believe that all the others were rotten, and agreed that unless the others were reformed, there was something very unsound in itself.

The ball at the Duchesse de Tarascon's was a brilliant event. The summer was far advanced; many of the Parisian holiday-makers had returned to the capital, but the season had not commenced, and a ball at that time of year was a very unwonted event. But there was a special occasion for this fete,—a marriage between a niece of the Duchesse and the son of a great official in high favour at the Imperial Court.

The dinner at Louvier's broke up early, and the music for the second waltz was sounding when Enguerrand, Alain, and the Vicomte de Mauleon ascended the stairs. Raoul did not accompany them; he went very rarely to any balls,—never to one given by an Imperialist, however nearly related to him the Imperialist might be. But in the sweet indulgence of his good-nature, he had no blame for those who did go,—not for Enguerrand, still less, of course, for Alain.

Something too might well here be said as to his feeling towards Victor de Mauleon. He had joined in the family acquittal of that kinsman as to the grave charge of the jewels; the proofs of innocence thereon seemed to him unequivocal and decisive, therefore he had called on the Vicomte and acquiesced in all formal civilities shown to him. But such acts of justice to a fellow-gentilhomme and a kinsman duly performed, he desired to see as little as possible of the Vicomte de Mauleon. He reasoned thus: "Of every charge which society made against this man he is guiltless; but of all the claims to admiration which society accorded to him before it erroneously condemned, there are none which make me covet his friendship, or suffice to dispel doubts as to what he may be when society once more receives him. And the man is so captivating that I should dread his influence over myself did I see much of him."

Raoul kept his reasonings to himself, for he had that sort of charity which indisposes an amiable man to be severe on bygone offences. In the eyes of Enguerrand and Alain, and such young votaries of the mode as they could influence, Victor de Mauleon assumed almost heroic proportions. In the affair which had inflicted on him a calumny so odious, it was clear that he had acted with chivalrous delicacy of honour. And the turbulence and recklessness of his earlier years, redeemed as they were, in the traditions of his contemporaries, by courage and generosity, were not offences to which young Frenchmen are inclined to be harsh. All question as to the mode in which his life might have been passed during his long absence from the capital was merged in the respect due to the only facts known, and these were clearly proved in his pieces justificatives: First, that he had served under another name in the ranks of the army in Algiers; had distinguished himself there for signal valour, and received, with promotion, the decoration of the cross. His real name was known only to his colonel, and on quitting the service, the colonel placed in his hands a letter of warm eulogy on his conduct, and identifying him as Victor de Mauleon. Secondly, that in California he had saved a wealthy family from midnight murder, fighting single-handed against and overmastering three ruffians, and declining all other reward from those he had preserved than a written attestation of their gratitude. In all countries, valour ranks high in the list of virtues; in no country does it so absolve from vices as it does in France.

But as yet Victor de Mauleon's vindication was only known by a few, and those belonging to the gayer circles of life. How he might be judged by the sober middle class, which constitutes the most important section of public opinion to a candidate for political trusts and distinctions, was another question.

The Duchesse stood at the door to receive her visitors. Duplessis was seated near the entrance, by the side of a distinguished member of the Imperial Government, with whom he was carrying on a whispered conversation. The eye of the financier, however, turned towards the doorway as Alain and Enguerrand entered, and passing over their familiar faces, fixed itself attentively on that of a mach older man whom Enguerrand was presenting to the Duchesse, and in whom Duplessis rightly divined the

Vicomte de Mauleon. Certainly if no one could have recognized M. Lebeau in the stately personage who had visited Louvier, still less could one who had heard of the wild feats of the roi des viveurs in his youth reconcile belief in such tales with the quiet modesty of mien which distinguished the cavalier now replying, with bended head and subdued accents, to the courteous welcome of the brilliant hostess. But for such difference in attributes between the past and the present De Mauleon, Duplessis had been prepared by the conversation at the Maison Doree. And now, as the Vicomte, yielding his place by the Duchesse to some new-comer, glided on, and, leaning against a column, contemplated the gay scene before him with that expression of countenance, half sarcastic, half mournful, with which men regard, after long estrangement, the scenes of departed joys, Duplessis felt that no change in that man had impaired the force of character which had made him the hero of reckless coevals. Though wearing no beard, not even a mustache, there was something emphatically masculine in the contour of the close-shaven cheek and resolute jaw; in a forehead broad at the temples, and protuberant in those organs over the eyebrows which are said to be significant of quick perception and ready action; in the lips, when in repose compressed, perhaps somewhat stern in their expression, but pliant and mobile when speaking, and wonderfully fascinating when they smiled. Altogether, about this Victor de Mauleon there was a nameless distinction, apart from that of conventional elegance. You would have said, "That is a man of some marked individuality, an eminence of some kind in himself." You would not be surprised to hear that he was a party-leader, a skilled diplomatist, a daring soldier, an adventurous traveller; but you would not guess him to be a student, an author, an artist.

While Duplessis thus observed the Vicomte de Mauleon, all the while seeming to lend an attentive ear to the whispered voice of the Minister by his side, Alain passed on into the ball-room. He was fresh enough to feel the exhilaration of the dance. Enguerrand (who had survived that excitement, and who habitually deserted any assembly at an early hour for the cigar and whist of his club) had made his way to De Mauleon, and there stationed himself. The lion of one generation has always a mixed feeling of curiosity and respect for the lion of a generation before him, and the young Vandemar had conceived a strong and almost an affectionate interest in this discrowned king of that realm in fashion which, once lost, is never to be regained; for it is only Youth that can hold its sceptre and command its subjects.

"In this crowd, Vicomte," said Enguerrand, "there must be many old acquaintances of yours?"

"Perhaps so, but as yet I have only seen new faces."

As he thus spoke, a middle-aged man, decorated with the grand cross of the Legion and half-a-dozen foreign orders, lending his arm to a lady of the same age radiant in diamonds, passed by towards the ball-room, and in some sudden swerve of his person, occasioned by a pause of his companion to adjust her train, he accidentally brushed against De Mauleon, whom he had not before noticed. Turning round to apologize for his awkwardness, he encountered the full gaze of the Vicomte, started, changed countenance, and hurried on his companion.

"Do you not recognize his Excellency?" said Enguerrand, smiling. "His cannot be a new face to you."

"Is it the Baron de Lacy?" asked De Mauleon.

"The Baron de Lacy, now Comte d'Epinay, ambassador at the Court of ——-, and, if report speak true, likely soon to exchange that post for the porte feuille of Minister."

"He has got on in life since I saw him last, the little Baron. He was then my devoted imitator, and I was not proud of the imitation."

"He has got on by always clinging to the skirts of some one stronger than himself,—to yours, I dare say, when, being a parvenu despite his usurped title of baron, he aspired to the entree into clubs and salons. The entree thus obtained, the rest followed easily; he became a millionaire through a wife's dot, and an ambassador through the wife's lover, who is a power in the State."

"But he must have substance in himself. Empty bags can not be made to stand upright. Ah! unless I mistake, I see some one I knew better. Yon pale, thin man, also with the grand cross—surely that is Alfred Hennequin. Is he too a decorated Imperialist? I left him a socialistic Republican."

"But, I presume, even then an eloquent avocat. He got into the Chamber, spoke well, defended the coup-d'etat. He has just been made Prefet of the great department of the a popular appointment. He bears a high character. Pray renew your acquaintance with him; he is coming this way."

"Will so grave a dignitary renew acquaintance with me? I doubt it."

But as De Mauleon said this, he moved from the column, and advanced towards the Prefet. Enguerrand followed him, and saw the Vicomte extend his hand to his old acquaintance.

The Prefet stared, and said, with frigid courtesy, "Pardon me,—some mistake."

"Allow me, Monsieur Hennequin," said Enguerrand, interposing, and wishing good-naturedly to save De Mauleon the awkwardness of introducing himself,—"allow me to reintroduce you to my kinsman, whom the lapse of years may well excuse you for forgetting, the Vicomte de Mauleon."

Still the Prefet did not accept the hand. He bowed with formal ceremony, said, "I was not aware that Monsieur le Vicomte had returned to Paris," and moving to the doorway, made his salutation to the hostess and disappeared.

"The insolent!" muttered Enguerrand.

"Hush!" said De Mauleon, quietly, "I can fight no more duels,—especially with a Prefet. But I own I am weak enough to feel hurt at such a reception from Hennequin, for he owed me some obligations,—small, perhaps, but still they were such as might have made me select him, rather than Louvier, as the vindicator of my name, had I known him to be so high placed. But a man who has raised himself into an authority may well be excused for forgetting a friend whose character needs defence. I forgive him."

There was something pathetic in the Vicomte's tone which touched Enguerrand's warm if light heart. But De Mauleon did not allow him time to answer. He went on quickly through an opening in the gay crowd, which immediately closed behind him, and Enguerrand saw him no more that evening.

Duplessis ere this had quitted his seat by the Minister, drawn thence by a young and very pretty girl resigned to his charge by a cavalier with whom she had been dancing. She was the only daughter of Duplessis, and he valued her even more than the millions he had made at the Bourse. "The Princess," she said, "has been swept off in the train of some German Royalty; so, petit pere, I must impose myself on thee."

The Princess, a Russian of high rank, was the chaperon that evening of Mademoiselle Valerie Duplessis.

"And I suppose I must take thee back into the ballroom," said the financier, smiling proudly, "and find thee partners."

"I don't want your aid for that, Monsieur; except this quadrille, my list is pretty well filled up."

"And I hope the partners will be pleasant. Let me know who they are," he whispered, as they threaded their way into the ball-room.

The girl glanced at her tablet.

"Well, the first on the list is milord somebody, with an unpronounceable English name."

"Beau cavalier?"

"No; ugly, old too; thirty at least."

Duplessis felt relieved. He did not wish his daughter to fall in love with an Englishman.

"And the next?"

"The next?" she said hesitatingly, and he observed that a soft blush accompanied the hesitation.

"Yes, the next. Not English too?"

"Oh, no; the Marquis de Rochebriant."

"Ah! who presented him to thee?"

"Thy friend, petit pere, M. de Braze."

Duplessis again glanced at his daughter's face; it was bent over her bouquet.

"Is he ugly also?"

"Ugly!" exclaimed the girl, indignantly; "why, he is—" she checked herself and turned away her head.

Duplessis became thoughtful. He was glad that he had accompanied his child into the ball-room; he would stay there, and keep watch on her and Rochebriant also.

Up to that moment he had felt a dislike to Rochebriant. That young noble's too obvious pride of race had nettled him, not the less that the financier himself was vain of his ancestry. Perhaps he still disliked Alain, but the dislike was now accompanied with a certain, not hostile, interest; and if he became connected with the race, the pride in it might grow contagious.

They had not been long in the ball-room before Alain came up to claim his promised partner. In saluting Duplessis, his manner was the same as usual, not more cordial, not less ceremoniously distant. A man so able as the financier cannot be without quick knowledge of the human heart.

"If disposed to fall in love with Valerie," thought Duplessis, "he would have taken more pains to please her father. Well, thank heaven, there are better matches to be found for her than a noble without fortune and a Legitimist without career."

In fact, Alain felt no more for Valerie than for any other pretty girl in the room. In talking with the Vicomte de Braze in the intervals of the dance, he had made some passing remark on her beauty. De Braze had said, "Yes, she is charming; I will present you," and hastened to do so before Rochebriant even learned her name. So introduced, he could but invite her to give him her first disengaged dance, and when that was fixed, he had retired, without entering into conversation.

Now, as they took their places in the quadrille, he felt that effort of speech had become a duty, if not a pleasure; and of course, he began with the first commonplace which presented itself to his mind.

"Do you not think it a very pleasant ball, Mademoiselle?"

"Yes," dropped, in almost inaudible reply, from Valerie's rosy lips.

"And not over-crowded, as most balls are?"

Valerie's lips again moved, but this time quite inaudibly. The obligations of the figure now caused a pause. Alain racked his brains and began,

"They tell me the last season was more than usually gay; of that I cannot judge, for it was well-nigh over when I came to Paris for the first time."

Valerie looked up with a more animated expression than her childlike face had yet shown, and said, this time distinctly, "This is my first ball, Monsieur le Marquis."

"One has only to look at Mademoiselle to divine that fact," replied Alain, gallantly.

Again the conversation was interrupted by the dance; but the ice between the two was now broken; and when the quadrille was concluded, and Rochebriant led the fair Valerie back to her father's side, she felt as if she had been listening to the music of the spheres, and that the music had now suddenly stopped. Alain, alas for her! was under no such pleasing illusion. Her talk had seemed to him artless indeed, but very insipid, compared with the brilliant conversation of the wedded Parisiennes with whom he more habitually danced; and it was with rather a sensation of relief that he made his parting bow, and receded into the crowd of bystanders.

Meanwhile De Mauleon had quitted the assemblage, walking slowly through the deserted streets towards his apartment. The civilities he had met at Louvier's dinner-party, and the marked distinction paid to him by kinsmen of rank and position so unequivocal as Alain and Enguerrand, had softened his mood and cheered his spirits. He had begun to question himself whether a fair opening to his political ambition was really forbidden to him under the existent order of things, whether it necessitated the employment of such dangerous tools as those to which anger and despair had reconciled his intellect. But the pointed way in which he had been shunned or slighted by the two men who belonged to political life—two men who in youth had looked up to himself, and whose dazzling career of honours was identified with the Imperial system—reanimated his fiercer passions and his more perilous designs. The frigid accost of Hennequin more especially galled him; it wounded not only his pride but his heart; it had the venom of ingratitude, and it is the peculiar privilege of ingratitude to wound hearts that have learned to harden themselves to the hate or contempt of men to whom no services have been rendered. In some private affair concerning his property, De Mauleon had had occasion to consult Hennequin, then a rising young avocat. Out of that consultation a friendship had sprung up, despite the differing habits and social grades of the two men. One day, calling on Hennequin, he found him in a state of great nervous excitement. The avocat had received a public insult in the salon of a noble, to whom De Mauleon had introduced him, from a man who pretended to the hand of a young lady to whom Hennequin was attached, and indeed almost affianced. The man was a notorious spadassin,—a duellist little less renowned for skill in all weapons than De Mauleon himself. The affair had been such that Hennequin's friends assured him he had no choice but to challenge this bravo. Hennequin, brave enough at the bar, was no hero before sword-point or pistol. He was utterly ignorant of the use of either weapon; his death in the encounter with an antagonist so formidable seemed to him certain, and life was so precious,—an honourable and distinguished career opening before him, marriage with the woman he loved. Still he had the Frenchman's point of honour. He had been told that he must fight; well, then, he must. He asked De Mauleon to be one of his seconds, and in asking him, sank in his chair, covered his face with his hands, and burst into tears.

"Wait till to-morrow," said De Mauleon; "take no step till then. Meanwhile, you are in my hands, and I answer for your honour."

On leaving Hennequin, Victor sought the spadassin at the club of which they were both members, and contrived, without reference to Hennequin, to pick a quarrel with him. A challenge ensued; a duel with swords took place the next morning. De Mauleon disarmed and wounded his antagonist, not gravely, but sufficiently to terminate the encounter. He assisted to convey the wounded man to his apartment, and planted himself by his bedside, as if he were a friend.

"Why on earth did you fasten a quarrel on me?" asked the spadassin; "and why, having done so, did you spare my life; for your sword was at my heart when you shifted its point, and pierced my shoulder?"

"I will tell you, and in so doing, beg you to accept my friendship hereafter, on one condition. In the course of the day, write or dictate a few civil words of apology to M. Hennequin. Ma foi! every one will praise you for a generosity so becoming in a man who has given such proofs of courage and skill to an avocat who has never handled a sword nor fired a pistol."

That same day De Mauleon remitted to Hennequin an apology for heated words freely retracted, which satisfied all his friends. For the service thus rendered by De Mauleon, Hennequin declared himself everlastingly indebted. In fact, he entirely owed to that friend his life, his marriage, his honour, his career.

"And now," thought De Mauleon, "now, when he could so easily requite me,—now he will not even take my hand. Is human nature itself at war with me?"

# CHAPTER III.

Nothing could be simpler than the apartment of the Vicomte de Mauleon, in the second story of a quiet old-fashioned street. It had been furnished at small cost out of his savings. Yet, on the whole, it evinced the good taste of a man who had once been among the exquisites of the polite world. You felt that you were in the apartment of a gentleman, and a gentleman of somewhat severe tastes, and of sober matured years. He was sitting the next morning in the room which he used as a private study. Along the walls were arranged dwarf bookcases, as yet occupied by few books, most of them books of reference, others cheap editions of the French classics in prose—no poets, no romance-writers, with a few Latin authors also in prose,—Cicero, Sallust, Tacitus. He was engaged at his desk writing,—a book with its leaves open before him, "Paul Louis Courier," that model of political irony and masculine style of composition. There was a ring at his door-bell. The Vicomte kept no servant. He rose and answered the summons. He recoiled a few paces on recognizing his visitor in M. Hennequin.

The Prefet this time did not withdraw his hand; he extended it, but it was with a certain awkwardness and timidity. "I thought it my duty to call on you, Vicomte, thus early, having already seen M. Enguerrand de Vandemar. He has shown me the copies of the pieces which were inspected by your distinguished kinsmen, and which completely clear you of the charge that—grant me your pardon when I say—seemed to me still to remain unanswered when I had the honour to meet you last night."

"It appears to me, Monsieur Hennequin, that you, as an avocat so eminent, might have convinced yourself very readily of that fact."

"Monsieur le Vicomte, I was in Switzerland with my wife at the time of the unfortunate affair in which you were involved."

"But when you returned to Paris, you might perhaps have deigned to make inquiries so affecting the honour of one you had called a friend, and for whom you had professed"—De Mauleon paused; he disdained to add—"an eternal gratitude."

Hennequin coloured slightly, but replied with self-possession.

"I certainly did inquire. I did hear that the charge against you with regard to the abstraction of the jewels was withdrawn, that you were therefore acquitted by law; but I heard also that society did not acquit you, and that, finding this, you had quitted France. Pardon me again, no one would listen to me when I attempted to speak on your behalf but now that so many years have elapsed, that the story is imperfectly remembered, that relations so high-placed receive you so cordially,—now I rejoice to think that you will have no difficulty in regaining a social position never really lost, but for a time resigned."

"I am duly sensible of the friendly joy you express. I was reading the other day in a lively author some pleasant remarks on the effects of medisance or calumny upon our impressionable Parisian public. 'If,' says the writer, 'I found myself accused of having put the two towers of Notre Dame into my waistcoat-pocket I should not dream of defending myself; I should take to flight. And,' adds the writer, 'if my best friend were under the same accusation, I should be so afraid of being considered his accomplice that I should put my best friend outside the door.' Perhaps, Monsieur Hennequin, I was seized with the first alarm. Why should I blame you if seized with the second? Happily, this good city of Paris has its reactions. And you can now offer me your hand. Paris has by this time discovered that the two towers of Notre Dame are not in my pocket."

There was a pause. De Mauleon had resettled himself at his desk, bending over his papers, and his manner seemed to imply that he considered the conversation at an end.

But a pang of shame, of remorse, of tender remembrance, shot across the heart of the decorous, worldly, self-seeking man, who owed all that he now was to the ci-devant vaurien before him. Again he stretched forth his hand, and this time grasped De Mauleon's warmly. "Forgive me," he said, feelingly and hoarsely; "forgive me, I was to blame. By character, and perhaps by the necessities of my career, I am over-timid to public opinion, public scandal. Forgive me. Say if in anything now I can requite, though but slightly, the service I owe you."

De Mauleon looked steadily at the Prefet, and said slowly, "Would you serve me in turn? Are you sincere?"

The Prefet hesitated a moment, then answered firmly, "Yes."

"Well, then, what I ask of you is a frank opinion,—not as lawyer, not as Prefet, but as a man who knows the present state of French society. Give that opinion without respect to my feelings one way or other. Let it emanate solely from your practised judgment."

"Be it so," said Hennequin, wondering what was to come. De Mauleon resumed, "As you may remember, during my former career I had no political ambition. I did not meddle with politics. In the troubled times that immediately succeeded the fall of Louis Philippe I was but an epicurean looker-on. Grant that, so far as admission to the salons is concerned, I shall encounter no difficulty in regaining position; but as regards the Chamber, public life, a political career, can I have my fair opening under the Empire? You pause. Answer as you have promised, frankly."

"The difficulties in the way of a political career would be very great."

"Insuperable?"

"I fear so. Of course, in my capacity of Prefet, I have no small influence in my department in support of a Government candidate. But I do not think that the Imperial Government could, at this time especially, in which it must be very cautious in selecting its candidates, be induced to recommend you. The affair of the jewels would be raked up; your vindication disputed, denied; the fact that for so many years you have acquiesced in that charge without taking steps to refute it; your antecedents, even apart from that charge; your present want of property (M. Enguerrand tells me your income is but moderate); the absence of all previous repute in public life. No; relinquish the idea of political contest,—it would expose you to inevitable mortifications, to a failure that would even jeopardize the admission to the salons which you are now gaining. You could not be a Government candidate."

"Granted. I may have no desire to be one; but an opposition candidate, one of the Liberal party?"

"As an Imperialist," said Hennequin, smiling gravely, "and holding the office I do, it would not become me to encourage a candidate against the Emperor's Government. But speaking with the frankness you solicit, I should say that your chances there are infinitely worse. The Opposition are in a pitiful minority,—the most eminent of the Liberals can scarcely gain seats for themselves; great local popularity or property, high established repute for established patriotism, or proved talents of oratory and statesmanship, are essential qualifications for a seat in the Opposition; and even these do not suffice for a third of the persons who possess them. Be again what you were before,—the hero of salons remote from the turbulent vulgarity of politics."

"I am answered. Thank you once more. The service I rendered you once is requited now."

"No, indeed,—no; but will you dine with me quietly today, and allow me to present to you my wife and two children, born since we parted? I say to-day, for to-morrow I return to my Prefecture."

"I am infinitely obliged by your invitation, but to-day I dine with the Comte de Beauvilliers to meet some of the Corps Diplomatique. I must make good my place in the salons, since you so clearly show me that I have no chance of one in the Legislature—unless—"

"Unless what?"

"Unless there happen one of those revolutions in which the scum comes uppermost."

"No fear of that. The subterranean barracks and railway have ended forever the rise of the scum, the reign of the canaille and its barricades."

"Adieu, my dear Hennequin. My respectful hommages a Madame."

After that day the writing of Pierre Firmin in "Le Sens Commun," though still keeping within the pale of the law, became more decidedly hostile to the Imperial system, still without committing their author to any definite programme of the sort of government that should succeed it.

# CHAPTER IV.

The weeks glided on. Isaura's manuscript bad passed into print; it came out in the French fashion of feuilletons,—a small detachment at a time. A previous flourish of trumpets by Savarin and the clique at his command insured it attention, if not from the general public, at least from critical and literary coteries. Before the fourth instalment appeared it had outgrown the patronage of the coteries; it seized hold of the public. It was not in the last school in fashion; incidents were not crowded and violent,—they were few and simple, rather appertaining to an elder school, in which poetry of sentiment and grace of diction prevailed. That very resemblance to old favourites gave it the attraction of novelty. In a word, it excited a pleased admiration, and great curiosity was felt as to the authorship. When it oozed out that it was by the young lady whose future success in the musical world had been so sanguinely predicted by all who had heard her sing, the interest wonderfully increased. Petitions to be introduced to her acquaintance were showered upon Savarin. Before she scarcely realized her dawning fame, she was drawn from her quiet home and retired habits; she was fetee and courted in the literary circle of which Savarin was a chief. That circle touched, on one side, Bohemia; on the other, that realm of politer fashion which, in every intellectual metropolis, but especially in Paris, seeks to gain borrowed light from luminaries in art and letters. But the very admiration she obtained somewhat depressed, somewhat troubled her; after all, it did not differ from that which was at her command as a singer.

On the one hand, she shrank instinctively from the caresses of female authors and the familiar greetings of male authors, who frankly lived in philosophical disdain of the conventions respected by sober, decorous mortals. On the other hand, in the civilities of those who, while they courted a rising celebrity, still held their habitual existence apart from the artistic world, there was a certain air of condescension, of patronage, towards the young stranger with no other protector but Signora Venosta, the ci-devant public singer, and who had made her debut in a journal edited by M. Gustave Rameau, which, however disguised by exaggerated terms of praise, wounded her pride of woman in flattering her vanity as author. Among this latter set were wealthy, high-born men, who addressed her as woman—as woman beautiful and young—with words of gallantry that implied love, but certainly no thought of marriage,—many of the most ardent were indeed married already. But once launched into the thick of Parisian hospitalities, it was difficult to draw back. The Venosta wept at the thought of missing some lively soiree, and Savarin laughed at her shrinking fastidiousness as that of a child's ignorance of the world. But still she had her mornings to herself; and in those mornings, devoted to the continuance of her work (for the commencement was in print before a third was completed), she forgot the commonplace world that received her in the evenings. Insensibly to herself the tone of this work had changed as it proceeded. It had begun seriously indeed, but in the seriousness there was a certain latent joy. It might be the joy of having found vent of utterance; it might be rather a joy still more latent, inspired by the remembrance of Graham's words and looks, and by the thought that she had renounced all idea of the professional career which he had evidently disapproved. Life then seemed to her a bright possession. We have seen that she had begun her roman without planning how it should end. She had, however, then meant it to end, somehow or other, happily. Now the lustre had gone from life; the tone of the work was saddened; it foreboded a tragic close. But for the general reader it became, with every chapter, still more interesting; the poor child had a singularly musical gift of style,—a music which lent itself naturally to pathos. Every very young writer knows how his work, if one of feeling, will colour itself from the views of some truth in his innermost self; and in proportion as it does so, how his absorption in the work increases, till it becomes part and parcel of his own mind and heart. The presence of a hidden sorrow may change the fate of the beings he has created, and guide to the grave those whom, in a happier vein, he would have united at the altar. It is not till a later stage of experience and art that the writer escapes from the influence of his individual personality, and lives in existences that take no colourings from his own. Genius usually must pass through the subjective process before it gains the objective. Even a Shakspeare represents himself in the Sonnets before no trace of himself is visible in a Falstaff or a Lear.

No news of the Englishman,—not a word. Isaura could not but feel that in his words, his looks, that day in her own garden, and those yet happier days at Enghien, there had been more than friendship; there had been love,—love enough to justify her own pride in whispering to herself, "And I love too." But then that last parting! how changed he was! how cold! She conjectured that jealousy of Rameau might, in some degree, account for the coldness when he first entered the room, but surely not when he left; surely not when she had overpassed the reserve of her sex, and implied by signs rarely misconstrued by those who love that he had no cause for jealousy of another. Yet he had gone,—parted with her pointedly as a friend, a mere friend. How foolish she had been to think this rich ambitious foreigner could ever have meant to be more! In the occupation of her work she thought to banish his image; but in that work the image was never absent; there were passages in which she pleadingly addressed it, and then would cease abruptly, stifled by passionate tears. Still she fancied that the work would reunite them; that in its pages he would hear her voice and comprehend her heart. And thus all praise of the work became very, very dear to her.

At last, after many weeks, Savarin heard from Graham. The letter was dated Aix-la-Chapelle, at which the Englishman said he might yet be some time detained. In the letter Graham spoke chiefly of the new journal: in polite compliment of Savarin's own effusions; in mixed praise and condemnation of the political and social articles signed Pierre Firmin,—praise of their intellectual power, condemnation of their moral cynicism.

> *"The writer," he said, "reminds me of a passage in which Montesquieu compares the heathen philosophers to those plants which the earth produces in places that have never seen the heavens. The soil of his experience does not grow a single belief; and as no community can exist without a belief of some kind, so a politician without belief can but help to destroy; he cannot reconstruct. Such writers corrupt a society; they do not reform a system."*

He closed his letter with a reference to Isaura:

> *"Do, in your reply, my dear Savarin, tell me something about your friends Signora Venosta and the Signorina, whose work, so far as yet published, I have read with admiring astonishment at the power of a female writer so young to rival the veteran practitioners of fiction in the creation of interest in imaginary characters, and in sentiments which, if they appear somewhat over-romantic and exaggerated, still touch very fine chords in human nature not awakened in our trite every-day existence. I presume that the beauty of the roman has been duly appreciated by a public so refined as the Parisian, and that the name of the author is generally known. No doubt she is now much the rage of the literary circles, and her career as a writer may be considered fixed. Pray present my congratulations to the Signorina when you see her."*

Savarin had been in receipt of this letter some days before he called on Isaura, and carelessly showed it to her. She took it to the window to read, in order to conceal the trembling of her hands. In a few minutes she returned it silently.

"Those Englishmen," said Savarin, "have not the heart of compliment. I am by no means flattered by what he says of my trifles, and I dare say you are still less pleased with this chilly praise of your charming tale; but the man means to be civil."

"Certainly," said Isaura, smiling faintly.

"Only think of Rameau!" resumed Savarin. "On the strength of his salary in the 'Sens Commun,' and on the chateaux en Espagne which he constructs thereon, he has already furnished an apartment in the Chaussee d'Antin, and talks of setting up a coupe in order to maintain the dignity of letters when he goes to dine with the duchesses who are some day or other to invite him. Yet I admire his self-confidence, though I laugh at it. A man gets on by a spring in his own mechanism, and he should always keep it wound up. Rameau will make a figure. I used to pity him; I begin to respect. Nothing succeeds like success. But I see I am spoiling your morning. Au revoir, mon enfant."

Left alone, Isaura brooded in a sort of mournful wonderment over the words referring to herself in Graham's letter. Read though but once, she knew them by heart. What! did he consider those characters she had represented as wholly imaginary? In one—the most prominent, the most attractive—could he detect no likeness to himself? What! did he consider so "over-romantic and exaggerated" sentiments which couched appeals from her heart to his? Alas! in matters of sentiment it is the misfortune of us men that even the most refined of us often grate upon some sentiment in a woman, though she may not be romantic,—not romantic at all, as people go,—some sentiment which she thought must be so obvious if we cared a straw about her, and which, though we prize her above the Indies, is by our dim, horn-eyed, masculine vision undiscernible. It may be something in itself the airiest of trifles: the anniversary of a day in which the first kiss was interchanged, nay, of a violet gathered, a misunderstanding cleared up; and of that anniversary we remember no more than we do of our bells and coral. But she—she remembers it; it is no bells and coral to her. Of course, much is to be said in excuse of man, brute though he be. Consider the multiplicity of his occupations, the practical nature of his cares. But granting the validity of all such excuse, there is in man an original obtuseness of fibre as regards sentiment in comparison with the delicacy of woman's. It comes, perhaps, from the same hardness of constitution which forbids us the luxury of ready tears. Thus it is very difficult for the wisest man to understand thoroughly a woman. Goethe says somewhere that the highest genius in man must have much of the woman in it. If this be true, the highest genius alone in man can comprehend and explain the nature of woman, because it is not remote from him, but an integral part of his masculine self. I am not sure, however, that it necessitates the highest genius, but rather a special idiosyncrasy in genius which the highest may or may not have. I think Sophocles a higher genius than Euripides; but Euripides has that idiosyncrasy, and Sophocles not. I doubt whether women would accept Goethe as their interpreter with the same readiness with which they would accept Schiller. Shakspeare, no doubt, excels all poets in the comprehension of women, in his sympathy with them in the woman-part of his nature which Goethe ascribes to the highest genius; but, putting aside that "monster," I do not remember any English poet whom we should consider conspicuously eminent in that lore, unless it be the prose poet, nowadays generally underrated and little read, who wrote the letters of Clarissa Harlowe. I say all this in vindication of Graham Vane, if, though a very clever man in his way, and by no means uninstructed in human nature, he had utterly failed in comprehending the mysteries which to this poor woman-child seemed to need no key for one who really loved her. But we have said somewhere before in this book that music speaks in a language which cannot explain itself except in music. So speaks, in the human heart, much which is akin to music. Fiction (that is, poetry, whether in form of rhyme or prose) speaks thus pretty often. A reader must be more commonplace than, I trust, my gentle readers are, if he suppose that when Isaura symbolized the real hero of her thoughts in the fabled hero of her romance, she depicted him as one of whom the world could say, "That is Graham Vane." I doubt if even a male poet would so vulgarize any woman whom he thoroughly reverenced and loved. She is too sacred to him to be thus unveiled to the public stare; as the sweetest of all ancient love-poets says well—

*"Qui sapit in tacito gaudeat ille sinu."*

But a girl, a girl in her first untold timid love, to let the world know, "that is the man I love and would die for!"—if such a girl be, she has no touch of the true woman-genius, and certainly she and Isaura have nothing in common. Well, then, in Isaura's invented hero, though she saw the archetypal form of Graham Vane,—saw him as in her young, vague, romantic dreams idealized, beautified, transfigured,—he would have been the vainest of men if he had seen therein the reflection of himself. On the contrary he said, in the spirit of that jealousy to which he was too prone, "Alas! this, then, is some ideal, already seen perhaps, compared to which how commonplace am I!" and thus persuading himself, no wonder that the sentiments surrounding this unrecognized archetype appeared to him over-romantic. His taste acknowledged the beauty of form which clothed them; his heart envied the ideal that inspired them. But they seemed so remote from him; they put the dreamland of the writer farther and farther from his workday real life.

In this frame of mind, then, he had written to Savarin, and the answer he received hardened it still more. Savarin had replied, as was his laudable wont in correspondence, the very day he received Graham's letter, and therefore before he had even seen Isaura. In his reply, he spoke much of the success her work had obtained; of the invitations showered upon her, and the sensation she caused in the salons; of her future career, with hope that she might even rival Madame de Grantmesnil some day, when her ideas became emboldened by maturer experience, and a closer study of that model of eloquent style,—saying that the young editor was evidently becoming enamoured of his fair contributor; and that Madame Savarin had ventured the prediction that the Signorina's roman would end in the death of the heroine, and the marriage of the writer.

# CHAPTER V.

And still the weeks glided on: autumn succeeded to summer, the winter to autumn; the season of Paris was at its height. The wondrous capital seemed to repay its Imperial embellisher by the splendour and the joy of its fetes. But the smiles on the face of Paris were hypocritical and hollow. The Empire itself had passed out of fashion. Grave men and impartial observers felt anxious. Napoleon had renounced les ideas Napoleoniennes. He was passing into the category of constitutional sovereigns, and reigning, not by his old undivided prestige, but by the grace of party. The press was free to circulate complaints as to the past and demands as to the future, beneath which the present reeled, ominous of earthquake. People asked themselves if it were possible that the Empire could co-exist with forms of government not imperial, yet not genuinely constitutional, with a majority daily yielding to a minority. The basis of universal suffrage was sapped. About this time the articles in the "Sens Commun" signed Pierre Firmin were creating not only considerable sensation, but marked effect on opinion; and the sale of the journal was immense.

Necessarily the repute and the position of Gustave Rameau, as the avowed editor of this potent journal, rose with its success. Nor only his repute and position; bank-notes of considerable value were transmitted to him by the publisher, with the brief statement that they were sent by the sole proprietor of the paper as the editor's fair share of profit. The proprietor was never named, but Rameau took it for granted that it was M. Lebeau. M. Lebeau he had never seen since the day he had brought him the list of contributors, and was then referred to the publisher, whom he supposed M. Lebeau had secured, and received the first quarter of his salary in advance. The salary was a trifle compared to the extra profits thus generously volunteered. He called at Lebeau's office, and saw only the clerk, who said that his chef was abroad.

Prosperity produced a marked change for the better, if not in the substance of Rameau's character, at least in his manners and social converse. He no longer exhibited that restless envy of rivals, which is the most repulsive symptom of vanity diseased. He pardoned Isaura her success; nay, he was even pleased at it. The nature of her work did not clash with his own kind of writing. It was so thoroughly woman like that one could not compare it to a man's. Moreover, that success had contributed largely to the profits by which he had benefited, and to his renown as editor of the journal which accorded place to this new-found genius. But there was a deeper and more potent cause for sympathy with the success of his fair young contributor. He had imperceptibly glided into love with her,—a love very different from that with which poor Julie Caumartin flattered herself she had inspired the young poet. Isaura was one of those women for whom, even in natures the least chivalric, love, however ardent, cannot fail to be accompanied with a certain reverence,—the reverence with which the ancient knighthood, in its love for women, honoured the ideal purity of womanhood itself. Till then Rameau had never revered any one.

On her side, brought so frequently into communication with the young conductor of the journal in which she wrote, Isaura entertained for him a friendly, almost sister-like affection.

I do not think that, even if she had never known the Englishman, she would have really become in love with Rameau, despite the picturesque beauty of his countenance and the congeniality of literary pursuits; but perhaps she might have fancied herself in love with him. And till one, whether man or woman, has known real love, fancy is readily mistaken for it. But little as she had seen of Graham, and that little not in itself wholly favourable to him, she knew in her heart of hearts that his image would never be replaced by one equally dear. Perhaps in those qualities that placed him in opposition to her she felt his attractions. The poetical in woman exaggerates the worth of the practical in man. Still for Rameau her exquisitely kind and sympathizing nature conceived one of those sentiments which in woman are almost angel-like. We have seen in her letters to Madame de Grantmesnil that from the first he inspired her with a compassionate interest; then the compassion was checked by her perception of his more unamiable and envious attributes. But now those attributes, if still existent, had ceased to be apparent to her, and the compassion became unalloyed. Indeed, it was thus so far increased that it was impossible for any friendly observer to look at the beautiful face of this youth, prematurely wasted and worn, without the kindliness of pity. His prosperity had brightened and sweetened the expression of that face, but it had not effaced the vestiges of decay; rather perhaps deepened them, for the duties of his post necessitated a regular labour, to which he had been unaccustomed, and the regular labour necessitated, or seemed to him to necessitate, an increase of fatal stimulants. He imbibed absinthe with everything he drank, and to absinthe he united opium. This, of course, Isaura knew not, any more than she knew of his liaison with the "Ondine" of his muse; she saw only the increasing delicacy of his face and form, contrasted by his increased geniality and liveliness of spirits, and the contrast saddened her. Intellectually, too, she felt for him compassion. She recognized and respected in him the yearnings of a genius too weak to perform a tithe of what, in the arrogance of youth, it promised to its ambition. She saw, too, those struggles between a higher and a lower self, to which a weak degree of genius united with a strong degree of arrogance is so often subjected. Perhaps she overestimated the degree of genius, and what, if rightly guided, it could do; but she did, in the desire of her own heavenlier instinct, aspire to guide it heavenward. And as if she were twenty years older than himself, she obeyed that desire in remonstrating and warning and urging, and the young man took all these "preachments" with a pleased submissive patience. Such, as the new year dawned upon the grave of the old one, was the position between these two. And nothing more was heard from Graham Vane.

# CHAPTER VI.

It has now become due to Graham Vane, and to his place in the estimation of my readers, to explain somewhat more distinctly the nature of the quest in prosecution of which he had sought the aid of the Parisian police, and under an assumed name made the acquaintance of M. Lebeau.

The best way of discharging this duty will perhaps be to place before the reader the contents of the letter which passed under Graham's eyes on the day in which the heart of the writer ceased to beat.

(Confidential. To be opened immediately after my death, and before the perusal of my will.—Richard King.)

TO GRAHAM VANE, Esq.

My DEAR GRAHAM,—By the direction on the envelope of this letter, "Before the perusal of my will," I have wished to save you from the disappointment you would naturally experience if you learned my bequest without being prevised of the conditions which I am about to impose upon your honour. You will see ere you conclude this letter that you are the only man living to whom I could intrust the secret it contains and the task it enjoins.

You are aware that I was not born to the fortune that passed to me by the death of a distant relation, who had, in my earlier youth, children of his own. I was an only son, left an orphan at the age of sixteen with a very slender pittance. My guardians designed me for the medical profession. I began my studies at Edinburgh, and was sent to Paris to complete them, It so chanced that there I lodged in the same house with an artist named Auguste Duval, who, failing to gain his livelihood as a painter, in what—for his style was ambitious—is termed the Historical School, had accepted the humbler calling of a drawing-master. He had practised in that branch of the profession for several years at Tours, having a good clientele among English families settled there. This clientele, as he frankly confessed, he had lost from some irregularities of conduct. He was not a bad man, but of convivial temper, and easily led into temptation. He had removed to Paris a few months before I made his acquaintance. He obtained a few pupils, and often lost them as soon as gained. He was unpunctual and addicted to drink. But he had a small pension, accorded to him, he was wont to say mysteriously, by some high-born kinsfolk, too proud to own connection with a drawing-master, and on the condition that he should never name them. He never did name them to me, and I do not know to this day whether the story of this noble relationship was true or false. A pension, however, he did receive quarterly from some person or other, and it was an unhappy provision for him. It tended to make him an idler in his proper calling; and whenever he received the payment he spent it in debauch, to the neglect, while it lasted, of his pupils. This man had residing with him a young daughter, singularly beautiful. You may divine the rest. I fell in love with her,—a love deepened by the compassion with which she inspired me. Her father left her so frequently that, living on the same floor, we saw much of each other. Parent and child were often in great need,—lacking even fuel or food. Of course I assisted them to the utmost of my scanty means Much as I was fascinated by Louise Duval, I was not blind to great defects in her character. She was capricious, vain, aware of her beauty, and sighing for the pleasures or the gauds beyond her reach. I knew that she did not love me,—there was little, indeed, to captivate her fancy in a poor, thread-bare medical student,—and yet I fondly imagined that my own persevering devotion would at length win her affections, I spoke to her father more than once of my hope some day to make Louise my wife. This hope, I must frankly acknowledge, he never encouraged. On the contrary, he treated it with scorn,—"His child with her beauty would look much higher;" but be continued all the same to accept my assistance, and to sanction my visits. At length my slender purse was pretty well exhausted, and the luckless drawing-master was so harassed with petty debts that further credit became impossible. At this time I happened to hear from a fellow-student that his sister, who was the principal of a lady's school in Cheltenham, bad commissioned him to look out for a first-rate teacher of drawing with whom her elder pupils could converse in French, but who should be sufficiently acquainted with English to make his instructions intelligible to the young. The salary was liberal, the school large and of high repute, and his appointment to it would open to an able teacher no inconsiderable connection among private families. I communicated this intelligence to Duval. He caught at it eagerly. He had learned at Tours to speak English fluently; and as his professional skill was of high order, and he was popular with several eminent artists, he obtained certificates as to his talents, which my fellow-student forwarded to England with specimens of Duval's drawings. In a few days the offer of an engagement arrived, was accepted, and Duval and his daughter set out for Cheltenham. At the eve of their departure, Louise, profoundly dejected at the prospect of banishment to a foreign country, and placing no trust in her father's reform to steady habits, evinced a tenderness for me hitherto new; she wept bitterly; she allowed me to believe that her tears flowed at the thought of parting with me, and even besought me to accompany them to Cheltenham, if only for a few days. You may suppose how delightedly I complied with the request. Duval had been about a week at the watering place, and was discharging the duties he had undertaken with such unwonted steadiness and regularity that I began sorrowfully to feel I had no longer an excuse for not returning to my studies at Paris, when the poor teacher was seized with a fit of paralysis. He lost the power of movement, and his mind was affected. The medical attendant called in said that he might linger thus for some time, but that, even if he recovered his intellect, which was more than doubtful, he would never be able to resume his profession. I could not leave Louise in circumstances so distressing,—I remained. The little money Duval had brought from Paris was now exhausted; and when the day on which he had been in the habit of receiving his quarter's pension came round, Louise was unable even to conjecture how it was to be applied for. It seems he had always gone for it in person; but to whom he went was a secret which he had never divulged, and at this critical juncture his mind was too enfeebled even to comprehend us when we inquired. I had already drawn from the small capital on the interest of which I had maintained myself; I now drew out most of the remainder. But this was a resource that could not last long. Nor could I, without seriously compromising Louise's character, be constantly in the house with a girl so young, and whose sole legitimate protector was thus afflicted. There seemed but one alternative to that of abandoning her altogether,—namely, to make her my wife, to conclude the studies necessary to obtain my diploma, and purchase some partnership in a small country practice with the scanty surplus that might be left of my capital. I placed this option before Louise timidly, for I could not bear the thought of forcing her inclinations. She seemed much moved by what she called my generosity: she consented; we were married. I was, as you may conceive, wholly ignorant of French law. We were married according to the English ceremony and the Protestant ritual. Shortly after our marriage we all three returned to Paris, taking an apartment in a quarter remote from that in which we had before lodged, in order to avoid any, harassment to which such small creditors as Duval had left behind him might subject us. I resumed my studies with redoubled energy, and Louise was necessarily left much alone with her poor father in the daytime. The defects in her character became more and more visible. She reproached me for the solitude to which I condemned her; our poverty galled her; she had no kind greeting for me when I returned at evening, wearied out. Before marriage she had not loved me; after marriage, alas! I fear she hated. We had been returned to Paris some months when poor Duval died; he had never recovered his faculties, nor had we ever learned from whom his pension had been received. Very soon after her father's death I observed a singular change in the humour and manner of Louise. She was no longer peevish, irascible, reproachful; but taciturn and thoughtful. She seemed to me under the influence of some suppressed excitement, her cheeks flushed and her eye abstracted. At length, one evening when I returned I found her gone. She did not come back that night nor the next day. It was impossible for me to conjecture what had become of her. She had no friends, so far as I knew; no one had visited at our squalid apartment. The poor house in which we lodged had no concierge whom I could question; but the ground-floor was occupied by a small tobacconist's shop, and the woman at the counter told me that for some days before my wife's disappearance, she had observed her pass the shop-window in going out in the afternoon and returning towards the evening. Two terrible conjectures beset me either in her walk she had met some admirer, with whom she had fled; or, unable to bear the companionship and poverty of a union which she had begun to loathe, she had gone forth to drown herself in the Seine. On the third day from her flight I received the letter I enclose. Possibly the handwriting may serve you as a guide in the mission I intrust to you.

> *MONSIEUR,—You have deceived me vilely,—taken advantage of my inexperienced youth and friendless position to decoy me into an illegal marriage. My only consolation under my calamity and disgrace is, that I am at least free from a detested bond. You will not see me again,—it is idle to attempt to do so. I have obtained refuge with relations whom I have been fortunate enough to discover, and to whom I intrust my fate; and even if you could learn the shelter I have sought, and have the audacity to molest me, you would but subject yourself to the chastisement you so richly deserve.*
>
> Louise DUVAL.

At the perusal of this cold-hearted, ungrateful letter, the love I had felt for this woman—already much shaken by her wayward and perverse temper—vanished from my heart, never to return. But as an honest man, my conscience was terribly stung. Could it be possible that I had unknowingly deceived her,—that our marriage was not legal? When I recovered from the stun which was the first effect of her letter, I sought the opinion of an avoue in the neighbourbood, named Sartiges, and to my dismay, I learned that while I, marrying according to the customs of my own country, was legally bound to Louise in England, and could not marry another, the marriage was in all ways illegal for her,—being without the consent of her relations while she was under age; without the ceremonials of the Roman Catholic Church,—to which, though I never heard any profession of religious belief from her or her father, it might fairly be presumed that she belonged; and, above all, without the form of civil contract which is indispensable to the legal marriage of a French subject.

The avoue said that the marriage, therefore, in itself was null, and that Louise could, without incurring legal penalties for bigamy, marry again in France according to the French laws; but that under the circumstances it was probable that her next of kin would apply on her behalf to the proper court for the formal annulment of the marriage, which would be the most effectual mode of saving her from any molestation on my part, and remove all possible questions hereafter as to her single state and absolute right to remarry. I had better remain quiet, and wait for intimation of further proceedings. I knew not what else to do, and necessarily submitted.

From this wretched listlessness of mind, alternated now by vehement resentment against Louise, now by the reproach of my own sense of honour in leaving that honour in so questionable a point of view, I was aroused by a letter from the distant kinsman by whom hitherto I had been so neglected. In the previous year he had lost one of his two children; the other was just dead. No nearer relation now surviving stood between me and my chance of inheritance from him. He wrote word of his domestic affliction with a manly sorrow which touched me, said that his health was failing, and begged me, as soon as possible, to come and visit him in Scotland. I went, and continued to reside with him till his death, some months afterwards. By his will I succeeded to his ample fortune on condition of taking his name.

As soon as the affairs connected with this inheritance permitted, I returned to Paris, and again saw M. Sartiges. I had never heard from Louise, nor from any one connected with her since the letter you have read. No steps had been taken to annul the marriage, and sufficient time had elapsed to render it improbable that such steps would be taken now; but if no such steps were taken, however free from the marriage-bond Louise might be, it clearly remained binding on myself.

At my request, M. Sartiges took the most vigorous measures that occurred to him to ascertain where Louise was, and what and who was the relation with whom she asserted she had found refuge. The police were employed; advertisements were issued, concealing names, but sufficiently clear to be intelligible to Louise if they came under her eye, and to the effect that if any informality in our marriage existed, she was implored for her own sake to remove it by a second ceremonial—answer to be addressed to the avoue. No answer came; the police had hitherto failed of discovering her, but were sanguine of success, when a few weeks after these advertisements a packet reached M. Sartiges, enclosing the certificates annexed to this letter, of the death of Louise Duval at Munich. The certificates, as you will see, are to appearance officially attested and unquestionably genuine. So they were considered by M. Sartiges as well as by myself. Here, then, all inquiry ceased; the police were dismissed. I was free. By little and little I overcame the painful impressions which my ill-starred union and the announcement of Louise's early death bequeathed. Rich, and of active mind, I learned to dismiss the trials of my youth as a gloomy dream. I entered into public life; I made myself a creditable position; became acquainted with your aunt; we were wedded, and the beauty of her nature embellished mine. Alas, alas! two years after our marriage—nearly five years after I had received the certificates of Louise's death—I and your aunt made a summer excursion into the country of the Rhine; on our return we rested at Aix-la-Chapelle. One day while there I was walking alone in the environs of the town, when, on the road, a little girl, seemingly about five years old, in chase of a butterfly, stumbled and fell just before my feet; I took her up, and as she was crying more from the shock of the fall than any actual hurt, I was still trying my best to comfort her, when a lady some paces behind her came up, and in taking the child from my arms as I was bending over her, thanked me in a voice that made my heart stand still. I looked up, and beheld Louise.

It was not till I had convulsively clasped her hand and uttered her name that she recognized me. I was, no doubt, the more altered of the two,—prosperity and happiness had left little trace of the needy, care worn, threadbare student. But if she were the last to recognize, she was the first to recover self-possession. The expression of her face became hard and set. I cannot pretend to repeat with any verbal accuracy the brief converse that took place between us, as she placed the child on the grass bank beside the path, bade her stay there quietly, and walked on with me some paces as if she did not wish the child to hear what was said.

The purport of what passed was to this effect: She refused to explain the certificates of her death further than that, becoming aware of what she called the "persecution" of the advertisements issued and inquiries instituted, she had caused those documents to be sent to the address given in the advertisement, in order to terminate all further molestation. But how they could have been obtained, or by what art so ingeniously forged as to deceive the acuteness of a practised lawyer, I know not to this day. She declared, indeed, that she was now happy, in easy circumstances, and that if I wished to make some reparation for the wrong I had done her, it would be to leave her in peace; and in case—which was not likely—we ever met again, to regard and treat her as a stranger; that she, on her part, never would molest me, and that the certified death of Louise Duval left me as free to marry again as she considered herself to be.

My mind was so confused, so bewildered, while she thus talked, that I did not attempt to interrupt her. The blow had so crushed me that I scarcely struggled under it; only, as she turned to leave me, I suddenly recollected that the child, when taken from my arms, had called her "Maman," and, judging by the apparent age of the child, it must have been born but a few months after Louise had left me,—that it must be mine. And so, in my dreary woe, I faltered out, "But what of your infant? Surely that has on me a claim that you relinquish for yourself. You were not unfaithful to me while you deemed you were my wife?"

"Heavens! can you insult me by such a doubt? No!" she cried out, impulsively and haughtily. "But as I was not legally your wife, the child is not legally yours; it is mine, and only mine. Nevertheless, if you wish to claim it"—here she paused as in doubt. I saw at once that she was prepared to resign to me the child if I had urged her to do so. I must own, with a pang of remorse, that I recoiled from such a proposal. What could I do with the child? How explain to my wife the cause of my interest in it? If only a natural child of mine, I should have shrunk from owning to Janet a youthful error. But as it was,—the child by a former marriage, the former wife still living!—my blood ran cold with dread. And if I did take the child, invent what story I might as to its parentage, should I not expose myself, expose Janet, to terrible constant danger? The mother's natural affection might urge her at any time to seek tidings of the child, and in so doing she might easily discover my new name, and, perhaps years hence, establish on me her own claim.

No, I could not risk such perils. I replied sullenly, "You say rightly; the child is yours,—only yours." I was about to add an offer of pecuniary provision for it, but Louise had already turned scornfully towards the bank on which she had left the infant. I saw her snatch from the child's hand some wild flowers the poor thing had been gathering; and how often have I thought of the rude way in which she did it,—not as a mother who loves her child. Just then other passengers appeared on the road; two of them I knew,—an English couple very intimate with Lady Janet and myself. They stopped to accost me, while Louise passed by with the infant towards the town. I turned in the opposite direction, and strove to collect my thoughts. Terrible as was the discovery thus suddenly made, it was evident that Louise had as strong an interest as myself to conceal it. There was little chance that it would ever be divulged. Her dress and that of the child were those of persons in the richer classes of life. After all, doubtless, the child needed not pecuniary assistance from me, and was surely best off under the mother's care. Thus I sought to comfort and to delude myself.

The next day Janet and I left Aix-la-Chapelle and returned to England. But it was impossible for me to banish the dreadful thought that Janet was not legally my wife; that could she even guess the secret lodged in my breast she would be lost to me forever, even though she died of the separation (you know well how tenderly she loved me). My nature underwent a silent revolution. I had previously cherished the ambition common to most men in public life,—the ambition for fame, for place, for power. That ambition left me; I shrank from the thought of becoming too well known, lest Louise or her connections, as yet ignorant of my new name, might more easily learn what the world knew; namely that I had previously borne another name,—the name of her husband,—and finding me wealthy and honoured, might hereafter be tempted to claim for herself or her daughter the ties she adjured for both while she deemed me poor and despised. But partly my conscience, partly the influence of the angel by my side, compelled me to seek whatever means of doing good to others position and circumstances placed at my disposal. I was alarmed when even such quiet exercise of mind and fortune acquired a sort of celebrity. How pain fully I shrank from it! The world attributed my dread of publicity to unaffected modesty. The world praised me, and I knew myself an impostor. But the years stole on. I heard no more of Louise or her child, and my fears gradually subsided. Yet I was consoled when the two children born to me by Janet died in their infancy. Had they lived, who can tell whether something might not have transpired to prove them illegitimate.

I must hasten on. At last came the great and crushing calamity of my life,—I lost the woman who was my all in all. At least she was spared the discovery that would have deprived me of the right of tending her deathbed, and leaving within her tomb a place vacant for myself.

But after the first agonies that followed her loss, the conscience I had so long sought to tranquillize became terribly reproachful. Louise had forfeited all right to my consideration, but my guiltless child had not done so. Did it live still? If so, was it not the heir to my fortunes,—the only child left to me? True, I have the absolute right to dispose of my wealth: it is not in land; it is not entailed: but was not the daughter I had forsaken morally the first claimant; was no reparation due to her? You remember that my physician ordered me, some little time after your aunt's death, to seek a temporary change of scene. I obeyed, and went away no one knew whither. Well, I repaired to Paris; there I sought M. Sartiges, the avoue. I found he had been long dead. I discovered his executors, and inquired if any papers or correspondence between Richard Macdonald and himself many years ago were in existence. All such documents, with others not returned to correspondents at his decease, had been burned by his desire. No possible clew to the whereabouts of Louise, should any have been gained since I last saw her, was left. What then to do I knew not. I did not dare to make inquiries through strangers, which, if discovering my child, might also bring to light a marriage that would have dishonoured the memory of my lost saint. I returned to England, feeling that my days were numbered. It is to you that I transmit the task of those researches which I could not institute. I bequeath to you, with the exception of trifling legacies and donations to public charities, the whole of my fortune; but you will understand by this letter that it is to be held on a trust which I cannot specify in my will. I could not, without dishonouring the venerated name of your aunt, indicate as the heiress of my wealth a child by a wife living at the time I married Janet. I cannot form any words for such a devise which would not arouse gossip and suspicion, and furnish ultimately a clew to the discovery I would shun. I calculate that, after all deductions, the sum that will devolve to you will be about L220,000. That which I mean to be absolutely and at once yours is the comparatively trifling legacy of L20,000. If Louise's child be not living, or if you find full reason to suppose that despite appearances the child is not mine, the whole of my fortune lapses to you; but should Louise be surviving and need pecuniary aid, you will contrive that she may have such an annuity as you may deem fitting, without learning whence it come. You perceive that it is your object, if possible, even more than mine, to preserve free from slur the name and memory of her who was to you a second mother. All ends we desire would be accomplished could you, on discovering my lost child, feel that, without constraining your inclinations, you could make her your wife. She would then naturally share with you my fortune, and all claims of justice and duty would be quietly appeased. She would now be of age suitable to yours. When I saw her at Aix she gave promise of inheriting no small share of her mother's beauty. If Louise's assurance of her easy circumstances were true, her daughter has possibly been educated and reared with tenderness and care. You have already assured me that you have no prior attachment. But if, on discovering this child, you find her already married, or one whom you could not love nor esteem, I leave it implicitly to your honour and judgment to determine what share of the L200,000 left in your hands should be consigned to her. She may have been corrupted by her mother's principles. She may—Heaven forbid!—have fallen into evil courses, and wealth would be misspent in her hands. In that case a competence sufficing to save her from further degradation, from the temptations of poverty, would be all that I desire you to devote from my wealth. On the contrary, you may find in her one who, in all respects, ought to be my chief inheritor. All this I leave in full confidence to you, as being, of all the men I know, the one who unites the highest sense of honour with the largest share of practical sense and knowledge of life. The main difficulty, whatever this lost girl may derive from my substance, will be in devising some means to convey it to her so that neither she nor those around her may trace the bequest to me. She can never be acknowledged as my child,—never! Your reverence for the beloved dead forbids that. This difficulty your clear strong sense must overcome; mine is blinded by the shades of death. You too will deliberately consider how to institute the inquiries after mother and child so as not to betray our secret. This will require great caution. You will probably commence at Paris, through the agency of the police, to whom you will be very guarded in your communications. It is most unfortunate that I have no miniature of Louise, and that any description of her must be so vague that it may not serve to discover her; but such as it is, it may prevent your mistaking for her some other of her name. Louise was above the common height, and looked taller than she was, with the peculiar combination of very dark hair, very fair complexion, and light-gray eyes. She would now be somewhat under the age of forty. She was not without accomplishments, derived from the companionship with her father. She spoke English fluently; she drew with taste, and even with talent. You will see the prudence of confining research at first to Louise, rather than to the child who is the principal object of it; for it is not till you can ascertain what has become of her that you can trust the accuracy of any information respecting the daughter, whom I assume, perhaps after all erroneously, to be mine. Though Louise talked with such levity of holding herself free to marry, the birth of her child might be sufficient injury to her reputation to become a serious obstacle to such second nuptials, not having taken formal steps to annul her marriage with myself. If not thus remarried, there would be no reason why she should not resume her maiden name of Duval, as she did in the signature of her letter to me: finding that I had ceased to molest her by the inquiries, to elude which she had invented the false statement of her death. It seems probable, therefore, that she is residing somewhere in Paris, and in the name of Duval. Of course the burden of uncertainty as to your future cannot be left to oppress you for an indefinite length of time. If at the end, say, of two years, your researches have wholly failed, consider three-fourths of my whole fortune to have passed to you, and put by the fourth to accumulate, should the child afterwards be discovered, and satisfy your judgment as to her claims on me as her father. Should she not, it will be a reserve fund for your own children. But oh, if my child could be found in time! and oh, if she be all that could win your heart, and be the wife you would select from free choice! I can say no more. Pity me, and judge leniently of Janet's husband.

*R. K.*

The key to Graham's conduct is now given,—the deep sorrow that took him to the tomb of the aunt he so revered, and whose honoured memory was subjected to so great a risk; the slightness of change in his expenditure and mode of life, after an inheritance supposed to be so ample; the abnegation of his political ambition; the subject of his inquiries, and the cautious reserve imposed upon them; above all, the position towards Isaura in which he was so cruelly placed.

Certainly, his first thought in revolving the conditions of his trust had been that of marriage with this lost child of Richard King's, should she be discovered single, disengaged, and not repulsive to his inclinations. Tacitly he subscribed to the reasons for this course alleged by the deceased. It was the simplest and readiest plan of uniting justice to the rightful inheritor with care for a secret so important to the honour of his aunt, of Richard King himself,—his benefactor,—of the illustrious house from which Lady Janet had sprung. Perhaps, too, the consideration that by this course a fortune so useful to his career was secured was not without influence on the mind of a man naturally ambitious. But on that consideration he forbade himself to dwell. He put it away from him as a sin. Yet, to marriage with any one else, until his mission was fulfilled, and the uncertainty as to the extent of his fortune was dispelled, there interposed grave practical obstacles. How could he honestly present himself to a girl and to her parents in the light of a rich man, when in reality he might be but a poor man? How could he refer to any lawyer the conditions which rendered impossible any settlement that touched a shilling of the large sum which at any day he might have to transfer to another? Still, when once fully conspicuous how deep was the love with which Isaura had inspired him, the idea of wedlock with the daughter of Richard King, if she yet lived and was single, became inadmissible. The orphan condition of the young Italian smoothed away the obstacles to proposals of marriage which would have embarrassed his addresses to girls of his own rank, and with parents who would have demanded settlements. And if he had found Isaura alone on that day on which he had seen her last, he would doubtless have yielded to the voice of his heart, avowed his love, wooed her own, and committed both to the tie of betrothal. We have seen how rudely such yearnings of his heart were repelled on that last interview. His English prejudices were so deeply rooted, that, even if he had been wholly free from the trust bequeathed to him, he would have recoiled from marriage with a girl who, in the ardour for notoriety, could link herself with such associates as Gustave Rameau, by habits a Bohemian, and by principles a Socialist.

In flying from Paris, he embraced the resolve to banish all thought of wedding Isaura, and to devote himself sternly to the task which had so sacred a claim upon him. Not that he could endure the idea of marrying another, even if the lost heiress should be all that his heart could have worshipped, had that heart been his own to give; but he was impatient of the burden heaped on him,—of the fortune which might not be his, of the uncertainty which paralyzed all his ambitious schemes for the future.

Yet, strive as he would—and no man could strive more resolutely—he could not succeed in banishing the image of Isaura. It was with him always; and with it a sense of irreparable loss, of a terrible void, of a pining anguish.

And the success of his inquiries at Aix-la-Chapelle, while sufficient to detain him in the place, was so slight, and advanced by such slow degrees, that it furnished no continued occupation to his restless mind. M. Renard was acute and painstaking. But it was no easy matter to obtain any trace of a Parisian visitor to so popular a Spa so many years ago. The name Duval, too, was so common, that at Aix, as we have seen at Paris, time was wasted in the chase of a Duval who proved not to be the lost Louise. At last M. Renard chanced on a house in which, in the year 1849, two ladies from Paris had lodged for three weeks. One was named Madame Duval, the other Madame Marigny. They were both young, both very handsome, and much of the same height and colouring. But Madame Marigny was the handsomer of the two. Madame Duval frequented the gaming-tables and was apparently of very lively temper. Madame Marigny lived very quietly, rarely or never stirred out, and seemed in delicate health. She, however, quitted the apartment somewhat abruptly, and, to the best of the lodging-house-keeper's recollection, took rooms in the country near Aix—she could not remember where. About two months after the departure of Madame Marigny, Madame Duval also left Aix, and in company with a French gentleman who had visited her much of late,—a handsome man of striking appearance. The lodging house-keeper did not know what or who he was. She remembered that he used to be announced to Madame Duval by the name of M. Achille. Madame Duval had never been seen again by the lodging-house-keeper after she had left. But Madame Marigny she had once seen, nearly five years after she had quitted the lodgings,—seen her by chance at the railway station, recognized her at once, and accosted her, offering her the old apartment. Madame Marigny had, however, briefly replied that she was only at Aix for a few hours, and should quit it the same day.

The inquiry now turned towards Madame Marigny. The date on which the lodging-house-keeper had last seen her coincided with the year in which Richard King had met Louise. Possibly, therefore, she might have accompanied the latter to Aix at that time, and could, if found, give information as to her subsequent history and present whereabouts.

After a tedious search throughout all the environs of Aix, Graham himself came, by the merest accident, upon the vestiges of Louise's friend. He had been wandering alone in the country round Aix, when a violent thunderstorm drove him to ask shelter in the house of a small farmer, situated in a field, a little off the byway which he had taken. While waiting for the cessation of the storm, and drying his clothes by the fire in a room that adjoined the kitchen, he entered into conversation with the farmer's wife, a pleasant, well-mannered person, and made some complimentary observation on a small sketch of the house in water-colours that hung upon the wall. "Ah," said the farmer's wife, "that was done by a French lady who lodged here many years ago. She drew very prettily, poor thing."

"A lady who lodged here many years ago,—how many?"

"Well, I guess somewhere about twenty."

"Ah, indeed! Was it a Madame Marigny?"

"Bon Dieu! That was indeed her name. Did you know her? I should be so glad to hear she is well and—I hope—happy."

"I do not know where she is now, and am making inquiries to ascertain. Pray help me. How long did Madame Marigny lodge with you?"

"I think pretty well two months; yes, two months. She left a month after her confinement."

"She was confined here?"

"Yes. When she first came, I had no idea that she was enceinte. She had a pretty figure, and no one would have guessed it, in the way she wore her shawl. Indeed I only began to suspect it a few days before it happened; and that was so suddenly, that all was happily over before we could send for the accoucheur."

"And the child lived?—a girl or a boy?"

"A girl,—the prettiest baby."

"Did she take the child with her when she went?"

"No; it was put out to nurse with a niece of my husband who was confined about the same time. Madame paid liberally in advance, and continued to send money half-yearly, till she came herself and took away the little girl."

"When was that,—a little less than five years after she had left it?"

"Why, you know all about it, Monsieur; yes, not quite five years after. She did not come to see me, which I thought unkind, but she sent me, through my niece-in-law, a real gold watch and a shawl. Poor dear lady—

for lady she was all over,—with proud ways, and would not bear to be questioned. But I am sure she was none of your French light ones, but an honest wife like myself, though she never said so."

"And have you no idea where she was all the five years she was away, or where she went after reclaiming her child?"

"No, indeed, Monsieur."

"But her remittances for the infant must have been made by letters, and the letters would have had post-marks?"

"Well, I dare say; I am no scholar myself. But suppose you see Marie Hubert, that is my niece-in-law, perhaps she has kept the envelopes."

"Where does Madame Hubert live?"

"It is just a league off by the short path; you can't miss the way. Her husband has a bit of land of his own, but he is also a carrier—'Max Hubert, carrier,'—written over the door, just opposite the first church you get to. The rain has ceased, but it may be too far for you to-day."

"Not a bit of it. Many thanks."

"But if you find out the dear lady and see her, do tell her how pleased I should be to hear good news of her and the little one."

Graham strode on under the clearing skies to the house indicated. He found Madame Hubert at home, and ready to answer all questions; but, alas! she had not the envelopes. Madame Marigny, on removing the child, had asked for all the envelopes or letters, and carried them away with her. Madame Hubert, who was as little of a scholar as her aunt-in-law was, had never paid much attention to the post-marks on the envelopes; and the only one that she did remember was the first, that contained a bank-note, and that post-mark was "Vienna."

"But did not Madame Marigny's letters ever give you an address to which to write with news of her child?"

"I don't think she cared much for her child, Monsieur. She kissed it very coldly when she came to take it away. I told the poor infant that that was her own mamma; and Madame said, 'Yes, you may call me maman,' in a tone of voice—well, not at all like that of a mother. She brought with her a little bag which contained some fine clothes for the child, and was very impatient till the child had got them on."

"Are you quite sure it was the same lady who left the child?"

"Oh, there is no doubt of that. She was certainly tres belle, but I did not fancy her as aunt did. She carried her head very high, and looked rather scornful. However, I must say she behaved very generously."

"Still you have not answered my question whether her letters contained no address."

"She never wrote more than two letters. One enclosing the first remittance was but a few lines, saying that if the child was well and thriving, I need not write; but if it died or became dangerously ill, I might at any time write a line to Madame ——-, Poste Restante, Vienna. She was travelling about, but the letter would be sure to reach her sooner or later. The only other letter I had was to apprise me that she was coming to remove the child, and might be expected in three days after the receipt of her letter."

"And all the other communications from her were merely remittances in blank envelopes?"

"Exactly so."

Graham, finding he could learn no more, took his departure. On his way home, meditating the new idea that his adventure that day suggested, he resolved to proceed at once, accompanied by M. Renard, to Munich, and there learn what particulars could be yet ascertained respecting those certificates of the death of Louise Duval, to which (sharing Richard King's very natural belief that they had been skilfully forged) he had hitherto attached no importance.

# CHAPTER VII.

No satisfactory result attended the inquiries made at Munich save indeed this certainty,—the certificates attesting the decease of some person calling herself Louise Duval had not been forged. They were indubitably genuine. A lady bearing that name had arrived at one of the principal hotels late in the evening, and had there taken handsome rooms. She was attended by no servant, but accompanied by a gentleman, who, however, left the hotel as soon as he had seen her lodged to her satisfaction. The books of the hotel still retained the entry of her name,—Madame Duval, Francaise rentiere. On comparing the handwriting of this entry with the letter from Richard King's first wife, Graham found it to differ; but then it was not certain, though probable, that the entry had been written by the alleged Madame Duval herself. She was visited the next day by the same gentleman who had accompanied her on arriving. He dined and spent the evening with her. But no one at the hotel could remember what was the gentleman's name, nor even if he were announced by any name. He never called again. Two days afterwards, Madame Duval was taken ill; a doctor was sent for, and attended her till her death. This doctor was easily found. He remembered the case perfectly,—congestion of the lungs, apparently caused by cold caught on her journey. Fatal symptoms rapidly manifested themselves, and she died on the third day from the seizure. She was a young and handsome woman. He had asked her during her short illness if he should not write to her friends; if there were no one she would wish to be sent for. She replied that there was only one friend, to whom she had already written, and who would arrive in a day or two; and on inquiring, it appeared that she had written such a letter, and taken it herself to the post on the morning of the day she was taken ill.

She had in her purse not a large sum, but money enough to cover all her expenses, including those of her funeral, which, according to the law in force at the place, followed very quickly on her decease. The arrival of the friend to whom she had written being expected, her effects were, in the meanwhile, sealed up. The day after her death a letter arrived for her, which was opened. It was evidently written by a man, and apparently by a lover. It expressed an impassioned regret that the writer was unavoidably prevented returning to Munich so soon as he had hoped, but trusted to see his dear bouton de rose in the course of the following week; it was only signed Achille, and gave no address. Two or three days after, a lady, also young and handsome, arrived at the hotel, and inquired for Madame Duval. She was greatly shocked at hearing of her decease. When sufficiently recovered to bear being questioned as to Madame Duval's relations and position, she appeared confused; said, after much pressing, that she was no relation to the deceased; that she believed Madame Duval had no relations with whom she was on friendly terms,—at least she had never heard her speak of any; and that her own acquaintance with the deceased, though cordial, was very recent. She could or would not give any clew to the writer of the letter signed Achille, and she herself quitted Munich that evening, leaving the impression that Madame Duval had been one of those ladies who, in adopting a course of life at variance with conventional regulations, are repudiated by their relations, and probably drop even their rightful names.

Achille never appeared; but a few days after, a lawyer at Munich received a letter from another at Vienna, requesting, in compliance with a client's instructions, the formal certificates of Louise Duval's death. These were sent as directed, and nothing more about the ill-fated woman was heard of. After the expiration of the time required by law, the seals were removed from the effects, which consisted of two malles and a dressing-case. But they only contained the articles appertaining to a lady's wardrobe or toilet,—no letters, not even another note from Achille,—no clew, in short, to the family or antecedents of the deceased. What then had become of these effects, no one at the hotel could give a clear or satisfactory account. It was said by the mistress of the hotel, rather sullenly, that they had, she supposed, been sold by her predecessor, and by order of the authorities, for the benefit of the poor.

If the lady who had represented herself as Louise Duval's acquaintance had given her own name, which doubtless she did, no one recollected it. It was not entered in the books of the hotel, for she had not lodged there; nor did it appear that she had allowed time for formal examination by the civil authorities. In fact, it was clear that poor Louise Duval had been considered as an adventuress by the hotel-keeper and the medical attendant at Munich; and her death had excited so little interest, that it was strange that even so many particulars respecting it could be gleaned.

After a prolonged but fruitless stay at Munich, Graham and M. Renard repaired to Vienna; there, at least, Madame Marigny had given an address, and there she might be heard of.

At Vienna, however, no research availed to discover a trace of any such person; and in despair Graham returned to England in the January of 1870, and left the further prosecution of his inquiries to M. Renard, who, though obliged to transfer himself to Paris for a time, promised that he would leave no stone unturned for the discovery of Madame Marigny; and Graham trusted to that assurance when M. Renard, rejecting half of the large gratuity offered him, added, "Je suis Francais; this with me has ceased to be an affair of money; it has become an affair that involves my amour propre."

## CHAPTER VIII.

If Graham Vane had been before caressed and courted for himself, he was more than ever appreciated by polite society, now that he added the positive repute of wealth to that of a promising intellect. Fine ladies said that Graham Vane was a match for any girl. Eminent politicians listened to him with a more attentive respect, and invited him to selecter dinner-parties. His cousin the Duke urged him to announce his candidature for the county, and purchase back, at least, the old Stamm-schloss. But Graham obstinately refused to entertain either proposal, continued to live as economically as before in his old apartments, and bore with an astonishing meekness of resignation the unsolicited load of fashion heaped upon his shoulders. At heart he was restless and unhappy. The mission bequeathed to him by Richard King haunted his thoughts like a spectre not to be exorcised. Was his whole life to be passed in the weary sustainment of an imposture which in itself was gall and wormwood to a nature constitutionally frank and open? Was he forever to appear a rich man and live as a poor one? Was he till his deathbed to be deemed a sordid miser whenever he refused a just claim on his supposed wealth, and to feel his ambition excluded from the objects it earnestly coveted, and which he was forced to appear too much of an Epicurean philosopher to prize?

More torturing than all else to the man's innermost heart was the consciousness that he had not conquered, could not conquer, the yearning love with which Isaura had inspired him, and yet that against such love all his reasonings, all his prejudices, more stubbornly than ever were combined. In the French newspapers which he had glanced over while engaged in his researches in Germany-nay, in German critical journals themselves—he had seen so many notices of the young author,—highly eulogistic, it is true, but which to his peculiar notions were more offensive than if they had been sufficiently condemnatory of her work to discourage her from its repetition; notices which seemed to him the supreme impertinences which no man likes exhibited towards the woman to whom he would render the chivalrous homage of respect. Evidently this girl had become as much public property as if she had gone on the stage. Minute details of her personal appearance,—of the dimples on her cheek, of the whiteness of her arms, of her peculiar way of dressing her hair; anecdotes of her from childhood (of course invented, but how could Graham know that?); of the reasons why she had adopted the profession of author instead of that of the singer; of the sensation she had created in certain salons (to Graham, who knew Paris so well, salons in which he would not have liked his wife to appear); of the compliments paid to her by grands seigneurs noted for their liaisons with ballet-dancers, or by authors whose genius soared far beyond the flammantia maenia of a world confined by respect for one's neighbours' land-marks,—all this, which belongs to ground of personal gossip untouched by English critics of female writers, ground especially favoured by Continental, and, I am grieved to say, by American journalists,—all this was to the sensitive Englishman much what the minute inventory of Egeria's charms would have been to Numa Pompilius. The nymph, hallowed to him by secret devotion, was vulgarized by the noisy hands of the mob, and by the popular voices, which said, "We know more about Egeria than you do." And when he returned to England, and met with old friends familiar to Parisian life, who said, "of course you have read the Cicogna's roman. What do you think of it? Very fine writing, I dare say, but above me. I go in for 'Les Mysteres de Paris' or 'Monte Cristo;' but I even find Georges Sand a bore," then as a critic Graham Vane fired up, extolled the roman he would have given his ears for Isaura never to have written; but retired from the contest muttering inly, "How can I—I, Graham Vane—how can I be such an idiot; how can I in every hour of the twenty-four sigh to myself, 'What are other women to me? Isaura, Isaura!'"

# BOOK VII.

## CHAPTER I.

It is the first week in the month of May, 1870. Celebrities are of rapid growth in the salons of Paris. Gustave Rameau has gained the position for which he sighed. The journal he edits has increased its hold on the public, and his share of the profits has been liberally augmented by the secret proprietor. Rameau is acknowledged as a power in literary circles. And as critics belonging to the same clique praise each other in Paris, whatever they may do in communities more rigidly virtuous, his poetry has been declared by authorities in the press to be superior to that of Alfred de Musset in vigour—to that of Victor Hugo in refinement; neither of which assertions would much, perhaps, shock a cultivated understanding.

It is true that it (Gustave's poetry) has not gained a wide audience among the public. But with regard to poetry nowadays, there are plenty of persons who say as Dr. Johnson said of the verse of Spratt, "I would rather praise it than read."

At all events, Rameau was courted in gay and brilliant circles, and, following the general example of French litterateurs in fashion, lived well up to the income he received, had a delightful bachelor's apartment, furnished with artistic effect, spent largely on the adornment of his person, kept a coupe, and entertained profusely at the cafe Anglais and the Maison Doree. A reputation that inspired a graver and more unquiet interest had been created by the Vicomte de Mauleon. Recent articles in the Sens Commun, written under the name of Pierre Firmin on the discussions on the vexed question of the plebiscite, had given umbrage to the Government, and Rameau had received an intimation that he, as editor, was responsible for the compositions of the contributors to the journal he edited; and that though, so long as Pierre Firmin had kept his caustic spirit within proper bounds, the Government had winked at the evasion of the law which required every political article in a journal to be signed by the real name of its author, it could do so no longer. Pierre Firmin was apparently a nom de plume; if not, his identity must be proved, or Rameau would pay the penalty which his contributor seemed bent on incurring.

Rameau, much alarmed for the journal that might be suspended, and for himself who might be imprisoned, conveyed this information through the publisher to his correspondent Pierre Firmin, and received the next day an article signed Victor de Mauleon, in which the writer proclaimed himself to be one and the same with Pierre Firmin, and, taking a yet bolder tone than he had before assumed, dared the Government to attempt legal measures against him. The Government was prudent enough to disregard that haughty bravado, but Victor de Mauleon rose at once into political importance. He had already in his real name and his quiet way established a popular and respectable place in Parisian society. But if this revelation created him enemies whom he had not before provoked, he was now sufficiently acquitted, by tacit consent, of the sins formerly laid to his charge, to disdain the assaults of party wrath. His old reputation for personal courage and skill in sword and pistol served, indeed, to protect him from such charges as a Parisian journalist does not reply to with his pen. If he created some enemies, he created many more friends, or, at least, partisans and admirers. He only needed fine and imprisonment to become a popular hero.

A few days after he had thus proclaimed himself, Victor de Mauleon—who had before kept aloof from Rameau, and from salons at which he was likely to meet that distinguished minstrel—solicited his personal acquaintance, and asked him to breakfast.

Rameau joyfully went. He had a very natural curiosity to see the contributor whose articles had so mainly insured the sale of the Sens Commun.

In the dark-haired, keen-eyed, well-dressed, middle-aged man, with commanding port and courtly address, he failed to recognise any resemblance to the flaxen-wigged, long-coated, be-spectacled, shambling sexagenarian whom he had known as Lebeau. Only now and then a tone of voice struck him as familiar, but he could not recollect where he had heard the voice it resembled. The thought of Lebeau did not occur to him; if it had occurred it would only have struck him as a chance coincidence. Rameau, like most egotists, was rather a dull observer of men. His genius was not objective.

"I trust, Monsieur Rameau," said the Vicomte, as he and his guest were seated at the breakfast-table, "that you are not dissatisfied with the remuneration your eminent services in the journal have received."

"The proprietor, whoever he be, has behaved most liberally," answered Rameau.

"I take that compliment to myself, cher confrere; for though the expenses of starting the Sens Commun, and the caution money lodged, were found by a friend of mine, that was as a loan, which I have long since repaid, and the property in the journal is now exclusively mine. I have to thank you not only for your own brilliant contributions, but for those of the colleagues you secured. Monsieur Savarin's piquant criticisms were most valuable to us at starting. I regret to have lost his aid. But as he has set up a new journal of his own, even he has not wit enough to spare for another. A propos of our contributors, I shall ask you to present me to the fair author of The Artist's Daughter. I am of too prosaic a nature to appreciate justly the merits of a roman; but I have heard warm praise of this story from the young—they are the best judges of that kind of literature; and I can at least understand the worth of a contributor who trebled the sale of our journal. It is a misfortune to us, indeed, that her work is completed, but I trust that the sum sent to her through our publisher suffices to tempt her to favour us with another roman in series."

"Mademoiselle Cicogna," said Rameau, with a somewhat sharper intonation of his sharp voice, "has accepted for the republication of her roman in a separate form terms which attest the worth of her genius, and has had offers from other journals for a serial tale of even higher amount than the sum so generously sent to her through your publisher."

"Has she accepted them, Monsieur Rameau? If so, tant pis pour vous. Pardon me, I mean that your salary suffers in proportion as the Sens Commun declines in sale."

"She has not accepted them. I advised her not to do so until she could compare them with those offered by the proprietor of the Sens Commun."

"And your advice guides her? Ah, cher confrere, you are a happy man!—you have influence over this young aspirant to the fame of a De Stael or a Georges Sand."

"I flatter myself that I have some," answered Rameau, smiling loftily as he helped himself to another tumbler of. Volnay wine—excellent, but rather heady.

"So much the better. I leave you free to arrange terms with Mademoiselle Cicogna, higher than she can obtain elsewhere, and kindly contrive my own personal introduction to her—you have breakfasted already?—permit me to offer you a cigar—excuse me if I do not bear you company; I seldom smoke—never of a morning. Now to business, and the state of France. Take that easy-chair, seat yourself comfortably. So! Listen! If ever Mephistopheles revisit the earth, how he will laugh at Universal Suffrage and Vote by Ballot in an old country like France, as things to be admired by educated men, and adopted by friends of genuine freedom!"

"I don't understand you," said Rameau.

"In this respect at least, let me hope that I can furnish you with understanding.

"The Emperor has resorted to a plebiscite—viz., a vote by ballot and universal suffrage—as to certain popular changes which circumstances compel him to substitute for his former personal rule. Is there a single intelligent Liberal who is not against that plebiscite?—is there any such who does not know that the appeal of the Emperor to universal suffrage and vote by ballot must result in a triumph over all the variations of free thought, by the unity which belongs to Order, represented through an able man at the head of the State? The multitude never comprehend principles; principles are complex ideas; they comprehend a single idea, and the simplest idea is, a Name that rids their action of all responsibility to thought.

"Well, in France there are principles superabundant which you can pit against the principle of Imperial rule. But there is not one name you can pit against Napoleon the Third; therefore, I steer our little bark in the teeth of the popular gale when I denounce the plebiscite, and Le Sens Commun will necessarily fall in sale—it is beginning to fall already. We shall have the educated men with us, the rest against. In every country—even in China, where all are highly educated—a few must be yet more highly educated than the many. Monsieur Rameau, I desire to overthrow the Empire: in order to do that, it is not enough to have on my side the educated men, I must have the canaille—the canaille of Paris and of the manufacturing towns. But I use the canaille for my purpose—I don't mean to enthrone it. You comprehend?—the canaille quiescent is simply mud at the bottom of a stream; the canaille agitated is mud at the surface. But no man capable of three ideas builds the palaces and senates of civilised society out of mud, be it at the top or the bottom of an ocean. Can either you or I desire that the destinies of France shall be swayed by coxcombical artisans who think themselves superior to every man who writes grammar, and whose idea of a common-wealth is the confiscation of private property?" Rameau, thoroughly puzzled by this discourse, bowed his head, and replied whisperingly, "Proceed. You are against the Empire, yet against the populace!—What are you for? not, surely, the Legitimists?—are you Republican? Orleanist? or what?"

"Your questions are very pertinent," answered the Vicomte, courteously, "and my answer shall be very frank. I am against absolute rule, whether under a Buonaparte or a Bourbon. I am for a free State, whether under a constitutional hereditary sovereign like the English or Belgian, or whether, republican in name, it be less democratic than constitutional monarchy in practice, like the American. But as a man interested in the fate of le Sens Commun, I hold in profound disdain all crotchets for revolutionising the elements of Human Nature. Enough of this abstract talk. To the point. You are of course aware of the violent meetings held by the Socialists, nominally against the plebiscite, really against the Emperor himself?"

"Yes, I know at least that the working class are extremely discontented; the numerous strikes last month were not on a mere question of wages—they were against the existing forms of society. And the articles by Pierre Firmin which brought me into collision with the Government, seemed to differ from what you now say. They approve those strikes; they appeared to sympathise with the revolutionary meetings at Belleville and Montmartre."

"Of course—we use coarse tools for destroying; we cast them aside for finer ones when we want to reconstruct.

"I attended one of those meetings last night. See, I have a pass for all such assemblies, signed by some dolt who cannot even spell the name he assumes—'Pom-de-Tair.' A commissary of police sat yawning at the end of the orchestra, his secretary by his side, while the orators stammer out fragments of would-be thunderbolts. Commissary of police yawns more wearily than before, secretary disdains to use his pen, seizes his penknife and pares his nails. Up rises a wild-haired, weak-limbed silhouette of a man, and affecting a solemnity of mien which might have become the virtuous Guizot, moves this resolution: 'The French people condemns Charles Louis Napoleon the Third to the penalty of perpetual hard labour.' Then up rises the commissary of police and says quietly, 'I declare this meeting at an end.'

"Sensation among the audience—they gesticulate—they screech—they bellow—the commissary puts on his greatcoat—the secretary gives a last touch to his nails and pockets his penknife—the audience disperses—the silhouette of a man effaces itself—all is over."

"You describe the scene most wittily," said Rameau, laughing, but the laugh was constrained. A would-be cynic himself, there was a something grave and earnest in the real cynic that awed him.

"What conclusion do you draw from such a scene, cher poete" asked De Mauleon, fixing his keen quiet eyes on Rameau.

"What conclusion? Well, that—that—"

"Yes, continue."

"That the audience were sadly degenerated from the time when Mirabeau said to a Master of the Ceremonies, 'We are here by the power of the French people, and nothing but the point of the bayonet shall expel us.'"

"Spoken like a poet, a French poet. I suppose you admire M. Victor Hugo. Conceding that he would have employed a more sounding phraseology, comprising more absolute ignorance of men, times, and manners in unintelligible metaphor and melodramatic braggadocio, your answer might have been his; but pardon me if I add, it would not be that of Common Sense."

"Monsieur le Vicomte might rebuke me more politely," said Rameau, colouring high.

"Accept my apologies; I did not mean to rebuke, but to instruct. The times are not those of 1789. And Nature, ever repeating herself in the production of coxcombs and blockheads, never repeats herself in the production of Mirabeaus. The Empire is doomed—doomed, because it is hostile to the free play of intellect. Any Government that gives absolute preponderance to the many is hostile to intellect, for intellect is necessarily confined to the few.

"Intellect is the most revengeful of all the elements of society. It cares not what the materials through which it insinuates or forces its way to its seat.

"I accept the aid of Pom-de-Tair. I do not demean myself to the extent of writing articles that may favor the principles of Pom-de-Tair, signed in the name of Victor de Mauleon or of Pierre Firinin.

"I will beg you, my dear editor, to obtain clever, smart writers, who know nothing about Socialists and Internationalists, who therefore will not commit Le Sens Commun by advocating the doctrines of those idiots, but who will flatter the vanity of the canaille—vaguely; write any stuff they please about the renown of Paris, 'the eye of the world,' 'the sun of the European system,' &c., of the artisans of Paris as supplying soul to that eye and fuel to that sun—any blague of that sort—genre Victor Hugo; but nothing definite against life and property, nothing that may not be considered hereafter as the harmless extravagance of a poetic enthusiasm. You might write such articles yourself. In fine, I want to excite the multitude, and yet not to commit our journal to the contempt of the few. Nothing is to be admitted that may bring the law upon us except it be signed by my name. There may be a moment in which it would be desirable for somebody to be sent to prison: in that case, I allow no substitute—I go myself.

"Now you have my most secret thoughts. I intrust them to your judgment with entire confidence. Monsieur Lebeau gave you a high character, which you have hitherto deserved. By the way, have you seen anything lately of that bourgeois conspirator?"

"No, his professed business of letter-writer or agent is transferred to a clerk, who says M. Lebeau is abroad."

"Ah! I don't think that is true. I fancy I saw him the other evening gilding along the lanes of Belleville. He is too confirmed a conspirator to be long out of Paris; no place like Paris for seething brains."

"Have you known M. Lebeau long?" asked Rameau. "Ay, many years. We are both Norman by birth, as you may perceive by something broad in our accent."

"Ha! I knew your voice was familiar to me; certainly it does remind me of Lebeau's."

"Normans are like each other in many things besides voice and accent—obstinacy, for instance, in clinging to ideas once formed; this makes them good friends and steadfast enemies. I would advise no man to make an enemy of Lebeau.

"Au revoir, cher confrere. Do not forget to present me to Mademoiselle Cicogna."

# CHAPTER II.

On leaving De Mauleon and regaining his coupe, Rameau felt at once bewildered and humbled, for he was not prepared for the tone of careless superiority which the Vicomte assumed over him. He had expected to be much complimented, and he comprehended vaguely that he had been somewhat snubbed. He was not only irritated—he was bewildered; for De Mauleon's political disquisitions did not leave any clear or definite idea on his mind as to the principles which as editor of the Sens Commun he was to see adequately represented and carried out. In truth, Rameau was one of those numerous Parisian politicians who have read little and reflected less on the government of men and States. Envy is said by a great French writer to be the vice of Democracies. Envy certainly had made Rameau a democrat. He could talk and write glibly enough upon the themes of equality and fraternity, and was so far an ultra-democrat that he thought moderation the sign of a mediocre understanding.

De Mauleon's talk, therefore, terribly perplexed him. It was unlike anything he had heard before. Its revolutionary professions, accompanied with so much scorn for the multitude, and the things the multitude desired, were Greek to him. He was not shocked by the cynicism which placed wisdom in using the passions of mankind as tools for the interests of an individual; but he did not understand the frankness of its avowal.

Nevertheless the man had dominated over and subdued him. He recognized the power of his contributor without clearly analysing its nature—a power made up of large experience of life, of cold examination of doctrines that heated others—of patrician calm—of intellectual sneer—of collected confidence in self.

Besides, Rameau felt, with a nervous misgiving, that in this man, who so boldly proclaimed his contempt for the instruments he used, he had found a master. De Mauleon, then, was sole proprietor of the journal from which Rameau drew his resources; might at any time dismiss him; might at any time involve the journal in penalties which, even if Rameau could escape in his official capacity as editor, still might stop the Sens Commun, and with it Rameau's luxurious subsistence.

Altogether the visit to De Mauleon had been anything but a pleasant one. He sought, as the carriage rolled on, to turn his thoughts to more agreeable subjects, and the image of Isaura rose before him. To do him justice he had learned to love this girl as well as his nature would permit: he loved her with the whole strength of his imagination, and though his heart was somewhat cold, his imagination was very ardent. He loved her also with the whole strength of his vanity, and vanity was even a more preponderant organ of his system than imagination. To carry off as his prize one who had already achieved celebrity, whose beauty and fascination of manner were yet more acknowledged than her genius, would certainly be a glorious triumph.

Every Parisian of Rameau's stamp looks forward in marriage to a brilliant salon. What salon more brilliant than that which he and Isaura united could command? He had long conquered his early impulse of envy at Isaura's success,—in fact that success had become associated with his own, and had contributed greatly to his enrichment. So that to other motives of love he might add the prudential one of interest. Rameau well knew that his own vein of composition, however lauded by the cliques, and however unrivalled in his own eyes, was not one that brings much profit in the market. He compared himself to those poets who are too far in advance of their time to be quite as sure of bread and cheese as they are of immortal fame.

But he regarded Isaura's genius as of a lower order, and a thing in itself very marketable. Marry her, and the bread and cheese were so certain that he might elaborate as slowly as he pleased the verses destined to immortal fame. Then he should be independent of inferior creatures like Victor de Mauleon. But while Rameau convinced himself that he was passionately in love with Isaura, he could not satisfy himself that she was in love with him.

Though during the past year they had seen each other constantly, and their literary occupations had produced many sympathies between them—though he had intimated that many of his most eloquent love-poems were inspired by her—though he had asserted in prose, very pretty prose too, that she was all that youthful poets dream of,—yet she had hitherto treated such declarations with a playful laugh, accepting them as elegant compliments inspired by Parisian gallantry; and he felt an angry and sore foreboding that if he were to insist too seriously on the earnestness of their import and ask her plainly to be his wife, her refusal would be certain, and his visits to her house might be interdicted.

Still Isaura was unmarried, still she had refused offers of marriage from men higher placed than himself,—still he divined no one whom she could prefer. And as he now leaned back in his coupe he muttered to himself, "Oh, if I could but get rid of that little demon Julie, I would devote myself so completely to winning Isaura's heart that I must succeed!—but how to get rid of Julie? She so adores me, and is so headstrong! She is capable of going to Isaura—showing my letters—making such a scene!"

Here he checked the carriage at a cafe on the Boulevard—descended, imbibed two glasses of absinthe,—and then feeling much emboldened, remounted his coupe and directed the driver to Isaura's apartment.

# CHAPTER III.

Yes, celebrities are of rapid growth in the salons of Paris. Far more solid than that of Rameau, far more brilliant than that of De Mauleon, was the celebrity which Isaura had now acquired. She had been unable to retain the pretty suburban villa at A———. The owner wanted to alter and enlarge it for his own residence, and she had been persuaded by Signora Venosta, who was always sighing for fresh salons to conquer, to remove (towards the close of the previous year) to apartments in the centre of the Parisian beau monde. Without formally professing to receive, on one evening in the week her salon was open to those who had eagerly sought her acquaintance—comprising many stars in the world of fashion, as well as those in the world of art and letters. And as she had now wholly abandoned the idea of the profession for which her voice had been cultivated, she no longer shrank from the exercise of her surpassing gift of song for the delight of private friends. Her physician had withdrawn the interdict on such exercise. His skill, aided by the rich vitality of her constitution, had triumphed over all tendencies to the malady for which he had been consulted. To hear Isaura Cicogna sing in her own house was a privilege sought and prized by many who never read a word of her literary compositions. A good critic of a book is rare; but good judges of a voice are numberless. Adding this attraction of song to her youth, her beauty, her frank powers of converse—an innocent sweetness of manner free from all conventional affectation—and to the fresh novelty of a genius which inspired the young with enthusiast and beguiled the old to indulgence, it was no wonder that Isaura became a celebrity at Paris.

Perhaps it was a wonder that her head was not turned by the adulation that surrounded her. But I believe, be it said with diffidence, that a woman of mind so superior that the mind never pretends to efface the heart, is less intoxicated with flattery than a man equally exposed to it.

It is the strength of her heart that keeps her head sober. Isaura had never yet overcome her first romance of love; as yet, amid all her triumphs, there was not a day in which her thoughts did not wistfully, mournfully, fly back to those blessed moments in which she felt her cheek colour before a look, her heart beat at the sound of a footfall. Perhaps if there had been the customary finis to this young romance—the lover's deliberate renunciation, his formal farewell—the girl's pride would ere this have conquered her affection,—possibly—who knows?—replaced it.

But, reader, be you male or female, have you ever known this sore trial of affection and pride, that from some cause or other, to you mysterious, the dear intercourse to which you had accustomed the secret life of your life, abruptly ceases; you know that a something has come between you and the beloved which you cannot distinguish, cannot measure, cannot guess, and therefore cannot surmount; and you say to yourself at the dead of solitary night, "Oh for an explanation! Oh for one meeting more! All might be so easily set right; or if not, I should know the worst, and knowing it, could conquer!"

This trial was Isaura's. There had been no explanation, no last farewell between her and Graham. She divined—no woman lightly makes a mistake there—that he loved her! She knew that this dread something had intervened between her and him when he took leave of her before others so many months ago; that this dread something still continued—what was it? She was certain that it would vanish, could they but once meet again and not before others. Oh for such a meeting!

She could not herself destroy hope. She could not marry another. She would have no heart to give to another while he was free, while in doubt if his heart was still her own. And thus her pride did not help her to conquer her affection.

Of Graham Vane she heard occasionally. He had ceased to correspond with Savarin; but among those who most frequented her salon were the Morleys. Americans so well educated and so well placed as the Morleys knew something about every Englishman of the social station of Graham Vane. Isaura learned from them that Graham, after a tour on the Continent, had returned to England at the commencement of the year, had been invited to stand for Parliament, had refused, that his name was in the list published by the Morning Post of the elite whose arrivals in London, or whose presence at dinner-tables, is recorded as an event. That the Athenaeum had mentioned a rumour that Graham Vane was the author of a political pamphlet which, published anonymously, had made no inconsiderable sensation. Isaura sent to England for that pamphlet: the subject was somewhat dry, and the style, though clear and vigorous, was scarcely of the eloquence which wins the admiration of women; and yet she learned every word of it by heart.

We know how little she dreamed that the celebrity which she hailed as an approach to him was daily making her more remote. The sweet labours she undertook for that celebrity continued to be sweetened yet more by secret associations with the absent one. How many of the passages most admired could never have been written had he been never known!

And she blessed those labours the more that they upheld her from the absolute feebleness of sickened reverie, beguiled her from the gnawing torture of unsatisfied conjecture. She did comply with Madame de Grantmesnil's command—did pass from the dusty beaten road of life into green fields and along flowery river-banks, and did enjoy that ideal by-world.

But still the one image which reigned over her human heart moved beside her in the gardens of fairyland.

# CHAPTER IV.

Isaura was seated in her pretty salon, with the Venosta, M. Savarin, the Morleys, and the financier Louvier, when Rameau was announced.

"Ha!" cried Savarin, "we were just discussing a matter which nearly concerns you, cher poete. I have not seen you since the announcement that Pierre Firmin is no other than Victor de Mauleon. Ma foi, that worthy seems likely to be as dangerous with his pen as he was once with his sword. The article in which he revealed himself makes a sharp lunge on the Government. 'Take care of yourself. When hawks and nightingales fly together the hawk may escape, and the nightingale complain of the barbarity of kings, in a cage: 'flebiliter gemens infelix avis.''"

"He is not fit to conduct a journal," replied Rameau, magniloquently, "who will not brave a danger for his body in defence of the right to infinity for his thought."

"Bravo!" said Mrs. Morley, clapping her pretty hands. "That speech reminds me of home. The French are very much like the Americans in their style of oratory."

"So," said Louvier, "my old friend the Vicomte has come out as a writer, a politician, a philosopher; I feel hurt that he kept this secret from me despite our intimacy. I suppose you knew it from the first, M. Rameau?"

"No, I was as much taken by surprise as the rest of the world. You have long known M. de Mauleon?"

"Yes, I may say we began life together—that is, much at the same time."

"What is he like in appearance?" asked Mrs. Morley. "The ladies thought him very handsome when he was young," replied Louvier. "He is still a fine-looking man, about my height."

"I should like to know him!" cried Mrs. Morley, "if only to tease that husband of mine. He refuses me the dearest of woman's rights.—I can't make him jealous."

"You may have the opportunity of knowing this ci-devant Lovelace very soon," said Rameau, "for he has begged me to present him to Mademoiselle

Cicogna, and I will ask her permission to do so, on Thursday evening when she receives."

Isaura, who had hitherto attended very listlessly to the conversation, bowed assent. "Any friend of yours will be welcome. But I own the articles signed in the name of Pierre Firmin do not prepossess me in favour of their author."

"Why so?" asked Louvier; "surely you are not an Imperialist?"

"Nay, I do not pretend to be a politician at all, but there is something in the writing of Pierre Firmin that pains and chills me."

"Yet the secret of its popularity," said Savarin, "is that it says what every one says—only better."

"I see now that it is exactly that which displeases me; it is the Paris talk condensed into epigram: the graver it is the less it elevates—the lighter it is, the more it saddens."

"That is meant to hit me," said Savarin, with his sunny laugh—"me whom you call cynical."

"No, dear M. Savarin; for above all your cynicism is genuine gaiety, and below it solid kindness. You have that which I do not find in M. de Mauleon's writing, nor often in the talk of the salon—you have youthfulness."

"Youthfulness at sixty—flatterer!"

"Genius does not count its years by the almanac," said Mrs. Morley. "I know what Isaura means—she is quite right; there is a breath of winter in M. de Mauleon's style, and an odour of fallen leaves. Not that his diction wants vigour; on the contrary, it is crisp with hoar-frost. But the sentiments conveyed by the diction are those of a nature sear and withered. And it is in this combination of brisk words and decayed feelings that his writing represents the talk and mind of Paris. He and Paris are always fault-finding: fault-finding is the attribute of old age."

Colonel Morley looked round with pride, as much as to say, "Clever talker my wife."

Savarin understood that look, and replied to it courteously. "Madame has a gift of expression which Emile de Girardin can scarcely surpass. But when she blames us for fault-finding, can she expect the friends of liberty to praise the present style of things?"

"I should be obliged to the friends of liberty," said the Colonel, drily, "to tell me how that state of things is to be mended. I find no enthusiasm for the Orleanists, none for a Republic; people sneer at religion; no belief in a cause, no adherence to an opinion. But the worst of it is that, like all people who are blases, the Parisians are eager for strange excitement, and ready to listen to any oracle who promises a relief from indifferentism. This it is which makes the Press more dangerous in France than it is in any other country. Elsewhere the Press sometimes leads, sometimes follows, public opinion. Here there is no public opinion to consult, and instead of opinion the Press represents passion."

"My dear Colonel Morley," said Savarin, "I hear you very often say that a Frenchman cannot understand America. Permit me to observe that an American cannot understand France—or at least Paris. Apropos of Paris that is a large speculation of yours, Louvier, in the new suburb."

"And a very sound one; I advise you to invest in it. I can secure you at present 5 per cent. on the rental; that is nothing—the houses will be worth double when the Rue de Louvier is completed."

"Alas! I have no money; my new journal absorbs all my capital."

"Shall I transfer the money I hold for you, Signorina, and add to them whatever you may have made by your delightful roman, as yet lying idle, to this investment? I cannot say more in its favour than this: I have embarked a very large portion of my capital in the Rue de Louvier, and I flatter myself that I am not one of those men who persuade their friends to do a foolish thing by setting them the example."

"Whatever you advise on such a subject," said Isaura, graciously, "is sure to be as wise as it is kind!"

"You consent, then?"

"Certainly."

Here the Venosta, who had been listening with great attention to Louvier's commendation of this investment, drew him aside, and whispered in his ear: "I suppose, M. Louvier, that one can't put a little money-a very little money—poco-poco pocolino, into your street."

"Into my street! Ah, I understand—into the speculation of the Rue de Louvier! Certainly you can. Arrangements are made on purpose to suit the convenience of the smallest capitalists—from 500 francs upwards."

"And you feel quite sure that we shall double our money when the street is completed—I should not like to have my brains in my heels."

*["'Avere il cervello nella calcagna,"—viz., to act without prudent reflection.]*

"More than double it, I hope, long before the street is completed."

"I have saved a little money—very little. I have no relations, and I mean to leave it all to the Signorina; and if it could be doubled, why, there would be twice as much to leave her."

"So there would," said Louvier. "You can't do better than put it all into the Rue de Louvier. I will send you the necessary papers to-morrow, when I send hers to the Signorina."

Louvier here turned to address himself to Colonel Morley, but finding that degenerate son of America indisposed to get cent. per cent. for his money when offered by a Parisian, he very soon took his leave. The other visitors followed his example, except Rameau, who was left alone with the Venosta and Isaura. The former had no liking for Rameau, who showed her none of the attentions her innocent vanity demanded, and she soon took herself off to her own room to calculate the amount of her savings, and dream of the Rue de Louvier and "golden joys."

Rameau approaching his chair to Isaura's then commenced conversation, drily enough, upon pecuniary matters; acquitting himself of the mission with which De Mauleon had charged him, the request for a new work from her pen for the Sens Commun, and the terms that ought to be asked for compliance. The young lady-author shrank from this talk. Her private income, though modest, sufficed for her wants, and she felt a sensitive shame in the sale of her thoughts and fancies.

Putting hurriedly aside the mercantile aspect of the question, she said that she had no other work in her mind at present—that, whatever her vein of invention might be, it flowed at its own will, and could not be commanded.

"Nay," said Rameau, "this is not true. We fancy, in our hours of indolence, that we must wait for inspiration; but once force ourselves to work, and ideas spring forth at the wave of the pen. You may believe me here, I speak from experience: I, compelled to work, and in modes not to my taste—I do my task I know not how. I rub the lamp, 'the genius comes.'"

"I have read in some English author that motive power is necessary to continued labour: you have motive power, I have none."

"I do not quite understand you."

"I mean that a strong ruling motive is required to persist in any regular course of action that needs effort: the motive with the majority of men is the need of subsistence; with a large number (as in trades or professions), not actually want, but a desire of gain, and perhaps of distinction, in their calling: the desire of professional distinction expands into the longings for more comprehensive fame, more exalted honours, with the few who become great writers, soldiers, statesmen, orators."

"And do you mean to say you have no such motive?"

"None in the sting of want, none in the desire of gain."

"But fame?"

"Alas! I thought so once. I know not now—I begin to doubt if fame should be sought by women." This was said very dejectedly.

"Tut, dearest Signorina! what gadfly has stung you? Your doubt is a weakness unworthy of your intellect; and even were it not, genius is destiny and will be obeyed: you must write, despite yourself—and your writing must bring fame, whether you wish it or not."

Isaura was silent, her head drooped on her breast—there were tears in her downcast eyes.

Rameau took her hand, which she yielded to him passively, and clasping it in both his own, he rushed on impulsively—

"Oh, I know what these misgivings are when we feel ourselves solitary, unloved: how often have they been mine! But how different would labour be if shared and sympathised with by a congenial mind, by a heart that beats in unison with one's own!"

Isaura's breast heaved beneath her robe, she sighed softly.

"And then how sweet the fame of which the one we love is proud! how trifling becomes the pang of some malignant depreciation, which a word from the beloved one can soothe! O Signorina! O Isaura! are we not made for each other? Kindred pursuits, hopes, and fears in common; the same race to run, the same goal to win! I need a motive stronger than I have yet known for the persevering energy that insures success: supply to me that motive. Let me think that whatever I win in the strife of the world is a tribute to Isaura. No, do not seek to withdraw this hand, let me claim it as mine for life. I love you as man never loved before—do not reject my love."

They say the woman who hesitates is lost. Isaura hesitated, but was not yet lost. The words she listened to moved her deeply. Offers of marriage she had already received: one from a rich middle-aged noble, a devoted musical virtuoso; one from a young avocat fresh from the provinces, and somewhat calculating on her dot; one from a timid but enthusiastic admirer of her genius and her beauty, himself rich, handsome, of good birth, but with shy manners and faltering tongue.

But these had made their proposals with the formal respect habitual to French decorum in matrimonial proposals. Words so eloquently impassioned as Gustave Rameau's had never before thrilled her ears; Yes, she was deeply moved; and yet, by that very emotion she knew that it was not to the love of this wooer that her heart responded.

There is a circumstance in the history of courtship familiar to the experience of many women, that while the suitor is pleading his cause, his language may touch every fibre in the heart of his listener, yet substitute, as it were, another presence for his own. She may be saying to herself, "Oh that another had said those words!" and be dreaming of the other, while she hears the one. Thus it was with Isaura, and not till Rameau's voice had ceased did that dream pass away, and with a slight shiver she turned her face towards the wooer sadly and pityingly. "It cannot be," she said, in a low whisper; "I were not worthy of your love could I accept it. Forget that you have so spoken; let me still be a friend admiring your genius, interested in your career. I cannot be more. Forgive me if I unconsciously led you to think I could, I am so grieved to pain you."

"Am I to understand," said Rameau, coldly, for his amour propre was resentful, "that the proposals of another have been more fortunate than mine?" And he named the youngest and comeliest of those whom she had rejected. "Certainly not," said Isaura.

Rameau rose and went to the window, turning his face from her. In reality he was striving to collect his thoughts and decide on the course it were most prudent for him now to pursue. The fumes of the absinthe which had, despite his previous forebodings, emboldened him to hazard his avowal, had now subsided into the languid reaction which is generally consequent on that treacherous stimulus, a reaction not unfavourable to passionless reflection. He knew that if he said he could not conquer his love, he would still cling to hope, and trust to perseverance and time, he should compel Isaura to forbid his visits and break off their familiar intercourse. This would be fatal to the chance of yet winning her, and would also be of serious disadvantage to his more worldly interests. Her literary aid might become essential to the journal on which his fortunes depended; and at all events, in her conversation, in her encouragement, in her sympathy with the pains and joys of his career, he felt a support, a comfort, nay, an inspiration. For the spontaneous gush of her fresh thoughts and fancies served to recruit his own jaded ideas, and enlarge his own stinted range of invention. No, he could not commit himself to the risk of banishment from Isaura.

And mingled with meaner motives for discretion, there was one of which he was but vaguely conscious, purer and nobler. In the society of this girl, in whom whatever was strong and high in mental organisation became so sweetened into feminine grace by gentleness of temper and kindliness of disposition, Rameau felt himself a better man. The virgin-like dignity with which she moved, so untainted by a breath of scandal, amid salons in which the envy of virtues doubted sought to bring innocence itself into doubt, warmed into a genuine reverence the cynicism of his professed creed.

While with her, while under her chastening influence, he was sensible of a poetry infused within him far more true to the Camoenae than all he had elaborated into verse. In these moments he was ashamed of the vices he had courted as distractions. He imagined that with her all his own, it would be easy to reform.

No; to withdraw wholly from Isaura was to renounce his sole chance of redemption.

While these thoughts, which it takes so long to detail, passed rapidly through his brain, he felt a soft touch on his arm, and, turning his face slowly, encountered the tender, compassionate eyes of Isaura.

"Be consoled, dear friend," she said, with a smile, half cheering, half mournful. "Perhaps for all true artists the solitary lot is the best."

"I will try to think so," answered Rameau; "and meanwhile I thank you with a full heart for the sweetness with which you have checked my presumption—the presumption shall not be repeated. Gratefully I accept the friendship you deign to tender me. You bid me forget the words I uttered. Promise in turn that you will forget them—or at least consider them withdrawn. You will receive me still as friend?"

"As friend, surely: yes. Do we not both need friends?" She held out her hand as she spoke; he bent over it, kissed it with respect, and the interview thus closed.

# CHAPTER V.

It was late in the evening that day when a man who had the appearance of a decent bourgeois, in the lower grades of that comprehensive class, entered one of the streets in the Faubourg Montmartre, tenanted chiefly by artisans. He paused at the open doorway of a tall narrow house, and drew back as he heard footsteps descending a very gloomy staircase.

The light from a gas lamp on the street fell full on the face of the person thus quitting the house—the face of a young and handsome man, dressed with the quiet elegance which betokened one of higher rank or fashion than that neighbourhood was habituated to find among its visitors. The first comer retreated promptly into the shade, and, as by sudden impulse, drew his hat low down over his eyes.

The other man did not, however, observe him, went his way with a quick step along the street, and entered another house some yards distant.

"What can that pious Bourbonite do here?" muttered the first comer. "Can he be a conspirator? Diable! 'tis as dark as Erebus on that staircase."

Taking cautious hold of the banister, the man now ascended the stairs. On the landing of the first floor there was a gas lamp which threw upward a faint ray that finally died at the third story. But at that third story the man's journey ended; he pulled a bell at the door to the right, and in another moment or so the door was opened by a young woman of twenty-eight or thirty, dressed very simply, but with a certain neatness not often seen in the wives of artisans in the Faubourg Montmartre. Her face, which, though pale and delicate, retained much of the beauty of youth, became clouded as she recognised the visitor; evidently the visit was not welcome to her.

"Monsieur Lebeau again!" she exclaimed, shrinking back.

"At your service, chere dame. The goodman is of course at home? Ah, I catch sight of him," and sliding by the woman, M. Lebeau passed the narrow lobby in which she stood, through the open door conducting into the room in which Armand Monnier was seated, his chin propped on his hand, his elbow resting on a table, looking abstractedly into space. In a corner of the room two small children were playing languidly with a set of bone tablets, inscribed with the letters of the alphabet. But whatever the children were doing with the alphabet, they were certainly not learning to read from it.

The room was of fair size and height, and by no means barely or shabbily furnished. There was a pretty clock on the mantelpiece. On the wall were hung designs for the decoration of apartments, and shelves on which were ranged a few books.

The window was open, and on the sill were placed flowerpots; you could scent the odour they wafted into the room. Altogether it was an apartment suited to a skilled artisan earning high wages. From the room we are now in, branched on one side a small but commodious kitchen; on the other side, on which the door was screened by a portiere, with a border prettily worked by female hands—some years ago, for it was faded now—was a bedroom, communicating with one of less size in which the children slept. We do not enter those additional rooms, but it may be well here to mention them as indications of the comfortable state of an intelligent skilled artisan of Paris, who thinks he can better that state by some revolution which may ruin his employer.

Monnier started up at the entrance of Lebeau, and his face showed that he did not share the dislike to the visit which that of the female partner of his life had evinced. On the contrary, his smile was cordial, and there was a hearty ring in the voice which cried out—

"I am glad to see you—something to do? Eh!"

"Always ready to work for liberty, mon brave."

"I hope so: what's in the wind now?"

"O Armand, be prudent—be prudent!" cried the woman, piteously. "Do not lead him into further mischief, Monsieur Lebeau;" as she faltered forth the last words, she bowed her head over the two little ones, and her voice died in sobs.

"Monnier," said Lebeau, gravely, "Madame is right. I ought not to lead you into further mischief; there are three in the room who have better claims on you than—"

"The cause of millions," interrupted Monnier.

"No."

He approached the woman and took up one of the children very tenderly, stroking back its curls and kissing the face, which, if before surprised and saddened by the mother's sob, now smiled gaily under the father's kiss.

"Canst thou doubt, my Heloise," said the artisan, mildly, "that whatever I do thou and these are not uppermost in my thoughts? I act for thine interest and theirs—the world as it exists is the foe of you three. The world I would replace it by will be more friendly."

The poor woman made no reply, but as he drew her towards him, she leant her head upon his breast and wept quietly. Monnier led her thus from the room, whispering words of soothing. The children followed the parents into the adjoining chamber. In a few minutes Monnier returned, shutting the door behind him, and drawing the portiere close.

"You will excuse me, Citizen, and my poor wife—wife she is to me and to all who visit here, though the law says she is not."

"I respect Madame the more for her dislike to myself," said Lebeau, with a somewhat melancholy smile.

"Not dislike to you personally, Citizen, but dislike to the business which she connects with your visits, and she is more than usually agitated on that subject this evening, because, just before you came, another visitor had produced a great effect on her feelings—poor dear Heloise!"

"Indeed! how?"

"Well, I was employed in the winter in redecorating the salon, and boudoir, of Madame de Vandemar; her son, M. Raoul, took great interest in superintending the details. He would sometimes talk to me very civilly, not only on my work, but on other matters. It seems that Madame now wants something done to the salle-a-manger, and asked old Gerard—my late master, you know—to send me. Of course he said that was impossible—for, though I was satisfied with my own wages, I had induced his other men to strike, and was one of the ringleaders in the recent strike of artisans in general—a dangerous man, and he would have nothing more to do with me. So M. Raoul came to see and talk to me—scarce gone before you rang at the bell—you might have almost met him on the stairs."

"I saw a beau monsieur come out of the house. And so his talk has affected Madame."

"Very much; it was quite brother-like. He is one of the religious set, and they always get at the weak side of the soft sex."

"Ay," said Lebeau, thoughtfully; "if religion were banished from the laws of men, it would still find a refuge in the hearts of women. But Raoul de Vandemar did not presume to preach to Madame upon the sin of loving you and your children?"

"I should like to have heard him preach to her," cried Monnier, fiercely. "No, he only tried to reason with me about matters he could not understand."

"Strikes?"

"Well, not exactly strikes—he did not contend that we workmen had not full right to combine and to strike for obtaining fairer money's worth for our work; but he tried to persuade me that where, as in my case, it was not a matter of wages, but of political principle—of war against capitalists—I could but injure myself and mislead others. He wanted to reconcile me to old Gerard, or to let him find me employment elsewhere; and when I told him that my honour forbade me to make terms for myself till those with whom I was joined were satisfied, he said, 'But if this lasts much longer, your children will not look so rosy;' then poor Heloise began to wring her hands and cry, and he took me aside and wanted to press money on me—as a loan. He spoke so kindly that I could not be angry; but when he found I would take nothing, he asked me about some families in the street of whom he had a list, and who, he was informed, were in great distress. That is true; I am feeding some of them myself out of my savings. You see, this young Monsieur belongs to a society of men, many as young as he is, which visits the poor and dispenses charity. I did not feel I had a right to refuse aid for others, and I told him where his money would be best spent. I suppose he went there when he left me."

"I know the society you mean, that of St. Francois de Sales. It comprises some of the most ancient of that old noblesse to which the ouvriers in the great Revolution were so remorseless."

"We ouvriers are wiser now; we see that in assailing them, we gave ourselves worse tyrants in the new aristocracy of the capitalists. Our quarrel now is that of artisans against employers."

"Of course, I am aware of that; but to leave general politics, tell me frankly, How has the strike affected you as yet? I mean in purse? Can you stand its pressure? If not, you are above the false pride of not taking help from me, a fellow-conspirator, though you were justified in refusing it when offered by Raoul de Vandemar, the servant of the Church."

"Pardon, I refuse aid from any one, except for the common cause. But do not fear for me, I am not pinched as yet. I have had high wages for some years, and since I and Heloise came together, I have not wasted a sous out of doors, except in the way of public duty, such as making converts at the Jean Jacques and elsewhere; a glass of beer and a pipe don't cost much. And Heloise is such a house-wife, so thrifty, scolds me if I buy her a ribbon, poor love! No wonder that I would pull down a society that dares to scoff at her—dares to say she is not my wife, and her children are base born. No, I have some savings left yet. War to society, war to the knife!"

"Monnier," said Lebeau, in a voice that evinced emotion, "listen to me: I have received injuries from society which, when they were fresh, half-maddened me—that is twenty years ago. I would then have thrown myself into any plot against society that proffered revenge; but society, my friend, is a wall of very strong masonry, as it now stands; it may be sapped in the course of a thousand years, but stormed in a day—no. You dash your head against it—you scatter your brains, and you dislodge a stone. Society smiles in scorn, effaces the stain, and replaces the stone. I no longer war against society. I do war against a system in that society which is hostile to me—systems in France are easily overthrown. I say this because I want to use you, and I do not want to deceive."

"Deceive me, bah! You are an honest man," cried Monnier; and he seized Lebeau's hand, and shook it with warmth and vigour.

"But for you I should have been a mere grumbler. No doubt I should have cried out where the shoe pinched, and railed against laws that vex me; but from the moment you first talked to me I became a new man. You taught me to act, as Rousseau and Madame de Grantmesnil had taught me to think and to feel. There is my brother, a grumbler too, but professes to have a wiser head than mine. He is always warning me against you—against joining a strike—against doing any thing to endanger my skin. I always went by his advice till you taught me that it was well enough for women to talk and complain; men should dare and do."

"Nevertheless," said Lebeau, "your brother is a safer counsellor to a pere de famille than I. I repeat what I have so often said before: I desire, and I resolve, that the Empire of M. Bonaparte shall be overthrown. I see many concurrent circumstances to render that desire and resolve of practicable fulfilment. You desire and resolve the same thing. Up to that point we can work together. I have encouraged your action only so far as it served my design; but I separate from you the moment you would ask me to aid your design in the hazard of experiments which the world has never yet favoured, and trust me, Monnier, the world never will favour."

"That remains to be seen," said Monnier, with compressed, obstinate lips. "Forgive me, but you are not young; you belong to an old school."

"Poor young man!" said Lebeau, readjusting his spectacles, "I recognise in you the genius of Paris, be the genius good or evil. Paris is never warned by experience. Be it so. I want you so much, your enthusiasm is so fiery, that I can concede no more to the mere sentiment which makes me say to myself, 'It is a shame to use this great-hearted, wrong-headed creature for my personal ends.' I come at once to the point—that is, the matter on which I seek you this evening. At my suggestion, you have been a ringleader in strikes which have terribly shaken the Imperial system, more than its Ministers deem; now I want a man like you to assist in a bold demonstration against the Imperial resort to a rural priest-ridden suffrage, on the part of the enlightened working class of Paris."

"Good!" said Monnier.

"In a day or two the result of the plebiscite will be known. The result of universal suffrage will be enormously in favour of the desire expressed by one man."

"I don't believe it," said Monnier, stoutly. "France cannot be so hoodwinked by the priests."

"Take what I say for granted," resumed Lebeau, calmly. "On the 8th of this month we shall know the amount of the majority—some millions of French votes. I want Paris to separate itself from France, and declare against those blundering millions. I want an emeute, or rather a menacing demonstration—not a premature revolution, mind. You must avoid bloodshed."

"It is easy to say that beforehand; but when a crowd of men once meets in the streets of Paris—"

"It can do much by meeting, and cherishing resentment if the meeting be dispersed by an armed force, which it would be waste of life to resist."

"We shall see when the time comes," said Monnier, with a fierce gleam in his bold eyes.

"I tell you, all that is required at this moment is an evident protest of the artisans of Paris against the votes of the 'rurals' of France. Do you comprehend me?"

"I think so; if not, I obey. What we ouvriers want is what we have not got—a head to dictate action to us."

"See to this, then. Rouse the men you can command. I will take care that you have plentiful aid from foreigners. We may trust to the confreres of our council to enlist Poles and Italians; Gaspard le Noy will turn out the volunteer rioters at his command. Let the emeute be within, say a week, after the vote of the plebiscite is taken. You will need that time to prepare."

"Be contented—it shall be done."

"Good night, then." Lebeau leisurely took up his hat and drew on his gloves—then, as if struck by a sudden thought, he turned briskly on the artisan and said in quick blunt tones:

"Armand Monnier, explain to me why it is that you—a Parisian artisan, the type of a class the most insubordinate, the most self-conceited that exists on the face of earth—take without question, with so docile a submission, the orders of a man who plainly tells you he does not sympathise in your ultimate objects, of whom you really know very little, and whose views you candidly own you think are those of an old and obsolete school of political reasoners."

"You puzzle me to explain," said Monnier, with an ingenuous laugh, that brightened up features stern and hard, though comely when in repose. "Partly, because you are so straightforward, and do not talk blague; partly, because I don't think the class I belong to would stir an inch unless we had a leader of another class—and you give me at least that leader. Again, you go to that first stage which we all agree to take, and—well, do you want me to explain more?"

"Yes."

"Et bien! you have warned me, like an honest man; like an honest man I warn you. That first step we take together; I want to go a step further; you retreat, you say, 'No:' I reply you are committed; that further step you must take, or I cry 'Traitre!—au la lanterne!' You talk of 'superior experience:' bah! what does experience really tell you? Do you suppose that Philippe Egalite, when he began to plot against Louis XVI., meant to vote for his kinsman's execution by the guillotine? Do you suppose that Robespierre, when he commenced his career as the foe of capital punishment, foresaw that he should be the Minister of the Reign of Terror? Not a bit of it. Each was committed by his use of those he designed for his tools: so must you be—or you perish."

Lebeau, leaning against the door, heard the frank avowal he had courted without betraying a change of countenance. But when Armand Monnier had done, a slight movement of his lips showed emotion; was it of fear or disdain?

"Monnier," he said, gently; "I am so much obliged to you for the manly speech you have made. The scruples which my conscience had before entertained are dispelled. I dreaded lest I, a declared wolf, might seduce into peril an innocent sheep. I see I have to deal with a wolf of younger vigour and sharper fangs than myself, so much the better: obey my orders now; leave it to time to say whether I obey yours later. Au revoir."

# CHAPTER VI.

Isaura's apartment, on the following Thursday evening, was more filled than usual. Besides her habitual devotees in the artistic or literary world, there were diplomatists and deputies commixed with many fair chiefs of la jeunesse doree; amongst the latter the brilliant Enguerrand de Vandemar, who, deeming the acquaintance of every celebrity essential to his own celebrity in either Carthage, the beau monde, or the demi-monde, had, two Thursdays before, made Louvier attend her soiree and present him. Louvier, though gathering to his own salons authors and artists, very rarely favoured their rooms with his presence; he did not adorn Isaura's party that evening. But Duplessis was there, in compensation. It had chanced that Valerie had met Isaura at some house in the past winter, and conceived an enthusiastic affection for her: since then, Valerie came very often to see her, and made a point of dragging with her to Isaura's Thursday reunions her obedient father. Soirees, musical or literary, were not much in his line; but he had no pleasure like that of pleasing his spoilt child. Our old friend Frederic Lemercier was also one of Isaura's guests that night. He had become more and more intimate with Duplessis, and Duplessis had introduced him to the fair Valerie as "un jeune homme plein de moyens, qui ira loin."

Savarin was there of course, and brought with him an English gentleman of the name of Bevil, as well known at Paris as in London—invited everywhere—popular everywhere,—one of those welcome contributors to the luxuries of civilised society who trade in gossip, sparing no pains to get the pick of it, and exchanging it liberally sometimes for a haunch of venison, sometimes for a cup of tea. His gossip not being adulterated with malice was in high repute for genuine worth.

If Bevil said, "This story is a fact," you no more thought of doubting him than you would doubt Rothschild if he said, "This is Lafitte of '48."

Mr. Bevil was at present on a very short stay at Paris, and, naturally wishing to make the most of his time, he did not tarry beside Savarin, but, after being introduced to Isaura, flitted here and there through the assembly.

*"Apis Matinae—*
*More modoque—*
*Grata carpentis thyma"—*

The bee proffers honey, but bears a sting.

The room was at its fullest when Gustave Rameau entered, accompanied by Monsieur de Mauleon.

Isaura was agreeably surprised by the impression made on her by the Vicomte's appearance and manner. His writings, and such as she had heard of his earlier repute, had prepared her to see a man decidedly old, of withered aspect and sardonic smile—aggressive in demeanour—forward or contemptuous in his very politeness—a Mephistopheles engrafted on the stem of a Don Juan. She was startled by the sight of one who, despite his forty-eight years—and at Paris a man is generally older at forty-eight than he is elsewhere—seemed in the zenith of ripened manhood—startled yet more by the singular modesty of a deportment too thoroughly high-bred not to be quietly simple—startled most by a melancholy expression in eyes that could be at times soft, though always so keen, and in the grave pathetic smile which seemed to disarm censure of past faults in saying, "I have known sorrows."

He did not follow up his introduction to his young hostess by any of the insipid phrases of compliment to which she was accustomed; but, after expressing in grateful terms his thanks for the honour she had permitted Rameau to confer on him, he moved aside, as if he had no right to detain her from other guests more worthy her notice, towards the doorway, taking his place by Enguerrand amidst a group of men of whom Duplessis was the central figure.

At that time—the first week in May, 1870—all who were then in Paris will remember that there were two subjects uppermost in the mouths of men: first, the plebiscite; secondly, the conspiracy to murder the Emperor—which the disaffected considered to be a mere fable, a pretence got up in time to serve the plebiscite and prop the Empire.

Upon this latter subject Duplessis had been expressing himself with unwonted animation. A loyal and earnest Imperialist, it was only with effort that he could repress his scorn of that meanest sort of gossip which is fond of ascribing petty motives to eminent men.

To him nothing could be more clearly evident than the reality of this conspiracy, and he had no tolerance for the malignant absurdity of maintaining that the Emperor or his Ministers could be silly and wicked enough to accuse seventy-two persons of a crime which the police had been instructed to invent.

As De Mauleon approached, the financier brought his speech to an abrupt close. He knew in the Vicomte de Mauleon the writer of articles which had endangered the Government, and aimed no pointless shafts against its Imperial head.

"My cousin," said Enguerrand, gaily, as he exchanged a cordial shake of the hand with Victor, "I congratulate you on the fame of journalist, into which you have vaulted, armed cap-a pie, like a knight of old into his saddle; but I don't sympathise with the means you have taken to arrive at that renown. I am not myself an Imperialist—a Vandemar can be scarcely that. But if I am compelled to be on board a ship, I don't wish to take out its planks and let in an ocean, when all offered to me instead is a crazy tub and a rotten rope."

"Tres bien," said Duplessis, in Parliamentary tone and phrase.

"But," said De Mauleon, with his calm smile, "would you like the captain of the ship, when the sky darkened and the sea rose, to ask the common sailors 'whether they approved his conduct on altering his course or shortening his sail'? Better trust to a crazy tub and a rotten rope than to a ship in which the captain consults a plebiscite."

"Monsieur," said Duplessis, "your metaphor is ill chosen no metaphor indeed is needed. The head of the State was chosen by the voice of the people, and, when required to change the form of administration which the people had sanctioned, and inclined to do so from motives the most patriotic and liberal, he is bound again to consult the people from whom he holds his power. It is not, however, of the plebiscite we were conversing, so much as of the atrocious conspiracy of assassins—so happily discovered in time. I presume that Monsieur de Mauleon must share the indignation which true Frenchmen of every party must feel against a combination united by the purpose of murder."

The Vicomte bowed as in assent. "But do you believe," asked a Liberal Depute, "that such a combination existed, except in the visions of the police or the cabinet of a Minister?"

Duplessis looked keenly at De Mauleon while this question was put to him. Belief or disbelief in the conspiracy was with him, and with many, the test by which a sanguinary revolutionist was distinguished from an honest politician.

"Ma foi," answered De Mauleon, shrugging his shoulders, "I have only one belief left; but that is boundless. I believe in the folly of mankind in general, and of Frenchmen in particular. That seventy-two men should plot the assassination of a sovereign on whose life interests so numerous and so watchful depend, and imagine they could keep a secret which any drunkard amongst them would blab out, any tatterdemalion would sell, is a betise so gross that I think it highly probable. But pardon me if I look upon the politics of Paris much as I do upon its mud—one must pass through it when one walks in the street. One changes one's shoes before entering the salon. A word with you, Enguerrand,"—and taking his kinsman's arm he drew him aside from the circle. "What has become of your brother? I see nothing of him now."

"Oh, Raoul," answered Enguerrand, throwing himself on a couch in a recess, and making room for De Mauleon beside him—"Raoul is devoting himself to the distressed ouvriers who have chosen to withdraw from work. When he fails to persuade them to return, he forces food and fuel on their wives and children. My good mother encourages him in this costly undertaking, and no one but you who believe in the infinity of human folly would credit me when I tell you that his eloquence has drawn from me all the argent de poche I get from our shop. As for himself, he has sold his horses, and even grudges a cab-fare, saying, 'That is a meal for a family.' Ah! if he had but gone into the Church, what a saint would have deserved canonisation!"

"Do not lament—he will probably have what is a better claim than mere saintship on Heaven—martyrdom," said De Mauleon, with a smile in which sarcasm disappeared in melancholy. "Poor Raoul!—and what of my other cousin, the beau Marquis? Several months ago his Legitimist faith seemed vacillating—he talked to me very fairly about the duties a Frenchman owed to France, and hinted that he should place his sword at the command of Napoleon III. I have not yet heard of him as a soldat de France—I hear a great deal of him as a viveur de Paris."

"Don't you know why his desire for a military career was frost-bitten?"

"No! why?"

"Alain came from Bretagne profoundly ignorant of most things known to a gamin of Paris. When he conscientiously overcame the scruples natural to one of his name and told the Duchesse de Tarascon that he was ready to fight under the flag of France whatever its colour, he had a vague reminiscence of ancestral Rochebriants earning early laurels at the head of their regiments. At all events he assumed as a matter of course that he, in the first rank as gentilhomme, would enter the army, if as a sous-lieutenant, still as gentilhomme. But when told that, as he had been at no military college, he could only enter the ranks as a private soldier—herd with private soldiers—for at least two years before, passing through the grade of corporal, his birth, education, habits of life could, with great favour, raise him to the station of a sous-lieutenant, you may conceive that the martial ardour of a Rochebriant was somewhat cooled."

"If he knew what the dormitory of French privates is, and how difficult a man well educated well brought up, finds it, first, to endure the coarsest ribaldry and the loudest blasphemy, and then, having endured and been compelled to share them, ever enforce obedience and discipline as a superior among those with whom just before he was an equal, his ardour would not have been merely cooled—it would have been changed into despair for the armies of France, if hereafter they are met by those whose officers have been trained to be officers from the outset and have imbibed from their cradle an education not taught to the boy-pedants from school—the two-fold education how with courtesy to command, how with dignity to obey. To return to Rochebriant, such salons as I frequent are somewhat formal—as befits my grave years and my modest income; I may add, now that you know my vocation, befits me also as a man who seeks rather to be instructed than amused. In those salons I did, last year sometimes, however, meet Rochebriant—as I sometimes still meet you; but of late he has deserted such sober reunions, and I hear with pain that he is drifting among those rocks against which my own youth was shipwrecked. Is the report true?"

"I fear," said Enguerrand, reluctantly, "that at least the report is not unfounded. And my conscience accuses me of having been to blame in the first instance. You see, when Alain made terms with Louvier by which he obtained a very fair income, if prudently managed, I naturally wished that a man of so many claims to social distinction, and who represents the oldest branch of my family, should take his right place in our world of Paris. I gladly therefore presented him to the houses and the men most a la mode—advised him as to the sort of establishment, in apartments, horses, &c., which it appeared to me that he might reasonably afford—I mean such as, with his means, I should have prescribed to myself—"

"Ah! I understand. But you, dear Enguerrand, are a born Parisian, every inch of you: and a born Parisian is, whatever be thought to the contrary, the best manager in the world. He alone achieves the difficult art of uniting thrift with show. It is your Provincial who comes to Paris in the freshness of undimmed youth, who sows his whole life on its barren streets. I guess the rest: Alain is ruined." Enguerrand, who certainly was so far a born Parisian that with all his shrewdness and savoir faire, he had a wonderfully sympathetic heart, very easily moved, one way or the other—Enguerrand winced at his elder kinsman's words complimentarily reproachful, and said in unwonted tones of humility: "Cousin, you are cruel, but you are in the right. I did not calculate sufficiently on the chances of Alain's head being turned. Hear my excuse. He seemed to me so much more thoughtful than most at our age are, so much more stately and proud; well, also so much more pure, so impressed with the responsibilities of station, so bent on retaining the old lands in Bretagne; by habit and rearing so simple and self-denying,—that I took it for granted he was proof against stronger temptations than those which a light nature like my own puts aside with a laugh. And at first I had no reason to think myself deceived, when, some months ago, I heard that he was getting into debt, losing at play, paying court to female vampires, who drain the life-blood of those on whom they fasten their fatal lips. Oh, then I spoke to him earnestly!"

"And in vain?"

"In vain. A certain Chevalier de Finisterre, whom you may have heard of—"

"Certainly, and met; a friend of Louvier's—"

"The same man—has obtained over him an influence which so far subdues mine, that he almost challenged me when I told him his friend was a scamp. In fine, though Alain and I have not actually quarrelled, we pass each other with, 'Bon jour, mon ami.'"

"Hum! My dear Enguerrand, you have done all you could. Flies will be flies, and spiders, spiders, till the earth is destroyed by a comet. Nay, I met a distinguished naturalist in America who maintained that we shall find flies and spiders in the next world."

"You have been in America? Ah, true—I remember, California!"

"Where have I not been? Tush! music—shall I hear our fair hostess sing?"

"I am afraid not to-night: because Madame S—————— is to favour us, and the Signorina makes it a rule not to sing at her own house when professional artists do. You must hear the Cicogna quietly some day; such a voice, nothing like it."

Madame S————-, who, since she had learned that there was no cause to apprehend that Isaura might become her professional rival, conceived for her a wonderful affection, and willingly contributed her magnificent gifts of song to the charms of Isaura's salon, now began a fragment from I Puritani, which held the audience as silent as the ghosts listening to Sappho, and when it was over, several of the guests slipped away, especially those who disliked music, and feared Madame S————- might begin again. Enguerrand was not one of such soulless recreants, but he had many other places to go to. Besides, Madame S———— was no novelty to him.

De Mauleon now approached Isaura, who was seated next to Valerie, and after well-merited encomium on Madame S———'s performance, slid into some critical comparisons between that singer and those of a former generation, which interested Isaura, and evinced to her quick perceptions that kind of love for music which has been refined by more knowledge of the art than is common to mere amateurs.

"You have studied music, Monsieur de Mauleon," she said. "Do you not perform yourself?"

"I? No. But music has always had a fatal attraction for me. I ascribe half the errors of my life to that temperament which makes me too fascinated by harmonies—too revolted by discords."

"I should have thought such a temperament would have led from errors—are not errors discords?"

"To the inner sense, yes; but to the outer sense not always. Virtues are often harsh to the ear—errors very sweet-voiced. The sirens did not sing out of tune. Better to stop one's ears than glide on Scylla or be merged into Charybdis."

"Monsieur," cried Valerie, with a pretty brusquerie which became her well, "you talk like a Vandal."

"It is, I think, by Mademoiselle Duplessis that I have the honour to be rebuked. Is Monsieur your father very susceptible to music?"

"Well, I cannot say that he cares much for it. But then his mind is so practical—"

"And his life so successful. No Scylla, no Charybdis for him. However, Mademoiselle, I am not quite the Vandal you suppose, I do not say that susceptibility to the influence of music may not be safe, nay, healthful, to others it was not so to me in my youth. It can do me no harm now."

Here Duplessis came up and whispered his daughter "it was time to leave; they had promised the Duchesse de Tarascon to assist at the soiree she gave that night." Valerie took her father's arm with a brightening smile and a heightened colour. Alain de Rochebriant might probably be at the Duchesse's.

"Are you not going also to the Hotel de Tarascon, M. de Mauleon?" asked Duplessis.

"No; I was never there but once. The Duchesse is an Imperialist, at once devoted and acute, and no doubt very soon divined my lack of faith in her idols."

Duplessis frowned, and hastily led Valerie away.

In a few minutes the room was comparatively deserted. De Mauleon, however, lingered by the side of Isaura till all the other guests were gone.

Even then he lingered still, and renewed the interrupted conversation with her, the Venosta joining therein; and so agreeable did he make himself to her Italian tastes by a sort of bitter-sweet wisdom like that of her native proverbs—comprising much knowledge of mankind on the unflattering side of humanity in that form of pleasantry which has a latent sentiment of pathos—that the Venosta exclaimed, "Surely you must have been brought up in Florence!"

There was that in De Mauleon's talk hostile to all which we call romance that excited the imagination of Isaura, and compelled her instinctive love for whatever is more sweet, more beautiful, more ennobling on the many sides of human life, to oppose what she deemed the paradoxes of a man who had taught himself to belie even his own nature. She became eloquent, and her countenance, which in ordinary moments owed much of its beauty to an expression of meditative gentleness, was now lighted up by the energy of earnest conviction—the enthusiasm of an impassioned zeal.

Gradually De Mauleon relaxed his share in the dialogue, and listened to her, rapt and dreamily as in his fiery youth he had listened to the songs of the sirens. No siren Isaura! She was defending her own cause, though unconsciously—defending the vocation of art as the embellisher of external nature, and more than embellisher of the nature which dwells crude, but plastic in the soul of man: indeed therein the creator of a new nature, strengthened, expanded, and brightened in proportion as it accumulates the ideas that tend beyond the boundaries of the visible and material nature, which is finite; for ever seeking in the unseen and the spiritual the goals in the infinite which it is their instinct to divine. "That which you contemptuously call romance," said Isaura, "is not essential only to poets and artists. The most real side of every life, from the earliest dawn of mind in the infant, is the romantic."

"When the child is weaving flower-chains, chasing butterflies, or sitting apart and dreaming what it will do in the future, is not that the child's real life, and yet is it not also the romantic?"

"But there comes a time when we weave no flower-chains, and chase no butterflies."

"Is it so?—still on one side of life, flowers and butterflies may be found to the last; and at least to the last are there no dreams of the future? Have you no such dreams at this moment? and without the romance of such dreams, would there be any reality to human life which could distinguish it from the life of the weed that rots on Lethe?"

"Alas, Mademoiselle," said De Mauleon, rising to take leave, "your argument must rest without answer. I would not, if I could, confute the beautiful belief that belongs to youth, fusing into one rainbow all the tints that can colour the world. But the Signora Venosta will acknowledge the truth of an old saying expressed in every civilised language, but best, perhaps in that of the Florentine—'You might as well physic the dead as instruct the old.'"

"But you are not old!" said the Venosta, with Florentine politeness,—"you! not a grey hair."

"'Tis not by the grey of the hair that one knows the age of the heart," answered De Mauleon, in another paraphrase of Italian proverb, and he was gone.

As he walked homeward, through deserted streets, Victor de Mauleon thought to himself, "Poor girl, how I pity her! married to a Gustave Rameau—married to any man—nothing in the nature of man, be he the best and the cleverest, can ever realise the dream of a girl who is pure and has genius. Ah, is not the converse true? What girl, the best and the cleverest, comes up to the ideal of even a commonplace man—if he ever dreamed of an ideal!"

Then he paused, and in a moment or so afterwards his thought knew such questionings no more. It turned upon personalities, on stratagems and plots, on ambition. The man had more than his share of that peculiar susceptibility which is one of the characteristics of his countrymen—susceptibility to immediate impulse—susceptibility to fleeting impressions. It was a key to many mysteries in his character when he owned his subjection to the influence of music, and in music recognised not the seraph's harp, but the siren's song. If you could have permanently fixed Victor de Mauleon in one of the good moments of his life—even now—some moment of exquisite kindness—of superb generosity—of dauntless courage—you would have secured a very rare specimen of noble humanity. But so to fix him was impossible.

That impulse of the moment vanished the moment after; swept aside by the force of his very talents—talents concentrated by his intense sense of individuality—sense of wrongs or of rights—interests or objects personal to himself. He extended the royal saying, "L'etat, c'est moi," to words far more grandiloquent. "The universe, 'tis I." The Venosta would have understood him and smiled approvingly, if he had said with good-humoured laugh, "I dead, the world is dead!" That is an Italian proverb, and means much the same thing.

# BOOK VIII.

## CHAPTER I.

On the 8th of May the vote of the plebiscite was recorded,—between seven and eight millions of Frenchmen in support of the Imperial programme—in plain words, of the Emperor himself—against a minority of 1,500,000. But among the 1,500,000 were the old throne-shakers-those who compose and those who lead the mob of Paris. On the 14th, as Rameau was about to quit the editorial bureau of his printing-office, a note was brought in to him which strongly excited his nervous system. It contained a request to see him forthwith, signed by those two distinguished foreign members of the Secret Council of Ten, Thaddeus Loubinsky and Leonardo Raselli.

The meetings of that Council had been so long suspended that Rameau had almost forgotten its existence. He gave orders to admit the conspirators. The two men entered, the Pole, tall, stalwart, and with martial stride—the Italian, small, emaciated, with skulking, noiseless, cat-like step, both looking wondrous threadbare, and in that state called "shabby genteel," which belongs to the man who cannot work for his livelihood, and assumes a superiority over the man who can. Their outward appearance was in notable discord with that of the poet-politician—he all new in the last fashions of Parisian elegance, and redolent of Parisian prosperity and extrait de Mousseline!

"Confrere," said the Pole, seating himself on the edge of the table, while the Italian leaned against the mantelpiece, and glanced round the room with furtive eye, as if to detect its innermost secrets, or decide where safest to drop a Lucifer-match for its conflagration,—"confrere," said the Pole, "your country needs you—"

"Rather the cause of all countries," interposed the Italian softly,—"Humanity."

"Please to explain yourselves; but stay, wait a moment," said Rameau; and rising, he went to the door, opened it, looked forth, ascertained that the coast was clear, then reclosed the door as cautiously as a prudent man closes his pocket whenever shabby-genteel visitors appeal to him in the cause of his country, still more if they appeal in that of Humanity.

"Confrere," said the Pole, "this day a movement is to be made—a demonstration on behalf of your country—"

"Of Humanity," again softly interposed the Italian. "Attend and share it," said the Pole.

"Pardon me," said Rameau, "I do not know what you mean. I am now the editor of a journal in which the proprietor does not countenance violence; and if you come to me as a member of the Council, you must be aware that I should obey no orders but that of its president, whom I—I have not seen for nearly a year; indeed I know not if the Council still exists."

"The Council exists, and with it the obligation it imposes," replied Thaddeus.

"Pampered with luxury," here the Pole raised his voice, "do you dare to reject the voice of Poverty and Freedom?"

"Hush, dear but too vehement confrere," murmured the bland Italian; "permit me to dispel the reasonable doubts of our confrere," and he took out of his breast-pocket a paper which he presented to Rameau; on it were written these words:

"This evening May 24th. Demonstration.—Faubourg du Temple.—Watch events, under orders of A. M. Bid the youngest member take that first opportunity to test nerves and discretion. He is not to act, but to observe."

No name was appended to this instruction, but a cipher intelligible to all members of the Council as significant of its president, Jean Lebeau.

"If I err not," said the Italian, "Citizen Rameau is our youngest confrere."

Rameau paused. The penalties for disobedience to an order of the President of the Council were too formidable to be disregarded. There could be no doubt that,—though his name was not mentioned, he, Rameau, was accurately designated as the youngest member of the Council. Still, however he might have owed his present position to the recommendation of Lebeau, there was nothing in the conversation of M. de Mauleon which would warrant participation in a popular emeute by the editor of a journal belonging to that mocker of the mob. Ah! but—and here again he glanced over the paper—he was asked "not to act; but to observe." To observe was the duty of a journalist. He might go to the demonstration as De Mauleon confessed he had gone to the Communist Club, a philosophical spectator.

"You do not disobey this order?" said the Pole, crossing his arms.

"I shall certainly go into the Faubourg du Temple this evening," answered Rameau, drily, "I have business that way."

"Bon!" said the Pole; "I did not think you would fail us, though you do edit a journal which says not a word on the duties that bind the French people to the resuscitation of Poland."

"And is not pronounced in decided accents upon the cause of the human race," put in the Italian, whispering.

"I do not write the political articles in Le Seas Commun," answered Rameau; "and I suppose that our president is satisfied with them since he recommended me to the preference of the person who does. Have you more to say? Pardon me, my time is precious, for it does not belong to me."

"Eno'!" said the Italian, "we will detain you no longer." Here, with a bow and a smile, he glided towards the door.

"Confrere," muttered the Pole, lingering, "you must have become very rich!—do not forget the wrongs of Poland—I am their Representative—I—speaking in that character, not as myself individually—I have not breakfasted!"

Rameau, too thoroughly Parisian not to be as lavish of his own money as he was envious of another's, slipped some pieces of gold in the Pole's hand. The Pole's bosom heaved with manly emotion: "These pieces bear the effigies of the tyrant—I accept them as redeemed from disgrace by their uses to Freedom."

"Share them with Signor Raselli in the name of the same cause," whispered Rameau, with a smile he might have plagiarised from De Mauleon.

The Italian, whose ear was inured to whispers, heard and turned round as he stood at the threshold.

"No, confrere of France—no, confrere of Poland—I am Italian. All ways to take the life of an enemy are honourable—no way is honourable which begs money from a friend."

An hour or so later, Rameau was driven in his comfortable coupe to the Faubourg du Temple.

Suddenly, at the angle of a street, his coachman was stopped—a rough-looking man appeared at the door—__"Descends, mon petit bourgeois__." Behind the rough-looking man were menacing faces.

Rameau was not physically a coward—very few Frenchmen are, still fewer Parisians; and still fewer no matter what their birthplace, the men whom we call vain—the men who over-much covet distinction, and over-much dread reproach.

"Why should I descend at your summons?" said Rameau, haughtily. "Bah! Coachman, drive on!"

The rough-looking man opened the door, and silently extended a hand to Rameau, saying gently: "Take my advice, mon bourgeois. Get out—we want your carriage. It is a day of barricades—every little helps, even your coupe!"

While this man spoke others gesticulated; some shrieked out, "He is an employer! he thinks he can drive over the employed!"

Some leader of the crowd—a Parisian crowd always has a classical leader, who has never read the classics—thundered forth, "Tarquin's car! Down with Tarquin!" Therewith came a yell, "A la lanterne—Tarquin!"

We Anglo-Saxons, of the old country or the new, are not familiarised to the dread roar of a populace delighted to have a Roman authority for tearing us to pieces; still Americans know what is Lynch law. Rameau was in danger of Lynch law, when suddenly a face not unknown to him interposed between himself and the rough-looking man.

"Ha!" cried this new comer, "my young confrere, Gustave Rameau, welcome! Citizens, make way. I answer for this patriot—I, Armand Monnier. He comes to help use! Is this the way you receive him?" Then in a low voice to Rameau, "Come out. Give your coupe to the barricade. What matters such rubbish? Trust to me—I expected you. Hist!—Lebeau bids me see that you are safe." Rameau then, seeking to drape himself in majesty,—as the aristocrats of journalism in a city wherein no other aristocracy is recognised naturally and commendably do, when ignorance combined with physical strength asserts itself to be a power, beside which the power of knowledge is what a learned poodle is to a tiger—Rameau then descended from his coupe, and said to this Titan of labour, as a French marquis might have said to his valet, and as, when the French marquis has become a ghost of the past, the man who keeps a coupe says to the man who mends its wheels, "Honest fellow, I trust you."

Monnier led the journalist through the mob to the rear of the barricade hastily constructed. Here were assembled very motley groups.

The majority were ragged boys, the gamins of Paris, commingled with several women of no reputable appearance, some dingily, some gaudily apparelled. The crowd did not appear as if the business in hand was a very serious one. Amidst the din of voices the sounds of laughter rose predominant, jests and bon mots flew from lip to lip. The astonishing good-humour of the Parisians was not yet excited into the ferocity that grows out of it by a street contest. It was less like a popular emeute than a gathering of schoolboys, bent not less on fun than on mischief. But, still, amid this gayer crowd were sinister, lowering faces; the fiercest were not those of the very poor, but rather of artisans, who, to judge by their dress, seemed well off of men belonging to yet higher grades. Rameau distinguished amongst these the medecin des pauvres, the philosophical atheist, sundry young, long-haired artists, middle aged writers for the Republican press, in close neighbourhood with ruffians of villainous aspect, who might have been newly returned from the galleys. None were regularly armed; still revolvers and muskets and long knives were by no means unfrequently interspersed among the rioters. The whole scene was to Rameau a confused panorama, and the dissonant tumult of yells and laughter, of menace and joke, began rapidly to act on his impressionable nerves. He felt that which is the prevalent character of a Parisian riot—the intoxication of an impulsive sympathy; coming there as a reluctant spectator, if action commenced he would have been borne readily into the thick of the action—he could not have helped it; already he grew impatient of the suspense of strife. Monnier having deposited him safely with his back to a wall, at the corner of a street handy for flight, if flight became expedient, had left him for several minutes, having business elsewhere. Suddenly the whisper of the Italian stole into his ear—"These men are fools. This is not the way to do business; this does not hurt the robber of Nice—Garibaldi's Nice: they should have left it to me."

"What would you do?"

"I have invented a new machine," whispered the Friend of humanity; "it would remove all at one blow—lion and lioness, whelp and jackals—and then the Revolution if you will! not this paltry tumult. The cause of the human race is being frittered away. I am disgusted with Lebeau. Thrones are not overturned by gamins."

Before Rameau could answer, Monnier rejoined him. The artisan's face was overcast—his lips compressed, yet quivering with indignation. "Brother," he said to Rameau, "to-day the cause is betrayed"—(the word trahi was just then coming into vogue at Paris)—"the blouses I counted on are recreant. I have just learned that all is quiet in the other quartiers where the rising was to have been simultaneous with this. We are in a guet-apens—the soldiers will be down on us in a few minutes; hark! don't you hear the distant tramp? Nothing for us but to die like men. Our blood will be avenged later. Here," and he thrust a revolver into Rameau's hand. Then with a lusty voice that rang through the crowd, he shouted "Vive le peuple!" The rioters caught and re-echoed the cry, mingled with other cries,' "Vive la Republique!" "Vive le drapeau rouge!"

The shouts were yet at their full when a strong hand grasped Monnier's arm, and a clear, deep, but low voice thrilled through his ear: "Obey! I warned you. No fight to-day. Time not ripe. All that is needed is done—do not undo it. Hist! the sergens de ville are force enough to disperse the swarm of those gnats. Behind the sergens come soldiers who will not fraternise. Lose not one life to-day. The morrow when we shall need every man—nay, every gamin—will dawn soon. Answer not. Obey!" The same strong hand quitting its hold on Monnier, then seized Rameau by the wrist, and the same deep voice said, "Come with me." Rameau, turning in amaze, not unmixed with anger, saw beside him a tall man with sombrero hat pressed close over his head, and in the blouse of a labourer, but through such disguise he recognized the pale grey whiskers and green spectacles of Lebeau. He yielded passively to the grasp that led him away down the deserted street at the angle.

At the further end of that street, however, was heard the steady thud of hoofs.

"The soldiers are taking the mob at its rear," said Lebeau, calmly; "we have not a moment to lose—this way," and he plunged into a dismal court, then into a labyrinth of lanes, followed mechanically by Rameau. They issued at last on the Boulevards, in which the usual loungers were quietly sauntering, wholly unconscious of the riot elsewhere. "Now, take that fiacre and go home; write down your impressions of what you have seen, and take your MS. to M. de Mauleon." Lebeau here quitted him.

Meanwhile all happened as Lebeau had predicted. The sergens de ville showed themselves in front of the barricades, a small troop of mounted soldiers appeared in the rear. The mob greeted the first with yells and a shower of stones; at the sight of the last they fled in all directions; and the sergens de ville, calmly scaling the barricades, carried off in triumph, as prisoners of war, 4 gamins, 3 women, and 1 Irishman loudly protesting innocence, and shrieking "Murther!" So ended the first inglorious rise against the plebiscite and the Empire, on the 14th of May, 1870.

From Isaura Cicogna to Madame de Grantmesnil. Saturday. May 21.

"I am still, dearest Eulalie, under the excitement of impressions wholly new to me. I have this day witnessed one of those scenes which take us out of our private life, not into the world of fiction, but of history, in which we live as in the life of a nation. You know how intimate I have become with Valerie Duplessis. She is in herself so charming in her combination of petulant wilfulness and guileless naivete, that she might sit as a model for one of your exquisite heroines. Her father, who is in great favour at Court, had tickets for the Salle des Etats of the Louvre today—when, as the journals will tell you, the results of the plebiscite were formally announced to the Emperor—and I accompanied him and Valerie. I felt, on entering the hall, as if I had been living for months in an atmosphere of false rumours, for those I chiefly meet in the circles of artists and men of letters, and the wits and flaneurs who haunt such circles, are nearly all hostile to the Emperor. They agree, at least, in asserting the decline of his popularity—the failure of his intellectual powers; in predicting his downfall—deriding the notion of a successor in his son. Well, I know not how to reconcile these statements with the spectacle I have beheld to-day.

"In the chorus of acclamation amidst which the Emperor entered the hall, it seemed as if one heard the voice of the France he had just appealed to. If the Fates are really weaving woe and shame in his woof, it is in hues which, to mortal eyes, seem brilliant with glory and joy.

"You will read the address of the President of the Corps Legislatif; I wonder how it will strike you! I own fairly that me it wholly carried away. At each sentiment I murmured to myself, 'Is not this true? and, if true, are France and human nature ungrateful?'

"'It is now,' said the President, 'eighteen years since France, wearied with confusion, and anxious for security, confiding in your genuis and the Napoleonic dynasty, placed in your hands, together with the Imperial Crown, the authority which the public necessity demanded.' Then the address proceeded to enumerate the blessings that ensued—social order speedily restored—the welfare of all classes of society promoted—advances in commerce and manufactures to an extent hitherto unknown. Is not this true? and, if so, are you, noble daughter of France, ungrateful?

"Then came words which touched me deeply—me, who, knowing nothing of politics, still feel the link that unites Art to Freedom: 'But from the first your Majesty has looked forward to the time when this concentration of power would no longer correspond to the aspirations of a tranquil and reassured country, and, foreseeing the progress of modern society, you proclaimed that 'Liberty must be the crowning of the edifice.'' Passing then over the previous gradual advances in popular government, the President came to the 'present self-abnegation, unprecedented in history,' and to the vindication of that plebiscite which I have heard so assailed—viz., Fidelity to the great principle upon which the throne was founded, required that so important a modification of a power bestowed by the people should not be made without the participation of the people themselves. Then, enumerating the millions who had welcomed the new form of government—the President paused a second or two, as if with suppressed emotion—and every one present held his breath, till, in a deeper voice, through which there ran a quiver that thrilled through the hall, he concluded with—'France is with you; France places the cause of liberty under the protection of your dynasty and the great bodies of the State.' Is France with him? I know not; but if the malcontents of France had been in the hall at that moment, I believe they would have felt the power of that wonderful sympathy which compels all the hearts in great audiences to beat in accord, and would have answered, 'It is true.'

"All eyes now fixed on the Emperor, and I noticed few eyes which were not moist with tears. You know that calm unrevealing face of his—a face which sometimes disappoints expectation. But there is that in it which I have seen in no other, but which I can imagine to have been common to the Romans of old, the dignity that arises from self-control—an expression which seems removed from the elation of joy, the depression of sorrow—not unbecoming to one who has known great vicissitudes of Fortune, and is prepared alike for her frowns or her smiles.

"I had looked at that face while M. Schneider was reading the address—it moved not a muscle, it might have been a face of marble. Even when at moments the words were drowned in applause and the Empress, striving at equal composure, still allowed us to see a movement of her eye lids, a tremble on her lips. The boy at his right, heir to his dynasty, had his looks fixed on the President, as if eagerly swallowing each word in the address, save once or twice, when he looked around the hall curiously, and with a smile as a mere child might look. He struck me as a mere child. Next to the Prince was one of those countenances which once seen are never to be forgotten—the true Napoleonic type, brooding, thoughtful, ominous, beautiful. But not with the serene energy that characterises the head of the first Napoleon when Emperor, and wholly without the restless eagerness for action which is stamped in the lean outline of Napoleon when First Consul: no—in Prince Napoleon there is a beauty to which, as woman, I could never give my heart—were I a man, the intellect that would not command my trust. But, nevertheless, in beauty, it is signal, and in that beauty the expression of intellect is predominant.

"Oh, dear Eulalie, how I am digressing! The Emperor spoke—and believe me, Eulalie, whatever the journals or your compatriots may insinuate, there is in that man no sign of declining intellect or failing health. I care not what may be his years, but that man is in mind and in health as young as Caesar when he crossed the Rubicon.

"The old cling to the past—they do not go forward to the future. There was no going back in that speech of the Emperor. There was something grand and something young in the modesty with which he put aside all references to that which his Empire had done in the past, and said with a simple earnestness of manner which I cannot adequately describe—

"'We must more than ever look fearlessly forward to the future. Who can be opposed to the progressive march of a regime founded by a great people in the midst of political disturbance, and which now is fortified by liberty?'

"As he closed, the walls of that vast hall seemed to rock with an applause that must have been heard on the other side of the Seine.

"'Vive l'Empereur!'" "'Vive l'Imperatrice!'" "'Vive le Prince Imperial!'"—and the last cry was yet more prolonged than the others, as if to affirm the dynasty.

"Certainly I can imagine no Court in the old days of chivalry more splendid than the audience in that grand hall of the Louvre. To the right of the throne all the ambassadors of the civilised world in the blaze of their rich costumes and manifold orders. In the gallery at the left, yet more behind, the dresses and jewels of the dames d'honneur and of the great officers of State. And when the Empress rose to depart, certainly my fancy cannot picture a more queenlike image, or one that seemed more in unison with the representation of royal pomp and power. The very dress, of colour which would have been fatal to the beauty of most women equally fair—a deep golden colour—(Valerie profanely called it buff)—seemed so to suit the splendour of the ceremony and the day; it seemed as if that stately form stood in the midst of a sunlight reflected from itself. Day seemed darkened when that sunlight passed away.

"I fear you will think I have suddenly grown servile to the gauds and shows of mere royalty. I ask myself if that be so—I think not. Surely it is a higher sense of greatness which has been impressed on me by the pageant of to-day I feel as if there were brought vividly before me the majesty of France, through the representation of the ruler she has crowned.

"I feel also as if there, in that hall, I found a refuge from all the warring contests in which no two seem to me in agreement as to the sort of government to be established in place of the present. The 'Liberty' clamoured for by one would cut the throat of the 'Liberty' worshipped by another.

"I see a thousand phantom forms of LIBERTY—but only one living symbol of ORDER—that which spoke from a throne to-day."

Isaura left her letter uncompleted. On the following Monday she was present at a crowded soiree given by M. Louvier. Among the guests were some of the most eminent leaders of the Opposition, including that vivacious master of sharp sayings, M. P———, whom Savarin entitled "the

French Sheridan;" if laws could be framed in epigrams he would be also the French Solon.

There, too, was Victor de Mauleon, regarded by the Republican party with equal admiration and distrust. For the distrust, he himself pleasantly accounted in talk with Savarin.

"How can I expect to be trusted? I represent 'Common Sense;' every Parisian likes Common Sense in print, and cries 'Je suis trahi' when Common Sense is to be put into action."

A group of admiring listeners had collected round one (perhaps the most brilliant) of those oratorical lawyers by whom, in France, the respect for all laws has been so often talked away: he was speaking of the Saturday's ceremonial with eloquent indignation. It was a mockery to France to talk of her placing Liberty under the protection of the Empire.

There was a flagrant token of the military force under which civil freedom was held in the very dress of the Emperor and his insignificant son: the first in the uniform of a General of Division; the second, forsooth, in that of a sous-lieutenant. The other liberal chiefs chimed in: "The army," said one, "was an absurd expense; it must be put down:" "The world was grown too civilised for war," said another: "The Empress was priest-ridden," said a third: "Churches might be tolerated; Voltaire built a church, but a church simply to the God of Nature, not of priestcraft,"—and so on.

Isaura, whom any sneer at religion pained and revolted, here turned away from the orators to whom she had before been listening with earnest attention, and her eyes fell on the countenance of De Mauleon, who was seated opposite.

The countenance startled her, its expression was so angrily scornful; that expression, however, vanished at once as De Mauleon's eyes met her own, and drawing his chair near to her, he said, smiling: "Your look tells me that I almost frightened you by the ill-bred frankness with which my face must have betrayed my anger, at hearing such imbecile twaddle from men who aspire to govern our turbulent France. You remember that after Lisbon was destroyed by an earthquake a quack advertised 'pills against earthquakes.' These messieurs are not so cunning as the quack; he did not name the ingredients of his pills."

"But, M. de Mauleon," said Isaura, "if you, being opposed to the Empire, think so ill of the wisdom of those who would destroy it, are you prepared with remedies for earthquakes more efficacious than their pills?"

"I reply as a famous English statesman, when in opposition, replied to a somewhat similar question,—'I don't prescribe till I'm called in.'"

"To judge by the seven millions and a half whose votes were announced on Saturday, and by the enthusiasm with which the Emperor was greeted, there is too little fear of an earthquake for a good trade of the pills of these messieurs, or for fair play to the remedies you will not disclose till called in."

"Ah, Mademoiselle! playful wit from lips not formed for politics makes me forget all about emperors and earthquakes. Pardon that commonplace compliment—remember I am a Frenchman, and cannot help being frivolous."

"You rebuke my presumption too gently. True, I ought not to intrude political subjects on one like you—I understand so little about them—but this is my excuse, I do so desire to know more."

M. de Mauleon paused, and looked at her earnestly with a kindly, half compassionate look, wholly free from the impertinence of gallantry. "Young poetess," he said, softly, "you care for politics. Happy, indeed, is he—and whether he succeed or fail in his ambition abroad, proud should he be of an ambition crowned at home—he who has made you desire to know more of politics!"

The girl felt the blood surge to her temples. How could she have been so self-confessed? She made no reply, nor did M. de Mauleon seem to expect one; with that rare delicacy of high breeding which appears in France to belong to a former generation, he changed his tone, and went on as if there had been no interruption to the question her words implied.

"You think the Empire secure—that it is menaced by on earthquake? You deceive yourself. The Emperor began with a fatal mistake, but a mistake it needs many years to discover. He disdained the slow natural process of adjustment between demand and supply—employer and workmen. He desired—no ignoble ambition—to make Paris the wonder of the world, the eternal monument of his reign. In so doing, he sought to create artificial modes of content for revolutionary workmen. Never has any ruler had such tender heed of manual labour to the disparagement of intellectual culture. Paris is embellished; Paris is the wonder of the world; other great towns have followed its example; they, too, have their rows of palaces and temples. Well, the time comes when the magician can no longer give work to the spirits he raises; then they must fall on him and rend: out of the very houses he built for the better habitation of workmen will flock the malcontents who cry, 'Down with the Empire!' On the 21st of May you witnessed the pompous ceremony which announces to the Empire a vast majority of votes, that will be utterly useless to it except as food for gunpowder in the times that are at hand. Seven days before, on the 14th of May, there was a riot in the Faubourg d'Temple—easily put down—you scarcely hear of it. That riot was not the less necessary to those who would warn the Empire that it is mortal. True, the riot disperses—but it is unpunished; riot unpunished is a revolution begun. The earthquake is nearer than you think; and for that earthquake what are the pills you quacks advertise? They prate of an age too enlightened for war; they would mutilate the army—nay, disband it if they could—with Prussia next door to France. Prussia, desiring, not unreasonably, to take that place in the world which France now holds, will never challenge France; if she did, she would be too much in the wrong to find a second: Prussia knowing that she has to do with the vainest, the most conceited, the rashest antagonist that ever flourished a rapier in the face of a spadassin—Prussia will make France challenge her.

"And how do ces messieurs deal with the French army? Do they dare to say to the ministers, 'Reform it'? Do they dare say, 'Prefer for men whose first duty it is to obey, discipline to equality—insist on the distinction between the officer and the private, and never confound it; Prussian officers are well-educated gentlemen, see that yours are'? Oh no; they are democrats too stanch not to fraternise with an armed mob; they content themselves with grudging an extra sou to the Commissariat, and winking at the millions fraudulently pocketed by some 'Liberal contractor.' Dieu des dieux! France to be beaten, not as at Waterloo by hosts combined, but in fair duel by a single foe! Oh, the shame! the shame! But as the French army is now organised, beaten she must be, if she meets the march of the German."

"You appal me with your sinister predictions," said Isaura; "but, happily, there is no sign of war. M. Duplessis, who is in the confidence of the Emperor, told us only the other day that Napoleon, on learning the result of the plebiscite, said: 'The foreign journalists who have been insisting that the Empire cannot coexist with free institutions, will no longer hint that it can be safely assailed from without.' And more than ever I may say L'Empire c'est la paix!"

Monsieur de Mauleon shrugged his shoulders. "The old story—Troy and the wooden horse."

"Tell me, M. de Mauleon, why do you, who so despise the Opposition, join with it in opposing the Empire?"

"Mademoiselle, the Empire opposes me; while it lasts I cannot be even a Depute; when it is gone, Heaven knows that I may be, perhaps Dictator; one thing, you may rely upon, that I would, if not Dictator myself, support any man who was better fitted for that task."

"Better fitted to destroy the liberty which he pretended to fight for."

"Not exactly so," replied M. de Mauleon, imperturbably—"better fitted to establish a good government in lieu of the bad one he had fought against, and the much worse governments that would seek to turn France into a madhouse, and make the maddest of the inmates the mad doctor!" He turned away, and here their conversation ended.

But it so impressed Isaura, that the same night she concluded her letter to Madame de Grantmesnil, by giving a sketch of its substance, prefaced by an ingenuous confession that she felt less sanguine confidence in the importance of the applauses which had greeted the Emperor at the Saturday's ceremonial, and ending thus: "I can but confusedly transcribe the words of this singular man, and can give you no notion of the manner and the voice which made them eloquent. Tell me, can there be any truth in his gloomy predictions? I try not to think so, but they seem to rest over that brilliant hall of the Louvre like an ominous thunder-cloud."

# CHAPTER II.

The Marquis de Rochebriant was seated in his pleasant apartment, glancing carelessly at the envelopes of many notes and letters lying yet unopened on his breakfast-table. He had risen late at noon, for he had not gone to bed till dawn. The night had been spent at his club—over the card-table—by no means to the pecuniary advantage of the Marquis. The reader will have learned, through the conversation recorded in a former chapter between De Mauleon and Enguerrand de Vandemar, that the austere Seigneur Breton had become a fast viveur of Paris. He had long since spent the remnant of Louvier's premium of L10,000., and he owed a year's interest. For this last there was an excuse. M. Collot, the contractor to whom he had been advised to sell the yearly fall of his forest-trees, had removed the trees, but had never paid a sou beyond the preliminary deposit; so that the revenue, out of which the mortgagee should be paid his interest, was not forthcoming. Alain had instructed M. Hebert to press the contractor; the contractor had replied, that if not pressed he could soon settle all claims—if pressed, he must declare himself bankrupt. The Chevalier de Finisterre had laughed at the alarm which Alain conceived when he first found himself in the condition of debtor for a sum he could not pay—creditor for a sum he could not recover.

"Bagatelle!" said the Chevalier. "Tschu! Collot, if you give him time, is as safe as the Bank of France, and Louvier knows it. Louvier will not trouble you—Louvier, the best fellow in the world! I'll call on him and explain matters."

It is to be presumed that the Chevalier did so explain; for though both at the first, and quite recently at the second default of payment, Alain received letters from M. Louvier's professional agent, as reminders of interest due, and as requests for its payment, the Chevalier assured him that these applications were formalities of convention—that Louvier, in fact, knew nothing about them; and when dining with the great financier himself, and cordially welcomed and called "Mon cher," Alain had taken him aside and commenced explanation and excuse, Louvier had cut him short. "Peste!

don't mention such trifles. There is such a thing as business—that concerns my agent; such a thing as friendship—that concerns me. Allez!"

Thus M. de Rochebriant, confiding in debtor and in creditor, had suffered twelve months to glide by without much heed of either, and more than live up to an income amply sufficient indeed for the wants of an ordinary bachelor, but needing more careful thrift than could well be expected from the head of one of the most illustrious houses in France, cast so young into the vortex of the most expensive capital in the world.

The poor Marquis glided into the grooves that slant downward, much as the French Marquis of tradition was wont to glide; not that he appeared to live extravagantly, but he needed all he had for his pocket-money, and had lost that dread of being in debt which he had brought up from the purer atmosphere of Bretagne.

But there were some debts which; of course, a Rochebriant must pay—debts of honour—and Alain had, on the previous night, incurred such a debt and must pay it that day. He had been strongly tempted, when the debt rose to the figure it had attained, to risk a change of luck; but whatever his imprudence, he was incapable of dishonesty. If the luck did not change, and he lost more, he would be without means to meet his obligations. As the debt now stood, he calculated that he could just discharge it by the sale of his coupe and horses. It is no wonder he left his letters unopened, however charming they might be; he was quite sure they would contain no cheque which would enable him to pay his debt and retain his equipage.

The door opened, and the valet announced M. le Chevalier de Finisterre—a man with smooth countenance and air distinque, a pleasant voice and perpetual smile.

"Well, mon cher," cried the Chevalier, "I hope that you recovered the favour of Fortune before you quitted her green table last night. When I left she seemed very cross with you."

"And so continued to the end," answered Alain, with well-simulated gaiety—much too bon gentilhomme to betray rage or anguish for pecuniary loss.

"After all," said de Finisterre, lighting his cigarette, "the uncertain goddess could not do you much harm; the stakes were small, and your adversary, the Prince, never goes double or quits."

"Nor I either. 'Small,' however, is a word of relative import; the stakes might be small to you, to me large. Entre nous, cher ami, I am at the end of my purse, and I have only this consolation-I am cured of play: not that

I leave the complaint, the complaint leaves me; it can no more feed on me than a fever can feed on a skeleton."

"Are you serious?"

"As serious as a mourner who has just buried his all."

"His all? Tut, with such an estate as Rochebriant!"

For the first time in that talk Alain's countenance became overcast.

"And how long will Rochebriant be mine? You know that I hold it at the mercy of the mortgagee, whose interest has not been paid, and who could if, he so pleased, issue notice, take proceedings—that—"

"Peste!" interrupted de Finisterre; "Louvier take proceedings! Louvier, the best fellow in the world! But don't I see his handwriting on that envelope? No doubt an invitation to dinner."

Alain took up the letter thus singled forth from a miscellany of epistles, some in female handwritings, unsealed but ingeniously twisted into Gordian knots—some also in female handwritings, carefully sealed—others in ill-looking envelopes, addressed in bold, legible, clerk-like caligraphy. Taken altogether, these epistles had a character in common; they betokened the correspondence of a viveur, regarded from the female side as young, handsome, well-born—on the male side, as a viveur who had forgotten to pay his hosier and tailor.

Louvier wrote a small, not very intelligible, but very masculine hand, as most men who think cautiously and act promptly do write. The letter ran thus:

"Cher petit Marquis" (at that commencement Alain haughtily raised his head and bit his lips).

> *"CHER PETIT MARQUIS,—It is an age since I have seen you. No doubt my humble soirees are too dull for a beau seigueur so courted. I forgive you. Would I were a beau seigneur at your age! Alas! I am only a commonplace man of business, growing old, too. Aloft from the world in which I dwell, you can scarcely be aware that I have embarked a great part of my capital in building speculations. There is a Rue de Louvier that runs its drains right through my purse. I am obliged to call in the moneys due to me. My agent informs me that I am just 7000 louis short of the total I need—all other debts being paid in—and that there is a trifle more than 7000 louis owned to me as interest on my hypotheque on Rochebriant: kindly pay into his hands before the end of this week*

*that sum. You have been too lenient to Collot, who must owe you more than that. Send agent to him. Desole to trouble you, and am au desespoir to think that my own pressing necessities compel me to urge you to take so much trouble. Mais que faire? The Rue de Louvier stops the way, and I must leave it to my agent to clear it.*

*"Accept all my excuses, with the assurance of my sentiments the most cordial. PAUL LOUVIER."*

Alain tossed the letter to De Finisterre. "Read that from the best fellow in the world."

The Chevalier laid down his cigarette and read. "Diable!" he said, when he returned the letter and resumed the cigarette—"Diable! Louvier must be much pressed for money, or he would not have written in this strain. What does it matter? Collot owes you more than 7000 louis. Let your lawyer get them, and go to sleep with both ears on your pillow."

"Ah! you think Collot can pay if he will?"

"Ah! foi! did not M. Gandrin tell you that M. Collot was safe to buy your wood at more money than any one else would give?"

"Certainly," said Alain, comforted. "Gandrin left that impression on my mind. I will set him on the man. All will come right, I dare say; but if it does not come right, what would Louvier do?"

"Louvier do!" answered Finisterre, reflectively. "Well do you ask my opinion and advice?"

"Earnestly, I ask."

"Honestly, then, I answer. I am a little on the Bourse myself—most Parisians are. Louvier has made a gigantic speculation in this new street, and with so many other irons in the fire he must want all the money he can get at. I dare say that if you do not pay him what you owe, he must leave it to his agent to take steps for announcing the sale of Rochebriant. But he detests scandal; he hates the notion of being severe; rather than that, in spite of his difficulties, he will buy Rochebriant of you at a better price than it can command at public sale. Sell it to him. Appeal to him to act generously, and you will flatter him. You will get more than the old place is worth. Invest the surplus—live as you have done, or better—and marry an heiress. Morbleu! a Marquis de Rochebriant, if he were sixty years old, would rank high in the matrimonial market. The more the democrats have sought to impoverish titles and laugh down historical names, the more do rich democrat fathers-in-law seek to decorate their daughters with titles and give their grandchildren the heritage of historical names. You look shocked, pauvre anti. Let us hope, then, that Collot will pay. Set your dog—I mean your lawyer—at him; seize him by the throat!"

Before Alain had recovered from the stately silence with which he had heard this very practical counsel, the valet again appeared, and ushered in M. Frederic Lemercier.

There was no cordial acquaintance between the visitors. Lemercier was chafed at finding himself supplanted in Alain's intimate companionship by so new a friend, and De Finisterre affected to regard Lemercier as a would-be exquisite of low birth and bad taste.

Alain, too, was a little discomposed at the sight of Lemercier, remembering the wise cautious which that old college friend had wasted on him at the commencement of his Parisian career, and smitten with vain remorse that the cautions had been so arrogantly slighted.

It was with some timidity that he extended his hand to Frederic, and he was surprised as well as moved by the more than usual warmth with which it was grasped by the friend he had long neglected. Such affectionate greeting was scarcely in keeping with the pride which characterised Frederic Lemercier.

"Ma foi!" said the Chevalier, glancing towards the clock, "how time flies! I had no idea it was so late. I must leave you now, my dear Rochebriant. Perhaps we shall meet at the club later—I dine there to-day. Au plaisir, M. Lemercier."

# CHAPTER III.

When the door had closed on the Chevalier, Frederic's countenance became very grave. Drawing his chair near to Alain, he said: "We have not seen much of each other lately,—nay, no excuses; I am well aware that it could scarcely be otherwise. Paris has grown so large and so subdivided into sets, that the best friends belonging to different sets become as divided as if the Atlantic flowed between them. I come to-day in consequence of something I have just heard from Duplessis. Tell me, have you got the money for the wood you sold to M. Collot a year ago?"

"No," said Alain, falteringly.

"Good heavens! none of it?"

"Only the deposit of ten per cent., which of course I spent, for it formed the greater part of my income. What of Collot? Is he really unsafe?"

"He is ruined, and has fled the country. His flight was the talk of the Bourse this morning. Duplessis told me of it."

Alain's face paled. "How is Louvier to be paid? Read that letter!"

Lemercier rapidly scanned his eye over the contents of Louvier's letter.

"It is true, then, that you owe this man a year's interest—more than 7,000 louis?"

"Somewhat more—yes. But that is not the first care that troubles me—Rochebriant may be lost, but with it not my honour. I owe the Russian Prince 300 louis, lost to him last night at ecarte. I must find a purchaser for my coupe and horses; they cost me 600 louis last year,—do you know any one who will give me three?"

"Pooh! I will give you six; your alezan alone is worth half the money!"

"My dear Frederic, I will not sell them to you on any account. But you have so many friends—"

"Who would give their soul to say, 'I bought these horses of Rochebriant.' Of course I do. Ha! young Rameau, you are acquainted with him?"

"Rameau! I never heard of him!"

"Vanity of vanities, then what is fame? Rameau is the editor of Le Sens Commun. You read that journal?"

"Yes, it has clever articles, and I remember how I was absorbed in the eloquent romance which appeared in it."

"Ah! by the Signora Cicogna, with whom I think you were somewhat smitten last year."

"Last year—was I? How a year can alter a man! But my debt to the Prince. What has Le Sens Commun to do with my horses?"

"I met Rameau at Savarin's the other evening. He was making himself out a hero and a martyr! his coupe had been taken from him to assist in a barricade in that senseless emeute ten days ago; the coupe got smashed, the horses disappeared. He will buy one of your horses and coupe.

"Leave it to me! I know where to dispose of the other two horses. At what hour do you want the money?"

"Before I go to dinner at the club."

"You shall have it within two hours; but you must not dine at the club to-day. I have a note from Duplessis to invite you to dine with him to-day!"

"Duplessis! I know so little of him!"

"You should know him better. He is the only man who can give you sound advice as to this difficulty with Louvier; and he will give it the more carefully and zealously because he has that enmity to Louvier which one rival financier has to another. I dine with him too. We shall find an occasion to consult him quietly; he speaks of you most kindly. What a lovely girl his daughter is!"

"I dare say. Ah! I wish I had been less absurdly fastidious. I wish I had entered the army as a private soldier six months ago; I should have been a corporal by this time! Still it is not too late. When Rochebriant is gone, I can yet say with the Mouszquetaire in the melodrame: 'I am rich—I have my honour and my sword!'"

"Nonsense! Rochebriant shall be saved; meanwhile I hasten to Rameau. Au revoir, at the Hotel Duplessis—seven o'clock."

Lemercier went, and in less than two hours sent the Marquis bank-notes for 600 louis, requesting an order for the delivery of the horses and carriage.

That order written and signed, Alain hastened to acquit himself of his debt of honour, and contemplating his probable ruin with a lighter heart presented himself at the Hotel Duplessis.

Duplessis made no pretensions to vie with the magnificent existence of Louvier. His house, though agreeably situated and flatteringly styled the Hotel Duplessis, was of moderate size, very unostentatiously furnished; nor was it accustomed to receive the brilliant motley crowds which assembled in the salons of the elder financier.

Before that year, indeed, Duplessis had confined such entertainments as he gave to quiet men of business, or a few of the more devoted and loyal partisans of the Imperial dynasty; but since Valerie came to live with him he had extended his hospitalities to wider and livelier circles, including some celebrities in the world of art and letters as well as of fashion. Of the party assembled that evening at dinner were Isaura, with the Signora Venosta, one of the Imperial Ministers, the Colonel whom Alain had already met at Lemercier's supper, Deputes (ardent Imperialists), and the Duchesse de Tarascon; these, with Alain and Frederic, made up the party. The conversation was not particularly gay. Duplessis himself, though an exceedingly well-read and able man, had not the genial accomplishments of a brilliant host. Constitutionally grave and habitually taciturn—though there were moments in which he was roused out of his wonted self into eloquence or wit—he seemed to-day absorbed in some engrossing train of thought. The Minister, the Deputes and the Duchesse de Tarascon talked politics, and ridiculed the trumpery emeute of the 14th; exulted in the success of the plebiscite; and admitting, with indignation, the growing strength of Prussia, and—with scarcely less indignation, but more contempt, censuring the selfish egotism of England in disregarding the due equilibrium of the European balance of power,—hinted at the necessity of annexing Belgium as a set-off against the results of Sadowa.

Alain found himself seated next to Isaura—to the woman who had so captivated his eye and fancy on his first arrival in Paris.

Remembering his last conversation with Graham nearly a year ago, he felt some curiosity to ascertain whether the rich Englishman had proposed to her, and if so, been refused or accepted.

The first words that passed between them were trite enough, but after a little pause in the talk, Alain said:

"I think Mademoiselle and myself have an acquaintance in common-Monsieur Vane, a distinguished Englishman. Do you know if he be in Paris at present? I have not seen him for many months."

"I believe he is in London; at least, Colonel Morley met the other day a friend of his who said so."

Though Isaura strove to speak in a tone of indifference, Alain's ear detected a ring of pain in her voice; and watching her countenance, he was impressed with a saddened change in its expression. He was touched, and his curiosity was mingled with a gentler interest as he said "When I last saw M. Vane I should have judged him to be too much under the spell of an enchantress to remain long without the pale of the circle she draws around her."

Isaura turned her face quickly towards the speaker, and her lips moved, but she said nothing audibly.

"Can there have been quarrel or misunderstanding?" thought Alain; and after that question his heart asked itself, "Supposing Isaura were free, her affections disengaged, could he wish to woo and to win her?" and his heart answered—"Eighteen months ago thou wert nearer to her than now. Thou wert removed from her for ever when thou didst accept the world as a barrier between you; then, poor as thou wert, thou wouldst have preferred her to riches. Thou went then sensible only of the ingenuous impulses of youth, but the moment thou saidst, 'I am Rochebriant, and having once owned the claims of birth and station, I cannot renounce them for love, Isaura became but a dream. Now that ruin stares thee in the face—now that thou must grapple with the sternest difficulties of adverse fate—thou hast lost the poetry of sentiment which could alone give to that dream the colours and the form of human life." He could not again think of that fair creature as a prize that he might even dare to covet. And as he met her inquiring eyes, and saw her quivering lip, he felt instinctively that Graham was dear to her, and that the tender interest with which she inspired himself was untroubled by one pang of jealousy. He resumed:

"Yes, the last time I saw the Englishman he spoke with such respectful homage of one lady, whose hand he would deem it the highest reward of ambition to secure, that I cannot but feel deep compassion for him if that ambition has been foiled; and thus only do I account for his absence from Paris."

"You are an intimate friend of Mr. Vane's?"

"No, indeed, I have not that honour; our acquaintance is but slight, but it impressed me with the idea of a man of vigorous intellect, frank temper, and perfect honour."

Isaura's face brightened with the joy we feel when we hear the praise of those we love.

At this moment, Duplessis, who had been observing the Italian and the young Marquis, for the first time during dinner, broke silence.

"Mademoiselle," he said, addressing Isaura across the table, "I hope I have not been correctly informed that your literary triumph has induced you to forego the career in which all the best judges concur that your successes would be not less brilliant; surely one art does not exclude another."

Elated by Alain's report of Graham's words, by the conviction that these words applied to herself, and by the thought that her renunciation of the stage removed a barrier between them, Isaura answered, with a sort of enthusiasm:

"I know not, M. Duplessis, if one art excludes another; if there be desire to excel in each. But I have long lost all desire to excel in the art you refer to, and resigned all idea of the career in which it opens."

"So M. Vane told me," said Alain, in a whisper.

"When?"

"Last year—on the day that he spoke in terms of admiration so merited of the lady whom M. Duplessis has just had the honour to address."

All this while, Valerie, who was seated at the further end of the table beside the Minister, who had taken her in to dinner, had been watching, with eyes, the anxious tearful sorrow of which none but her father had noticed, the low-voiced confidence between Alain and the friend, whom till that day she had so enthusiastically loved. Hitherto she had been answering in monosyllables all attempts of the great man to draw her into conversation; but now, observing how Isaura blushed and looked down, that strange faculty in women, which we men call dissimulation, and which in them is truthfulness to their own nature, enabled her to carry off the sharpest anguish she had ever experienced, by a sudden burst of levity of spirit. She caught up some commonplace the Minister had adapted to what he considered the poverty of her understanding, with a quickness of satire which startled that grave man, and he gazed at her astonished. Up to that moment he had secretly admired her as a girl well brought up—as girls fresh from a French convent are supposed to be; now, hearing her brilliant rejoinder to his stupid observation, he said inly: "Dame! the low birth of a financier's daughter shows itself."

But, being a clever man himself, her retort put him on his mettle, and he became, to his own amazement, brilliant himself. With that matchless quickness which belongs to Parisians, the guests around him seized the new esprit de conversation which had been evoked between the statesman and the childlike girl beside him; and as they caught up the ball, lightly flung among them, they thought within themselves how much more sparkling the financier's pretty, lively daughter was than that dark-eyed young muse, of whom all the journalists of Paris were writing in a chorus of welcome and applause, and who seemed not to have a word to say worth listening to, except to the handsome young Marquis, whom, no doubt, she wished to fascinate.

Valerie fairly outshone Isaura in intellect and in wit; and neither Valerie nor Isaura cared, to the value of a bean-straw, about that distinction. Each was thinking only of the prize which the humblest peasant women have in common with the most brilliantly accomplished of their sex—the heart of a man beloved.

# CHAPTER IV.

On the Continent generally, as we all know, men do not sit drinking wine together after the ladies retire. So when the signal was given all the guests adjourned to the salon; and Alain quitted Isaura to gain the ear of the Duchesse de Tarascon.

"It is long—at, least long for Paris life," said the Marquis—"since my first visit to you, in company with Enguerrand de Vandemar. Much that you then said rested on my mind, disturbing the prejudices I took from Bretagne."

"I am proud to hear it, my kinsman."

"You know that I would have taken military service under the Emperor, but for the regulation which would have compelled me to enter the ranks as a private soldier."

"I sympathise with that scruple; but you are aware that the Emperor himself could not have ventured to make any exception even in your favour."

"Certainly not. I repent me of my pride; perhaps I may enlist still in some regiment sent to Algiers."

"No; there are other ways in which a Rochebriant can serve a throne. There will be an office at Court vacant soon, which would not misbecome your birth."

"Pardon me; a soldier serves his country—a courtier owns a master; and I cannot take the livery of the Emperor, though I could wear the uniform of France."

"Your distinction is childish, my kinsman," said the Duchesse, impetuously. "You talk as if the Emperor had an interest apart from the nation. I tell you that he has not a corner of his heart—not even one reserved for his son and his dynasty—in which the thought of France does not predominate."

"I do not presume, Madame la Duchesse, to question the truth of what you say; but I have no reason to suppose that the same thought does not predominate in the heart of the Bourbon. The Bourbon would be the first to say to me: 'If France needs your sword against her foes, let it not rest in the scabbard.' But would the Bourbon say, 'The place of a Rochebriant is among the valetaille of the Corsican's successor'?"

"Alas for poor France!" said the Duchesse; "and alas for men like you, my proud cousin, if the Corsican's successors or successor be—"

"Henry V." interrupted Alain, with a brightening eye. "Dreamer! No; some descendant of the mob-kings who gave Bourbons and nobles to the guillotine."

While the Duchesse and Alain were thus conversing, Isaura had seated herself by Valerie, and, unconscious of the offence she had given, addressed her in those pretty caressing terms with which young-lady friends are wont to compliment each other; but Valerie answered curtly or sarcastically, and turned aside to converse with the Minister. A few minutes more, and the party began to break up. Lemercier, however, detained Alain, whispering, "Duplessis will see us on your business so soon as the other guests have gone."

# CHAPTER V.

"Monsieur le Marquis," said Duplessis, when the salon was cleared of all but himself and the two friends, "Lemercier has confided to me the state of your affairs in connection with M. Louvier, and flatters me by thinking my advice may be of some service; if so, command me."

"I shall most gratefully accept your advice," answered Alain, "but I fear my condition defies even your ability and skill."

"Permit me to hope not, and to ask a few necessary questions. M. Louvier has constituted himself your sole mortgagee; to what amount, at what interest, and from what annual proceeds is the interest paid?"

Herewith Alain gave details already furnished to the reader. Duplessis listened, and noted down the replies.

"I see it all," he said, when Alain had finished. "M. Louvier had predetermined to possess himself of your estate: he makes himself mortgagee at a rate of interest so low, that I tell you fairly, at the present value of money, I doubt if you could find any capitalist who would accept the transfer of the mortgage at the same rate. This is not like Louvier, unless he had an object to gain, and that object is your land. The revenue from your estate is derived chiefly from wood, out of which the interest due to Louvier is to be paid. M. Gandrin, in a skilfully-guarded letter, encourages you to sell the wood from your forests to a man who offers you several thousand francs more than it could command from customary buyers. I say nothing against M. Gandrin, but every man who knows Paris as I do, knows that M. Louvier can put, and has put, a great deal of money into M. Gandrin's pocket. The purchaser of your wood does not pay more than his deposit, and has just left the country insolvent. Your purchaser, M. Collot, was an adventurous speculator; he would have bought anything at any price, provided he had time to pay; if his speculations had been lucky he would have paid. M. Louvier knew, as I knew, that M. Collot was a gambler, and the chances were that he would not pay. M. Louvier allows a year's interest on his hypotheque to become due-notice thereof duly given to you by his agent—now you come under the operation of the law. Of course, you know what the law is?"

"Not exactly," answered Alain, feeling frostbitten by the congealing words of his counsellor; "but I take it for granted that if I cannot pay the interest of a sum borrowed on my property, that property itself is forfeited."

"No, not quite that—the law is mild. If the interest which should be paid half-yearly remains unpaid at the end of a year, the mortgagee has a right to be impatient, has he not?"

"Certainly he has."

"Well, then, on fait un commandement tendant de saisie immobiliere, viz: The mortgagee gives a notice that the property shall be put up for sale. Then it is put up for sale, and in most cases the mortgagee buys it in. Here, certainly, no competitors in the mere business way would vie with Louvier; the mortgage at three and a half per cent. covers more than the estate is apparently worth. Ah! but stop, M. le Marquis; the notice is not yet served: the whole process would take six months from the day it is served to the taking possession after the sale; in the meanwhile, if you pay the interest due, the action drops. Courage, M. le Marquis! Hope yet, if you condescend to call me friend."

"And me," cried Lemercier; "I will sell out of my railway shares to-morrow-see to it, Duplessis—enough to pay off the damnable interest. See to it, mon ami."

"Agree to that, M. le Marquis, and you are safe for another year," said Duplessis, folding up the paper on which he had made his notes, but fixing on Alain quiet eyes half concealed under drooping lids.

"Agree to that!" cried Rochebriant, rising—"agree to allow even my worst enemy to pay for me moneys I could never hope to repay—agree to allow the oldest and most confiding friends to do so—M. Duplessis, never! If I carried the porter's knot of an Auverguat, I should still remain gentilhomme and Breton."

Duplessis, habitually the driest of men, rose with a moistened eye and flushing cheek—"Monsieur le Marquis, vouchsafe me the honour to shake hands with you. I, too, am by descent gentilhomme, by profession a speculator on the Bourse. In both capacities I approve the sentiment you have uttered. Certainly, if our friend Frederic lent you 7000 Louis or so this year, it would be impossible for you even to foresee the year in which you could repay it; but,"—here Duplessis paused a minute, and then lowering the tone of his voice, which had been somewhat vehement and enthusiastic, into that of a colloquial good-fellowship, equally rare to the measured reserve of the financier, he asked, with a lively twinkle of his grey eye, "Did you never hear, Marquis, of a little encounter between me and M. Louvier?"

"Encounter at arms—does Louvier fight?" asked Alain, innocently.

"In his own way he is always fighting; but I speak metaphorically. You see this small house of mine—so pinched in by the houses next to it that I can neither get space for a ball-room for Valerie, nor a dining-room for more than a friendly party like that which has honoured me to-day. Eh bien! I bought this house a few years ago, meaning to buy the one next to it and throw the two into one. I went to the proprietor of the next house, who, as I knew, wished to sell. 'Aha,' he thought, 'this is the rich Monsieur Duplessis;' and he asked me 2000 louis more than the house was worth. We men of business cannot bear to be too much cheated; a little cheating we submit to—much cheating raises our gall. Bref—this was on Monday. I offered the man 1000 louis above the fair price, and gave him till Thursday to decide. Somehow or other Louvier hears of this. 'Hillo!' says Louvier, 'here is a financier who desires a hotel to vie with mine!' He goes on Wednesday to my next-door neighbour. 'Friend, you want to sell your house. I want to buy—the price?' The proprietor, who does not know him by sight, says: 'It is as good as sold. M. Duplessis and I shall agree.' 'Bah! What sum did you ask M. Duplessis?' He names the sum; 2000 louis more than he can get elsewhere. 'But M. Duplessis will give me the sum.' 'You ask too little. I will give 3000. A fig for M. Duplessis. I am Monsieur Louvier.' So when I call on Thursday the house is sold. I reconcile myself easily enough to the loss of space for a larger dining-room; but though Valerie was then a child at a convent, I was sadly disconcerted by the thought that I could have no salle de bal ready for her when she came to reside with me. Well, I say to myself, patience; I owe M. Louvier a good turn; my time to pay him off will come. It does come, and very soon. M. Louvier buys an estate near Paris—builds a superb villa. Close to his property is a rising forest ground for sale. He goes to the proprietor: says the proprietor to himself, 'The great Louvier wants this,' and adds 5000 louis to its market price. Louvier, like myself, can't bear to be cheated egregiously. Louvier offers 2000 louis more than the man could fairly get, and leaves him till Saturday to consider. I hear of this—speculators hear of everything. On Friday night I go to the man and I give him 6000 louis, where he had asked 5000. Fancy Louvier's face the next day! But there my revenge only begins," continued Duplessis, chuckling inwardly. "My forest looks down on the villa he is building. I only wait till his villa is built, in order to send to my architect and say, Build me a villa at least twice as grand as M. Louvier's, then clear away the forest trees, so that every morning he may see my palace dwarfing into insignificance his own."

"Bravo!" cried Lemercier, clapping his hands. Lemercier had the spirit of party, and felt for Duplessis against Louvier much as in England Whig feels against Tory, or vice versa.

"Perhaps now," resumed Duplessis, more soberly,—"perhaps now, M. le Marquis, you may understand why I humiliate you by no sense of obligation if I say that M. Louvier shall not be the Seigneur de Rochebriant if I can help it. Give me a line of introduction to your Breton lawyer and to Mademoiselle your aunt—let me have your letters early to-morrow. I will take the afternoon train. I know not how many days I may be absent, but I shall not return till I have carefully examined the nature and conditions of your property. If I see my way to save your estate, and give a mauvais quart d'heure to Louvier, so much the better for you, M. le Marquis; if I cannot, I will say frankly, 'Make the best terms you can with your creditor.'"

"Nothing can be more delicately generous than the way you put it," said Alain; "but pardon me, if I say that the pleasantry with which you narrate your grudge against M. Louvier does not answer its purpose in diminishing my sense of obligation." So, linking his arm in Lemercier's, Alain made his bow and withdrew.

When his guests had gone, Duplessis remained seated in meditation—apparently pleasant meditation, for he smiled while indulging it; he then passed through the reception-rooms to one at the far end appropriated to Valerie as a boudoir or morning-room, adjoining her bed-chamber; he knocked gently at the door, and, all remaining silent within, he opened it noiselessly and entered. Valerie was reclining on the sofa near the window-her head drooping, her hands clasped on her knees. Duplessis neared her with tender stealthy steps, passed his arm round her, and drew her head towards his bosom. "Child!" he murmured; "my child, my only one!"

At that soft loving voice, Valerie flung her arms round him, and wept aloud like an infant in trouble. He seated himself beside her, and wisely suffered her to weep on, till her passion had exhausted itself; he then said, half fondly, half chillingly: "Have you forgotten our conversation only three days ago? Have you forgotten that I then drew forth the secret of your heart? Have you forgotten what I promised you in return for your confidence? and a promise to you have I ever yet broken?"

"Father! father! I am so wretched and so ashamed of myself for being wretched! Forgive me. No, I do not forget your promise; but who can promise to dispose of the heart of another? and that heart will never be mine. But bear with me a little, I shall soon recover."

"Valerie, when I made you the promise you now think I cannot keep, I spoke only from that conviction of power to promote the happiness of a child which nature implants in the heart of parents; and it may be also from the experience of my own strength of will, since that which I have willed I have always won. Now I speak on yet surer ground. Before the year is out you shall be the beloved wife of Alain de Rochebriant. Dry your tears and smile on me, Valerie. If you will not see in me mother and father both, I have double love for you, motherless child of her who shared the poverty of my youth, and did not live to enjoy the wealth which I hold as a trust for that heir to mine all which she left me."

As this man thus spoke you would scarcely have recognized in him the old saturnine Duplessis, his countenance became so beautified by the one soft feeling which care and contest, ambition and money-seeking, had left unaltered in his heart. Perhaps there is no country in which the love of parent and child, especially of father and daughter, is so strong as it is in France; even in the most arid soil, among the avaricious, even among the profligate, it forces itself into flower. Other loves fade away: in the heart of the true Frenchman that parent love blooms to the last. Valerie felt the presence of that love as a divine protecting guardianship. She sank on her knees and covered his hand with grateful kisses.

"Do not torture yourself, my child, with jealous fears of the fair Italian. Her lot and Alain de Rochebriant's can never unite; and whatever you may think of their whispered converse, Alain's heart at this moment is too filled with anxious troubles to leave one spot in it accessible even to a frivolous gallantry. It is for us to remove these troubles; and then, when he turns his eyes towards you, it will be with the gaze of one who beholds his happiness. You do not weep now, Valerie!"

# BOOK IX.

## CHAPTER I.

On waking some morning, have you ever felt, reader, as if a change for the brighter in the world, without and within you, had suddenly come to pass-some new glory has been given to the sunshine, some fresh balm to the air-you feel younger, and happier, and lighter, in the very beat of your heart-you almost fancy you hear the chime of some spiritual music far off, as if in the deeps of heaven? You are not at first conscious how, or wherefore, this change has been brought about. Is it the effect of a dream in the gone sleep, that has made this morning so different from mornings that have dawned before? And while vaguely asking yourself that question, you become aware that the cause is no mere illusion, that it has its substance in words spoken by living lips, in things that belong to the work-day world.

It was thus that Isaura woke the morning after the conversation with Alain de Rochebriant, and as certain words, then spoken, echoed back on her ear, she knew why she was so happy, why the world was so changed.

In those words she heard the voice of Graham Vane—nor she had not deceived herself—she was loved! she was loved! What mattered that long cold interval of absence? She had not forgotten—she could not believe that absence had brought forgetfulness. There are moments when we insist on judging another's heart by our own. All would be explained some day—all would come right.

How lovely was the face that reflected itself in the glass as she stood before it, smoothing back her long hair, murmuring sweet snatches of Italian love-song, and blushing with sweeter love-thoughts as she sang! All that had passed in that year so critical to her outer life—the authorship, the fame, the public career, the popular praise—vanished from her mind as a vapour that rolls from the face of a lake to which the sunlight restores the smile of a brightened heaven.

She was more the girl now than she had ever been since the day on which she sat reading Tasso on the craggy shore of Sorrento.

Singing still as she passed from her chamber, and entering the sitting-room, which fronted the east, and seemed bathed in the sunbeams of deepening May, she took her bird from its cage, and stopped her song to cover it with kisses, which perhaps yearned for vent somewhere.

Later in the day she went out to visit Valerie. Recalling the altered manner of her young friend, her sweet nature became troubled. She divined that Valerie had conceived some jealous pain which she longed to heal; she could not bear the thought of leaving any one that day unhappy. Ignorant before of the girl's feelings towards Alain, she now partly guessed them—one woman who loves in secret is clairvoyante as to such secrets in another.

Valerie received her visitor with a coldness she did not attempt to disguise. Not seeming to notice this, Isaura commenced the conversation with frank mention of Rochebriant. "I have to thank you so much, dear Valerie, for a pleasure you could not anticipate—that of talking about an absent friend, and hearing the praise he deserved from one so capable of appreciating excellence as M. de Rochebriant appears to be."

"You were talking to M. de Rochebriant of an absent friend—ah! you seemed indeed very much interested in the conversation—"

"Do not wonder at that, Valerie; and do not grudge me the happiest moments I have known for months."

"In talking with M. de Rochebriant! No doubt, Mademoiselle Cicogna, you found him very charming."

To her surprise and indignation, Valerie here felt the arm of Isaura tenderly entwining her waist, and her face drawn towards Isaura's sisterly kiss.

"Listen to me, naughty child-listen and believe. M. de Rochebriant can never be charming to me—never touch a chord in my heart or my fancy except as friend to another, or—kiss me in your turn, Valerie—as suitor to yourself."

Valerie here drew back her pretty childlike head, gazed keenly a moment into Isaura's eyes, felt convinced by the limpid candour of their unmistakable honesty, and flinging herself on her friend's bosom, kissed her passionately, and burst into tears.

The complete reconciliation between the two girls was thus peacefully effected; and then Isaura had to listen, at no small length, to the confidences poured into her ears by Valerie, who was fortunately too engrossed by her own hopes and doubts to exact confidences in return. Valerie's was one of those impulsive eager natures that longs for a confidante. Not so Isaura's.

Only when Valerie had unburthened her heart, and been soothed and caressed into happy trust in the future, did she recall Isaura's explanatory words, and said, archly: "And your absent friend? Tell me about him. Is he as handsome as Alain?"

"Nay," said Isaura, rising to take up the mantle and hat she had laid aside on entering, "they say that the colour of a flower is in our vision, not in the leaves." Then with a grave melancholy in the look she fixed upon Valerie, she added: "Rather than distrust of me should occasion you pain, I have pained myself, in making clear to you the reason why I felt interest in M. de Rochebriant's conversation. In turn, I ask of you a favour—do not on this point question me farther. There are some things in our past which influence the present, but to which we dare not assign a future—on which we cannot talk to another. What soothsayer can tell us if the dream of a yesterday will be renewed on the night of a morrow? All is said—we trust one another, dearest."

# CHAPTER II.

That evening the Morleys looked in at Isaura's on their way to a crowded assembly at the house of one of those rich Americans, who were then outvying the English residents at Paris in the good graces of Parisian society. I think the Americans get on better with the French than the English do—I mean the higher class of Americans. They spend more money; their men speak French better; the women are better dressed, and, as a general rule, have read more largely, and converse more frankly. Mrs. Morley's affection for Isaura had increased during the last few months. As so notable an advocate of the ascendancy of her sex, she felt a sort of grateful pride in the accomplishments and growing renown of so youthful a member of the oppressed sisterhood. But, apart from that sentiment, she had conceived a tender mother-like interest for the girl who stood in the world so utterly devoid of family ties, so destitute of that household guardianship and protection which, with all her assertion of the strength and dignity of woman, and all her opinions as to woman's right of absolute emancipation from the conventions fabricated by the selfishness of man, Mrs. Morley was too sensible not to value for the individual, though she deemed it not needed for the mass. Her great desire was that Isaura should marry well, and soon. American women usually marry so young that it seemed to Mrs. Morley an anomaly in social life, that one so gifted in mind and person as Isaura should already have passed the age in which the belles of the great Republic are enthroned as wives and consecrated as mothers. We have seen that in the past year she had selected from our unworthy but necessary sex, Graham Vane as a suitable spouse to her young friend. She had divined the state of his heart—she had more than suspicions of the state of Isaura's. She was exceedingly perplexed and exceedingly chafed at the Englishman's strange disregard to his happiness and her own projects. She had counted, all this past winter, on his return to Paris; and she became convinced that some misunderstanding, possibly some lover's quarrel, was the cause of his protracted absence, and a cause that, if ascertained, could be removed. A good opportunity now presented itself—Colonel Morley was going to London the next day. He had business there which would detain him at least a week. He would see Graham; and as she considered her husband the shrewdest and wisest person in the world—I mean of the male sex—she had no doubt of his being able to turn Graham's mind thoroughly inside out, and ascertain his exact feelings and intentions. If the Englishman, thus assayed, were found of base metal, then, at least, Mrs. Morley would be free to cast him altogether aside, and coin for the uses of the matrimonial market some nobler effigy in purer gold.

"My dear child," said Mrs. Morley, in a low voice, nestling herself close to Isaura, while the Colonel, duly instructed, drew off the Venosta, "have you heard anything lately of our pleasant friend Mr. Vane?"

You can guess with what artful design Mrs. Morley put that question point-blank, fixing keen eyes on Isaura while she put it. She saw the heightened colour, the quivering lip of the girl thus abruptly appealed to, and she said inly: "I was right—she loves him!"

"I heard of Mr. Vane last night—accidentally."

"Is he coming to Paris soon?"

"Not that I know of. How charmingly that wreath becomes you! it suits the earrings so well, too."

"Frank chose it; he has good taste for a man. I trust him with my commissions to Hunt and Roskell's but I limit him as to price, he is so extravagant—men are, when they make presents. They seem to think we value things according to their cost. They would gorge us with jewels, and let us starve for want of a smile. Not that Frank is so bad as the rest of them. But a propos of Mr. Vane—Frank will be sure to see him, and scold him well for deserting us all. I should not be surprised if he brought the deserter back with him, for I send a little note by Frank, inviting him to pay us a visit. We have spare rooms in our apartments."

Isaura's heart heaved beneath her robe, but she replied in a tone of astonishing indifference: "I believe this is the height of the London season, and Mr. Vane would probably be too engaged to profit even by an invitation so tempting."

"Nous verrons. How pleased he will be to hear of your triumphs! He admired you so much before you were famous: what will be his admiration now! men are so vain—they care for us so much more when people praise us. But till we have put the creatures in their proper place, we must take them for what they are."

Here the Venosta, with whom the poor Colonel had exhausted all the arts at his command for chaining her attention, could be no longer withheld from approaching Mrs. Morley, and venting her admiration of that lady's wreath, earrings, robes, flounces. This dazzling apparition had on her the effect which a candle has on a moth—she fluttered round it, and longed to absorb herself in its blaze. But the wreath especially fascinated her—a wreath which no prudent lady with colourings less pure, and features less exquisitely delicate than the pretty champion of the rights of women, could have fancied on her own brows without a shudder. But the Venosta in such matters was not prudent. "It can't be dear," she cried piteously, extending her arms towards Isaura. "I must have one exactly like. Who made it? Cara signora, give me the address."

"Ask the Colonel, dear Madame; he chose and bought it," and Mrs. Morley glanced significantly at her well-tutored Frank.

"Madame," said the Colonel, speaking in English, which he usually did with the Venosta—who valued herself on knowing that language and was flattered to be addressed in it—while he amused himself by introducing into its forms the dainty Americanisms with which he puzzled the Britisher—he might well puzzle the Florentine,—"Madame, I am too anxious for the appearance of my wife to submit to the test of a rival schemer like yourself in the same apparel. With all the homage due to a sex of which I am enthused dreadful, I decline to designate the florist from whom I purchased Mrs. Morley's head-fixings."

"Wicked man!" cried the Venosta, shaking her finger at him coquettishly. "You are jealous! Fie! a man should never be jealous of a woman's rivalry with women;" and then, with a cynicism that might have become a greybeard, she added, "but of his own sex every man should be jealous—though of his dearest friend. Isn't it so, Colonello?"

The Colonel looked puzzled, bowed, and made no reply. "That only shows," said Mrs. Morley, rising, "what villains the Colonel has the misfortune to call friends and fellow-men."

"I fear it is time to go," said Frank, glancing at the clock.

In theory the most rebellious, in practice the most obedient, of wives, Mrs. Morley here kissed Isaura, resettled her crinoline, and shaking hands with the Venosta, retreated to the door.

"I shall have the wreath yet," cried the Venosta, impishly. "La speranza e fenamina" (Hope is female).

"Alas!" said Isaura, half mournfully, half smiling, "alas! do you not remember what the poet replied when asked what disease was most mortal?—'the hectic fever caught from the chill of hope.'"

# CHAPTER III.

Graham Vane was musing very gloomily in his solitary apartment one morning, when his servant announced Colonel Morley.

He received his visitor with more than the cordiality with which every English politician receives an American citizen. Graham liked the Colonel too well for what he was in himself to need any national title to his esteem. After some preliminary questions and answers as to the health of Mrs. Morley, the length of the Colonel's stay in London, what day he could dine with Graham at Richmond or Gravesend, the Colonel took up the ball. "We have been reckoning to see you at Paris, sir, for the last six months."

"I am very much flattered to hear that you have thought of me at all; but I am not aware of having warranted the expectation you so kindly express."

"I guess you must have said something to my wife which led her to do more than expect—to reckon on your return. And, by the way, sir, I am charged to deliver to you this note from her, and to back the request it contains that you will avail yourself of the offer. Without summarising the points I do so."

Graham glanced over the note addressed to him

> *"DEAR MR. VANE,—Do you forget how beautiful the environs of Paris*
> *are in May and June? how charming it was last year at the lake of Enghien? how gay were our little dinners out of doors in the garden arbours, with the Savarins and the fair Italian, and her incomparably amusing chaperon? Frank has my orders to bring you back to renew these happy days, while the birds are in their first song, and the leaves are in their youngest green. I have prepared your rooms chez nous—a chamber that looks out on the Champs Elysees, and a quiet cabinet de travail at the back, in which you can read, write, or sulk undisturbed. Come, and we will again visit Enghien and Montmorency. Don't talk of engagements. If man proposes, woman disposes. Hesitate not—obey. Your sincere little friend, Lizzy."*

"My dear Morley," said Graham, with emotion, "I cannot find words to thank your wife sufficiently for an invitation so graciously conveyed. Alas! I cannot accept it."

"Why?" asked the Colonel, drily.

"I have too much to do in London."

"Is that the true reason, or am I to suspicion that there is anything, sir, which makes you dislike a visit to Paris?"

The Americans enjoy the reputation of being the frankest putters of questions whom liberty of speech has yet educated into la recherche de la verite, and certainly Colonel Morley in this instance did not impair the national reputation.

Graham Vane's brow slightly contracted, and he bit his lip as if stung by a sudden pang; but after a moment's pause, he answered with a good-humoured smile:

"No man who has taste enough to admire the most beautiful city, and appreciate the charms of the most brilliant society in the world, can dislike Paris."

"My dear sir, I did not ask you if you disliked Paris, but if there were anything that made you dislike coming back to it on a visit."

"What a notion! and what a cross-examiner you would have made if you had been called to the bar! Surely, my dear friend, you can understand that when a man has in one place business which he cannot neglect, he may decline going to another place, whatever pleasure it would give him to do so. By the way, there is a great ball at one of the Ministers' to-night; you should go there, and I will point out to you all those English notabilities in whom Americans naturally take interest. I will call for you at eleven o'clock. Lord ———, who is a connection of mine, would be charmed to know you."

Morley hesitated; but when Graham said, "How your wife will scold you if you lose such an opportunity of telling her whether the Duchess of —— is as beautiful as report says, and whether Gladstone or Disraeli seems to your phrenological science to have the finer head!" the Colonel gave in, and it was settled that Graham should call for him at the Langham Hotel.

That matter arranged, Graham probably hoped that his inquisitive visitor would take leave for the present, but the Colonel evinced no such intention. On the contrary, settling himself more at ease in his arm-chair, he said, "if I remember aright, you do not object to the odour of tobacco?"

Graham rose and presented to his visitor a cigar-box which he took from the mantelpiece.

The Colonel shook his head, and withdrew from his breast pocket a leather case, from which he extracted a gigantic regalia; this he lighted from a gold match-box in the shape of a locket attached to his watch-chain, and took two or three preliminary puffs, with his head thrown back and his eyes meditatively intent upon the ceiling.

We know already that strange whim of the Colonel's (than whom, if he so pleased, no man could speak purer English as spoken by the Britisher) to assert the dignity of the American citizen by copious use of expressions and phrases familiar to the lips of the governing class of the great Republic—delicacies of speech which he would have carefully shunned in the polite circles of the Fifth Avenue in New York. Now the Colonel was much too experienced a man of the world not to be aware that the commission with which his Lizzy had charged him was an exceedingly delicate one; and it occurred to his mother wit that the best way to acquit himself of it, so as to avoid the risk of giving or of receiving serious affront, would be to push that whim of his into more than wonted exaggeration. Thus he could more decidedly and briefly come to the point; and should he, in doing so, appear too meddlesome, rather provoke a laugh than a frown-retiring from the ground with the honours due to a humorist. Accordingly, in his deepest nasal intonation, and withdrawing his eyes from the ceiling, he began:

"You have not asked, sir, after the signorina, or as we popularly call her, Mademoiselle Cicogna?"

"Have I not? I hope she is quite well, and her lively companion, Signora Venosta."

"They are not sick, sir; or at least they were not so last night when my wife and I had the pleasure to see them. Of course you have read Mademoiselle Cicogna's book—a bright performance, sir, age considered."

"Certainly, I have read the book; it is full of unquestionable genius. Is Mademoiselle writing another? But of course she is."

"I am not aware of the fact, sir. It may be predicated; such a mind cannot remain inactive; and I know from M. Savarin and that rising young man Gustave Rameau, that the publishers bid high for her brains considerable. Two translations have already appeared in our country. Her fame, sir, will be world-wide. She may be another George Sand, or at least another Eulalie Grantmesnil."

Graham's cheek became as white as the paper I write on. He inclined his head as in assent, but without a word. The Colonel continued:

"We ought to be very proud of her acquaintance, sir. I think you detected her gifts while they were yet unconjectured. My wife says so. You must be gratified to remember that, sir—clear grit, sir, and no mistake."

"I certainly more than once have said to Mrs. Morley, that I esteemed Mademoiselle's powers so highly that I hoped she would never become a stage-singer and actress. But this M. Rameau? You say he is a rising man. It struck me when at Paris that he was one of those charlatans with a great deal of conceit and very little information, who are always found in scores on the ultra-Liberal side of politics;-possibly I was mistaken."

"He is the responsible editor of Le Sens Commun, in which talented periodical Mademoiselle Cicogna's book was first raised."

"Of course, I know that; a journal which, so far as I have looked into its political or social articles, certainly written by a cleverer and an older man than M. Rameau, is for unsettling all things and settling nothing. We have writers of that kind among ourselves—I have no sympathy with them. To me it seems that when a man says, 'Off with your head,' he ought to let us know what other head he would put on our shoulders, and by what process the change of heads shall be effected. Honestly speaking, if you and your charming wife are intimate friends and admirers of Mademoiselle Cicogna, I think you could not do her a greater service than that of detaching her from all connection with men like M. Rameau, and journals like La Sens Commun."

The Colonel here withdrew his cigar from his lips, lowered his head to a level with Graham's, and relaxing into an arch significant smile, said: "Start to Paris, and dissuade her yourself. Start—go ahead—don't be shy—don't seesaw on the beam of speculation. You will have more influence with that young female than we can boast." Never was England in greater danger of quarrel with America than at that moment; but Graham curbed his first wrathful impulse, and replied coldly:

"It seems to me, Colonel, that you, though very unconsciously, derogate from the respect due to Mademoiselle Cicogna. That the counsel of a married couple like yourself and Mrs. Morley should be freely given to and duly heeded by a girl deprived of her natural advisers in parents, is a reasonable and honourable supposition; but to imply that the most influential adviser of a young lady so situated is a young single man, in no way related to her, appears to me a dereliction of that regard to the dignity of her sex which is the chivalrous characteristic of your countrymen—and to Mademoiselle Cicogna herself, a surmise which she would be justified in resenting as an impertinence."

"I deny both allegations," replied the Colonel serenely. "I maintain that a single man whips all connubial creation when it comes to gallantising a single young woman; and that no young lady would be justified in resenting as impertinence my friendly suggestion to the single man so deserving of her consideration as I estimate you to be, to solicit the right to advise her for life. And that's a caution."

Here the Colonel resumed his regalia, and again gazed intent on the ceiling.

"Advise her for life! You mean, I presume, as a candidate for her hand."

"You don't Turkey now. Well, I guess, you are not wide of the mark there, sir."

"You do me infinite honour, but I do not presume so far."

"So, so—not as yet. Before a man who is not without gumption runs himself for Congress, he likes to calculate how the votes will run. Well, sir, suppose we are in caucus, and let us discuss the chances of the election with closed doors."

Graham could not help smiling at the persistent officiousness of his visitor, but his smile was a very sad one.

"Pray change the subject, my dear Colonel Morley—it is not a pleasant one to me; and as regards Mademoiselle Cicogna, can you think it would not shock her to suppose that her name was dragged into the discussions you would provoke, even with closed doors?"

"Sir," replied the Colonel, imperturbably, "since the doors are closed, there is no one, unless it be a spirit-listener under the table, who can wire to Mademoiselle Cicogna the substance of debate. And, for my part, I do not believe in spiritual manifestations. Fact is, that I have the most amicable sentiments towards both parties, and if there is a misunderstanding which is opposed to the union of the States, I wish to remove it while yet in time. Now, let us suppose that you decline to be a candidate; there are plenty of others who will run; and as an elector must choose one representative or other, so a gal must choose one husband or other. And then you only repent when it is too late. It is a great thing to be first in the field. Let us approximate to the point; the chances seem good-will you run? Yes or no?"

"I repeat, Colonel Morley, that I entertain no such presumption."

The Colonel here, rising, extended his hand, which Graham shook with constrained cordiality, and then leisurely walked to the door; there he paused, as if struck by a new thought, and said gravely, in his natural tone of voice, "You have nothing to say, sir, against the young lady's character and honour?"

"I!—heavens, no! Colonel Morley, such a question insults me."

The Colonel resumed his deepest nasal bass: "It is only, then, because you don't fancy her now so much as you did last year—fact, you are soured on her and fly off the handle. Such things do happen. The same thing has happened to myself, sir. In my days of celibacy, there was a gal at Saratoga whom I gallantised, and whom, while I was at Saratoga, I thought Heaven had made to be Mrs. Morley: I was on the very point of telling her so, when I was suddenly called off to Philadelphia; and at Philadelphia, sir, I found that Heaven had made another Mrs. Morley. I state this fact, sir, though I seldom talk of my own affairs, even when willing to tender my advice in the affairs of another, in order to prove that I do not intend to censure you if Heaven has served you in the same manner. Sir, a man may go blind for one gal when he is not yet dry behind the ears, and then, when his eyes are skinned, go in for one better. All things mortal meet with a change, as my sisters little boy said when, at the age of eight, he quitted the Methodys and turned Shaker. Threep and argue as we may, you and I are both mortals—more's the pity. Good morning, sir (glancing at the clock, which proclaimed the hour of 3 P.M.),—I err—good evening."

By the post that day the Colonel transmitted a condensed and laconic report of his conversation with Graham Vane. I can state its substance in yet fewer words. He wrote word that Graham positively declined the invitation to Paris; that he had then, agreeably to Lizzy's instruction, ventilated the Englishman, in the most delicate terms, as to his intentions with regard to Isaura, and that no intentions at all existed. The sooner all thoughts of him were relinquished, as a new suitor on the ground, the better it would be for the young lady's happiness in the only state in which happiness should be, if not found, at least sought, whether by maid or man.

Mrs. Morley was extremely put out by this untoward result of the diplomacy she had intrusted to the Colonel; and when, the next day, came a very courteous letter from Graham, thanking her gratefully for the kindness of her invitation, and expressing his regret briefly, though cordially, at his inability to profit by it, without the most distant allusion to the subject which the Colonel had brought on the tapis, or even requesting his compliments to the Signoras Venosta and Cicogna, she was more than put out, more than resentful,—she was deeply grieved. Being, however, one of those gallant heroes of womankind who do not give in at the first defeat, she began to doubt whether Frank had not rather overstrained the delicacy which he said he had put into his "soundings." He ought to have been more explicit.

Meanwhile she resolved to call on Isaura, and, without mentioning Graham's refusal of her invitation, endeavour to ascertain whether the attachment which she felt persuaded the girl secretly cherished for this recalcitrant Englishman were something more than the first romantic fancy—whether it were sufficiently deep to justify farther effort on Mrs. Morley's part to bring it to a prosperous issue.

She found Isaura at home and alone; and, to do her justice, she exhibited wonderful tact in the fulfilment of the task she had set herself. Forming her judgment by manner and look—not words—she returned home, convinced that she ought to seize the opportunity afforded to her by Graham's letter. It was one to which she might very naturally reply, and in that reply she might convey the object at her heart more felicitously than the Colonel had done. "The cleverest man is," she said to herself, "stupid compared to an ordinary woman in the real business of life, which does not consist of fighting and moneymaking."

Now there was one point she had ascertained by words in her visit to Isaura—a point on which all might depend. She had asked Isaura when and where she had seen Graham last; and when Isaura had given her that information, and she learned it was on the eventful day on which Isaura gave her consent to the publication of her MS. if approved by Savarin, in the journal to be set up by the handsome-faced young author, she leapt to the conclusion that Graham had been seized with no unnatural jealousy, and was still under the illusive glamoury of that green-eyed fiend. She was confirmed in this notion, not altogether an unsound one, when asking with apparent carelessness, "And in that last interview, did you see any change in Mr. Vane's manner, especially when he took leave?"

Isaura turned away pale, and involuntarily clasping her hands-as women do when they would suppress pain-replied, in a low murmur, "His manner was changed."

Accordingly, Mrs. Morley sat down and wrote the following letter:

"DEAR MR. VANE,—I am very angry indeed with you for refusing my invitation—I had so counted on you, and I don't believe a word of your excuse. Engagements! To balls and dinners, I suppose, as if you were not much too clever to care about such silly attempts to enjoy solitude in crowds. And as to what you men call business, you have no right to have any business at all. You are not in commerce; you are not in Parliament; you told me yourself that you had no great landed estates to give you trouble; you are rich, without any necessity to take pains to remain rich, or to become richer; you have no business in the world except to please yourself: and when you will not come to Paris to see one of your truest friends—which I certainly am—it simply means, that no matter how such a visit would please me, it does not please yourself. I call that abominably rude and ungrateful.

"But I am not writing merely to scold you. I have something else on my mind, and it must come out. Certainly, when you were at Paris last year you did admire, above all other young ladies, Isaura Cicogna. And I honoured you for doing so. I know no other young lady to be called her equal. Well, if you admired her then, what would you do now if you met her? Then she was but a girl—very brilliant, very charming, it is true—but undeveloped, untested. Now she is a woman, a princess among women, but retaining all that is most lovable in a girl; so courted, yet so simple—so gifted, yet so innocent. Her head is not a bit turned by all the flattery that surrounds her. Come and judge for yourself. I still hold the door of the rooms destined to you open for repentance.

"My dear Mr. Vane, do not think me a silly match-making little woman, when I write to you thus, a coeur ouvert.

"I like you so much that I would fain secure to you the rarest prize which life is ever likely to offer to your ambition. Where can you hope to find another Isaura? Among the stateliest daughters of your English dukes, where is there one whom a proud man would be more proud to show to the world, saying, 'She is mine!' where one more distinguished—I will not say by mere beauty, there she might be eclipsed—but by sweetness and dignity combined—in aspect, manner, every movement, every smile?

"And you, who are yourself so clever, so well read—you who would be so lonely with a wife who was not your companion, with whom you could not converse on equal terms of intellect,—my dear friend, where could you find a companion in whom you would not miss the poet-soul of Isaura? Of course I should not dare to obtrude all these questionings on your innermost reflection, if I had not some idea, right or wrong, that since the days when at Enghien and Montmorency, seeing you and Isaura side by side, I whispered to Frank, 'So should those two be through life,' some cloud has passed between your eyes and the future on which they gazed. Cannot that cloud be dispelled? Were you so unjust to yourself as to be jealous of a rival, perhaps of a Gustave Rameau? I write to you frankly—answer me frankly; and if you answer, 'Mrs. Morley, I don't know, what you mean; I admired Mademoiselle Cicogna as I might admire any other pretty, accomplished girl, but it is really nothing to me whether she marries Gustave Rameau or any one else,'—why, then, burn this letter—forget that it has been written; and may you never know the pang of remorseful sigh, if, in the days to come, you see her—whose name in that case I should profane did I repeat it—the comrade of another man's mind, the half of another man's heart, the pride and delight of another man's blissful home."

# CHAPTER IV.

There is somewhere in Lord Lytton's writings—writings so numerous that I may be pardoned if I cannot remember where-a critical definition of the difference between dramatic and narrative art of story, instanced by that marvellous passage in the loftiest of Sir Walter Scott's works, in which all the anguish of Ravenswood on the night before he has to meet Lucy's brother in mortal combat is conveyed without the spoken words required in tragedy. It is only to be conjectured by the tramp of his heavy boots to and fro all the night long in his solitary chamber, heard below by the faithful Caleb. The drama could not have allowed that treatment; the drama must have put into words, as "soliloquy," agonies which the non-dramatic narrator knows that no soliloquy can describe. Humbly do I imitate, then, the great master of narrative in declining to put into words the conflict between love and reason that tortured the heart of Graham Vane when, dropping noiselessly the letter I have just transcribed, he covered his face with his hands and remained—I know not how long—in the same position, his head bowed, not a sound escaping from his lips.

He did not stir from his rooms that day; and had there been a Caleb's faithful ear to listen, his tread, too, might have been heard all that sleepless night passing to and fro, but pausing oft, along his solitary floors.

Possibly love would have borne down all opposing seasonings, doubts, and prejudices, but for incidents that occurred the following evening. On that evening Graham dined en famille with his cousins the Altons. After dinner, the Duke produced the design for a cenotaph inscribed to the memory of his aunt, Lady Janet King, which he proposed to place in the family chapel at Alton.

"I know," said the Duke, kindly, "you would wish the old house from which she sprang to preserve some such record of her who loved you as her son; and even putting you out of the question, it gratifies me to attest the claim of our family to a daughter who continues to be famous for her goodness, and made the goodness so lovable that envy forgave it for being famous. It was a pang to me when poor Richard King decided on placing her tomb among strangers; but in conceding his rights as to her resting-place, I retain mine to her name,—Nostris liberis virtutis exemplar."

Graham wrung his cousin's hand-he could not speak, choked by suppressed tears.

The Duchess, who loved and honoured Lady Janet almost as much as did her husband, fairly sobbed aloud. She had, indeed, reason for grateful memories of the deceased: there had been some obstacles to her marriage with the man who had won her heart, arising from political differences and family feuds between their parents, which the gentle meditation of Lady Janet had smoothed away. And never did union founded on mutual and ardent love more belie the assertions of the great Bichat (esteemed by Dr. Buckle the finest intellect which practical philosophy has exhibited since Aristotle), that "Love is a sort of fever which does not last beyond two years," than that between those eccentric specimens of a class denounced as frivolous and artless by philosophers, English and French, who have certainly never heard of Bichat.

When the emotion the Duke had exhibited was calmed down, his wife pushed towards Graham a sheet of paper, inscribed with the epitaph composed by his hand. "Is it not beautiful," she said, falteringly—"not a word too much or too little?"

Graham read the inscription slowly, and with very dimmed eyes. It deserved the praise bestowed on it; for the Duke, though a shy and awkward speaker, was an incisive and graceful writer.

Yet, in his innermost self, Graham shivered when he read that epitaph, it expressed so emphatically the reverential nature of the love which Lady Janet had inspired—the genial influences which the holiness of a character so active in doing good had diffused around it. It brought vividly before Graham that image of perfect spotless womanhood. And a voice within him asked, "Would that cenotaph be placed amid the monuments of an illustrious lineage if the secret known to thee could transpire? What though the lost one were really as unsullied by sin as the world deems, would the name now treasured as an heirloom not be a memory of gall and a sound of shame?"

He remained so silent after putting down the inscription, that the Duke said modestly: "My dear Graham, I see that you do not like what I have written. Your pen is much more practised than mine. If I did not ask you to compose the epitaph, it was because I thought it would please you more in coming, as a spontaneous tribute due to her, from the representative of her family. But will you correct my sketch, or give me another according to your own ideas?"

"I see not a word to alter," said Graham; "forgive me if my silence wronged my emotion; the truest eloquence is that which holds us too mute for applause."

"I knew you would like it. Leopold is always so disposed to underrate himself," said the duchess, whose hand was resting fondly on her husband's shoulder. "Epitaphs are so difficult to write-especially epitaphs on women of whom in life the least said the better. Janet was the only woman I ever knew whom one could praise in safety."

"Well expressed," said the Duke, smiling: "and I wish you would make that safety clear to some lady friends of yours, to whom it might serve as a lesson. Proof against every breath of scandal herself, Janet King never uttered and never encouraged one ill-natured word against another. But I am afraid, my dear fellow, that I must leave you to a tete-a-tete with Eleanor. You know that I must be at the House this evening—I only paired till half-past nine."

"I will walk down to the House with you, if you are going on foot."

"No," said the Duchess; "you must resign yourself to me for at least half an hour. I was looking over your aunt's letters to-day, and I found one which I wish to show you; it is all about yourself, and written within the last few months of her life." Here she put her arm into Graham's, and led him into her own private drawing-room, which, though others might call it a boudoir, she dignified by the name of her study. The Duke remained for some minutes thoughtfully leaning his arm on the mantelpiece. It was no unimportant debate in the Lords that night, and on a subject in which he took great interest, and the details of which he had thoroughly mastered. He had been requested to speak, if only a few words, for his high character and his reputation for good sense gave weight to the mere utterance of his opinion. But though no one had more moral courage in action, the Duke had a terror at the very thought of addressing an audience, which made him despise himself.

"Ah!" he muttered, "if Graham Vane were but in Parliament, I could trust him to say exactly what I would rather be swallowed up by an earthquake than stand up and say for myself. But now he has got money he seems to think of nothing but saving it."

# CHAPTER V.

The letter from Lady Janet, which the Duchess took from the desk and placed in Graham's hand, was in strange coincidence with the subject that for the last twenty-four hours had absorbed his thoughts and tortured his heart. Speaking of him in terms of affectionate eulogy, the writer proceeded to confide her earnest wish that he should not longer delay that change in life which, concentrating so much that is vague in the desires and aspirations of man, leaves his heart and his mind, made serene by the contentment of home, free for the steadfast consolidation of their warmth and their light upon the ennobling duties that unite the individual to his race.

"There is no one," wrote Lady Janet, "whose character and career a felicitous choice in marriage can have greater influence over than this dear adopted son of mine. I do not fear that in any case he will be liable to the errors of his brilliant father. His early reverse of fortune here seems to me one of those blessings which Heaven conceals in the form of affliction. For in youth, the genial freshness of his gay animal spirits, a native generosity mingled with desire of display and thirst for applause, made me somewhat alarmed for his future. But, though he still retains these attributes of character, they are no longer predominant; they are modified and chastened. He has learned prudence. But what I now fear most for him is that which he does not show in the world, which neither Leopold nor you seem to detect,—it is an exceeding sensitiveness of pride. I know not how else to describe it. It is so interwoven with the highest qualities, that I sometimes dread injury to them could it be torn away from the faultier ones which it supports.

"It is interwoven with that lofty independence of spirit which has made him refuse openings the most alluring to his ambition; it communicates a touching grandeur to his self-denying thrift; it makes him so tenacious of his word once given, so cautious before he gives it. Public life to him is essential; without it he would be incomplete; and yet I sigh to think that whatever success he may achieve in it will be attended with proportionate pain. Calumny goes side by side with fame, and courting fame as a man, he is as thin-skinned to calumny as a woman.

"The wife for Graham should have qualities, not taken individually, uncommon in English wives, but in combination somewhat rare.

"She must have mind enough to appreciate his—not to clash with it. She must be fitted with sympathies to be his dearest companion, his confidante in the hopes and fears which the slightest want of sympathy would make him keep ever afterwards pent within his breast. In herself worthy of distinction, she must merge all distinction in his. You have met in the world men who, marrying professed beauties, or professed literary geniuses, are spoken of as the husband of the beautiful Mrs. A———, or of the clever Mrs. B———: can you fancy Graham Vane in the reflected light of one of those husbands? I trembled last year when I thought he was attracted by a face which the artists raved about, and again by a tongue which dropped bons mots that went the round of the club. I was relieved, when, sounding him, he said, laughingly, 'No, dear aunt, I should be one sore from head to foot if I married a wife that was talked about for anything but goodness.'

"No,—Graham Vane will have pains sharp enough if he live to be talked about himself. But that tenderest half of himself, the bearer of the name he would make, and for the dignity of which he alone would be responsible,—if that were the town talk, he would curse the hour he gave any one the right to take on herself his man's burden of calumny and fame. I know not which I should pity the most, Graham Vane or his wife.

"Do you understand me, dearest Eleanor? No doubt you do so far, that you comprehend that the women whom men most admire are not the women we, as women ourselves, would wish our sons or brothers to marry. But perhaps you do not comprehend my cause of fear, which is this—for in such matters men do not see as we women do—Graham abhors, in the girls of our time, frivolity and insipidity. Very rightly, you will say. True, but then he is too likely to be allured by contrasts. I have seen him attracted by the very girls we recoil from more than we do from those we allow to be frivolous and insipid. I accused him of admiration for a certain young lady whom you call 'odious,' and whom the slang that has come into vogue calls 'fast;' and I was not satisfied with his answer, 'Certainly I admire her; she is not a doll—she has ideas.' I would rather of the two see Graham married to what men call a doll, than to a girl with ideas which are distasteful to women."

Lady Janet then went on to question the Duchess about a Miss Asterisk, with whom this tale will have nothing to do, but who, from the little which Lady Janet had seen of her, might possess all the requisites that fastidious correspondent would exact for the wife of her adopted son.

This Miss Asterisk had been introduced into the London world by the Duchess. The Duchess had replied to Lady Janet, that if earth could be ransacked, a more suitable wife for Graham Vane than Miss Asterisk could not be found; she was well born—an heiress; the estates she inherited were in the county of—(viz., the county in which the ancestors of D'Altons and Vanes had for centuries established their whereabout). Miss Asterisk was pretty enough to please any man's eye, but not with the beauty of which artists rave; well informed enough to be companion to a well-informed man, but certainly not witty enough to supply bons mots to the clubs. Miss Asterisk was one of those women of whom a husband might be proud, yet with whom a husband would feel safe from being talked about.

And in submitting the letter we have read to Graham's eye, the Duchess had the cause of Miss Asterisk pointedly in view. Miss Asterisk had confided to her friend, that, of all men she had seen, Mr. Graham Vane was the one she would feel the least inclined to refuse.

So when Graham Vane returned the letter to the Duchess, simply saying, "How well my dear aunt divined what is weakest in me!" the Duchess replied quickly, "Miss Asterisk dines here to-morrow; pray come; you would like her if you knew more of her."

"To-morrow I am engaged—an American friend of mine dines with me; but 'tis no matter, for I shall never feel more for Miss Asterisk than I feel for Mont Blanc."

# CHAPTER VI.

On leaving his cousin's house Graham walked on, he scarce knew or cared whither, the image of the beloved dead so forcibly recalled the solemnity of the mission with which he had been intrusted, and which hitherto he had failed to fulfil. What if the only mode by which he could, without causing questions and suspicions that might result in dragging to day the terrible nature of the trust he held, enrich the daughter of Richard King, repair all wrong hitherto done to her, and guard the sanctity of Lady Janet's home,—should be in that union which Richard King had commended to him while his heart was yet free? In such a case, would not gratitude to the dead, duty to the living, make that union imperative at whatever sacrifice of happiness to himself? The two years to which Richard King had limited the suspense of research were not yet expired. Then, too, that letter of Lady Janet's,—so tenderly anxious for his future, so clear-sighted as to the elements of his own character in its strength or its infirmities—combined with graver causes to withhold his heart from its yearning impulse, and—no, not steel it against Isaura, but forbid it to realise, in the fair creature and creator of romance, his ideal of the woman to whom an earnest, sagacious, aspiring man commits all the destinies involved in the serene dignity of his hearth. He could not but own that this gifted author—this eager seeker after fame—this brilliant and bold competitor with men on their own stormy battle-ground-was the very person from whom Lady Janet would have warned away his choice. She (Isaura) merge her own distinctions in a husband's;—she leave exclusively to him the burden of fame and calumny!—she shun "to be talked about!" she who could feel her life to be a success or a failure, according to the extent and the loudness of the talk which it courted!

While these thoughts racked his mind, a kindly hand was laid on his arm, and a cheery voice accosted him. "Well met, my dear Vane! I see we are bound to the same place; there will be a good gathering to-night."

"What do you mean, Bevil? I am going nowhere, except to my own quiet rooms."

"Pooh! Come in here at least for a few minutes,"—and Bevil drew him up to the door-step of a house close by, where, on certain evenings, a well-known club drew together men who seldom meet so familiarly elsewhere—

men of all callings; a club especially favoured by wits, authors, and the flaneurs of polite society.

Graham shook his head, about to refuse, when Bevil added, "I have just come from Paris, and can give you the last news, literary, political, and social. By the way, I saw Savarin the other night at the Cicogna's—he introduced me there." Graham winced; he was spelled by the music of a name, and followed his acquaintance into the crowded room, and, after returning many greetings and nods, withdrew into a remote corner, and motioned Bevil to a seat beside him.

"So you met Savarin? Where, did you say?"

"At the house of the new lady-author—I hate the word authoress—Mademoiselle Cicogna! Of course you have read her book?"

"Yes."

"Full of fine things, is it not?—though somewhat highflown and sentimental: however, nothing succeeds like success. No book has been more talked about at Paris: the only thing more talked about is the lady-author herself."

"Indeed, and how?"

"She doesn't look twenty, a mere girl—of that kind of beauty which so arrests the eye that you pass by other faces to gaze on it, and the dullest stranger would ask, 'Who, and what is she?' A girl, I say, like that—who lives as independently as if she were a middle-aged widow, receives every week (she has her Thursdays), with no other chaperon than an old ci-devant Italian singing woman, dressed like a guy—must set Parisian tongues into play even if she had not written the crack book of the season."

"Mademoiselle Cicogna receives on Thursdays,—no harm in that; and if she have no other chaperon than the Italian lady you mention, it is because Mademoiselle Cicogna is an orphan, and having a fortune, such as it is, of her own, I do not see why she should not live as independently as many an unmarried woman in London placed under similar circumstances. I suppose she receives chiefly persons in the literary or artistic world, and if they are all as respectable as the Savarins, I do not think ill-nature itself could find fault with her social circle."

"Ah! you know the Cicogna, I presume. I am sure I did not wish to say anything that could offend her best friends, only I do think it is a pity she is not married, poor girl!"

"Mademoiselle Cicogna, accomplished, beautiful, of good birth (the Cicogna's rank among the oldest of Lombard families), is not likely to want offers."

"Offers of marriage,—h'm—well, I dare say, from authors and artists. You know Paris better even than I do, but I don't suppose authors and artists there make the most desirable husbands; and I scarcely know a marriage in France between a man-author and lady-author which does not end in the deadliest of all animosities—that of wounded amour propre. Perhaps the man admires his own genius too much to do proper homage to his wife's."

"But the choice of Mademoiselle Cicogna need not be restricted to the pale of authorship—doubtless she has many admirers beyond that quarrelsome borderland."

"Certainly-countless adorers. Enguerrand de Vandemar—you know that diamond of dandies?"

"Perfectly—is he an admirer?"

"Cela va sans dire—he told me that though she was not the handsomest woman in Paris, all other women looked less handsome since he had seen her. But, of course, French lady-killers like Enguerrand, when it comes to marriage, leave it to their parents to choose their wives and arrange the terms of the contract. Talking of lady-killers, I beheld amid the throng at Mademoiselle Cicogna's the ci-devant Lovelace whom I remember some twenty-three years ago as the darling of wives and the terror of husbands-Victor de Mauleon."

"Victor de Mauleon at Mademoiselle Cicogna's!—what, is that man restored to society?"

"Ah! you are thinking of the ugly old story about the jewels—oh, yes, he has got over that; all his grand relations, the Vandemars, Beauvilliers, Rochebriant, and others, took him by the hand when he reappeared at Paris last year; and though I believe he is still avoided by many, he is courted by still more—and avoided, I fancy, rather from political than social causes. The Imperialist set, of course, execrate and prescribe him. You know he is the writer of those biting articles signed Pierre Firmin in the Sens Commun; and I am told he is the proprietor of that very clever journal, which has become a power."

"So, so—that is the journal in which Mademoiselle Cicogna's roman first appeared. So, so—Victor de Mauleon one of her associates, her counsellor and friend—ah!"

"No, I didn't say that; on the contrary, he was presented to her the first time the evening I was at the house. I saw that young silk-haired coxcomb, Gustave Rameau, introduce him to her. You don't perhaps know Rameau, editor of the Sens Commun—writes poems and criticisms. They say he is a Red Republican, but De Mauleon keeps truculent French politics subdued if not suppressed in his cynical journal. Somebody told me that the Cicogna is very much in love with Rameau; certainly he has a handsome face of his own, and that is the reason why she was so rude to the Russian Prince X— —-."

"How rude! Did the Prince propose to her?"

"Propose! you forget—he is married. Don't you know the Princess? Still there are other kinds of proposals than those of marriage which a rich Russian prince may venture to make to a pretty novelist brought up for the stage."

"Bevil!" cried Graham, grasping the man's arm fiercely, "how dare you?"

"My dear boy," said Bevil, very much astonished, "I really did not know that your interest in the young lady was so great. If I have wounded you in relating a mere on dit picked up at the Jockey Club, I beg you a thousand pardons. I dare say there was not a word of truth in it."

"Not a word of truth, you may be sure, if the on dit was injurious to Mademoiselle Cicogna. It is true, I have a strong interest in her; any man—any gentleman—would have such interest in a girl so brilliant and seemingly so friendless. It shames one of human nature to think that the reward which the world makes to those who elevate its platitudes, brighten its dulness, delight its leisure, is Slander! I have had the honour to make the acquaintance of this lady before she became a 'celebrity,' and I have never met in my paths through life a purer heart or a nobler nature. What is the wretched on dit you condescend to circulate? Permit me to add:

"'He who repeats a slander shares the crime.'"

"Upon my honour, my dear Vane," said Bevil seriously (he did not want for spirit), "I hardly know you this evening. It is not because duelling is out of fashion that a man should allow himself to speak in a tone that gives offence to another who intended none; and if duelling is out of fashion in England, it is still possible in France.—Entre nous, I would rather cross the Channel with you than submit to language that conveys unmerited insult."

Graham's cheek, before ashen pale, flushed into dark red. "I understand you," he said quietly, "and will be at Boulogne to-morrow."

"Graham Vane," replied Bevil, with much dignity, "you and I have known each other a great many years, and neither of us has cause to question the courage of the other; but I am much older than yourself—permit me to take the melancholy advantage of seniority. A duel between us in consequence of careless words said about a lady in no way connected with either, would be a cruel injury to her; a duel on grounds so slight would little injure me—a man about town, who would not sit an hour in the House of Commons if you paid him a thousand pounds a minute. But you, Graham Vane—you whose destiny it is to canvass electors and make laws—would it not be an injury to you to be questioned at the hustings why you broke the law, and why you sought another man's life? Come, come! shake hands and consider all that seconds, if we chose them, would exact, is said, every affront on either side retracted, every apology on either side made."

"Bevil, you disarm and conquer me. I spoke like a hotheaded fool; forget it—forgive. But—but—I can listen calmly now—what is that on dit?"

"One that thoroughly bears out your own very manly upholding of the poor young orphan, whose name I shall never again mention without such respect as would satisfy her most sensitive champion. It was said that the Prince X——— boasted that before a week was out Mademoiselle Cicogna should appear in his carriage at the Bois de Boulogne, and wear at the opera diamonds he had sent to her; that this boast was enforced by a wager, and the terms of the wager compelled the Prince to confess the means he had taken to succeed, and produce the evidence that he had lost or won. According to this on dit, the Prince had written to Mademoiselle Cicogna, and the letter had been accompanied by a parure that cost him half a million of francs; that the diamonds had been sent back with a few words of such scorn as a queen might address to an upstart lackey. But, my dear Vane, it is a mournful position for the girl to receive such offers; and you must agree with me in wishing she were safely married, even to Monsieur Rameau, coxcomb though he be. Let us hope that they will be an exception to French authors, male and female, in general, and live like turtle-doves."

# CHAPTER VII.

A few days after the date of the last chapter, Colonel Morley returned to Paris. He had dined with Graham at Greenwich, had met him afterwards in society, and paid him a farewell visit on the day before the Colonel's departure; but the name of Isaura Cicogna had not again been uttered by either. Morley was surprised that his wife did not question him minutely as to the mode in which he had executed her delicate commission, and the manner as well as words with which Graham had replied to his "ventilations." But his Lizzy cut him short when he began his recital:

"I don't want to hear anything more about the man. He has thrown away a prize richer than his ambition will ever gain, even if it gained him a throne."

"That it can't gain him in the old country. The people are loyal to the present dynasty, whatever you may be told to the contrary."

"Don't be so horribly literal, Frank; that subject is done with. How was the Duchess of — — — dressed?"

But when the Colonel had retired to what the French call the cabinet de traivail—and which he more accurately termed his "smoke den"—and there indulged in the cigar which, despite his American citizenship, was forbidden in the drawing-room of the tyrant who ruled his life, Mrs. Morley took from her desk a letter received three days before, and brooded over it intently, studying every word. When she had thus reperused it, her tears fell upon the page. "Poor Isaura!" she muttered—"poor Isaura! I know she loves him—and how deeply a nature like hers can love! But I must break it to her. If I did not, she would remain nursing a vain dream, and refuse every chance of real happiness for the sake of nursing it." Then she mechanically folded up the letter—I need not say it was from Graham Vane—restored it to the desk, and remained musing till the Colonel looked in at the door and said peremptorily, "Very late—come to bed."

The next day Madame Savarin called on Isaura.

"Chere enfant," said she, "I have bad news for you. Poor Gustave is very ill—an attack of the lungs and fever; you know how delicate he is."

"I am sincerely grieved," said Isaura, in earnest tender tones; "it must be a very sudden attack: he was here last Thursday."

"The malady only declared itself yesterday morning, but surely you must have observed how ill he has been looking for several days past? It pained me to see him."

"I did not notice any change in him," said Isaura, somewhat conscience-stricken. Wrapt in her own happy thoughts, she would not have noticed change in faces yet more familiar to her than that of her young admirer.

"Isaura," said Madame Savarin, "I suspect there are moral causes for our friend's failing health. Why should I disguise my meaning? You know well how madly he is in love with you, and have you denied him hope?"

"I like M. Rameau as a friend; I admire him—at times I pity him."

"Pity is akin to love."

"I doubt the truth of that saying, at all events as you apply it now. I could not love M. Rameau; I never gave him cause to think I could."

"I wish for both your sakes that you could make me a different answer; for his sake, because, knowing his faults and failings, I am persuaded that they would vanish in a companionship so pure, so elevating as yours: you could make him not only so much happier but so much better a man. Hush! let me go on, let me come to yourself,—I say for your sake I wish it. Your pursuits, your ambition, are akin to his; you should not marry one who could not sympathise with you in these. If you did, he might either restrict the exercise of your genius or be chafed at its display. The only authoress I ever knew whose married lot was serenely happy to the last, was the greatest of English poetesses married to a great English poet. You cannot, you ought not, to devote yourself to the splendid career to which your genius irresistibly impels you, without that counsel, that support, that protection, which a husband alone can give. My dear child, as the wife myself of a man of letters, and familiarised to all the gossip, all the scandal, to which they who give their names to the public are exposed, I declare that if I had a daughter who inherited Savarin's talents, and was ambitious of attaining to his renown, I would rather shut her up in a convent than let her publish a book that was in every one's hands until she had sheltered her name under that of a husband; and if I say this of my child, with a father so wise in the world's ways, and so popularly respected as my bon homme, what must I feel to be essential to your safety, poor stranger in our land! poor solitary orphan! with no other advice or guardian than the singing mistress whom you touchingly call 'Madre!' I see how I distress and pain you—I cannot help it. Listen! The other evening Savarin came back from his favourite cafe in a state of excitement that made me think he came to announce a revolution. It was about you; he stormed, he wept—actually wept—my philosophical laughing Savarin. He had just heard of that atrocious wager made by a Russian barbarian. Every one praised you for the contempt with which you had treated the savage's insolence. But that you should have been submitted to such an insult without one male friend who had the right to resent and chastise it,—you cannot think how Savarin was chafed and galled. You know how he admires, but you cannot guess how he reveres you; and since then he says to me every day: 'That girl must not remain single. Better marry any man who has a heart to defend a wife's honour and the nerve to fire a pistol: every Frenchman has those qualifications!'"

Here Isaura could no longer restrain her emotions; she burst into sobs so vehement, so convulsive, that Madame Savarin became alarmed; but when she attempted to embrace and soothe her, Isaura recoiled with a visible shudder, and gasping out, "Cruel, cruel!" turned to the door, and rushed to her own room.

A few minutes afterwards a maid entered the salon with a message to Madame Savarin that Mademoiselle was so unwell that she must beg Madame to excuse her return to the salon.

Later in the day Mrs. Morley called, but Isaura would not see her.

Meanwhile poor Rameau was stretched on his sick-bed, and in sharp struggle between life and death. It is difficult to disentangle, one by one, all the threads in a nature so complex as Rameau's; but if we may hazard a conjecture, the grief of disappointed love was not the immediate cause of his illness, and yet it had much to do with it. The goad of Isaura's refusal had driven him into seeking distraction in excesses which a stronger frame could not have courted with impunity. The man was thoroughly Parisian in many things, but especially in impatience of any trouble. Did love trouble him—love could be drowned in absinthe; and too much absinthe may be a more immediate cause of congested lungs than the love which the absinthe had lulled to sleep.

His bedside was not watched by hirelings. When first taken thus ill—too ill to attend to his editorial duties—information was conveyed to the publisher of the Sens Commun, and in consequence of that information, Victor de Mauleon came to see the sick man. By his bed he found Savarin, who had called, as it were by chance, and seen the doctor, who had said, "It is grave. He must be well nursed." Savarin whispered to De Mauleon, "Shall we call in a professional nurse, or a soeur de charite?"

De Mauleon replied, also in a whisper, "Somebody told me that the man had a mother."

It was true—Savarin had forgotten it. Rameau never mentioned his parents—he was not proud of them.

They belonged to a lower class of the bourgeoisie, retired shopkeepers, and a Red Republican is sworn to hate of the bourgeoisie, high or low; while a beautiful young author pushing his way into the Chaussee d'Antin does not proclaim to the world that his parents had sold hosiery in the Rue St. Denis.

Nevertheless Savarin knew that Rameau had such parents still living, and took the hint. Two hours afterwards Rameau was leaning his burning forehead on his mother's breast.

The next morning the doctor said to the mother, "You are worth ten of me. If you can stay here we shall pull him through."

"Stay here!—my own boy!" cried indignantly the poor mother.

# CHAPTER VIII.

The day which had inflicted on Isaura so keen an anguish was marked by a great trial in the life of Alain de Rochebriant.

In the morning he received the notice "of un commandement tendant a saisie immobiliere," on the part of his creditor, M. Louvier; in plain English, an announcement that his property at Rochebriant would be put up to public sale on a certain day, in case all debts due to the mortgagee were not paid before. An hour afterwards came a note from Duplessis stating that "he had returned from Bretagne on the previous evening, and would be very happy to see the Marquis de Rochebriant before two o'clock, if not inconvenient to call."

Alain put the "commandement" into his pocket, and repaired to the Hotel Duplessis.

The financier received him with very cordial civility. Then he began: "I am happy to say I left your excellent aunt in very good health. She honoured the letter of introduction to her which I owe to your politeness with the most amiable hospitalities; she insisted on my removing from the auberge at which I first put up and becoming a guest under your venerable roof-tree—a most agreeable lady, and a most interesting chateau."

"I fear your accommodation was in striking contrast to your comforts at Paris; my chateau is only interesting to an antiquarian enamoured of ruins."

"Pardon me, 'ruins' is an exaggerated expression. I do not say that the chateau does not want some repairs, but they would not be costly; the outer walls are strong enough to defy time for centuries to come, and a few internal decorations and some modern additions of furniture would make the old manoir a home fit for a prince. I have been over the whole estate, too, with the worthy M. Hebert,—a superb property."

"Which M. Louvier appears to appreciate," said Alain, with a somewhat melancholy smile, extending to Duplessis the menacing notice.

Duplessis glanced at it, and said drily: "M. Louvier knows what he is about. But I think we had better put an immediate stop to formalities which must be painful to a creditor so benevolent. I do not presume to offer to pay the interest due on the security you can give for the repayment. If you refused that offer from so old a friend as Lemercier, of course you could not accept it from me. I make another proposal, to which you can scarcely object. I do not like to give my scheming rival on the Bourse the triumph of so profoundly planned a speculation. Aid me to defeat him. Let me take the mortgage on myself, and become sole mortgagee—hush!—on this condition,—that there should be an entire union of interests between us two; that I should be at liberty to make the improvements I desire, and when the improvements be made, there should be a fair arrangement as to the proportion of profits due to me as mortgagee and improver, to you as original owner. Attend, my dear Marquis,—I am speaking as a mere man of business. I see my way to adding more than a third, I might even say a half—to the present revenues of Rochbriant. The woods have been sadly neglected, drainage alone would add greatly to their produce. Your orchards might be rendered magnificent supplies to Paris with better cultivation. Lastly, I would devote to building purposes or to market gardens all the lands round the two towns of ——— and —————. I think I can lay my hands on suitable speculators for these last experiments. In a word, though the market value of Rochebriant, as it now stands, would not be equivalent to the debt on it, in five or six years it could be made worth—well, I will not say how much—but we shall be both well satisfied with the result. Meanwhile, if you allow me to find purchasers for your timber, and if you will not suffer the Chevalier de Finisterre to regulate your expenses, you need have no fear that the interest due to me will not be regularly paid, even though I shall be compelled, for the first year or two at least, to ask a higher rate of interest than Louvier exacted—say a quarter per cent. more; and in suggesting that, you will comprehend that this is now a matter of business between us, and not of friendship."

Alain turned his head aside to conceal his emotion, and then, with the quick affectionate impulse of the genuine French nature, threw himself on the financier's breast and kissed him on both cheeks.

"You save me! you save the home and the tombs of my ancestors! Thank you I cannot; but I believe in God—I pray—I will pray for you as for a father; and if ever," he hurried on in broken words, "I am mean enough to squander on idle luxuries one franc that I should save for the debt due to you, chide me as a father would chide a graceless son."

Moved as Alain was, Duplessis was moved yet more deeply. "What father would not be proud of such a son? Ah, if I had such a one!" he said softly. Then, quickly recovering his wonted composure, he added, with the sardonic smile which often chilled his friends and alarmed his foes, "Monsieur Louvier is about to pass that which I ventured to promise him, a 'mauvais quart-d'heure.' Lend me that commandement tendant a saisie. I must be off to my avoue with instructions. If you have no better engagement, pray dine with me to-day and accompany Valerie and myself to the opera."

I need not say that Alain accepted the invitation. How happy Valerie was that evening!

# CHAPTER IX.

The next day Duplessis was surprised by a visit from M. Louvier—that magnate of millionaires had never before set foot in the house of his younger and less famous rival.

The burly man entered the room with a face much flushed, and with more than his usual mixture of jovial brusquerie and opulent swagger.

"Startled to see me, I dare say," began Louvier, as soon as the door was closed. "I have this morning received a communication from your agent containing a cheque for the interest due to me from M. Rochebriant, and a formal notice of your intention to pay off the principal on behalf of that popinjay prodigal. Though we two have not hitherto been the best friends in the world, I thought it fair to a man in your station to come to you direct and say, 'Cher confrere, what swindler has bubbled you? You don't know the real condition of this Breton property, or you would never so throw away your millions. The property is not worth the mortgage I have on it by 30,000 louis."

"Then, M. Louvier, you will be 30,000 louis the richer if I take the mortgage off your hands."

"I can afford the loss—no offence—better than you can; and I may have fancies which I don't mind paying for, but which cannot influence another. See, I have brought with me the exact schedule of all details respecting this property. You need not question their accuracy; they have been arranged by the Marquis's own agents, M. Gandrin and M. Hebert. They contain, you will perceive, every possible item of revenue, down to an apple-tree. Now, look at that, and tell me if you are justified in lending such a sum on such a property."

"Thank you very much for an interest in my affairs that I scarcely ventured to expect M. Louvier to entertain; but I see that I have a duplicate of this paper, furnished to me very honestly by M. Hebert himself. Besides, I, too, have fancies which I don't mind paying for, and among them may be a fancy for the lands of Rochebriant."

"Look you, Duplessis, when a man like me asks a favour, you may be sure that he has the power to repay it. Let me have my whim here, and ask anything you like from me in return!"

"Desole not to oblige you, but this has become not only a whim of mine, but a matter of honour; and honour you know, my dear M. Louvier, is the first principle of sound finance. I have myself, after careful inspection of the Rochebriant property, volunteered to its owner to advance the money to pay off your hypotheque; and what would be said on the Bourse if Lucien Duplessis failed in an obligation?"

"I think I can guess what will one day be said of Lucien Duplessis if he make an irrevocable enemy of Paul Louvier. Corbleu! mon cher, a man of thrice your capital, who watched every speculation of yours with a hostile eye, might some beau jour make even you a bankrupt!"

"Forewarned, forearmed!" replied Duplessis, imperturbably, "Fas est ab hoste doceri,—I mean, 'It is right to be taught by an enemy;' and I never remember the day when you were otherwise, and yet I am not a bankrupt, though I receive you in a house which, thanks to you, is so modest in point of size!"

"Bah! that was a mistake of mine,—and, ha! ha! you had your revenge there—that forest!"

"Well, as a peace offering, I will give you up the forest, and content my ambition as a landed proprietor with this bad speculation of Rochebriant!"

"Confound the forest, I don't care for it now! I can sell my place for more than it has cost me to one of your imperial favourites. Build a palace in your forest. Let me have Rochebriant, and name your terms."

"A thousand pardons! but I have already had the honour to inform you, that I have contracted an obligation which does not allow me to listen to terms."

As a serpent, that, after all crawlings and windings, rears itself on end, Louvier rose, crest erect:

"So then it is finished. I came here disposed to offer peace—you refuse, and declare war."

"Not at all, I do not declare war; I accept it if forced on me."

"Is that your last word, M. Duplessis?"

"Monsieur Louvier, it is."

"Bon jour!"

And Louvier strode to the door; here he paused: "Take a day to consider."

"Not a moment."

"Your servant, Monsieur,—your very humble servant." Louvier vanished.

Duplessis leaned his large thoughtful forehead on his thin nervous hand. "This loan will pinch me," he muttered. "I must be very wary now with such a foe. Well, why should I care to be rich? Valerie's dot, Valerie's happiness, are secured."

# CHAPTER X.

Madame Savarin wrote a very kind and very apologetic letter to Isaura, but no answer was returned to it. Madame Savarin did not venture to communicate to her husband the substance of a conversation which had ended so painfully. He had, in theory, a delicacy of tact, which, if he did not always exhibit it in practice, made him a very severe critic of its deficiency in others. Therefore, unconscious of the offence given, he made a point of calling at Isaura's apartments, and leaving word with her servant that "he was sure she would be pleased to hear M. Rameau was somewhat better, though still in danger."

It was not till the third day after her interview with Madame Savarin that Isaura left her own room,—she did so to receive Mrs. Morley.

The fair American was shocked to see the change in Isaura's countenance. She was very pale, and with that indescribable appearance of exhaustion which betrays continued want of sleep; her soft eyes were dim, the play of her lips was gone, her light step weary and languid.

"My poor darling!" cried Mrs. Morley, embracing her, "you have indeed been ill! What is the matter?—who attends you?"

"I need no physician, it was but a passing cold—the air of Paris is very trying. Never mind me, dear—what is the last news?"

Therewith Mrs. Morley ran glibly through the principal topics of the hour: the breach threatened between M. Ollivier and his former liberal partisans; the tone unexpectedly taken by M. de Girardin; the speculations as to the result of the trial of the alleged conspirators against the Emperor's life, which was fixed to take place towards the end of that month of June,—all matters of no slight importance to the interests of an empire. Sunk deep into the recesses of her fauteuil, Isaura seemed to listen quietly, till, when a pause came, she said in cold clear tones:

"And Mr. Graham Vane—he has refused your invitation?"

"I am sorry to say he has—he is so engaged in London."

"I knew he had refused," said Isaura, with a low bitter laugh.

"How? who told you?"

"My own good sense told me. One may have good sense, though one is a poor scribbler."

"Don't talk in that way; it is beneath you to angle for compliments."

"Compliments, ah! And so Mr. Vane has refused to come to Paris; never mind, he will come next year. I shall not be in Paris then. Did Colonel Morley see Mr. Vane?"

"Oh, yes; two or three times."

"He is well?"

"Quite well, I believe—at least Frank did not say to the contrary; but, from what I hear, he is not the person I took him for. Many people told Frank that he is much changed since he came into his fortune—is grown very stingy, quite miserly indeed; declines even a seat in Parliament because of the expense. It is astonishing how money does spoil a man."

"He had come into his fortune when he was here. Money had not spoiled him then."

Isaura paused, pressing her hands tightly together; then she suddenly rose to her feet, the colour on her cheek mantling and receding rapidly, and fixing on her startled visitor eyes no longer dim, but with something half fierce, half imploring in the passion of their gaze, said: "Your husband spoke of me to Mr. Vane: I know he did. What did Mr. Vane answer? Do not evade my question. The truth! the truth! I only ask the truth!"

"Give me your hand; sit here beside me, dearest child."

"Child!—no, I am a woman!—weak as a woman, but strong as a woman too!—The truth!"

Mrs. Morley had come prepared to carry out the resolution she had formed and "break" to Isaura "the truth," that which the girl now demanded. But then she had meant to break the truth in her own gentle, gradual way. Thus suddenly called upon, her courage failed her. She burst into tears. Isaura gazed at her dry-eyed.

"Your tears answer me. Mr. Vane has heard that I have been insulted. A man like him does not stoop to love for a woman who has known an insult. I do not blame him; I honour him the more—he is right."

"No-no-no!—you insulted! Who dared to insult you? (Mrs. Morley had never heard the story about the Russian Prince.) Mr. Vane spoke to Frank, and writes of you to me as of one whom it is impossible not to admire, to respect; but—I cannot say it—you will have the truth,—there, read and judge for yourself." And Mrs. Morley drew forth and thrust into Isaura's hands the letter she had concealed from her husband. The letter was not very long; it began with expressions of warm gratitude to Mrs. Morley, not for her invitation only, but for the interest she had conceived in his happiness. It went on thus "I join with my whole heart in all that you say, with such eloquent justice, of the mental and personal gifts so bounteously lavished by nature on the young lady whom you name.

"No one can feel more sensible than I of the charm of so exquisite a loveliness; no one can more sincerely join in the belief that the praise which greets the commencement of her career is but the whisper of the praise that will cheer its progress with louder and louder plaudits.

"He only would be worthy of her hand, who, if not equal to herself in genius, would feel raised into partnership with it by sympathy with its objects and joy in its triumphs. For myself, the same pain with which I should have learned she had adopted the profession which she originally contemplated, saddened and stung me when, choosing a career that confers a renown yet more lasting than the stage, she no less left behind her the peaceful immunities of private life. Were I even free to consult only my own heart in the choice of the one sole partner of my destinies (which I cannot at present honestly say that I am, though I had expected to be so ere this, when I last saw you at Paris); could I even hope—which I have no right to do—that I could chain to myself any private portion of thoughts which now flow into the large channels by which poets enrich the blood of the world,—still (I say it in self-reproach, it may be the fault of my English rearing, it may rather be the fault of an egotism peculiar to myself)—still I doubt if I could render happy any woman whose world could not be narrowed to the Home that she adorned and blessed.

"And yet not even the jealous tyranny of man's love could dare to say to natures like hers of whom we speak, 'Limit to the household glory of one the light which genius has placed in its firmament for the use and enjoyment of all.'"

"I thank you so much," said Isaura, calmly; "suspense makes a woman so weak—certainty so strong." Mechanically she smoothed and refolded the letter—mechanically, with slow, lingering hands—then she extended it to her friend, smiling.

"Nay, will you not keep it yourself?" said Mrs. Morley. "The more you examine the narrow-minded prejudices, the English arrogant man's jealous dread of superiority—nay, of equality—in the woman he 'can only value as he does his house or his horse, because she is his exclusive property, the more you will be rejoiced to find yourself free for a more worthy choice. Keep the letter; read it till you feel for the writer forgiveness and disdain."

Isaura took back the letter, and leaned her cheek on her hand, looking dreamily into space. It was some moments before she replied, and her words then had no reference to Mrs. Morley's consolatory exhortation.

"He was so pleased when he learned that I renounced the career on which I had set my ambition. I thought he would have been so pleased when I sought in another career to raise myself nearer to his level—I see now how sadly I was mistaken. All that perplexed me before in him is explained. I did not guess how foolishly I had deceived myself till three days ago,—then I did guess it; and it was that guess which tortured me so terribly that I could not keep my heart to myself when I saw you to-day; in spite of all womanly pride it would force its way—to the truth.

"Hush! I must tell you what was said to me by another friend of mine—a good friend, a wise and kind one. Yet I was so angry when she said it that I thought I could never see her more."

"My sweet darling! who was this friend, and what did she say to you?"

"The friend was Madame Savarin."

"No woman loves you more except myself—and she said?"

"That she would have suffered no daughter of hers to commit her name to the talk of the world as I have done—be exposed to the risk of insult as I have been—until she had the shelter and protection denied to me. And I have thus overleaped the bound that a prudent mother would prescribe to her child, have become one whose hand men do not seek, unless they themselves take the same roads to notoriety. Do you not think she was right?"

"Not as you so morbidly put it, silly girl,—certainly not right. But I do wish that you had the shelter and protection which Madame Savarin meant to express; I do wish that you were happily married to one very different from Mr. Vane—one who would be more proud of your genius than of your beauty—one who would say, 'My name, safer far in its enduring nobility than those that depend on titles and lands—which are held on the tenure of the popular breath—must be honoured by posterity, for She has deigned to make it hers. No democratic revolution can disennoble me."

"Ay, ay, you believe that men will be found to think with complacency that they owe to a wife a name they could not achieve for themselves. Possibly there are such men. Where?—among those that are already united by sympathies in the same callings, the same labours, the same hopes and fears with the women who have left behind them the privacies of home. Madame de Grantmesnil was wrong. Artists should wed with artists. True—true!"

Here she passed her hand over her forehead—it was a pretty way of hers when seeking to concentrate thought—and was silent a moment or so.

"Did you ever feel," she then asked dreamily, "that there are moments in life when a dark curtain seems to fall over one's past that a day before was so clear, so blended with the present? One cannot any longer look behind; the gaze is attracted onward, and a track of fire flashes upon the future,—the future which yesterday was invisible. There is a line by some English poet—Mr. Vane once quoted it, not to me, but to M. Savarin, and in illustration of his argument, that the most complicated recesses of thought are best reached by the simplest forms of expression. I said to myself, 'I will study that truth if ever I take to literature as I have taken to song;' and—yes—it was that evening that the ambition fatal to woman fixed on me its relentless fangs—at Enghien—we were on the lake—the sun was setting."

"But you do not tell me the line that so impressed you," said Mrs. Morley, with a woman's kindly tact.

"The line—which line? Oh, I remember; the line was this:

"'I see as from a tower the end of all."

"And now—kiss me, dearest—never a word again to me about this conversation: never a word about Mr. Vane—the dark curtain has fallen on the past."

# CHAPTER XI.

Men and women are much more like each other in certain large elements of character than is generally supposed, but it is that very resemblance which makes their differences the more incomprehensible to each other; just as in politics, theology, or that most disputatious of all things disputable, metaphysics, the nearer the reasoners approach each other in points that to an uncritical bystander seem the most important, the more sure they are to start off in opposite directions upon reaching the speck of a pin-prick.

Now there are certain grand meeting-places between man and woman—the grandest of all is on the ground of love, and yet here also is the great field of quarrel. And here the teller of a tale such as mine ought, if he is sufficiently wise to be humble, to know that it is almost profanation if, as man, he presumes to enter the penetralia of a woman's innermost heart, and repeat, as a man would repeat, all the vibrations of sound which the heart of a woman sends forth undistinguishable even to her own ear.

I know Isaura as intimately as if I had rocked her in her cradle, played with her in her childhood, educated and trained her in her youth; and yet I can no more tell you faithfully what passed in her mind during the forty-eight hours that intervened between her conversation with that American lady and her reappearance in some commonplace drawing-room, than I can tell you what the Man in the Moon might feel if the sun that his world reflected were blotted out of creation.

I can only say that when she reappeared in that commonplace drawing-room world, there was a change in her face not very perceptible to the ordinary observer. If anything, to his eye she was handsomer—the eye was brighter—the complexion (always lustrous, though somewhat pale, the limpid paleness that suits so well with dark hair) was yet more lustrous,—it was flushed into delicate rose hues—hues that still better suit with dark hair. What, then, was the change, and change not for the better? The lips, once so pensively sweet, had grown hard; on the brow that had seemed to laugh when the lips did, there was no longer sympathy between brow and lip; there was scarcely seen a fine threadlike line that in a few years would be a furrow on the space between the eyes; the voice was not so tenderly soft; the step was haughtier. What all such change denoted it is for a woman to decide-I can only guess. In the mean while, Mademoiselle Cicogna had sent her servant daily to inquire after M. Rameau. That, I think, she would have done under any circumstances. Meanwhile, too, she had called on Madame Savarin—made it up with her—sealed the reconciliation by a cold kiss. That, too, under any circumstances, I think she would have done—under some circumstances the kiss might have been less cold.

There was one thing unwonted in her habits. I mention it, though it is only a woman who can say if it means anything worth noticing.

For six days she had left a letter from Madame de Grantmesnil unanswered. With Madame de Grantmesnil was connected the whole of her innermost life—from the day when the lonely desolate child had seen, beyond the dusty thoroughfares of life, gleams of the faery land in poetry and art-onward through her restless, dreamy, aspiring youth-onward—onward—till now, through all that constitutes the glorious reality that we call romance.

Never before had she left for two days unanswered letters which were to her as Sibylline leaves to some unquiet neophyte yearning for solutions to enigmas suggested whether by the world without or by the soul within. For six days Madame de Grantmesnil's letter remained unanswered, unread, neglected, thrust out of sight; just as when some imperious necessity compels us to grapple with a world that is, we cast aside the romance which, in our holiday hours, had beguiled us to a world with which we have interests and sympathies no more.

# CHAPTER XII.

Gustave recovered, but slowly. The physician pronounced him out of all immediate danger, but said frankly to him, and somewhat more guardedly to his parents, "There is ample cause to beware." "Look you, my young friend," he added to Rameau, "mere brain-work seldom kills a man once accustomed to it like you; but heart-work, and stomach-work, and nerve-work, added to brain-work, may soon consign to the coffin a frame ten times more robust than yours. Write as much as you will—that is your vocation; but it is not your vocation to drink absinthe—to preside at orgies in the Maison Doree. Regulate yourself, and not after the fashion of the fabulous Don Juan. Marry—live soberly and quietly—and you may survive the grandchildren of viveurs. Go on as you have done, and before the year is out you are in Pere la Chaise."

Rameau listened languidly, but with a profound conviction that the physician thoroughly understood his case.

Lying helpless on his bed, he had no desire for orgies at the Maison Doree; with parched lips thirsty for innocent tisane of lime-blossoms, the thought of absinthe was as odious to him as the liquid fire of Phlegethon. If ever sinner became suddenly convinced that there was a good deal to be said in favour of a moral life, that sinner at the moment I speak of was Gustave Rameau: Certainly a moral life—'Domus et placens uxor',—was essential to the poet who, aspiring to immortal glory, was condemned to the ailments of a very perishable frame.

"Ah," he murmured plaintively to himself, "that girl Isaura can have no true sympathy with genius! It is no ordinary man that she will kill in me!"

And so murmuring he fell asleep. When he woke and found his head pillowed on his mother's breast, it was much as a sensitive, delicate man may wake after having drunk too much the night before. Repentant, mournful, maudlin, he began to weep, and in the course of his weeping he confided to his mother the secret of his heart.

Isaura had refused him—that refusal had made him desperate.

"Ah! with Isaura how changed would be his habits! how pure! how healthful!" His mother listened fondly, and did her best to comfort him and cheer his drooping spirits.

She told him of Isaura's messages of inquiry duly twice a day. Rameau, who knew more about women in general, and Isaura in particular, than his mother conjectured, shook his head mournfully. "She could not do less," he said. "Has no one offered to do more?"—he thought of Julie when he asked that—Madame Rameau hesitated.

The poor Parisians! it is the mode to preach against them; and before my book closes, I shall have to preach—no, not to preach, but to imply—plenty of faults to consider and amend. Meanwhile I try my best to take them, as the philosophy of life tells us to take other people, for what they are.

I do not think the domestic relations of the Parisian bourgeoisie are as bad as they are said to be in French novels. Madame Rameau is not an uncommon type of her class. She had been when she first married singularly handsome. It was from her that Gustave inherited his beauty; and her husband was a very ordinary type of the French shopkeeper—very plain, by no means intellectual, but gay, good-humoured, devotedly attached to his wife, and with implicit trust in her conjugal virtue. Never was trust better placed. There was not a happier nor a more faithful couple in the quartier in which they resided. Madame Rameau hesitated when her boy, thinking of Julie, asked if no one had done more than send to inquire after him as Isaura had done.

After that hesitating pause she said, "Yes—a young lady calling herself Mademoiselle Julie Caumartin wished to instal herself here as your nurse. When I said, 'But I am his mother—he needs no other nurses,' she would have retreated, and looked ashamed—poor thing! I don't blame her if she loved my son. But, my son, I say this,—if you love her, don't talk to me about that Mademoiselle Cicogna; and if you love Mademoiselle Cicogna, why, then your father will take care that the poor girl who loved you not knowing that you loved another is not left to the temptation of penury."

Rameau's pale lips withered into a phantom-like sneer! Julie! the resplendent Julie!—true, only a ballet-dancer, but whose equipage in the Bois had once been the envy of duchesses—Julie! who had sacrificed fortune for his sake—who, freed from him, could have millionaires again at her feet!—Julie! to be saved from penury, as a shopkeeper would save an erring nursemaid—Julie! the irrepressible Julie! who had written to him, the day before his illness, in a pen dipped, not in ink, but in blood from a vein she had opened in her arm:

> *"Traitor!—I have not seen thee for three days. Dost thou dare to love another? If so, I care not how thou attempt to conceal it—woe to her! Ingrat! woe to thee! Love is not love, unless, when betrayed by Love, it appeals to death. Answer me quick—quick.*

*JULIE."*

Poor Gustave thought of that letter and groaned. Certainly his mother was right—he ought to get rid of Julie; but he did not clearly see how Julie was to be got rid of. He replied to Madame Rameau peevishly, "Don't trouble your head about Mademoiselle Caumartin; she is in no want of money. Of course, if I could hope for Isaura—but, alas! I dare not hope. Give me my tisane."

When the doctor called next day, he looked grave, and, drawing Madame Rameau into the next room, he said, "We are not getting on so well as I had hoped; the fever is gone, but there is much to apprehend from the debility left behind. His spirits are sadly depressed." Then added the doctor, pleasantly, and with that wonderful insight into our complex humanity in which physicians excel poets, and in which Parisian physicians are not excelled by any physicians in the world: "Can't you think of any bit of good news—that 'M. Thiers raves about your son's last poem! that 'it is a question among the Academicians between him and Jules Janin'—or that 'the beautiful Duchesse de ———- has been placed in a lunatic asylum because she has gone mad for love of a certain young Red Republican whose name begins with R.'—can't you think of any bit of similar good news? If you can, it will be a tonic to the relaxed state of your dear boy's amour propre, compared to which all the drugs in the Pharmacopoeia are moonshine and water; and meanwhile be sure to remove him to your own house, and out of the reach of his giddy young friends, as soon as you possibly can."

When that great authority thus left his patient's case in the hands of the mother, she said, "The boy shall be saved."

# CHAPTER XIII.

Isaura was seated beside the Venosta,—to whom, of late, she seemed to cling with greater fondness than ever,—working at some piece of embroidery—a labour from which she had been estranged for years; but now she had taken writing, reading, music, into passionate disgust. Isaura was thus seated, silently intent upon her work, and the Venosta in full talk, when the servant announced Madame Rameau.

The name startled both; the Venosta had never heard that the poet had a mother living, and immediately jumped to the conclusion that Madame Rameau must be a wife he had hitherto kept unrevealed. And when a woman, still very handsome, with a countenance grave and sad, entered the salon, the Venosta murmured, "The husband's perfidy reveals itself on a wife's face," and took out her handkerchief in preparation for sympathising tears.

"Mademoiselle," said the visitor, halting, with eyes fixed on Isaura. "Pardon my intrusion-my son has the honour to be known to you. Every one who knows him must share in my sorrow—so young—so promising, and in such danger—my poor boy!" Madame Rameau stopped abruptly. Her tears forced their way—she turned aside to conceal them.

In her twofold condition of being—womanhood and genius—Isaura was too largely endowed with that quickness of sympathy which distinguishes woman from man, and genius from talent, not to be wondrously susceptible to pity.

Already she had wound her arm round the grieving mother—already drawn her to the seat from which she herself had risen—and bending over her had said some words—true, conventional enough in themselves,—but cooed forth in a voice the softest I ever expect to hear, save in dreams, on this side of the grave.

Madame Rameau swept her hand over her eyes, glanced round the room, and noticing the Venosta in dressing-robe and slippers, staring with those Italian eyes, in seeming so quietly innocent, in reality so searchingly shrewd, she whispered pleadingly, "May I speak to you a few minutes alone?" This was not a request that Isaura could refuse, though she was embarrassed and troubled by the surmise of Madame Rameau's object in asking it; accordingly she led her visitor into the adjoining room, and making an apologetic sign to the Venosta, closed the door.

# CHAPTER XIV.

When they were alone, Madame Rameau took Isaura's hand in both her own, and, gazing wistfully into her face, said, "No wonder you are so loved—yours is the beauty that sinks into the hearts and rests there. I prize my boy more, now that I have seen you. But, oh, Mademoiselle! pardon me—do not withdraw your hand—pardon the mother who comes from the sick-bed of her only son and asks if you will assist to save him! A word from you is life or death to him!"

"Nay, nay, do not speak thus, Madame; your son knows how much I value, how sincerely I return, his friendship; but—but," she paused a moment, and continued sadly and with tearful eyes—"I have no heart to give to him-to any one."

"I do not—I would not if I dared—ask what it would be violence to yourself to promise. I do not ask you to bid me return to my son and say, 'Hope and recover,' but let me take some healing message from your lips. If I understand your words rightly, I at least may say that you do not give to another the hopes you, deny to him?"

"So far you understand me rightly, Madame. It has been said, that romance-writers give away so much of their hearts to heroes or heroines of their own creation, that they leave nothing worth the giving to human beings like themselves. Perhaps it is so; yet, Madame," added Isaura, with a smile of exquisite sweetness in its melancholy, "I have heart enough left to feel for you."

Madame Rameau was touched. "Ah, Mademoiselle, I do not believe in the saying you have quoted. But I must not abuse your goodness by pressing further upon you subjects from which you shrink. Only one word more: you know that my husband and I are but quiet tradesfolks, not in the society, nor aspiring to it, to which my son's talents have raised himself; yet dare I ask that you will not close here the acquaintance that I have obtruded on you?—dare I ask, that I may, now and then, call on you—that now and then I may see you at my own home? Believe that I would not here ask anything which your own mother would disapprove if she overlooked disparities of station. Humble as our home is, slander never passed its threshold."

"Ah, Madame, I and the Signora Venosta, whom in our Italian tongue I call mother, can but feel honoured and grateful whenever it pleases you to receive visits from us."

"It would be a base return for such gracious compliance with my request if I concealed from you the reason why I pray Heaven to bless you for that answer. The physician says that it may be long before my son is sufficiently convalescent to dispense with a mother's care, and resume his former life and occupation in the great world. It is everything for us if we can coax him into coming under our own roof-tree. This is difficult to do. It is natural for a young man launched into the world to like his own chez lui. Then what will happen to Gustave? He, lonely and heart-stricken, will ask friends, young as himself, but far stronger, to come and cheer him; or he will seek to distract his thoughts by the overwork of his brain; in either case he is doomed. But I have stronger motives yet to fix him a while at our hearth. This is just the moment, once lost never to be regained, when soothing companionship, gentle reproachless advice, can fix him lastingly in the habits and modes of life which will banish all fears of his future from the hearts of his parents. You at least honour him with friendship, with kindly interest—you at least would desire to wean him from all that a friend may disapprove or lament—a creature whom Providence meant to be good, and perhaps great. If I say to him, 'It will be long before you can go out and see your friends, but at my house your friends shall come and see you—among them Signora Venosta and Mademoiselle Cicogna will now and then drop in'—my victory is gained, and my son is saved."

"Madame," said Isaura, half sobbing, "what a blessing to have a mother like you! Love so noble ennobles those who hear its voice. Tell your son how ardently I wish him to be well, and to fulfil more than the promise of his genius; tell him also this—how I envy him his mother."

# CHAPTER XV.

It needs no length of words to inform thee, my intelligent reader, be thou man or woman—but more especially woman—of the consequences following each other, as wave follows wave in a tide, that resulted from the interview with which my last chapter closed. Gustave is removed to his parents' house; he remains for weeks confined within doors, or, on sunny days, takes an hour or so in his own carriage, drawn by the horse bought from Rochebriant, into by-roads remote from the fashionable world; Isaura visits his mother, liking, respecting, influenced by her more and more; in those visits she sits beside the sofa on which Rameau reclines. Gradually, gently—more and more by his mother's lips—is impressed on her the belief that it is in her power to save a human life, and to animate its career towards those goals which are never based wholly upon earth in the earnest eyes of genius, or perhaps in the yet more upward vision of pure-souled believing woman.

And Gustave himself, as he passes through the slow stages of convalescence, seems so gratefully to ascribe to her every step in his progress—seems so gently softened in character—seems so refined from the old affectations, so ennobled above the old cynicism—and, above all, so needing her presence, so sunless without it, that—well, need I finish the sentence?—the reader will complete what I leave unsaid.

Enough, that one day Isaura returned home from a visit at Madame Rameau's with the knowledge that her hand was pledged—her future life disposed of; and that, escaping from the Venosta, whom she so fondly, and in her hunger for a mother's love, called Madre, the girl shut herself up in her own room with locked doors.

Ah, poor child! ah, sweet-voiced Isaura! whose delicate image I feel myself too rude and too hard to transfer to this page in the purity of its outlines, and the blended softnesses of its hues—thou who, when saying things serious in the words men use, saidst them with a seriousness so charming, and with looks so feminine—thou, of whom no man I ever knew was quite worthy—ah, poor, simple, miserable girl, as I see thee now in the solitude of that white-curtained virginal room; hast thou, then, merged at last thy peculiar star into the cluster of all these commonplace girls whose lips have said "Ay," when their hearts said "No"?—thou, O brilliant Isaura! thou, O motherless child!

She had sunk into her chair—her own favourite chair, the covering of it had been embroidered by Madame de Grantmesnil, and bestowed on her as a birthday present last year—the year in which she had first learned what it is to love—the year in which she had first learned what it is to strive for fame. And somehow uniting, as many young people do, love and fame in dreams of the future, that silken seat had been to her as the Tripod of Delphi was to the Pythian: she had taken to it, as it were intuitively, in all those hours, whether of joy or sorrow, when youth seeks to prophesy, and does but dream.

There she sat now, in a sort of stupor—a sort of dreary bewilderment—the illusion of the Pythian gone—desire of dream and of prophecy alike extinct—pressing her hands together, and muttering to herself, "What has happened?—what have I done?"

Three hours later you would not have recognised the same face that you see now. For then the bravery, the honour, the loyalty of the girl's nature had asserted their command. Her promise had been given to one man—it could not be recalled. Thought itself of any other man must be banished. On her hearth lay ashes and tinder—the last remains of every treasured note from Graham Vane; of the hoarded newspaper extracts that contained his name; of the dry treatise he had published, and which had made the lovely romance-writer first desire "to know something about politics." Ay, if the treatise had been upon fox-hunting, she would have desired "to know something about" that! Above all, yet distinguishable from the rest—as the sparks still upon stem and leaf here and there faintly glowed and twinkled—the withered flowers which recorded that happy hour in the arbour, and the walks of the forsaken garden—the hour in which she had so blissfully pledged herself to renounce that career in art wherein fame would have been secured, but which would not have united Fame with Love—in dreams evermore over now.

# BOOK X.

## CHAPTER I.

Graham Vane had heard nothing for months from M. Renard, when one morning he received the letter I translate:

"MONSIEUR,—I am happy to inform you that I have at last obtained one piece of information which may lead to a more important discovery. When we parted after our fruitless research in Vienna, we had both concurred in the persuasion that, for some reason known only to the two ladies themselves, Madame Marigny and Madame Duval had exchanged names—that it was Madame Marigny who had deceased in the name of Madame Duval, and Madame Duval who had survived in that of Marigny.

"It was clear to me that the beau Monsieur who had visited the false Duval must have been cognisant of this exchange of name, and that, if his name and whereabouts could be ascertained, he, in all probability, would know what had become of the lady who is the object of our research; and after the lapse of so many years he would probably have very slight motive to preserve the concealment of facts which might, no doubt, have been convenient at the time. The lover of the soi-disant Mademoiselle Duval was by such accounts as we could gain a man of some rank—very possibly a married man; and the liaison, in short, was one of those which, while they last, necessitate precautions and secrecy.

"Therefore, dismissing all attempts at further trace of the missing lady, I resolved to return to Vienna as soon as the business that recalled me to Paris was concluded, and devote myself exclusively to the search after the amorous and mysterious Monsieur.

"I did not state this determination to you, because, possibly, I might be in error—or, if not in error, at least too sanguine in my expectations—and it is best to avoid disappointing an honourable client.

"One thing was clear, that, at the time of the soi-disant Duval's decease, the beau Monsieur was at Vienna.

"It appeared also tolerably clear that when the lady friend of the deceased quitted Munich so privately, it was to Vienna she repaired, and from Vienna comes the letter demanding the certificates of Madame Duval's death. Pardon me, if I remind you of all these circumstances no doubt fresh in your recollection. I repeat them in order to justify the conclusions to which they led me.

"I could not, however, get permission to absent myself from Paris for the time I might require till the end of last April. I had meanwhile sought all private means of ascertaining what Frenchmen of rank and station were in that capital in the autumn of 1849. Among the list of the very few such Messieurs I fixed upon one as the most likely to be the mysterious Achille—Achille was, indeed, his nom de bapteme.

"A man of intrigue—a bonnes fortunes—of lavish expenditure withal; very tenacious of his dignity, and avoiding any petty scandals by which it might be lowered; just the man who, in some passing affair of gallantry with a lady of doubtful repute, would never have signed his titular designation to a letter, and would have kept himself as much incognito as he could. But this man was dead—had been dead some years. He had not died at Vienna—never visited that capital for some years before his death. He was then, and had long been, the ami de la maison of one of those grandes dames of whose intimacy grands seigneurs are not ashamed. They parade there the bonnes fortunes they conceal elsewhere. Monsieur and the grande dame were at Baden when the former died. Now, Monsieur, a Don Juan of that stamp is pretty sure always to have a confidential Leporello. If I could find Leporello alive I might learn the secrets not to be extracted from a Don Juan defunct. I ascertained, in truth, both at Vienna, to which I first repaired in order to verify the renseignements I had obtained at Paris, and at Baden, to which I then bent my way, that this brilliant noble had a favourite valet who had lived with him from his youth—an Italian, who had contrived in the course of his service to lay by savings enough to set up a hotel somewhere in Italy, supposed to be Pisa. To Pisa I repaired, but the man had left some years; his hotel had not prospered—he had left in debt. No one could say what had become of him. At last, after a long and tedious research, I found him installed as manager of a small hotel at Genoa—a pleasant fellow enough; and after friendly intercourse with him (of course I lodged at his hotel), I easily led him to talk of his earlier life and adventures, and especially of his former master, of whose splendid career in the army of 'La Belle Deesse' he was not a little proud. It was not very easy to get him to the particular subject in question. In fact, the affair with the poor false Duval had been so brief and undistinguished an episode in his master's life, that it was not without a strain of memory that he reached it.

"By little and little, however, in the course of two or three evenings, and by the aid of many flasks of Orviette or bottles of Lacrima (wines, Monsieur, that I do not commend to any one who desires to keep his stomach sound and his secrets safe), I gathered these particulars.

"Our Don Juan, since the loss of a wife in the first year of marriage, had rarely visited Paris where he had a domicile—his ancestral hotel there he had sold.

"But happening to visit that capital of Europe a few months before we come to our dates at Aix-la-Chapelle, he made acquaintance with Madame Marigny, a natural daughter of high-placed parents, by whom, of course, she had never been acknowledged, but who had contrived that she should receive a good education at a convent; and on leaving it also contrived that an old soldier of fortune—which means an officer without fortune—who had served in Algiers with some distinction, should offer her his hand, and add the modest dot they assigned her to his yet more modest income. They contrived also that she should understand the offer must be accepted. Thus Mademoiselle 'Quelque Chose' became Madame Marigny, and she, on her part, contrived that a year or so later she should be left a widow. After a marriage, of course the parents washed their hands of her—they had done their duty. At the time Don Juan made this lady's acquaintance nothing could be said against her character; but the milliners and butchers had begun to imply that they would rather have her money than trust to her character. Don Juan fell in love with her, satisfied the immediate claims of milliner and butcher, and when they quitted Paris it was agreed that they should meet later at Aix-la-Chapelle. But when he resorted to that sultry and, to my mind, unalluring spa, he was surprised by a line from her saying that she had changed her name of Marigny for that of Duval.

"'I recollect,' said Leporello, 'that two days afterwards my master said to me, 'Caution and secrecy. Don't mention my name at the house to which I may send you with any note for Madame Duval. I don't announce my name when I call. La petite Marigny has exchanged her name for that of Louise Duval; and I find that there is a Louise Duval here, her friend, who is niece to a relation of my own, and a terrible relation to quarrel with—a dead shot and unrivalled swordsman—Victor de Mauleon. My master was brave enough, but he enjoyed life, and he did not think la petite Marigny worth being killed for.'

"Leporello remembered very little of what followed. All he did remember is that Don Juan, when at Vienna, said to him one morning, looking less gay than usual, 'It is finished with ca petite Marigny-she is no more.' Then he ordered his bath, wrote a note, and said with tears in his eyes, 'Take this to Mademoiselle Celeste; not to be compared to la petite Marigny; but la petite Celeste is still alive.' Ah, Monsieur! if only any man in France could be as proud of his ruler as that Italian was of my countrymen! Alas! we Frenchmen are all made to command—or at least we think ourselves so—and we are insulted by one who says to us, 'Serve and obey.' Nowadays, in France, we find all Don Juans and no Leporellos.

"After strenuous exertions upon my part to recall to Leporello's mind the important question whether he had ever seen the true Duval, passing under the name of Marigny—whether she had not presented herself to his master at Vienna or elsewhere—he rubbed his forehead, and drew from it these reminiscences.

"'On the day that his Excellency,'—Leporello generally so styled his master—'Excellency,' as you are aware, is the title an Italian would give to Satan if taking his wages, told me that la petite Marigny was no more, he had received previously a lady veiled and mantled, whom I did not recognise as any one I had seen before, but I noticed her way of carrying herself—haughtily—her head thrown back; and I thought to myself, that lady is one of his grandes dames. She did call again two or three times, never announcing her name; then she did not reappear. She might be Madame Duval—I can't say.'

"'But did you never hear his Excellency speak of the real Duval after that time?'

"'No—non mi ricordo—I don't remember.'

"'Nor of some living Madame Marigny, though the real one was dead?'

"'Stop, I do recollect; not that he ever named such a person to me, but that I have posted letters for him to a Madame Marigny—oh, yes! even years after the said petite Marigny was dead; and once I did venture to say, 'Pardon me, Eccellenza, but may I ask if that poor lady is really dead, since I have to prepay this letter to her?'"

"'Oh,' said he, 'Madame Marigny! Of course the one you know is dead, but there are others of the same name; this lady is of my family. Indeed, her house, though noble in itself, recognises the representative of mine as its head, and I am too bon prince not to acknowledge and serve any one who branches out of my own tree.'"

"A day after this last conversation on the subject, Leporello said to me: 'My friend, you certainly have some interest in ascertaining what became of the lady who took the name of Marigny (I state this frankly, Monsieur, to show how difficult even for one so prudent as I am to beat about a bush long but what you let people know the sort of bird you are in search of).

"'Well,' said I, 'she does interest me. I knew something of that Victor de Mauleon, whom his Excellency did not wish to quarrel with; and it would be a kindly act to her relation if one could learn what became of Louise Duval.'

"'I can put you on the way of learning all that his Excellency was likely to have known of her through correspondence. I have often heard him quote, with praise, a saying so clever that it might have been Italian, "Never write, never burn;" that is, never commit yourself by a letter—keep all letters that could put others in your power. All the letters he received were carefully kept and labelled. I sent them to his son in four large trunks. His son, no doubt, has them still.'

"Now, however, I have exhausted my budget. I arrived at Paris last night. I strongly advise you to come hither at once, if you still desire to prosecute your search.

"You, Monsieur, can do what I could not venture to do; you can ask the son of Don Juan if, amid the correspondence of his father, which he may have preserved, there be any signed Marigny or Duval—any, in short, which can throw light on this very obscure complication of circumstances. A grand seigneur would naturally be more complaisant to a man of your station than he would be to an agent of police. Don Juan's son, inheriting his father's title, is Monsieur le Marquis de Rochebriant; and permit me to add, that at this moment, as the journals doubtless inform you, all Paris resounds with the rumour of the coming war; and Monsieur de Rochebriant—who is, as I have ascertained, now in Paris—it may be difficult to find anywhere on earth a month or two hence.—I have the honour, with profound consideration, &c., &c., RENARD."

The day after the receipt of this letter Graham Vane was in Paris.

# CHAPTER II.

Among things indescribable is that which is called "Agitation" in Paris—"Agitation" without riot or violence—showing itself by no disorderly act, no turbulent outburst. Perhaps the cafes are more crowded; passengers in the streets stop each other more often, and converse in small knots and groups; yet, on the whole, there is little externally to show how loudly the heart of Paris is beating. A traveller may be passing through quiet landscapes, unconscious that a great battle is going on some miles off, but if he will stop and put his ear to the ground he will recognise by a certain indescribable vibration, the voice of the cannon.

But at Paris an acute observer need not stop and put his ear to the ground; he feels within himself a vibration—a mysterious inward sympathy which communicates to the individual a conscious thrill—when the passions of the multitude are stirred, no matter how silently.

Tortoni's cafe was thronged when Duplessis and Frederic Lemercier entered it: it was in vain to order breakfast; no table was vacant either within the rooms or under the awnings without.

But they could not retreat so quickly as they had entered. On catching sight of the financier several men rose and gathered round him, eagerly questioning:

"What do you think, Duplessis? Will any insult to France put a drop of warm blood into the frigid veins of that miserable Ollivier?"

"It is not yet clear that France has been insulted, Messieurs," replied Duplessis, phlegmatically.

"Bah! Not insulted! The very nomination of a Hohenzollern to the crown of Spain was an insult—what would you have more?"

"I tell you what it is, Duplessis," said the Vicomte de Breze, whose habitual light good temper seemed exchanged for insolent swagger—"I tell you what it is, your friend the Emperor has no more courage than a chicken. He is grown old, and infirm, and lazy; he knows that he can't even mount on horseback. But if, before this day week, he has not declared war on the Prussians, he will be lucky if he can get off as quietly as poor Louis Philippe did under shelter of his umbrella, and ticketed 'Schmidt.' Or could you not, M. Duplessis, send him back to London in a bill of exchange?"

"For a man of your literary repute, M. le Vicomte," said Duplessis, "you indulge in a strange confusion of metaphors. But, pardon me, I came here to breakfast, and I cannot remain to quarrel. Come, Lemercier, let us take our chance of a cutlet at the Trois Freres."

"Fox, Fox," cried Lemercier, whistling to a poodle that had followed him into the cafe, and, frightened by the sudden movement and loud voices of the habitues, had taken refuge under the table.

"Your dog is poltron," said De Breze; "call him Nap." At this stroke of humour there was a general laugh, in the midst of which Duplessis escaped, and Frederic, having discovered and caught his dog, followed with that animal tenderly clasped in his arms.

"I would not lose Fox for a great deal," said Lemercier with effusion; "a pledge of love and fidelity from an English lady the most distinguished: the lady left me—the dog remains."

Duplessis smiled grimly: "What a thoroughbred Parisian you are, my dear Frederic! I believe if the tramp of the last angel were sounding, the Parisians would be divided into two sets: one would be singing the Marseillaise, and parading the red flag; the other would be shrugging their shoulders and saying, 'Bah! as if le Bon Dieu would have the bad taste to injure Paris—the Seat of the Graces, the School of the Arts, the Fountain of Reason, the Eye of the World;' and so be found by the destroying angel caressing poodles and making bons mots about les femmes."

"And quite right, too," said Lemercier, complacently; "what other people in the world could retain lightness of heart under circumstances so unpleasant? But why do you take things so solemnly? Of course there will be war idle now to talk of explanations and excuses. When a Frenchman says, 'I am insulted,' he is not going to be told that he is not insulted. He means fighting, and not apologising. But what if there be war? Our brave soldiers beat the Prussians—take the Rhine—return to Paris covered with laurels; a new Boulevard de Berlin eclipses the Boulevard Sebastopol. By the way, Duplessis, a Boulevard de Berlin will be a good speculation—better than the Rue de Louvier. Ah! is not that my English friend, Grarm Varn?" here, quitting the arm of Duplessis, Lemercier stopped a gentleman who was about to pass him unnoticing. "Bon jour, mon ami! how long have you been at Paris?"

"I only arrived last evening," answered Graham, "and my stay will be so short that it is a piece of good luck, my dear Lemercier, to meet with you, and exchange a cordial shake of the hand."

"We are just going to breakfast at the Trois Freres—Duplessis and I—pray join us."

"With great pleasure—ah, M. Duplessis, I shall be glad to hear from you that the Emperor will be firm enough to check the advances of that martial fever which, to judge by the persons I meet, seems to threaten delirium."

Duplessis looked very keenly at Graham's face, as he replied slowly: "The English, at least, ought to know that when the Emperor by his last reforms resigned his personal authority for constitutional monarchy, it ceased to be a question whether he could or could not be firm in matters that belonged to the Cabinet and the Chambers. I presume that if Monsieur Gladstone advised Queen Victoria to declare war upon the Emperor of Russia, backed by a vast majority in Parliament, you would think me very ignorant of constitutional monarchy and Parliamentary government if I said, 'I hope Queen Victoria will resist that martial fever.'"

"You rebuke me very fairly, M. Duplessis, if you can show me that the two cases are analogous; but we do not understand in England that, despite his last reforms, the Emperor has so abnegated his individual ascendency, that his will, clearly and resolutely expressed, would not prevail in his Council and silence opposition in the Chambers. Is it so? I ask for information."

The three men were walking on towards the Palais Royal side by side while this conversation proceeded.

"That all depends," replied Duplessis, "upon what may be the increase of popular excitement at Paris. If it slackens, the Emperor, no doubt, could turn to wise account that favourable pause in the fever. But if it continues to swell, and Paris cries, 'War,' in a voice as loud as it cried to Louis Philippe 'Revolution,' do you think that the Emperor could impose on his ministers the wisdom of peace? His ministers would be too terrified by the clamour to undertake the responsibility of opposing it—they would resign. Where is the Emperor to find another Cabinet? a peace Cabinet? What and who are the orators for peace?—whom a handful!—who? Gambetta, Jules Favre, avowed Republicans,—would they even accept the post of ministers to Louis Napoleon? If they did, would not their first step be the abolition of the Empire? Napoleon is therefore so far a constitutional monarch in the same sense as Queen Victoria, that the popular will in the country (and in France in such matters Paris is the country) controls the Chambers, controls the Cabinet; and against the Cabinet the Emperor could not contend. I say nothing of the army—a power in France unknown to you in England, which would certainly fraternise with no peace party. If war is proclaimed,—let England blame it if she will—she can't lament it more than I should: but let England blame the nation; let her blame, if she please, the form of the government, which rests upon popular suffrage; but do not let her blame our sovereign more than the French would blame her own, if compelled by the conditions on which she holds her crown to sign a declaration of war, which vast majorities in a Parliament just elected, and a Council of Ministers whom she could not practically replace, enforced upon her will."

"Your observations, M. Duplessis, impress me strongly, and add to the deep anxieties with which, in common with all my countrymen, I regard the menacing aspect of the present hour. Let us hope the best. Our Government, I know, is exerting itself to the utmost verge of its power, to remove every just ground of offence that the unfortunate nomination of a German Prince to the Spanish throne could not fail to have given to French statesmen."

"I am glad you concede that such a nomination was a just ground of offence," said Lemercier, rather bitterly; "for I have met Englishmen who asserted that France had no right to resent any choice of a sovereign that Spain might make."

"Englishmen in general are not very reflective politicians in foreign affairs," said Graham; "but those who are must see that France could not, without alarm the most justifiable, contemplate a cordon of hostile states being drawn around her on all sides,—Germany, is, itself so formidable since the field of Sadowa, on the east; a German prince in the southwest; the not improbable alliance between Prussia and the Italian kingdom, already so alienated from the France to which it owed so much. If England would be uneasy were a great maritime power possessed of Antwerp, how much more uneasy might France justly be if Prussia could add the armies of Spain to those of Germany, and launch them both upon France. But that cause of alarm is over—the Hohenzollern is withdrawn. Let us hope for the best."

The three men had now seated themselves at a table in the Trois Freres, and Lemercier volunteered the task of inspecting the menu and ordering the repast, still keeping guard on Fox.

"Observe that man," said Duplessis, pointing towards a gentleman who had just entered; "the other day he was the popular hero—now, in the excitement of threatened war, he is permitted to order his bifteck uncongratulated, uncaressed; such is fame at Paris! here to-day and gone to-morrow."

"How did the man become famous?"

"He is a painter, and refused a decoration—the only French painter who ever did."

"And why refuse?"

"Because he is more stared at as the man who refused than he would have been as the man who accepted. If ever the Red Republicans have their day, those among them most certain of human condemnation will be the coxcombs who have gone mad for the desire of human applause."

"You are a profound philosopher, M. Duplessis."

"I hope not—I have an especial contempt for philosophers. Pardon me a moment—I see a man to whom I would say a word or two."

Duplessis crossed over to another table to speak to a middle-aged man of somewhat remarkable countenance, with the red ribbon in his buttonhole, in whom Graham recognised an ex-minister of the Emperor, differing from most of those at that day in his Cabinet, in the reputation of being loyal to his master and courageous against a mob. Left thus alone with Lemercier, Graham said:

"Pray tell me where I can find your friend the Marquis de Rochebriant. I called at his apartment this morning, and I was told that he had gone on some visit into the country, taking his valet, and the concierge could not give me his address. I thought myself so lucky on meeting with you, who are sure to know."

"No, I do not; it is some days since I saw Alain. But Duplessis will be sure to know." Here the financier rejoined them.

"Mon cher, Grarm Varn wants to know for what Sabine shades Rochebriant has deserted the 'fumum opes strepitumque' of the capital."

"Ah! the Marquis is a friend of yours, Monsieur?"

"I can scarcely boast that honour, but he is an acquaintance whom I should be very glad to see again."

"At this moment he is at the Duchesse de Tarascon's country-house near Fontainebleau; I had a hurried line from him two days ago stating that he was going there on her urgent invitation. But he may return to-morrow; at all events he dines with me on the 8th, and I shall be charmed if you will do me the honour to meet him at my house."

"It is an invitation too agreeable to refuse, and I thank you very much for it."

Nothing worth recording passed further in conversation between Graham and the two Frenchmen. He left them smoking their cigars in the garden, and walked homeward by the Rue de Rivoli. As he was passing beside the Magasin du Louvre he stopped, and made way for a lady crossing quickly out of the shop towards her carriage at the door. Glancing at him with a slight inclination of her head in acknowledgment of his courtesy, the lady recognised his features,—

"Ah, Mr. Vane!" she cried, almost joyfully—"you are then at Paris, though you have not come to see me."

"I only arrived last night, dear Mrs. Morley," said Graham, rather embarrassed, "and only on some matters of business which unexpectedly summoned me. My stay will probably be very short."

"In that case let me rob you of a few minutes—no, not rob you even of them; I can take you wherever you want to go, and as my carriage moves more quickly than you do on foot, I shall save you the minutes instead of robbing you of them."

"You are most kind, but I was only going to my hotel, which is close by."

"Then you have no excuse for not taking a short drive with me in the Champs Elysees—come."

Thus bidden, Graham could not civilly disobey. He handed the fair American into her carriage, and seated himself by her side.

# CHAPTER III.

"Mr. Vane, I feel as if I had many apologies to make for the interest in your life which my letter to you so indiscreetly betrayed."

"Oh, Mrs. Morley! you cannot guess how deeply that interest touched me."

"I should not have presumed so far," continued Mrs. Morley, unheeding the interruption, "if I had not been altogether in error as to the nature of your sentiments in a certain quarter. In this you must blame my American rearing. With us there are many flirtations between boys and girls which come to nothing; but when in my country a man like you meets with a woman like Mademoiselle Cicogna, there cannot be flirtation. His attentions, his looks, his manner, reveal to the eyes of those who care enough for him to watch, one of two things—either he coldly admires and esteems, or he loves with his whole heart and soul a woman worthy to inspire such a love. Well, I did watch, and I was absurdly mistaken. I imagined that I saw love, and rejoiced for the sake of both of you to think so. I know that in all countries, our own as well as yours, love is so morbidly sensitive and jealous that it is always apt to invent imaginary foes to itself. Esteem and admiration never do that. I thought that some misunderstanding, easily removed by the intervention of a third person, might have impeded the impulse of two hearts towards each other—and so I wrote. I had assumed that you loved—I am humbled to the last degree—you only admired and esteemed."

"Your irony is very keen, Mrs. Morley, and to you it may seem very just."

"Don't call me Mrs. Morley in that haughty tone of voice,—can't you talk to me as you would talk to a friend? You only esteemed and admired—there is an end of it."

"No, there is not an end of it," cried Graham, giving way to an impetuosity of passion, which rarely, indeed, before another, escaped his self-control; "the end of it to me is a life out of which is ever stricken such love as I could feel for woman. To me true love can only come once. It came with my first look on that fatal face—it has never left me in thought by day, in dreams by night. The end of it to me is farewell to all such happiness as the one love of a life can promise—but—"

"But what?" asked Mrs. Morley, softly, and very much moved by the passionate earnestness of Graham's voice and words.

"But," he continued with a forced smile, "we Englishmen are trained to the resistance of absolute authority; we cannot submit all the elements that make up our being to the sway of a single despot. Love is the painter of existence, it should not be its sculptor."

"I do not understand the metaphor."

"Love colours our life, it should not chisel its form."

"My dear Mr. Vane, that is very cleverly said, but the human heart is too large and too restless to be quietly packed up in an aphorism. Do you mean to tell me that if you found you had destroyed Isaura Cicogna's happiness as well as resigned your own, that thought would not somewhat deform the very shape you would give to your life? Is it colour alone that your life would lose?"

"Ah, Mrs. Morley, do not lower your friend into an ordinary girl in whom idleness exaggerates the strength of any fancy over which it dreamily broods. Isaura Cicogna has her occupations—her genius—her fame—her career. Honestly speaking, I think that in these she will find a happiness that no quiet hearth could bestow. I will say no more. I feel persuaded that were we two united I could not make her happy. With the irresistible impulse that urges the genius of the writer towards its vent in public sympathy and applause, she would chafe if I said, 'Be contented to be wholly mine.' And if I said it not, and felt I had no right to say it, and allowed the full scope to her natural ambition, what then? She would chafe yet more to find that I had no fellowship in her aims and ends—that where I should feel pride, I felt humiliation. It would be so; I cannot help it, 'tis my nature."

"So be it then. When, next year perhaps, you visit Paris, you will be safe from my officious interference! Isaura will be the wife of another."

Graham pressed his hand to his heart with the sudden movement of one who feels there an agonising spasm—his cheek, his very lips were bloodless.

"I told you," he said bitterly, "that your fears of my influence over the happiness of one so gifted, and so strong in such gifts, were groundless; you allow that I should be very soon forgotten?"

"I allow no such thing—I wish I could. But do you know so little of a woman's heart (and in matters of heart, I never yet heard that genius had a talisman against emotion),—do you know so little of a woman's heart as not to know that the very moment in which she may accept a marriage the least fitted to render her happy, is that in which she has lost all hope of happiness in another?"

"Is it indeed so?" murmured Graham—"Ay, I can conceive it."

"And have you so little comprehension of the necessities which that fame, that career to which you allow she is impelled by the instincts of genius, impose on this girl, young, beautiful, fatherless, motherless? No matter how pure her life, can she guard it from the slander of envious tongues? Will not all her truest friends—would not you, if you were her brother—press upon her by all the arguments that have most weight with the woman who asserts independence in her modes of life, and yet is wise enough to know that the world can only judge of virtue by its shadow—reputation, not to dispense with the protection which a husband can alone secure? And that is why I warn you, if it be yet time, that in resigning your own happiness you may destroy Isaura's. She will wed another, but she will not be happy. What a chimera or dread your egotism as man conjures up! Oh! forsooth, the qualities that charm and delight a world are to unfit a woman to be helpmate to a man. Fie on you!—fie!"

Whatever answer Graham might have made to these impassioned reproaches was here checked.

Two men on horseback stopped the carriage. One was Enguerrand de Vandemar, the other was the Algerine Colonel whom we met at the supper given at the Maison Doree by Frederic Lemercier.

"Pardon, Madame Morley," said Enguerrand; "but there are symptoms of a mob-epidemic a little further up the fever began at Belleville, and is threatening the health of the Champs Elysees. Don't be alarmed—it may be nothing, though it may be much. In Paris, one can never calculate an hour beforehand the exact progress of a politico-epidemic fever. At present I say, 'Bah! a pack of ragged boys, gamins de Paris;' but my friend the Colonel, twisting his moustache en souriant amerement, says, 'It is the indignation of Paris at the apathy of the Government under insult to the honour of France;' and Heaven only knows how rapidly French gamins grow into giants when Colonels talk about the indignation of Paris and the honour of France!"

"But what has happened?" asked Mrs. Morley, turning to the Colonel.

"Madame," replied the warrior, "it is rumoured that the King of Prussia has turned his back upon the ambassador of France; and that the pekin who is for peace at any price—M. Ollivier—will say tomorrow in the Chamber, that France submits to a slap in the face."

"Please, Monsieur de Vandemar, to tell my coachman to drive home," said Mrs. Morley.

The carriage turned and went homeward. The Colonel lifted his hat, and rode back to see what the gamins were about. Enguerrand, who had no interest in the gamins, and who looked on the Colonel as a bore, rode by the side of the carriage.

"Is there anything serious in this?" asked Mrs. Morley.

"At this moment, nothing. What it may be this hour to-morrow I cannot say. Ah! Monsieur Vane, bon jour I did not recognise you at first. Once, in a visit at the chateau of one of your distinguished countrymen, I saw two game-cocks turned out facing each other: they needed no pretext for quarrelling—neither do France and Prussia—no matter which game-cock gave the last offence, the two game-cocks must have it out. All that Ollivier can do, if he be wise, is to see that the French cock has his steel spurs as long as the Prussians. But this I do say, that if Ollivier attempts to put the French cock back into its bag, the Empire is gone in forty-eight hours. That to me is a trifle—I care nothing for the Empire; but that which is not a trifle is anarchy and chaos. Better war and the Empire than peace and Jules Favre. But let us seize the present hour, Mr. Vane; whatever happens to-morrow, shall we dine together to-day? Name your restaurant."

"I am so grieved," answered Graham, rousing himself, "I am here only on business, and engaged all the evening."

"What a wonderful thing is this life of ours!" said Enguerrand. "The destiny of France at this moment hangs on a thread—I, a Frenchman, say to an English friend, 'Let us dine—a cutlet to-day and a fig for to-morrow;' and my English friend, distinguished native of a country with which we have the closest alliance, tells me that in this crisis of France he has business to attend to! My father is quite right; he accepts the Voltairean philosophy, and cries, Vivent les indifferents!"

"My dear M. de Vandemar," said Graham, "in every country you will find the same thing. All individuals massed together constitute public life. Each individual has a life of his own, the claims and the habits and the needs of which do not suppress his sympathies with public life, but imperiously overrule them. Mrs. Morley, permit me to pull the check-string—I get out here."

"I like that man," said Enguerrand, as he continued to ride by the fair American, "in language and esprit he is so French."

"I use to like him better than you can," answered Mrs. Morley, "but in prejudice and stupidity he is so English. As it seems you are disengaged, come and partake, pot au feu, with Frank and me."

"Charmed to do so," answered the cleverest and best bred of all Parisian beaux garcons, "but forgive me if I quit you soon. This poor France! Entre nous, I am very uneasy about the Parisian fever. I must run away after dinner to clubs and cafes to learn the last bulletins."

"We have nothing like that French Legitimist in the States," said the fair American to herself, "unless we should ever be so silly as to make Legitimists of the ruined gentlemen of the South."

Meanwhile Graham Vane went slowly back to his apartment. No false excuse had he made to Enguerrand; this evening was devoted to M. Renard, who told him little he had not known before; but his private life overruled his public, and all that night he, professed politician, thought sleeplessly, not over the crisis to France, which might alter the conditions of Europe, but the talk on his private life of that intermeddling American woman.

# CHAPTER IV.

The next day, Wednesday, July 6th, commenced one of those eras in the world's history in which private life would vainly boast that it overrules Life Public. How many private lives does such a terrible time influence, absorb, darken with sorrow, crush into graves?

It was the day when the Duc de Gramont uttered the fatal speech which determined the die between peace and war. No one not at Paris on that day can conceive the popular enthusiasm with which that speech was hailed—the greater because the warlike tone of it was not anticipated; because there had been a rumour amidst circles the best informed that a speech of pacific moderation was to be the result of the Imperial Council. Rapturous indeed were the applauses with which the sentences that breathed haughty defiance were hailed by the Assembly. The ladies in the tribune rose with one accord, waving their handkerchiefs. Tall, stalwart, dark, with Roman features and lofty presence, the Minister of France seemed to say with Catiline in the fine tragedy: "Lo! where I stand, I am war!"

Paris had been hungering for some hero of the hour—the Duc de Gramont became at once raised to that eminence. All the journals, save the very few which were friendly to peace, because hostile to the Emperor, resounded with praise, not only of the speech, but of the speaker. It is with a melancholy sense of amusement that one recalls now to mind those organs of public opinion—with what romantic fondness they dwelt on the personal graces of the man who had at last given voice to the chivalry of France: "The charming gravity of his countenance—the mysterious expression of his eye!"

As the crowd poured from the Chambers, Victor de Mauleon and Savarin, who had been among the listeners, encountered.

"No chance for my friends the Orleanists now," said Savarin. "You who mock at all parties are, I suppose, at heart for the Republican—small chance, too, for that."

"I do not agree with you. Violent impulses have quick reactions."

"But what reaction could shake the Emperor after he returns a conqueror, bringing in his pocket the left bank of the Rhine?"

"None—when he does that. Will he do it? Does he himself think he will do it? I doubt—"

"Doubt the French army against the Prussian?"

"Against the German people united—yes, very much."

"But war will disunite the German people. Bavaria will surely assist us—Hanover will rise against the spoliator—Austria at our first successes must shake off her present enforced neutrality?"

"You have not been in Germany, and I have. What yesterday was a Prussian army, to-morrow will be a German population; far exceeding our own in numbers, in hardihood of body, in cultivated intellect, in military discipline. But talk of something else. How is my ex-editor—poor Gustave Rameau?"

"Still very weak, but on the mend. You may have him back in his office soon."

"Impossible! even in his sick-bed his vanity was more vigorous than ever. He issued a war-song, which has gone the round of the war journals signed by his own name. He must have known very well that the name of such a Tyrtaeus cannot reappear as the editor of Le Sens Commun; that in launching his little firebrand he burned all vessels that could waft him back to the port he had quitted. But I dare say he has done well for his own interests; I doubt if Le Sens Commun can much longer hold its ground in the midst of the prevalent lunacy."

"What! it has lost subscribers?—gone off in sale already, since it declared for peace?"

"Of course it has; and after the article which, if I live over to-night, will appear to-morrow, I should wonder if it sell enough to cover the cost of the print and paper."

"Martyr to principle! I revere, but I do not envy thee."

"Martyrdom is not my ambition. If Louis Napoleon be defeated, what then? Perhaps he may be the martyr; and the Favres and Gambettas may roast their own eggs on the gridiron they heat for his majesty."

Here an English gentleman, who was the very able correspondent to a very eminent journal, and in that capacity had made acquaintance with De Mauleon, joined the two Frenchmen; Savarin, however, after an exchange of salutations, went his way.

"May I ask a frank answer to a somewhat rude question, M. le Vicomte?" said the Englishman. "Suppose that the Imperial Government had to-day given in their adhesion to the peace party, how long would it have been before their orators in the Chamber and their organs in the press would have said that France was governed by poltrons?"

"Probably for most of the twenty-four hours. But there are a few who are honest in their convictions; of that few I am one."

"And would have supported the Emperor and his Government?"

"No, Monsieur—I do not say that."

"Then the Emperor would have turned many friends into enemies, and no enemies into friends."

"Monsieur—you in England know that a party in opposition is not propitiated when the party in power steals its measures. Ha!—pardon me, who is that gentleman, evidently your countryman, whom I see yonder talking to the Secretary of your Embassy?"

"He.—Mr. Vane-Graham Vane. Do you not know him? He has been much in Paris, attached to our Embassy formerly; a clever man—much is expected from him."

"Ah! I think I have seen him before, but am not quite sure. Did you say Vane? I once knew a Monsieur Vane, a distinguished parliamentary orator."

"That gentleman is his son—would you like to be introduced to him?"

"Not to-day—I am in some hurry." Here Victor lifted his hat in parting salutation, and as he walked away cast at Graham another glance keen and scrutinising. "I have seen that man before," he muttered, "where?—when?—can it be only a family likeness to the father? No, the features are different; the profile is—ha!—Mr. Lamb, Mr. Lamb—but why call himself by that name?—why disguised?—what can he have to do with poor Louise? Bah—these are not questions I can think of now. This war—this war—can it yet be prevented? How it will prostrate all the plans my ambition so carefully schemed! Oh!—at least if I were but in the Chamber. Perhaps I yet may be before the war is ended—the Clavignys have great interest in their department."

# CHAPTER V.

Graham had left a note with Rochebriant's concierge requesting an interview on the Marquis's return to Paris, and on the evening after the day just commemorated he received a line, saying that Alain had come back, and would be at home at nine o'clock. Graham found himself in the Breton's apartment punctually at the hour indicated.

Alain was in high spirits: he burst at once into enthusiastic exclamations on the virtual announcement of war.

"Congratulate me, mon cher!" he cried—"the news was a joyous surprise to me. Only so recently as yesterday morning I was under the gloomy apprehension that the Imperial Cabinet would continue to back Ollivier's craven declaration 'that France had not been affronted!' The Duchesse de Tarascon, at whose campagne I was a guest, is (as you doubtless know) very much in the confidence of the Tuileries. On the first signs of war, I wrote to her, saying that whatever the objections of my pride to enter the army as a private in time of peace, such objections ceased on the moment when all distinctions of France must vanish in the eyes of sons eager to defend her banners. The Duchesse in reply begged me to come to her campagne and talk over the matter. I went; she then said that if war should break out it was the intention to organise the Mobiles and officer them with men of birth and education, irrespective of previous military service, and in that case I might count on my epaulets. But only two nights ago she received a letter—I know not of course from whom—evidently from some high authority—that induced her to think the moderation of the Council would avert the war, and leave the swords of the Mobiles in their sheaths. I suspect the decision of yesterday must have been a very sudden one. Ce cher Gramont! See what it is to have a well-born man in a sovereign's councils."

"If war must come, I at least wish all renown to yourself. But—"

"Oh! spare me your 'buts'; the English are always too full of them where her own interests do not appeal to her. She had no 'buts' for war in India or a march into Abyssinia."

Alain spoke petulantly; at that moment the French were very much irritated by the monitory tone of the English journals. Graham prudently avoided the chance of rousing the wrath of a young hero yearning for his epaulets.

"I am English enough," said he, with good-humoured courtesy, "to care for English interests; and England has no interest abroad dearer to her than the welfare and dignity of France. And now let me tell you why I presumed on an acquaintance less intimate than I could desire, to solicit this interview on a matter which concerns myself, and in which you could perhaps render me a considerable service."

"If I can, count it rendered; move to this sofa—join me in a cigar, and let us talk at ease comme de vieux amis, whose fathers or brothers might have fought side by side in the Crimea." Graham removed to the sofa beside Rochebriant, and after one or two whiffs laid aside the cigar and began:

"Among the correspondence which Monsieur your father has left, are there any letters of no distant date signed Marigny—Madame Marigny? Pardon me, I should state my motive in putting this question. I am intrusted with a charge, the fulfilment of which may prove to the benefit of this lady or her child; such fulfilment is a task imposed upon my honour. But all the researches to discover this lady which I have instituted stop at a certain date, with this information,—viz., that she corresponded occasionally with the late Marquis de Rochebriant; that he habitually preserved the letters of his correspondents; and that these letters were severally transmitted to you at his decease."

Alain's face had taken a very grave expression while Graham spoke, and he now replied with a mixture of haughtiness and embarrassment:

"The boxes containing the letters my father received and preserved were sent to me as you say—the larger portion of them were from ladies—sorted and labelled, so that in glancing at any letter in each packet I could judge of the general tenor of these in the same packet without the necessity of reading them. All packets of that kind, Monsieur Vane, I burned. I do not remember any letters signed 'Marigny!"

"I perfectly understand, my dear Marquis, that you would destroy all letters which your father himself would have destroyed if his last illness had been sufficiently prolonged. But I do not think the letters I mean would have come under that classification; probably they were short, and on matters of business relating to some third person—some person, for instance, of the name of Louise, or of Duval!"

"Stop! let me think. I have a vague remembrance of one or two letters which rather perplexed me, they were labelled, 'Louise D—. Mem.: to make further inquiries as to the fate of her uncle.'"

"Marquis, these are the letters I seek. Thank heaven, you have not destroyed them?"

"No; there was no reason why I should destroy, though I really cannot state precisely any reason why I kept them. I have a very vague recollection of their existence."

"I entreat you to allow me at least a glance at the handwriting, and compare it with that of a letter I have about me; and if the several handwritings correspond, I would ask you to let me have the address, which, according to your father's memorandum, will be found in the letters you have preserved."

"To compliance with such a request I not only cannot demur, but perhaps it may free me from some responsibility which I might have thought the letters devolved upon my executorship. I am sure they did not concern the honour of any woman of any family, for in that case I must have burned them."

"Ah, Marquis, shake hands there! In such concord between man and man, there is more entente cordiale between England and France than there was at Sebastopol. Now let me compare the handwritings."

"The box that contained the letters is not here—I left it at Rochebriant; I will telegraph to my aunt to send it; the day after to-morrow it will no doubt arrive. Breakfast with me that day—say at one o'clock, and after breakfast the Box!"

"How can I thank you?"

"Thank me! but you said your honour was concerned in your request—requests affecting honour between men comma il faut is a ceremony of course, like a bow between them. One bows, the other returns the bow—no thanks on either side. Now that we have done with that matter, let me say that I thought your wish for our interview originated in a very different cause."

"What could that be?"

"Nay, do you not recollect that last talk between us, when with such loyalty you spoke to me about Mademoiselle Cicogna, and supposing that there might be rivalship between us, retracted all that you might have before said to warn me against fostering the sentiment with which she had inspired me; even at the first slight glance of a face which cannot be lightly forgotten by those who have once seen it."

"I recollect perfectly every word of that talk, Marquis," answered Graham, calmly, but with his hand concealed within his vest and pressed tightly to his heart. The warning of Mrs. Morley flashed upon him. "Was this the man to seize the prize he had put aside—this man, younger than himself—handsomer than himself—higher in rank?"

"I recollect that talk, Marquis! Well, what then?"

"In my self-conceit I supposed that you might have heard how much I admired Mademoiselle Cicogna—how, having not long since met her at the house of Duplessis (who by the way writes me word that I shall meet you chez lui tomorrow), I have since sought her society wherever there was a chance to find it. You may have heard, at our club, or elsewhere, how I adore her genius—how, I say, that nothing so Breton—that is, so pure and so lofty—has appeared and won readers since the days of Chateaubriand,—and—you, knowing that les absents ont toujours tort, come to me and ask Monsieur de Rochebriant, Are we rivals? I expected a challenge—you relieve my mind—you abandon the field to me?"

At the first I warned the reader how improved from his old mauvaise honte a year or so of Paris life would make our beau Marquis. How a year or two of London life with its horsey slang and its fast girls of the period would have vulgarised an English Rochebriant! Graham gnawed his lips and replied quietly, "I do not challenge! Am I to congratulate you?"

"No, that brilliant victory is not for me. I thought that was made clear in the conversation I have referred to. But if you have done me the honour to be jealous I am exceedingly flattered. Speaking, seriously, if I admired Mademoiselle Cicogna when you and I last met, the admiration is increased by the respect with which I regard a character so simply noble. How many women older than she would have been spoiled by the adulation that has followed her literary success!—how few women so young, placed in a position so critical, having the courage to lead a life so independent, would have maintained the dignity of their character free from a single indiscretion! I speak not from my own knowledge, but from the report of all, who would be pleased enough to censure if they could find a cause. Good society is the paradise of mauvaises langues."

Graham caught Alain's hand and pressed it, but made no answer.

The young Marquis continued:

"You will pardon me for speaking thus freely in the way that I would wish any friend to speak of the demoiselle who might become my wife. I owe you much, not only for the loyalty with which you address me in reference to this young lady, but for words affecting my own position in France, which sank deep into my mind—saved me from deeming myself a proscrit in my own land—filled me with a manly ambition, not stifled amidst the thick of many effeminate follies—and, in fact, led me to the career which is about to open before me, and in which my ancestors have left me no undistinguished examples. Let us speak, then, a coeur ouvert, as one friend to another. Has there been any misunderstanding between you and Mademoiselle Cicogna which has delayed your return to Paris? If so, is it over now?"

"There has been no such misunderstanding."

"Do you doubt whether the sentiments you expressed in regard to her when we met last year, are returned?"

"I have no right to conjecture her sentiments. You mistake altogether."

"I do not believe that I am dunce enough to mistake your feelings towards Mademoiselle—they may be read in your face at this moment. Of course I do not presume to hazard a conjecture as to those of Mademoiselle towards yourself. But when I met her not long since at the house of Duplessis, with whose daughter she is intimate, I chanced to speak to her of you; and if I may judge, by looks and manner, I chose no displeasing theme. You turn away—I offend you?"

"Offend!—no, indeed; but on this subject I am not prepared to converse. I came to Paris on matters of business much complicated and which ought to absorb my attention. I cannot longer trespass on your evening. The day after to-morrow, then, I will be with you at one o'clock."

"Yes, I hope then to have the letters you wish to consult; and, meanwhile, we meet to-morrow at the Hotel Duplessis."

# CHAPTER VI.

Graham had scarcely quitted Alain, and the young Marquis was about to saunter forth to his club, when Duplessis was announced.

These two men had naturally seen much of each other since Duplessis had returned from Bretagne and delivered Alain from the gripe of Louvier. Scarcely a day had passed but what Alain had been summoned to enter into the financier's plans for the aggrandisement of the Rochebriant estates, and delicately made to feel that he had become a partner in speculations, which, thanks to the capital and the abilities Duplessis brought to bear, seemed likely to result in the ultimate freedom of his property from all burdens, and the restoration of his inheritance to a splendour correspondent with the dignity of his rank.

On the plea that his mornings were chiefly devoted to professional business, Duplessis arranged that these consultations should take place in the evenings. From those consultations Valerie was not banished; Duplessis took her into the council as a matter of course. "Valerie," said the financier to Alain, "though so young, has a very clear head for business, and she is so interested in all that interests myself, that even where I do not take her opinion, I at least feel my own made livelier and brighter by her sympathy."

So the girl was in the habit of taking her work or her book into the cabinet de travail, and never obtruding a suggestion unasked, still, when appealed to, speaking with a modest good sense which justified her father's confidence and praise; and a propos of her book, she had taken Chateaubriand into peculiar favour. Alain had respectfully presented to her beautifully bound copies of Atala and Ls Genie du Christianisme; it is astonishing, indeed, how he had already contrived to regulate her tastes in literature. The charms of those quiet family evenings had stolen into the young Breton's heart.

He yearned for none of the gayer reunions in which he had before sought for a pleasure that his nature had not found; for, amidst the amusements of Paris, Alain remained intensely Breton—viz., formed eminently for the simple joys of domestic life, associating the sacred hearthstone with the antique religion of his fathers; gathering round it all the images of pure and noble affections which the romance of a poetic temperament had evoked from the solitude which had surrounded a melancholy boyhood-an uncontaminated youth.

Duplessis entered abruptly, and with a countenance much disturbed from its wonted saturnine composure.

"Marquis, what is this I have just heard from the Duchesse de Tarascon? Can it be? You ask military service in this ill-omened war?—you?"

"My dear and best friend," said Alain, very much startled, "I should have thought that you, of all men in the world, would have most approved of my request—you, so devoted an Imperialist—you, indignant that the representative of one of these families, which the First Napoleon so eagerly and so vainly courted, should ask for the grade of sous-lieutenant in the armies of Napoleon the Third—you, who of all men know how ruined are the fortunes of a Rochebriant—you, feel surprised that he clings to the noblest heritage his ancestors have left to him—their sword! I do not understand you."

"Marquis," said Duplessis, seating himself, and regarding Alain with a look in which were blended the sort of admiration and the sort of contempt with which a practical man of the world, who, having himself gone through certain credulous follies, has learned to despise the follies, but retains a reminiscence of sympathy with the fools they bewitch, "Marquis, pardon me; you talk finely, but you do not talk common sense. I should be extremely pleased if your Legitimist scruples had allowed you to solicit, or rather to accept, a civil appointment not unsuited to your rank, under the ablest sovereign, as a civilian, to whom France can look for rational liberty combined with established order. Such openings to a suitable career you have rejected; but who on earth could expect you, never trained to military service, to draw a sword hitherto sacred to the Bourbons, on behalf of a cause which the madness, I do not say of France but of Paris, has enforced on a sovereign against whom you would fight to-morrow if you had a chance of placing the descendant of Henry IV. on his throne."

"I am not about to fight for any sovereign, but for my country against the foreigner."

"An excellent answer if the foreigner had invaded your country; but it seems that your country is going to invade the foreigner—a very different thing. Chut! all this discussion is most painful to me. I feel for the Emperor a personal loyalty, and for the hazards he is about to encounter a prophetic dread, as an ancestor of yours might have felt for Francis I. could he have foreseen Pavia. Let us talk of ourselves and the effect the war should have upon our individual action. You are aware, of course, that, though M. Louvier has had notice of our intention to pay off his mortgage, that intention cannot be carried into effect for six months; if the money be not then forthcoming his hold on Rochebriant remains unshaken—the sum is large."

"Alas! yes."

"The war must greatly disturb the money-market, affect many speculative adventures and operations when at the very moment credit may be most needed. It is absolutely necessary that I should be daily at my post on the Bourse, and hourly watch the ebb and flow of events. Under these circumstances I had counted, permit me to count still, on your presence in Bretagne. We have already begun negotiations on a somewhat extensive scale, whether as regards the improvement of forests and orchards, or the plans for building allotments, as soon as the lands are free for disposal—for all these the eye of a master is required. I entreat you, then, to take up your residence at Rochebriant."

"My dear friend, this is but a kindly and delicate mode of relieving me from the dangers of war. I have, as you must be conscious, no practical knowledge of business. Hebert can be implicitly trusted, and will carry out your views with a zeal equal to mine, and with infinitely more ability."

"Marquis, pray neither to Hercules nor to Hebert; if you wish to get your own cart out of the ruts, put your own shoulder to the wheel."

Alain coloured high, unaccustomed to be so bluntly addressed, but he replied with a kind of dignified meekness: "I shall ever remain grateful for what you have done, and wish to do for me. But, assuming that you suppose rightly, the estates of Rochebriant would, in your hands, become a profitable investment, and more than redeem the mortgage, and the sum you have paid Louvier on my account, let it pass to you irrespectively of me. I shall console myself in the knowledge that the old place will be restored, and those who honoured its old owners prosper in hands so strong, guided by a heart so generous."

Duplessis was deeply affected by these simple words; they seized him on the tenderest side of his character—for his heart was generous, and no one, except his lost wife and his loving child, had ever before discovered it to be so. Has it ever happened to you, reader, to be appreciated on the one point of the good or the great that is in you—on which secretly you value yourself most—but for which nobody, not admitted into your heart of hearts, has given you credit? If that has happened to you, judge what Duplessis felt when the fittest representative of that divine chivalry which, if sometimes deficient in head, owes all that exalts it to riches of heart, spoke thus to the professional moneymaker, whose qualities of head were so acknowledged that a compliment to them would be a hollow impertinence, and whose qualities of heart had never yet received a compliment!

Duplessis started from his seat and embraced Alain, murmuring, "Listen to me, I love you—I never had a son—be mine—Rochebriant shall be my daughter's dot."

Alain returned the embrace, and then recoiling, said: "Father, your first desire must be honour for your son. You have guessed my secret—I have learned to love Valerie. Seeing her out in the world, she seemed like other girls, fair and commonplace—seeing her—at your house, I have said to myself, 'There is the one girl fairer than all others in my eyes, and the one individual to whom all other girls are commonplace.'"

"Is that true?—is it?"

"True! does a gentilhomme ever lie? And out of that love for her has grown this immovable desire to be something worthy of her—something that may lift me from the vulgar platform of men who owe all to ancestors, nothing to themselves. Do you suppose for one moment that I, saved from ruin and penury by Valerie's father, could be base enough to say to her, 'In return be Madame la Marquise de Rochebriant'? Do you suppose that I, whom you would love and respect as son, could come to you and say: 'I am oppressed by your favours—I am crippled with debts—give me your millions and we are quits.' No, Duplessis! You, so well descended yourself—so superior as man amongst men that you would have won name and position had you been born the son of a shoeblack,—you would eternally despise the noble who, in days when all that we Bretons deem holy in noblesse are subjected to ridicule and contempt, should so vilely forget the only motto which the scutcheons of all gentilhommes have in common, 'Noblesse oblige.' War, with all its perils and all its grandeur,—war lifts on high the banners of France,—war, in which every ancestor of mine whom I care to recall aggrandised the name that descends to me. Let me then do as those before me have done; let me prove that I am worth something in myself, and then you and I are equals; and I can say with no humbled crest, 'Your benefits are accepted:' the man who has fought not ignobly for France may aspire to the hand of her daughter. Give me Valerie; as to her dot,—be it so, Rochebriant,—it will pass to her children."

"Alain! Alain! my friend! my son!—but if you fall."

"Valerie will give you a nobler son."

Duplessis moved away, sighing heavily; but he said no more in deprecation of Alain's martial resolves.

A Frenchman, however practical, however worldly, however philosophical he may be, who does not sympathise with the follies of honour—who does not concede indulgence to the hot blood of youth when he says, "My country is insulted and her banner is unfurled," may certainly be a man of excellent common sense; but if such men had been in the majority, Gaul would never have been France—Gaul would have been a province of Germany.

And as Duplessis walked homeward—he the calmest and most far-seeing of all authorities on the Bourse—the man who, excepting only De Mauleon, most decidedly deemed the cause of the war a blunder, and most forebodingly anticipated its issues, caught the prevalent enthusiasm. Everywhere he was stopped by cordial hands, everywhere met by congratulating smiles. "How right you have been, Duplessis, when you have laughed at those who have said, 'The Emperor is ill, decrepit, done up.'"

"Vive l'Empereur! at least we shall be face to face with those insolent Prussians!"

Before he arrived at his home, passing along the Boulevards, greeted by all the groups enjoying the cool night air before the cafes, Duplessis had caught the war epidemic.

Entering his hotel, he went at once to Valerie's chamber. "Sleep well to-night, child; Alain has told me that he adores thee, and if he will go to the war, it is that he may lay his laurels at thy feet. Bless thee, my child, thou couldst not have made a nobler choice."

Whether, after these words, Valerie slept well or not 'tis not for me to say; but if she did sleep, I venture to guess that her dreams were rose-coloured.

# CHAPTER VII.

All the earlier part of that next day, Graham Vane remained in-doors—a lovely day at Paris that 8th of July, and with that summer day all hearts at Paris were in unison. Discontent was charmed into enthusiasm—Belleville and Montmartre forgot the visions of Communism and Socialism and other "isms" not to be realised except in some undiscovered Atlantis!

The Emperor was the idol of the day—the names of Jules Favre and Gambetta were by-words of scorn. Even Armand Monnier, still out of work, beginning to feel the pinch of want, and fierce for any revolution that might turn topsy-turvy the conditions of labour,—even Armand Monnier was found among groups that were laying immortelles at the foot of the column in the Place Vendome, and heard to say to a fellow malcontent, with eyes uplifted to the statue of the First Napoleon, "Do you not feel at this moment that no Frenchman can be long angry with the Little Corporal? He denied La Liberte, but he gave La Gloire."

Heeding not the stir of the world without, Graham was compelling into one resolve the doubts and scruples which had so long warred against the heart which they ravaged, but could not wholly subdue.

The conversations with Mrs. Morley and Rochebriant had placed in a light in which he had not before regarded it, the image of Isaura.

He had reasoned from the starting-point of his love for her, and had sought to convince himself that against that love it was his duty to strive.

But now a new question was addressed to his conscience as well as to his heart. What though he had never formally declared to her his affection—never, in open words, wooed her as his own—never even hinted to her the hopes of a union which at one time he had fondly entertained,—still was it true that his love had been too transparent not to be detected by her, and not to have led her on to return it?

Certainly he had, as we know, divined that he was not indifferent to her: at Enghien, a year ago, that he had gained her esteem, and perhaps interested her fancy.

We know also how he had tried to persuade himself that the artistic temperament, especially when developed in women, is too elastic to suffer the things of real life to have lasting influence over happiness or sorrow,—that in the pursuits in which her thought and imagination found employ, in the excitement they sustained, and the fame to which they conduced, Isaura would be readily consoled for a momentary pang of disappointed affection. And that a man so alien as himself, both by nature and by habit, from the artistic world, was the very last person who could maintain deep and permanent impression on her actual life or her ideal dreams. But what if, as he gathered from the words of the fair American—what if, in all these assumptions, she was wholly mistaken? What if, in previously revealing his own heart, he had decoyed hers—what if, by a desertion she had no right to anticipate, he had blighted her future? What if this brilliant child of genius could love as warmly, as deeply, as enduringly as any simple village girl to whom there is no poetry except love? If this were so—what became the first claim on his honour, his conscience, his duty?

The force which but a few days ago his reasonings had given to the arguments that forbade him to think of Isaura, became weaker and weaker, as now in an altered mood of reflection he resummoned and reweighed them.

All those prejudices—which had seemed to him such rational common-sense truths, when translated from his own mind into the words of Lady Janet's letter,—was not Mrs. Morley right in denouncing them as the crotchets of an insolent egotism? Was it not rather to the favour than to the disparagement of Isaura, regarded even in the man's narrow-minded view of woman's dignity, that this orphan girl could, with character so unscathed, pass through the trying ordeal of the public babble, the public gaze-command alike the esteem of a woman so pure as Mrs. Morley, the reverence of a man so chivalrously sensitive to honour as Alain de Rochebriant?

Musing thus, Graham's countenance at last brightened—a glorious joy entered into and possessed him. He felt as a man who had burst asunder the swathes and trammels which had kept him galled and miserable with the sense of captivity, and from which some wizard spell that took strength from his own superstition had forbidden to struggle.

He was free!—and that freedom was rapture!—yes, his resolve was taken.

The day was now far advanced. He should have just time before the dinner with Duplessis to drive to A———, where he still supposed Isaura resided. How, as his fiacre rolled along the well-remembered road—how completely he lived in that world of romance of which he denied himself to be a denizen.

Arrived at the little villa, he found it occupied only by workmen—it was under repair. No one could tell him to what residence the ladies who occupied it the last year had removed.

"I shall learn from Mrs. Morley," thought Graham, and at her house he called in going back, but Mrs. Morley was not at home; he had only just time, after regaining his apartment, to change his dress for the dinner to which he was invited. As it was, he arrived late, and while apologising to his host for his want of punctuality, his tongue faltered. At the farther end of the room he saw a face, paler and thinner than when he had seen it last—a face across which a something of grief had gone.

The servant announced that dinner was served.

"Mr. Vane," said Duplessis, "will you take into dinner Mademoiselle Cicogna?"

# BOOK XI.

## CHAPTER I.

Amoung the frets and checks to the course that "never did run smooth," there is one which is sufficiently frequent, for many a reader will remember the irritation it caused him. You have counted on a meeting with the beloved one unwitnessed by others, an interchange of confessions and vows which others may not hear. You have arranged almost the words in which your innermost heart is to be expressed; pictured to yourself the very looks by which those words will have their sweetest reply. The scene you have thus imagined appears to you vivid and distinct, as if foreshown in a magic glass. And suddenly, after long absence, the meeting takes place in the midst of a common companionship: nothing that you wished to say can be said. The scene you pictured is painted out by the irony of Chance; and groups and backgrounds of which you had never dreamed start forth from the disappointing canvas. Happy if that be all! But sometimes, by a strange, subtle intuition, you feel that the person herself is changed; and sympathetic with that change, a terrible chill comes over your own heart.

Before Graham had taken his seat at the table beside Isaura, he felt that she was changed to him. He felt it by her very touch as their hands met at the first greeting,—by the tone of her voice in the few words that passed between them,—by the absence of all glow in the smile which had once lit up her face, as a burst of sunshine lights up a day in spring, and gives a richer gladness of colour to all its blooms. Once seated side by side they remained for some moments silent. Indeed, it would have been rather difficult for anything less than the wonderful intelligence of lovers between whom no wall can prevent the stolen interchange of tokens, to have ventured private talk of their own amid the excited converse which seemed all eyes, all tongues, all ears, admitting no one present to abstract himself from the common emotion. Englishmen do not recognise the old classic law which limited the number of guests, where banquets are meant to be pleasant, to that of the Nine-Muses. They invite guests so numerous, and so shy of launching talk across the table, that you may talk to the person next to you not less secure from listeners than you would be in talking with the stranger whom you met at a well in the Sahara. It is not so, except on state occasions, at Paris. Difficult there to retire into solitude with your next neighbour. The guests collected by Duplessis completed with himself the number of the Sacred Nine—the host, Valerie, Rochebriant, Graham, Isaura, Signora Venosta, La Duchesse de Tarascon, the wealthy and high-born Imperialist, Prince — — — —, and last and least, one who shall be nameless.

I have read somewhere, perhaps in one of the books which American superstition dedicates to the mysteries of Spiritualism, how a gifted seer, technically styled medium, sees at the opera a box which to other eyes appears untenanted and empty, but to him is full of ghosts, well dressed in costume de-regle, gazing on the boards and listening to the music. Like such ghosts are certain beings whom I call Lookers-on. Though still living, they have no share in the life they survey, they come as from another world to hear and to see what is passing in ours. In ours they lived once, but that troubled sort of life they have survived. Still we amuse them as stage-players and puppets amuse ourselves. One of these Lookers-on completed the party at the house of Duplessis.

How lively, how animated the talk was at the financier's pleasant table that day, the 8th of July! The excitement of the coming war made itself loud in every Gallic voice, and kindled in every Gallic eye. Appeals at every second minute were made, sometimes courteous, sometimes sarcastic, to the Englishman—promising son of an eminent statesman, and native of a country in which France is always coveting an ally, and always suspecting an enemy. Certainly Graham could not have found a less propitious moment for asking Isaura if she really were changed. And certainly the honour of Great Britain was never less ably represented (that is saying a great deal) than it was on this occasion by the young man reared to diplomacy and aspiring to Parliamentary distinction. He answered all questions with a constrained voice and an insipid smile,—all questions pointedly addressed to him as to what demonstrations of admiring sympathy with the gallantry of France might be expected from the English Government and people; what his acquaintance with the German races led him to suppose would be the effect on the Southern States of the first defeat of the Prussians; whether the man called Moltke was not a mere strategist on paper, a crotchety pedant; whether, if Belgium became so enamoured of the glories of France as to solicit fusion with her people, England would have a right to offer any objection,&c., &c. I do not think that during that festival Graham once thought one-millionth so much about the fates of Prussia and France as he did think, "Why is that girl so changed to me? Merciful heaven! is she lost to my life?"

By training, by habit, even by passion, the man was a genuine politician, cosmopolitan as well as patriotic, accustomed to consider what effect every vibration in that balance of European power, which no deep thinker can despise, must have on the destinies of civilised humanity, and on those of the nation to which he belongs. But are there not moments in life when the human heart suddenly narrows the circumference to which its emotions are extended? As the ebb of a tide, it retreats from the shores it had covered on its flow, drawing on with contracted waves the treasure-trove it has selected to hoard amid its deeps.

# CHAPTER II.

On quitting the dining-room, the Duchesse de Tarascon said to her host, on whose arm she was leaning, "Of course you and I must go with the stream. But is not all the fine talk that has passed to-day at your table, and in which we too have joined, a sort of hypocrisy? I may say this to you; I would say it to no other."

"And I say to you, Madame la Duchesse, that which I would say to no other. Thinking over it as I sit alone, I find myself making a 'terrible hazard;' but when I go abroad and become infected by the general enthusiasm, I pluck up gaiety of spirit, and whisper to myself, 'True, but it may be an enormous gain.' To get the left bank of the Rhine is a trifle; but to check in our next neighbour a growth which a few years hence would overtop us,—that is no trifle. And, be the gain worth the hazard or not, could the Emperor, could any Government likely to hold its own for a week, have declined to take the chance of the die?"

The Duchesse mused a moment, and meanwhile the two seated themselves on a divan in the corner of the salon. Then she said very slowly—

"No Government that held its tenure on popular suffrage could have done so. But if the Emperor had retained the personal authority which once allowed the intellect of one man to control and direct the passions of many, I think the war would have been averted. I have reason to know that the Emperor gave his emphatic support to the least bellicose members of the Council, and that Gramont's speech did not contain the passage that precipitates hostilities when the Council in which it was framed broke up. These fatal Ministers found the Chamber, and the reports of the popular excitement which could not be resisted without imminent danger of revolution. It is Paris that has forced the war on the Emperor. But enough of this subject. What must be, must, and, as you say, the gain may be greater than the hazard. I come to something else you whispered to me before we went in to dinner,—a sort of complaint which wounds me sensibly. You say I had assisted to a choice of danger and possibly of death a very distant connection of mine, who might have been a very near connection of yours. You mean Alain de Rochebriant?"

"Yes; I accept him as a suitor for the hand of my only daughter."

"I am so glad, not for your sake so much as for his. No one can know him well without appreciating in him the finest qualities of the finest order of the French noble; but having known your pretty Valerie so long, my congratulations are for the man who can win her. Meanwhile, hear my explanation: when I promised Alain any interest I can command for the grade of officer in a regiment of Mobiles, I knew not that he had formed, or was likely to form, ties or duties to keep him at home. I withdraw my promise."

"No, Duchesse, fulfil it. I should be disloyal indeed if I robbed a sovereign under whose tranquil and prosperous reign I have acquired, with no dishonour, the fortune which Order proffers to Commerce, of one gallant defender in the hour of need. And, speaking frankly, if Alain were really my son, I think I am Frenchman enough to remember that France is my mother."

"Say no more, my friend—say no more," cried the Duchesse, with the warm blood of the heart rushing through all the delicate coatings of pearl-powder. "If every Frenchman felt as you do; if in this Paris of ours all hostilities of class may merge in the one thought of the common country; if in French hearts there yet thrills the same sentiment as that which, in the terrible days when all other ties were rent asunder, revered France as mother, and rallied her sons to her aid against the confederacy of Europe,—why, then, we need not grow pale with dismay at the sight of a Prussian needle-gun. Hist! look yonder: is not that a tableau of Youth in Arcady? Worlds rage around, and Love, unconcerned, whispers to Love!" The Duchesse here pointed to a corner of the adjoining room in which Alain and Valerie sat apart, he whispering into her ear; her cheek downcast, and, even seen at that distance, brightened by the delicate tenderness of its blushes.

# CHAPTER III.

But in that small assembly there were two who did not attract the notice of Duplessis or of the lady of the Imperial Court. While the Prince —— and the placid Looker-on were engaged at a contest of ecarte, with the lively Venosta, for the gallery, interposing criticisms and admonitions, Isaura was listlessly turning over a collection of photographs, strewed on a table that stood near to an open window in the remoter angle of the room, communicating with a long and wide balcony filled partially with flowers and overlooking the Champs Elysees, softly lit up by the innumerable summer stars. Suddenly a whisper, the command of which she could not resist, thrilled through her ear, and sent the blood rushing back to her heart.

"Do you remember that evening at Enghien? how I said that our imagination could not carry us beyond the question whether we two should be gazing together that night twelve months on that star which each of us had singled out from the hosts of heaven? That was the 8th of July. It is the 8th of July once more. Come and seek for our chosen star—come. I have something to say, which say I must. Come."

Mechanically, as it were,—mechanically, as they tell us the Somnambulist obeys the Mesmeriser,—Isaura obeyed that summons. In a kind of dreamy submission she followed his steps, and found herself on the balcony, flowers around her and stars above, by the side of the man who had been to her that being ever surrounded by flowers and lighted by stars,—the ideal of Romance to the heart of virgin Woman.

"Isaura," said the Englishman, softly. At the sound of her own name for the first time heard from those lips, every nerve in her frame quivered. "Isaura, I have tried to live without you. I cannot. You are all in all to me: without you it seems to me as if earth had no flowers, and even heaven had withdrawn its stars. Are there differences between us, differences of taste, of sentiments, of habits, of thought? Only let me hope that you can love me a tenth part so much as I love you, and such differences cease to be discord. Love harmonises all sounds, blends all colours into its own divine oneness of heart and soul. Look up! is not the star which this time last year invited our gaze above, is it not still there? Does it not still invite our gaze? Isaura, speak!"

"Hush, hush, hush,"—the girl could say no more, but she recoiled from his side.

The recoil did not wound him: there was no hate in it. He advanced, he caught her hand, and continued, in one of those voices which become so musical in summer nights under starry skies:

"Isaura, there is one name which I can never utter without a reverence due to the religion which binds earth to heaven—a name which to man should be the symbol of life cheered and beautified, exalted, hallowed. That name is 'wife.' Will you take that name from me?"

And still Isaura made no reply. She stood mute, and cold, and rigid as a statue of marble. At length, as if consciousness had been arrested and was struggling back, she sighed heavily, and passed her hands slowly over her forehead.

"Mockery, mockery," she said then, with a smile half bitter, half plaintive, on her colourless lips. "Did you wait to ask me that question till you knew what my answer must be? I have pledged the name of wife to another."

"No, no; you say that to rebuke, to punish me! Unsay it! unsay it!"

Isaura beheld the anguish of his face with bewildered eyes. "How can my words pain you?" she said, drearily. "Did you not write that I had unfitted myself to be wife to you?"

"I?"

"That I had left behind me the peaceful immunities of private life? I felt you were so right! Yes! I am affianced to one who thinks that in spite of that misfortune—"

"Stop, I command you—stop! You saw my letter to Mrs. Morley. I have not had one moment free from torture and remorse since I wrote it. But whatever in that letter you might justly resent—"

"I did not resent—"

Graham heard not the interruption, but hurried on. "You would forgive could you read my heart. No matter. Every sentiment in that letter, except those which conveyed admiration, I retract. Be mine, and instead of presuming to check in you the irresistible impulse of genius to the first place in the head or the heart of the world, I teach myself to encourage, to share, to exult in it. Do you know what a difference there is between the absent one and the present one—between the distant image against whom our doubts, our fears, our suspicions, raise up hosts of imaginary giants, barriers of visionary walls, and the beloved face before the sight of which the hosts are fled, the walls are vanished? Isaura, we meet again. You know now from my own lips that I love you. I think your lips will not deny that you love me. You say that you are affianced to another. Tell the man frankly, honestly, that you mistook your heart. It is not yours to give. Save yourself, save him, from a union in which there can be no happiness."

"It is too late," said Isaura, with hollow tones, but with no trace of vacillating weakness on her brow and lips. "Did I say now to that other one, 'I break the faith that I pledged to you,' I should kill him, body and soul. Slight thing though I be, to him I am all in all; to you, Mr. Vane, to you a memory—the memory of one whom a year, perhaps a month, hence, you will rejoice to think you have escaped."

She passed from him—passed away from the flowers and the starlight; and when Graham,—recovering from the stun of her crushing words, and with the haughty mien and stop of the man who goes forth from the ruin of his hopes, leaning for support upon his pride,—when Graham re-entered the room, all the guests had departed save only Alain, who was still exchanging whispered words with Valerie.

# CHAPTER IV.

The next day, at the hour appointed, Graham entered Alain's apartment. "I am glad to tell you," said the Marquis, gaily, "that the box has arrived, and we will very soon examine its contents. Breakfast claims precedence." During the meal Alain was in gay spirits, and did not at first notice the gloomy countenance and abstracted mood of his guest. At length, surprised at the dull response to his lively sallies on the part of a man generally so pleasant in the frankness of his speech, and the cordial ring of his sympathetic laugh, it occurred to him that the change in Graham must be ascribed to something that had gone wrong in the meeting with Isaura the evening before; and remembering the curtness with which Graham had implied disinclination to converse about the fair Italian, he felt perplexed how to reconcile the impulse of his good nature with the discretion imposed on his good-breeding. At all events, a compliment to the lady whom Graham had so admired could do no harm.

"How well Mademoiselle Cicogna looked last night!"

"Did she? It seemed to me that, in health at least, she did not look very well. Have you heard what day M. Thiers will speak on the war?"

"Thiers? No. Who cares about Thiers? Thank heaven his day is past! I don't know any unmarried woman in Paris, not even Valerie—I mean Mademoiselle Duplessis—who has so exquisite a taste in dress as Mademoiselle Cicogna. Generally speaking, the taste of a female author is atrocious."

"Really—I did not observe her dress. I am no critic on subjects so dainty as the dress of ladies, or the tastes of female authors."

"Pardon me," said the beau Marquis, gravely. "As to dress, I think that so essential a thing in the mind of woman, that no man who cares about women ought to disdain critical study of it. In woman, refinement of character is never found in vulgarity of dress. I have only observed that truth since I came up from Bretagne."

"I presume, my dear Marquis, that you may have read in Bretagne books which very few not being professed scholars have ever read at Paris; and possibly you may remember that Horace ascribes the most exquisite refinement in dress, denoted by the untranslatable words, 'simplex munditiis,' to a lady who was not less distinguished by the ease and rapidity with which she could change her affection. Of course that allusion does not apply to Mademoiselle Cicogna, but there are many other exquisitely dressed ladies at Paris of whom an ill-fated admirer

*'fidem*
*Mutatosque deos flebit.'*

"Now, with your permission, we will adjourn to the box of letters."

The box being produced and unlocked, Alain looked with conscientious care at its contents before he passed over to Graham's inspection a few epistles, in which the Englishman immediately detected the same handwriting as that of the letter from Louise which Richard King had bequeathed to him.

They were arranged and numbered chronologically.

*LETTER I.*

*DEAR M. LE MARQUIS,—How can I thank you sufficiently for obtaining and remitting to me those certificates? You are too aware of the unhappy episode in my life not to know how inestimable is the service you render me. I am saved all further molestation from the man who had indeed no right over my freedom, but whose persecution might compel me to the scandal and disgrace of an appeal to the law for protection, and the avowal of the illegal marriage into which I was duped. I would rather be torn limb from limb by wild horses, like the Queen in the history books, than dishonour myself and the ancestry which I may at least claim on the mother's side, by proclaiming that I had lived with that low Englishman as his wife, when I was only—O heavens, I cannot conclude the sentence!*

*"No, Mons. le Marquis, I am in no want of the pecuniary aid you so generously wish to press on me. Though I know not where to address my poor dear uncle,—though I doubt, even if I did, whether I could venture to confide to him the secret known only to yourself as to the name I now bear—and if he hear of me at all he must believe me dead,—yet I have enough left of the money he last remitted to me for present support; and when that fails, I think, what with my knowledge of English and such other slender accomplishments as I possess, I could maintain myself as a teacher or governess in some German family. At all events, I will write to you again soon, and I entreat you to let me know all you can learn about my uncle. I feel so grateful to you for your just disbelief of the horrible calumny*

*which must be so intolerably galling to a man so proud, and, whatever his errors, so incapable of a baseness.*

*"Direct to me Poste restante, Augsburg.*

*"Yours with all consideration,*

*LETTER II.*

(Seven months after the date of Letter 1.)

*"AUGSBURG.*

*"DEAR M. LE MARQUIS,—I thank you for your kind little note informing me of the pains you have taken, as yet with no result, to ascertain what has become of my unfortunate uncle. My life since I last wrote has been a very quiet one. I have been teaching among a few families here; and among my pupils are two little girls of very high birth. They have taken so great a fancy to me that their mother has just asked me to come and reside at their house as governess. What wonderfully kind hearts those Germans have,—so simple, so truthful! They raise no troublesome questions,—accept my own story implicitly." Here follow a few commonplace sentences about the German character, and a postscript. "I go into my new home next week. When you hear more of my uncle, direct to me at the Countess von Rudesheim, Schloss ————, near Berlin."*

"Rudesheim!" Could this be the relation, possibly the wife, of the Count von Rudesheim with whom Graham had formed acquaintance last year?
LETTER III.

(Between three and four years after the date of the last.)

*"You startle me indeed, dear M. le Marquis. My uncle said to have been recognised in Algeria under another name, a soldier in the Algerian army? My dear, proud, luxurious uncle! Ah, I cannot believe it, any more than you do: but I long eagerly for such further news as you can learn of him. For myself, I shall perhaps surprise you when I say I am about to be married. Nothing can exceed the amiable kindness I have received from the Rudesheims since I have been in their house. For the last year especially I have been treated on equal terms as one of the family. Among the habitual visitors at the house is a gentleman of noble birth, but not of rank too high, nor of fortune too great, to make a marriage with the French widowed governess a misalliance. I am sure that he loves me sincerely; and he is the only man I ever met whose love I have cared to win. We are to be married in the course of the year.*

*Of course he is ignorant of my painful history, and will never learn it. And after all, Louise D— — is dead. In the home to which I am about to remove, there is no probability that the wretched Englishman can ever cross my path. My secret is as safe with you as in the grave that holds her whom in the name of Louise D— — you once loved. Henceforth I shall trouble you no more with my letters; but if you hear anything decisively authentic of my uncle's fate, write me a line at any time, directed as before to Madame — —, enclosed to the Countess von Rudesheim.*

*"And accept, for all the kindness you have ever shown me, as to one whom you did not disdain to call a kinswoman, the assurance of my undying gratitude. In the alliance she now makes, your kinswoman does not discredit the name through which she is connected with the yet loftier line of Rochebriant."*

To this letter the late Marquis had appended in pencil. "Of course Rochebriant never denies the claim of a kinswoman, even though a drawing-master's daughter. Beautiful creature, Louise, but a termagant. I could not love Venus if she were a termagant. L.'s head turned by the unlucky discovery that her mother was noble. In one form or other, every woman has the same disease—vanity. Name of her intended not mentioned—easily found out."

The next letter was dated May 7, 1859, on black-edged paper, and contained but these lines: "I was much comforted by your kind visit yesterday, dear Marquis. My affliction has been heavy: but for the last two years my poor husband's conduct has rendered my life unhappy, and I am recovering the shock of his sudden death. It is true that I and the children are left very ill provided for; but I cannot accept your generous offer of aid. Have no fear as to my future fate. Adieu, my dear Marquis! This will reach you just before you start for Naples. Bon voyage." There was no address on this note-no postmark on the envelope-evidently sent by hand.

The last note, dated 1861, March 20, was briefer than its predecessor. "I have taken your advice, dear Marquis; and, overcoming all scruples, I have accepted his kind offer, on the condition that I am never to be taken to England. I had no option in this marriage. I can now own to you that my poverty had become urgent.—Yours, with inalienable gratitude. This last note, too, was without postmark, and was evidently sent by hand.

"There are no other letters, then, from this writer?" asked Graham; "and no further clue as to her existence?"

"None that I have discovered; and I see now why I preserved these letters. There is nothing in their contents not creditable to my poor father. They show how capable he was of good-natured disinterested kindness towards even a distant relation of whom he could certainly not have been proud, judging not only by his own pencilled note, or by the writer's condition as a governess, but by her loose sentiments as to the marriage tie. I have not the slightest idea who she could be. I never at least heard of one connected, however distantly, with my family, whom I could identify with the writer of these letters."

"I may hold them a short time in my possession?"

"Pardon me a preliminary question. If I may venture to form a conjecture, the object of your search must be connected with your countryman, whom the lady politely calls the 'wretched Englishman;' but I own I should not like to lend, through these letters, a pretence to any steps that may lead to a scandal in which my father's name or that of any member of my family could be mixed up."

"Marquis, it is to prevent the possibility of all scandal that I ask you to trust these letters to my discretion."

"Foi de gentilhomme?"

"Foi de gentilhomme!"

"Take them. When and where shall we meet again?"

"Soon, I trust; but I must leave Paris this evening. I am bound to Berlin in quest of this Countess von Rudesheim: and I fear that in a very few days intercourse between France and the German frontier will be closed upon travellers."

After a few more words not worth recording, the two young men shook hands and parted.

# CHAPTER V.

It was with an interest languid and listless indeed, compared with that which he would have felt a day before, that Graham mused over the remarkable advances towards the discovery of Louise Duval which were made in the letters he had perused. She had married, then, first a foreigner, whom she spoke of as noble, and whose name and residence could be easily found through the Countess von Rudesheim. The marriage did not seem to have been a happy one. Left a widow in reduced circumstances, she had married again, evidently without affection. She was living so late as 1861, and she had children living is 1859: was the child referred to by Richard King one of them?

The tone and style of the letters served to throw some light on the character of the writer: they evinced pride, stubborn self-will, and unamiable hardness of nature; but her rejection of all pecuniary aid from a man like the late Marquis de Rochebriant betokened a certain dignity of sentiment. She was evidently, whatever her strange ideas about her first marriage with Richard King, no vulgar woman of gallantry; and there must have been some sort of charm about her to have excited a friendly interest in a kinsman so remote, and a man of pleasure so selfish, as her high-born correspondent.

But what now, so far as concerned his own happiness, was the hope, the probable certainty, of a speedy fulfilment of the trust bequeathed to him? Whether the result, in the death of the mother, and more especially of the child, left him rich, or, if the last survived, reduced his fortune to a modest independence, Isaura was equally lost to him, and fortune became valueless. But his first emotions on recovering from the shock of hearing from Isaura's lips that she was irrevocably affianced to another, were not those of self-reproach. They were those of intense bitterness against her who, if really so much attached to him as he had been led to hope, could within so brief a time reconcile her heart to marriage with another. This bitterness was no doubt unjust; but I believe it to be natural to men of a nature so proud and of affections so intense as Graham's, under similar defeats of hope. Resentment is the first impulse in a man loving with the whole ardour of his soul, rejected, no matter why or wherefore, by the woman by whom he had cause to believe he himself was beloved; and though Graham's standard of honour was certainly the reverse of low, yet man does not view honour in the same light as woman does, when involved in analogous difficulties of position. Graham conscientiously thought that if Isaura so loved him as to render distasteful an engagement to another which could only very recently have been contracted, it would be more honourable frankly so to tell the accepted suitor than to leave him in ignorance that her heart was estranged. But these engagements are very solemn things with girls like Isaura, and hers was no ordinary obligation of woman-honour. Had the accepted one been superior in rank-fortune—all that flatters the ambition of woman in the choice of marriage; had he been resolute, and strong, and self-dependent amid the trials and perils of life—then possibly the woman's honour might find excuse in escaping the penalties of its pledge. But the poor, ailing, infirm, morbid boy-poet, who looked to her as his saving angel in body, in mind, and soul-to say to him, "Give me back my freedom," would be to abandon him to death and to sin. But Graham could not of course divine why what he as a man thought right was to Isaura as woman impossible: and he returned to his old prejudiced notion that there is no real depth and ardour of affection for human lovers in the poetess whose mind and heart are devoted to the creation of imaginary heroes. Absorbed in reverie, he took his way slowly and with downcast looks towards the British embassy, at which it was well to ascertain whether the impending war yet necessitated special passports for Germany.

"Bon-jour, cher ami," said a pleasant voice; "and how long have you been at Paris?"

"Oh, my dear M. Savarin! charmed to see you looking so well! Madame well too, I trust? My kindest regards to her. I have been in Paris but a day or two, and I leave this evening."

"So soon? The war frightens you away, I suppose. Which way are you going now?"

"To the British embassy."

"Well, I will go with you so far—it is in my own direction. I have to call at the charming Italian's with my congratulations—on news I only heard this morning."

"You mean Mademoiselle Cicogna—and the news that demands congratulations—her approaching marriage!"

"Mon Dieu! when could you have heard of that?"

"Last night at the house of M. Duplessis."

"Parbleu! I shall scold her well for confiding to her new friend Valerie the secret she kept from her old friends, my wife and myself."

"By the way," said Graham, with a tone of admirably-feigned indifference, "who is the happy man? That part of the secret I did not hear."

"Can't you guess?" "NO."

"Gustave Rameau."

"Ah!" Graham almost shrieked, so sharp and shrill was his cry. "Ah! I ought indeed to have guessed that!"

"Madame Savarin, I fancy, helped to make up the marriage. I hope it may turn out well; certainly it will be his salvation. May it be for her happiness!"

"No doubt of that! Two poets-born for each other, I dare say. Adieu, my dear Savarin! Here we are at the embassy."

# CHAPTER VI.

That evening Graham found himself in the coupe of the express train to Strasbourg. He had sent to engage the whole coupe to himself, but that was impossible. One place was bespoken as far as C— — —-, after which Graham might prosecute his journey alone on paying for the three places.

When he took his seat another man was in the further corner whom he scarcely noticed. The train shot rapidly on for some leagues. Profound silence in the coupe, save at moments those heavy impatient sighs that came from the very depths of the heart, and of which he who sighs is unconscious, burst from the Englishman's lips, and drew on him the observant side-glance of his fellow-traveller.

At length the fellow-traveller said in very good English, though with French accent, "Would you object, sir, to my lighting my little carriage-lantern? I am in the habit of reading in the night train, and the wretched lamp they give us does not permit that. But if you wish to sleep, and my lantern would prevent you doing so, consider my request unasked."

"You are most courteous, sir. Pray light your lantern—that will not interfere with my sleep."

As Graham thus answered, far away from the place and the moment as his thoughts were, it yet faintly struck him that he had heard that voice before.

The man produced a small lantern, which he attached to the window-sill, and drew forth from a small leathern bag sundry newspapers and pamphlets. Graham flung himself back, and in a minute or so again came his sigh.

"Allow me to offer you those evening journals—you may not have had time to read them before starting," said the fellow-traveller, leaning forward, and extending the newspapers with one hand, while with the other he lifted his lantern. Graham turned, and the faces of the two men were close to each other—Graham with his travelling-cap drawn over his brows, the other with head uncovered.

"Monsieur Lebeau!"

"Bon soir, Mr. Lamb!"

Again silence for a moment or so. Monsieur Lebeau then broke it—

"I think, Mr. Lamb, that in better society than that of the Faubourg Montmartre you are known under another name." Graham had no heart then for the stage-play of a part, and answered, with quiet haughtiness, "Possibly—and what name?"

"Graham Vane. And, sir," continued Lebeau, with a haughtiness equally quiet, but somewhat more menacing, "since we two gentlemen find ourselves thus close, do I ask too much if I inquire why you condescend to seek my acquaintance in disguise?"

"Monsieur le Vicomte de Mauleon, when you talk of disguise, is it too much to inquire why my acquaintance was accepted by Monsieur Lebeau?"

"Ha! Then you confess that it was Victor de Mauleon whom you sought when you first visited the cafe Jean Jacques?"

"Frankly I confess it."

Monsieur Lebeau drew himself back, and seemed to reflect.

"I see! Solely for the purpose of learning whether Victor de Mauleon could give you any information about Louise Duval. Is it so?"

"Monsieur le Vicomte, you say truly."

Again M. Lebeau paused as if in reflection; and Graham, in that state of mind when a man who may most despise and detest the practice of duelling, may yet feel a thrill of delight if some homicide would be good enough to put him out of his misery, flung aside his cap, lifted his broad frank forehead, and stamped his foot impatiently as if to provoke a quarrel.

M. Lebeau lowered his spectacles, and, with those calm, keen, searching eyes of his, gazed at the Englishman.

"It strikes me," he said, with a smile, the fascination of which not even those faded whiskers could disguise—"it strikes me that there are two ways in which gentlemen such as you and I are can converse: firstly, with reservation and guard against each other; secondly, with perfect openness. Perhaps of the two I have more need of reservation and wary guard against any stranger than you have. Allow me to propose the alternative—perfect openness. What say you?" and he extended his hand.

"Perfect openness," answered Graham, softened into sudden liking for this once terrible swordsman, and shaking, as an Englishman shakes, the hand held out to him in peace by the man from whom he had anticipated quarrel.

"Permit me now, before you address any questions to me, to put one to you. How did you learn that Victor de Mauleon was identical with Jean Lebeau?"

"I heard that from an agent of the police."

"Ah!"

"Whom I consulted as to the means of ascertaining whether Louise Duval was alive,—if so, where she could be found."

"I thank you very much for your information. I had no notion that the police of Paris had divined the original alias of poor Monsieur Lebeau, though something occurred at Lyons which made me suspect it. Strange that the Government, knowing through the police that Victor de Mauleon, a writer they had no reason to favour, had been in so humble a position, should never, even in their official journals, have thought it prudent to say so! But, now I think of it, what if they had? They could prove nothing against Jean Lebeau. They could but say, 'Jean Lebeau is suspected to be too warm a lover of liberty, too earnest a friend of the people, and Jean Lebeau is the editor of La Sens Commun.' Why, that assertion would have made Victor de Mauleon the hero of the Reds, the last thing a prudent Government could desire. I thank you cordially for your frank reply. Now, what question would you put to me?"

"In one word, all you can tell me about Louise Duval."

"You shall have it. I had heard vaguely in my young days that a half-sister of mine by my father's first marriage with Mademoiselle de Beauvilliers had—when in advanced middle life he married a second time—conceived a dislike for her mother-in-law, and, being of age, with an independent fortune of her own, had quitted the house, taken up her residence with an elderly female relative, and there had contracted a marriage with a man who gave her lessons in drawing. After that marriage, which my father in vain tried to prevent, my sister was renounced by her family. That was all I knew till, after I came into my inheritance by the death of both my parents, I learned from my father's confidential lawyer that the drawing-master, M. Duval, had soon dissipated his wife's fortune, become a widower with one child—a girl—and fallen into great distress. He came to my father, begging for pecuniary aid. My father, though by no means rich, consented to allow him a yearly pension, on condition that he never revealed to his child her connection with our family. The man agreed to the condition, and called at my father's lawyer quarterly for his annuity. But the lawyer informed me that this deduction from my income had ceased, that M. Duval had not for a year called or sent for the sum due to him, and that he must therefore be dead. One day my valet informed me that a young lady wished to see me—in those days young ladies very often called on me. I desired her to be shown in. There entered a young creature, almost of my own age, who, to my amazement saluted me as uncle. This was the child of my half-sister. Her father had been dead several months, fulfilling very faithfully the condition on which he had held his pension, and the girl never dreaming of the claims that, if wise, poor child, she ought not to have cared for, viz.,—to that obsolete useless pauper birthright, a branch on the family tree of a French noble. But in pinch of circumstance, and from female curiosity, hunting among the papers her father had left for some clue to the reasons for the pension he had received, she found letters from her mother, letters from my father, which indisputably proved that she was grandchild to the fue Vicomte de Mauleon, and niece to myself. Her story as told to me was very pitiable. Conceiving herself to be nothing higher in birth than daughter to this drawing-master, at his death, poor, penniless orphan that she was, she had accepted the hand of an English student of medicine whom she did not care for. Miserable with this man, on finding by the documents I refer to that she was my niece, she came to me for comfort and counsel. What counsel could I or any man give to her but to make the best of what had happened, and live with her husband? But then she started another question. It seems that she had been talking with some one, I think her landlady, or some other woman with whom she had made acquaintance—was she legally married to this man? Had he not entrapped her ignorance into a false marriage? This became a grave question, and I sent at once to my lawyer. On hearing the circumstances, he at once declared that the marriage was not legal according to the laws of France. But, doubtless, her English soi-disant husband was not cognisant of the French law, and a legal marriage could, with his assent, be at once solemnised. Monsieur Vane, I cannot find words to convey to you the joy that poor girl showed in her face and in her words when she learned that she was not bound to pass her life with that man as his wife. It was in vain to talk and reason with her. Then arose the other question, scarcely less important. True, the marriage was not legal, but would it not be better on all accounts to take steps to have it formally annulled, thus freeing her from the harassment of any claim the Englishman might advance, and enabling her to establish the facts in a right position, not injurious to her honour in the eyes of any future suitor to her hand? She would not hear of such a proposal. She declared that she could not bring to the family she pined to re-enter the scandal of disgrace. To allow that she had made such a misalliance would be bad enough in itself; but to proclaim to the world that, though nominally the wife, she had in fact been only the mistress of this medical student—she would rather throw herself into the Seine. All she desired was to fund some refuge, some hiding-place for a time, whence she could write to the man informing him that he had no lawful hold on her. Doubtless he would not seek then to molest her. He would return to his own country, and be effaced from her life. And then, her story unknown, she might form a more suitable alliance. Fiery young creature though she was—true De Mauleon in being so fiery—she interested me strongly. I should say that she was wonderfully handsome; and though imperfectly educated, and brought up in circumstances so lowly, there was nothing common about her—a certain je ne sais quoi of stateliness and race. At all events she did with me what she wished. I agreed to aid her desire of a refuge and hiding-place. Of course I could not lodge her in my own apartment, but I induced a female relation of her mother's, an old lady living at Versailles, to receive her, stating her birth, but of course concealing her illegal marriage.

"From time to time I went to see her. But one day I found this restless bright-plumaged bird flown. Among the ladies who visited at her relative's house was a certain Madame Marigny, a very pretty young widow. Madame Marigny and Louise formed a sudden and intimate friendship. The widow was moving from Versailles into an apartment at Paris, and invited Louise to share it. She had consented. I was not pleased at this; for the widow was too young, and too much of a coquette, to be a safe companion to Louise. But though professing much gratitude and great regard for me, I had no power of controlling the poor girl's actions. Her nominal husband, meanwhile, had left France, and nothing more was heard or known of him. I saw that the best thing that could possibly befall Louise was marriage with some one rich enough to gratify her taste for luxury and pomp; and that if such a marriage offered itself, she might be induced to free it from all possible embarrassment by procuring the annulment of the former, from which she had hitherto shrunk in such revolt. This opportunity presented itself. A man already rich, and in a career that promised to make him infinitely richer, an associate of mine in those days when I was rapidly squandering the remnant of my inheritance—this man saw her at the opera in company with Madame Marigny, fell violently in love with her, and ascertaining her relationship to me, besought an introduction. I was delighted to give it; and, to say the truth, I was then so reduced to the bottom of my casket, I felt that it was becoming impossible for me to continue the aid I had hitherto given to Louise, and—what then would become of her? I thought it fair to tell Louvier—"

"Louvier—the financier?"

"Ah, that was a slip of the tongue, but no matter; there is no reason for concealing his name. I thought it right, I say, to tell Louvier confidentially the history of the unfortunate illegal marriage. It did not damp his ardour. He wooed her to the best of his power, but she evidently took him into great dislike. One day she sent for me in much excitement, showed me some advertisements in the French journals which, though not naming her, evidently pointed at her, and must have been dictated by her soi-disant husband. The advertisements might certainly lead to her discovery if she remained in Paris. She entreated my consent to remove elsewhere. Madame Marigny had her own reason for leaving Paris, and would accompany her. I supplied her with the necessary means, and a day or two afterwards she and her friend departed, as I understood, for Brussels. I received no letter from her; and my own affairs so seriously pre-occupied me, that poor Louise might have passed altogether out of my thoughts, had it not been for the suitor she had left in despair behind. Louvier besought me to ascertain her address; but I could give him no, other clue to it than that she said she was going to Brussels, but should soon remove to some quiet village. It was not for a long time—I can't remember how long—it might be several weeks, perhaps two or three months, that I received a short note from her stating that she waited for a small remittance, the last she would accept from me, as she was resolved, so soon as her health would permit, to find means to maintain herself—and telling me to direct to her, Poste restante, Aix-la-Chapelle. I sent her the sum she asked, perhaps a little more, but with a confession reluctantly wrung from me that I was a ruined man; and I urged her to think very seriously before she refused the competence and position which a union with M. Louvier would insure.

"This last consideration so pressed on me that, when Louvier called on me, I think that day or the nests I gave him Louise's note, and told him that, if he were still as much in love with her as ever, les absents ont toujours tort, and he had better go to Aix-la-Chapelle and find her out; that he had my hearty approval of his wooing, and consent to his marriage, though I still urged the wisdom and fairness, if she would take the preliminary step—which, after all, the French law frees as much as possible from pain and scandal—of annulling the irregular marriage into which her childlike youth had been decoyed.

"Louvier left me for Aix-la-Chapelle. The very next day came that cruel affliction which made me a prey to the most intolerable calumny, which robbed me of every friend, which sent me forth from my native country penniless, and resolved to be nameless—until—until—well, until my hour could come again—every dog, if not hanged, has its day;—when that affliction befell me, I quitted France, heard no more of Louvier nor of Louise; indeed, no letter addressed to me at Paris would have reached—"

The man paused here, evidently with painful emotion. He resumed in the quiet matter-of-fact way in which he had commenced his narrative.

"Louise had altogether faded out of my remembrance until your question revived it. As it happened, the question came at the moment when I meditated resuming my real name and social position. In so doing, I should of course come in contact with my old acquaintance Louvier; and the name of Louise was necessarily associated with us. I called on him, and made myself known. The slight information I gave you as to my niece was gleaned from him.

"I may now say more. It appears that when he arrived at Aix-la-Chapelle he found that Louise Duval had left it a day or two previously, and according to scandal had been for some time courted by a wealthy and noble lover, whom she had gone to Munich to meet. Louvier believed this tale: quitted Aix indignantly, and never heard more of her. The probability is, M. Vane, that she must have been long dead. But if living still, I feel quite sure that she will communicate with me some day or other. Now that I have reappeared in Paris in my own name—entered into a career that, for good or for evil, must ere long bring my name very noisily before the public—Louise cannot fail to hear of my existence and my whereabouts; and unless I am utterly mistaken as to her character, she will assuredly inform me of her own. Oblige me with your address, and in that case I will let you know. Of course I take for granted the assurance you gave me last year, that you only desire to discover her in order to render her some benefit, not to injure or molest her?"

"Certainly. To that assurance I pledge my honour. Any letter with which you may favour me had better be directed to my London address; here is my card. But, M. le Vicomte, there is one point on which pray pardon me if I question you still. Had you no suspicion that there was one reason why this lady might have quitted Paris so hastily, and have so shrunk from the thought of a marriage so advantageous, in a worldly point of view, as that with M. Louvier,—namely, that she anticipated the probability of becoming the mother of a child by the man whom she refused to acknowledge as a husband?"

"That idea did not strike me until you asked me if she had a child. Should your conjecture be correct, it would obviously increase her repugnance to apply for the annulment of her illegal marriage. But if Louise is still living and comes across me, I do not doubt that, the motives for concealment no longer operating, she will confide to me the truth. Since we have been talking together thus frankly, I suppose I may fairly ask whether I do not guess correctly in supposing that this soi-disant husband, whose name I forget,—Mac—something, perhaps, Scotch-I think she said he was Ecossais,—is dead and has left by will some legacy to Louise and any child she may have borne to him?"

"Not exactly so. The man, as you say, is dead; but he bequeathed no legacy to the lady who did not hold herself married to him. But there are those connected with him who, knowing the history, think that some compensation is due for the wrong so unconsciously done to her, and yet more to any issue of a marriage not meant to be irregular or illegal. Permit me now to explain why I sought you in another guise and name than my own. I could scarcely place in M. Lebeau the confidence which I now unreservedly place in the Vicomte de Mauleon."

"Cela va sans dire. You believed, then, that calumny about the jewels; you do not believe it now?"

"Now! my amazement is, that any one who had known you could believe it."

"Oh, how often, and with tears of rage in my exile—my wanderings—have I asked that question of myself! That rage has ceased; and I have but one feeling left for that credulous, fickle Paris, of which one day I was the idol, the next the byword. Well, a man sometimes plays chess more skilfully for having been long a mere bystander. He understands better how to move, and when to sacrifice the pieces. Politics, M. Vane, is the only exciting game left to me at my years. At yours, there is still that of love. How time flies! we are nearing the station at which I descend. I have kinsfolk of my mother's in these districts. They are not Imperialists; they are said to be powerful in the department. But before I apply to them in my own name, I think it prudent that M. Lebeau should quietly ascertain what is their real strength, and what would be the prospects of success if Victor de Mauleon offered himself as depute at the next election. Wish him joy, M. Vane! If he succeed, you will hear of him some day crowned in the Capitol, or hurled from the Tarpeian rock."

Here the train stopped. The false Lebeau gathered up his papers, readjusted his spectacles and his bag, descended lightly, and, pressing Graham's hand as he paused at the door, said, "Be sure I will not forget your address if I have anything to say. Bon voyage!"

# CHAPTER VII.

Graham continued his journey to Strasbourg. On arriving there he felt very unwell. Strong though his frame was, the anguish and self-struggle through which he had passed since the day he had received in London Mrs. Morley's letter, till that on which he had finally resolved on his course of conduct at Paris, and the shock which had annihilated his hopes in Isaura's rejection, had combined to exhaust its endurance, and fever had already commenced when he took his place in the coupe. If there be a thing which a man should not do when his system is undermined, and his pulse between 90 and 100, it is to travel all night by a railway express. Nevertheless, as the Englishman's will was yet stronger than his frame, he would not give himself more than an hour's rest, and again started for Berlin. Long before he got to Berlin, the will failed him—as well as the frame. He was lifted out of the carriage, taken to a hotel in a small German town, and six hours afterwards he was delirious. It was fortunate for him that under such circumstances plenty of money and Scott's circular-notes for some hundreds were found in his pocketbook, so that he did not fail to receive attentive nursing and skilful medical treatment. There, for the present, I must leave him—leave him for how long? But any village apothecary could say that fever such as his must run its course. He was still in bed, and very dimly—and that but at times—conscious, when the German armies were gathering round the penfold of Sedan.

# CHAPTER VIII.

When the news of the disastrous day at Sedan reached Paris, the first effect was that of timid consternation. There were a few cries of Decheance! fewer still of Vive la Republique among the motley crowds; but they were faint, and chiefly by ragged gamins. A small body repaired to Trochu and offered him the sceptre, which he politely declined. A more important and respectable body—for it comprised the majority of the Corps Legislatif—urged Palikao to accept the temporary dictatorship, which the War Minister declined with equal politeness. In both these overtures it was clear that the impulse of the proposers was towards any form of government rather than republican. The sergens de ville were sufficient that day to put down riot. They did make a charge on a mob, which immediately ran away.

The morning of that day the Council of Ten were summoned by Lebeau—minus only Rameau, who was still too unwell to attend, and the Belgian, not then at Paris; but their place was supplied by the two travelling members, who had been absent from the meeting before recorded. These were conspirators better known in history than those I have before described; professional conspirators—personages who from their youth upwards had done little else but conspire. Following the discreet plan pursued elsewhere throughout this humble work, I give their names other than they bore. One, a very swarthy and ill-favoured man, between forty and fifty, I call Paul Grimm—by origin a German, but by rearing and character French; from the hair on his head, staring up rough and ragged as a bramblebush, to the soles of small narrow feet, shod with dainty care, he was a personal coxcomb, and spent all he could spare on his dress. A clever man, not ill-educated—a vehement and effective speaker at a club. Vanity and an amorous temperament had made him a conspirator, since he fancied he interested the ladies more in that capacity than any other. His companion, Edgar Ferrier, would have been a journalist, only hitherto his opinions had found no readers; the opinions were those of Marat. He rejoiced in thinking that his hour for glory, so long deferred, had now arrived. He was thoroughly sincere: his father and grandfather had died in a madhouse. Both these men, insignificant in ordinary times, were likely to become of terrible importance in the crisis of a revolution. They both had great power with the elements that form a Parisian mob. The instructions given to these members of the Council by Lebeau were brief: they were summed up in the one word, Decheance. The formidable nature of a council apparently so meanly constituted became strikingly evident at that moment, because it was so small in number, while each one of these could put in movement a large section of the populace; secondly, because, unlike a revolutionary club or a numerous association, no time was wasted in idle speeches, and all were under the orders of one man of clear head and resolute purpose; and thirdly, and above all, because one man supplied the treasury, and money for an object desired was liberally given and promptly at hand. The meeting did not last ten minutes, and about two hours afterwards its effects were visible. From Montmartre and Belleville and Montretout poured streams of ouvriers, with whom Armand Monnier was a chief, and the Medecin des Pauvres an oracle. Grimm and Ferrier headed other detachments that startled the well-dressed idlers on the Boulevards. The stalwart figure of the Pole was seen on the Place de la Concorde, towering amidst other refugees, amid which glided the Italian champion of humanity. The cry of Decheance became louder. But as yet there were only few cries of Vive la Republique!—such a cry was not on the orders issued by Lebeau. At midnight the crowd round the hall of the Corps Legislatif is large: cries of La Dechaeance loud—a few cries, very feeble, of Vive la Republique!

What followed on the 4th—the marvellous audacity with which half-a-dozen lawyers belonging to a pitiful minority in a Chamber elected by universal suffrage walked into the Hotel de Ville and said, "The Republic is established, and we are its Government," history has told too recently for me to narrate. On the evening of the 5th the Council of Ten met again: the Pole; the Italian radiant; Grimm and Ferrier much excited and rather drunk; the Medecin des Pauvres thoughtful; and Armand Monnier gloomy. A rumour has spread that General Trochu, in accepting the charge imposed on him, has exacted from the Government the solemn assurance of respect for God, and for the rights of Family and Property. The Atheist is very indignant at the assent of the Government to the first proposition; Monnier equal indignant at the assent to the second and third. What has that honest ouvrier conspired for?—what has he suffered for?—of late nearly starved for?—but to marry another man's wife, getting rid of his own, and to legalise a participation in the property of his employer,—and now he is no better off than before. "There must be another revolution," he whispers to the Atheist.

"Certainly," whispers back the Atheist; "he who desires to better this world must destroy all belief in another." The conclave was assembled when Lebeau entered by the private door. He took his place at the head of the table; and, fixing on the group eyes that emitted a cold gleam through the spectacles, thus spoke:

"Messieurs, or Citoyens, which ye will—I no longer call ye confreres—you have disobeyed or blundered my instructions. On such an occasion disobedience and blunder are crimes equally heinous."

Angry murmurs.

"Silence! Do not add mutiny to your other offences. My instructions were simple and short. Aid in the abolition of the Empire. Do not aid in any senseless cry for a Republic or any other form of government. Leave that to the Legislature. What have you done? You swelled the crowd that invaded the Corps Ligislatif. You, Dombinsky, not even a Frenchman, dare to mount the President's rostrum, and brawl forth your senseless jargon. You, Edgar Ferrier, from whom I expected better, ascend the tribune, and invite the ruffians in the crowd to march to the prisons and release the convicts; and all of you swell the mob at the Hotel de Ville, and inaugurate the reign of folly by creating an oligarchy of lawyers to resist the march of triumphal armies. Messieurs, I have done with you. You are summoned for the last time: the Council is dissolved."

With these words Lebeau put on his hat, and turned to depart. But the Pole, who was seated near him, sprang to his feet, exclaiming, "Traitor, thou shalt not escape! Comrades, he wants to sell us!"

"I have a right to sell you at least, for I bought you, and a very bad bargain I made," said Lebeau, in a tone of withering sarcasm.

"Liar!" cried the Pole, and seized Lebeau by the left hand, while with the right he drew forth a revolver. Ferrier and Grimm, shouting, "A bas le renegat!" would have rushed forward in support of the Pole, but Monnier thrust himself between them and their intended victim, crying with a voice that dominated their yell, "Back!—we are not assassins." Before he had finished the sentence the Pole was on his knees. With a vigour which no one could have expected from the seeming sexagenarian, Lebeau had caught the right arm of his assailant, twisted it back so mercilessly as almost to dislocate elbow and shoulder joint. One barrel of the revolver discharged itself harmlessly against the opposite wall, and the pistol itself then fell from the unnerved hand of the would-be assassin; and what with the pain and the sudden shock, the stalwart Dombinsky fell in the attitude of a suppliant at the feet of his unlooked-for vanquisher.

Lebeau released his hold, possessed himself of the pistol, pointing the barrels towards Edgar Ferrier, who stood with mouth agape and lifted arm arrested, and said quietly: "Monsieur, have the goodness to open that window." Ferrier mechanically obeyed. "Now, hireling," continued Lebeau, addressing the vanquished Pole, "choose between the door and the window."

"Go, my friend," whispered the Italian. The Pole did not utter a word; but rising nimbly, and rubbing his arm, stalked to the door. There he paused a moment and said, "I retire overpowered by numbers," and vanished.

"Messieurs," resumed Lebeau, calmly, "I repeat that the Council is dissolved. In fact its object is fulfilled more abruptly than any of us foresaw, and by means which I at least had been too long out of Paris to divine as possible. I now see that every aberration of reason is possible to the Parisians. The object that united us was the fall of the Empire. As I have always frankly told you, with that object achieved, separation commences. Each of us has his own crotchet, which differs from the other man's. Pursue yours as you will—I pursue mine—you will find Jean Lebeau no more in Paris: il s'eface. Au plaisir, mais pas au revoir."

He retreated to the masked door and disappeared.

Marc le Roux, the porter or custos of that ruinous council-hall, alarmed at the explosion of the pistol, had hurried into the room, and now stood unheeded by the door with mouth agape, while Lebeau thus curtly dissolved the assembly. But when the president vanished through the secret doorway, Le Roux also retreated. Hastily descending the stairs, he made as quickly as his legs could carry him for the mouth of the alley in the rear of the house, through which he knew that Lebeau must pass. He arrived, panting and breathless, in time to catch hold of the ex-president's arm. "Pardon, citizen," stammered he, "but do I understand that you have sent the Council of Ten to the devil?"

"I? Certainly not, my good Paul; I dismiss them to go where they like. If they prefer the direction you name, it is their own choice. I declined to accompany them, and I advise you not to do so."

"But, citizen, have you considered what is to become of Madame? Is she to be turned out of the lodge? Are my wages to stop, and Madame to be left without a crust to put into her soup?"

"Not so bad as that; I have just paid the rent of the baraque for three months in advance, and there is your quarter's pay, in advance also. My kind regards to Madame, and tell her to keep your skin safe from the schemes of these lunatics." Thrusting some pieces of gold into the hands of the porter, Lebeau nodded his adieu, and hastened along his way.

Absorbed in his own reflections, he did not turn to look behind. But if he had, he could not have detected the dark form of the porter, creeping in the deep shadow of the streets with distant but watchful footsteps.

# CHAPTER IX.

The conspirators, when left by their president, dispersed in deep, not noisy resentment. They were indeed too stunned for loud demonstration; and belonging to different grades of life, and entertaining different opinions, their confidence in each other seemed lost now that the chief who had brought and kept them together was withdrawn from their union. The Italian and the Atheist slunk away, whispering to each other. Grimm reproached Ferrier for deserting Dombinsky and obeying Lebeau. Ferrier accused Grimm of his German origin, and hinted at denouncing him as a Prussian spy. Gaspard le Noy linked his arm in Monnier's, and when they had gained the dark street without, leading into a labyrinth of desolate lanes, the Medicin des Pauvres said to the mechanic: "You are a brave fellow, Monnier. Lebeau owes you a good turn. But for your cry, 'We are not assassins,' the Pole might not have been left without support. No atmosphere is so infectious as that in which we breathe the same air of revenge: when the violence of one man puts into action the anger or suspicion of others, they become like a pack of hounds, which follow the spring of the first hound, whether on the wild boar or their own master. Even I, who am by no means hot-headed, had my hand on my case-knife when the word 'assassin' rebuked and disarmed me."

"Nevertheless," said Monnier, gloomily, "I half repent the impulse which made me interfere to save that man. Better he should die than live to betray the cause we allowed him to lead."

"Nay, mon ami, speaking candidly, we must confess that he never from the first pretended to advocate the cause for which you conspired. On the contrary, he always said that with the fall of the Empire our union would cease, and each become free to choose his own way towards his own after-objects."

"Yes," answered Armand, reluctantly; "he said that to me privately, with still greater plainness than he said it to the Council. But I answered as plainly."

"How?"

"I told him that the man who takes the first step in a revolution, and persuades others to go along with him, cannot in safety stand still or retreat when the next step is to be taken. It is 'en avant' or 'a la lanterne.' So it shall be with him. Shall a fellow-being avail himself of the power over my mind which he derives from superior education or experience,—break into wild fragments my life, heretofore tranquil, orderly, happy,—make use of my opinions, which were then but harmless desires, to serve his own purpose, which was hostile to the opinions he roused into action,—say to me, 'Give yourself up to destroy the first obstacle in the way of securing a form of society which your inclinations prefer,' and then, that first obstacle destroyed, cry, 'Halt! I go with you no further; I will not help you to piece together the life I have induced you to shatter; I will not aid you to substitute for the society that pained you the society that would please; I leave you, struggling, bewildered, maddened, in the midst of chaos within and without you'? Shall a fellow-being do this, and vanish with a mocking cry: 'Tool! I have had enough of thee; I cast thee aside as worthless lumber'? Ah! let him beware! The tool is of iron, and can be shaped to edge and point." The passion with which this rough eloquence was uttered, and the fierce sinister expression that had come over a countenance habitually open and manly, even when grave and stern, alarmed and startled Le Noy. "Pooh, my friend!" he said, rather falteringly, "you are too excited now to think justly. Go home and kiss your children. Never do anything that may make them shrink from their father. And as to Lebeau, try and forget him. He says he shall disappear from Paris. I believe him. It is clear to me that the man is not what he seemed to us. No man of sixty could by so easy a sleight of hand have brought that giant Pole to his knee. If Lebeau reappear it will be in some other form. Did you notice that in the momentary struggle his flaxen wig got disturbed, and beneath it I saw a dark curl. I suspect that the man is not only younger than he seemed, but of higher rank—a conspirator against one throne, perhaps, in order to be minister under another. There are such men."

Before Monnier, who seemed struck by these conjectures, collected his thoughts to answer, a tall man in the dress of a sous lieutenant stopped under a dim gas-lamp, and, catching sight of the artisan's face, seized him by the hand, exclaiming, "Armand, mon frere! well met; strange times, eh? Come and discuss them at the cafe de Lyon yonder over a bowl of punch. I'll stand treat."

"Agreed, dear Charles."

"And if this monsieur is a friend of yours, perhaps he will join us."

"You are too obliging, Monsieur," answered Le Noy, not ill-pleased to get rid of his excited companion; "but it has been a busy day with me, and I am only fit for bed. Be abstinent of the punch, Armand. You are feverish already. Good-night, Messieurs."

The cafe de Lyon, in vogue among the National Guard of the quartier, was but a few yards off, and the brothers turned towards it arm in arm. "Who is the friend?" asked Charles; "I don't remember to have seen him with thee before."

"He belongs to the medical craft—a good patriot and a kind man—attends the poor gratuitously. Yes, Charles, these are strange times; what dost thou think will come of them?"

They had now entered the cafe; and Charles had ordered the punch, and seated himself at a vacant table before he replied. "What will come of these times? I will tell thee. National deliverance and regeneration through the ascendency of the National Guard."

"Eh? I don't take," said Armand, bewildered.

"Probably not," answered Charles, with an air of compassionate conceit; "thou art a dreamer, but I am a politician." He tapped his forehead significantly. "At this custom-house, ideas are examined before they are passed."

Armand gazed at his brother wistfully, and with a defence he rarely manifested towards any one who disputed his own claims to superior intelligence. Charles was a few years older than Monnier; he was of large build; he had shaggy lowering eyebrows, a long obstinate upper lip, the face of a man who was accustomed to lay down the law. Inordinate self-esteem often gives that character to a physiognomy otherwise commonplace. Charles passed for a deep thinker in his own set, which was a very different set from Armand's—not among workmen but small shopkeepers. He had risen in life to a grade beyond Armand's; he had always looked to the main chance, married the widow of a hosier and glover much older than himself, and in her right was a very respectable tradesman, comfortably well off; a Liberal, of course, but a Liberal bourgeois, equally against those above him and those below. Needless to add that he had no sympathy with his brother's socialistic opinions. Still he loved that brother as well as he could love any one except himself. And Armand, who was very affectionate, and with whom family ties were very strong, returned that love with ample interest; and though so fiercely at war with the class to which Charles belonged, was secretly proud of having a brother who was of that class. So in England I have known the most violent antagonist of the landed aristocracy—himself a cobbler—who interrupts a discourse on the crimes of the aristocracy by saying, "Though I myself descend from a county family."

In an evil day Charles Monnier, enrolled in the National Guard, had received promotion in that patriotic corps. From that date he began to neglect his shop, to criticise military matters, and to think that if merit had fair play he should be a Cincinnatus or a Washington, he had not decided which.

"Yes," resumed Charles, ladling out the punch, "thou hast wit enough to perceive that our generals are imbeciles or traitors; that gredin Bonaparte has sold the army for ten millions of francs to Bismarck, and I have no doubt that Wimpffen has his share of the bargain. McMahon was wounded conveniently, and has his own terms for it. The regular army is nowhere. Thou wilt see—thou wilt see—they will not stop the march of the Prussians. Trochu will be obliged to come to the National Guard. Then we shall say, 'General, give us our terms, and go to sleep.'

"I shall be summoned to the council of war. I have my plan. I explain it—'tis accepted—it succeeds. I am placed in supreme command—the Prussians are chased back to their sour-krout. And I—well—I don't like to boast, but thou'lt see—thou'lt see—what will happen."

"And thy plan, Charles—thou hast formed it already?"

"Ay, ay,—the really military genius is prompt, mon petit Armand—a flash of the brain. Hark ye! Let the Vandals come to Paris and invest it. Whatever their numbers on paper, I don't care a button; they can only have a few thousands at any given point in the vast circumference of the capital. Any fool must grant that—thou must grant it eh?"

"It seems just."

"Of course. Well, then, we proceed by sorties of 200,000 men repeated every other day, and in twelve days the Prussians are in full flight. The country rises on their flight—they are cut to pieces. I depose Trochu—the National Guard elects the Saviour of France. I have a place in my eye for thee. Thou art superb as a decorator—thou shalt be Minister des Beaux Arts. But keep clear of the canaille. No more strikes then—thou wilt be an employer—respect thy future order."

*[Charles Monnier seems to have indiscreetly blabbed out his "idea," for it was plagiarised afterwards at a meeting of the National Guards in the Salle de la Bourse by Citizen Rochebrune (slain 19th January, 1871, in the affair of Montretout). The plan, which he developed nearly in the same words as Charles Monnier, was received with lively applause; and at the close of his speech it was proposed to name at once Citizen Rochebrune General of the National Guard, an honour which, unhappily for his country, the citizen had the modesty to decline.]*

Armand smiled mournfully. Though of intellect which, had it been disciplined, was far superior to his brother's, it was so estranged from practical opinions, so warped, so heated, so flawed and cracked in parts, that he did not see the ridicule of Charles's braggadocio. Charles had succeeded in life, Armand had failed; and Armand believed in the worldly wisdom of the elder born. But he was far too sincere for any bribe to tempt him to forsake his creed and betray his opinions. And he knew that it must be a very different revolution from that which his brother contemplated, that could allow him to marry another man's wife, and his "order" to confiscate other people's property.

"Don't talk of strikes, Charles. What is done is done. I was led into heading a strike, not on my own account, for I was well paid and well off, but for the sake of my fellow-workmen. I may regret now what I did, for the sake of Marie and the little ones. But it is an affair of honour, and I cannot withdraw from the cause till my order, as thou namest my class, has its rights."

"Bah! thou wilt think better of it when thou art an employer. Thou hast suffered enough already. Remember that I warned thee against that old fellow in spectacles whom I met once at thy house. I told thee he would lead thee into mischief, and then leave thee to get out of it. I saw through him. I have a head! Va!"

"Thou wert a true prophet—he has duped me. But in moving me he has set others in movement; and I suspect he will find he has duped himself. Time will show."

Here the brothers were joined by some loungers belonging to the National Guard. The talk became general, the potations large. Towards daybreak Armand reeled home, drunk for the first time in his life. He was one of those whom drink makes violent. Marie had been sitting up for him, alarmed at his lengthened absence. But when she would have thrown herself on his breast, her pale face and her passionate sobs enraged him. He flung her aside roughly. From that night the man's nature was changed. If, as a physiognomist has said, each man has in him a portion of the wild beast, which is suppressed by mild civilising circumstances, and comes uppermost when self-control is lost, the nature of many an honest workman, humane and tender-hearted as the best of us, commenced a change into the wild beast that raged through the civil war of the Communists, on the day when half-a-dozen Incapables, with no more claim to represent the people of Paris than half-a-dozen monkeys would have, were allowed to elect themselves to supreme power, and in the very fact of that election released all the elements of passion, and destroyed all the bulwarks of order.

# CHAPTER X.

No man perhaps had more earnestly sought and more passionately striven for the fall of the Empire than Victor de Mauleon; and perhaps no man was more dissatisfied and disappointed by the immediate consequences of that fall, In first conspiring against the Empire, he had naturally enough, in common with all the more intelligent enemies of the dynasty, presumed that its fate would be worked out by the normal effect of civil causes—the alienation of the educated classes, the discontent of the artisans, the eloquence of the press and of popular meetings, strengthened in proportion as the Emperor had been compelled to relax the former checks upon the license of either. And De Mauleon had no less naturally concluded that there would be time given for the preparation of a legitimate and rational form of government to succeed that which was destroyed. For, as has been hinted or implied, this remarkable man was not merely an instigator of revolution through the Secret Council, and the turbulent agencies set in movement through the lower strata of society;—he was also in confidential communication with men eminent for wealth, station, and political repute, from whom he obtained the funds necessary for the darker purposes of conspiracy, into the elaboration of which they did not inquire; and these men, though belonging like himself to the Liberal party, were no hot-blooded democrats. Most of them were in favour of constitutional monarchy; all of them for forms of government very different from any republic in which socialists or communists could find themselves uppermost. Among these politicians were persons ambitious and able, who, in scheming for the fall of the Empire, had been prepared to undertake the task of conducting to ends compatible with modern civilisation the revolution they were willing to allow a mob at Paris to commence. The opening of the war necessarily suspended their designs. How completely the events of the 4th September mocked the calculations of their ablest minds, and paralysed the action of their most energetic spirits, will appear in the conversation I am about to record. It takes place between Victor de Mauleon and the personage to whom he had addressed the letter written on the night before the interview with Louvier, in which Victor had announced his intention of reappearing in Paris in his proper name and rank. I shall designate this correspondent as vaguely as possible; let me call him the Incognito. He may yet play so considerable a part in the history of France as a potent representative of the political philosophy of De Tocqueville—that is, of Liberal principles incompatible with the absolute power either of a sovereign or a populace, and resolutely opposed to experiments on the foundations of civilised society—that it would be unfair to himself and his partisans if, in a work like this, a word were said that could lead malignant conjecture to his identity with any special chief of the opinions of which I here present him only as a type.

The Incognito, entering Victor's apartment:

"My dear friend, even if I had not received your telegram, I should have hastened hither on the news of this astounding revolution. It is only in Paris that such a tragedy could be followed by such a farce. You were on the spot—a spectator. Explain it if you can."

DE MAULEON.—"I was more than a spectator; I was an actor. Hiss me—I deserve it. When the terrible news from Sedan reached Paris, in the midst of the general stun and bewilderment I noticed a hesitating timidity among all those who had wares in their shops and a good coat on their backs. They feared that to proclaim the Empire defunct would be to install the Red Republic with all its paroxysm of impulsive rage and all its theories of wholesale confiscation. But since it was impossible for the object we had in view to let slip the occasion of deposing the dynasty which stood in its way, it was necessary to lose no time in using the revolutionary part of the populace for that purpose. I assisted in doing so; my excuse is this—that in a time of crisis a man of action must go straight to his immediate object, and in so doing employ the instruments at his command. I made, however, one error in judgment which admits no excuse: I relied on all I had heard, and all I had observed, of the character of Trochu, and I was deceived, in common, I believe, with all his admirers, and three parts of the educated classes of Paris."

INCOGNITO.—"I should have been equally deceived! Trochu's conduct is a riddle that I doubt if he himself can ever solve. He was master of the position; he had the military force in his hands if he combined with Palikao, which, whatever the jealousies between the two, it was his absolute duty to do. He had a great prestige—"

DE MAULEON.—"And for the moment a still greater popularity. His ipse dixit could have determined the wavering and confused spirits of the population. I was prepared for his abandonment of the Emperor—even of the Empress and the Regency. But how could I imagine that he, the man of moderate politics, of Orleanistic leanings, the clever writer, the fine talker, the chivalrous soldier, the religious Breton, could abandon everything that was legal, everything that could save France against the enemy, and Paris against civil discord; that he would connive at the annihilation of the Senate, of the popular Assembly, of every form of Government that could be recognised as legitimate at home or abroad, accept service under men whose doctrines were opposed to all his antecedents, all his professed opinions, and inaugurate a chaos under the name of a Republic!"

INCOGNITO.—"How, indeed? How suppose that the National Assembly, just elected by a majority of seven millions and a half, could be hurried into a conjuring-bog, and reappear as the travesty of a Venetian oligarchy, composed of half-a-dozen of its most unpopular members! The sole excuse for Trochu is, that he deemed all other considerations insignificant compared with the defence of Paris, and the united action of the nation against the invaders. But if that were his honest desire in siding with this monstrous usurpation of power, he did everything by which the desire could be frustrated. Had there been any provisional body composed of men known and esteemed, elected by the Chambers, supported by Trochu and the troops at his back, there would have been a rallying-point for the patriotism of the provinces; and in the wise suspense of any constitution to succeed that Government until the enemy were chased from the field, all partisans—Imperialists, Legitimists, Orleanists, Republicans—would have equally adjourned their differences. But a democratic Republic, proclaimed by a Parisian mob for a nation in which sincere democratic Republicans are a handful, in contempt of an Assembly chosen by the country at large; headed by men in whom the provinces have no trust, and for whom their own representatives are violently cashiered;—can you conceive such a combination of wet blankets supplied by the irony of Fate for the extinction of every spark of ardour in the population from which armies are to be gathered in haste, at the beck of usupers they distrust and despise? Paris has excelled itself in folly. Hungering for peace, it proclaims a Government which has no legal power to treat for it. Shrieking out for allies among the monarchies, it annihilates the hope of obtaining them; its sole chance of escape from siege, famine, and bombardment, is in the immediate and impassioned sympathy of the provinces; and it revives all the grudges which the provinces have long sullenly felt against the domineering pretensions of the capital, and invokes the rural populations, which comprise the pith and sinew of armies, in the name of men whom I verily believe they detest still more than they do the Prussians. Victor, it is enough to make one despair of his country! All beyond the hour seems anarchy and ruin."

"Not so!" exclaimed De Mauleon. "Everything comes to him who knows how to wait. The Empire is destroyed; the usurpation that follows it has no roots. It will but serve to expedite the establishment of such a condition as we have meditated and planned—a constitution adapted to our age and our people, not based wholly on untried experiments, taking the best from nations that do not allow Freedom and Order to be the sport of any popular breeze. From the American Republic we must borrow the only safeguards against the fickleness of the universal suffrage which, though it was madness to concede in any ancient community, once conceded cannot be safely abolished,—viz., the salutary law that no article of the Constitution, once settled, can be altered without the consent of two-thirds of the legislative body. By this law we insure permanence, and that concomitant love for institutions which is engendered by time and custom. Secondly, the formation of a senate on such principles as may secure to it in all times of danger a confidence and respect which counteract in public opinion the rashness and heat of the popular assembly. On what principles that senate should be formed, with what functions invested, what share of the executive—especially in foreign affairs, declarations of war, or treaties of peace—should be accorded to it, will no doubt need the most deliberate care of the ablest minds. But a senate I thus sketch has alone rescued America from the rashness of counsel incident to a democratic Chamber; and it is still more essential to France, with still more favourable elements for its creation. From England we must borrow the great principle that has alone saved her from revolution—that the head of the State can do no wrong. He leads no armies, he presides over no Cabinet. All responsibility rests with his advisers; and where we upset a dynasty, England changes an administration. Whether the head of the State should have the title of sovereign or president, whether he be hereditary or elected, is a question of minor importance impossible now to determine, but on which I heartily concur with you that hereditary monarchy is infinitely better adapted to the habits of Frenchmen, to their love of show and of honours—and infinitely more preservative from all the dangers which result from constant elections to such a dignity, with parties so heated, and pretenders to the rank so numerous—than any principle by which a popular demagogue or a successful general is enabled to destroy the institutions he is elected to guard. On these fundamental doctrines for the regeneration of France I think we are agreed. And I believe when the moment arrives to promulgate them, through an expounder of weight like yourself, they will rapidly commend themselves to the intellect of France. For they belong to common sense; and in the ultimate prevalence of common-sense I have a faith which I refuse to medievalists who would restore the right divine; and still more to fanatical quacks, who imagine that the worship of the Deity, the ties of family, and the rights of property are errors at variance with the progress of society. Qui vivera, verra."

INCOGNITO.—"In the outlines of the policy you so ably enunciate I heartily concur. But if France is, I will not say to be regenerated, but to have fair play among the nations of Europe, I add one or two items to the programme. France must be saved from Paris, not by subterranean barracks and trains, the impotence of which we see to-day with a general in command of the military force, but by conceding to France its proportionate share of the power now monopolised by Paris. All this system of centralisation, equally tyrannical and corrupt, must be eradicated. Talk of examples from America, of which I know little—from England, of which I know much,—what can we more advantageously borrow from England than that diffusion of all her moral and social power which forbids the congestion of blood in one vital part? Decentralise! decentralise! decentralise! will be my incessant cry, if ever the time comes when my cry will be heard. France can never be a genuine France until Paris has no more influence over the destinies of France than London has over those of England. But on this theme I could go on till midnight. Now to the immediate point: what do you advise me to do in this crisis, and what do you propose to do yourself?"

De Mauleon put his hand to his brow, and remained a few moments silent and thoughtful. At last he looked up with that decided expression of face which was not the least among his many attributes for influence over those with whom he came into contact.

"For you, on whom so much of the future depends, my advice is brief—have nothing to do with the present. All who join this present mockery of a Government will share the fall that attends it—a fall from which one or two of their body may possibly recover by casting blame on their confreres,—you never could. But it is not for you to oppose that Government with an enemy on its march to Paris. You are not a soldier; military command is not in your rode. The issue of events is uncertain; but whatever it be, the men in power cannot conduct a prosperous war nor obtain an honourable peace. Hereafter you may be the Deus ex machina. No personage of that rank and with that mission appears till the end of the play: we are only in the first act. Leave Paris at once, and abstain from all action."

INCOGNITO (dejectedly).—"I cannot deny the soundness of your advice, though in accepting it I feel unutterably saddened. Still you, the calmest and shrewdest observer among my friends, think there is cause for hope, not despair. Victor, I have more than most men to make life pleasant, but I would lay down life at this moment with you. You know me well enough to be sure that I utter no melodramatic fiction when I say that I love my country as a young man loves the ideal of his dreams—with my whole mind and heart and soul! and the thought that I cannot now aid her in the hour of her mortal trial is—is—"

The man's voice broke down, and he turned aside, veiling his face with a hand that trembled.

DE MAULEON—"Courage—patience! All Frenchmen have the first; set them an example they much need in the second. I, too, love my country, though I owe to it little enough, heaven knows. I suppose love of country is inherent in all who are not Internationalists. They profess only to love humanity, by which, if they mean anything practical, they mean a rise in wages."

INCOGNITO (rousing himself, and with a half smile). "Always cynical, Victor—always belying yourself. But now that you have advised my course, what will be your own? Accompany me, and wait for better times."

"No, noble friend; our positions are different. Yours is made—mine yet to make. But for this war I think I could have secured a seat in the Chamber. As I wrote you, I found that my kinsfolk were of much influence in their department, and that my restitution to my social grade, and the repute I had made as an Orleanist, inclined them to forget my youthful errors and to assist my career. But the Chamber ceases to exist. My journal I shall drop. I cannot support the Government; it is not a moment to oppose it. My prudent course is silence."

INCOGNITO.—"But is not your journal essential to your support?"

DE MAULEON.—"Fortunately not. Its profits enabled me to lay by for the rainy day that has come; and having reimbursed you and all friends the sums necessary to start it, I stand clear of all debt, and, for my slender wants, a rich man. If I continued the journal I should be beggared; for there would be no readers to Common Sense in this interval of lunacy. Nevertheless, during this interval, I trust to other ways for winning a name that will open my rightful path of ambition whenever we again have a legislature in which Common Sense can be heard."

INCOGNITO.—"But how win that name, silenced as a writer?"

DE MAULEON.—"You forget that I have fought in Algeria. In a few days Paris will be in a state of siege; and then—and then," he added, and very quietly dilated on the renown of a patriot or the grave of a soldier.

"I envy you the chance of either," said the Incognito; and after a few more brief words he departed, his hat drawn over his brows, and entering a hired carriage which he had left at the corner of the quiet street, was consigned to the station du ————, just in time for the next train.

# CHAPTER XI.

Victor dressed and went out. The streets were crowded. Workmen were everywhere employed in the childish operation of removing all insignia, and obliterating all names that showed where an Empire had existed. One greasy citizen, mounted on a ladder, was effacing the words "Boulevard Haussman," and substituting for Haussman, "Victor Hugo."

Suddenly De Mauleon came on a group of blouses, interspersed with women holding babies and ragged boys holding stones, collected round a well-dressed slender man, at whom they were hooting and gesticulating, with menaces of doing something much worse. By an easy effort of his strong frame the Vicomte pushed his way through the tormentors, and gave his arm to their intended victim.

"Monsieur, allow me to walk home with you." Therewith the shrieks and shouts and gesticulations increased. "Another impertinent! Another traitor! Drown him! Drown them both! To the Seine! To the Seine!" A burly fellow rushed forward, and the rest made a plunging push. The outstretched arm of De Mauleon kept the ringleader at bay. "Mes enfans," cried Victor with a calm clear voice, "I am not an Imperialist. Many of you have read the articles signed Pierre Firmin, written against the tyrant Bonaparte when he was at the height of his power. I am Pierre Firmin—make way for me." Probably not one in the crowd had ever read a word written by Pierre Firmin, nor even heard of the name. But they did not like to own ignorance; and that burly fellow did not like to encounter that arm of iron which touched his throat. So he cried out, "Oh! if you are the great Pierre Firmin, that alters the case. Make way for the patriot Pierre!"

"But," shrieked a virago, thrusting her baby into De Mauleon's face, "the other is the Imperialist, the capitalist, the vile Duplessis. At least we will have him."

De Mauleon suddenly snatched the baby from her, and said, with imperturbable good temper, "Exchange of prisoners. I resign the man, and I keep the baby."

No one who does not know the humours of a Parisian mob can comprehend the suddenness of popular change, or the magical mastery over crowds which is effected by quiet courage and a ready joke. The group was appeased at once. Even the virago laughed; and when De Mauleon restored the infant to her arms, with a gold piece thrust into its tiny clasp, she eyed the gold, and cried, "God bless you, citizen!" The two gentlemen made their way safely now.

"M. de Mauleon," said Duplessis, "I know not how to thank you. Without your seasonable aid I should have been in great danger of life; and—would you believe it?—the woman who denounced and set the mob on me was one of the objects of a charity which I weekly dispense to the poor."

"Of course I believe that. At the Red clubs no crime is more denounced than that of charity. It is the 'fraud against Egalite'—a vile trick of the capitalist to save to himself the millions he ought to share with all by giving a sou to one. Meanwhile, take my advice, M. Duplessis, and quit Paris with your young daughter. This is no place for rich Imperialists at present."

"I perceived that before to-day's adventure. I distrust the looks of my very servants, and shall depart with Valerie this evening for Bretagne."

"Ah! I heard from Louvier that you propose to pay off his mortgage on Rochebriant, and make yourself sole proprietor of my young kinsman's property."

"I trust you only believe half what you hear. I mean to save Rochebriant from Louvier, and consign it, free of charge, to your kinsman, as the dot of his bride, my daughter."

"I rejoice to learn such good news for the head of my house. But Alain himself—is he not with the prisoners of war?"

"No, thank heaven. He went forth an officer of a regiment of Parisian Mobiles—went full of sanguine confidence; he came back with his regiment in mournful despondency. The undiscipline of his regiment, of the Parisian Mobiles generally, appears incredible. Their insolent disobedience to their officers, their ribald scoffs at their general—oh, it is sickening to speak of it! Alain distinguished himself by repressing a mutiny and is honoured by a signal compliment from the commander in a letter of recommendation to Palikao. But Palikao is nobody now. Alain has already been sent into Bretagne, commissioned to assist in organising a corps of Mobiles in his neighbourhood. Trochu, as you know, is a Breton. Alain is confident of the good conduct of the Bretons. What will Louvier do? He is an arch Republican; is he pleased now he has got what he wanted?"

"I suppose he is pleased, for he is terribly frightened. Fright is one of the great enjoyments of a Parisian. Good day. Your path to your hotel is clear now. Remember me kindly to Alain."

De Mauleon continued his way through streets sometimes deserted, sometimes thronged. At the commencement of the Rue de Florentin he encountered the brothers Vandemar walking arm in arm.

"Ha, De Mauleon!" cried Enguerrand; "what is the last minute's news?"

"I can't guess. Nobody knows at Paris how soon one folly swallows up another. Saturn here is always devouring one or other of his children."

"They say that Vinoy, after a most masterly retreat, is almost at our gates with 80,000 men."

"And this day twelvemonth we may know what he does with them."

Here Raoul, who seemed absorbed in gloomy reflections, halted before the hotel in which the Contessa di Rimini lodged, and with a nod to his brother, and a polite, if not cordial salutation to Victor, entered the porte cochere.

"Your brother seems out of spirits,—a pleasing contrast to the uproarious mirth with which Parisians welcome the advance of calamity."

"Raoul, as you know, is deeply religious. He regards the defeat we have sustained, and the peril that threatens us, as the beginning of a divine chastisement, justly incurred by our sins—I mean, the sins of Paris. In vain my father reminds him of Voltaire's story, in which the ship goes down with a fripon on board. In order to punish the fripon, the honest folks are drowned."

"Is your father going to remain on board the ship, and share the fate of the other honest folks?"

"Pas si bete. He is off to Dieppe for sea-bathing. He says that Paris has grown so dirty since the 4th September, that it is only fit for the feet of the Unwashed. He wished my mother to accompany him; but she replies, 'No; there are already too many wounded not to need plenty of nurses.' She is assisting to inaugurate a society of ladies in aid of the Soeurs de Charite. Like Raoul, she is devout, but she has not his superstitions. Still his superstitions are the natural reaction of a singularly earnest and pure nature from the frivolity and corruption which, when kneaded well up together with a slice of sarcasm, Paris calls philosophy."

"And what, my dear Enguerrand, do you propose to do?"

"That depends on whether we are really besieged. If so, of course I become a soldier."

"I hope not a National Guard?"

"I care not in what name I fight, so that I fight for France."

As Enguerrand said these simple words, his whole countenance, seemed changed. The crest rose; his eyes sparkled; the fair and delicate beauty which had made him the darling of women—the joyous sweetness of expression and dainty grace of high breeding which made him the most popular companion to men,—were exalted in a masculine nobleness of aspect, from which a painter might have taken hints for a study of the young Achilles separated for ever from effeminate companionship at the sight of the weapons of war. De Mauleon gazed on him admiringly. We have seen that he shared the sentiments uttered—had resolved on the same course of action. But it was with the tempered warmth of a man who seeks to divest his thoughts and his purpose of the ardour of romance, and who, in serving his country, calculates on the gains to his own ambition. Nevertheless he admired in Enguerrand the image of his own impulsive and fiery youth.

"And you, I presume," resumed Enguerrand, "will fight too, but rather with pen than with sword."

"Pens will now only be dipped in red ink, and commonsense never writes in that colour; as for the sword, I have passed the age of forty-five, at which military service halts. But if some experience in active service, some knowledge of the art by which soldiers are disciplined and led, will be deemed sufficient title to a post of command, however modest the grade be, I shall not be wanting among the defenders of Paris."

"My brave dear Vicomte, if you are past the age to serve, you are in the ripest age to command; and with the testimonials and the cross you won in Algeria, your application for employment will be received with gratitude by any general so able as Trochu."

"I don't know whether I shall apply to Trochu. I would rather be elected to command even by the Mobiles or the National Guard, of whom I have just spoken disparagingly; and no doubt both corps will soon claim and win the right to choose their officers. But if elected, no matter by whom, I shall make a preliminary condition; the men under me shall train, and drill, and obey,—soldiers of a very different kind from the youthful Pekins nourished on absinthe and self-conceit, and applauding that Bombastes Furioso, M. Hugo, when he assures the enemy that Paris will draw an idea from its scabbard. But here comes Savarin. Bon jour, my dear poet."

"Don't say good day. An evil day for journalists and writers who do not out-Herod Blanqui and Pyat. I know not how I shall get bread and cheese. My poor suburban villa is to be pulled down by way of securing Paris; my journal will be suppressed by way of establishing the liberty of the press. I ventured to suggest that the people of France should have some choice in the form of their government."

"That was very indiscreet, my poor Savarin," said Victor; "I wonder your printing-office has not been pulled down. We are now at the moment when wise men hold their tongues."

"Perhaps so, M. de Mauleon. It might have been wiser for all of us, you as well as myself, if we had not allowed our tongues to be so free before this moment arrived. We live to learn; and if we ever have what may be called a passable government again, in which we may say pretty much what we like, there is one thing I will not do, I will not undermine that government without seeing a very clear way to the government that is to follow it. What say you, Pierre Firmin?"

"Frankly, I say that I deserve your rebuke," answered De Mauleon thoughtfully. "But, of course, you are going to take or send Madame Savarin out of Paris."

"Certainly. We have made a very pleasant party for our hegira this evening-among others the Morleys. Morley is terribly disgusted. A Red Republican slapped him on the shoulder and said, 'American, we have a republic as well as you.' 'Pretty much you know about republics,' growled Morley; 'a French republic is as much like ours as a baboon is like a man.' On which the Red roused the mob, who dragged the American off to the nearest station of the National Guard, where he was accused of being a Prussian spy. With some difficulty, and lots of brag about the sanctity of the stars and stripes, he escaped with a reprimand, and caution how to behave himself in future. So he quits a city in which there no longer exists freedom of speech. My wife hoped to induce Mademoiselle Cicogna to accompany us; I grieve to say she refuses. You know she is engaged in marriage to Gustave Rameau; and his mother dreads the effect that these Red Clubs and his own vanity may have upon his excitable temperament if the influence of Mademoiselle Cicogna be withdrawn."

"How could a creature so exquisite as Isaura Cicogna ever find fascination in Gustave Rameau!" exclaimed Enguerrand.

"A woman like her," answered De Mauleon, "always finds a fascination in self-sacrifice."

"I think you divine the truth," said Savarin, rather mournfully. "But I must bid you good-bye. May we live to shake hands reunis sons des meilleurs auspices."

Here Savarin hurried off, and the other two men strolled into the Champs Elysees, which were crowded with loungers, gay and careless, as if there had been no disaster at Sedan, no overthrow of an Empire, no enemy on its road to Paris.

In fact the Parisians, at once the most incredulous and the most credulous of all populations, believed that the Prussians would never be so impertinent as to come in sight of the gates. Something would occur to stop them! The king had declared he did not war on Frenchmen, but on the Emperor: the Emperor gone, the war was over. A democratic republic was instituted. A horrible thing in its way, it is true; but how could the Pandour tyrant brave the infection of democratic doctrines among his own barbarian armies? Were not placards, addressed to our "German brethren," posted upon the walls of Paris, exhorting the Pandours to fraternise with their fellow-creatures? Was not Victor Hugo going to publish "a letter to the German people"? Had not Jules Favre graciously offered peace, with the assurance that "France would not cede a stone of her fortresses—an inch of her territory? She would pardon the invaders and not march upon Berlin!" To all these, and many more such incontestable proofs, that the idea of a siege was moonshine, did Enguerrand and Victor listen as they joined group after group of their fellow-countrymen: nor did Paris cease to harbour such pleasing illusions, amusing itself with piously laying crowns at the foot of the statue of Strasbourg, swearing "they would be worthy of their Alsatian brethren," till on the 19th of September the last telegram was received, and Paris was cut of from the rest of the world by the iron line of the Prussian invaders. "Tranquil and terrible," says Victor Hugo, "she awaits the invasion! A volcano needs no assistance."

# CHAPTER XII.

We left Graham Vane slowly recovering from the attack of fever which had arrested his journey to Berlin in quest of the Count von Rudesheimn. He was, however, saved the prosecution of that journey, and his direction turned back to France by a German newspaper which informed him that the King of Prussia was at Rheims, and that the Count von Rudesheim was among the eminent personages gathered there around their sovereign. In conversing the same day with the kindly doctor who attended him, Graham ascertained that this German noble held a high command in the German armies, and bore a no less distinguished reputation as a wise political counsellor than he had earned as a military chief. As soon as he was able to travel, and indeed before the good doctor sanctioned his departure, Graham took his way to Rheims, uncertain, however, whether the Count would still be found there. I spare the details of his journey, interesting as they were. On reaching the famous and, in the eyes of Legitimists, the sacred city, the Englishman had no difficulty in ascertaining the house, not far from the cathedral, in which the Count von Rudesheim had taken his temporary abode. Walking towards it from the small hotel in which he had been lucky enough to find a room disengaged—slowly, for he was still feeble—he was struck by the quiet conduct of the German soldiery, and, save in their appearance, the peaceful aspect of the streets. Indeed, there was an air of festive gaiety about the place, as in an English town in which some popular regiment is quartered. The German soldiers thronged the shops, buying largely; lounged into the cafes; here and there attempted flirtations with the grisettes, who laughed at their French and blushed at their compliments; and in their good-humoured, somewhat bashful cheeriness, there was no trace of the insolence of conquest.

But as Graham neared the precincts of the cathedral his ear caught a grave and solemn music, which he at first supposed to come from within the building. But as he paused and looked round, he saw a group of the German military, on whose stalwart forms and fair manly earnest faces the setting sun cast its calm lingering rays. They were chanting, in voices not loud but deep, Luther's majestic hymn:

"Nun danket alle Gott." The chant awed even the ragged beggar boys who had followed the Englishman, as they followed any stranger, would have followed King William himself, whining for alms. "What a type of the difference between the two nations!" thought Graham; "the Marseillaise, and Luther's Hymn!" While thus meditating and listening, a man in a general's uniform came slowly out of the cathedral, with his hands clasped behind his back, and his head bent slightly downwards. He, too, paused on hearing the hymn; then unclasped his hand and beckoned to one of the officers, to whom approaching he whispered a word or two, and passed on towards the Episcopal palace. The hymn hushed, and the singers quietly dispersed. Graham divined rightly that the general had thought a hymn thanking the God of battles might wound the feelings of the inhabitants of the vanquished city—not, however, that any of them were likely to understand the language in which the thanks were uttered. Graham followed the measured steps of the general, whose hands were again clasped behind his back—the musing habit of Von Moltke, as it had been of Napoleon the First. Continuing his way, the Englishman soon reached the house in which the Count von Rudesheim was lodged, and, sending in his card, was admitted at once through an anteroom in which sate two young men, subaltern officers apparently employed in draughting maps, into the presence of the Count.

"Pardon me," said Graham, after the first conventional salutation, "if I interrupt you for a moment or so in the midst of events so grave, on a matter that must seem to you very trivial."

"Nay," answered the Count, "there is nothing so trivial in this world but what there will be some one to whom it is important. Say how I can serve you."

"I think, M. le Comte, that you once received in your household, as teacher or governess, a French lady, Madame Marigny."

"Yes, I remember her well—a very handsome woman. My wife and daughter took great interest in her. She was married out of my house."

"Exactly—and to whom?"

"An Italian of good birth, who was then employed by the Austrian Government in some minor post, and subsequently promoted to a better one in the Italian dominion, which then belonged to the house of Hapsburg, after which we lost sight of him and his wife."

"An Italian—what was his name?"

"Ludovico Cicogna."

"Cicogna!" exclaimed Graham, turning very pale. "Are you sure that was the name?"

"Certainly. He was a cadet of a very noble house, and disowned by relations too patriotic to forgive him for accepting employment under the Austrian Government."

"Can you not give me the address of the place in Italy to which he was transferred on leaving Austria?"

"No; but if the information be necessary to you, it can be obtained easily at Milan, where the head of the family resides, or indeed in Vienna, through any ministerial bureau."

"Pardon me one or two questions more. Had Madame Marigny any children by a former husband?"

"Not that I know of: I never heard so. Signor Cicogna was a widower, and had, if I remember right, children by his first wife, who was also a Frenchwoman. Before he obtained office in Austria, he resided, I believe, in France. I do not remember how many children he had by his first wife. I never saw them. Our acquaintance began at the baths of Toplitz, where he saw and fell violently in love with Madame Marigny. After their marriage, they went to his post, which was somewhere, I think, in the Tyrol. We saw no more of them; but my wife and daughter kept up a correspondence with the Signora Cicogna for a short time. It ceased altogether when she removed into Italy."

"You do not even know if the Signora is still living?"

"No."

"Her husband, I am told, is dead."

"Indeed! I am concerned to hear it. A good-looking, lively, clever man. I fear he must have lost all income when the Austrian dominions passed to the house of Savoy."

"Many thanks for your information. I can detain you no longer," said Graham, rising.

"Nay, I am not very busy at this moment; but I fear we Germans have plenty of work on our hands."

"I had hoped that, now the French Emperor, against whom your king made war, was set aside, his Prussian majesty would make peace with the French people."

"Most willingly would he do so if the French people would let him. But it must be through a French Government legally chosen by the people. And they have chosen none! A mob at Paris sets up a provisional administration, that commences by declaring that it will not give up 'an inch of its territory nor a stone of its fortresses.' No terms of peace can be made with such men holding such talk." After a few words more over the state of public affairs,—in which Graham expressed the English side of affairs, which was all for generosity to the vanquished; and the Count argued much more ably on the German, which was all for security against the aggressions of a people that would not admit itself to be vanquished,—the short interview closed.

As Graham at night pursued his journey to Vienna, there came into his mind Isaura's song of the Neapolitan fisherman. Had he, too, been blind to the image on the rock? Was it possible that all the while he had been resisting the impulse of his heart, until the discharge of the mission entrusted to him freed his choice and decided his fortunes, the very person of whom he was in search had been before him, then to be for ever won, lost to him now for ever? Could Isaura Cicogna be the child of Louise Duval by Richard King? She could not have been her child by Cicogna: the dates forbade that hypothesis. Isaura must have been five years old when Louise married the Italian. Arrived at Milan, Graham quickly ascertained that the post to which Ludovico Cicogna had been removed was in Verona, and that he had there died eight years ago. Nothing was to be learned as to his family or his circumstances at the time of his death. The people of whose history we know the least are the relations we refuse to acknowledge. Graham continued his journey to Verona. There he found on inquiry that the Cicognas had occupied an apartment in a house which stood at the outskirts of the town and had been since pulled down to make way for some public improvements. But his closest inquiries could gain him no satisfactory answers to the all-important questions as to Ludovico Cicogna's family. His political alienation from the Italian cause, which was nowhere more ardently espoused than at Verona, had rendered him very unpopular. He visited at no Italian houses. Such society as he had was confined to the Austrian military within the Quadrilateral or at Venice, to which city he made frequent excursions: was said to lead there a free and gay life, very displeasing to the Signora, whom he left in Verona. She was but little seen, and faintly remembered as very handsome and proud-looking. Yes, there were children—a girl, and a boy several years younger than the girl; but whether she was the child of the Signora by a former marriage, or whether the Signora was only the child's stepmother, no one could say. The usual clue, in such doubtful matters obtainable through servants, was here missing. The Cicognas had only kept two servants, and both were Austrian subjects, who had long left the country,—their very names forgotten.

Graham now called to mind the Englishman Selby, for whom Isaura had such grateful affection, as supplying to her the place of her father. This must have been the Englishman whom Louise Duval had married after Cicogna's death. It would be no difficult task, surely, to ascertain where he had resided. Easy enough to ascertain all that Graham wanted to know from Isaura herself, if a letter could reach her. But, as he knew by the journals, Paris was now invested—cut off from all communication with the world beyond. Too irritable, anxious, and impatient to wait for the close of the siege, though he never suspected it could last so long as it did, he hastened to Venice, and there learned through the British consul that the late Mr. Selby was a learned antiquarian, an accomplished general scholar, a fanatico in music, a man of gentle temper though reserved manners; had at one time lived much at Venice: after his marriage with the Signora Cicogna he had taken up his abode near Florence. To Florence Graham now went. He found the villa on the skirts of Fiesole at which Mr. Selby had resided. The peasant who had officiated as gardener and shareholder in the profits of vines and figs, was still, with his wife, living on the place. Both man and wife remembered the Inglese well; spoke of him with great affection, of his wife with great dislike. They said her manners were very haughty, her temper very violent; that she led the Inglese a very unhappy life; that there were a girl and a boy, both hers by a former marriage; but when closely questioned whether they were sure that the girl was the Signora's child by the former husband, or whether she was not the child of that husband by a former wife, they could not tell; they could only say that both were called by the same name—Cicogna; that the boy was the Signora's favourite—that indeed she seemed wrapt up in him; that he died of a rapid decline a few months after Mr. Selby had hired the place, and that shortly after his death the Signora left the place and never returned to it; that it was little more than a year that she had lived with her husband before this final separation took place. The girl remained with Mr. Selby, who cherished and loved her as his own child. Her Christian name was Isaura, the boy's Luigi. A few years later, Mr. Selby left the villa and went to Naples, where they heard he had died. They could give no information as to what had become of his wife: Since the death of her boy that lady had become very much changed—her spirits quite broken, no longer violent. She would sit alone and weep bitterly. The only person out of her family she would receive was the priest; till the boy's death she had never seen the priest, nor been known to attend divine service.

"Was the priest living?"

"Oh, no; he had been dead two years. A most excellent man—a saint," said the peasant's wife.

"Good priests are like good women," said the peasant, drily; "there are plenty of them, but they are all underground."

On which remark the wife tried to box his ears. The contadino had become a freethinker since the accession of the house of Savoy. His wife remained a good Catholic. Said the peasant as, escaping from his wife, he walked into the high-road with Graham, "My belief, Eccellenza, is, that the priest did all the mischief."

"What mischief?"

"Persuaded the Signora to leave her husband. The Inglese was not a Catholic. I heard the priest call him a heretic. And the padre, who, though not so bad as some of his cloth, was a meddling bigot, thought it perhaps best for her soul that it should part company with a heretic's person. I can't say for sure, but I think that was it. The padre seemed to triumph when the Signora was gone." Graham mused. The peasant's supposition was not improbable. A woman such as Louise Duval appeared to be—of vehement passions and ill-regulated mind—was just one of those who, in a moment of great sorrow, and estranged from the ordinary household affections, feel, though but imperfectly, the necessity of a religion, and, ever in extremes, pass at once from indifferentism into superstition.

Arrived at Naples, Graham heard little of Selby except as a literary recluse, whose only distraction from books was the operatic stage. But he heard much of Isaura; of the kindness which Madame de Grantmesnil had shown to her, when left by Selby's death alone in the world; of the interest which the friendship and the warm eulogies of one so eminent as the great French writer had created for Isaura in the artistic circles; of the intense sensation her appearance, her voice, her universal genius, had made in that society, and the brilliant hopes of her subsequent career on the stage the cognoscenti had formed. No one knew anything of her mother; no one entertained a doubt that Isaura was by birth a Cicogna. Graham could not learn the present whereabouts of Madame de Grantmesnil. She had long left Naples, and had been last heard of at Genoa; was supposed to have returned to France a little before the war. In France she had no fixed residence.

The simplest mode of obtaining authentic information whether Isaura was the daughter of Ludovico Cicogna by his first wife—namely, by registration of her birth—failed him; because, as von Rudesheim had said, his first wife was a Frenchwoman. The children had been born somewhere in France, no one could even guess where. No one had ever seen the first wife, who had never appeared in Italy, nor had even heard what was her maiden name.

Graham, meanwhile, was not aware that Isaura was still in the besieged city, whether or not already married to Gustave Rameau; so large a number of the women had quitted Paris before the siege began, that he had reason to hope she was among them. He heard through an American that the Morleys had gone to England before the Prussian investment; perhaps Isaura had gone with them. He wrote to Mrs. Morley, inclosing his letter to the Minister of the United States at the Court of St. James's, and while still at Naples received her answer. It was short, and malignantly bitter. "Both myself and Madame Savarin, backed by Signora Venosta, earnestly entreated Mademoiselle Cicogna to quit Paris, to accompany us to England. Her devotion to her affianced husband would not permit her to listen to us. It is only an Englishman who could suppose Isaura Cicogna to be one of those women who do not insist on sharing the perils of those they love. You ask whether she was the daughter of Ludovico Cicogna by his former marriage, or of his second wife by him. I cannot answer. I don't even know whether Signor Cicogna ever had a former wife. Isaura Cicogna never spoke to me of her parents. Permit me to ask—what business is it of yours now? Is it the English pride that makes you wish to learn whether on both sides she is of noble family? How can that discovery alter your relations towards the affianced bride of another?"

On receipt of this letter, Graham quitted Naples, and shortly afterwards found himself at Versailles. He obtained permission to establish himself there, though the English were by no means popular. Thus near to Isaura, thus sternly separated from her, Graham awaited the close of the siege. Few among those at Versailles believed that the Parisians would endure it much longer. Surely they would capitulate before the bombardment, which the Germans themselves disliked to contemplate as a last resource, could commence.

In his own mind Graham was convinced that Isaura was the child of Richard King. It seemed to him probable that Louise Duval, unable to assign any real name to the daughter of the marriage she disowned,—neither the name borne by the repudiated husband, nor her own maiden name,—would, on taking her daughter to her new home, have induced Cicogna to give the child his name, or that after Cicogna's death she herself had so designated the girl. A dispassionate confidant, could Graham have admitted any confidant whatever, might have suggested the more than equal probability that Isaura was Cicogna's daughter by his former espousal. But then what could have become of Richard King's child? To part with the fortune in his hands, to relinquish all the ambitious dreams which belonged to it, cost Graham Vane no pang: but he writhed with indignant grief when he thought that the wealth of Richard King's heiress was to pass to the hands of Gustave

Rameau,—that this was to be the end of his researches—this the result of the sacrifice his sense of honour imposed on him. And now that there was the probability that he must convey to Isaura this large inheritance, the practical difficulty of inventing some reason for such a donation, which he had, while at a distance made light of, became seriously apparent. How could he say to Isaura that he had L200,000. in trust for her, without naming any one so devising it? Still more, how constitute himself her guardian, so as to secure it to herself, independently of her husband? Perhaps Isaura was too infatuated with Rameau, or too romantically unselfish, to permit the fortune so mysteriously conveyed being exclusively appropriated to herself. And if she were already married to Rameau, and if he were armed with the right to inquire into the source of this fortune, how exposed to the risks of disclosure would become the secret Graham sought to conceal. Such a secret affecting the memory of the sacred dead, affixing a shame on the scutcheon of the living, in the irreverent hands of a Gustave Rameau,—it was too dreadful to contemplate such a hazard. And yet, if Isaura were the missing heiress, could Graham Vane admit any excuse for basely withholding from her, for coolly retaining to himself the wealth for which he was responsible? Yet, torturing as were these communings with himself, they were mild in their torture compared to the ever-growing anguish of the thought that in any case the only woman he had ever loved—ever could love,—who might but for his own scruples and prejudices have been the partner of his life, was perhaps now actually the wife of another, and, as such, in what terrible danger! Famine within the walls of the doomed city: without, the engines of death waiting for a signal. So near to her, and yet so far! So willing to die for her, if for her he could not live: and with all his devotion, all his intellect, all his wealth, so powerless!

## CHAPTER XIII.

It is now the middle of November-a Sunday. The day has been mild, and is drawing towards its close. The Parisians have been enjoying the sunshine. Under the leafless trees in the public gardens and the Champs Elysees children have been at play. On the Boulevards the old elegance of gaiety is succeeded by a livelier animation. Itinerant musicians gather round them ragged groups. Fortune-tellers are in great request, especially among the once brilliant Laises and Thaises, now looking more shabby, to whom they predict the speedy restoration of Nabobs and Russians, and golden joys. Yonder Punch is achieving a victory over the Evil One, who wears the Prussian spiked helmet, and whose face has been recently beautified into a resemblance to Bismarck. Punch draws to his show a laughing audience of Moblots and recruits to the new companies of the National Guard. Members of the once formidable police, now threadbare and hunger-pinched, stand side by side with unfortunate beggars and sinister-looking patriots who have served their time in the jails or galleys.

Uniforms of all variety are conspicuous—the only evidence visible of an enemy at the walls. But the aspects of the wearers of warlike accoutrements are debonnaire and smiling, as of revellers on a holiday of peace. Among these defenders of their country, at the door of a crowded cafe, stands Frederic Lemercier, superb in the costume, bran-new, of a National Guard,—his dog Fox tranquilly reposing on its haunches, with eyes fixed upon its fellow-dog philosophically musing on the edge of Punch's show, whose master is engaged in the conquest of the Bismarck fiend.

"Lemercier," cried the Vicomte de Breze, approaching the cafe, "I scarcely recognise you in that martial guise. You look magnifique—the galons become you. Peste! an officer already?"

"The National Guards and Mobiles are permitted to choose their own officers, as you are aware. I have been elected, but to subaltern grade, by the warlike patriots of my department. Enguerrand de Vandemar is elected a captain of the Mobiles in his, and Victor de Mauleon is appointed to the command of a battalion of the National Guards. But I soar above jealousy at such a moment,—

*"'Rome a choisi mon bras; je n'examine rien.'"*

"You have no right to be jealous. De Mauldon has had experience and won distinction in actual service, and from all I hear is doing wonders with his men—has got them not only to keep but to love drill. I heard no less an authority than General V—— say that if all the officers of the National Guard were like De Mauleon, that body would give an example of discipline to the line."

"I say nothing as to the promotion of a real soldier like the Vicomte—but a Parisian dandy like Euguerrand de Vande—"

"You forget that Enguerrand received a military education—an advantage denied to you."

"What does that matter? Who cares for education nowadays? Besides, have I not been training ever since the 4th of September, to say nothing of the hard work on the ramparts?"

"Parlez moi de cela it is indeed hard work on the ramparts. Infandum dolorem quorum pars magna fui. Take the day duty. What with rising at seven o'clock, and being drilled between a middle-aged and corpulent grocer on one side and a meagre beardless barber's apprentice on the other; what with going to the bastions at eleven, and seeing half one's companions drunk before twelve; what with trying to keep their fists off one's face when one politely asks them not to call one's general a traitor or a poltroon,—the work of the ramparts would be insupportable, if I did not take a pack of cards with me, and enjoy a quiet rubber with three other heroes in some sequestered corner. As for night work, nothing short of the indomitable fortitude of a Parisian could sustain it; the tents made expressly not to be waterproof, like the groves of the Muses,

*"' per*
*Quos et aquea subeant et aurae.'*

A fellow-companion of mine tucks himself up on my rug, and pillows his head on my knapsack. I remonstrate—he swears—the other heroes wake up and threaten to thrash us both; and just when peace is made, and one hopes for a wink of sleep, a detachment of spectators, chiefly gamins, coming to see that all is safe in the camp, strike up the Marseillaise. Ah, the world will ring to the end of time with the sublime attitude of Paris in the face of the Vandal invaders, especially when it learns that the very shoes we stand in are made of cardboard. In vain we complain. The contractor for shoes is a staunch Republican, and jobs by right divine. May I ask if you have dined yet?"

"Heavens! no, it is too early. But I am excessively hungry. I had only a quarter of jugged cat for breakfast, and the brute was tough. In reply to your question, may I put another—Did you lay in plenty of stores?"

"Stores? no; I am a bachelor, and rely on the stores of my married friends."

"Poor De Breze! I sympathise with you, for I am in the same boat, and dinner invitations have become monstrous rare."

"Oh, but you are so confoundedly rich! What to you are forty francs for a rabbit, or eighty francs for a turkey?"

"Well, I suppose I am rich, but I have no money, and the ungrateful restaurants will not give me credit. They don't believe in better days."

"How can you want money?"

"Very naturally. I had invested my capital famously-the best speculations—partly in house rents, partly in company shares; and houses pay no rents, and nobody will buy company shares. I had 1,000 napoleons on hand, it is true, when Duplessis left Paris—much more, I thought, than I could possibly need, for I never believed in the siege. But during the first few weeks I played at whist with bad luck, and since then so many old friends have borrowed of me that I doubt if I have 200 francs left. I have despatched four letters to Duplessis by pigeon and balloon, entreating him to send me 25,000 francs by some trusty fellow who will pierce the Prussian lines. I have had two answers: 1st, that he will find a man; 2nd, that the man is found and on his way. Trust to that man, my dear friend, and meanwhile lend me 200 francs."

"Mon cher, desole to refuse; but I was about to ask you to share your 200 francs with me who live chiefly by my pen; and that resource is cut off. Still, il faut vivre—one must dine."

"That is a fact, and we will dine together to-day at my expense; limited liability, though—eight francs a head."

"Generous Monsieur, I accept. Meanwhile let us take a turn towards the Madeleine."

The two Parisians quit the cafe, and proceed up the Boulevard. On their way they encounter Savarin. "Why," said De Breze, "I thought you had left Paris with Madame."

"So I did, and deposited her safely with the Morleys at Boulogne. These kind Americans were going to England, and they took her with them. But I quit Paris! No: I am old; I am growing obese. I have always been short-sighted. I can neither wield a sword nor handle a musket. But Paris needs defenders; and every moment I was away from her I sighed to myself, 'il faut etre la!' I returned before the Vandals had possessed themselves of our railways, the convoi overcrowded with men like myself, who had removed wives and families; and when we asked each other why we went back, every answer was the same, 'il faut etre la.' No, poor child, no—I have nothing to give you."

These last words were addressed to a woman young and handsome, with a dress that a few weeks ago might have been admired for taste and elegance by the lady leaders of the ton, but was now darned, and dirty, and draggled.

"Monsieur, I did not stop you to ask for alms. You do not seem to remember me, M. Savarin."

"But I do," said Lemercier, "surely I address Mademoiselle Julie Caumartin."

"Ah, excuse me, le petit Frederic," said Julie with a sickly attempt at coquettish sprightliness; "I had no eyes except for M. Savarin."

"And why only for me, my poor child?" asked the kindhearted author.

"Hush!" She drew him aside. "Because you can give me news of that monster Gustave. It is not true, it cannot be true, that he is going to be married?"

"Nay, surely, Mademoiselle, all connection between you and young Rameau has ceased for months—ceased from the date of that illness in July which nearly carried him off."

"I resigned him to the care of his mother," said the girl; "but when he no longer needs a mother, he belongs to me. Oh, consider, M. Savarin, for his sake I refused the most splendid offers! When he sought me, I had my coupe, my opera-box, my cachemires, my jewels. The Russians—the English—vied for my smiles. But I loved the man. I never loved before: I shall never love again; and after the sacrifices I have made for him, nothing shall induce me to give him up. Tell me, I entreat, my dear M. Savarin, where he is hiding. He has left the parental roof, and they refused there to give me his address."

"My poor girl, don't be mechante. It is quite true that Gustave Rameau is engaged to be married; and any attempt of yours to create scandal—"

"Monsieur," interrupted Julie, vehemently, "don't talk to me about scandal! The man is mine, and no one else shall have him. His address?"

"Mademoiselle," cried Savarin, angrily, "find it out for yourself." Then—repentant of rudeness to one so young and so desolate—he added, in mild expostulatory accents: "Come, come, ma belle enfant, be reasonable: Gustave is no loss. He is reduced to poverty."

"So much the better. When he was well off I never cost him more than a supper at the Maison Doree; and if he is poor he shall marry me, and I will support him!"

"You!—and how?"

"By my profession when peace comes; and meanwhile I have offers from a cafe to recite warlike songs. Ah! you shake your head incredulously. The ballet-dancer recite verses? Yes! he taught me to recite his own Soyez bon pour moi. M. Savarin! do say where I can find mon homme."

"No."

"That is your last word?"

"It is."

The girl drew her thin shawl round her and hurried off. Savarin rejoined his friends. "Is that the way you console yourself for the absence of Madame?" asked De Breze, drily.

"Fie!" cried Savarin, indignantly; "such bad jokes are ill-timed. What strange mixtures of good and bad, of noble and base, every stratum of Paris life contains! There is that poor girl, in one way contemptible, no doubt, and yet in another way she has an element of grandeur. On the whole, at Paris, the women, with all their faults, are of finer mould than the men."

"French gallantry has always admitted that truth," said Lemercier. "Fox, Fox, Fox." Uttering this cry, he darted forward after the dog, who had strayed a few yards to salute another dog led by a string, and caught the animal in his arms. "Pardon me," he exclaimed, returning to his friends, "but there are so many snares for dogs at present. They are just coming into fashion for roasts, and Fox is so plump."

"I thought," said Savarin, "that it was resolved at all the sporting clubs that, be the pinch of famine ever so keen, the friend of man should not be eaten."

"That was while the beef lasted; but since we have come to cats, who shall predict immunity to dogs? Quid intactum nefasti linquimus? Nothing is sacred from the hand of rapine."

The church of the Madeleine now stood before them. Moblots were playing pitch-and-toss on its steps.

"I don't wish you to accompany me, Messieurs," said Lemercier, apologetically, "but I am going to enter the church."

"To pray?" asked De Breze, in profound astonishment. "Not exactly; but I want to speak to my friend Rochebriant, and I know I shall find him there."

"Praying?" again asked De Breze.

"Yes."

"That is curious—a young Parisian exquisite at prayer—that is worth seeing. Let us enter, too, Savarin."

They enter the church. It is filled, and even the sceptical De Breze is impressed and awed by the sight. An intense fervour pervades the congregation. The majority, it is true, are women, many of them in deep mourning, and many of their faces mourning deeper than the dress. Everywhere may be seen gushing tears, and everywhere faintly heard the sound of stifled sighs. Besides the women are men of all ages—young, middle-aged, old, with heads bowed and hands clasped, pale, grave, and earnest. Most of them were evidently of the superior grade of life—nobles, and the higher bourgeoisie: few of the ouvrier class, very few, and these were of an earlier generation. I except soldiers, of whom there were many, from the provincial Mobiles, chiefly Bretons; you know the Breton soldiers by the little cross worn on their kepis.

Among them Lemercier at once distinguished the noble countenance of Alain de Rochebriant. De Breze and Savarin looked at each other with solemn eyes. I know not when either had last been within a church; perhaps both were startled to find that religion still existed in Paris—and largely exist it does, though little seen on the surface of society, little to be estimated by the articles of journals and the reports of foreigners. Unhappily, those among whom it exists are not the ruling class—are of the classes that are dominated over and obscured in every country the moment the populace becomes master. And at that moment the journals chiefly read were warring more against the Deity than the Prussians—were denouncing soldiers who attended mass. "The Gospel certainly makes a bad soldier," writes the patriot Pyat.

Lemercier knelt down quietly. The other two men crept noiselessly out, and stood waiting for him on the steps, watching the Moblots (Parisian Moblots) at play.

"I should not wait for the roturier if he had not promised me a roti," said the Vicomte de Breze, with a pitiful attempt at the patrician wit of the ancien regime.

Savarin shrugged his shoulders. "I am not included in the invitation," said he, "and therefore free to depart. I must go and look up a former confrere who was an enthusiastic Red Republican, and I fear does not get so much to eat since he has no longer an Emperor to abuse."

So Savarin went away. A few minutes afterwards Lemercier emerged from the church with Alain.

# CHAPTER XIV.

"I knew I should find you in the Madeleine," said Lemercier, "and I wished much to know when you had news from Duplessis. He and your fair fiancee are with your aunt still staying at Rochebriant?"

"Certainly. A pigeon arrived this morning with a few lines. All well there."

"And Duplessis thinks, despite the war, that he shall be able, when the time comes, to pay Louvier the mortgage-sum?"

"He never doubts that. His credit in London is so good. But of course all works of improvement are stopped."

"Pray did he mention me?—anything about the messenger who was to pierce the Prussian lines?"

"What! has the man not arrived? It is two weeks since he left."

"The Uhlans have no doubt shot him—the assassins, and drunk up my 25,000 francs—the thieves."

"I hope not. But in case of delay, Duplessis tells me I am to remit to you 2,000 francs for your present wants. I will send them to you this evening."

"How the deuce do you possess such a sum?"

"I came from Brittany with a purse well filled. Of course I could have no scruples in accepting money from my destined father-in-law."

"And you can spare this sum?"

"Certainly—the State now provides for me; I am in command of a Breton company."

"True. Come and dine with me and De Breze."

"Alas! I cannot. I have to see both the Vandemars before I return to the camp for the night. And now-hush—come this way (drawing Frederic further from De Breze), I have famous news for you. A sortie on a grand scale is imminent; in a few days we may hope for it."

"I have heard that so often that I am incredulous."

"Take it as a fact now."

"What! Trochu has at last matured his plan?"

"He has changed its original design, which was to cut through the Prussian lines to Rouen, occupying there the richest country for supplies, guarding the left bank of the Seine and a watercourse to convoy them to Paris. The incidents of war prevented that: he has a better plan now. The victory of the army of the Loire at Orleans opens a new enterprise. We shall cut our way through the Prussians, join that army, and with united forces fall on the enemy at the rear. Keep this a secret as yet, but rejoice with me that we shall prove to the invaders what men who fight for their native soil can do under the protection of Heaven."

"Fox, Fox, mon cheri," said Lemercier, as he walked towards the cafe Riche with De Breze; "thou shalt have a festin de Balthazar under the protection of Heaven."

# CHAPTER XV.

On leaving Lemercier and De Breze, Savarin regained the Boulevard, and pausing every now and then to exchange a few words with acquaintances—the acquaintances of the genial author were numerous—turned into the quartier Chaussee d'Antin, and gaining a small neat house, with a richly-ornamented facade, mounted very clean, well-kept stairs to a third story. On one of the doors on the landing-place was nailed a card, inscribed, "Gustave Rameau, homme de lettres." Certainly it is not usual in Paris thus to afficher one's self as a "man of letters"? But Genius scorns what is usual. Had not Victor Hugo left in the hotel-books on the Rhine his designation "homme de lettres"? Did not the heir to one of the loftiest houses in the peerage of England, and who was also a first-rate amateur in painting, inscribe on his studio when in Italy, "—artiste"? Such examples, no doubt, were familiar to Gustave Rameau, and "homme de lettres" was on the scrap of pasteboard nailed to his door.

Savarin rang; the door opened, and Gustave appeared. The poet was, of course, picturesquely attired. In his day of fashion he had worn within doors a very pretty fanciful costume, designed after portraits of the young Raffaelle; that costume he had preserved—he wore it now. It looked very threadbare, and the pourpoint very soiled. But the beauty of the poet's face had survived the lustre of the garments. True, thanks to absinthe, the cheeks had become somewhat puffy and bloated. Grey was distinctly visible in the long ebon tresses. But still the beauty of the face was of that rare type which a Thorwaldsen or a Gibson seeking a model for a Narcissus would have longed to fix into marble.

Gustave received his former chief with a certain air of reserved dignity; led him into his chamber, only divided by a curtain from his accommodation for washing and slumber, and placed him in an arm-chair beside a drowsy fire—fuel had already become very dear.

"Gustave," said Savarin, "are you in a mood favourable to a little serious talk?"

"Serious talk from M. Savarin is a novelty too great not to command my profoundest interest."

"Thank you,—and to begin: I who know the world and mankind advise you, who do not, never to meet a man who wishes to do you a kindness with an ungracious sarcasm. Irony is a weapon I ought to be skilled in, but weapons are used against enemies, and it is only a tyro who flourishes his rapier in the face of his friends."

"I was not aware that M. Savarin still permitted me to regard him as a friend."

"Because I discharged the duties of friend—remonstrated, advised, and warned. However, let bygones be bygones. I entreated you not to quit the safe shelter of the paternal roof. You insisted on doing so. I entreated you not to send to one of the most ferocious of the Red, or rather, the Communistic, journals, articles, very eloquent, no doubt, but which would most seriously injure you in the eyes of quiet, orderly people, and compromise your future literary career for the sake of a temporary flash in the pan during a very evanescent period of revolutionary excitement. You scorned my adjurations, but at all events you had the grace not to append your true name to those truculent effusions. In literature, if literature revive in France, we two are henceforth separated. But I do not forego the friendly interest I took in you in the days when you were so continually in my house. My wife, who liked you so cordially, implored me to look after you during her absence from Paris, and, enfin, mon pauvre garcon, it would grieve me very much if, when she comes back, I had to say to her, 'Gustave Rameau has thrown away the chance of redemption and of happiness which you deemed was secure to him.' A l'oeil malade, la lumiere nuit."

So saying, he held out his hand kindly.

Gustave, who was far from deficient in affectionate or tender impulses, took the hand respectfully, and pressed it warmly.

"Forgive me if I have been ungracious, M. Savarin, and vouchsafe to hear my explanation."

"Willingly, mon garcon."

"When I became convalescent, well enough to leave my father's house, there were circumstances which compelled me to do so. A young man accustomed to the life of a garcon can't be always tied to his mother's apron-strings."

"Especially if the apron-pocket does not contain a bottle of absinthe," said Savarin, drily. "You may well colour and try to look angry; but I know that the doctor strictly forbade the use of that deadly liqueur, and enjoined your mother to keep strict watch on your liability to its temptations. And hence one cause of your ennui under the paternal roof. But if there you could not imbibe absinthe, you were privileged to enjoy a much diviner intoxication. There you could have the foretaste of domestic bliss,—the society of the girl you loved, and who was pledged to become your wife. Speak frankly. Did not that society itself begin to be wearisome?"

"No," cried Gustave, eagerly, "it was not wearisome—"

"Yes, but—"

"But it could not be all-sufficing to a soul of fire like mine."

"Hem," murmured Savarin—"a soul of fire! This is very interesting; pray go on."

"The calm, cold, sister-like affection of a childish undeveloped nature, which knew no passion except for art, and was really so little emancipated from the nursery as to take for serious truth all the old myths of religion—such companionship may be very soothing and pleasant when one is lying on one's sofa, and must live by rule, but when one regains the vigour of youth and health—"

"Do not pause," said Savarin, gazing with more compassion than envy on that melancholy impersonation of youth and health. "When one regains that vigour of which I myself have no recollection, what happens?"

"The thirst for excitement, the goads of ambition, the irresistible claims which the world urges upon genius, return."

"And that genius, finding itself at the North Pole amid Cimmerian darkness in the atmosphere of a childish intellect—in other words, the society of a pure-minded virgin, who, though a good romance-writer, writes nothing but what a virgin may read, and, though a bel esprit, says her prayers and goes to church—then genius—well, pardon my ignorance, what does genius do?"

"Oh, M. Savarin, M. Savarin! don't let us talk any more. There is no sympathy between us. I cannot bear that bloodless, mocking, cynical mode of dealing with grand emotions, which belongs to the generation of the Doctrinaires. I am not a Thiers or a Guizot."

"Good heavens! who ever accused you of being either? I did not mean to be cynical. Mademoiselle Cicogna has often said I am, but I did not think you would. Pardon me. I quite agree with the philosopher who asserted that the wisdom of the past was an imposture, that the meanest intellect now living is wiser than the greatest intellect which is buried in Pere la Chaise; because the dwarf who follows the giant, when perched on the shoulders of the giant, sees farther than the giant ever could. Allez. I go in for your generation. I abandon Guizot and Thiers. Do condescend and explain to my dull understanding, as the inferior mortal of a former age, what are the grand emotions which impel a soul of fire in your wiser generation. The thirst of excitement—what excitement? The goads of ambition—what ambition?"

"A new social system is struggling from the dissolving elements of the old one, as, in the fables of priestcraft, the soul frees itself from the body which has become ripe for the grave. Of that new system I aspire to be a champion—a leader. Behold the excitement that allures me, the ambition that goads."

"Thank you," said Savarin, meekly; "I am answered. I recognise the dwarf perched on the back of the giant. Quitting these lofty themes, I venture to address to you now one simple matter-of-fact question: How about Mademoiselle Cicogna? Do you think you can induce her to transplant herself to the new social system, which I presume will abolish, among other obsolete myths, the institution of marriage?"

"M. Savarin, your question offends me. Theoretically I am opposed to the existing superstitions that encumber the very simple principle by which may be united two persons so long as they desire the union, and separated so soon as the union becomes distasteful to either. But I am perfectly aware that such theories would revolt a young lady like Mademoiselle Cicogna. I have never even named them to her, and our engagement holds good."

"Engagement of marriage? No period for the ceremony fixed?"

"That is not my fault. I urged it on Isaura with all earnestness before I left my father's house."

"That was long after the siege had begun. Listen to me, Gustave. No persuasion of mine or my wife's, nor Mrs. Morley's, could induce Isaura to quit Paris while it was yet time. She said very simply that, having pledged her truth and hand to you, it would be treason to honour and duty if she should allow any considerations for herself to be even discussed so long as you needed her presence. You were then still suffering, and, though convalescent, not without danger of a relapse. And your mother said to her—I heard the words: ''Tis not for his bodily health I could dare to ask you to stay, when every man who can afford it is sending away his wife, sisters, daughters. As for that, I should suffice to tend him; but if you go, I resign all hope for the health of his mind and his soul.' I think at Paris there may be female poets and artists whom that sort of argument would not have much influenced. But it so happens that Isaura is not a Parisienne. She believes in those old myths which you think fatal to sympathies with yourself; and those old myths also lead her to believe that where a woman has promised she will devote her life to a man, she cannot forsake him when told by his mother that she is necessary to the health of his mind and his soul. Stay. Before you interrupt me, let me finish what I have to say. It appears that, so soon as your bodily health was improved, you felt that your mind and your soul could take care of themselves; and certainly it seems to me that Isaura Cicogna is no longer of the smallest use to either."

Rameau was evidently much disconcerted by this speech. He saw what Savarin was driving at—the renunciation of all bond between Isaura and himself. He was not prepared for such renunciation. He still felt for the Italian as much of love as he could feel for any woman who did not kneel at his feet, as at those of Apollo condescending to the homage of Arcadian maids. But on the one hand, he felt that many circumstances had occurred since the disaster at Sedan to render Isaura a very much less desirable partie than she had been when he had first wrung from her the pledge of betrothal. In the palmy times of a Government in which literature and art commanded station and insured fortune, Isaura, whether as authoress or singer, was a brilliant marriage for Gustave Rameau. She had also then an assured and competent, if modest, income. But when times change, people change with them. As the income for the moment (and Heaven only can say how long that moment might last), Isaura's income had disappeared. It will be recollected that Louvier had invested her whole fortune in the houses to be built in the street called after his name. No houses, even when built, paid any rent now. Louvier had quitted Paris; and Isaura could only be subsisting upon such small sum as she might have had in hand before the siege commenced. All career in such literature and art as Isaura adorned was at a dead stop. Now, to do Rameau justice, he was by no means an avaricious or mercenary man. But he yearned for modes of life to which money was essential. He liked his "comforts;" and his comforts included the luxuries of elegance and show-comforts not to be attained by marriage with Isaura under existing circumstances.

Nevertheless it is quite true that he had urged her to marry him at once, before he had quitted his father's house; and her modest shrinking from such proposal, however excellent the reasons for delay in the national calamities of the time, as well as the poverty which the calamity threatened, had greatly wounded his amour propre. He had always felt that her affection for him was not love; and though he could reconcile himself to that conviction when many solid advantages were attached to the prize of her love, and when he was ill, and penitent, and maudlin, and the calm affection of a saint seemed to him infinitely preferable to the vehement passion of a sinner,—yet when Isaura was only Isaura by herself—Isaura minus all the et cetera which had previously been taken into account—the want of adoration for himself very much lessened her value.

Still, though he acquiesced in the delayed fulfilment of the engagement with Isaura, he had no thought of withdrawing from the engagement itself, and after a slight pause he replied: "You do me great injustice if you suppose that the occupations to which I devote myself render me less sensible to the merits of Mademoiselle Cicogna, or less eager for our union. On the contrary, I will confide to you—as a man of the world—one main reason why I quitted my father's house, and why I desire to keep my present address a secret. Mademoiselle Caumartin conceived for me a passion—a caprice—which was very flattering for a time, but which latterly became very troublesome. Figure to yourself—she daily came to our house while I was lying ill, and with the greatest difficulty my mother got her out of it. That was not all. She pestered me with letters containing all sorts of threats—nay, actually kept watch at the house; and one day when I entered the carriage with my mother and Signora Venosta for a drive in the Bois (meaning to call for Isaura by the way), she darted to the carriage-door, caught my hand, and would have made a scene if the coachman had given her leave to do so. Luckily he had the tact to whip on his horses, and we escaped. I had some little difficulty in convincing the Signora Venosta that the girl was crazed. But I felt the danger I incurred of her coming upon me some moment when in company with Isaura, and so I left my father's house; and naturally wishing to steer clear of this vehement little demon till I am safely married, I keep my address a secret from all who are likely to tell her of it."

"You do wisely if you are really afraid of her, and cannot trust your nerves to say to her plainly, 'I am engaged to be married; all is at an end between us. Do not force me to employ the police to protect myself from unwelcome importunities.'"

"Honestly speaking, I doubt if I have the nerve to do that, and I doubt still more if it would be of any avail. It is very ennuayant to be so passionately loved; but, que voulez vous? It is my fate."

"Poor martyr! I condole with you: and, to say truth, it was chiefly to warn you of Mademoiselle Caumartin's pertinacity that I call this evening."

Here Savarin related the particulars of his rencontre with Julie, and concluded by saying: "I suppose I may take your word of honour that you will firmly resist all temptation to renew a connection which would be so incompatible with the respect due to your fiancee? Fatherless and protectorless as Isaura is, I feel bound to act as a virtual guardian to one in whom my wife takes so deep an interest, and to whom, as she thinks, she had some hand in bringing about your engagement: she is committed to no small responsibilities. Do not allow poor Julie, whom I sincerely pity, to force on me the unpleasant duty of warning your fiancee of the dangers to which she might be subjected by marriage with an Adonis whose fate it is to be so profoundly beloved by the sex in general, and ballet nymphs in particular."

"There is no chance of so disagreeable a duty being incumbent on you, M. Savarin. Of course, what I myself have told you in confidence is sacred."

"Certainly. There are things in the life of a garcon before marriage which would be an affront to the modesty of his fiancee to communicate and discuss. But then those things must belong exclusively to the past and cast no shadow over the future. I will not interrupt you further. No doubt you have work for the night before you. Do the Red journalists for whom you write pay enough to support you in these terribly dear times?"

"Scarcely. But I look forward to wealth and fame in the future. And you?"

"I just escape starvation. If the siege last much longer, it is not of the gout I shall die. Good-night to you."

# CHAPTER XVI.

Isaura had, as we have seen, been hitherto saved by the siege and its consequences from the fulfilment of her engagement to Gustave Rameau; and since he had quitted his father's house she had not only seen less of him, but a certain chill crept into his converse in the visits he paid to her. The compassionate feeling his illness had excited, confirmed by the unwonted gentleness of his mood, and the short-lived remorse with which he spoke of his past faults and follies, necessarily faded away in proportion as he regained that kind of febrile strength which was his normal state of health, and with it the arrogant self-assertion which was ingrained in his character. But it was now more than ever that she became aware of the antagonism between all that constituted his inner life and her own. It was not that he volunteered in her presence the express utterance of those opinions, social or religious, which he addressed to the public in the truculent journal to which, under a nom de plume, he was the most inflammatory contributor. Whether it was that he shrank from insulting the ears of the pure virgin whom he had wooed as wife with avowals of his disdain of marriage bonds, or perhaps from shocking yet more her womanly humanity and her religious faith by cries for the blood of anti-republican traitors and the downfall of Christian altars; or whether he yet clung, though with relapsing affection, to the hold which her promise had imposed on him, and felt that that hold would be for ever gone, and that she would recoil from his side in terror and dismay, if she once learned that the man who had implored her to be his saving angel from the comparatively mild errors of youth, had so belied his assurance, so mocked her credulity, as deliberately to enter into active warfare against all that he knew her sentiments regarded as noble and her conscience received as divine: despite the suppression of avowed doctrine on his part, the total want of sympathy between these antagonistic natures made itself felt by both—more promptly felt by Isaura. If Gustave did not frankly announce to her in that terrible time (when all that a little later broke out on the side of the Communists was more or less forcing ominous way to the lips of those who talked with confidence to each other, whether to approve or to condemn) the associates with whom he was leagued, the path to which he had committed his career—still for her instincts for genuine Art—which for its development needs the serenity of peace, which for its ideal needs dreams that soar into the Infinite—Gustave had only the scornful sneer of the man who identifies with his ambition the violent upset of all that civilisation has established in this world, and the blank negation of all that patient hope and heroic aspiration which humanity carries on into the next.

On his side, Gustave Rameau, who was not without certain fine and delicate attributes in a complicated nature over which the personal vanity and the mobile temperament of the Parisian reigned supreme, chafed at the restraints imposed on him. No matter what a man's doctrines may be—however abominable you and I may deem them—man desires to find, in the dearest fellowship he can establish, that sympathy in the woman his choice singles out from her sex-deference to his opinions, sympathy with his objects, as man. So, too, Gustave's sense of honour and according to his own Parisian code that sense was keen—became exquisitely stung by the thought that he was compelled to play the part of a mean dissimulator to the girl for whose opinions he had the profoundest contempt. How could these two, betrothed to each other, not feel, though without coming to open dissension, that between them had flowed the inlet of water by which they had been riven asunder? What man, if he can imagine himself a Gustave Rameau, can blame the revolutionist absorbed in ambitious projects for turning the pyramid of society topsy-turvy, if he shrank more and more from the companionship of a betrothed with whom he could not venture to exchange three words without caution and reserve? And what woman can blame an Isaura if she felt a sensation of relief at the very neglect of the affianced whom she had compassionated and could never love?

Possibly the reader may best judge of the state of Isaura's mind at this time by a few brief extracts from an imperfect fragmentary journal, in which, amid saddened and lonely hours, she held converse with herself.

"One day at Enghien I listened silently to a conversation between M. Savarin and the Englishman, who sought to explain the conception of duty in which the German poet has given such noble utterance to the thoughts of the German philosopher—viz., that moral aspiration has the same goal as the artistic,—the attainment to the calm delight wherein the pain of effort disappears in the content of achievement. Thus in life, as in art, it is through discipline that we arrive at freedom, and duty only completes itself when all motives, all actions, are attuned into one harmonious whole, and it is not striven for as duty, but enjoyed as happiness. M. Savarin treated this theory with the mockery with which the French wit is ever apt to treat what it terms German mysticism. According to him, duty must always be a hard and difficult struggle; and he said laughingly, 'Whenever a man says, "I have done my duty," it is with a long face and a mournful sigh.'

"Ah, how devoutly I listened to the Englishman! how harshly the Frenchman's irony jarred upon my ears! And yet now, in the duty that life imposes on me, to fulfil which I strain every power vouchsafed to my nature, and seek to crush down every impulse that rebels, where is the promised calm, where any approach to the content of achievement? Contemplating the way before me, the Beautiful even of Art has vanished. I see but cloud and desert. Can this which I assume to be duty really be so? Ah, is it not sin even to ask my heart that question?

"Madame Rameau is very angry with her son for his neglect both of his parents and of me. I have had to take his part against her. I would not have him lose their love. Poor Gustave! But when Madame Rameau suddenly said to-day: 'I erred in seeking the union between thee and Gustave. Retract thy promise; in doing so thou wilt be justified,'—oh, the strange joy that flashed upon me as she spoke. Am I justified? Am I? Oh, if that Englishman had never crossed my path! Oh, if I had never loved! or if in the last time we met he had not asked for my love, and confessed his own! Then, I think, I could honestly reconcile my conscience with my longings, and say to Gustave, 'We do not suit each other; be we both released!' But now-is it that Gustave is really changed from what he was, when in despondence at my own lot, and in pitying belief that I might brighten and exalt his, I plighted my troth to him? or is it not rather that the choice I thus voluntarily made became so intolerable a thought the moment I knew I was beloved and sought by another; and from that moment I lost the strength I had before,—strength to silence the voice at my own heart? What! is it the image of that other one which is persuading me to be false?—to exaggerate the failings, to be blind to the merits of him who has a right to say, 'I am what I was when thou didst pledge thyself to take me for better or for worse'?

"Gustave has been here after an absence of several days. He was not alone. The good Abbe Vertpre and Madame de Vandemar, with her son, M. Raoul, were present. They had come on matters connected with our ambulance. They do not know of my engagement to Gustave; and seeing him in the uniform of a National Guard, the Abbe courteously addressed to him some questions as to the possibility of checking the terrible increase of the vice of intoxication, so alien till of late to the habits of the Parisians, and becoming fatal to discipline and bodily endurance,—could the number of the cantines on the ramparts be more limited? Gustave answered with rudeness and bitter sarcasm, 'Before priests could be critics in military matters they must undertake military service themselves.'

"The Abbe replied with unalterable good-humour, 'But, in order to criticise the effects of drunkenness, must one get drunk one's self?' Gustave was put out, and retired into a corner of the room, keeping sullen silence till my other visitors left.

"Then before I could myself express the pain his words and manner had given me, he said abruptly, 'I wonder how you can tolerate the tartuferie which may amuse on the comic stage, but in the tragedy of these times is revolting.' This speech roused my anger, and the conversation that ensued was the gravest that had ever passed between us.

"If Gustave were of stronger nature and more concentrated will, I believe that the only feelings I should have for him would be antipathy and dread. But it is his very weaknesses and inconsistencies that secure to him a certain tenderness of interest. I think he could never be judged without great indulgence by women; there is in him so much of the child,—wayward, irritating one moment, and the next penitent, affectionate. One feels as if persistence in evil were impossible to one so delicate both in mind and form. That peculiar order of genius to which he belongs seems as if it ought to be so estranged from all directions, violent or coarse. When in poetry he seeks to utter some audacious and defying sentiment, the substance melts away in daintiness of expression, in soft, lute-like strains of slender music. And when he has stung, angered, revolted my heart the most, suddenly he subsides into such pathetic gentleness, such tearful remorse, that I feel as if resentment to one so helpless, desertion of one who must fall without the support of a friendly hand, were a selfish cruelty. It seems to me as if I were dragged towards a precipice by a sickly child clinging to my robe.

"But in this last conversation with him, his language in regard to subjects I hold most sacred drew forth from me words which startled him, and which may avail to save him from that worst insanity of human minds,—the mimicry of the Titans who would have dethroned a God to restore a Chaos. I told him frankly that I had only promised to share his fate on my faith in his assurance of my power to guide it heavenward; and that if the opinions he announced were seriously entertained, and put forth in defiance of heaven itself, we were separated for ever. I told him how earnestly, in the calamities of the time, my own soul had sought to take refuge in thoughts and hopes beyond the earth; and how deeply many a sentiment that in former days passed by me with a smile in the light talk of the salons, now shocked me as an outrage on the reverence which the mortal child owes to the Divine Father. I owned to him how much of comfort, of sustainment, of thought and aspiration, elevated beyond the sphere of Art in which I had hitherto sought the purest air, the loftiest goal, I owed to intercourse with minds like those of the Abbe de Vertpre; and how painfully I felt as if I were guilty of ingratitude when he compelled me to listen to insults on those whom I recognised as benefactors.

"I wished to speak sternly; but it is my great misfortune, my prevalent weakness, that I cannot be stern when I ought to be. It is with me in life as in art. I never could on the stage have taken the part of a Norma or a Medea. If I attempt in fiction a character which deserves condemnation, I am untrue to poetic justice. I cannot condemn and execute; I can but compassionate and pardon the creature I myself have created. I was never in the real world stern but to one; and then, alas! it was because I loved where I could no longer love with honour; and I, knowing my weakness, had terror lest I should yield.

"So Gustave did not comprehend from my voice, my manner, how gravely I was in earnest. But, himself softened, affected to tears, he confessed his own faults—ceased to argue in order to praise; and—and—uttering protestations seemingly the most sincere, he left me bound to him still—bound to him still—woe is me!"

It is true that Isaura had come more directly under the influence of religion than she had been in the earlier dates of this narrative. There is a time in the lives of most of us, and especially in the lives of women, when, despondent of all joy in an earthly future, and tortured by conflicts between inclination and duty, we transfer all the passion and fervour of our troubled souls to enthusiastic yearnings for the Divine Love; seeking to rebaptise ourselves in the fountain of its mercy, taking thence the only hopes that can cheer, the only strength that can sustain us. Such a time had come to Isaura. Formerly she had escaped from the griefs of the work-a-day world into the garden-land of Art. Now, Art had grown unwelcome to her, almost hateful. Gone was the spell from the garden-land; its flowers were faded, its paths were stony, its sunshine had vanished in mist and rain. There are two voices of Nature in the soul of the genuine artist,—that is, of him who, because he can create, comprehends the necessity of the great Creator. Those voices are never both silent. When one is hushed, the other becomes distinctly audible. The one speaks to him of Art, the other of Religion.

At that period several societies for the relief and tendance of the wounded had been formed by the women of Paris,—the earliest, if I mistake not, by ladies of the highest rank—amongst whom were the Comtesse de Vandemar and the Contessa di Rimini—though it necessarily included others of stations less elevated. To this society, at the request of Alain de Rochebriant and of Enguerrand, Isaura had eagerly attached herself. It occupied much of her time; and in connection with it she was brought much into sympathetic acquaintance with Raoul de Vandemar—the most zealous and active member of that Society of St. Francois de Sales, to which belonged other young nobles of the Legitimist creed. The passion of Raoul's life was the relief of human suffering. In him was personified the ideal of Christian charity. I think all, or most of us, have known what it is to pass under the influence of a nature that is so far akin to ours that it desires to become something better and higher than it is—that desire being paramount in ourselves—but seeks to be that something in ways not akin to, but remote from, the ways in which we seek it. When this contact happens, either one nature, by the mere force of will, subjugates and absorbs the other, or both, while preserving their own individuality, apart and independent, enrich themselves by mutual interchange, and the asperities which differences of taste and sentiment in detail might otherwise provoke melt in the sympathy which unites spirits striving with equal earnestness to rise nearer to the unseen and unattainable Source, which they equally recognise as Divine.

Perhaps, had these two persons met a year ago in the ordinary intercourse of the world, neither would have detected the sympathy of which I speak. Raoul was not without the prejudice against artists and writers of romance, that is shared by many who cherish the persuasion that all is vanity which does not concentrate imagination and intellect in the destinies of the soul hereafter; and Isaura might have excited his compassion, certainly not his reverence. While to her, his views on all that seeks to render the actual life attractive and embellished, through the accomplishments of Muse and Grace, would have seemed the narrow-minded asceticism of a bigot. But now, amid the direful calamities of the time, the beauty of both natures became visible to each. To the eyes of Isaura tenderness became predominant in the monastic self-denial of Raoul. To the eyes of Raoul, devotion became predominant in the gentle thoughtfulness of Isaura. Their intercourse was in ambulance and hospital-in care for the wounded, in prayer for the dying. Ah! it is easy to declaim against the frivolities and vices of Parisian society as they appear on the surface; and, in revolutionary times, it is the very worst of Paris that ascends in scum to the top. But descend below the surface, even in that demoralising suspense of order, and nowhere on earth might the angel have beheld the image of humanity more amply vindicating its claim to the heritage of heaven.

# CHAPTER XVII.

The warning announcement of some great effort on the part of the besieged, which Alain had given to Lemercier, was soon to be fulfilled.

For some days the principal thoroughfares were ominously lined with military convois. The loungers on the Boulevards stopped to gaze on the long defiles of troops and cannons, commissariat conveyances, and, saddening accompaniments! the vehicles of various ambulances for the removal of the wounded. With what glee the loungers said to each other "Enfin!" Among all the troops that Paris sent forth, none were so popular as those which Paris had not nurtured—the sailors. From the moment they arrived, the sailors had been the pets of the capital. They soon proved themselves the most notable contrast to that force which Paris herself had produced—the National Guard. Their frames were hardy, their habits active, their discipline perfect, their manners mild and polite. "Oh, if all our troops were like these!" was the common exclamation of the Parisians.

At last burst forth upon Paris the proclamations of General Trochu and General Ducrot; the first brief, calm, and Breton-like, ending with "Putting our trust in God. March on for our country:" the second more detailed, more candidly stating obstacles and difficulties, but fiery with eloquent enthusiasm, not unsupported by military statistics, in the 400 cannon, two-thirds of which were of the largest calibre, that no material object could resist; more than 150,000 soldiers, all well armed, well equipped, abundantly provided with munitions, and all (j'en a l'espoir) animated by an irresistible ardour. "For me," concludes the General, "I am resolved. I swear before you, before the whole nation, that I will not re-enter Paris except as dead or victorious."

At these proclamations, who then at Paris does not recall the burst of enthusiasm that stirred the surface? Trochu became once more popular; even the Communistic or atheistic journals refrained from complaining that he attended mass, and invited his countrymen to trust in God. Ducrot was more than popular—he was adored.

The several companies in which De Mauleon and Enguerrand served departed towards their post early on the same morning, that of the 28th. All the previous night, while Enguerrand was buried in profound slumber,

Raoul remained in his brother's room; sometimes on his knees before the ivory crucifix which had been their mother's last birthday gift to her youngest son—sometimes seated beside the bed in profound and devout meditation. At daybreak, Madame de Vandemar stole into the chamber. Unconscious of his brother's watch, he had asked her to wake him in good time, for the young man was a sound sleeper. Shading the candle she bore with one hand, with the other she drew aside the curtain, and looked at Enguerrand's calm fair face, its lips parted in the happy smile which seemed to carry joy with it wherever its sunshine played. Her tears fell noiselessly on her darling's cheek; she then knelt down and prayed for strength. As she rose she felt Raoul's arm around her; they looked at each other in silence; then she bowed her head and wakened Enguerrand with her lips. "Pas de querelle, mes amis," he murmured, opening his sweet blue eyes drowsily. "Ah, it was a dream! I thought Jules and Emile [two young friends of his] were worrying each other; and you know, dear Raoul, that I am the most officious of peacemakers. Time to rise, is it? No peacemaking to-day. Kiss me again, mother, and say 'Bless thee.'"

"Bless thee, bless thee, my child," cried the mother, wrapping her arms passionately round him, and in tones choked with sobs.

"Now leave me, maman," said Enguerrand, resorting to the infantine ordinary name, which he had not used for years. "Raoul, stay and help me to dress. I must be tres beau to-day. I shall join thee at breakfast, maman. Early for such repast, but l'appetit vient en mangeant. Mind the coffee is hot."

Enguerrand, always careful of each detail of dress, was especially so that morning, and especially gay, humming the old air, "Partant pour la Syrie." But his gaiety was checked when Raoul, taking from his breast a holy talisman, which he habitually wore there, suspended it with loving hands round his brother's neck. It was a small crystal set in Byzantine filigree; imbedded in it was a small splinter of wood, said by pious tradition to be a relic of the Divine Cross. It had been for centuries in the family of the Contessa di Rimini, and was given by her to Raoul, the only gift she had ever made him, as an emblem of the sinless purity of the affection that united those two souls in the bonds of the beautiful belief.

"She bade me transfer it to thee to-day, my brother," said Raoul, simply; "and now without a pang I can gird on thee thy soldier's sword."

Enguerrand clasped his brother in his arms, and kissed him with passionate fervour. "Oh, Raoul, how I love thee! how good thou hast ever been to me! how many sins thou hast saved me from! how indulgent thou hast been to those from which thou couldst not save! Think on that, my brother, in case we do not meet again on earth."

"Hush, hush, Enguerrand! No gloomy forebodings now! Come, come hither, my half of life, my sunny half of life!" and uttering these words, he led Enguerrand towards the crucifix, and there, in deeper and more solemn voice, said, "Let us pray." So the brothers knelt side by side, and Raoul prayed aloud as only such souls can pray.

When they descended into the salon where breakfast was set out, they found assembled several of their relations, and some of Enguerrand's young friends not engaged in the sortie. One or two of the latter, indeed, were disabled from fighting by wounds in former fields; they left their sick-beds to bid him good-bye. Unspeakable was the affection this genial nature inspired in all who came into the circle of its winning magic; and when, tearing himself from them, he descended the stair, and passed with light step through the Porte cochere, there was a crowd around the house—so widely had his popularity spread among even the lower classes, from which the Mobiles in his regiment were chiefly composed. He departed to the place of rendezvous amid a chorus of exhilarating cheers.

Not thus lovingly tended on, not thus cordially greeted, was that equal idol of a former generation, Victor de Mauleon. No pious friend prayed beside his couch, no loving kiss waked him from his slumbers. At the grey of the November dawn he rose from a sleep which had no smiling dreams, with that mysterious instinct of punctual will which cannot even go to sleep without fixing beforehand the exact moment in which sleep shall end. He, too, like Enguerrand, dressed himself with care—unlike Enguerrand, with care strictly soldier-like. Then, seeing he had some little time yet before him, he rapidly revisited the pigeonholes and drawers in which might be found by prying eyes anything he would deny to them curiosity. All that he found of this sort were some letters in female handwriting, tied together with faded ribbon, relics of earlier days, and treasured throughout later vicissitudes; letters from the English girl to whom he had briefly referred in his confession to Louvier,—the only girl he had ever wooed as his wife. She was the only daughter of highborn Roman Catholics, residing at the time of his youth in Paris. Reluctantly they had assented to his proposals; joyfully they had retracted their assent when his affairs had become so involved; yet possibly the motive that led him to his most ruinous excesses—the gambling of the turf—had been caused by the wild hope of a nature, then fatally sanguine, to retrieve the fortune that might suffice to satisfy the parents. But during his permitted courtship the lovers had corresponded. Her letters were full of warm, if innocent, tenderness—till came the last cold farewell.

The family had long ago returned to England; he concluded, of course, that she had married another.

Near to these letters lay the papers which had served to vindicate his honour in that old affair, in which the unsought love of another had brought on him shame and affliction. As his eye fell on the last, he muttered to him self, "I kept these, to clear my repute. Can I keep those, when, if found, they might compromise the repute of her who might have been my wife had I been worthy of her? She is doubtless now another's; or, if dead,—honour never dies." He pressed his lips to the letters with a passionate, lingering, mournful kiss; then, raking up the ashes of yesterday's fire, and rekindling them, he placed thereon those leaves of a melancholy romance in his past, and watched them slowly, reluctantly smoulder away into tinder. Then he opened a drawer in which lay the only paper of a political character which he had preserved. All that related to plots or conspiracies in which his agency had committed others, it was his habit to destroy as soon as received. For the sole document thus treasured he alone was responsible; it was an outline of his ideal for the future constitution of France, accompanied with elaborate arguments, the heads of which his conversation with the Incognito made known to the reader. Of the soundness of this political programme, whatever its merits or faults (a question on which I presume no judgment), he had an intense conviction. He glanced rapidly over its contents, did not alter a word, sealed it up in an envelope, inscribed, "My Legacy to my Countrymen." The papers refuting a calumny relating solely to himself he carried into the battle-field, placed next to his heart,—significant of a Frenchman's love of honour in this world—as the relic placed round the neck of Enguerrand by his pious brother was emblematic of the Christian hope of mercy in the next.

# CHAPTER XVIII.

The streets swarmed with the populace troops as they passed to their destination. Among those of the Mobiles who especially caught the eye were two companies in which Enguerrand de Vandemar and Victor de Mauleon commanded. In the first were many young men of good family, or in the higher ranks of the bourgeoisie, known to numerous lookers-on; there was something inspiriting in their gay aspects, and in the easy carelessness of their march. Mixed with this company, however, and forming of course the bulk of it, were those who belonged to the lower classes of the population; and though they too might seem gay to an ordinary observer, the gaiety was forced. Many of them were evidently not quite sober; and there was a disorderly want of soldiership in their mien and armament which inspired distrust among such vieux moustaches as, too old for other service than that of the ramparts, mixed here and there among the crowd.

But when De Mauleon's company passed, the vieux moustaches impulsively touched each other. They recognised the march of well-drilled men; the countenances grave and severe, the eyes not looking on this side and that for admiration, the step regularly timed; and conspicuous among these men the tall stature and calm front of the leader.

"These fellows will fight well," growled a vieux moustache, "where did they fish out their leader?"

"Don't you know?" said a bourgeois. "Victor de Mauleon. He won the cross in Algeria for bravery. I recollect him when I was very young; the very devil for women and fighting."

"I wish there were more such devils for fighting and fewer for women," growled again le vieux moustache.

One incessant roar of cannon all the night of the 29th. The populace had learned the names of the French cannons, and fancied they could distinguish the several sounds of their thunder. "There spits 'Josephine'!" shouts an invalid sailor. "There howls our own 'Populace'!" cries a Red Republican from Belleville.

*[The "Populace" had been contributed to the artillery,*
*sou a sou, by the working class.]*

"There sings 'Le Chatiment'!" laughed Gustave Rameau, who was now become an enthusiastic admirer of the Victor Hugo he had before affected to despise. And all the while, mingled with the roar of the cannon, came, far and near from the streets, from the ramparts, the gusts of song—song sometimes heroic, sometimes obscene, more often carelessly joyous. The news of General Vinoy's success during the early part of the day had been damped by the evening report of Ducrot's delay in crossing the swollen Marne. But the spirits of the Parisians rallied from a momentary depression on the excitement at night of that concert of martial music.

During that night, close under the guns of the double redoubt of Gravelle and La Faisanderie, eight pontoon-bridges were thrown over the Marne; and at daybreak the first column of the third army under Blanchard and Renoult crossed with all their artillery, and, covered by the fire of the double redoubts, of the forts of Vincennes, Nogent, Rossuey, and the batteries of Mont Avron, had an hour before noon carried the village of Champingy, and the first echelon of the important plateau of Villiers, and were already commencing the work of intrenchment, when, rallying from the amaze of a defeat, the German forces burst upon them, sustained by fresh batteries. The Prussian pieces of artillery established at Chennevieres and at Neuilly opened fire with deadly execution; while a numerous infantry, descending from the intrenchments of Villiers, charged upon the troops under Renoult. Among the French in that strife were Enguerrand and the Mobiles of which he was in command. Dismayed by the unexpected fire, these Mobiles gave way, as indeed did many of the line. Enguerrand rushed forward to the front: "On, mes enfans, on! What will our mothers and wives say of us if we fly? Vive la France!—On!" Among those of the better class in that company there rose a shout of applause, but it found no sympathy among the rest. They wavered, they turned. "Will you suffer me to go on alone, countrymen?" cried Enguerrand; and alone he rushed on towards the Prussian line—rushed, and fell, mortally wounded, by a musket-ball. "Revenge, revenge!" shouted some of the foremost; "Revenge!" shouted those in the rear; and, so shouting, turned on their heels and fled. But ere they could disperse they encountered the march, steadfast though rapid, of the troop led by Victor de Mauleon. "Poltroons!" he thundered, with the sonorous depth of his strong voice, "halt and turn, or my men shall fire on you as deserters."

"Va, citoyen," said one fugitive, an officer-popularly elected, because he was the loudest brawler in the club of the Salle Favre,—we have seen him before—Charles, the brother of Armand Monnier;—"men can't fight when they despise their generals. It is our generals who are poltroons and fools both."

"Carry my answer to the ghosts of cowards," cried De Mauldon, and shot the man dead.

His followers, startled and cowed by the deed, and the voice and the look of the death-giver, halted. The officers, who had at first yielded to the panic of their men, took fresh courage, and finally led the bulk of the troop back to their post "enlevis a la baionette," to use the phrase of a candid historian of that day.

Day, on the whole, not inglorious to France. It was the first, if it was the last, really important success of the besieged. They remained masters of the ground, the Prussians leaving to them the wounded and the dead.

That night what crowds thronged from Paris to the top of the Montmartre heights, from the observatory on which the celebrated inventor Bazin had lighted up, with some magical electric machine, all the plain of Gennevilliers from Mont Valerien to the Fort de la Briche! The splendour of the blaze wrapped the great city;—distinctly above the roofs of the houses soared the Dome des Invalides, the spires of Notre Dame, the giant turrets of the Tuileries;—and died away on resting on the infames scapulos Acroceraunia, the "thunder crags" of the heights occupied by the invading army.

Lemercier, De Breze, and the elder Rameau—who, despite his peaceful habits and grey hairs, insisted on joining in the aid of la patrie—were among the National Guards attached to the Fort de la Briche and the neighbouring eminence, and they met in conversation.

"What a victory we have had!" said the old Rameau.

"Rather mortifying to your son, M. Rameau," said LeMercier.

"Mortifying to my son, sir!—the victory of his countrymen. What do you mean?"

"I had the honour to hear M. Gustave the other night at the club de la Vengeance."

"Bon Dieu! do you frequent those tragic reunions?" asked De Breze.

"They are not at all tragic: they are the only comedies left us, as one must amuse one's self somewhere, and the club de la Vengeance is the prettiest thing of the sort going. I quite understand why it should fascinate a poet like your son, M. Rameau. It is held in a salle de cafe chantant—style Louis Quinze—decorated with a pastoral scene from Watteau. I and my dog Fox drop in. We hear your son haranguing. In what poetical sentences he despaired of the Republic! The Government (he called them les charlatans de l'Hotel de Ville) were imbeciles. They pretended to inaugurate a revolution, and did not employ the most obvious of revolutionary means. There Fox and I pricked up our ears: what were those means? Your son proceeded to explain: 'All mankind were to be appealed to against individual interests. The commerce of luxury was to be abolished. Clearly luxury was not at the command of all mankind. Cafes and theatres were to be closed for ever—all mankind could not go to cafes and theatres. It was idle to expect the masses to combine for anything in which the masses had not an interest in common. The masses had no interest in any property that did not belong to the masses. Programmes of the society to be founded, called the Ligue Cosmopolite Democratique, should be sent at once into all the States of the civilised world—how? by balloons. Money corrupts the world as now composed: but the money at the command of the masses could buy all the monarchs and courtiers and priests of the universe.' At that sentiment, vehemently delivered, the applauses were frantic, and Fox in his excitement began to bark. At the sound of his bark one man cried out, 'That's a Prussian!' another, 'Down with the spy!' another, 'There's an aristo present—he keeps alive a dog which would be a week's meal for a family!' I snatch up Fox at the last cry, and clasp him to a bosom protected by the uniform of the National Guard.

"When the hubbub had subsided, your son, M. Rameau, proceeded, quitting mankind in general, and arriving at the question in particular most interesting to his audience—the mobilisation of the National Guard; that is, the call upon men who like talking and hate fighting to talk less and fight more. 'It was the sheerest tyranny to select a certain number of free citizens to be butchered. If the fight was for the mass, there ought to be la levee en masse. If one did not compel everybody to fight, why should anybody fight?' Here the applause again became vehement, and Fox again became indiscreet. I subdued Fox's bark into a squeak by pulling his ears. 'What!' cries your poet-son, 'la levee en masse gives us fifteen millions of soldiers, with which we could crush, not Prussia alone, but the whole of Europe. (Immense sensation.) Let us, then, resolve that the charlatans of the Hotel de Ville are incapable of delivering us from the Prussians; that they are deposed; that the Ligue of the Democratie Cosmopolite is installed; that meanwhile the Commune shall be voted the Provisional Government, and shall order the Prussians to retire within three days from the soil of Paris.'

"Pardon me this long description, my dear M. Rameau, but I trust I have satisfactorily explained why victory obtained in the teeth of his eloquent opinions, if gratifying to him as a Frenchman, must be mortifying to him as a politician."

The old Rameau sighed, hung his head, and crept away. While, amid this holiday illumination, the Parisians enjoyed the panorama before them, the Freres Chretiens and the attendants of the various ambulances were moving along the battle-plains; the first in their large-brimmed hats and sable garbs, the last in strange motley costume, many of them in glittering uniform—all alike in their serene indifference to danger; often pausing to pick up among the dead their own brethren who had been slaughtered in the midst of their task. Now and then they came on sinister forms apparently engaged in the same duty of tending the wounded and dead, but in truth murderous plunderers, to whom the dead and the dying were equal harvests. Did the wounded man attempt to resist the foul hands searching for their spoil, they added another wound more immediately mortal, grinning as they completed on the dead the robbery they had commenced on the dying.

Raoul de Vandemar had been all the earlier part of the day with the assistants of the ambulance over which he presided, attached to the battalions of the National Guard in a quarter remote from that in which his brother had fought and fallen. When those troops, later in the day, were driven from the Montmedy plateau, which they had at first carried, Raoul repassed towards the plateau at Villiers, on which the dead lay thickest. On the way he heard a vague report of the panic which had dispersed the Mobiles of whom Enguerrand was in command, and of Enguerrand's vain attempt to inspirit them. But his fate was not known. There, at midnight, Raoul is still searching among the ghastly heaps and pools of blood, lighted from afar by the blaze from the observatory of Montmartre, and more near at hand by the bivouac fires extended along the banks to the left of the Marne, while everywhere about the field flitted the lanterns of the Frere Chretiens. Suddenly, in the dimness of a spot cast into shadow by an incompleted earthwork, he observed a small sinister figure perched on the breast of some wounded soldier, evidently not to succour. He sprang forward and seized a hideous-looking urchin, scarcely twelve years old, who held in one hand a small crystal locket, set in filigree gold, torn from the soldier's breast, and lifted high in the other a long case-knife. At a glance Raoul recognised the holy relic he had given to Enguerrand, and, flinging the precocious murderer to be seized by his assistants, he cast himself beside his brother. Enguerrand still breathed, and his languid eyes brightened as he knew the dear familiar face. He tried to speak, but his voice failed, and he shook his head sadly, but still with a faint smile on his lips. They lifted him tenderly, and placed him on a litter. The movement, gentle as it was, brought back pain, and with the pain strength to mutter, "My mother—-I would see her once more."

As at daybreak the loungers on Montmartre and the ramparts descended into the streets—most windows in which were open, as they had been all night, with anxious female faces peering palely down-they saw the conveyances of the ambulances coming dismally along, and many an eye turned wistfully towards the litter on which lay the idol of the pleasure-loving Paris, with the dark, bareheaded figure walking beside it,—onwards, onwards, till it reached the Hotel de Vandemar, and a woman's cry was heard at the entrance—the mother's cry, "My son! my son!"

# BOOK XII.

## CHAPTER I.

The last book closed with the success of the Parisian sortie on the 30th of November, to be followed by the terrible engagements no less honourable to French valour, on the 2nd of December. There was the sanguine belief that deliverance was at hand; that Trochu would break through the circle of iron, and effect that junction with the army of Aurelles de Paladine which would compel the Germans to raise the investment;—belief rudely shaken by Ducrot's proclamation of the 4th, to explain the recrossing of the Marne, and the abandonment of the positions conquered, but not altogether dispelled till von Moltke's letter to Trochu on the 5th announcing the defeat of the army of the Loire and the recapture of Orleans. Even then the Parisians did not lose hope of succour; and even after the desperate and fruitless sortie against Le Bourget on the 21st, it was not without witticisms on defeat and predictions of triumph, that Winter and Famine settled sullenly on the city.

Our narrative reopens with the last period of the siege.

It was during these dreadful days, that if the vilest and the most hideous aspects of the Parisian population showed themselves at the worst, so all its loveliest, its noblest, its holiest characteristics—unnoticed by ordinary observers in the prosperous days of the capital—became conspicuously prominent. The higher classes, including the remnant of the old noblesse, had, during the whole siege, exhibited qualities in notable contrast to those assigned them by the enemies of aristocracy. Their sons had been foremost among those soldiers who never calumniated a leader, never fled before a foe; their women had been among the most zealous and the most tender nurses of the ambulances they had founded and served; their houses had been freely opened, whether to the families exiled from the suburbs, or in supplement to the hospitals. The amount of relief they afforded unostentatiously, out of means that shared the general failure of accustomed resource, when the famine commenced, would be scarcely credible if stated. Admirable, too, were the fortitude and resignation of the genuine Parisian bourgeoisie,—the thrifty tradesfolk and small rentiers,—that class in which, to judge of its timidity when opposed to a mob, courage is not the most conspicuous virtue. Courage became so now—courage to bear hourly increasing privation, and to suppress every murmur of suffering that would discredit their patriotism, and invoke "peace at any price." It was on this class that the calamities of the siege now pressed the most heavily. The stagnation of trade, and the stoppage of the rents, in which they had invested their savings, reduced many of them to actual want. Those only of their number who obtained the pay of one-and-a-half franc a day as National Guards, could be sure to escape from starvation. But this pay had already begun to demoralise the receivers. Scanty for supply of food, it was ample for supply of drink. And drunkenness, hitherto rare in that rank of the Parisians, became a prevalent vice, aggravated in the case of a National Guard, when it wholly unfitted him for the duties he undertook, especially such National Guards as were raised from the most turbulent democracy of the working class.

But of all that population; there were two sections in which the most beautiful elements of our human nature were most touchingly manifest—the women and the priesthood, including in the latter denomination all the various brotherhoods and societies which religion formed and inspired.

It was on the 27th of December that Frederic Lemercier stood gazing wistfully on a military report affixed to a blank wall, which stated that "the enemy, worn out by a resistance of over one hundred days," had commenced the bombardment. Poor Frederic was sadly altered; he had escaped the Prussian's guns, but not the Parisian winter—the severest known for twenty years. He was one of the many frozen at their posts—brought back to the ambulance with Fox in his bosom trying to keep him warm. He had only lately been sent forth as convalescent,—ambulances were too crowded to retain a patient longer than absolutely needful,—and had been hunger-pinched and frost-pinched ever since. The luxurious Frederic had still, somewhere or other, a capital yielding above three thousand a year, and of which he could not now realise a franc, the title-deeds to various investments being in the hands of Duplessis, the most trustworthy of friends, the most upright of men, but who was in Bretagne, and could not be got at. And the time had come at Paris when you could not get trust for a pound of horse-flesh, or a daily supply of fuel. And Frederic Lemercier, who had long since spent the 2000 francs borrowed from Alain (not ignobly, but somewhat ostentatiously, in feasting any acquaintance who wanted a feast), and who had sold to any one who could afford to speculate on such dainty luxuries,—clocks, bronzes, amber-mounted pipes,—all that had made the envied garniture of his bachelor's apartment—Frederic Lemercier was, so far as the task of keeping body and soul together, worse off than any English pauper who can apply to the Union. Of course he might have claimed his half-pay of thirty sous as a National Guard. But he little knows the true Parisian who imagines a seigneur of the Chaussee d'Antin, the oracle of those with whom he lived, and one who knew life so well that he had preached prudence to a seigneur of the Faubourg like Alain de Rochebriant, stooping to apply for the wages of thirty sons. Rations were only obtained by the wonderful patience of women, who had children to whom they were both saints and martyrs. The hours, the weary hours, one had to wait before one could get one's place on the line for the distribution of that atrocious black bread, defeated men,—defeated most wives if only for husbands, were defied only by mothers and daughters. Literally speaking, Lemercier was starving. Alain had been badly wounded in the sortie of the 21st, and was laid up in an ambulance. Even if he could have been got at, he had probably nothing left to bestow upon Lemercier.

Lemercier gazed on the announcement of the bombardment, and the Parisian gaiety, which some French historian of the siege calls douce philosophie, lingering on him still, he said, audibly, turning round to any stranger who heard: "Happiest of mortals that we are! Under the present Government we are never warned of anything disagreeable that can happen; we are only told of it when it has happened, and then as rather pleasant than otherwise. I get up. I meet a civil gendarme. 'What is that firing? which of our provincial armies is taking Prussia in the rear? 'Monsieur,' says the gendarme, 'it is the Prussian Krupp guns.' I look at the proclamation, and my fears varnish,—my heart is relieved. I read that the bombardment is a sure sign that the enemy is worn out."

Some of the men grouped round Frederic ducked their heads in terror; others, who knew that the thunderbolt launched from the plateau of Avron would not fall on the pavements of Paris, laughed and joked. But in front, with no sign of terror, no sound of laughter, stretched, moving inch by inch, the female procession towards the bakery in which the morsel of bread for their infants was doled out.

"Hist, mon ami," said a deep voice beside Lemercier. "Look at those women, and do not wound their ears by a jest."

Lemercier, offended by that rebuke, though too susceptible to good emotions not to recognise its justice, tried with feeble fingers to turn up his moustache, and to turn a defiant crest upon the rebuker. He was rather startled to see the tall martial form at his side, and to recognise Victor de Mauleon. "Don't you think, M. Lemercier," resumed the Vicomte, half sadly, "that these women are worthy of better husbands and sons than are commonly found among the soldiers whose uniform we wear?"

"The National Guard! You ought not to sneer at them, Vicomte,—you whose troop covered itself with glory on the great days of Villiers and Champigny,—you in whose praise even the grumblers of Paris became eloquent, and in whom a future Marshal of France is foretold."

"But, alas! more than half of my poor troop was left on the battle-field, or is now wrestling for mangled remains of life in the ambulances. And the new recruits with which I took the field on the 21st are not likely to cover themselves with glory, or to insure their commander the baton of a marshal."

"Ay, I heard when I was in the hospital that you had publicly shamed some of these recruits, and declared that you would rather resign than lead them again to battle."

"True; and at this moment, for so doing, I am the man most hated by the rabble who supplied those recruits." The men, while thus conversing, had moved slowly on, and were now in front of a large cafe, from the interior of which came the sound of loud bravos and clappings of hands. Lemercier's curiosity was excited. "For what can be that applause?" he said; "let us look in and see." The room was thronged. In the distance, on a small raised platform, stood a girl dressed in faded theatrical finery, making her obeisance to the crowd.

"Heavens!" exclaimed Frederic—"can I trust my eyes? Surely that is the once superb Julie: has she been dancing here?"

One of the loungers, evidently belonging to the same world as Lemercier, overheard the question and answered politely: "No, Monsieur: she has been reciting verses, and really declaims very well, considering it is not her vocation. She has given us extracts from Victor Hugo and De Musset: and crowned all with a patriotic hymn by Gustave Rameau,—her old lover, if gossip be true." Meanwhile De Mauleon, who at first had glanced over the scene with his usual air of calm and cold indifference, became suddenly struck by the girl's beautiful face, and gazed on it with a look of startled surprise.

"Who and what did you say that poor fair creature is, M. Lemercier?"

"She is a Mademoiselle Julie Caumartin, and was a very popular coryphee. She has hereditary right to be a good dancer, as the daughter of a once more famous ornament of the ballet, la belle Leonie—whom you must have seen in your young days."

"Of course. Leonie—she married a M. Surville, a silly bourgeois gentilhomme, who earned the hatred of Paris by taking her off the stage. So that is her daughter I see no likeness to her mother—much handsomer. Why does she call herself Caumartin?"

"Oh," said Frederic, "a melancholy but trite story."

"Leonie was left a widow, and died in want. What could the poor young daughter do? She found a rich protector, who had influence to get her an appointment in the ballet: and there she did as most girls so circumstanced do—appeared under an assumed name, which she has since kept."

"I understand," said Victor, compassionately. "Poor thing! she has quitted the platform, and is coming this way, evidently to speak to you. I saw her eyes brighten as she caught sight of your face."

Lemercier attempted a languid air of modest self-complacency as the girl now approached him. "Bonjour, M. Frederic! Ah, mon Dieu! how thin you have grown! You have been ill?"

"The hardships of a military life, Mademoiselle. Ah, for the beaux fours and the peace we insisted on destroying under the Empire which we destroyed for listening to us! But you thrive well, I trust. I have seen you better dressed, but never in greater beauty."

The girl blushed as she replied, "Do you really think as you speak?"

"I could not speak more sincerely if I lived in the legendary House of Glass."

The girl clutched his arm, and said in suppressed tones, "Where is Gustave?"

"Gustave Rameau? I have no idea. Do you never see him now?"

"Never,—perhaps I never shall see him again; but when you do meet him, say that Julie owes to him her livelihood. An honest livelihood, Monsieur. He taught her to love verses—told her how to recite them. I am engaged at this cafe—you will find me here the same hour every day, in case—in case—You are good and kind, and will come and tell me that Gustave is well and happy even if he forgets me. Au revoir! Stop, you do look, my poor Frederic, as if—as if—pardon me, Monsieur Lemercier, is there anything I can do? Will you condescend to borrow from me? I am in funds."

Lemercier at that offer was nearly moved to tears. Famished though he was, he could not, however, have touched that girl's earnings.

"You are an angel of goodness, Mademoiselle! Ah, how I envy Gustave Rameau! No, I don't want aid. I am always a—rentier."

"Bien! and if you see Gustave, you will not forget."

"Rely on me. Come away," he said to De Mauleon; "I don't want to hear that girl repeat the sort of bombast the poets indite nowadays. It is fustian; and that girl may have a brain of feather, but she has a heart of gold."

"True," said Victor, as they regained the street. "I overheard what she said to you. What an incomprehensible thing is a woman! how more incomprehensible still is a woman's love! Ah, pardon me; I must leave you. I see in the procession a poor woman known to me in better days."

De Mauleon walked towards the woman he spoke of—one of the long procession to the bakery—a child clinging to her robe. A pale grief-worn woman, still young, but with the weariness of age on her face, and the shadow of death on her child's.

"I think I see Madame Monnier," said De Mauleon, softly.

She turned and looked at him drearily. A year ago, she would have blushed if addressed by a stranger in a name not lawfully hers.

"Well," she said, in hollow accents broken by cough; "I don't know you, Monsieur."

"Poor woman!" he resumed, walking beside her as she moved slowly on, while the eyes of other women in the procession stared at him hungrily. "And your child looks ill too. It is your youngest?"

"My only one! The others are in Pere la Chaise. There are but few children alive in my street now. God has been very merciful, and taken them to Himself."

De Mauleon recalled the scene of a neat comfortable apartment, and the healthful happy children at play on the floor. The mortality among the little ones, especially in the quartier occupied by the working classes, had of late been terrible. The want of food, of fuel, the intense severity of the weather, had swept them off as by a pestilence.

"And Monnier—what of him? No doubt he is a National Guard, and has his pay?"

The woman made no answer, but hung down her head. She was stifling a sob. Till then her eyes seemed to have exhausted the last source of tears.

"He lives still?" continued Victor, pityingly: "he is not wounded?"

"No: he is well—in health; thank you kindly, Monsieur."

"But his pay is not enough to help you, and of course he can get no work. Excuse me if I stopped you. It is because I owed Armand Monnier a little debt for work, and I am ashamed to say that it quite escaped my memory in these terrible events. Allow me, Madame, to pay it to you," and he thrust his purse into her hand. "I think this contains about the sum I owed; if more or less, we will settle the difference later. Take care of yourself."

He was turning away when the woman caught hold of him.

"Stay, Monsieur. May Heaven bless you!—but—but tell me what name I am to give to Armand. I can't think of any one who owed him money. It must have been before that dreadful strike, the beginning of all our woes. Ah, if it were allowed to curse any one, I fear my last breath would not be a prayer."

"You would curse the strike, or the master who did not forgive Armand's share in it?"

"No, no,—the cruel man who talked him into it—into all that has changed the best workman, the kindest heart—the—the—" again her voice died in sobs.

"And who was that man?" asked De Mauleon, falteringly.

"His name was Lebeau. If you were a poor man, I should say 'Shun him.'"

"I have heard of the name you mention; but if we mean the same person, Monnier cannot have met him lately. He has not been in Paris since the siege."

"I suppose not, the coward! He ruined us—us who were so happy before; and then, as Armand says, cast us away as instruments he had done with. But—but if you do know him, and do see him again, tell him—tell him not to complete his wrong—not to bring murder on Armand's soul. For Armand isn't what he was—and has become, oh, so violent! I dare not take this money without saying who gave it. He would not take money as alms from an aristocrat. Hush! he beat me for taking money from the good Monsieur Raoul de Vandemar—my poor Armand beat me!"

De Mauleon shuddered. "Say that it is from a customer whose rooms he decorated in his spare hours on his own account before the strike,—Monsieur ————;" here he uttered indistinctly some unpronounceable name and hurried off, soon lost as the streets grew darker. Amid groups of a higher order of men-military men, nobles, ci-devant deputies—among such ones his name stood very high. Not only his bravery in the recent sorties had been signal, but a strong belief in his military talents had become prevalent; and conjoined with the name he had before established as a political writer, and the remembrance of the vigour and sagacity with which he had opposed the war, he seemed certain, when peace and order became established, of a brilliant position and career in a future administration: not less because he had steadfastly kept aloof from the existing Government, which it was rumoured, rightly or erroneously, that he had been solicited to join; and from every combination of the various democratic or discontented factions.

Quitting these more distinguished associates, he took his way alone towards the ramparts. The day was closing; the thunders of the cannon were dying down.

He passed by a wine-shop round which were gathered many of the worse specimens of the Moblots and National Guards, mostly drunk, and loudly talking in vehement abuse of generals and officers and commissariat. By one of the men, as he came under the glare of a petroleum lamp (there was gas no longer in the dismal city), he was recognised as the commander who had dared to insist on discipline, and disgrace honest patriots who claimed to themselves the sole option between fight and flight. The man was one of those patriots—one of the new recruits whom Victor had shamed and dismissed for mutiny and cowardice. He made a drunken plunge at his former chief, shouting, "A bas Pai-isto! Comrades, this is the coquin De Mauleon who is paid by the Prussians for getting us killed: a la lanterne!" "A la lanterne!" stammered and hiccupped others of the group; but they did not stir to execute their threat. Dimly seen as the stern face and sinewy form of the threatened man was by their drowsied eyes, the name of De Mauleon, the man without fear of a foe, and without ruth for a mutineer, sufficed to protect him from outrage; and with a slight movement of his arm that sent his denouncer reeling against the lamp-post, De Mauleon passed on:—when another man, in the uniform of a National Guard, bounded from the door of the tavern, crying with a loud voice, "Who said De Mauleon?—let me look on him:" and Victor, who had strode on with slow lion-like steps, cleaving the crowd, turned, and saw before him in the gleaming light a face, in which the bold frank, intelligent aspect of former days was lost in a wild, reckless, savage expression—the face of Armand Monnier.

"Ha! are you really Victor de Mauleon?" asked Monnier, not fiercely, but under his breath,—in that sort of stage whisper which is the natural utterance of excited men under the mingled influence of potent drink and hoarded rage.

"Certainly; I am Victor de Mauleon."

"And you were in command of the—company of the National Guard on the 30th of November at Champigny and Villiers?"

"I was."

"And you shot with your own hand an officer belonging to another company who refused to join yours?"

"I shot a cowardly soldier who ran away from the enemy, and seemed a ringleader of other runaways; and in so doing, I saved from dishonour the best part of his comrades."

"The man was no coward. He was an enlightened Frenchman, and worth fifty of such aristos as you; and he knew better than his officers that he was to be led to an idle slaughter. Idle—I say idle. What was France the better, how was Paris the safer, for the senseless butchery of that day? You mutinied against a wiser general than Saint Trochu when you murdered that mutineer."

"Armand Monnier, you are not quite sober to-night, or I would argue with you that question. But you no doubt are brave: how and why do you take the part of a runaway?"

"How and why? He was my brother, and you own you murdered him: my brother—the sagest head in Paris. If I had listened to him, I should not be,—bah!—no matter now what I am."

"I could not know he was your brother; but if he had been mine I would have done the same."

Here Victor's lip quivered, for Monnier griped him by the arm, and looked him in the face with wild stony eyes. "I recollect that voice! Yet—yet—you say you are a noble, a Vicomte—Victor de Mauleon, and you shot my brother!"

Here he passed his left hand rapidly over his forehead. The fumes of wine still clouded his mind, but rays of intelligence broke through the cloud. Suddenly he said in a loud, and calm, and natural voice:

"Mons. le Vicomte, you accost me as Armand Monnier—pray how do you know my name?"

"How should I not know it? I have looked into the meetings of the 'Clubs rouges.' I have heard you speak, and naturally asked your name. Bon soir M. Monnier! When you reflect in cooler moments, you will see that if patriots excuse Brutus for first dishonouring and then executing his own son, an officer charged to defend his country may be surely pardoned for slaying a runaway to whom he was no relation, when in slaying he saved the man's name and kindred from dishonour—unless, indeed, you insist on telling the world why he was slain."

"I know your voice—I know it. Every sound becomes clearer to my ear. And if—"

But while Monnier thus spoke, De Mauleon had hastened on. Monnier looked round, saw him gone, but did not pursue. He was just intoxicated enough to know that his footsteps were not steady, and he turned back to the wine-shop and asked surlily for more wine. Could you have seen him then as he leant swinging himself to and fro against the wall,—had you known the man two years ago, you would have been a brute if you felt disgust. You could only have felt that profound compassion with which we gaze on a great royalty fallen. For the grandest of all royalties is that which takes its crown from Nature, needing no accident of birth. And Nature made the mind of Armand Monnier king-like; endowed it with lofty scorn of meanness and falsehood and dishonour, with warmth and tenderness of heart which had glow enough to spare from ties of kindred and hearth and home, to extend to those distant circles of humanity over which royal natures would fain extend the shadow of their sceptre.

How had the royalty of the man's nature fallen thus? Royalty rarely falls from its own constitutional faults. It falls when, ceasing to be royal, it becomes subservient to bad advisers. And what bad advisers, always appealing to his better qualities and so enlisting his worser, had discrowned this mechanic?

"A little knowledge is a dangerous thing," says the old-fashioned poet.

"Not so," says the modern philosopher; "a little knowledge; is safer than no knowledge." Possibly, as all individuals and all communities must go through the stage of a little knowledge before they can arrive at that of much knowledge, the philosopher's assertion may be right in the long-run, and applied to humankind in general. But there is a period, as there is a class, in which a little knowledge tends to terrible demoralisation. And Armand Monnier lived in that period and was one of that class. The little knowledge that his mind, impulsive and ardent, had picked up out of books that warred with the great foundations of existing society, had originated in ill advices. A man stored with much knowledge would never have let Madame de Grantmesnil's denunciations of marriage rites, or Louis Blane's vindication of Robespierre as the representative of the working against the middle class, influence his practical life. He would have assessed such opinions at their real worth; and whatever that worth might seem to him, would not to such opinions have committed the conduct of his life. Opinion is not fateful: conduct is. A little knowledge crazes an earnest, warm-blooded, powerful creature like Armand Monnier into a fanatic. He takes an opinion which pleases him as a revelation from the gods; that opinion shapes his conduct; that conduct is his fate. Woe to the philosopher who serenely flings before the little knowledge of the artisan dogmas as harmless as the Atlantis of Plato if only to be discussed by philosophers, and deadly as the torches of Ate if seized as articles of a creed by fanatics! But thrice woe to the artisan who makes himself the zealot of the Dogma!

Poor Armand acts on the opinions he adopts; proves his contempt for the marriage state by living with the wife of another; resents, as natures so inherently manly must do, the Society that visits on her his defiance of its laws; throws himself, head foremost, against that society altogether; necessarily joins all who have other reasons for hostility to Society; he himself having every inducement not to join indiscriminate strikes—high wages, a liberal employer, ample savings, the certainty of soon becoming employer himself. No; that is not enough to the fanatic: he persists on being dupe and victim. He, this great king of labour, crowned by Nature, and cursed with that degree of little knowledge which does not comprehend how much more is required before a schoolboy would admit it to be knowledge at all,—he rushes into the maddest of all speculations—that of the artisan with little knowledge and enormous faith—that which intrusts the safety and repose and dignity of life to some ambitious adventurer, who uses his warm heart for the adventurer's frigid purpose, much as the lawyer-government of September used the Communists,—much as, in every revolution of France, a Bertrand has used a Raton—much as, till the sound of the last trumpet, men very much worse than Victor de Mauleon will use men very much better than Armand Monnier, if the Armand Monniers disdain the modesty of an Isaac Newton on hearing that a theorem to which he had given all the strength of his patient intellect was disputed: "It may be so;" meaning, I suppose, that it requires a large amount of experience ascertained before a man of much knowledge becomes that which a man of little knowledge is at a jump-the fanatic of an experiment untried.

## CHAPTER II.

Scarcely had De Mauleon quitted Lemercier before the latter was joined by two loungers scarcely less famished than himself—Savarin and De Breze. Like himself, too, both had been sufferers from illness, though not of a nature to be consigned to an hospital. All manner of diseases then had combined to form the pestilence which filled the streets with unregarded hearses—bronchitis, pneumonia, smallpox, a strange sort of spurious dysentery much more speedily fatal than the genuine. The three men, a year before so sleek, looked like ghosts under the withering sky; yet all three retained embers of the native Parisian humour, which their very breath on meeting sufficed to kindle up into jubilant sparks or rapid flashes.

"There are two consolations," said Savarin, as the friends strolled or rather crawled towards the Boulevards—"two consolations for the gourmet and for the proprietor in these days of trial for the gourmand, because the price of truffles is come down."

"Truffles!" gasped De Breze, with watering mouth; "impossible! They are gone with the age of gold."

"Not so. I speak on the best authority—my laundress; for she attends the succursale in the Rue de Chateaudun; and if the poor woman, being, luckily for me, a childless widow, gets a morsel she can spare, she sells it to me."

"Sells it!" feebly exclaimed Lemercier. "Croesus! you have money then, and can buy?"

"Sells it—on credit! I am to pension her for life if I live to have money again. Don't interrupt me. This honest woman goes this morning to the succursale. I promise myself a delicious bifteck of horse. She gains the succursale, and the employee informs her that there is nothing left in his store except—truffles. A glut of those in the market allows him to offer her a bargain-seven francs la boite. Send me seven francs, De Breze, and you shall share the banquet."

De Breze shook his head expressively.

"But," resumed Savarin, "though credit exists no more except with my laundress, upon terms of which the usury is necessarily proportioned to the risk, yet, as I had the honour before to observe, there is comfort for the proprietor. The instinct of property is imperishable."

"Not in the house where I lodge," said Lemercier. "Two soldiers were billeted there; and during my stay in the ambulance they enter my rooms, and cart away all of the little furniture left there, except a bed and a table. Brought before a court-martial, they defend themselves by saying, 'The rooms were abandoned.' The excuse was held valid. They were let off with a reprimand and a promise to restore what was not already disposed of. They have restored me another table and four chairs."

"Nevertheless, they had the instinct of property, though erroneously developed, otherwise they would not have deemed any excuse for their act necessary. Now for my instance of the inherent tenacity of that instinct. A worthy citizen in want of fuel sees a door in a garden wall, and naturally carries off the door. He is apprehended by a gendarme who sees the act. 'Voleur,' he cries to the gendarme, 'do you want to rob me of my property?' 'That door your property? I saw you take it away.' 'You confess,' cries the citizen, triumphantly—'you confess that it is my property; for you saw me appropriate it.' Thus you see how imperishable is the instinct of property. No sooner does it disappear as yours than it reappears as mine."

"I would laugh if I could," said Lemercier, "but such a convulsion would be fatal. Dieu des dieux, how empty I am!" He reeled as he spoke, and clung to De Breze for support. De Breze had the reputation of being the most selfish of men. But at that moment, when a generous man might be excused for being selfish enough to desire to keep the little that he had for his own reprieve from starvation, this egotist became superb. "Friends," he cried, with enthusiasm, "I have something yet in my pocket; we will dine, all three of us."

"Dine!" faltered Lemercier. "Dine! I have not dined since I left the hospital. I breakfasted yesterday—on two mice upon toast. Dainty, but not nutritious. And I shared them with Fox."

"Fox! Fox lives still, then?" cried De Breze, startled.

"In a sort of way he does. But one mouse since yesterday morning is not much; and he can't expect that every day."

"Why don't you take him out?" asked Savarin. "Give him a chance of picking up a bone somewhere."

"I dare not; he would be picked up himself. Dogs are getting very valuable: they sell for 50 francs apiece. Come, De Breze, where are we to dine?"

"I and Savarin can dine at the London Tavern upon rat pate or jugged cat. But it would be impertinence to invite a satrap like yourself who has a whole dog in his larder—a dish of 50 francs—a dish for a king. Adieu, my dear Frederic. Allons, Savarin."

"I feasted you on better meats than dog when I could afford it," said Frederic, plaintively; "and the first time you invite me you retract the invitation. Be it so. Bon appetit."

"Bah!" said De Breze, catching Frederic's arm as he turned to depart. "Of course I was but jesting. Only another day, when my pockets will be empty, do think what an excellent thing a roasted dog is, and make up your mind while Fox has still some little flesh on his bones."

"Flesh!" said Savarin, detaining them. "Look! See how right Voltaire was in saying, 'Amusement is the first necessity of civilised man.' Paris can do without bread Paris still retains Polichinello."

He pointed to the puppet-show, round which a crowd, not of children alone, but of men-middle-aged and old-were collected; while sous were dropped into the tin handed round by a squalid boy.

"And, mon ami," whispered De Breze to Lemercier, with the voice of a tempting fiend, "observe how Punch is without his dog."

It was true. The dog was gone,—its place supplied by a melancholy emaciated cat.

Frederic crawled towards the squalid boy. "What has become of Punch's dog?"

"We ate him last Sunday. Next Sunday we shall have the cat in a pie," said the urchin, with a sensual smack of the lips.

"O Fox! Fox!" murmured Frederic, as the three men went slowly down through the darkening streets—the roar of the Prussian guns heard afar, while distinct and near rang the laugh of the idlers round the Punch without a dog.

# CHAPTER III.

While De Breze and his friends were feasting at the cafe Anglais, and faring better than the host had promised—for the bill of fare comprised such luxuries as ass, mule, peas, fried potatoes, and champagne (champagne in some mysterious way was inexhaustible during the time of famine)—a very different group had assembled in the rooms of Isaura Cicogna. She and the Venosta had hitherto escaped the extreme destitution to which many richer persons had been reduced. It is true that Isaura's fortune placed in the hands of the absent Louvier, and invested in the new street that was to have been, brought no return. It was true that in that street the Venosta, dreaming of cent. per cent., had invested all her savings. But the Venosta, at the first announcement of war, had insisted on retaining in hand a small sum from the amount Isaura had received from her "roman," that might suffice for current expenses, and with yet more acute foresight had laid in stores of provisions and fuel immediately after the probability of a siege became apparent. But even the provident mind of the Venosta had never foreseen that the siege would endure so long, or that the prices of all articles of necessity would rise so high. And meanwhile all resources—money, fuel, provisions—had been largely drawn upon by the charity and benevolence of Isaura, without much remonstrance on the part of the Venosta, whose nature was very accessible to pity. Unfortunately, too, of late money and provisions had failed to Monsieur and Madame Rameau, their income consisting partly of rents no longer paid, and the profits of a sleeping partnership in the old shop, from which custom had departed; so that they came to share the fireside and meals at the rooms of their son's fiancee with little scruple, because utterly unaware that the money retained and the provisions stored by the Venosta were now nearly exhausted.

The patriotic ardour which had first induced the elder Rameau to volunteer his services as a National Guard had been ere this cooled if not suppressed, first by the hardships of the duty, and then by the disorderly conduct of his associates, and their ribald talk and obscene songs. He was much beyond the age at which he could be registered. His son was, however, compelled to become his substitute, though from his sickly health and delicate frame attached to that portion of the National Guard which took no part in actual engagements, and was supposed to do work on the ramparts and maintain order in the city.

In that duty, so opposed to his tastes and habits, Gustave signalised himself as one of the loudest declaimers against the imbecility of the Government, and in the demand for immediate and energetic action, no matter at what loss of life, on the part of all—except the heroic force to which he himself was attached. Still, despite his military labours, Gustave found leisure to contribute to Red journals, and his contributions paid him tolerably well. To do him justice, his parents concealed from him the extent of their destitution; they, on their part, not aware that he was so able to assist them, rather fearing that he himself had nothing else for support but his scanty pay as a National Guard. In fact, of late the parents and son had seen little of each other. M. Rameau, though a Liberal politician, was Liberal as a tradesman, not as a Red Republican or a Socialist. And, though little heeding his son's theories while the Empire secured him from the practical effect of them, he was now as sincerely frightened at the chance of the Communists becoming rampant as most of the Parisian tradesmen were. Madame Rameau, on her side, though she had the dislike to aristocrats which was prevalent with her class, was a stanch Roman Catholic; and seeing in the disasters that had befallen her country the punishment justly incurred by its sins, could not but be shocked by the opinions of Gustave, though she little knew that he was the author of certain articles in certain journals, in which these opinions were proclaimed with a vehemence far exceeding that which they assumed in his conversation. She had spoken to him with warm anger, mixed with passionate tears, on his irreligious principles; and from that moment Gustave shunned to give her another opportunity of insulting his pride and depreciating his wisdom.

Partly to avoid meeting his parents, partly because he recoiled almost as much from the ennui of meeting the other visitors at her apartments—the Paris ladies associated with her in the ambulance, Raoul de Vandeniar, whom he especially hated, and the Abbe Vertpre, who had recently come into intimate friendship with both the Italian ladies—his visits to Isaura had become exceedingly rare. He made his incessant military duties the pretext for absenting himself; and now, on this evening, there were gathered round Isaura's hearth—on which burned almost the last of the hoarded fuel—the Venosta, the two Rameaus, the Abbe Vertpre, who was attached as confessor to the society of which Isaura was so zealous a member. The old priest and the young poetess had become dear friends. There is in the nature of a woman (and especially of a woman at once so gifted and so childlike as Isaura, combining an innate tendency towards faith with a restless inquisitiveness of intellect, which is always suggesting query or doubt) a craving for something afar from the sphere of her sorrow, which can only be obtained through that "bridal of the earth and sky" which we call religion.

And hence, to natures like Isaura's, that link between the woman and the priest, which the philosophy of France has never been able to dissever.

"It is growing late," said Madame Rameau; "I am beginning to feel uneasy. Our dear Isaura is not yet returned."

"You need be under no apprehension," said the Abby. "The ladies attached to the ambulance of which she is so tender and zealous a sister incur no risk. There are always brave men related to the sick and wounded who see to the safe return of the women. My poor Raoul visits that ambulance daily. His kinsman, M. de Rochebriant, is there among the wounded."

"Not seriously hurt, I hope," said the Venosta; "not disfigured? He was so handsome; it is only the ugly warrior whom a scar on the face improves."

"Don't be alarmed, Signora; the Prussian guns spared his face. His wounds in themselves were not dangerous, but he lost a good deal of blood. Raoul and the Christian brothers found him insensible among a heap of the slain."

"M. de Vandemar seems to have very soon recovered the shock of his poor brother's death," said Madame Rameau. "There is very little heart in an aristocrat."

The Abbe's mild brow contracted. "Have more charity, my daughter. It is because Raoul's sorrow for his lost brother is so deep and so holy that he devotes himself more than ever to the service of the Father which is in heaven. He said, a day or two after the burial, when plans for a monument to Enguerrand were submitted to him: 'May my prayer be vouchsafed, and my life be a memorial of him more acceptable to his gentle spirit than monuments of bronze or marble. May I be divinely guided and sustained in my desire to do such good acts as he would have done had he been spared longer to earth. And whenever tempted to weary, may my conscience whisper, Betray not the trust left to thee by thy brother, lest thou be not reunited to him at last.'"

"Pardon me, pardon!" murmured Madame Rameau humbly, while the Venosta burst into tears.

The Abbe, though a most sincere and earnest ecclesiastic, was a cheery and genial man of the world; and, in order to relieve Madame Rameau from the painful self-reproach he had before excited, he turned the conversation. "I must beware, however," he said, with his pleasant laugh, "as to the company in which I interfere in family questions; and especially in which I defend my poor Raoul from any charge brought against him. For some good friend this day sent me a terrible organ of communistic philosophy, in which we humble priests are very roughly handled, and I myself am especially singled out by name as a pestilent intermeddler in the affairs of private households. I am said to set the women against the brave men who are friends of the people, and am cautioned by very truculent threats to cease from such villainous practices." And here, with a dry humour that turned into ridicule what would otherwise have excited disgust and indignation among his listeners, he read aloud passages replete with the sort of false eloquence which was then the vogue among the Red journals. In these passages, not only the Abbe was pointed out for popular execration, but Raoul de Vandemar, though not expressly named, was clearly indicated as a pupil of the Abbe's, the type of a lay Jesuit.

The Venosta alone did not share in the contemptuous laughter with which the inflated style of these diatribes inspired the Rameaus. Her simple Italian mind was horror-stricken by language which the Abbe treated with ridicule.

"Ah!" said M. Rameau, "I guess the author—that firebrand Felix Pyat."

"No," answered the Abbe; "the writer signs himself by the name of a more learned atheist—Diderot le jeune." Here the door opened, and Raoul entered, accompanying Isaura. A change had come over the face of the young Vandemar since his brother's death. The lines about the mouth had deepened, the cheeks had lost their rounded contour and grown somewhat hollow. But the expression was as serene as ever, perhaps even less pensively melancholy. His whole aspect was that of a man who has sorrowed, but been supported in sorrow; perhaps it was more sweet-certainly it was more lofty.

And, as if there were in the atmosphere of his presence something that communicated the likeness of his own soul to others, since Isaura had been brought into his companionship, her own lovely face had caught the expression that prevailed in his—that, too, had become more sweet—that, too, had become more lofty.

The friendship that had grown up between these two young mourners was of a very rare nature. It had in it no sentiment that could ever warm into the passion of human love. Indeed, had Isaura's heart been free to give away, love for Raoul de Vandemar would have seemed to her a profanation. He was never more priestly than when he was most tender. And the tenderness of Raoul towards her was that of some saint-like nature towards the acolyte whom it attracted upwards. He had once, just before Enguerrand's death, spoken to Isaura with a touching candour as to his own predilection for a monastic life. "The worldly avocations that open useful and honourable careers for others have no charm for me. I care not for riches nor power, nor honours nor fame. The austerities of the conventual life have no terror for me; on the contrary, they have a charm, for with them are abstraction from earth and meditation on heaven. In earlier years I might, like other men, have cherished dreams of human love, and felicity in married life, but for the sort of veneration with which I regarded one to whom I owe—humanly speaking—whatever of good there may be in me. Just when first taking my place among the society of young men who banish from their life all thought of another, I came under the influence of a woman who taught me to see that holiness was beauty. She gradually associated me with her acts of benevolence, and from her I learned to love God too well not to be indulgent to his creatures. I know not whether the attachment I felt to her could have been inspired in one who had not from childhood conceived a romance, not perhaps justified by history, for the ideal images of chivalry. My feeling for her at first was that of the pure and poetic homage which a young knight was permitted, sans reproche, to render to some fair queen or chatelaine, whose colours he wore in the lists, whose spotless repute he would have perilled his life to defend. But soon even that sentiment, pure as it was, became chastened from all breath of earthly love, in proportion as the admiration refined itself into reverence. She has often urged me to marry, but I have no bride on this earth. I do but want to see Enguerrand happily married, and then I quit the world for the cloister."

But after Enguerrand's death, Raoul resigned all idea of the convent. That evening, as he attended to their homes Isaura and the other ladies at to the ambulance, he said, in answer to inquiries about his mother, "She is resigned and calm. I have promised her I will not, while she lives, bury her other son: I renounce my dreams of the monastery."

Raoul did not remain many minutes at Isaura's. The Abbe accompanied him on his way home. "I have a request to make to you," said the former; "you know, of course, your distant cousin the Vicomte de Mauleon?"

"Yes. Not so well as I ought, for Enguerrand liked him."

"Well enough, at all events, to call on him with a request which I am commissioned to make, but it might come better from you as a kinsman. I am a stranger to him, and I know not whether a man of that sort would not regard as an officious intermeddling any communication made to him by a priest. The matter, however, is a very simple one. At the convent of ———- there is a poor nun who is, I fear, dying. She has an intense desire to see M. de Mauleon, whom she declares to be her uncle, and her only surviving relative. The laws of the convent are not too austere to prevent the interview she seeks in such a case. I should add that I am not acquainted with her previous history. I am not the confessor of the sisterhood; he, poor man, was badly wounded by a chance ball a few days ago when attached to an ambulance on the ramparts. As soon as the surgeon would allow him to see any one, he sent for me, and bade me go to the nun I speak of—Sister Ursula. It seems that he had informed her that M. de Mauleon was at Paris, and had promised to ascertain his address. His wound had prevented his doing so, but he trusted to me to procure the information. I am well acquainted with the Superieure of the convent, and I flatter myself that she holds me in esteem. I had therefore no difficulty to obtain her permission to see this poor nun, which I did this evening. She implored me for the peace of her soul to lose no time in finding out M. de Mauleon's address, and entreating him to visit her. Lest he should demur, I was to give him the name by which he had known her in the world—Louise Duval. Of course I obeyed. The address of a man who has so distinguished himself in this unhappy siege I very easily obtained, and repaired at once to M. de Mauleon's apartment. I there learned that he was from home, and it was uncertain whether he would not spend the night on the ramparts."

"I will not fail to see him early in the morning," said Raoul, "and execute your commission."

# CHAPTER IV.

M. Mauleon was somewhat surprised by Raoul's visit the next morning. He had no great liking for a kinsman whose politely distant reserve towards him, in contrast to poor Euguerrand's genial heartiness, had much wounded his sensitive self-respect; nor could he comprehend the religious scruples which forbade Raoul to take a soldier's share in the battle-field, though in seeking there to save the lives of others so fearlessly hazarding his own life.

"Pardon," said Raoul, with his sweet mournful smile, "the unseasonable hour at which I disturb you. But your duties on the ramparts and mine in the hospital begin early, and I have promised the Abbe Vertpre to communicate a message of a nature which perhaps you may deem pressing." He proceeded at once to repeat what the Abbe had communicated to him the night before relative to the illness and the request of the nun.

"Louise Duval!" exclaimed the Vicomte, "discovered at last, and a religieuse! Ah! I now understand why she never sought me out when I reappeared at Paris. Tidings of that sort do not penetrate the walls of a convent. I am greatly obliged to you, M. de Vandemar, for the trouble you have so kindly taken. This poor nun is related to me, and I will at once obey the summons. But this convent des ———- I am ashamed to say I know not where it is. A long way off, I suppose?"

"Allow me to be your guide," said Raoul; "I should take it as a favour to be allowed to see a little more of a man whom my lost brother held in such esteem."

Victor was touched by this conciliatory speech, and in a few minutes more the two men were on their way to the convent on the other side of the Seine.

Victor commenced the conversation by a warm and heartfelt tribute to Euguerrand's character and memory. "I never," he said, "knew a nature more rich in the most endearing qualities of youth; so gentle, so high-spirited, rendering every virtue more attractive, and redeeming such few faults or foibles as youth so situated and so tempted cannot wholly escape, with an urbanity not conventional, not artificial, but reflected from the frankness of a genial temper and the tenderness of a generous heart. Be comforted for his loss, my kinsman. A brave death was the proper crown of that beautiful life."

Raoul made no answer, but pressed gratefully the arm now linked within his own. The companions walked on in silence; Victor's mind settling on the visit he was about to make to the niece so long mysteriously lost, and now so unexpectedly found. Louise had inspired him with a certain interest from her beauty and force of character, but never with any warm affection. He felt relieved to find that her life had found its close in the sanctuary of the convent. He had never divested himself of a certain fear, inspired by Louvier's statement that she might live to bring scandal and disgrace on the name he had with so much difficulty, and after so lengthened an anguish, partially cleared in his own person.

Raoul left De Mauleon at the gate of the convent, and took his way towards the hospitals where he visited, and the poor whom he relieved.

Victor was conducted silently into the convent parloir; and, after waiting there several minutes, the door opened, and the Superieure entered. As she advanced towards him, with stately step and solemn visage, De Mauleon recoiled, and uttered a half-suppressed exclamation that partook both of amaze and awe. Could it be possible? Was this majestic woman, with the grave impassible aspect, once the ardent girl whose tender letters he had cherished through stormy years, and only burned on the night before the most perilous of his battle-fields? This the one, the sole one, whom in his younger dreams he had seen as his destined wife? It was so—it was. Doubt vanished when he heard her voice; and yet how different every tone, every accent, from those of the low, soft, thrilling music that had breathed in the voice of old!

"M. de Mauleon," said the Superieure, calmly, "I grieve to sadden you by very mournful intelligence. Yesterday evening, when the Abbe undertook to convey to you the request of our Sister Ursula, although she was beyond mortal hope of recovery—as otherwise you will conceive that I could not have relaxed the rules of this house so as to sanction your visit—there was no apprehension of immediate danger. It was believed that her sufferings would be prolonged for some days. I saw her late last night before retiring to my cell, and she seemed even stronger than she had been for the last week. A sister remained at watch in her cell. Towards morning she fell into apparently quiet sleep, and in that sleep she passed away." The Superieure here crossed herself, and murmured pious words in Latin. "Dead! my poor niece!" said Victor, feelingly, roused from his stun at the first sight of the Superieure by her measured tones, and the melancholy information she so composedly conveyed to him. "I cannot, then, even learn why she so wished to see me once more,—or what she might have requested at my hands!"

"Pardon, M. le Vicomte. Such sorrowful consolation I have resolved to afford you, not without scruples of conscience, but not without sanction of the excellent Abbe Vertpre, whom I summoned early this morning to decide my duties in the sacred office I hold. As soon as Sister Ursula heard of your return to Paris, she obtained my permission to address to you a letter, subjected, when finished, to my perusal and sanction. She felt that she had much on her mind which her feeble state might forbid her to make known to you in conversation with 'sufficient fulness; and as she could only have seen you in presence of one of the sisters she imagined that there would also be less restraint in a written communication. In fine, her request was that, when you called, I might first place this letter in your hands, and allow you time to read it, before being admitted to her presence; when a few words conveying your promise to attend to the wishes with which you would then be acquainted, would suffice for an interview in her exhausted condition. Do I make myself understood?"

"Certainly, Madame,—and the letter?"

"She had concluded last evening; and when I took leave of her later in the night, she placed it in my hands for approval. M. le Vicomte, it pains me to say that there is much in the tone of that letter which I grieve for and condemn. And it was my intention to point this out to our sister at morning, and tell her that passages must be altered before I could give to you the letter. Her sudden decease deprived me of this opportunity. I could not, of course, alter or erase a line—a word. My only option was to suppress the letter altogether, or give it you intact. The Abbe thinks that, on the whole, my duty does not forbid the dictate of my own impulse—my own feelings; and I now place this letter in your hands."

De Mauleon took a packet, unsealed, from the thin white fingers of the Superieure; and as he bent to receive it, lifted towards her eyes eloquent with sorrowful, humble pathos, in which it was impossible for the heart of a woman who had loved not to see a reference to the past which the lips did not dare to utter.

A faint, scarce-perceptible blush stole over the marble cheek of the nun. But, with an exquisite delicacy, in which survived the woman while reigned the nun, she replied to the appeal.

"M. Victor de Mauleon, before, having thus met, we part for ever, permit a poor religieuse to say with what joy—a joy rendered happier because it was tearful—I have learned through the Abbe Vertpre that the honour which, as between man and man, no one who had once known you could ever doubt, you have lived to vindicate from calumny."

"Ah; you have heard that—at last, at last!"

"I repeat—of the honour thus deferred, I never doubted." The Superieure hurried on. "Greater joy it has been to me to hear from the same venerable source that, while found bravest among the defenders of your country, you are clear from all alliance with the assailants of your God. Continue so, continue so, Victor de Mauleon."

She retreated to the door, and then turned towards him with a look in which all the marble had melted away, adding, with words more formally nunlike, yet unmistakably womanlike, than those which had gone before, "That to the last you may be true to God, is a prayer never by me omitted."

She spoke, and vanished.

In a kind of dim and dreamlike bewilderment, Victor de Mauleon found himself without the walls of the convent. Mechanically, as a man does when the routine of his life is presented to him, from the first Minister of State to the poor clown at a suburban theatre, doomed to appear at their posts, to prose on a Beer Bill, or grin through a horse-collar, though their hearts are bleeding at every pore with some household or secret affliction,—mechanically De Mauldon went his way towards the ramparts, at a section of which he daily drilled his raw recruits. Proverbial for his severity towards those who offended, for the cordiality of his praise of those who pleased his soldierly judgment, no change of his demeanour was visible that morning, save that he might be somewhat milder to the one, somewhat less hearty to the other. This routine duty done, he passed slowly towards a more deserted because a more exposed part of the defences, and seated himself on the frozen sward alone. The cannon thundered around him. He heard unconsciously: from time to time an obus hissed and splintered close at his feet;—he saw with abstracted eye. His soul was with the past; and, brooding over all that in the past lay buried there, came over him a conviction of the vanity of the human earth-bounded objects for which we burn or freeze, far more absolute than had grown out of the worldly cynicism connected with his worldly ambition. The sight of that face, associated with the one pure romance of his reckless youth, the face of one so estranged, so serenely aloft from all memories of youth, of romance, of passion, smote him in the midst of the new hopes of the new career, as the look on the skull of the woman he had so loved and so mourned, when disburied from her grave, smote the brilliant noble who became the stern reformer of La Trappe. And while thus gloomily meditating, the letter of the poor Louise Duval was forgotten. She whose existence had so troubled, and crossed, and partly marred the lives of others,—she, scarcely dead, and already forgotten by her nearest kin. Well—had she not forgotten, put wholly out of her mind, all that was due to those much nearer to her than is an uncle to a niece?

The short, bitter, sunless day was advancing towards its decline before Victor roused himself with a quick impatient start from his reverie, and took forth the letter from the dead nun.

It began with expressions of gratitude, of joy at the thought that she should see him again before she died, thank him for his past kindness, and receive, she trusted, his assurance that he would attend to her last remorseful injunctions. I pass over much that followed in the explanation of events in her life sufficiently known to the reader. She stated, as the strongest reason why she had refused the hand of Louvier, her knowledge that she should in due time become a mother—a fact concealed from Victor, secure that he would then urge her not to annul her informal marriage, but rather insist on the ceremonies that would render it valid. She touched briefly on her confidential intimacy with Madame Marigny, the exchange of name and papers, her confinement in the neighbourhood of Aix, the child left to the care of the nurse, the journey to Munich to find the false Louise Duval was no more. The documents obtained through the agency of her easy-tempered kinsman, the late Marquis de Rochebriant, and her subsequent domestication in the house of the von Rudesheims,—all this it is needless to do more here than briefly recapitulate. The letter then went on: "While thus kindly treated by the family with whom nominally a governess, I was on the terms of a friend with Signor Ludovico Cicogna, an Italian of noble birth. He was the only man I ever cared for. I loved him with frail human passion. I could not tell him, my true history. I could not tell him that I had a child; such intelligence would have made him renounce me at once. He had a daughter, still but an infant, by a former marriage, then brought up in France. He wished to take her to his house, and his second wife to supply the place of her mother. What was I to do with the child I had left near Aix? While doubtful and distracted, I read an advertisement in the journals to the effect that a French lady, then staying in Coblentz, wished to adopt a female child not exceeding the age of six: the child to be wholly resigned to her by the parents, she undertaking to rear and provide for it as her own. I resolved to go to Coblentz at once. I did so. I saw this lady. She seemed in affluent circumstances, yet young, but a confirmed invalid, confined the greater part of the day to her sofa by some malady of the spine. She told me very frankly her story. She had been a professional dancer on the stage, had married respectably, quitted the stage, become a widow, and shortly afterwards been seized with the complaint that would probably for life keep her a secluded prisoner in her room. Thus afflicted, and without tie, interest, or object in the world, she conceived the idea of adopting a child that she might bring up to tend and cherish her as a daughter. In this, the imperative condition was that the child should never be sought by the parents. She was pleased by my manner and appearance: she did not wish her adopted daughter to be the child of peasants. She asked me for no references,—made no inquiries. She said cordially that she wished for no knowledge that, through any indiscretion of her own, communicated to the child might lead her to seek the discovery of her real parents. In fine, I left Coblentz on the understanding that I was to bring the infant, and if it pleased Madame Surville, the agreement was concluded.

"I then repaired to Aix. I saw the child. Alas! unnatural mother that I was, the sight only more vividly brought before me the sense of my own perilous position. Yet the child was lovely! a likeness of myself, but lovelier far, for it was a pure, innocent, gentle loveliness. And they told her to call me 'Maman.' Oh, did I not relent when I heard that name? No; it jarred on my ear as a word of reproach and shame. In walking with the infant towards the railway station, imagine my dismay when suddenly I met the man who had been taught to believe me dead. I soon discovered that his dismay was equal to my own,—that I had nothing to fear from his desire to claim me. It did occur to me for a moment to resign his child to him. But when he shrank reluctantly from a half suggestion to that effect, my pride was wounded, my conscience absolved. And, after all, it might be unsafe to my future to leave with him any motive for tracing me. I left him hastily. I have never seen nor heard of him more. I took the child to Coblentz. Madame Surville was charmed with its prettiness and prattle,—charmed still more when I rebuked the poor infant for calling me 'Maman,' and said, 'Thy real mother is here.' Freed from my trouble, I returned to the kind German roof I had quitted, and shortly after became the wife of Ludovico Cicogna.

"My punishment soon began. His was a light, fickle, pleasure-hunting nature. He soon grew weary of me. My very love made me unamiable to him. I became irritable, jealous, exacting. His daughter, who now came to live with us, was another subject of discord. I knew that he loved her better than me. I became a harsh step-mother; and Ludovico's reproaches, vehemently made, nursed all my angriest passions. But a son of this new marriage was born to myself. My pretty Luigi! how my heart became wrapt up in him! Nursing him, I forgot resentment against his father. Well, poor Cicogna fell ill and died. I mourned him sincerely; but my boy was left. Poverty then fell on me,—poverty extreme. Cicogna's sole income was derived from a post in the Austrian dominion in Italy, and ceased with it. He received a small pension in compensation; that died with him.

"At this time, an Englishman, with whom Ludovico had made acquaintance in Venice, and who visited often at our house in Verona, offered me his hand. He had taken an extraordinary liking to Isaura, Cicogna's daughter by his first marriage. But I think his proposal was dictated partly by compassion for me, and more by affection for her. For the sake of my boy Luigi I married him. He was a good man, of retired learned habits with which I had no sympathy. His companionship overwhelmed me with ennui. But I bore it patiently for Luigi's sake. God saw that my heart was as much as ever estranged from Him, and He took away my all on earth—my boy. Then in my desolation I turned to our Holy Church for comfort. I found a friend in the priest, my confessor. I was startled to learn from him how guilty I had been—was still. Pushing to an extreme the doctrines of the Church, he would not allow that my first marriage, though null by law, was void in the eyes of Heaven. Was not the death of the child I so cherished a penalty due to my sin towards the child I had abandoned?

"These thoughts pressed on me night and day. With the consent and approval of the good priest, I determined to quit the roof of M. Selby, and to devote myself to the discovery of my forsaken Julie.

"I had a painful interview with M. Selby. I announced my intention to separate from him. I alleged as a reason my conscientious repugnance to live with a professed heretic—an enemy to our Holy Church. When M. Selby found that he could not shake my resolution, he lent himself to it with the forbearance and generosity which he had always exhibited. On our marriage he had settled on me five thousand pounds, to be absolutely mine in the event of his death. He now proposed to concede to me the interest on that capital during his life, and he undertook the charge of my step-daughter Isaura, and secured to her all the rest he had to leave; such landed property as he possessed in England passing to a distant relative.

"So we parted, not with hostility—tears were shed on both sides. I set out for Coblentz. Madame Surville had long since quitted that town, devoting some years to the round of various mineral spas in vain hope of cure. Not without some difficulty I traced her to her last residence in the neighbourhood of Paris, but she was then no more—her death accelerated by the shock occasioned by the loss of her whole fortune, which she had been induced to place in one of the numerous fraudulent companies by which so many have been ruined. Julie, who was with her at the time of her death, had disappeared shortly after it—none could tell me whither; but from such hints as I could gather, the poor child, thus left destitute, had been betrayed into sinful courses.

"Probably I might yet by searching inquiry have found her out; you will say it was my duty at least to institute such inquiry. No doubt; I now remorsefully feel that it was. I did not think so at the time. The Italian priest had given me a few letters of introduction to French ladies with whom, when they had sojourned at Florence, he had made acquaintance. These ladies were very strict devotees, formal observers of those decorums by which devotion proclaims itself to the world. They had received me not only with kindness but with marked respect. They chose to exalt into the noblest self-sacrifice the act of my leaving M. Selby's house. Exaggerating the simple cause assigned to it in the priest's letter, they represented me as quitting a luxurious home and an idolising husband rather than continue intimate intercourse with the enemy of my religion. This new sort of flattery intoxicated me with its fumes. I recoiled from the thought of shattering the pedestal to which I had found myself elevated. What if I should discover my daughter in one from the touch of whose robe these holy women would recoil as from the rags of a leper! No; it would be impossible for me to own her—impossible for me to give her the shelter of my roof. Nay, if discovered to hold any commune with such an outcast, no explanation, no excuse short of the actual truth, would avail with these austere judges of human error. And the actual truth would be yet deeper disgrace. I reasoned away my conscience. If I looked for example in the circles in which I had obtained reverential place, I could find no instance in which a girl who had fallen from virtue was not repudiated by her nearest relatives. Nay, when I thought of my own mother, had not her father refused to see her, to acknowledge her child, from no other offence than that of a misalliance which wounded the family pride? That pride, alas! was in my blood—my sole inheritance from the family I sprang from.

"Thus it went on, till I had grave symptoms of a disease which rendered the duration of my life uncertain. My conscience awoke and tortured me. I resolved to take the veil. Vanity and pride again! My resolution was applauded by those whose opinion had so swayed my mind and my conduct. Before I retired into the convent from which I write, I made legal provision as to the bulk of the fortune which, by the death of M. Selby, has become absolutely at my disposal. One thousand pounds amply sufficed for dotation to the convent: the other four thousand pounds are given in trust to the eminent notary, M. Nadaud, Rue ———. On applying to him, you will find that the sum, with the accumulated interest, is bequeathed to you,—a tribute of gratitude for the assistance you afforded me in the time of your own need, and the kindness with which you acknowledged our relationship and commiserated my misfortunes.

"But oh, my uncle, find out—a man can do so with a facility not accorded to a woman—what has become of this poor Julie, and devote what you may deem right and just of the sum thus bequeathed to place her above want and temptation. In doing so, I know you will respect my name: I would not have it dishonour you, indeed.

"I have been employed in writing this long letter since the day I heard you were in Paris. It has exhausted the feeble remnants of my strength. It will be given to you before the interview I at once dread and long for, and in that interview you will not rebuke me. Will you, my kind uncle? No, you will only soothe and pity!

"Would that I were worthy to pray for others, that I might add, 'May the Saints have you in their keeping and lead you to faith in the Holy Church, which has power to absolve from sins those who repent as I do.'"

The letter dropped from Victor's hand. He took it up, smoothed it mechanically, and with a dim, abstracted, be wildered, pitiful wonder. Well might the Superieure have hesitated to allow confessions, betraying a mind so little regulated by genuine religious faith, to pass into other hands. Evidently it was the paramount duty of rescuing from want or from sin the writer's forsaken child, that had overborne all other considerations in the mind of the Woman and the Priest she consulted.

Throughout that letter, what a strange perversion of understanding! what a half-unconscious confusion of wrong and right!—the duty marked out so obvious and so neglected; even the religious sentiment awakened by the conscience so dividing itself from the moral instinct! the dread of being thought less religious by obscure comparative strangers stronger than the moral obligation to discover and reclaim the child for whose errors, if she had erred, the mother who so selfishly forsook her was alone responsible! even at the last, at the approach of death, the love for a name she had never made a self-sacrifice to preserve unstained; and that concluding exhortation,—that reliance on a repentance in which there was so qualified a reparation!

More would Victor de Mauldon have wondered had he known those points of similarity in character, and in the nature of their final bequests, between Louise Duval and the husband she had deserted. By one of those singular coincidences which, if this work be judged by the ordinary rules presented to the ordinary novel-reader, a critic would not unjustly impute to defective invention in the author, the provision for this child, deprived of its natural parents during their lives, is left to the discretion and honour of trustees, accompanied on the part of the consecrated Louise and "the blameless King," with the injunction of respect to their worldly reputations—two parents so opposite in condition, in creed, in disposition, yet assimilating in that point of individual character in which it touches the wide vague circle of human opinion. For this, indeed, the excuses of Richard King are strong, inasmuch as the secrecy he sought was for the sake, not of his own memory, but that of her whom the world knew only as his honoured wife. The conduct of Louise admits no such excuse; she dies as she had lived; an Egotist. But, whatever the motives of the parents, what is the fate of the deserted child? What revenge does the worldly opinion, which the parents would escape for themselves, inflict on the innocent infant to whom the bulk of their worldly possessions is to be clandestinely conveyed? Would all the gold of Ophir be compensation enough for her?

Slowly De Mauleon roused himself, and turned from the solitary place where he had been seated to a more crowded part of the ramparts. He passed a group of young Moblots, with flowers wreathed round their gun-barrels. "If," said one of them gaily, "Paris wants bread, it never wants flowers." His companions laughed merrily, and burst out into a scurrile song in ridicule of St. Trochu. Just then an obus fell a few yards before the group. The sound only for a moment drowned the song, but the splinters struck a man in a coarse, ragged dress, who had stopped to listen to the singers. At his sharp cry, two men hastened to his side: one was Victor de Mauleon; the other was a surgeon, who quitted another group of idlers—National Guards—attracted by the shriek that summoned his professional aid. The poor man was terribly wounded. The surgeon, glancing at De Mauleon, shrugged his shoulders, and muttered, "Past help!" The sufferer turned his haggard eyes on the Vicomte, and gasped out, "M. de Mauleon?"

"That is my name," answered Victor, surprised, and not immediately recognising the sufferer.

"Hist, Jean Lebeau!—look at me: you recollect me now,—Mart le Roux, concierge to the Secret Council. Ay, I found out who you were long ago—followed you home from the last meeting you broke up. But I did not betray you, or you would have been murdered long since. Beware of the old set—beware of—of—" Here his voice broke off into shrill exclamations of pain. Curbing his last agonies with a powerful effort, he faltered forth, "You owe me a service—see to the little one at home—she is starving." The death-rale came on; in a few moments he was no more.

Victor gave orders for the removal of the corpse, and hurried away. The surgeon, who had changed countenance when he overheard the name in which the dying man had addressed De Mauleon, gazed silently after De Mauleon's retreating form, and then, also quitting the dead, rejoined the group he had quitted. Some of those who composed it acquired evil renown later in the war of the Communists, and came to disastrous ends: among that number the Pole Loubinsky and other members of the Secret Council. The Italian Raselli was there too, but, subtler than his French confreres, he divined the fate of the Communists, and glided from it—safe now in his native land, destined there, no doubt, to the funereal honours and lasting renown which Italy bestows on the dust of her sons who have advocated assassination out of love for the human race.

Amid this group, too, was a National Guard, strayed from his proper post, and stretched on the frozen ground; and, early though the hour, in the profound sleep of intoxication.

"So," said Loubinsky, "you have found your errand in vain, Citizen le Noy; another victim to the imbecility of our generals."

"And partly one of us," replied the Medecin des Pauvres. "You remember poor le Roux, who kept the old baraque where the Council of Ten used to meet? Yonder he lies."

"Don't talk of the Council of Ten. What fools and dupes we were made by that vieux gredin, Jean Lebeau! How I wish I could meet him again!"

Gaspard le Noy smiled sarcastically. "So much the worse for you, if you did. A muscular and a ruthless fellow is that Jean Lebeau!" Therewith he turned to the drunken sleeper and woke him up with a shake and a kick. "Armand—Armand Monnier, I say, rise, rub your eyes. What if you are called to your post? What if you are shamed as a deserter and a coward?"

Armand turned, rose with an effort from the recumbent to the sitting posture, and stared dizzily in the face of the Medecin des Pauvres.

"I was dreaming that I had caught by the throat," said Armand, wildly, "the aristo who shot my brother; and lo, there were two men, Victor de Mauleon and Jean Lebeau."

"Ah! there is something in dreams," said the surgeon. "Once in a thousand times a dream comes true."

# CHAPTER V.

The time now came when all provision of food or of fuel failed the modest household of Isaura; and there was not only herself and the Venosta to feed and warm—there were the servants whom they had brought from Italy, and had not the heart now to dismiss to the 'certainty of famine. True, one of the three, the man, had returned to his native land before the commencement of the siege; but the two women had remained. They supported themselves now as they could on the meagre rations accorded by the Government. Still Isaura attended the ambulance to which she was attached. From the ladies associated with her she could readily have obtained ample supplies: but they had no conception of her real state of destitution; and there was a false pride generally prevalent among the respectable classes, which Isaura shared, that concealed distress lest alms should be proffered.

The destitution of the household had been carefully concealed from the parents of Gustave Rameau, until, one day, Madame Rameau, entering at the hour at which she generally, and her husband sometimes, came for a place by the fireside and a seat at the board, found on the one only ashes, on the other a ration of the black nauseous compound which had become the substitute for bread.

Isaura was absent on her duties at the ambulance hospital,—purposely absent, for she shrank from the bitter task of making clear to the friends of her betrothed the impossibility of continuing the aid to their support which their son had neglected to contribute; and still more from the comment which she knew they would make on his conduct, in absenting himself so wholly of late, and in the time of such trial and pressure, both from them and from herself. Truly, she rejoiced at that absence so far as it affected herself. Every hour of the day she silently asked her conscience whether she were not now absolved from a promise won from her only by an assurance that she had power to influence for good the life that now voluntarily separated itself from her own. As she had never loved Gustave, so she felt no resentment at the indifference his conduct manifested. On the contrary, she hailed it as a sign that the annulment of their betrothal would be as welcome to him as to herself. And if so, she could restore to him the sort of compassionate friendship she had learned to cherish in the hour of his illness and repentance. She had resolved to seize the first opportunity he afforded to her of speaking to him with frank and truthful plainness. But, meanwhile, her gentle nature recoiled from the confession of her resolve to appeal to Gustave himself for the rupture of their engagement.

Thus the Venosta alone received Madame Rameau; and while that lady was still gazing round her with an emotion too deep for immediate utterance, her husband entered with an expression of face new to him—the look of a man who has been stung to anger, and who has braced his mind to some stern determination. This altered countenance of the good-tempered bourgeois was not, however, noticed by the two women. The Venosta did not even raise her eyes to it, as with humbled accents she said, "Pardon, dear Monsieur, pardon, Madame, our want of hospitality; it is not our hearts that fail. We kept our state from you as long as we could. Now it speaks for itself; 'la fame e una bretta festin.'"

"Oh, Madame! and oh, my poor Isaura!" cried Madame Rameau, bursting into tears. "So we have been all this time a burden on you,—aided to bring such want on you! How can we ever be forgiven? And my son—to leave us thus,—not even to tell us where to find him!"

"Do not degrade us, my wife," said M. Rameau, with unexpected dignity, "by a word to imply that we would stoop to sue for support to our ungrateful child. No, we will not starve! I am strong enough still to find food for you. I will apply for restoration to the National Guard. They have augmented the pay to married men; it is now nearly two francs and a half a-day to a pere de famille, and on that pay we all can at least live. Courage, my wife! I will go at once for employment. Many men older than I am are at watch on the ramparts, and will march to the battle on the next sortie."

"It shall not be so," exclaimed Madame Rameau, vehemently, and winding her arm round her husband's neck. "I loved my son better than thee once—more shame to me. Now, I would rather lose twenty such sons than peril thy life, my Jacques! Madame," she continued, turning to the Venosta, "thou wert wiser than I. Thou wert ever opposed to the union between thy young friend and my son. I felt sore with thee for it—a mother is so selfish when she puts herself in the place of her child. I thought that only through marriage with one so pure, so noble, so holy, Gustave could be saved from sin and evil. I am deceived. A man so heartless to his parents, so neglectful of his affianced, is not to be redeemed. I brought about this betrothal: tell Isaura that I release her from it. I have watched her closely since she was entrapped into it. I know how miserable the thought of it has made her, though, in her sublime devotion to her plighted word, she sought to conceal from me the real state of her heart. If the betrothal bring such sorrow, what would the union do! Tell her this from me. Come, Jacques, come away!"

"Stay, Madame!" exclaimed the Venosta, her excitable nature much affected by this honest outburst of feeling. "It is true that I did oppose, so far as I could, my poor Piccola's engagement with M. Gustave. But I dare not do your bidding. Isaura would not listen to me. And let us be just! M. Gustave may be able satisfactorily to explain his seeming indifference and neglect. His health is always very delicate; perhaps he may be again dangerously ill. He serves in the National Guard; perhaps—" she paused, but the mother conjectured the word left unsaid, and, clasping her hands, cried out in anguish, "Perhaps dead!—and we have wronged him! Oh, Jacques, Jacques! how shall we find out-how discover our boy? Who can tell us where to search? at the hospital—or in the cemeteries?" At the last word she dropped into a seat, and her whole frame shook with her sobs.

Jacques approached her tenderly, and kneeling by her side, said:

"No, m'amie, comfort thyself, if it be indeed comfort to learn that thy son is alive and well. For my part, I know not if I would not rather he had died in his innocent childhood. I have seen him—spoken to him. I know where he is to be found."

"You do, and concealed it from me? Oh, Jacques!"

"Listen to me, wife, and you, too, Madame; for what I have to say should be made known to Mademoiselle Cicogna. Some time since, on the night of the famous sortie, when at my post on the ramparts, I was told that Gustave had joined himself to the most violent of the Red Republicans, and had uttered at the Club de la Vengeance sentiments, of which I will only say that I, his father and a Frenchman, hung my head with shame when they were repeated to me. I resolved to go to the club myself. I did. I heard him speak—heard him denounce Christianity as the instrument of tyrants."

"Ah!" cried the two women, with a simultaneous shudder.

"When the assembly broke up, I waylaid him at the door. I spoke to him seriously. I told him what anguish such announcement of blasphemous opinions would inflict on his pious mother. I told him I should deem it my duty to inform Mademoiselle Cicogna, and warn her against the union on which he had told us his heart was bent. He appeared sincerely moved by what I said; implored me to keep silence towards his mother and his betrothed; and promised, on that condition, to relinquish at once what he called 'his career as an orator,' and appear no more at such execrable clubs. On this understanding I held my tongue. Why, with such other causes of grief and suffering, should I tell thee, poor wife, of a sin that I hoped thy son had repented and would not repeat? And Gustave kept his word. He has never, so far as I know, attended, at least spoken, at the Red clubs since that evening."

"Thank heaven so far," murmured Madame Rameau.

"So far, yes; but hear more. A little time after I thus met him he changed his lodging, and did not confide to us his new address, giving as a reason to us that he wished to avoid a clue to his discovery by that pertinacious Mademoiselle Julie."

Rameau had here sunk his voice into a whisper, intended only for his wife, but the ear of the Venosta was fine enough to catch the sound, and she repeated, "Mademoiselle Julie! Santa Maria! who is she?"

"Oh!" said M. Rameau, with a shrug of his shoulders, and with true Parisian sangfroid as to such matters of morality, "a trifle not worth considering. Of course, a good-looking garcon like Gustave must have his little affairs of the heart before he settles for life. Unluckily, amongst those of Gustave was one with a violent-tempered girl who persecuted him when he left her, and he naturally wished to avoid all chance of a silly scandal, if only out of respect to the dignity of his fiancee. But I found that was not the true motive, or at least the only one, for concealment. Prepare yourself, my poor wife. Thou hast heard of these terrible journals which the decheance has let loose upon us. Our unhappy boy is the principal writer of one of the worst of them, under the name of 'Diderot le Jeune.'"

"What!" cried the Venosta. "That monster! The good Abbe Vertpre was telling us of the writings with that name attached to them. The Abbe himself is denounced by name as one of those meddling priests who are to be constrained to serve as soldiers or pointed out to the vengeance of the canaille. Isaura's fiancee a blasphemer!"

"Hush, hush!" said Madame Rameau, rising, very pale but self-collected. "How do you know this, Jacques?"

"From the lips of Gustave himself. I heard first of it yesterday from one of the young reprobates with whom he used to be familiar, and who even complimented me on the rising fame of my son, and praised the eloquence of his article that day. But I would not believe him. I bought the journal—here it is; saw the name and address of the printer—went this morning to the office—was there told that 'Diderot le Jeune' was within revising the press—stationed myself by the street door, and when Gustave came out I seized his arm, and asked him to say Yes or No if he was the author of this infamous article,—this, which I now hold in my hand. He owned the authorship with pride; talked wildly of the great man he was—of the great things he was to do; said that, in hitherto concealing his true name, he had done all he could to defer to the bigoted prejudices of his parents and his fiancee; and that if genius, like fire, would find its way out, he could not help it; that a time was rapidly coming when his opinions would be uppermost; that since October the Communists were gaining ascendancy, and only waited the end of the siege to put down the present Government, and with it all hypocrisies and shams, religious or social. My wife, he was rude to me, insulting! but he had been drinking—that made him incautious: and he continued to walk by my side towards his own lodging, on reaching which he ironically invited me to enter, saying, 'I should meet there men who would soon argue me out of my obsolete notions.' You may go to him, wife, now, if you please. I will not, nor will I take from him a crust of bread. I came hither, determined to tell the young lady all this, if I found her at home. I should be a dishonoured man if I suffered her to be cheated into misery.

"There, Madame Venosta, there! Take that journal, show it to Mademoiselle; and report to her all I have said."

M. Rameau, habitually the mildest of men, had, in talking, worked himself up into positive fury.

His wife, calmer but more deeply affected, made a piteous sign to the Venosta not to say more; and without other salutation or adieu took her husband's arm, and led him from the house.

# CHAPTER VI.

Obtaining from her husband Gustave's address, Madame Rameau hastened to her son's apartment alone through the darkling streets. The house in which he lodged was in a different quarter from that in which Isaura had visited him. Then, the street selected was still in the centre of the beau monde—now, it was within the precincts of that section of the many-faced capital in which the beau monde was held in detestation or scorn; still the house had certain pretensions, boasting a courtyard and a porter's lodge. Madame Rameau, instructed to mount au second, found the door ajar, and, entering, perceived on the table of the little salon the remains of a feast which, however untempting it might have been in happier times, contrasted strongly with the meagre fare of which Gustave's parents had deemed themselves fortunate to partake at the board of his betrothed; remnants of those viands which offered to the inquisitive epicure an experiment in food much too costly for the popular stomach—dainty morsels of elephant, hippopotamus, and wolf, interspersed with half-emptied bottles of varied and high-priced wines. Passing these evidences of unseasonable extravagance with a mute sentiment of anger and disgust, Madame Rameau penetrated into a small cabinet, the door of which was also ajar, and saw her son stretched on his bed half dressed, breathing heavily in the sleep which follows intoxication. She did not attempt to disturb him. She placed herself quietly by his side, gazing mournfully on the face which she had once so proudly contemplated, now haggard and faded,—still strangely beautiful, though it was the beauty of ruin.

From time to time he stirred uneasily, and muttered broken words, in which fragments of his own delicately-worded verse were incoherently mixed up with ribald slang, addressed to imaginary companions. In his dreams he was evidently living over again his late revel, with episodical diversions into the poet-world, of which he was rather a vagrant nomad than a settled cultivator. Then she would silently bathe his feverish temples with the perfumed water she found on his dressing-table. And so she watched till, in the middle of the night, he woke up, and recovered the possession of his reason with a quickness that surprised Madame Rameau. He was, indeed, one of those men in whom excess of drink, when slept off, is succeeded by extreme mildness, the effect of nervous exhaustion, and by a dejected repentance, which, to his mother, seemed a propitious lucidity of the moral sense.

Certainly on seeing her he threw himself on her breast, and began to shed tears. Madame Rameau had not the heart to reproach him sternly. But by gentle degrees she made him comprehend the pain he had given to his father, and the destitution in which he had deserted his parents and his affianced. In his present mood Gustave was deeply affected by these representations. He excused himself feebly by dwelling on the excitement of the times, the preoccupation of his mind, the example of his companions; but with his excuses he mingled passionate expressions of remorse, and before daybreak mother and son were completely reconciled. Then he fell into a tranquil sleep; and Madame Rameau, quite worn out, slept also in the chair beside him, her arm around his neck. He awoke before she did at a late hour in the morning; and stealing from her arm, went to his escritoire, and took forth what money he found there, half of which he poured into her lap, kissing her till she awoke.

"Mother," he said, "henceforth I will work for thee and my father. Take this trifle now; the rest I reserve for Isaura."

"Joy! I have found my boy again. But Isaura, I fear that she will not take thy money, and all thought of her must also be abandoned."

Gustave had already turned to his looking-glass, and was arranging with care his dark ringlets: his personal vanity—his remorse appeased by this pecuniary oblation—had revived.

"No," he said gaily, "I don't think I shall abandon her; and it is not likely, when she sees and hears me, that she can wish to abandon me! Now let us breakfast, and then I will go at once to her."

In the mean while, Isaura, on her return to her apartment at the wintry nightfall, found a cart stationed at the door, and the Venosta on the threshold, superintending the removal of various articles of furniture—indeed, all such articles as were not absolutely required.

"Oh, Piccola!" she said, with an attempt at cheerfulness, "I did not expect thee back so soon. Hush! I have made a famous bargain. I have found a broker to buy these things which we don't want just at present, and can replace by new and prettier things when the siege is over and we get our money. The broker pays down on the nail and thou wilt not go to bed without supper. There are no ills which are not more supportable after food."

Isaura smiled faintly, kissed the Venosta's cheek, and ascended with weary steps to the sitting-room. There she seated herself quietly, looking with abstracted eyes round the bare dismantled space by the light of the single candle.

When the Venosta re-entered, she was followed by the servants, bringing in a daintier meal than they had known for days—a genuine rabbit, potatoes, marrons glaces, a bottle of wine, and a pannier of wood. The fire was soon lighted, the Venosta plying the bellows. It was not till this banquet, of which Isaura, faint as she was, scarcely partook, had been remitted to the two Italian women-servants, and another log been thrown on the hearth, that the Venosta opened the subject which was pressing on her heart. She did this with a joyous smile, taking both Isaura's hands in her own, and stroking them fondly.

"My child, I have such good news for thee! Thou hast escaped—thou art free!" and then she related all that M. Rameau had said, and finished by producing the copy of Gustave's unhallowed journal.

When she had read the latter, which she did with compressed lips and varying colour, the girl fell on her knees—not to thank Heaven that she would now escape a union from which her soul so recoiled—not that she was indeed free, but to pray, with tears rolling down her cheeks, that God would yet save to Himself, and to good ends, the soul that she had failed to bring to Him. All previous irritation against Gustave was gone: all had melted into an ineffable compassion.

# CHAPTER VII.

When, a little before noon, Gustave was admitted by the servant into Isaura's salon, its desolate condition, stripped of all its pretty feminine elegancies, struck him with a sense of discomfort to himself which superseded any more remorseful sentiment. The day was intensely cold: the single log on the hearth did not burn; there were only two or three chairs in the room; even the carpet, which had been of gaily coloured Aubusson, was gone. His teeth chattered; and he only replied by a dreary nod to the servant who informed him that Madame Venosta was gone out, and Mademoiselle had not yet quitted her own room.

If there be a thing which a true Parisian of Rameau's stamp associates with love of woman, it is a certain sort of elegant surroundings, a pretty boudoir, a cheery hearth, an easy fauteuil. In the absence of such attributes, "fuyit retro Venus." If the Englishman invented the word comfort, it is the Parisian who most thoroughly comprehends the thing. And he resents the loss of it in any house where he has been accustomed to look for it, as a personal wrong to his feelings.

Left for some minutes alone, Gustave occupied himself with kindling the log, and muttering, "Par tous les diables, quel chien de rhume je vais attraper?" He turned as he heard the rustle of a robe and a light slow step. Isaura stood before him. Her aspect startled him. He had come prepared to expect grave displeasure and a frigid reception. But the expression of Isaura's face was more kindly, more gentle, more tender, than he had seen it since the day she had accepted his suit.

Knowing from his mother what his father had said to his prejudice, he thought within himself, "After all, the poor girl loves me better than I thought. She is sensible and enlightened; she cannot pretend to dictate an opinion to a man like me."

He approached with a complacent self-assured mien, and took her hand, which she yielded to him quietly, leading her to one of the few remaining chairs, and seating himself beside her.

"Dear Isaura," he said, talking rapidly all the while he performed this ceremony, "I need not assure you of my utter ignorance of the state to which the imbecility of our Government, and the cowardice, or rather the treachery, of our generals, has reduced you. I only heard of it late last night from my mother. I hasten to claim my right to share with you the humble resources which I have saved by the intellectual labours that have absorbed all such moments as my military drudgeries left to the talents which, even at such a moment, paralysing minds less energetic, have sustained me:"—and therewith he poured several pieces of gold and silver on the table beside her chair.

"Gustave," then said Isaura, "I am well pleased that you thus prove that I was not mistaken when I thought and said that, despite all appearances, all errors, your heart was good. Oh, do but follow its true impulses, and—"

"Its impulses lead me ever to thy feet," interrupted Gustave, with a fervour which sounded somewhat theatrical and hollow.

The girl smiled, not bitterly, not mockingly; but Gustave did not like the smile.

"Poor Gustave," she said, with a melancholy pathos in her soft voice, "do you not understand that the time has come when such commonplace compliments ill suit our altered positions to each other? Nay, listen to me patiently; and let not my words in this last interview pain you to recall. If either of us be to blame in the engagement hastily contracted, it is I. Gustave, when you, exaggerating in your imagination the nature of your sentiments for me, said with such earnestness that on my consent to our union depended your health, your life, your career; that if I withheld that consent you were lost, and in despair would seek distraction from thought in all from which your friends, your mother, the duties imposed upon Genius for the good of Man to the ends of God, should withhold and save you—when you said all this, and I believed it, I felt as if Heaven commanded me not to desert the soul which appealed to me in the crisis of its struggle and peril. Gustave, I repent; I was to blame."

"How to blame?"

"I overrated my power over your heart: I overrated still more, perhaps, my power over my own."

"Ah, your own! I understand now. You did not love me?"

"I never said that I loved you in the sense in which you use the word. I told you that the love which you have described in your verse, and which," she added, falteringly, with heightened colour and with hands tightly clasped, "I have conceived possible in my dreams, it was not mine to give. You declared you were satisfied with such affection as I could bestow. Hush! let me go on. You said that affection would increase, would become love, in proportion as I knew you more. It has not done so. Nay, it passed away; even before this time of trial and of grief, I became aware how different from the love you professed was the neglect which needs no excuse, for it did not pain me."

"You are cruel indeed, Mademoiselle."

"No, indeed, I am kind. I wish you to feel no pang at our parting. Truly I had resolved, when the siege terminated, and the time to speak frankly of our engagement came, to tell you that I shrank from the thought of a union between us; and that it was for the happiness of both that our promises should be mutually cancelled. The moment has come sooner than I thought. Even had I loved you, Gustave, as deeply as—as well as the beings of Romance love, I would not dare to wed one who calls upon mortals to deny God, demolish His altars, treat His worship as a crime. No; I would sooner die of a broken heart, that I might the sooner be one of those souls privileged to pray the Divine Intercessor for merciful light on those beloved and left dark on earth."

"Isaura!" exclaimed Gustave, his mobile temperament impressed, not by the words of Isaura, but by the passionate earnestness with which they were uttered, and by the exquisite spiritual beauty which her face took from the combined sweetness and fervour of its devout expression,—"Isaura, I merit your censure, your sentence of condemnation; but do not ask me to give back your plighted troth. I have not the strength to do so. More than ever, more than when first pledged to me, I need the aid, the companionship, of my guardian angel. You were that to me once; abandon me not now. In these terrible times of revolution, excitable natures catch madness from each other. A writer in the heat of his passion says much that he does not mean to be literally taken, which in cooler moments he repents and retracts. Consider, too, the pressure of want, of hunger. It is the opinions that you so condemn which alone at this moment supply bread to the writer. But say you will yet pardon me,—yet give me trial if I offend no more—if I withdraw my aid to any attacks on your views, your religion—if I say, 'Thy God shall be my God, and thy people shall be my people.'"

"Alas!" said Isaura, softly, "ask thyself if those be words which I can believe again. Hush!" she continued, checking his answer with a more kindling countenance and more impassioned voice. "Are they, after all, the words that man should address to woman? Is it on the strength of Woman that Man should rely? Is it to her that he should say, 'Dictate my opinions on all that belongs to the Mind of man; change the doctrines that I have thoughtfully formed and honestly advocate; teach me how to act on earth, clear all my doubts as to my hopes of heaven'? No, Gustave; in this task man never should repose on woman. Thou are honest at this moment, my poor friend; but could I believe thee to-day, thou wouldst laugh tomorrow at what woman can be made to believe."

Stung to the quick by the truth of Isaura's accusation, Gustave exclaimed with vehemence: "All that thou sayest is false, and thou knowest it. The influence of woman on man for good or for evil defies reasoning. It does mould his deeds on earth; it does either make or mar all that future which lies between his life and his gravestone, and of whatsoever may lie beyond the grave. Give me up now, and thou art responsible for me, for all I do, it may be against all that thou deemest holy. Keep thy troth yet awhile, and test me. If I come to thee showing how I could have injured, and how for thy dear sake I have spared, nay, aided, all that thou dost believe and reverence, then wilt thou dare to say, 'Go thy ways alone—I forsake thee!'"

Isaura turned aside her face, but she held out her hand—it was as cold as death. He knew that she had so far yielded, and his vanity exulted: he smiled in secret triumph as he pressed his kiss on that icy hand and was gone.

"This is duty—it must be duty," said Isaura to herself. "But where is the buoyant delight that belongs to a duty achieved?—where? oh where?" And then she stole with drooping head and heavy step into her own room, fell on her knees, and prayed.

# CHAPTER VIII.

In vain persons, be they male or female, there is a complacent self-satisfaction in any momentary personal success, however little that success may conduce to—nay, however much it may militate against—the objects to which their vanity itself devotes its more permanent desires. A vain woman may be very anxious to win A———, the magnificent, as a partner for life; and yet feel a certain triumph when a glance of her eye has made an evening's conquest of the pitiful B————, although by that achievement she incurs the imminent hazard of losing A——— altogether. So, when Gustave Rameau quitted Isaura, his first feeling was that of triumph. His eloquence had subdued her will; she had not finally discarded him. But as he wandered abstractedly in the biting air, his self-complacency was succeeded by mortification and discontent. He felt that he had committed himself to promises which he was by no means prepared to keep. True, the promises were vague in words; but in substance they were perfectly clear—"to spare, nay, to aid all that Isaura esteemed and reverenced." How was this possible to him? How could he suddenly change the whole character of his writings?—how become the defender of marriage and property, of church and religion?—how proclaim himself so utter an apostate? If he did, how become a leader of the fresh revolution? how escape being its victim? Cease to write altogether?

But then how live? His pen was his sole subsistence, save 30 sous a-day as a National Guard—30 sous a day to him, who, in order to be Sybarite in tastes, was Spartan in doctrine. Nothing better just at that moment than Spartan doctrine, "Live on black broth and fight the enemy." And the journalists in vogue so thrived upon that patriotic sentiment, that they were the last persons compelled to drink the black broth or to fight the enemy.

"Those women are such idiots when they meddle in politics," grumbled between his teeth the enthusiastic advocate of Woman's Rights on all matters of love. "And," he continued, soliloquising, "it is not as if the girl had any large or decent dot; it is not as if she said, 'In return for the sacrifice of your popularity, your prospects, your opinions, I give you not only a devoted heart, but an excellent table and a capital fire and plenty of pocket-money.' Sacre bleu! when I think of that frozen salon, and possibly the leg of a mouse for dinner, and a virtuous homily by way of grace, the prospect is not alluring; and the girl herself is not so pretty as she was—grown very thin. Sur mon ame, I think she asks too much—far more than she is worth. No, No; I had better have accepted her dismissal. Elle n'est pas digne de moi."

Just as he arrived at that conclusion, Gustave Rameau felt the touch of a light, a soft, a warm, yet a firm hand, on his aria. He turned, and beheld the face of the woman whom, through so many dreary weeks, he had sought to shun—the face of Julie Caumartin. Julie was not, as Savarin had seen her, looking pinched and wan, with faded robes, nor, as when met in the cafe by Lemercier, in the faded robes of a theatre. Julie never looked more beautiful, more radiant, than she did now; and there was a wonderful heartfelt fondness in her voice when she cried, "Mon homme! mon homme! seul homme au monde a mon coeur, Gustave, cheri adore! I have found thee-at last—at last!" Gustave gazed upon her, stupefied. Involuntarily his eye glanced from the freshness of bloom in her face which the intense cold of the atmosphere only seemed to heighten into purer health, to her dress, which was new and handsome—black—he did not know that it was mourning—the cloak trimmed with costly sables. Certainly it was no mendicant for alms who thus reminded the shivering Adonis of the claims of a pristine Venus. He stammered out her naive, "Julie!"—and then he stopped.

"Oui, ta Julie! Petit ingrat! how I have sought for thee! how I have hungered for the sight of thee! That monster Savarin! he would not give me any news of thee. That is ages ago. But at least Frederic Lemercier, whom I saw since, promised to remind thee that I lived still. He did not do so, or I should have seen thee—n'est ce, pas?"

"Certainly, certainly—only—chere amie—you know that—that—as I before announced to thee, I—I—was engaged in marriage—and—and—"

"But are you married?"

"No, no. Hark! Take care—is not that the hiss of an obus?"

"What then? Let it come! Would it might slay us both while my hand is in thine!"

"Ah!" muttered Gustave, inwardly, "what a difference! This is love! No preaching here! Elle est plus digne de moi que d'autre."

"No," he said, aloud, "I am not married. Marriage is at best a pitiful ceremony. But if you wished for news of me, surely you must have heard of my effect as an orator not despised in the Salle Favre. Since, I have withdrawn from that arena. But as a journalist I flatter myself that I have had a beau succes."

"Doubtless, doubtless, my Gustave, my Poet! Wherever thou art, thou must be first among men. But, alas it is my fault—my misfortune. I have not been in the midst of a world that perhaps rings of thy name."

"Not my name. Prudence compelled me to conceal that. Still, Genius pierces under any name. You might have discovered me under my nom de plume."

"Pardon me—I was always bete. But, oh! for so many weeks I was so poor—so destitute. I could go nowhere, except—don't be ashamed of me—except—"

"Yes? Go on."

"Except where I could get some money. At first to dance—you remember my bolero. Then I got a better engagement. Do you not remember that you taught me to recite verses? Had it been for myself alone, I might have been contented to starve. Without thee, what was life? But thou wilt recollect Madeleine, the old bonne who lived with me. Well, she had attended and cherished me since I was so high-lived with my mother. Mother! no; it seems that Madame Surville was not my mother after all. But, of course, I could not let my old Madeleine starve; and therefore, with a heart as heavy as lead, I danced and declaimed. My heart was not so heavy when I recited thy songs."

"My songs! Pauvre ange!" exclaimed the Poet.

"And then, too, I thought, 'Ah, this dreadful siege! He, too, may be poor—he may know want and hunger;' and so all I could save from Madeleine I put into a box for thee, in case thou shouldst come back to me some day. Mon homme, how could I go to the Salle Favre? How could I read journals, Gustave? But thou art not married, Gustave? Parole d'honneur?"

"Parole d'honneur! What does that matter?"

"Everything! Ah! I am not so mechante, so mauvaise tete as I was some months ago. If thou went married, I should say, 'Blessed and sacred be thy wife! Forget me.' But as it is, one word more. Dost thou love the young lady, whoever she be? or does she love thee so well that it would be sin in thee to talk trifles to Julie? Speak as honestly as if thou wert not a poet."

"Honestly, she never said she loved me. I never thought she did. But, you see, I was very ill, and my parents and friends and my physician said that it was right for me to arrange my life, and marry, and so forth. And the girl had money, and was a good match. In short, the thing was settled. But oh, Julie, she never learned my songs by heart! She did not love as thou mayst, and still dost. And—ah! well—now that we meet again—now that I look in thy face—now that I hear thy voice—No, I do not love her as I loved, and might yet love thee. But—but—"

"Well, but? oh, I guess. Thou seest me well dressed, no longer dancing and declaiming at cafes: and thou thinkest that Julie has disgraced herself? she is unfaithful?"

Gustave had not anticipated that frankness, nor was the idea which it expressed uppermost in his mind when he said, "but, but—" There were many buts all very confused, struggling through his mind as he spoke. However, he answered as a Parisian sceptic, not ill-bred, naturally would answer:

"My dear friend, my dear child" (the Parisian is very fond of the word child or enfant in addressing a woman), "I have never seen thee so beautiful as thou art now; and when thou tellest me that thou are no longer poor, and the proof of what thou sayest is visible in the furs, which, alas'. I cannot give thee, what am I to think?"

"Oh, mon homme, mon homme! thou art very spirituel, and that is why I loved thee. I am very bete, and that is excuse enough for thee if thou couldst not love me. But canst thou look me in the face and not know that my eyes could not meet thine as they do, if I had been faithless to thee even in a thought, when I so boldly touched thine arm? Viens chez moi, come and let me explain all. Only—only let me repeat, if another has rights over thee which forbid thee to come, say so kindly, and I will never trouble thee again."

Gustave had been hitherto walking slowly by the side of Julie, amidst the distant boom of the besiegers' cannon, while the short day began to close; and along the dreary boulevards sauntered idlers turning to look at the young, beautiful, well-dressed woman who seemed in such contrast to the capital whose former luxuries the "Ondine" of imperial Paris represented. He now offered his arm to Julie; and, quickening his pace, said, "There is no reason why I should refuse to attend thee home, and listen to the explanations thou dost generously condescend to volunteer."

# CHAPTER IX.

"Ah, indeed! what a difference! what a difference!" said Gustave to himself when he entered Julie's apartment. In her palmier days, when he had first made her acquaintance, the apartment no doubt had been infinitely more splendid, more abundant in silks and fringes and flowers and nicknacks; but never had it seemed so cheery and comfortable and home-like as now. What a contrast to Isaura's dismantled chilly salon! She drew him towards the hearth, on which, blazing though it was, she piled fresh billets, seated him in the easiest of easy-chairs, knelt beside him, and chafed his numbed hands in hers; and as her bright eyes fixed tenderly on his, she looked so young and so innocent! You would not then have called her the "Ondine of Paris."

But when, a little while after, revived by the genial warmth and moved by the charm of her beauty, Gustave passed his arm round her neck and sought to draw her on his lap, she slid from his embrace, shaking her head gently, and seated herself, with a pretty air of ceremonious decorum, at a little distance.

Gustave looked at her amazed.

"Causons," said she, gravely, "thou wouldst know why I am so well dressed, so comfortably lodged, and I am longing to explain to thee all. Some days ago I had just finished my performance at the cafe—, and was putting on my shawl, when a tall Monsieur, fort bel homme, with the air of a grand seigneur, entered the cafe, and approaching me politely, said, 'I think I have the honour to address Mademoiselle Julie Caumartin?' 'That is my name,' I said, surprised; and, looking at him more intently, I recognised his face. He had come into the cafe a few days before with thine old acquaintance Frederic Lemercier, and stood by when I asked Frederic to give me news of thee. 'Mademoiselle,' he continued, with a serious melancholy smile, 'I shall startle you when I say that I am appointed to act as your guardian by the last request of your mother.' 'Of Madame Surville?' 'Madame Surville adopted you, but was not your mother. We cannot talk at ease here. Allow me to request that you will accompany me to Monsieur ——-, the avoue. It is not very far from this—and by the way—I will tell you some news that may sadden, and some news that may rejoice.'

"There was an earnestness in the voice and look of this Monsieur that impressed me. He did not offer me his arm; but I walked by his side in the direction he chose. As we walked he told me in very few words that my mother had been separated from her husband, and for certain family reasons had found it so difficult to rear and provide for me herself, that she had accepted the offer of Madame Surville to adopt me as her own child. While he spoke, there came dimly back to me the remembrance of a lady who had taken me from my first home, when I had been, as I understood, at nurse, and left me with poor dear Madame Surville, saying, 'This is henceforth your mamma.'

"I never again saw that lady. It seems that many years afterwards my true mother desired to regain me. Madame Surville was then dead. She failed to trace me out, owing, alas! to my own faults and change of name. She then entered a nunnery, but, before doing so, assigned a sum of 100,000 francs to this gentleman, who was distantly connected with her, with full power to him to take it to himself, or give it to my use should he discover me, at his discretion. 'I ask you,' continued the Monsieur, 'to go with me to Mons. N———'s, because the sum is still in his hands. He will confirm my statement. All that I have now to say is this, If you accept my guardianship, if you obey implicitly my advice, I shall consider the interest of this sum which has accumulated since deposited with M. ——- due to you; and the capital will be your dot on marriage, if the marriage be with my consent.'"

Gustave had listened very attentively, and without interruption, until now; when he looked up, and said with his customary sneer, "Did your Monsieur, fort bel homme, you say, inform you of the value of the advice, rather of the commands, you were implicitly to obey?"

"Yes," answered Julie, "not then, but later. Let me go on. We arrived at M. N——-'s, an elderly grave man. He said that all he knew was that he held the money in trust for the Monsieur with me, to be given to him, with the accumulations of interest, on the death of the lady who had deposited it. If that Monsieur had instructions how to dispose of the money, they were not known to him. All he had to do was to transfer it absolutely to him on the proper certificate of the lady's death. So you see, Gustave, that the Monsieur could have kept all from me if he had liked."

"Your Monsieur is very generous. Perhaps you will now tell me his name."

"No; he forbids me to do it yet."

"And he took this apartment for you, and gave you money to buy that smart dress and these furs. Bah! mon enfant, why try to deceive me? Do I not know my Paris? A fort bel homme does not make himself guardian to a fort belle fine so young and fair as Mademoiselle Julie Caumartin without certain considerations which shall be nameless, like himself."

Julie's eyes flashed. "Ah, Gustave! ah, Monsieur!" she said, half angrily, half plaintively, "I see that my guardian knew you better than I did. Never mind; I will not reproach. Thou halt the right to despise me."

"Pardon! I did not mean to offend thee," said Gustave, somewhat disconcerted. "But own that thy story is strange; and this guardian, who knows me better than thou—does he know me at all? Didst thou speak to him of me?"

"How could I help it? He says that this terrible war, in which he takes an active part, makes his life uncertain from day to day. He wished to complete the trust bequeathed to him by seeing me safe in the love of some worthy man who"—she paused for a moment with an expression of compressed anguish, and then hurried on—"who would recognise what was good in me,—would never reproach me for—for—the past. I then said that my heart was thine: I could never marry any one but thee."

"Marry me," faltered Gustave—"marry!"

"And," continued the girl, not heeding his interruption, "he said thou wert not the husband he would choose for me: that thou wert not—no, I cannot wound thee by repeating what he said unkindly, unjustly. He bade me think of thee no more. I said again, that is impossible."

"But," resumed Rameau, with an affected laugh, "why think of anything so formidable as marriage? Thou lovest me, and—" He approached again, seeking to embrace her. She recoiled. "No, Gustave, no. I have sworn solemnly by the memory of my lost mother—O—that I will never sin again. I will never be to thee other than thy friend—or thy wife."

Before Gustave could reply to these words, which took him wholly by surprise, there was a ring at the outer door, and the old bonne ushered in Victor de Mauleon. He halted at the threshold, and his brow contracted.

"So you have already broken faith with me, Mademoiselle?"

"No, Monsieur, I have not broken faith," cried Julie; passionately. "I told you that I would not seek to find out Monsieur Rameau. I did not seek, but I met him unexpectedly. I owed to him an explanation. I invited him here to give that explanation. Without it, what would he have thought of me? Now he may go, and I will never admit him again without your sanction."

The Vicomte turned his stern look upon Gustave, who though, as we know, not wanting in personal courage, felt cowed by his false position; and his eye fell, quailed before De Mauleon's gaze.

"Leave us for a few minutes alone, Mademoiselle," said the Vicomte. "Nay, Julie," he added, in softened tones, "fear nothing. I, too, owe explanation—friendly explanation—to M. Rameau."

With his habitual courtesy towards women, he extended his hand to Julie, and led her from the room. Then, closing the door, he seated himself, and made a sign to Gustave to do the same.

"Monsieur," said De Mauleon, "excuse me if I detain you. A very few words will suffice for our present interview. I take it for granted that Mademoiselle has told you that she is no child of Madame Surville's: that her own mother bequeathed her to my protection and guardianship with a modest fortune which is at my disposal to give or withhold. The little I have seen already of Mademoiselle impresses me with sincere interest in her fate. I look with compassion on what she may have been in the past; I anticipate with hope what she may be in the future. I do not ask you to see her in either with my eyes. I say frankly that it is my intention, and I may add, my resolve, that the ward thus left to my charge shall be henceforth safe from the temptations that have seduced her poverty, her inexperience, her vanity, if you will, but have not yet corrupted her heart. Bref, I must request you to give me your word of honour that you will hold no further communication with her. I can allow no sinister influence to stand between her fate and honour."

"You speak well and nobly, M. le Vicomte," said Rameau, "and I give the promise you exact." He added, feelingly: "It is true her heart has never been corrupted that is good, affectionate, unselfish as a child's. J'ai l'honneur de vous saluer, M. le Vicomte."

He bowed with a dignity unusual to him, and tears were in his eyes as he passed by De Mauleon and gained the anteroom. There a side-door suddenly opened, and Julie's face, anxious, eager, looked forth.

Gustave paused: "Adieu, Mademoiselle! Adieu, though we may never meet again,—though our fates divide us,—believe me that I shall ever cherish your memory—and—"

The girl interrupted him, impulsively seizing his arm, and looking him in the face with a wild fixed stare. "Hush! dost thou mean to say that we are parted,—parted forever?"

"Alas!" said Gustave, "what option is before us? Your guardian rightly forbids my visits; and even were I free to offer you my hand, you yourself say that I am not a suitor he would approve."

Julie turned her eyes towards De Mauleon, who, following Gustave into the ante-room, stood silent and impassive, leaning against the wall.

He now understood and replied to the pathetic appeal in the girl's eyes.

"My young ward," he said, "M. Rameau expresses himself with propriety and truth. Suffer him to depart. He belongs to the former life; reconcile yourself to the new."

He advanced to take her hand, making a sign to Gustave to depart. But as he approached Julie, she uttered a weak piteous wail, and fell at his feet senseless. De Mauleon raised and carried her into her room, where he left her to the care of the old bonne. On re-entering the anteroom, he found Gustave still lingering by the outer door. "You will pardon me, Monsieur," he said to the Vicomte, "but in fact I feel so uneasy, so unhappy. Has she—? You see, you see that there is danger to her health, perhaps to her reason, in so abrupt a separation, so cruel a rupture between us. Let me call again, or I may not have strength to keep my promise."

De Mauleon remained a few minutes musing. Then he said in a whisper, "Come back into the salon. Let us talk frankly."

# CHAPTER X.

"M. Rameau," said De Mauleon, when the two men had reseated themselves in the salon, "I will honestly say that my desire is to rid myself as soon as I can of the trust of guardian to this young lady. Playing as I do with fortune, my only stake against her favours is my life. I feel as if it were my duty to see that Mademoiselle is not left alone and friendless in the world at my decease. I have in my mind for her a husband that I think in every way suitable: a handsome and brave young fellow in my battalion, of respectable birth, without any living relations to consult as to his choice. I have reason to believe that if Julie married him, she need never fear as a reproach to her antecedents. Her dot would suffice to enable him to realise his own wish of a country town in Normandy. And in that station, Paris and its temptations would soon pass from the poor child's thoughts, as an evil dream. But I cannot dispose of her hand without her own consent; and if she is to be reasoned out of her fancy for you, I have no time to devote to the task. I come to the point, You are not the man I would choose for her husband. But, evidently, you are the man she would choose. Are you disposed to marry her? You hesitate, very naturally; I have no right to demand an immediate answer to a question so serious. Perhaps you will think over it, and let me know in a day or two? I take it for granted that if you were, as I heard, engaged before the siege to marry the Signora Cicogna, that engagement is annulled?"

"Why take it for granted?" asked Gustave, perplexed. "Simply because I find you here. Nay, spare explanations and excuses. I quite understand that you were invited to come. But a man solemnly betrothed to a mademoiselle like the Signora Cicogna, in a time of such dire calamity and peril, could scarcely allow himself to be tempted to accept the invitation of one so beautiful, and so warmly attached to him, as is Mademoiselle Julie; and on witnessing the passionate strength of that attachment, say that he cannot keep a promise not to repeat his visits. But if I mistake, and you are still betrothed to the Signorina, of course all discussion is at an end."

Gustave hung his head in some shame, and in much bewildered doubt.

The practised observer of men's characters, and of shifting phases of mind, glanced at the poor poet's perturbed countenance with a half-smile of disdain.

"It is for you to judge how far the very love to you so ingenuously evinced by my ward—how far the reasons against marriage with one whose antecedents expose her to reproach—should influence one of your advanced opinions upon social ties. Such reasons do not appear to have with artists the same weight they have with the bourgeoisie. I have but to add that the husband of Julie will receive with her hand a dot of nearly 120,000 francs; and I have reason to believe that that fortune will be increased—how much, I cannot guess-when the cessation of the siege will allow communication with England. One word more. I should wish to rank the husband of my ward in the number of my friends. If he did not oppose the political opinions with which I identify my own career, I should be pleased to make any rise in the world achieved by me assist to the raising of himself. But my opinions, as during the time we were brought together you were made aware, are those of a practical man of the world, and have nothing in common with Communists, Socialists, Internationalists, or whatever sect would place the aged societies of Europe in Medea's caldron of youth. At a moment like the present, fanatics and dreamers so abound that the number of such sinners will necessitate a general amnesty when order is restored. What a poet so young as you may have written or said at such a time will be readily forgotten and forgiven a year or two hence, provided he does not put his notions into violent action. But if you choose to persevere in the views you now advocate, so be it. They will not make poor Julie less a believer in your wisdom and genius. Only they will separate you from me, and a day may come when I should have the painful duty of ordering you to be shot—Die meliora. Think over all I have thus frankly said. Give me your answer within forty-eight hours; and meanwhile hold no communication with my ward. I have the honour to wish you good-day."

# CHAPTER XI.

The short grim day was closing when Gustave, quitting Julie's apartment, again found himself in the streets. His thoughts were troubled and confused. He was the more affected by Julie's impassioned love for him, by the contrast with Isaura's words and manner in their recent interview. His own ancient fancy for the "Ondine of Paris" became revived by the difficulties between their ancient intercourse which her unexpected scruples and De Mauleon's guardianship interposed. A witty writer thus defines une passion, "une caprice inflamme par des obstacles." In the ordinary times of peace, Gustave, handsome, aspiring to reputable position in the beau monde, would not have admitted any considerations to compromise his station by marriage with a fagurante. But now the wild political doctrines he had embraced separated his ambition from that beau monde, and combined it with ascendancy over the revolutionists of the populace—a direction which he must abandon if he continued his suit to Isaura. Then, too, the immediate possession of Julie's dot was not without temptation to a man who was so fond of his personal comforts, and who did not see where to turn for a dinner, if, obedient to Isaura's "prejudices," he abandoned his profits as a writer in the revolutionary press. The inducements for withdrawal from the cause he had espoused, held out to him with so haughty a coldness by De Mauleon, were not wholly without force, though they irritated his self-esteem. He was dimly aware of the Vicomte's masculine talents for public life; and the high reputation he had already acquired among military authorities, and even among experienced and thoughtful civilians, had weight upon Gustave's impressionable temperament. But though De Mauleon's implied advice here coincided in much with the tacit compact he had made with Isaura, it alienated him more from Isaura herself, for Isaura did not bring to him the fortune which would enable him to suspend his lucubrations, watch the turn of events, and live at ease in the meanwhile; and the dot to be received with De Mauleon's ward had those advantages.

While thus meditating Gustave turned into one of the cantines still open, to brighten his intellect with a petit verre, and there he found the two colleagues in the extinct Council of Ten, Paul Grimm and Edgar Ferrier. With the last of these revolutionists Gustave had become intimately lie. They wrote in the same journal, and he willingly accepted a distraction from his self-conflict which Edgar offered him in a dinner at the cafe Riche, which still offered its hospitalities at no exorbitant price. At this repast, as the drink circulated, Gustave waxed confidential. He longed, poor youth, for an adviser. Could he marry a girl who had been a ballet-dancer, and who had come into an unexpected heritage? "Es-tu fou d'en douter?" cried Edgar. "What a sublime occasion to manifest thy scorn of the miserable banalities of the bourgeoisie! It will but increase thy moral power over the people. And then think of the money. What an aid to the cause! What a capital for the launch!—journal all thine own! Besides, when our principles triumph—as triumph they must—what would be marriage but a brief and futile ceremony, to be broken the moment thou hast cause to complain of thy wife or chafe at the bond? Only get the dot into thine own hands. L'amour passe—reste la cassette."

Though there was enough of good in the son of Madame Rameau to revolt at the precise words in which the counsel was given, still, as the fumes of the punch yet more addled his brains, the counsel itself was acceptable; and in that sort of maddened fury which intoxication produces in some excitable temperaments, as Gustave reeled home that night leaning on the arm of stouter Edgar Ferrier, he insisted on going out of his way to pass the house in which Isaura lived, and, pausing under her window, gasped out some verses of a wild song, then much in vogue among the votaries of Felix Pyat, in which everything that existent society deems sacred was reviled in the grossest ribaldry. Happily Isaura's ear heard it not. The girl was kneeling by her bedside absorbed in prayer.

# CHAPTER XII.

Three days after the evening thus spent by Gustave Rameau, Isaura was startled by a visit from M. de Mauleon. She had not seen him since the commencement of the siege, and she did not recognise him at first glance in his military uniform.

"I trust you will pardon my intrusion, Mademoiselle," he said, in the low sweet voice habitual to him in his gentler moods, "but I thought it became me to announce to you the decease of one who, I fear, did not discharge with much kindness the duties her connection with you imposed. Your father's second wife, afterwards Madame Selby, is no more. She died some days since in a convent to which she had retired."

Isaura had no cause to mourn the dead, but she felt a shock in the suddenness of this information; and in that sweet spirit of womanly compassion which entered so largely into her character, and made a part of her genius itself, she murmured tearfully, "The poor Signora! Why could I not have been with her in illness? She might then have learned to love me. And she died in a convent, you say? Ah, her religion was then sincere! Her end was peaceful?"

"Let us not doubt that, Mademoiselle. Certainly she lived to regret any former errors, and her last thought was directed towards such atonement as might be in her power. And it is that desire of atonement which now strangely mixes me up, Mademoiselle, in your destinies. In that desire for atonement, she left to my charge, as a kinsman distant indeed, but still, perhaps, the nearest with whom she was personally acquainted—a young ward. In accepting that trust, I find myself strangely compelled to hazard the risk of offending you."

"Offending me? How? Pray speak openly."

"In so doing, I must utter the name of Gustave Rameau."

Isaura turned pale and recoiled, but she did not speak. "Did he inform me rightly that, in the last interview with him three days ago, you expressed a strong desire that the engagement between him and yourself should cease; and that you only, and with reluctance, suspended your rejection of the suit he had pressed on you, in consequence of his entreaties, and of certain assurances as to the changed direction of the talents of which we will assume that he is possessed?"

"Well, well, Monsieur," exclaimed Isaura, her whole face brightening; "and you come on the part of Gustave Rameau to say that on reflection he does not hold me to our engagement—that in honour and in conscience I am free?"

"I see," answered De Mauleon, smiling, "that I am pardoned already. It would not pain you if such were my instructions in the embassy I undertake?"

"Pain me? No. But—"

"But what?"

"Must he persist in a course which will break his mother's heart, and make his father deplore the hour that he was born? Have you influence over him, M. de Mauleon? If so, will you not exert it for his good?"

"You interest yourself still in his fate, Mademoiselle?"

"How can I do otherwise? Did I not consent to share it when my heart shrank from the thought of our union? And now when, if I understand you rightly, I am free, I cannot but think of what was best in him."

"Alas! Mademoiselle, he is but one of many—a spoilt child of that Circe, imperial Paris. Everywhere I look around, I see but corruption. It was hidden by the halo which corruption itself engenders. The halo is gone, the corruption is visible. Where is the old French manhood? Banished from the heart, it comes out only at the tongue. Were our deeds like our words, Prussia would beg on her knee to be a province of France. Gustave is the fit poet for this generation. Vanity—desire to be known for something, no matter what, no matter by whom—that is the Parisian's leading motive power;—orator, soldier, poet, all alike. Utterers of fine phrases; despising knowledge, and toil, and discipline; railing against the Germans as barbarians, against their generals as traitors; against God for not taking their part. What can be done to weld this mass of hollow bubbles into the solid form of a nation—the nation it affects to be? What generation can be born out of the unmanly race, inebriate with brag and absinthe? Forgive me this tirade; I have been reviewing the battalion I command. As for Gustave Rameau,—if we survive the siege, and see once more a Government that can enforce order, and a public that will refuse renown for balderdash,—I should not be surprised if Gustave Rameau were among the prettiest imitators of Lamartine's early Meditations. Had he been born under Louis XIV. how loyal he would have been! What sacred tragedies in the style of Athalie he would have written, in the hope of an audience at Versailles! But I detain you from the letter I was charged to deliver you. I have done so purposely, that I might convince myself that you welcome that release which your too delicate sense of honour shrank too long from demanding."

Here he took forth and placed a letter in Isaura's hand; and, as if to allow her to read it unobserved, retired to the window recess.

Isaura glanced over the letter. It ran thus:

"I feel that it was only to your compassion that I owed your consent to my suit. Could I have doubted that before, your words when we last met sufficed to convince me. In my selfish pain at the moment, I committed a great wrong. I would have held you bound to a promise from which you desired to be free. Grant me pardon for that; and for all the faults by which I have offended you. In cancelling our engagement, let me hope that I may rejoice in your friendship, your remembrance of me, some gentle and kindly thought. My life may henceforth pass out of contact with yours; but you will ever dwell in my heart, an image pure and holy as the saints in whom you may well believe-they are of your own kindred."

"May I convey to Gustave Rameau any verbal reply to his letter?" asked De Mauleon, turning as she replaced the letter on the table.

"Only my wishes for his welfare. It might wound him if I added, my gratitude for the generous manner in which he has interpreted my heart, and acceded to its desires."

"Mademoiselle, accept my congratulations. My condolences are for the poor girl left to my guardianship. Unhappily she loves this man; and there are reasons why I cannot withhold my consent to her union with him, should he demand it, now that, in the letter remitted to you, he has accepted your dismissal. If I can keep him out of all the follies and all the evils into which he suffers his vanity to mislead his reason, I will do so;—would I might say, only in compliance with your compassionate injunctions. But henceforth the infatuation of my ward compels me to take some interest in his career. Adieu, Mademoiselle! I have no fear for your happiness now."

Left alone, Isaura stood as one transfigured. All the bloom of her youth seemed suddenly restored. Round her red lips the dimples opened, countless mirrors of one happy smile. "I am free, I am free," she murmured—"joy, joy!" and she passed from the room to seek the Venosta, singing clear, singing loud, as a bird that escapes from the cage and warbles to the heaven it regains the blissful tale of its release.

# CHAPTER XIII.

In proportion to the nearer roar of the besiegers' cannon, and the sharper gripe of famine within the walls, the Parisians seemed to increase their scorn for the skill of the enemy, and their faith in the sanctity of the capital. All false news was believed as truth; all truthful news abhorred as falsehood. Listen to the groups round the cafes. "The Prussian funds have fallen three per cent. at Berlin," says a threadbare ghost of the Bourse (he had been a clerk of Louvier's). "Ay," cries a National Guard, "read extracts from La Liberte. The barbarians are in despair. Nancy is threatened, Belfort is freed. Bourbaki is invading Baden. Our fleets are pointing their cannon upon Hamburg. Their country endangered, their retreat cut off, the sole hope of Bismarck and his trembling legions is to find a refuge in Paris. The increasing fury of the bombardment is a proof of their despair."

"In that case," whispered Savarin to De Breze, "suppose we send a flag of truce to Versailles with a message from Trochu that, on disgorging their conquests, ceding the left bank of the Rhine, and paying the expenses of the war, Paris, ever magnanimous to the vanquished; will allow the Prussians to retire."

"The Prussians! Retire!" cried Edgar Ferrier, catching the last word and glancing fiercely at Savarin. "What Prussian spy have we among us? Not one of the barbarians shall escape. We have but to dismiss the traitors who have usurped the government, proclaim the Commune and the rights of labour, and we give birth to a Hercules that even in its cradle can strangle the vipers."

Edgar Ferrier was the sole member of his political party among the group which he thus addressed; but such was the terror which the Communists already began to inspire among the bourgeoisie that no one volunteered a reply.

Savarin linked his arm in De Breze's, and prudently drew him off.

"I suspect," said the former, "that we shall soon have worse calamities to endure than the Prussian obus and the black loaf. The Communists will have their day."

"I shall be in my grave before then," said De Breze, in hollow accents. "It is twenty-four hours since I spent my last fifty sous on the purchase of a rat, and I burnt the legs of my bedstead for the fuel by which that quadruped was roasted."

"Entre nous, my poor friend, I am much in the same condition," said Savarin, with a ghastly attempt at his old pleasant laugh. "See how I am shrunken! My wife would be unfaithful to the Savarin of her dreams if she accepted a kiss from the slender gallant you behold in me. But I thought you were in the National Guard, and therefore had not to vanish into air."

"I was a National Guard, but I could not stand the hardships, and being above the age, I obtained my exemption. As to pay, I was then too proud to claim my wage of 1 franc 25 centimes. I should not be too proud now. Ah, blessed be Heaven! here comes Lemercier; he owes me a dinner—he shall pay it."

"Bon jour, my dear Frederic! How handsome you look in your kepi! Your uniform is brilliantly fresh from the soil of powder. What a contrast to the tatterdemalions of the Line!"

"I fear," said Lemercier, ruefully, "that my costume will not look so well a day or two hence. I have just had news that will no doubt seem very glorious—in the news papers. But then newspapers are not subjected to cannonballs."

"What do you mean?" answered De Breze.

"I met, as I emerged from my apartment a few minutes ago, that fire-eater, Victor de Mauleon, who always contrives to know what passes at headquarters. He told me that preparations are being made for a great sortie. Most probably the announcement will appear in a proclamation tomorrow, and our troops march forth to-morrow night. The National Guard (fools and asses who have been yelling out for decisive action) are to have their wish, and to be placed in the van of battle,—amongst the foremost, the battalion in which I am enrolled. Should this be our last meeting on earth, say that Frederic Lemercier has finished his part in life with eclat."

"Gallant friend," said De Breze, feebly seizing him by the arm, "if it be true that thy mortal career is menaced, die as thou hast lived. An honest man leaves no debt unpaid. Thou owest me a dinner."

"Alas! ask of me what is possible. I will give thee three, however, if I survive and regain my rentes. But today I have not even a mouse to share with Fox."

"Fox lives then?" cried De Breze, with sparkling hungry eyes.

"Yes. At present he is making the experiment how long an animal can live without food."

"Have mercy upon him, poor beast! Terminate his pangs by a noble death. Let him save thy friends and thyself from starving. For myself alone I do not plead; I am but an amateur in polite literature. But Savarin, the illustrious Savarin,—in criticism the French Longinus—in poetry the Parisian Horace—in social life the genius of gaiety in pantaloons,—contemplate his attenuated frame! Shall he perish for want of food while thou hast such superfluity in thy larder? I appeal to thy heart, thy conscience, thy patriotism. What, in the eyes of France, are a thousand Foxes compared to a single Savarin?"

"At this moment," sighed Savarin, "I could swallow anything, however nauseous, even thy flattery, De Breze. But, my friend Frederic, thou goest into battle—what will become of Fox if thou fall? Will he not be devoured by strangers? Surely it were a sweeter thought to his faithful heart to furnish a repast to thy friends?—his virtues acknowledged, his memory blest!"

"Thou dost look very lean, my poor Savarin! And how hospitable thou wert when yet plump!" said Frederic, pathetically. "And certainly, if I live, Fox will starve; if I am slain, Fox will be eaten. Yet, poor Fox, dear Fox, who lay on my breast when I was frostbitten. No; I have not the heart to order him to the spit for you. Urge it not."

"I will save thee that pang," cried De Breze. "We are close by thy rooms. Excuse me for a moment: I will run in and instruct thy bonne."

So saying, he sprang forward with an elasticity of step which no one could have anticipated from his previous languor. Frederic would have followed, but Savarin clung to him, whimpering: "Stay; I shall fall like an empty sack, without the support of thine arm, young hero. Pooh! of course De Breze is only joking—a pleasant joke. Hist! a secret: he has moneys, and means to give us once more a dinner at his own cost, pretending that we dine on thy dog. He was planning this when thou camest up. Let him have his joke, and we shall have a festin de Balthazar."

"Hein!" said Frederic, doubtfully; "thou art sure he has no designs upon Fox?"

"Certainly not, except in regaling us. Donkey is not bad, but it is 14 francs a pound. A pullet is excellent, but it is 30 francs. Trust to De Breze; we shall have donkey and pullet, and Fox shall feast upon the remains."

Before Frederic could reply, the two men were jostled and swept on by a sudden rush of a noisy crowd in their rear. They could but distinguish the words—Glorious news—victory—Faidherbe—Chanzy. But these words were sufficient to induce them to join willingly in the rush. They forgot their hunger; they forget Fox. As they were hurried on, they learned that there was a report of a complete defeat of the Prussians by Faidherbe near Amiens, of a still more decided one on the Loire by Chanzy. These generals, with armies flushed with triumph, were pressing on towards Paris to accelerate the destruction of the hated Germans. How the report arose no one exactly knew.

All believed it, and were making their way to the Hotel de Ville to hear it formally confirmed.

Alas! before, they got there they were met by another crowd returning, dejected but angry. No such news had reached the Government. Chanzy and Faidherbe were no doubt fighting bravely,—with every probability of success; but—

The Parisian imagination required no more. "We should always be defeating the enemy," said Savarin, "if there were not always a but;" and his audience, who, had he so expressed himself ten minutes before, would have torn him to pieces, now applauded the epigram; and with execrations on Trochu, mingled with many a peal of painful sarcastic laughter, vociferated and dispersed.

As the two friends sauntered back towards the part of the Boulevards on which De Breze had parted company with them, Savarin quitted Lemercier suddenly, and crossed the street to accost a small party of two ladies and two men who were on their way to the Madeleine. While he was exchanging a few words with them, a young couple, arm in arm, passed by Lemercier,—the man in the uniform of the National Guard-uniform as unsullied as Frederic's, but with as little of a military air as can well be conceived. His gait was slouching; his head bent downwards. He did not seem to listen to his companion, who was talking with quickness and vivacity, her fair face radiant with smiles. Lemercier looked at them as they passed by. "Sur mon ame," muttered Frederic to himself, "surely that is la belle Julie; and she has got back her truant poet at last."

While Lemercier thus soliloquised, Gustave, still looking down, was led across the street by his fair companion, and into the midst of the little group with whom Savarin had paused to speak. Accidentally brushing against Savarin himself, he raised his eyes with a start, about to mutter some conventional apology, when Julie felt the arm on which she leant tremble nervously. Before him stood Isaura, the Countess de Vandemar by her side; her two other companions, Raoul and the Abbe Vertpre, a step or two behind.

Gustave uncovered, bowed low, and stood mute and still for a moment, paralysed by surprise and the chill of a painful shame.

Julie's watchful eyes, following his, fixed themselves on the same face. On the instant she divined the truth. She beheld her to whom she had owed months of jealous agony, and over whom, poor child, she thought she had achieved a triumph. But the girl's heart was so instinctively good that the sense of triumph was merged in a sense of compassion. Her rival had lost Gustave. To Julie the loss of Gustave was the loss of all that makes life worth having. On her part, Isaura was moved not only by the beauty of Julie's countenance, but still more by the childlike ingenuousness of its expression.

So, for the first time in their lives, met the child and the stepchild of Louise Duval. Each so deserted, each so left alone and inexperienced amid the perils of the world, with fates so different, typifying orders of womanhood so opposed. Isaura was naturally the first to break the silence that weighed like a sensible load on all present.

She advanced towards Rameau, with sincere kindness in her look and tone.

"Accept my congratulations," she said, with a grave smile. "Your mother informed me last evening of your nuptials. Without doubt I see Madame Gustave Rameau;"—and she extended her hand towards Julie. The poor Ondine shrank back for a moment, blushing up to her temples. It was the first hand which a woman of spotless character had extended to her since she had lost the protection of Madame Surville. She touched it timidly, humbly, then drew her bridegroom on; and with head more downcast than Gustave, passed through the group without a word.

She did not speak to Gustave till they were out of sight and hearing of those they had left. Then, pressing his arm passionately, she said: "And that is the demoiselle thou halt resigned for me! Do not deny it. I am so glad to have seen her; it has done me so much good. How it has deepened, purified, my love for thee! I have but one return to make; but that is my whole life. Thou shalt never have cause to blame me—never—never!"

Savarin looked very grave and thoughtful when he rejoined Lemercier.

"Can I believe my eyes?" said Frederic. "Surely that was Julie Caumartin leaning on Gustave Rameau's arm! And had he the assurance, so accompanied, to salute Madame de Vandemar, and Mademoiselle Cicogna, to whom I understood he was affianced? Nay, did I not see Mademoiselle shake hands with the Ondine? or am I under one of the illusions which famine is said to engender in the brain?"

"I have not strength now to answer all these interrogatives. I have a story to tell; but I keep it for dinner. Let us hasten to thy apartment. De Breze is doubtless there waiting us."

# CHAPTER XIV.

Unprescient of the perils that awaited him, absorbed in the sense of existing discomfort, cold, and hunger, Fox lifted his mournful visage from his master's dressing-gown, in which he had encoiled his shivering frame, on the entrance of De Breze and the concierge of the house in which Lemercier had his apartment. Recognising the Vicomte as one of his master's acquaintances, he checked the first impulse that prompted him to essay a feeble bark, and permitted himself, with a petulant whine, to be extracted from his covering, and held in the arms of the murderous visitor.

"Dieu des dieux!" ejaculated De Breze, "how light the poor beast has become!" Here he pinched the sides and thighs of the victim. "Still," he said, "there is some flesh yet on these bones. You may grill the paws, fricassee the shoulders, and roast the rest. The rognons and the head accept for yourself as a perquisite." Here he transferred Fox to the arms of the concierge, adding, "Vite au besogne, mon ami."

"Yes, Monsieur. I must be quick about it while my wife is absent. She has a faiblesse for the brute. He must be on the spit before she returns."

"Be it so; and on the table in an hour—five o'clock precisely—I am famished."

The concierge disappeared with Fox. De Breze then amused himself by searching into Frederic's cupboards and buffets, from which he produced a cloth and utensils necessary for the repast. These he arranged with great neatness, and awaited in patience the moment of participation in the feast.

The hour of five had struck before Savarin and Frederio entered the salon; and at their sight De Breze dashed to the staircase and called out to the concierge to serve the dinner.

Frederic, though unconscious of the Thyestean nature of the banquet, still looked round for the dog; and, not perceiving him, began to call out, "Fox! Fox! where hast thou hidden thyself?"

"Tranquillise yourself," said De Breze. "Do not suppose that I have not...."

NOTE BY THE AUTHOR'S SON.—[See also Prefatory Note]—The hand that wrote thus far has left unwritten the last scene of the tragedy of poor Fox. In the deep where Prospero has dropped his wand are now irrevocably buried the humour and the pathos of this cynophagous banquet. One detail of it, however, which the author imparted to his son, may here be faintly indicated. Let the sympathising reader recognise all that is dramatic in the conflict between hunger and affection; let him recall to mind the lachrymose loving-kindness of his own post-prandial emotions after blissfully breaking some fast, less mercilessly prolonged, we will hope, than that of these besieged banqueters, and then, though unaided by the fancy which conceived so quaint a situation, he may perhaps imagine what tearful tenderness would fill the eyes of the kind-hearted Frederic, as they contemplate the well-picked bones of his sacrificed favourite on the plate before him; which he pushes away, sighing, "Ah, poor Fox! how he would have enjoyed those bones!"

The chapter immediately following this one also remains unfinished. It was not intended to close the narrative thus left uncompleted; but of those many and so various works which have not unworthily associated with almost every department of literature the name of a single English writer, it is CHAPTER THE LAST. Had the author lived to finish it, he would doubtless have added to his Iliad of the Siege of Paris its most epic episode, by here describing the mighty combat between those two princes of the Parisian Bourse, the magnanimous Duplessis and the redoubtable Louvier. Amongst the few other pages of the book which have been left unwritten, we must also reckon with regret some pages descriptive of the reconciliation between Graham Vane and Isaura Cicogna; but, fortunately for the satisfaction of every reader who may have followed thus far the fortunes of Die Parisians, all that our curiosity is chiefly interested to learn has been recorded in the Envoi, which was written before the completion of the novel.

We know not, indeed, what has become of these two Parisian types of a Beauty not of Holiness, the poor vain Poet of the Pave, and the good-hearted Ondine of the Gutter. It is obvious, from the absence of all allusion to them in Lemercier's letter to Vane, that they had passed out of the narrative before that letter was written. We must suppose the catastrophe of their fates to have been described, in some preceding chapter, by the author himself; who would assuredly not have left 141. Gustave Rameau in permanent pos session of his ill-merited and ill-ministered fortune. That French representative of the appropriately popular poetry of modern ideas, which prefers "the roses and raptures of vice" to "the lilies and languors of virtue," cannot have been irredeemably reconciled by the sweet savours of the domestic pot-au jeu, even when spiced with pungent whiffs of repudiated disreputability, to any selfish betrayal of the cause of universal social emancipation from the personal proprieties. If poor Julie Caumartin has perished in the siege of Paris, with all the grace of a self-wrought redemption still upon her, we shall doubtless deem her fate a happier one than any she could have found in prolonged existence as Madame Rameau; and a certain modicum of this world's good things will, in that case, have been rescued for worthier employment by Graham Vane. To that assurance nothing but Lemercier's description of the fate of Victor de Mauleon (which will be found in the Envoi) need be added for the satisfaction of our sense of poetic justice and if on the mimic stage, from which they now disappear, all these puppets have rightly played their parts in the drama of an empire's fall, each will have helped to "point a moral" as well as to "adorn a tale." Valete et plaudite!

# CHAPTER THE LAST.

Among the refugees which the convoi from Versailles disgorged on the Paris station were two men, who, in pushing through the crowd, came suddenly face to face with each other.

"Aha! Bon jour, M. Duplessis," said a burly voice. "Bon jour, M. Louvier," replied Duplessis.

"How long have you left Bretagne?"

"On the day that the news of the armistice reached it, in order to be able to enter Paris the first day its gates were open. And you—where have you been?"

"In London."

"Ah! in London!" said Duplessis, paling. "I knew I had an enemy there."

"Enemy! I? Bah! my dear Monsieur. What makes you think me your enemy?"

"I remember your threats."

"A propos of Rochebriant. By the way, when would it be convenient to you and the dear Marquis to let me into prompt possession of that property? You can no longer pretend to buy it as a dot for Mademoiselle Valerie."

"I know not that yet. It is true that all the financial operations attempted by my agent in London have failed. But I may recover myself yet, now that I re-enter Paris. In the mean time, we have still six months before us; for, as you will find—if you know it not already—the interest due to you has been lodged with Messrs. —— of ———, and you cannot foreclose, even if the law did not take into consideration the national calamities as between debtor and creditor."

"Quite true. But if you cannot buy the property it must pass into my hands in a very short time. And you and the Marquis had better come to an amicable arrangement with me. Apropos, I read in the Times newspaper that Alain was among the wounded in the sortie of December."

"Yes; we learnt that through a pigeon-post. We were afraid...."

# L'ENVOI.

The intelligent reader will perceive that the story I relate is virtually closed with the preceding chapter; though I rejoice to think that what may be called its plot does not find its denouement amidst the crimes and the frenzy of the Guerre des Communeaux. Fit subjects these, indeed, for the social annalist in times to come. When crimes that outrage humanity have their motive or their excuse in principles that demand the demolition of all upon which the civilisation of Europe has its basis-worship, property, and marriage—in order to reconstruct a new civilisation adapted to a new humanity, it is scarcely possible for the serenest contemporary to keep his mind in that state of abstract reasoning with which Philosophy deduces from some past evil some existent good. For my part, I believe that throughout the whole known history of mankind, even in epochs when reason is most misled and conscience most perverted, there runs visible, though fine and threadlike, the chain of destiny, which has its roots in the throne of an All-wise and an All-good; that in the wildest illusions by which muititudes are frenzied, there may be detected gleams of prophetic truths; that in the fiercest crimes which, like the disease of an epidemic, characterise a peculiar epoch under abnormal circumstances, there might be found instincts or aspirations towards some social virtues to be realised ages afterwards by happier generations, all tending to save man from despair of the future, were the whole society to unite for the joyless hour of his race in the abjuration of soul and the denial of God, because all irresistibly establishing that yearning towards an unseen future which is the leading attribute of soul, evincing the government of a divine Thought which evolves out of the discords of one age the harmonies of another, and, in the world within us as in the world without, enforces upon every unclouded reason the distinction between Providence and chance.

The account subjoined may suffice to say all that rests to be said of those individuals in whose fate, apart from the events or personages that belong to graver history, the reader of this work may have conceived an interest. It is translated from the letter of Frederic Lemercier to Graham Vane, dated June ——, a month after the defeat of the Communists.

"Dear and distinguished Englishman, whose name I honour but fail to pronounce, accept my cordial thanks for your interests in such remains of Frederic Lemercier as yet survive the ravages of Famine, Equality, Brotherhood, Petroleum, and the Rights of Labour. I did not desert my Paris when M. Thiers, 'parmula non bene relicta,' led his sagacious friends and his valiant troops to the groves of Versailles, and confided to us unarmed citizens the preservation of order and property from the insurgents whom he left in possession of our forts and cannon. I felt spellbound by the interest of the sinistoe melodrame, with its quick succession of scenic effects and the metropolis of the world for its stage. Taught by experience, I did not aspire to be an actor; and even as a spectator, I took care neither to hiss nor applaud. Imitating your happy England, I observed a strict neutrality; and, safe myself from danger, left my best friends to the care of the gods.

"As to political questions, I dare not commit myself to a conjecture. At this rouge et noir table, all I can say is, that whichever card turns up, it is either a red or a black one. One gamester gains for the moment by the loss of the other; the table eventually ruins both.

"No one believes that the present form of government can last; every one differs as to that which can. Raoul de Vandemar is immovably convinced of the restoration of the Bourbons. Savarin is meditating a new journal devoted to the cause of the Count of Paris. De Brew and the old Count de Passy, having in turn espoused and opposed every previous form of government, naturally go in for a perfectly novel experiment, and are for constitutional dictatorship under the Duc d'Aumale, which he is to hold at his own pleasure, and ultimately resign to his nephew the Count, under the mild title of a constitutional king;—that is, if it ever suits the pleasure of a dictator to depose himself. To me this seems the wildest of notions. If the Duc's administration were successful, the French would insist on keeping it; and if the uncle were unsuccessful, the nephew would not have a chance. Duplessis retains his faith in the Imperial dynasty; and that Imperialist party is much stronger than it appears on the surface. So many of the bourgeoisie recall with a sigh eighteen years of prosperous trade; so many of the military officers, so many of the civil officials, identify their career with the Napoleonic favour; and so many of the Priesthood, abhorring the Republic, always liable to pass into the hands of those who assail religion,—unwilling to admit the claim of the Orleanists, are at heart for the Empire.

"But I will tell you one secret. I and all the quiet folks like me (we are more numerous than any one violent faction) are willing to accept any form of government by which we have the best chance of keeping our coats on our backs. Liberte, Egalite, Fraternity, are gone quite out of fashion; and Mademoiselle—has abandoned her great chant of the Marseillaise, and is drawing tears from enlightened audiences by her pathetic delivery of 'O Richard! O mon roi!'"

"Now about the other friends of whom you ask for news.

"Wonders will never cease. Louvier and Duplessis are no longer deadly rivals. They have become sworn friends, and are meditating a great speculation in common, to commence as soon as the Prussian debt is paid off. Victor de Mauleon brought about this reconciliation in a single interview during the brief interregnum between the Peace and the Guerre des Communeaux. You know how sternly Louvier was bent upon seizing Alain de Rochebriant's estates. Can you conceive the true cause? Can you imagine it possible that a hardened money-maker like Louvier should ever allow himself to be actuated, one way or the other, by the romance of a sentimental wrong? Yet so it was. It seems that many years ago he was desperately in love with a girl who disappeared from his life, and whom he believed to have been seduced by the late Marquis de Rochebriant. It was in revenge for this supposed crime that he had made himself the principal mortgagee of the late Marquis; and, visiting the sins of the father on the son, had, under the infernal disguise of friendly interest, made himself sole mortgagee to Alain, upon terms apparently the most generous. The demon soon showed his griffe, and was about to foreclose, when Duplessis came to Alain's relief; and Rochebriant was to be Valerie's dot on her marriage with Alain. The Prussian war, of course, suspended all such plans, pecuniary and matrimonial. Duplessis, whose resources were terribly crippled by the war, attempted operations in London with a view of raising the sum necessary to pay off the mortgage;—found himself strangely frustrated and baffled. Louvier was in London, and defeated his rival's agent in every speculation. It became impossible for Duplessis to redeem the mortgage. The two men came to Paris with the peace. Louvier determined both to seize the Breton lands and to complete the ruin of Duplessis, when he learned from De Mauleon that he had spent half his life in a baseless illusion; that Alain's father was innocent of the crime for which his son was to suffer;—and Victor, with that strange power over men's minds which was so peculiar to him, talked Louvier into mercy if not into repentance. In short, the mortgage is to be paid off by instalments at the convenience of Duplessis. Alain's marriage with Valerie is to take place in a few weeks. The fournisseurs are already gone to fit up the old chateau for the bride, and Louvier is invited to the wedding.

"I have all this story from Alain, and from Duplessis himself. I tell the tale as 'twas told to me, with all the gloss of sentiment upon its woof. But between ourselves, I am too Parisian not to be sceptical as to the unalloyed amiability of sudden conversions. And I suspect that Louvier was no longer in a condition to indulge in the unprofitable whim of turning rural seigneur. He had sunk large sums and incurred great liabilities in the new street to be called after his name; and that street has been twice ravaged, first by the Prussian siege, and next by the Guerre des Communeaux; and I can detect many reasons why Louvier should deem it prudent not only to withdraw from the Rochebriant seizure, and make sure of peacefully recovering the capital lent on it, but establishing joint interest and quasi partnership with a financier so brilliant and successful as Armand Duplessis has hitherto been.

"Alain himself is not quite recovered from his wound, and is now at Rochebriant, nursed by his aunt and Valerie. I have promised to visit him next week. Raoul de Vandemar is still at Paris with his mother, saying, there is no place where one Christian man can be of such service. The old Count declines to come back, saying there is no place where a philosopher can be in such danger.

"I reserve as my last communication, in reply to your questions, that which is the gravest. You say that you saw in the public journals brief notice of the assassination of Victor de Mauleon; and you ask for such authentic particulars as I can give of that event, and of the motives of the assassin.

"I need not, of course, tell you how bravely the poor Vicomte behaved throughout the siege; but he made many enemies among the worst members of the National Guard by the severity of his discipline; and had he been caught by the mob the same day as Clement Thomas, who committed the same offence, would have certainly shared the fate of that general. Though elected a depute, he remained at Paris a few days after Thiers & Co. left it, in the hope of persuading the party of Order, including then no small portion of the National Guards, to take prompt and vigorous measures to defend the city against the Communists. Indignant at their pusillanimity, he then escaped to Versailles. There he more than confirmed the high reputation he had acquired during the siege, and impressed the ablest public men with the belief that he was destined to take a very leading part in the strife of party. When the Versailles troops entered Paris, he was, of course, among them in command of a battalion.

"He escaped safe through that horrible war of barricades, though no man more courted danger. He inspired his men with his own courage. It was not till the revolt was quenched on the evening of the 28th May that he met his death. The Versailles soldiers, naturally exasperated, were very prompt in seizing and shooting at once every passenger who looked like a foe. Some men under De Mauleon had seized upon one of these victims, and were hurrying him into the next street for execution, when, catching sight of the Vicomte, he screamed out, 'Lebeau, save me!'

"At that cry De Mauleon rushed forward, arrested his soldiers, cried, 'This man is innocent—a harmless physician. I answer for him.' As he thus spoke, a wounded Communist, lying in the gutter amidst a heap of the slain, dragged himself up, reeled towards De Mauleon, plunged a knife between his shoulders, and dropped down dead.

"The Vicomte was carried into a neighbouring house, from all the windows of which the tricolour was suspended; and the Medecin whom he had just saved from summary execution examined and dressed his wound. The Vicomte lingered for more than an hour, but expired in the effort to utter some words, the sense of which those about him endeavoured in vain to seize.

"It was from the Medecin that the name of the assassin and the motive for the crime were ascertained. The miscreant was a Red Republican and Socialist named Armand Monnier. He had been a very skilful workman, and earning, as such, high wages. But he thought fit to become an active revolutionary politician, first led into schemes for upsetting the world by the existing laws of marriage, which had inflicted on him one woman who ran away from him, but being still legally his wife, forbade him to marry another woman with whom he lived, and to whom he seems to have been passionately attached.

"These schemes, however, he did not put into any positive practice till he fell in with a certain Jean Lebeau, who exercised great influence over him, and by whom he was admitted into one of the secret revolutionary societies which had for their object the overthrow of the Empire. After that time his head became turned. The fall of the Empire put an end to the society he had joined: Lebeau dissolved it. During the siege Monnier was a sort of leader among the ouvriers; but as it advanced and famine commenced, he contracted the habit of intoxication. His children died of cold and hunger. The woman he lived with followed them to the grave. Then he seems to have become a ferocious madman, and to have been implicated in the worst crimes of the Communists. He cherished a wild desire of revenge against this Jean Lebeau, to whom he attributed all his calamities, and by whom, he said, his brother had been shot in the sortie of December.

"Here comes the strange part of the story. This Jean Lebeau is alleged to have been one and the same person with Victor de Mauleon. The Medecin I have named, and who is well known in Belleville and Montmartre as the Medecin des Pauvres, confesses that he belonged to the secret society organised by Lebeau; that the disguise the Vicomte assumed was so complete, that he should not have recognised his identity with the conspirator but for an accident. During the latter time of the bombardment, he, the *Medecin des*

*Pauvres*, was on the eastern ramparts, and his attention was suddenly called to a man mortally wounded by the splinter of a shell. While examining the nature of the wound; De Mauleon, who was also on the ramparts, came to the spot. The dying man said, 'M. le Vicomte, you owe me a service. My name is Marc le Roux. I was on the police before the war. When M. de. Mauleon reassumed his station, and was making himself obnoxious to the Emperor, I might have denounced him as Jean Lebeau the conspirator. I did not. The siege has reduced me to want. I have a child at home—a pet. Don't let her starve.' 'I will see to her,' said the Vicomte. Before we could get the man into the ambulance cart he expired.

"The Medecin who told this story I had the curiosity to see myself, and cross-question. I own I believe his statement. Whether De Mauleon did or did not conspire against a fallen dynasty, to which he owed no allegiance, can little, if at all, injure the reputation he has left behind of a very remarkable man—of great courage and great ability—who might have had a splendid career if he had survived. But, as Savarin says truly, the first bodies which the car of revolution crushes down are those which first harness themselves to it.

"Among De Mauleon's papers is the programme of a constitution fitted for France. How it got into Savarin's hands I know not. De Mauleon left no will, and no relations came forward to claim his papers. I asked Savarin to give me the heads of the plan, which he did. They are as follows:

"The American republic is the sole one worth studying, for it has lasted. The causes of its duration are in the checks to democratic fickleness and disorder. 1st. No law affecting the Constitution can be altered without the consent of two-thirds of Congress. 2nd. To counteract the impulses natural to a popular Assembly chosen by universal suffrage, the greater legislative powers, especially in foreign affairs, are vested in the Senate, which has even executive as well as legislative functions. 3rd. The Chief of the State, having elected his government, can maintain it independent of hostile majorities in either Assembly.

"'These three principles of safety to form the basis of any new constitution for France.

"'For France it is essential that the chief magistrate, under whatever title he assume, should be as irresponsible as an English sovereign. Therefore he should not preside at his councils; he should not lead his armies. The day for personal government is gone, even in Prussia. The safety for order in a State is that, when things go wrong, the Ministry changes, the State remains the same. In Europe, Republican institutions are safer where the chief magistrate is hereditary than where elective.'

"Savarin says these axioms are carried out at length, and argued with great ability.

"I am very grateful for your proffered hospitalities in England. Some day I shall accept them-viz., whenever I decide on domestic life, and the calm of the conjugal foyer. I have a penchant for an English Mees, and am not exacting as to the dot. Thirty thousand livres sterling would satisfy me—a trifle, I believe, to you rich islanders.

"Meanwhile I am naturally compelled to make up for the miseries of that horrible siege. Certain moralising journals tell us that, sobered by misfortunes, the Parisians are going to turn over a new leaf, become studious and reflective, despise pleasure and luxury, and live like German professors. Don't believe a word of it. My conviction is that, whatever may be said as to our frivolity, extravagance, &c., under the Empire, we shall be just the same under any form of government—the bravest, the most timid, the most ferocious, the kindest-hearted, the most irrational, the most intelligent, the most contradictory, the most consistent people whom Jove, taking counsel of Venus and the Graces, Mars and the Furies, ever created for the delight and terror of the world;—in a word, the Parisians.—Votre tout divoue, 'FREDERIC LEMERCIER.'"

It is a lovely noon on the bay of Sorrento, towards the close of the autumn of 1871. Upon the part of the craggy shore, to the left of the town, on which her first perusal of the loveliest poem in which the romance of Christian heroism has ever combined elevation of thought with silvery delicacies of speech, had charmed her childhood, reclined the young bride of Graham Vane. They were in the first month of their marriage. Isaura had not yet recovered from the effects of all that had preyed upon her life, from the hour in which she had deemed that in her pursuit of fame she had lost the love that had coloured her genius and inspired her dreams, to that in which....

The physicians consulted agreed in insisting on her passing the winter in a southern climate; and after their wedding, which took place in Florence, they thus came to Sorrento.

As Isaura is seated on the small smoothed rock, Graham reclines at her feet, his face upturned to hers with an inexpressible wistful anxiety in his impassioned tenderness. "You are sure you feel better and stronger since we have been here?"